TALES FROM WAKKEN WOOD

E. P. COWLEY

Tales from Wakken Wood

Illustrated by Jackie Richard

IGNATIUS PRESS SAN FRANCISCO

The characters and events in this book are fictional, and any resemblance to actual persons or events is coincidental.

Chapter 10 poetry quotation is from William Allingham, "The Fairies", 1883.

Chapter 17 poetry quotation is adapted from Dante Gabriel Rossetti, "Body's Beauty", 1866.

Chapter 27 song quotation is adapted from Beatrix Potter, *The Tale of Pigling Bland* (Frederick Warne & Co., 1913).

Chapter 48 quotation (Lila's incantation) is adapted from A. W. Moore, *The Folk-lore of the Isle of Man* (Brown & Son, 1891).

Cover illustration and title lettering by Timothy Jones

Cover design by John Herreid

ISBN 978-1-62164-800-0 (PB)
ISBN 978-1-64229-362-3 (eBook)
Library of Congress Control Number 2025936008
Printed in the United States of America ♾

To Mary
And to my children, and their children

CONTENTS

Part I

Part II

Part 1

I

Silver Freak

He ran like heck across the field, making for the oak tree. He knew he could swing himself up, out of reach.

Too late. Like a pack of outraged dogs, they caught him and threw him to the ground.

"Wolf boy!"

"Zombie freak!"

They punched his face, kicked his ribs, and whipped his legs with a leather belt. He sucked in his gut and covered his face.

Suddenly, their shouts turned to shrieks. Someone fell on top of him, swore, and jumped up. He opened one eye. Pixel. She stood near the tree beside a pile of rocks. Her aim was deadly. It wasn't the first time she'd come to his rescue.

Rolling over, he watched the boys run as she hurled rock after rock, few of them missing their targets. He sat up slowly, in time to see the last attacker disappear among the trees on the other side of the soccer field.

Pixel was small and wiry, skinny but tough, and she was a Rilson. No one messed with anyone from the Rilson tribe. "You look bad, Peter."

Dropping the last stone, she ran a hand through the short blond hair that stood up all over her head. Some kids called her Pixie. Never to her face. And he'd been dubbed "the Werewolf". He liked to think these names suggested the dynamic: material bodies always under the action of various physical, moral, or economic forces. That's what the dictionary said.

Gingerly he fingered the left side of his mouth. His upper lip was already swelling, and he felt a gash above his eyebrow. His jeans were torn and bloody. He took a deep breath and clutched his side, stifling a cry of pain.

"Bet they broke some ribs," Pixel said.

He nodded, the pain rising all over.

She helped him to his feet, and he followed her, limping across the field to her bicycle, which was propped against a tree. He straddled the seat, and she pedaled standing up, all the way to the hospital.

When Peter finally walked out of the emergency room, it was midnight. He'd sweet-talked the distracted nurse into discharging him. "My dad's in the car, just outside the door, but it'll take him a while to get in here because of the wheelchair." This was a bold-faced lie. Dad had neither a car nor a wheelchair. He was Martin Thornburg, ex-professor, who now supported his family by working as a quick-footed waiter at the all-night diner on 87th Street.

Now that he was bandaged and iced, Peter realized he was hungry. Most likely there was no food at home. If Mom had done the shopping, there'd be a fridge full of booze and a cupboard full of potato chips. He wanted more than chips.

Standing on the curb in front of the hospital, he remembered that Dad was *not* working the night shift at the diner. Good. Mrs. Murdle would be on, and she'd feed him first, ask questions later. Dad needn't know anything until tomorrow.

A police car cruised by slowly. Moving discreetly behind a parked minivan, Peter waited until the police passed, then moved off, headed for 87th Street.

With his medium height and brown hair, Peter liked to think of himself as an ordinary seventh grader. Sure, compared with the ragtag kids he went to school with, he was cast from a different mold; his history-professor dad had seen to that. Yet it wasn't his intellectual advantages that kept him from blending in with the crowd.

Strangers had two reactions to his face: Either they were afraid, or they wanted to beat him up. Mostly they were afraid and gave him a wide berth, which was why he didn't usually feel nervous walking down the street in the middle of the night. He'd learned to read people pretty well—a necessary survival skill—and knew when he was about to be attacked. He could run fast and had learned, long ago, that climbing a tree or a fire escape discouraged the average thickheaded bully. Yet today's assault had been different, the ferocity alarming.

The walk to the diner was about eight blocks. Limping, trying not to breathe too deeply, he kept to the shadows, knowing it was dangerous to walk the streets showing any sign of weakness, hoping he wouldn't have to run.

When he arrived, he found Pixel sitting at the counter, talking with Mrs. Murdle. "It's about time!" she said, turning to look him over.

"Oh, Peter!" Mrs. Murdle cried. "Look at your poor face!" She clucked and fussed over him, leading him to the cushioned bench of a booth. "Pixel told me you were attacked! But she didn't say you were beat to a pulp!"

"Did the police at the emergency room hassle you much?" Pixel asked.

Peter tried to sit down on the bench, but bending in the middle was painful, so he went to the counter and perched on a stool beside Pixel. "They asked a few questions, but then a woman came in with gunshot wounds, so they forgot about me."

"I told your dad you were coming over to my place after soccer practice, since it's Friday, to watch the Middle Earth movies," Pixel said. "Figured you wouldn't want him to know just yet."

"Why not?" Mrs. Murdle demanded.

"Mom's not doing so well right now," Peter said.

"Oh! That mother of yours!" Mrs. Murdle threw up her hands, then hurried behind the counter and called through the hatch, "Are you awake back there? We need a cheeseburger—hold the pickle—fries with ketchup and mayo mixed, and a slice of banana cream pie! Pronto!"

In a few minutes, Peter heard the sound of sizzling as the aroma of frying beef wafted into the dining area.

"Peter, honey," Mrs. Murdle said, "you really oughta be wearing tinted glasses all the time. It would keep folks from staring, you know." She took a small carton of milk from the fridge and set it down in front of him. "You can't help the way you were born, but people can't help the way they feel when they look at your eyes neither."

Leaning forward, he opened his eyes wide. Their silver, glittery metallic irises collected the light and reflected it back like small mirrors. "Don't my eyes give *you* the creeps, Mrs. Murdle?"

"No, darlin'," she said, looking right at him. "I've known you too long. I know what's behind 'em." She reached across the counter and tousled his hair as she used to when he was nine years old. Pulling away, he grinned but was comforted.

Banana cream pie was the best. Standing up at the counter now, because of the rib pain, Peter ate slowly. Mrs. Murdle and Pixel were still nattering on about tinted glasses, but it was a pointless discussion. He *had* tried wearing them. Once. On his first day of fourth grade at the new school. But almost as soon as he'd walked into class, the teacher made him take them off, and, of course, every person in the room sat up and stared. One or two girls gasped; boys began to titter. The whispering and ridicule began that day and had never let up.

At his *old* school, a private school where he didn't need to hide his eyes because his friends had known him since preschool, no one gave his freakiness a second thought. But life at the private school was a thing of the past. First, his older brother died in a bicycle accident, picked off by a driver who ran a red light. Mom was inconsolable and slipped into a depression that left her unable to speak for a long time. Dad had done everything he could for her, spent all their savings on doctors and treatment. His work, his research, fizzled, and eventually he lost tenure at the university. When their lovely house in the tree-lined neighborhood went up for sale and Dad took a job at the diner, the family descended into the real world.

That's how Peter thought of it. The real world was where most people lived, among Lang's tightly packed neighborhoods of ugly apartment buildings and littered streets. The old life of family vacations, a backyard, a basketball hoop, a garage with a car—all of it a dim, soft memory now. As he savored the last bite of banana cream, his mind came back to the present and he heard Pixel say, "She thought he should wear sunglasses too, and then she told me to take care of him."

"Who?" Peter looked at her thin face, its usually tough expression replaced by sudden embarrassment.

"I . . . I guess I never told you." Now her face was beet red.

"Told me what?" Peter put down his fork, and Mrs. Murdle swept his empty plate away.

"When you first came to our school. In the fourth grade. Remember?"

He nodded.

"I . . . I was scared of you. Because of your eyes. But when I told my granny about you, she . . . it was like she knew all about you. She got real fierce and said you were gonna get beat up here in Lang. Then she made me promise. To look out for you."

"And that's why you started talking to me the second week of fourth grade."

"Sure. But anyway, we were meant to be friends, no matter what Granny said."

"Yup. Thanks to you, I'm still here. Eating pie."

She laughed, and the deep blush faded until Mrs. Murdle said, "Well, I think you're grand, Pixel Rilson. That's the finest thing I've ever heard about your family!"

"Yeah. I'm the only Rilson *I* know without a criminal record."

Mrs. Murdle frowned. "Even your little brothers?"

"Well, the cops aren't after them yet, but they're always in trouble at school."

"Pixel, you just stay friends with Peter, and I expect you'll come out alright. He and his dad are the salt of the earth. But *you*, young man!" Mrs. Murdle put her hands on her hips. Peter, recognizing the mother-hen mood, stood up straight, prepared to take some medicine. "If you want to live much longer, you start wearing tinted glasses, you hear me?"

She would not let him go until she'd extracted a promise. Then he and Pixel went out and caught a bus to the neighborhood where they lived. There were few other passengers. As they sat down—Peter wincing in pain—Pixel said, "Wonder what your dad will say about the cuts on your face."

"He'll hunt those guys down. Kill them."

She snorted with laughter, and an old man sitting several seats ahead looked around. He frowned at them. Peter opened his eyes wide, and the man turned away quickly, then got off at the next stop.

"Sure," she said. "If Mr. Thornburg stops reading long enough, he could chuck books. Some of the big ones could kill."

"Never. Books are our friends."

She began to giggle. The bus driver looked up in the rearview mirror and shook his finger. "No trouble, you kids," he shouted. "I should turn you in. There's a curfew, you know."

"Seriously, Peter. He won't believe you tripped over your own feet. Not this time."

"He'll get me a guard dog. A black dog big as a baby elephant. I've been asking for one."

"No, he won't. He'll take you out of school."

He had no reply to this.

"I guess it won't matter. There's only two weeks left," she said quietly.

They rode the rest of the way in silence, getting off the bus in the glare of streetlights, at that hour of the morning when everything feels colder. They lived a block apart, in shabby apartment buildings that had stood on the south side of the city since before their parents were born. Walking along the sidewalk, Peter saw a rat slink out of the gutter into a bush. Across the street, an old man leaned against a wall, lighting a cigarette. Otherwise, there was no one about.

Then, abruptly, Pixel halted under a streetlamp and said, "I better tell you."

He stopped beside her in the circle of yellow light.

"I'm changing schools," she said quickly, keeping her eyes on the ground. "I'm leaving Lang."

He felt the air sucked out of his lungs. "Why?"

"I'm moving to Foyle."

"Foyle? On the island?"

"Is it on an island?"

"Yeah. Did your dad get a job there or something?"

"No. I'm going on my own." She shrugged. "It's a Rilson thing. Girls in the family go to Foyle sometime after they turn twelve. For blood treatments. I'll live with Aunt Kate. She's a nurse and takes care of everything."

He stared at her. "Do you have some kind of disease? You don't look sick to me."

She shrugged again.

"When are you leaving?"

"Sometime after school's out."

"When do you get back?"

"I don't know. I asked how long it would take, but Mom just started crying." Her gaze was fixed on a crack in the sidewalk. Then she glanced up, and Peter was surprised by the fear in her eyes. "I . . . I wish you were coming with me."

And somehow, he knew that he would.

❦ ❦ ❦

Pixel was right. The very next day, his dad pulled him out of school.

The sudden freedom of being at home would have been okay, but Mom was drinking a lot. She spent her mornings on the couch with all the dingy living-room curtains drawn. If she noticed his black eye and purple face, she didn't say so. Moving quietly around the apartment, he sometimes thought about the dim, soft past, when she'd been beautiful, always laughing or singing. He understood that she could never love him as she loved his older brother, Daniel, who hadn't had freak eyes.

Two days after he stopped going to school, Mom began coughing: a dry hack that gradually worsened. So it was that, a week after his own trip to the emergency room, he found himself there once again, this time with Mom. She was diagnosed with pneumonia and admitted to the hospital. Within a day or two, she stabilized, but the doctors kept her for a week. He watched his dad, going between the diner and the hospital, wearing himself out. Peter helped as much as he could by taking on all the housework, but there was nothing he could do for his mother. In her silence and despair, she had moved far beyond his reach.

❦ ❦ ❦

He sat in a booth at the diner, waiting for Pixel. She was leaving the following morning. He hadn't really believed it till she received a ferry ticket postmarked from Foyle. What *would* he do without her? She was his only friend in all of Lang.

The bell on the door tinkled as she entered. "Dad's in jail again," she said, sitting down on the opposite bench. "But Mom just got her paycheck and went to bail him out, so I'll get to say goodbye to him before I go."

"Go where?" Peter's dad, Martin Thornburg, appeared at their table wearing a white apron. He set down two glasses of water.

"To a place called Foyle. Didn't Peter tell you, Mr. Thornburg?"

"Visiting your family for the summer, are you?"

"Actually, it's a one-way ticket."

"Ah," he nodded. "The treatments. I see."

There was a slight pause, in which Peter saw the surprise on Pixel's face. "Mr. Thornburg, how do you know about the treatments?"

Before he could reply, Mrs. Murdle bustled over to their table. "Pixel! You leave tomorrow, don't you? Oh, we're gonna miss you so much!" Then all the regulars gathered around and before long, a going-away party was in full swing, complete with cheeseburgers, fries, and pie. Everyone toasted Pixel with orange juice, wishing her good luck, and then it was time to go. Her face suddenly drained of color, she said goodbye and walked quickly out the door, the bell tinkling as she left.

Peter watched her through the window as she crossed the street, not once looking back. She was going home to see her dad, to spend one more evening with her little brothers. Her mom was a mess, crying all the time. "I guess they *do* love me," she'd said, laughing a little, biting her lip. *We all love you*, Peter thought, as her small figure passed out of view. The empty twilight deepened over the hum and honking of traffic. The diner grew quiet. The regulars went home one by one.

Peter waited till Dad finished his shift; then they walked home together in the dark, passing under the streetlamps, through islands of yellow light. It was usually during these walks that Peter was questioned about his reading, but this evening, Dad was unusually silent. That was good. Mom was home from the hospital, and the empty bottles had appeared on the coffee table again. Better not to talk about it.

And then, three blocks from home, Dad stopped in the middle of the dark sidewalk and said, "Peter, you've heard me speak of my aunt Marj."

"Sure. The one who lives on the island. How far is she from Foyle?"

"About forty miles. Wakkenburg House is in the middle of a forest called Wakken Wood."

He nodded. Dad rarely spoke about his family, and never in front of Mom. With his lamp-like eyes, Peter searched his father's face, waiting.

"It's time for you to go there. To Wakkenburg. I've been in touch with Aunt Marj, and it's all arranged."

He was not surprised. Somehow, from the moment Pixel uttered the name Foyle, he had known this was coming. Yet all at once, the enormity of parting from Dad opened up like a black hole. "Come with me."

"I'll come when I can. When your mother is well."

"Come without her."

"You don't mean that."

Maybe he didn't. He respected Dad for sticking with her. "You can't just send me away. You need me here."

"Think I need looking after?"

"Yeah."

"How will you do that if people keep beating you up?"

"I'll take judo lessons. I'll get a giant guard dog."

"There's no money for either. Not just yet."

"We could afford to keep a dog if Mom stopped drinking."

"She'll stop someday."

"Sure. And you'll finish your book on that Lepanto battle and make tons of money, and everything will be just like it was."

"Nothing will ever be as it was," his dad said quietly.

There was nothing to say to that. Peter's eyes lit up Dad's tired face. "When do I leave?"

"First thing tomorrow."

"Right. Pixel will be surprised to see me."

"You didn't tell her about the island, did you? About our connection to it?"

"How could I? You never talk about it, so I don't know much. Anyway, it doesn't matter now." He turned his face away, fighting down a sudden anger. "I better get home. To pack."

"Peter." Dad spoke his name softly, an unbearable ache in his voice. He stood outside the light of the streetlamp, his head bowed. "Son." Reaching out, he gripped Peter's shoulder. "I've always known you'd end up on the island. I tried to tell myself we could keep you safe here, but I was wrong. You belong at Wakkenburg House. I knew it the moment you were born and opened your eyes."

"What do you mean?" Peter whispered.

"I can't explain. I don't understand it myself. But I think you'll find out when you get there."

❦ ❦ ❦

The next morning, before dawn, Peter and his father caught a bus to the docks. On the way through the city, Peter watched the sky begin to lighten high above the gray buildings. At the terminal, Dad bought a one-way ticket. Then he and Peter stood in the waiting area for foot passengers. Other people began to trickle in, laughing and talking, stacking their bags on black vinyl chairs.

"How did you know about the blood treatments?" Peter kept his eyes on the window, looking at the horizon of sea and sky but not really seeing it.

"Everyone in Foyle knows about them."

"Will she get well?"

"I don't know. No one outside the Rilson family has ever known what the treatments are or how long it takes to recover."

Peter nodded, unable to look at Dad, keeping his breathing shallow to fight back tears.

"Here. Write to me."

Dad held out a stack of postcards. It was his slightly frayed collection, some dating back to his college days in Oxford. There was a book of stamps under his thumb.

"I can't use those."

"Sure you can." Peter felt Dad push the postcards and stamps into the pocket of his jacket. "It's a beautiful arrangement. They'll be put to their proper use, and I'll get them all back. Better than email."

"Great-Aunt Marj doesn't have internet, does she?"

"No. If you want to send an email, you'll have to go to the library in Foyle. I doubt you'll get there often. Have you seen Pixel yet? Oh, there's the call for boarding."

"Say goodbye to Mom from me. Tell her … no, don't tell her anything."

He felt Dad's arms around him, hugging him tightly. When he let go, Peter stood there, looking at his father's face, unable to move, so Dad turned him around by the shoulders and sent him up the boarding ramp. Peter walked straight to the passenger deck, feeling a pain in his chest that he had not felt since his brother's death.

Once on deck, he stood at the rail looking toward the parking lot, hoping to see Dad on his way to the bus loop. Someone came to stand beside him, and he heard Pixel say, "Peter! What are you doing here?"

"Coming with you."

"But … but … how? Why?" She stood there with her mouth open, the duffel bag slipping from her shoulder.

He tried to grin but failed. "I'm not really sure myself."

The engine started, and a few minutes later, they were pulling away from the dock, under a bright sky. Gulls wheeled overhead, crying and scolding as the ferryboat plowed through the heaving sea, white foam churning in its wake. Pixel took Peter's hand and held on tight. Silently, they stood there, watching Lang grow smaller and smaller, until it was only a thin, dark line on the horizon. Already they were far from home, heading into a remote future they could not even guess at.

2

Seeing Things

Standing at the bow, Peter watched the ferry dock beside a very small village, little more than the terminal and one or two shops. There were a handful of vehicles in the parking lot. The sign above the loading platform said Orbsen Bay.

It had taken a day and a night to reach the island, and the berth had been uncomfortable. Besides that, he'd had the most vivid dreams. Of course, there was the usual one about the warrior riding a white horse over the sea. He'd been having that one all his life. But he'd also had a nightmare about a girl sleeping at the bottom of a lake. In the dream, she'd opened her eyes and they were silver, just like his. He shivered and rubbed his face. "Who's picking you up?" he asked, as Pixel came to stand beside him. She had gone to wash in the bathroom, and her short hair stood up all over her head like bristles.

"My aunt Kate. The nurse. Who's picking *you* up?"

He shrugged. "Great-Aunt Marj, I guess."

A voice over the intercom called for foot passengers to disembark. Peter and Pixel picked up their bags, walked off the ferry, and stood outside the small terminal, scanning the parking lot.

"I think that's her," Pixel said.

A woman got out of a black coupe and waved. She was blond and slight, an older version of Pixel, possibly in her late thirties.

"See you, Peter."

He watched her walk away with her shoulders hunched. During the long ferry ride, she had managed to hide her fear, never talking about the blood treatments. In fact, avoiding island topics altogether, she hadn't asked him about his relatives, which was good. He didn't know much. Only that he wouldn't be living in Foyle, and he hadn't told her that.

After fifteen minutes, the parking lot was empty. Peter sat down on the one bench, piling his bags at his feet. One or two of the dock workers eyed him sympathetically, but he kept his head down, trying not to meet anyone's gaze. He'd managed the entire ferry trip without incident, mainly because he'd avoided the crowds, keeping to himself in a quiet corner of the deck, hiding his eyes as well as his bruised face. No one but Pixel knew he was a freak being sent away from home.

Beside the bench, announcements and small posters were pinned to a signboard. One of these bore the title Principal Island Roads. Curious, Peter stood up to get a closer look.

It was only a partial map. Between the west and east coasts, thick lines indicated the roads, which were laid out in the shape of a long sock, the toe pointing south. At the end of the toe, a little line, like a dangling thread, marked the road to Orbsen Bay. From this point, the line that formed the sole of the sock went a little to the left and then up through the village of Foyle, situated near the southwest coast. This road was called Highway 20. Where the heel of the sock curved to the right, Highway 20 crossed Foyle Bridge and continued northward up the long leg, ending at the narrowed top of the sock, labeled "The Junction". North of the junction, a short road, unnamed, straggled off into nothing. At this convergence of three roads, Highway 20 ended and became Highway 21, which bent slightly south along the sock's cuff. At this upper end of the sock's leg—on the east coast—a town named Sweetwater was marked in large letters. Then Highway 21 continued straight south to the top of the toe, where it crossed another bridge, ending at Orbsen Bay. Between the two bridges, a thin blue line—the Glenfaba River—cut through the sock's foot.

The bottom part of the map was a bare outline, but no one had bothered to draw anything above Sweetwater. It was the oddest map he'd ever seen. It didn't inform tourists of anything but two towns, two highways, and part of a river.

"Aha! What have we here?"

Startled, Peter turned and looked into the face of a grubby old man smelling strongly of whiskey and sweat.

"Oh ho! What have we here indeed!" The man cackled idiotically, and Peter felt a hand clamp down on his arm. He twisted away, but the old man's grip was like iron. "Ha! You're not getting away from Mac. Oh no. We've been expecting *you*."

Just then, a long black hearse roared into the parking lot. Peter turned in time to see it careen wildly toward the terminal, headed straight for him. The old man squawked and released his grip, and Peter bolted over the back of the bench. Hearing the squeal of tires, he dropped to the ground and wrapped his arms around his head, but the impact never came. Instead, the engine shut off. Scrambling to his feet, he saw the front tire of the hearse sitting on the curb, inches from his baggage. A young man hopped out and looked at him.

"Thornburg! Peter Thornburg! Sorry I'm late! Throw your bags in the back, kid, and let's roll out!"

"Who the heck are you?"

"Foster. Your cousin, of course."

Peter looked into the man's eyes. They were blue as the sky. Too blue. "My dad never said anything about a cousin picking me up."

"Are you always this suspicious? Here, I've got the letter from your dad." Foster pulled a folded paper out of his shirt pocket and gave it to Peter.

Dear Aunt Marj,

Peter is coming alone. He'll arrive on July 10th. How shall I describe him? He looks like every other Thornburg child: dark hair, medium height. But I expect you'll know him by his eyes. I can only describe them as silver, like mercury, filled with light. Also, he's thinner than he should be.

I can't tell you how grateful I am that you're taking him now. Things are hard for him at school and harder at home. He is plagued by the usual bullies, as you warned he might be. At home, well . . . his mother's deep depression continues. I wrote to you about the death of our older son, Daniel. She does not understand her second son.

I wanted to come and help him settle in. It's been years since I've seen you. However, circumstances prevent my coming at this time.

I've explained nothing to Peter about the Thornburgs or the legends of Wakken Wood. I could never bring myself to burden him with all that family . . . history? If it weren't for the color of his eyes, I would certainly say myth.

He's a good boy. I hope he'll be safe with you. I'll come as soon as I can.

With love,
Martin

Peter felt the ache in his chest return. Dad must have written this letter a few weeks ago.

"Satisfied?" Foster said.

"Alright. Sorry. An old man tried to grab me. Then you came, driving like a maniac—"

"An old guy? Smells like whiskey?"

"Yeah. Called himself Mac."

"Well, well," Foster paused, staring into space. "Mac Rilson saw you first. That's unfortunate."

"That was Mac Rilson? I know the Rilsons, but I don't know you." Something about Foster struck a wrong chord. In his short life as a freak, Peter had learned to heed these inner warnings. "Did Great-Aunt Marj really send you?"

"Of course she did! Now get in the car. I'll take care of your bags."

Peter stuffed the letter in his pocket. A few minutes later, they were driving away from Orbsen Bay.

"Ever been to Foyle?" Foster asked.

"No."

"So you haven't met Aunt Marj or any other family?"

"No." Peter watched Foster warily, disliking his smug little smile, wishing Dad had been more explicit about family on the island.

"Auntie Marj sure kept you a secret." Foster was looking at Peter, not out the windshield, jiggling the steering wheel so that the hearse began weaving back and forth across the road. "I mean, we heard there was a cousin Martin with two kids, living in Lang, but I didn't know one of them was a Silver-eyed. You're the stuff of legends, kid."

"Look where you're going!" Instinctively, Peter ducked down as the hearse surged toward a ditch. Foster jerked the wheel to the left in the nick of time. From then on, he kept his eyes on the road, and the hearse in the right lane, though he was driving too fast. Even so, Peter relaxed a little and looked out the window at the densest forest he'd ever seen. Now and then they sped past a mailbox bearing a house number and driveways, sometimes paved, sometimes not. Between the trees, he caught glimpses of stone or clapboard houses set back from the road, surrounded by lawns and large gardens. After a while, the forest on the left gave way to rocks and high cliffs, and a few miles later, the cliffs gave way to fields, then houses. A sign flashed by: Welcome to Foyle. Beyond the houses, the sea spread out under the late-morning sun.

The two-lane road widened and became Main Street. They passed a library, a fire station, an auto shop, and a café. Foster was still driving too fast. Up ahead, Peter saw a man step into the crosswalk, but Foster didn't slow down.

"Hey!" Peter cried, just as Foster stomped on the brake pedal. The hearse squealed to a sudden stop, and Peter's head hit the dashboard.

"What's he doing?" Foster yelled.

With one hand on his forehead, Peter looked up in time to see the man in the crosswalk gesture angrily and hurry on. Then a woman ran out of the store on the corner, shouting and waving. She ran right up to the hearse and banged on the passenger window.

"Hey!" she shouted; then her mouth fell open.

Following her gaze, Peter turned and saw … no one. The driver's seat was empty. Foster was gone. The car door was still closed. Keys dangled from the ignition.

The woman ran around and opened the driver's side door. "Did you see …?" They looked at each other, as the engine idled. Finally, she said, "You're Peter."

"Yeah."

"Who was he?"

"Foster. My cousin. He picked me up to take me to … to …"

She slid into the driver's seat and shut the door. "I'm Annette Thornburg. I was supposed to meet you at the ferry, but I couldn't find the car. Or the letter your dad sent."

He stared at her worried face, the dark hair falling over her shoulders. Something about her was familiar. Then he realized that her gray eyes, the shape of her nose, her light olive skin and dark hair were the same as his father's. She could be a younger sister.

A car stopped behind them and honked. Silently, Annette shifted the car into gear and drove around the corner, pulling into the driveway behind the store. Then she parked and shut off the ignition. "Are you alright?" she asked.

Peter looked at her, then touched the small lump rising on his forehead. "I don't think so. First, a man tried to grab me; then that guy Foster just … he didn't know how to drive." Anger rose like a wave. He got out, slammed the door shut, and kicked the tire savagely. "I didn't want to come here!"

Through the window, he saw Annette slump in the seat and put her head down on the steering wheel. She sat there, as confused as he was. This, more than anything, assured him that she was okay. Then he looked up at the building and saw the sign over the back door: Thorny's Goods: Since 1891.

Annette got out of the car and led him through the back door into a bright, messy kitchen. "Mom! Dad!" she called. "Peter's here!"

An older woman entered the room, eager and expectant. She was slightly plump, with gray hair curling all around her face. A stout, jolly-looking man followed.

"Peter, this is my mom and dad, Mary and George Thornburg. Do you want to see their ID? And mine? I wouldn't blame you."

"Annette! That's no way to introduce us!" Mary said.

Then Annette told her what had happened.

George turned to Peter. "You say he called himself Foster and told you he's a cousin?"

"Could be some distant relation," Mary said.

"Peter, the Thornburgs are a numerous and complicated family, spread out all over the mainland," George explained. "Auntie Marj will no doubt show you the family tree sometime and try to teach you its ancient lineage. I'm the son of Marj's older brother, James, so we're cousins."

Their talk went on as if nothing unusual had happened, as if Foster's vanishing into thin air had passed from their minds.

"Well," said Mary, "we can't stand around talking about family all day. I'll make sandwiches. George, you'd better fill Marj's order."

The cousins began to bustle about, and before long, Peter found himself standing at the kitchen table, eating a sandwich, as Mary and Annette packed groceries into a box. George chattered away about relatives, and that was how Peter learned about Great-Uncle Edward, who also lived at Wakkenburg House.

For a moment, he felt wrapped in the warmth of this family. They welcomed him as a long-lost member of their clan. And yet he noticed that they didn't ask questions about his mother and father or his bruised face. No doubt they, too, had read the letter from his dad and were skirting around his family troubles, as one avoids walking through a puddle of antifreeze. One time he'd dipped the toe of his sneaker into a small puddle of antifreeze in the gutter. The next day there was a hole in the cloth.

"Do you know the Rilsons?" he asked at a pause in the conversation.

Everyone stopped what they were doing and looked at him.

"Sure. Oh sure," George said.

"Do *you* know the Rilsons?" Annette asked.

"I came on the ferry with my friend, Pixel Rilson," he said, suddenly aware of the tension in the room. "She came to live with relatives while she has blood treatments."

"Oh yes," Mary said. "The Rilson blood disease. Seems it affects only the girls. Poor things. I always wonder—"

"Well," George said, cutting her off. "I think we're about done here. Did you pack the coffee? Uncle Ed will be miffed if we don't!"

"I was wondering where the Rilsons live," Peter persisted. "I promised Pixel I'd visit her this summer, before we go back to school."

"It's a bit early to be thinkin' of school," George said. "You've got the whole summer before you! There's a lot to see around Foyle. Swimmin' holes, fishin'. Do you fish?"

"I never have," Peter admitted.

"Oh no!" Mary laughed. "Don't get George started on fishing!"

"Time to go," Annette said. "Auntie Marj is waiting."

They packed up the hearse, George talking all the while about fishing holes and fishing gear until, finally, Peter found himself once again in the passenger seat of the hearse, waving goodbye as Mary thrust a candy bar into his hand. Then Annette pulled onto Main Street, and he saw the old man who'd accosted him at the ferry terminal, standing on the sidewalk, scowling at someone.

"There's Mac Rilson."

"How do you know *him*?" Annette said.

"He's the one who tried to grab me at the terminal."

"I don't remember that," Annette said. "Good thing I got there when I did!"

He was about to correct her when he glanced at her face. She was smiling, her eyes on the road, completely oblivious of her mistake. He kept his mouth shut.

They drove in silence. When they passed the last house in Foyle, she said, "Peter, the Rilsons are a bad lot."

"Here too?"

"What do you mean 'here too'?"

"Well, in Lang they're pretty much all criminals, expect for Pixel and maybe a few of her relatives under ten years old."

"How in the world did you and Pixel become friends?"

"We're at the same school in Lang."

They passed a road sign: Leaving Foyle. Come Back Soon. A small signpost on the left said Glenfaba River. Crossing a stone bridge, they headed north.

As they entered a region of tall, dark forest, Annette said, "You have to understand, Peter. There's bad blood between the older Thornburgs and the Rilsons. They stay out of each other's way."

"You mean a family feud? I don't care about that. If Aunt Marj won't take me to see Pixel, I'll walk."

"It's a long way. Over forty miles."

"I'll get a horse. Or hitchhike. Anyway, I'll have to get to the library. I have a book addiction."

"You don't understand. The Thornburgs—"

"No. I don't understand the Thornburgs. I don't know any Thornburgs except my dad. He only sent me here because he thought a freak like me might be safer."

The ancient trees ticked by as they sped along the road. Peter was impressed by the huge boles of cedar and fir.

"Well," she finally said, "I'll have to help you. We'll visit Pixel together."

"When?"

"Next week. Maybe sooner." She smiled sadly, and he wondered why. His uneasiness about the blood treatments returned.

They lapsed into silence. The deep forest flanking the highway went on and on without a break, and they seemed to be the only thing moving in it. Now and then, sunlight glanced between the trees. At last, Peter said, "Why do you drive a hearse?"

"I borrowed it from Uncle Edward because my car's too small. I thought you'd have more luggage."

"Is Great-Uncle Edward in the funeral business or something?"

"No. He bought this hearse to cut expenses when he dies. That's what he said. He's never one to put more money in the pockets of the Rilsons than he has to."

"What do the Rilsons have to do with it?"

"They run the only funeral parlor on the island. In Sweetwater."

He couldn't help noticing that as they moved farther into the island's interior, Annette talked less. Back in the kitchen of Thorny's, she seemed so eager to tell him about family and he'd had the impression she was holding herself back, trying not to overwhelm him with information. Now she seemed reluctant to talk at all. He tried again. "Which way is Sweetwater from here?"

"The other side of the island. You must have noticed the turnoff to Highway 21 as you left the ferry terminal."

"Foster's driving was terrible. I was thinking more about staying alive."

"Who's Foster?" she said but then seemed to forget she'd asked the question and fell silent.

They hadn't seen another car since crossing the bridge out of Foyle. After a while, Peter said, "How big is this forest?"

"Wakken Wood takes up three-quarters of the island. It's all ancestral lands belonging to the Thornburgs. Didn't you know that?"

"Dad never talked about his family."

The trees on either side seemed to bend over the hearse as it sped over the highway. He had a fleeting sense of uneasiness, as if the forest were menacing, as if he and Annette were intruders in a world they knew nothing about. Then he glanced out the side window and saw a huge, dark shape moving through the trees, parallel with the road. "What's that? A bear?"

Startled, she took her foot off the gas, and the hearse slowed down fractionally. "We don't have bears on this island. Must be a deer. The island's full of deer." Then she sped up again.

It seemed like the wrong shape for a deer, but he was no wildlife expert, so he kept quiet and watched. Whatever it was, it could run as fast as the hearse. He glanced at the speedometer: seventy miles an hour.

"Here's the junction coming up. We're almost there," Annette said.

Peter saw the road sign: Sweetwater Exit, Right Lane. Annette made a left off the highway and turned onto Wakkenburg Road. He looked back and saw the huge black shape cross the highway, still keeping pace on the right, and he recognized a creature straight from his dreams. It was a huge black dog. Was he on an island where dreams come true? If so, it would be better to catch the next ferry to Lang.

From Wakkenburg Road, the hearse turned right onto a wooded lane, and the dog ran beside them with a long, loping gait, staying almost out of sight among the trees. Then the car shot out of the woods, between wide green lawns and flower beds ablaze with color. At the end of the drive stood a house bigger than anything Peter had imagined, as big as the mansions of Europe. Its gray stone walls and terraces gleamed in the sunlight.

Arresting as the sight was, Peter turned back to see whether the dog would follow and was just in time to see it stop at the abrupt edge of the woods and sit down on its haunches. He let out a short, tight breath.

"I know!" Annette laughed. "The woods end so suddenly, don't they? After miles and miles of closing in over our heads. It's like coming out of a long dark tunnel."

He nodded, gazing mutely at the square towers and parapets. How was it that he belonged here? Then, unbidden, a dazzling image flashed into his mind: Dad dressed all in white, holding a flaming sword. Or was it Dad? But there was no time to think. The hearse swept up the drive and stopped under the portico. He was here, and his father was far away, in Lang.

As soon as Great-Aunt Marj ushered him through the front door of Wakkenburg House, Peter noticed five wizened little faces staring at him from a landing at the top of the staircase, and he wasn't introduced to a single one. Annette didn't seem to notice them waving and winking. Distracted, he hardly took in Aunt Marj's gracious speech of welcome or Uncle Edward's gruff greeting.

He was led to a sunny sitting room, handed a cup of tea, and told to take a chair. Annette, buzzing about the room, gave Uncle Edward newspapers she'd brought from the store. Then a creature appeared at the old man's elbow, and Peter saw a gnarled hand reach out and swap the tea for coffee. Uncle Edward, his tall, lanky frame folded into a chintz armchair, never blinked an eye.

After supper, it was worse. Annette was gone, and as Peter toured the lower floor of the West Wing, trying to listen to Aunt Marj's explanations of this room or that painting, the strange faces peered at him from behind furniture, popping up at every turn, in every passage.

Only one of the creatures stood still and looked at him long and hard. It followed them, walking beside Aunt Marj as if listening to everything she said. It walked with them all the way to the door of his bedroom, where Aunt Marj left him to unpack and settle in. For all he knew, it was still standing outside in the passage.

Peter sat on the edge of his bed, looking at the thick rugs on the polished wood floor, the oaken furniture, the stone fireplace, and the old books standing thoughtfully in bays that lined one wall from floor to ceiling. He'd never had a room like this, not even in the old days before the funeral and the tiny apartment.

"This room has been waiting for you," Aunt Marj had told him, "and it belonged to the others like you. They lived a long time ago, but this room is always ready."

Others like me? Cripes! The silver eyes must be some sort of mutation, a bad string of DNA running through the family gene pool, surfacing now and then like some monstrous fish. And perhaps, with the eyes, came a sort of brainsickness that settled in slowly and began with visions of strange creatures.

As the dark of evening descended, the weight of homesickness bore down. Peter wanted to get away from this place and felt a sudden, overwhelming desire to run all the way to Orbsen Bay and get on the next ferry. Instead, he took the stack of postcards out of his bag.

He opened the drawer of the desk to look for a pen and was amazed to find a quill and an ink pot. For some reason, this made him angry, and he rummaged around until he found an old pencil. Shutting the drawer on historical relics he wasn't prepared to care about, he sat down to write.

Dear Dad,

I'm at Wakkenburg House. I met our cousins George, Mary, and Annette. Aunt Marj gave me a tour of the place. It's pretty big. Maybe you and Mom could come here and stay awhile. It would be a good place for her to rest. There are lots of old books in my room. Please come soon. Tell Mom hello from me.

Love,
Peter

P.S. There's a really big dog here, so one of my wishes came true.

He thought about crossing out the postscript. The dog must be a hallucination too. And what about Foster? Peter began to wonder whether Annette really *had* picked him up at the ferry.

It wasn't until he'd signed and stamped the postcard that he realized he couldn't just walk to the nearest mailbox. Suddenly, his postcard seemed urgent, and he decided to go downstairs and ask Aunt Marj about it.

As soon as he opened the door, he wished he hadn't. The creature who'd followed him to the bedroom was still standing in the passage. It looked a lot like a very small man, about his own height, with an unnaturally hairy, wrinkled face. It wore normal clothes: a shirt and trousers and brown shoes. Then it spoke. "I expect you want to post that letter?"

Peter stuffed the postcard in his back pocket. "I'm hallucinating. I'll close my eyes, and when I open them, you'll be gone, or you'll turn into a pink elephant or something." He shut his eyes, counted to ten, then looked again.

The little man rolled his eyes. "You humans are so limited."

Another creature came walking down the passage and stopped beside the first. It was obviously female, with wavy tresses but considerably less facial hair. "Norbert, you heard what Miss Marj said. This one's from the mainland. He won't know anything about us. You better explain."

Norbert sighed. "I don't suppose you'd do it for me, Muru? Since this boy's arrival, the others have taken a complete holiday! I really must go downstairs and try to restore order. Otherwise they'll let the fires go cold and there'll be no breakfast in the morning."

"Sure. Has Moody Doug arrived?"

"I expect so. Did you see the Moddey Dhoo, boy?"

Peter looked at them silently.

Norbert huffed. "You know. Big black dog. About the size of—"

"A baby elephant," Peter finished.

"Oh! You've seen him!" Muru exclaimed.

"Well he *is* hard to miss," Norbert snapped. "You take it from here, Muru. I'll let the dog in on my way downstairs. And Muru . . ."

"Yes?"

"Do persuade the boy to give you that letter he's wrinkling in his back pocket. I do so hate to let the Moddey Dhoo into the house for no good reason. He leaves mud on the carpets." Without another word, the little man turned and walked away down the passage.

"He'll warm up; you'll see," Muru said. "It's been a long time since one of you has lived here, and we're not used to being seen."

Peter stared at her.

"We're the Fennys. You know, the Fennodyree. Fennys for short. Ha ha."

He pinched himself. No, he wasn't asleep and dreaming. Probably he should go downstairs and ask Aunt Marj to call a doctor. A psychiatrist. That's what he needed.

"We do all the cooking and cleaning and gardening, and . . . and . . ." she faltered, obviously caught off guard by his silence. She tried again. "And now that you're here, and Moody Doug's come back, everything will be alright again. You'll see."

"I don't think so," he said aloud, but to himself. "I'm going insane."

Her shoulders sagged. "You really don't believe I'm here, do you?"

"You're not real."

"But you're talking to me!"

"I'm talking to myself, because I'm going crazy." He started to close the door, when he became aware of a heavy tread in the passage.

Before he had time to blink, he felt the rush of a large animal. Giant paws hit his shoulders, and a huge tongue licked his face. Then he was falling backward. His head hit the floor, and everything went black.

❦ ❦ ❦

He opened his eyes in a room illuminated by firelight. Shadows flickered over the high ceiling. *Where am I?* Then he saw an old woman leaning over the bed. She had short gray locks framing sea-gray eyes and a large, bony nose. Memory tumbled into place. "Aunt Marj."

She switched on the lamp at his bedside. "You've got a bump on the back of your head slightly larger than the one on your forehead."

The small woman, the Fenny called Muru, entered, bearing a tray with two mugs. Aunt Marj picked up one and gave it to Peter. "Mugwort tea. I don't know that you'll like the taste, but it will help you feel better." She took the other mug and sat down in a chair by the bed.

Peter looked from his aunt to Muru. "Um," he hesitated. "Did you see who brought the tea?"

"Yes. Didn't you?"

"Yeah. You ... you see them too? I'm not going nuts?"

"Well, I don't see them as you do. Not yet. You're blessed with the sight of the Silver-eyed. I see dim outlines, like shadows. But you're perfectly sane, Peter. I could see that the moment you walked in the door."

"Then ... they're all real?"

"Oh yes. Though, this afternoon you were so quiet I wasn't sure you *could* see the Fennys, which would be unusual for a Silver. So I didn't point them out because you might have thought *I* was crazy! Didn't your father read the Thornburg book to you?"

"*That* tome." Muru rolled her eyes.

"There's a Thornburg book?"

"Oh dear. Every Silver-eyed is supposed to have it all explained. I guess your father tried to warn me, but I really didn't think he'd told you absolutely nothing." She got up and went to the bookshelf.

It was then that he noticed the large black shape stretched across the hearthrug.

He sat up, and the great black dog raised its head and looked at him. Then it began to thump its tail, and the sound was like a large tree branch striking the floor. The dog rose, trotted over, and laid its head in Peter's lap.

“He’s the Moddey Dhoo,” Muru said, “but you can call him Moody Doug. Or just Moody for short. Everyone does.”

Hesitantly, Peter put his hand on the dog’s ridiculously big head. “Moody.” As soon as he said the name, the dog wagged his tail and sent the lamp on the nightstand crashing to the floor. Immediately, four Fennys ran into the room and swept up the glass. A fifth brought in a new lamp.

Aunt Marj, who was scanning the bookshelves, never turned a hair. “You see, dear, why we never put the good furniture in this room.”

“Better give him the letter, kid,” Muru said. “We’ll get no peace till you do.”

“Letter?”

“The one in your back pocket that you want to post. He’ll take it to Foyle for you.”

Peter pulled the postcard out of his pocket and held it out. Without hesitation, Moody took it in his teeth and trotted out the door.

“Well,” Aunt Marj said, coming back to the bedside empty-handed. “Man’s best friend.”

“You better drink that tea,” Muru said. “And if she’s gonna read from that book, I’m leaving. I’ve heard it read way too many times.”

“What did the Fenny say, Peter? I hear her voice, but the words aren’t clear.”

“She said she’s tired of hearing that book read aloud.”

“The Thornburg book? Oh well, I can’t find it. Anyway, you should rest. The Fenny will show you where to brush your teeth.”

She laid her hand on Peter's shoulder. "Feeling better now? Not so confused?"

"I . . . I don't know."

"Give it time, dear. I'm so glad you've come." She kissed the top of his head, then picked up her cup and left the room.

Ten minutes later he was settled for the night, sipping tea and looking at the fire. In his mind's eye, he saw Moody Doug running through the woods in the dark, faster than a deer, with the postcard clamped between his teeth. He thought of his father reading that postcard in a few days' time. He'd never guess how it had come to him, not in a million years. Or maybe he would. Peter looked around the room. Did his father already know about all this?

Muru came in and took his empty mug, then wished him good night and switched off the new lamp. Settling down among the soft pillows, Peter drifted into sleep.

❦ ❦ ❦

Crouched at the bottom of a lake, he looked up through the blue-green stillness. Little half-formed frogs darted across his vision. A woman's voice called, "Jen!" A few feet away, a young girl lay on a bed of iris leaves, strands of her dark hair undulating in the current. Suddenly, she opened silver eyes, which shone dully under the water, and pushed off from the mud, sinewy reeds catching at her ankles. He tried to follow but found himself stuck, rooted in the lake bed. All he could do was watch her swim away, higher and higher. Again, the lovely voice called, "Jen!" and a graceful hand broke through the water. The girl caught at the hand; her head and shoulders disappeared, then her legs and feet.

He was alone, tugging at his ankles, trying to get free of the slimy bottom as the agitated water grew murky. At last, with one final pull, his feet popped out and he pushed himself upward as the pain in his chest swelled. With a violent gasp, he broke the surface. He was floating in the middle of the sea, rising and falling on gentle swells. Hearing hoofbeats, he looked toward the far horizon and saw a man on a white horse ride straight out of the setting sun. The upraised sword in his hand flashed like a silver flame as he passed over the sea and disappeared into a land of dark wooded hills.

3

The Girl by the Lake

A mild breeze ruffled the waters of Granite Lake. Though it was only eleven miles north of Foyle, as the crow flies, there weren't any townsfolk living who had seen its wooded shores. That particular morning, the lake shone like a blue pear-shaped gem in the middle of the forest. On the grassy bank, at the south end, a young girl lay fast asleep. Long dark hair covered her pale face, and her fingers twitched slightly. Suddenly, she opened her eyes and sat up. "Let me go!" She looked around wildly but saw only the lake and the dark forest. A small striped creature on a low branch chattered at her, and she stood up.

A cool breeze lifted the hem of her skirt, and she tugged at the sleeves of her damp sweater, but they were too short. Wrapping her arms about herself, she looked into the forest, then down at the narrow strip of grass that divided the trees from the lake. "Mother?" she whispered. Then, a little louder, "Mother?" She waited, listening, but no one replied.

Brushing the hair out of her mouth, she felt something tickling the back of her neck and drew a long, slimy reed from the collar of her shirt. There were reeds and leaves tangled in her hair, and she spent a few moments pulling them out. Then she noticed the mud on her hands. Crouching down at the water's edge to wash, she saw, mirrored in the quiet lake, a girl with eyes like stars. "Who are you?" she said. The girl's mouth moved. She waved her hand, and the girl waved her hand. She stared at the face and the shining silver eyes. Then she stood up, shivering a little.

The face of a beautiful woman with golden hair and a cruel smile rose to the surface of her thoughts. Trembling, she remembered the pain of violent hands clutching her arms. Then, across the lake, a movement caught her eye. A tall figure came out of the woods and stood on the opposite shore. "Mother?" she said, squinting across the distance. "Mother!" she called, her heart swelling with relief.

"Wait!" a distant voice roared.

That wasn't Mother's voice. As she watched, unable to turn her eyes away, the figure began to sway, writhing this way and that. Guttural cries rent the air as the creature changed shape. The girl shrank back in horror. Then a triumphant whinny rent the air, and she saw the unmistakable shape of a large horse plunge into the water.

She stared at the empty shore. Then a little wavelet slapped the mud at her feet, and she saw two long furrows, pointed like an arrow, coming across the lake. In blind panic, she turned and ran into the dark forest as a path opened between the trees.

4

Blood Treatments

Pixel stood at the window of her third-floor bedroom and gazed absently at the street. She felt cold, though it was a warm day. The gabled Rilson house was charming, the kind of place in which she had always wanted to live. Everything was clean and white with soft curtains at the windows and a neatly mown lawn.

Aunt Kate was one of those slender blond beauties, dressed in an elegant skirt and blouse. After her initial greeting, she hadn't said a word during the car ride from the ferry terminal. Not a single question about Pixel's family and no attempt at small talk. When they arrived at the house, she'd hurried Pixel inside, introduced her to Cook, who was a distant relation, then taken her upstairs to the bedroom at the top of the house. In a few words, she explained that it was fine to explore the village and that the telephone was off-limits because of long-distance charges. Then she'd left Pixel to unpack.

I can't call home, but at least I'm not a prisoner, Pixel thought. She'd been afraid of being treated like an invalid.

It didn't take Pixel long to empty her duffel bag. All her clothes fit into two drawers of the small bureau. Having unpacked, she went downstairs to find her cousins. She'd met one or two of them at the odd family gathering, girls with long, swinging hair. There weren't many in the clan. The Rilson tribe tended toward boys who went on to populate Lang's leading correctional facilities.

At the bottom of the stairs, she met her aunt passing through the lower hallway. "Aunt Kate, where are the other girls?"

"What other girls?"

"My cousins. Dad told me about Clare and Bella. And Megan came last year."

"Oh. Right. Well, they don't live here now."

"They finished the treatments?"

"That's right. Now go to the dining room for lunch. I can't join you today, but Cook has made you a sandwich. And don't be late this afternoon."

"Late? For what?"

"Your first treatment, of course. Meet me right here at three o'clock. Don't forget."

"I don't feel sick."

"We don't wait for that, dear." Aunt Kate turned away and went down the passage toward the back of the house.

Pixel found the dining room, just off the front hall. It was a lovely room with a large, cloth-covered table and antique chairs. Looking out the long windows that faced Main Street, she saw a store called Thorny's directly across the road. There was hardly any traffic: Two cars lined up at a corner stop sign. One was a long black hearse. She squinted. Peter? Yes, he was sitting in the passenger's seat! A woman hurried around the front of the car and got in on the driver's side. The other car honked, and the hearse turned down the side street and pulled in behind the store.

"I bet Thorny's is short for Thornburg," Pixel said. Peter hadn't mentioned where his relatives lived, but it must be right across the street.

Then Cook came in with a tray of sandwiches, and Pixel sat down at the table.

After lunch, she went back to her room to change into shorts. There was enough time to explore the little town before her first blood treatment. First, she'd go over to Thorny's and see whether Peter wanted to come too.

She had just started down the stairs when a querulous voice broke into the quiet house. "I seen him, I tell you! A boy with silver eyes. There he was, sittin' at the dock. If you won't deliver my message, then let me upstairs. I'll tell him myself."

"That's enough!" Aunt Kate said, a note of warning in her voice. "You'd better leave now, before I call the police."

When Pixel reached the bottom of the stairs, her aunt was just closing the front door, and she glimpsed a man shuffling off the porch. "Who's that?" she asked.

Aunt Kate frowned. "That is Great-Uncle Mac. Best to stay out of his way. Are you off to explore?"

Pixel nodded.

"Back by three. Don't forget."

Aunt Kate opened the door again, and Pixel went out. Running lightly down the front steps, she crossed the lawn, but before she reached the sidewalk, a man grabbed her by the shoulder.

"Ha! You're the new Rilson girl come from Lang! I'd recognize you anywhere. You look just like the rest of 'em."

"Let me go!" She pulled away, but his hand went around her upper arm and held on tight.

"Just tell me if you rode the ferry that come in this mornin'."

She struggled under his grip. "Let go!"

He put his creased, unshaven face up close to hers, his breath smelling like whiskey. "Did you see a boy on that ferry? With silver eyes?"

"No!" She kicked out hard and walloped his shin. His battered hat fell off and he let go, cursing, as she darted across the road. Stopping in front of the store, she turned to look back and saw the hearse come around the corner with Peter in the passenger's seat. She wanted to wave and get his attention, but she didn't dare. The old man she'd kicked, who must be Uncle Mac, was standing on the front lawn, watching her. Plunking herself down on a wooden bench, she folded her arms and returned his stare, scowling. At last, he shuffled away down the other side of the street.

Feeling deflated by Peter's departure, she returned to the house, wondering where he had gone and when he'd be back.

At exactly three o'clock, Pixel met Aunt Kate in the front hall and followed her up the stairs to the treatment room on the second floor. First, she had to stand on a scale. "You're really underweight," her aunt said lightly. "I heard you have a cousin in Lang named Maxine. How old is she?"

"Ten. Why?"

"Timing. Sit down in that chair and put your arm on the table."

Pixel did as she was told, grimacing when her aunt tied a tourniquet above her elbow. Then Aunt Kate donned a pair of latex gloves and picked up a butterfly needle. "Just relax."

"What are you going to do? Am I getting medicine?"

"No. I'll draw a little blood. That's how these treatments go. We draw a little blood and have it tested. Then we'll know how to proceed."

Pixel felt the needle go in, hoping it would hurt less as the weeks went by. She watched Aunt Kate pluck two identical glass tubes from a rack on the table. Their labels said "6 ml". Deftly, her aunt attached one to the needle as Pixel thought about all the other girl cousins who had come before, wondering where they were. The first tube filled; while her aunt attached the second, Pixel thought about Peter. Somehow her thoughts always came back to Peter. *Why does Uncle Mac want him so badly? Can't be for anything good.*

Before long, Aunt Kate was slipping the needle out, and there were the two tubes on the table, full of blood. Something wrong with her blood.

❦ ❦ ❦

It was after midnight. Pixel was wide awake, listening to the crickets in the fields beyond, the creak and pop of old wooden beams, an occasional car passing along Main Street. Everyone else in the house had gone to bed hours ago. The night was warm, and everything was still. Too still.

She was used to the sound of sirens and garbage trucks; Dad coming home at three A.M. talking loudly and banging around in the kitchen; Mom's snoring and her brothers stumbling to the bathroom; the neighbor's stereo going till late; and the noise of lots more cars.

She heard a scraping sound from somewhere in the house, then the squeak of a door hinge. Must be Aunt Kate or Cook. They had rooms on the floor below.

Pixel lay there trying to guess, by the sound, who was up in the night, but what she heard was a slow, heavy tread that didn't sound like the women.

In her mind, she followed the footsteps along the length of the second-floor hallway. The bathroom was at the end, right near the stairs, but the footsteps didn't stop. Probably the person was headed down to the kitchen for a late-night snack.

Then she heard a clump on the stairs.

Slowly, the heavy footsteps mounted the steps to the third floor. *Clump, scrape, clump, scrape.* It sounded as if the person was dragging one foot.

Clump, scrape, clump, scrape. The footsteps reached the top of the stairs. Pixel sat up in bed. *Clump, scrape, clump, scrape.* The heavy tread came down the hall, and she felt the hair on her arms rise. *Clump, scrape, clump, scrape.* The footsteps stopped at the door of her room.

The only light shone up from Thorny's storefront across the street. In the dimness, she could see her white door. It wasn't locked. She held her breath, waiting. All within and without was very still. Even the crickets had stopped singing.

She wanted to get up and shout, "Who's there?" Or throw open the door and surprise whoever was lurking. It's what she would have done at home. But here, in this moment, she could hardly breathe. She felt her blood freeze as the presence on the other side of the door sucked her into a pitiful darkness. She sat there, paralyzed, waiting. Then slowly, the presence drew back. *Clump, scrape, clump, scrape.* It moved down the stairs and along the lower hallway. She heard a door shut, and then silence.

Trembling, ice cold, she shrank down under the blankets and lay staring out the window till dawn.

❦ ❦ ❦

Pixel slept way past breakfast, so it wasn't until lunch that she had a chance to talk to Cook.

"I heard someone walking around the house last night. It didn't sound like you or Aunt Kate."

"You must have been dreaming."

"I was wide awake."

Cook laughed. "Maybe it's spooks!"

"Whoever it was started on the second floor, then came upstairs and stood at my door."

Cook looked away and began setting silverware on the table. "It's just me and Kate on the second floor. Maybe Kate walks in her sleep! Ha ha!"

Pixel had a lot of experience with liars. She could tell Cook was holding something back, but she dropped the subject.

When she finished eating, she went quietly to the second floor and tiptoed along the hallway. At the far end, she found a stiff white curtain that, from a distance, had looked like a plain white wall. She stepped behind it and saw a short, narrow passage. Following it around a corner, she stood in the dim light, looking at a dark wooden door. A strong odor hung in the air. It reminded her of snakes.

A nameless fear crept over her mind. Instinct told her to run, but she mastered herself, turned around, and walked slowly out of the passage. Once past the curtain, she sprinted to the other end of the corridor, shut herself in the bathroom, and vomited her lunch into the toilet. Then she went downstairs and sat on the front porch for a while with her head between her knees.

She should go to her room and lie down, yet she couldn't bring herself to go back into the house. Instead, she got up and walked across the street to Thorny's Goods. She needed to find Peter.

Thorny's was a big log cabin, two stories high, with a peaked roof. There were curtains at the second-story windows, suggesting a cozy apartment. The windows fronting the street on the first floor were large and slightly dusty, sporting an array of goods: baseball mitts, spools of fishing line, cast-iron fry pans, and garden tools. The wooden door on the west end of the building bore one sign saying Open and another that said Bait for Sale. Pixel pushed open the door and heard a bell tinkle, just like the one at Mrs. Murdle's Diner.

Inside, under bright ceiling lights, she saw plank walls covered with old poster advertisements and framed landscapes. Beneath the posters were well-stocked shelves running the length of the room. A wooden checkout counter stood near the door, piled with an assortment of candy, cigarette lighters, and bottle-opener key chains. The back of the old metal cash register was covered with colored magnets. Pixel had never seen such a place.

The only person in the store was a young woman behind the counter, bent over an account book. She looked up. "Can I help you?"

"I ... I saw my friend come in here yesterday. Peter. Peter Thornburg. Does he live here?"

"No. I took him to my aunt's place. Up north at the Big House." The woman paused. "Your name is Pixel, right?"

"Did he tell you about me?"

"Yeah. I'm Annette, his cousin.

"Is the Big House very far?"

"It's a thirty-minute drive north. But I'll pick him up next week and bring him here to see you. Promise."

"Sure." She felt suddenly forlorn. "Okay, thanks."

"Do you want my aunt's phone number? I'm sure she won't mind if you call Peter."

Pixel hesitated. "I'm not allowed to use the phone at … at the house."

"Well, you can use our phone anytime. Do you want to call him now?"

She liked Annette, but for some reason, Pixel felt her confidence ebbing away. "Thanks, but I have another treatment pretty soon. I better go."

"Well, like I said, anytime."

Pixel walked out into the sunshine and stood on the curb, directly across the street from the Rilson house. It was a windy day. Looking up to her third-story bedroom, she saw the white curtain fluttering from the open window. The house was a quaint, old-fashioned place, painted white, with two peaked gables, but for some reason it puzzled her. To the left of the neatly trimmed front lawn, the driveway ended at a small carport, and on the other side of that, more grass. On the right, extending from the corner of the house, a tall laurel hedge grew in front of a high brick wall. The tops of dark evergreens were visible on the other side. A sudden gust swept the branches aside, and for a split second, Pixel saw a dark window and another roof beyond the wall.

"That's why," she whispered. "That's why the house seems bigger on the inside. I knew something was weird." Crossing the road, she walked up the drive, past Aunt Kate's car, and into the empty carport. At the back, she saw a white door and opened it.

"Oh!" she breathed, caught off guard by the wild beauty of the garden. A line of apple trees grew along the low stone wall at the very back, and rose vines in full bloom trailed along the ground. A small cement pond, half full of murky water, lay in the center of a weedy lawn. With sudden force, she was struck by the realization that in Lang she'd never seen leaves or grass so green or flowers of such vibrant colors. "I wish Mom and Dad could see this. Maybe they wouldn't be so sad and … and gray." "Gray" wasn't quite the right word, but she knew what she meant.

For a while, she walked all around the garden, gazing at the blooms whose names she did not know and the apple trees that stood like gnarled old men and women raising leafy arms to the sky. Unkempt though it was, to her it was an enchanted place surrounded by a mist of green and blue. Then, in the middle of the stone wall, she spied a little wooden gate that led from the back of the garden. Irresistibly drawn, she opened it and walked into a grove of white birch trees. This was the green haze above and beyond the apple trees that her eyes, unaccustomed to beauty, had not at first taken in as trees. She stood on a narrow track among the slender white trunks, pretty sure she'd just entered fairyland. Midsummer grass lapped her ankles as she walked through this magic place. If she'd seen a tall elf coming to meet her, she would not have been surprised.

Her curiosity about the hidden wing of the house forgotten, she followed the trail straight through the birch grove, all the way to the bluff above the sea. Here, a wider dirt track along the edge of the cliff served as a public pathway, and a set of wooden stairs went down to the beach. Standing at the edge of the fairy birch grove, she looked toward the bright expanse of sea and blue sky, feeling the wind whip at her clothes. Then, to her left, she saw a thick laurel hedge, just like the one at the front of the house, and her curiosity returned.

The hedge grew against the high brick wall that completely enclosed the hidden wing of the house and its copse of dark trees. At the farthest end of this secluded garden, Pixel found a gap in the thick hedge and, in the outer wall, a latchless iron door. Standing on the footpath, with her back to the sea, she hesitated. "What's in there?" she whispered. Then, "Who's in there?" Someone besides Aunt Kate or Cook, she was sure. And the only way in or out was through this black door or ... or through the part of the house hidden behind the white curtain. She shuddered. There was no way she'd go back through that curtain again. Just the thought of it made her queasy.

"Pixel!"

That was Aunt Kate. Was it already time for a blood treatment? Ducking into the gap, she crouched by the iron door. Her aunt called again, nearer this time. "Pixel!" She heard footsteps on the rocky ledge, then a sound like someone thumping on wood.

"Hello there, Kate Rilson. Lost one of your girls again?"

Peering around the hedge, Pixel saw an old woman at the top of the beach stairs. She held a wooden staff, which explained the thumping noise.

"What are you doing here?" Aunt Kate said in a peeved voice.

"I hope you don't mind my using your stairs," the old woman said. "Mine have gotten so rickety I don't quite trust them anymore."

"Then you better get them repaired."

Pixel inched forward to get a better look at the old woman. Something about the round, wrinkled face and cloud of white hair attracted her.

"I saw a newcomer on Main Street yesterday. By her blond hair, I'm guessing she's one of yours. What's her name?"

Aunt Kate took a step back, and Pixel could see her frowning profile. "I don't see what business it is of yours."

"I only asked her name."

"Pixel."

"Unusual," the old woman said, and she glanced toward the hedge and met Pixel's eye. Pixel pulled her head back.

"I thought she might be here at the beach," Aunt Kate replied, "but obviously not."

The woman did not reply, and there was a long silence. Was Aunt Kate still there? Then a soft voice said, "She's gone now. You can come out," and Pixel froze, looking up into the merry face. The woman winked and passed on, stumping slowly away along the bluff.

Pixel watched until she was out of sight, then went back toward the house. She'd better get upstairs to the treatment room. As she passed through the fairy grove, the enchantment entirely gone, she heard something. *Clump, scrape, clump, scrape.* She stopped by the hedge, her heart hammering. *Clump, scrape, clump, scrape.* The person was passing under the dark trees on the other side of the wall. She listened, paralyzed by fear. Then she heard a low laugh.

Like a hare released from a trap, she sprang away, running, without thinking of where she was going, out of the garden, down the drive, and away from the house. She tore along the sidewalk and barreled straight into the arms of a man.

"Whoa! Where are you going in such a hurry?"

Her heart still pumping with fear, she tried to get past him, but he held her firmly by the arm. She looked back, expecting to be followed, but the street was empty.

"You're Peter's friend. From Lang."

She looked at his face and saw strange eyes, the color of the bluest sky. "How do you know? Who are you? Let me go!"

"I'm Foster. Peter's cousin. Why were you running down the street like a wild woman? Did something scare you?"

"Yeah."

"Ah. Your blood treatments started. They don't waste time, do they?"

How did *he* know? Something about Foster made her want to kick him in the shins and run. But then he said, "You probably want to visit Peter. I can help you."

She stopped struggling and looked up into his expressionless face. "Really?"

His eyes turned inward and he let go of her arm. "Sure. I'll find you."

"Pixel!"

She looked back and saw Aunt Kate hurrying down the sidewalk.

"I gotta go," she said, turning to Foster, but he was gone. She looked around the street, but he was nowhere in sight. How could he just disappear like that?

"Pixel! I've been looking for you everywhere!"

"Did you ... did you see where that man went?"

"What man? You're late for your blood treatment. I shouldn't have to run around town looking for you!"

Aunt Kate began walking briskly back toward the house, and Pixel followed. They marched upstairs to the treatment room, past the bathroom and Cook's room on the right and Aunt Kate's room on the left. They were heading straight for the white curtain at the end of the corridor. Pixel felt a stab of panic; then her aunt opened the very last door on the right. As Pixel entered, her elbow brushed the curtain and she flinched. Standing in the treatment room, feeling cold, she sniffed the air but smelled only disinfectant. Hesitantly, she said, "Did the lab find out anything about my blood?"

"No." Aunt Kate jerked a drawer open. "More test material is needed. Every day for a while."

"Every day?" Pixel sank down onto the chair by the table. "Can't they tell if I have a disease from the blood you took yesterday?"

Her aunt frowned. "You have the disease. No question about that. Now hold your arm still." She applied the tourniquet, then donned a pair of latex gloves.

Pixel watched her take a glass vial, labeled "6 ml", from the rack, but only one tube this time. "I heard strange footsteps last night. Cook said it was spooks. Or you sleepwalking."

Aunt Kate started and dropped the tube on the floor. Sweeping the fragments aside with her foot, she took another. "It's Cook who sleepwalks. Now hold still."

She inserted the needle, and this time Pixel hardly felt it. The vial filled with blood, and then Aunt Kate was releasing the tourniquet, saying, "That's it. Same time tomorrow. And I don't want to have to come looking for you again."

Pixel stepped over the threshold, then turned back to ask a question, but the door shut in her face. She stood there, blinking. Then the door swung open.

"Why are you standing here?" Aunt Kate held the vial of blood in her hand.

"I ... I wanted to ask if I could visit my friend. Up north at the Big House. His cousin said he'd take me."

"You can't leave Foyle."

"But I ... I promise to be back in time for treatments."

Her aunt glanced sideways at the white curtain. "Cook will take you to Sweetwater sometime, but you can't go anywhere without one of us. In case you take a turn for the worse."

"But I don't feel sick."

"You *must* go to your room and lie down. Now. And after *every* treatment. If you don't, I'll take away your outdoor privileges."

"You ... you mean not leaving the house at all?"

"That's right."

Pixel stared at her aunt's stony expression and blank eyes. Instinctively, she stepped back, as if retreating from the edge of a sinkhole. Then she turned and walked blindly to the stairs. At the end of the corridor, she turned, expecting Aunt Kate to be at her heels. The hallway was empty, but the white curtain swayed as if someone had just passed through.

5

To Set Things Right

Peter opened his eyes and saw wooden beams in the ceiling. Where was he? "Dad?" A giant tongue licked his face, and a voice screeched, "Get out of here, you great lout! How many times do I have to tell you!"

Scrambling upright, Peter backed up against the headboard in time to see Muru whacking Moody Doug with a pillow. The great dog barked joyfully, and his tail knocked her over.

"Sit!" Peter shouted.

Moody's wagging tail swept the lamp from the bedside table.

"Not again!" Muru wailed.

Peter hopped out of bed as five Fennys ran into the room. Four of them cleaned up the glass, set a new lamp on the nightstand, and ran out.

The fifth fenny, Norbert, glared at him. "Boy, lamps don't grow on trees! We can't keep this dog in the house!"

"I thought he lived here."

"Of course not!" Norbert snapped. "He only appears when one of you does."

"Well, it's not my fault," Peter snapped back. "Doesn't he have a doghouse?"

Norbert continued to glare at Peter, but Muru said, "A what house?"

"A doghouse. You know. A house for a dog. In the backyard."

This statement was greeted by a short silence. To Peter's surprise, Muru said, "That's not a bad idea. Why hasn't anyone thought of it before?"

"Yes, and that idle garage crew could build it," Norbert mused. "Give them a useful occupation." He looked at Peter and for the first time seemed pleased. "Well, well. You may live up to your reputation after all. With your permission, I will take the dog outside and proceed with ordering the doghouse."

Peter stared. "Okay. Sure." To his amazement, Norbert bowed and left the room with Moody trotting meekly behind.

"Why did he ask *me* if it was okay?"

Muru began making the bed. "You people come and set things right. It's the task of the Silver-eyed."

"No way."

"Look, kid, you gotta find that Thornburg tome. But wait till I'm out of the room if you plan to read aloud like Jonas did. And you better change. I have a feeling the day's going to be pretty busy. You don't want things to start happening while you're still in pajamas."

She left the room, and Peter looked around helplessly. What in the world had he gotten into? Remembering the events of the night before, he fingered the lump on the back of his head, then felt the lump on his forehead. He needed to think things out, but as soon as he sat down in the nearest chair, the sound of shouting came through the open window.

Jumping to his feet, he looked out and saw Norbert and a crowd of Fennys chasing the giant dog across the grass. Moody stopped and began digging a hole right in the middle of the lawn.

"Good grief! He could dig to China in five minutes!" Peter threw off his pajamas, pulled on his clothes, and ran for the nearest door to the garden.

❦ ❦ ❦

Two days later, in the twilight before dawn, Peter sat at his desk, thinking about the doghouse that had taken shape on the back lawn. So far, it had a peaked roof and an arched doorway, and one of the Fennys was making a weathervane. Peter felt the fresh blisters on his palms. Life in Lang had not prepared him for swinging a hammer or giving orders. But it was good. He was beginning to feel as if he'd always lived here. Everyone at Wakkenburg was glad he'd come, except maybe Norbert—and Uncle Edward, who hardly spoke and never looked at him. Peter pulled open the desk drawer and took out the quill and pot of ink. He'd learn to use them. And he'd read the Thornburg book. Time to find out who he really was.

He picked up a regular pen, shut the drawer, then chose another postcard from the stack on the desk and wrote a few lines.

Dear Dad,

The dog I told you about follows me everywhere. His name is Moody. I wish you could see him. Tell Mom hi from me. And tell Mrs. Murdle that the food here is good. Thanks again for the postcards. This one of Magdalen Tower on May Day morning is pretty cool. Did you climb to the top? Things are fine but I wish you were here.

Peter

Yesterday, Aunt Marj had taken him shopping in Sweetwater. It was true that his Lang wardrobe was a bit threadbare. But he hated shopping, and she had made him wear dark glasses everywhere.

"Just a precaution, dear. So many of the island folks think we Thornburgs are a bit cuckoo. It wouldn't do to dredge up old rumors. And don't worry about money," she added. "You'll be inheriting the entire estate anyway. Actually, I think it might already be yours."

That thought startled him, and he went through the whole torturous shopping expedition, meekly acquiescing to anything Aunt Marj suggested.

Sometime during the night, the weather changed, and now it was raining hard. Peter got up from the desk and looked out the window to the west lawn. The sky was now a brighter gray, and in the growing light, he saw that the new doghouse had been painted white. After dressing quickly, he went outside, despite the rain, and walked all around the trim little building. It looked great. Too bad Moody wasn't here. Then he surveyed the garden, noting the blotches of white paint covering the gray stone walls of the house and a number of second-story windows. There must have been trouble with the new paint sprayer.

A door slammed, and Norbert came marching across the grass. "Look at the mess! This is your fault, boy!"

"Me? I wasn't even here!"

"Precisely! Good grief! Do you think I can manage them myself now that you've come?"

"I don't see what difference *I* make. Anyway, you said you'd get on fine without me."

"Clearly I was wrong. There's always a first time."

"Right. I'll help clean up," Peter said and went off to see the garage crew.

The rest of the morning, he stood in the rain with the Fennys, scrubbing at the paint on the walls of the house and thinking about the odd conversation he'd had with Aunt Marj the day before.

"Why can't we go shopping in Foyle?" he'd asked as they drove past the farms on Highway 21. "I could visit my friend."

"Because there are no clothing shops in Foyle anymore. Very few of any kind, really. Believe me, I'd *rather* go to Foyle. Spending the day in Rilson territory is *not* my favorite thing to do."

"Why are there so few shops in Foyle?"

"Because of the raids, dear."

"Raids? You mean like burglars or something?"

"That's right. They've been going on for a long time. Not very often, mind you. And that's why people in Foyle plant primroses near the front door, just as their grandparents and great-grandparents did."

"Primroses? Why?"

"To keep out the little people. The ones they believe are doing the raids, of course."

Hearing a loud rattle, Peter turned to see five Fennys hurrying across the lawn with an immensely long ladder, which they set up against the house. One of them scuttled up the rungs with a bucket and a brush just as the relentless drizzle turned into an outright downpour. Hoping the little guy wouldn't slip and fall, Peter went back to his work, but no matter how hard he scrubbed, or how hard it rained, the stone wall just wouldn't come clean. His shirt was soaked, and paint ran off his hands and dripped onto the grass.

Glancing at the Fenny beside him who was also scrubbing the wall but with far more success, he asked, "Furse, are there Fennys who live in the woods?" Renegade Fennys was the only explanation he could think of for Aunt Marj's strange story of mysterious bandits in Foyle.

Furse frowned. "No, sir, begging your pardon. It isn't natural for us to live anywhere but in a house where humans are."

"Then who raids Foyle?"

"It's not Fennys, sir." Furse paused. "My section of the wall is clean, sir. You can inspect it yourself. Shall I finish yours?"

"Well, if you wouldn't mind helping . . ."

Half an hour later, as Peter and the garage crew sat around the potbelly stove, passing a jug of berry juice, Norbert walked in, his dark eyes glittering. The jug disappeared and the whole crew with it.

"Clearly you haven't a brain in your head, boy," he said coldly. "Look at you! Wet to the skin and lolling about as if you have nine lives. If you so much as sniffle, Muru will flay you alive and I'll help her."

"We were just—"

"Into the house! Immediately!" Norbert said, pointing to the door.

Peter stood up to protest—he would not be ordered around like a small child by someone who was barely as tall as he was. Then Furse's face popped up behind the mower, grinning and winking. Another Fenny appeared behind Norbert's back, doing a dead-accurate impersonation. Keeping a straight face, Peter went meekly out the door as one of the crew stuck his head out of a barrel and mouthed the words *See you later.*

Norbert escorted him to the house in his cold, silent way and delivered him to the kitchen and a furious Muru.

"Norbert!" she shouted at the hastily retreating Head Fenny. "What do you think you're doing sending this boy out to work in the rain? Are you mad? It could have waited! It was just a little paint!"

Relieved that Muru's wrath wasn't directed at him, Peter looked around the kitchen for the first time. It was very large with a brown flagstone floor. Four Fennys worked at a stove where something that smelled delicious sizzled in a pan. A wooden table stood in the middle of the room with benches on either side. At its far end, a tattered armchair sat beside a hearth, where a little fire crackled. The table was piled with donuts and cake.

Moving toward the donuts, Peter suddenly realized that Muru was yelling at him.

"And what good are your silver eyes if you don't have enough backbone to stand up to that puffed-up excuse for a Head Fenny? How dare you let him order you around like that? Don't you have any brains at all? Here I am, wearing myself to the bone, taking care of your health, your looks—such as they are—your happiness, and even that oversized demented hound—"

"You've seen Moody?"

"And then you let Norbert—*Norbert!*—order you to work outside in the pouring rain!"

"I'm wondering where Moody is. Do you know?"

"Of course not! I only feed that giant flea-brained half-wit! Do you think I keep his schedule too? Are you listening to me at all?" she shrieked.

"Listen, Muru. I didn't know I *could* say no to Norbert. I thought he ran things around here."

"No, *you* run things around here!"

"Well, how am I supposed to know that when you're telling me what to do all the time?"

"Because you're here to set things right! I've told you! Are you deaf? And I suppose you haven't cracked that book open, have you? Running off to Sweetwater yesterday!"

Good grief. He'd been gone less than a day. Muru opened her mouth to say more when the door bumped open and Moody Doug trotted in, water streaming from his coat.

"*No!*" Muru shrieked as Moody shook himself.

"It's bad to stand around in wet clothes, Muru," Peter said, biting his lip to keep from laughing. Her wrinkly little face was frozen halfway between surprise and a scowl as water dripped from her hair and clothes.

Then Aunt Marj walked in. "Oh, here you are, Peter. I've been looking for you everywhere."

Moody rose and snuffled her hand. "Oh!" she gasped. "I felt that!" She reached up and stroked the big head. "I can feel his fur! And I can see him clearly again."

"Didn't you see him the other day?" Peter asked. "When he was in my room?"

"Just a general outline, like a shadow. And look! The Fennys! Why is everything clear now?"

"This is Muru," Peter said.

"Oh, Muru! How glad I am to see you!"

"It's because of the kid," Muru said, still scowling. "He stopped doubting. But he still better read that book."

"Oh, Peter," Aunt Marj scolded, "you're wet! Were you playing outside? What a silly thing to do."

"That's what I said." Muru began whacking at Moody Doug. "Out of the kitchen, hound!"

"Oh, I'll take him out. Let me." Aunt Marj laid her hand on Moody's neck. "Come along, dear. Isn't there a bone he could have?"

One of the Fennys offered a large beef bone.

"Oh, how lovely! Just the thing. Come now, Mr. Moody." And the great dog followed her out the door.

"You get out of those wet clothes," Muru said in a voice Peter dared not disobey. "Sit in that chair by the kitchen fire. Thrak," she said to one of the Fennys at the stove, "make sure he stays here till his hair is dry." Handing him a bathrobe that seemed to come out of thin air, she left the room. The kitchen Fennys disappeared too.

After peeling off his clothes and throwing them over a bench, Peter wrapped himself in the bathrobe, took a donut, and curled up in the armchair next to the hearth. Hearing the clunk of pans, he looked around and saw Thrak and the other Fennys back at work. They grinned at him. Thrak waved. A minute later, Aunt Marj returned.

"He's all settled in the new doghouse. With his bone." She sat down at the table, and immediately one of the Fennys brought her a cup of tea. "Thank you."

The same Fenny set a mug of hot cocoa and a plate of cakes and small sandwiches in front of Peter. "Thanks," Peter said, and the Fenny grinned.

"I was wondering," Aunt Marj began, "if you'd like to see Fenn House. It belongs to our family, and I try to go there once a month to make sure everything's alright. I'm pretty sure Fennys live there because someone's taking care of the place."

"Where is it?"

"North of here, on the other side of the marsh. It's on the map, remember?"

"What map?"

"The one hanging on the wall in your room, and then there's the map in the book." She paused. "I suppose you've been too busy to look at either. The Fennys do depend on you. There hasn't been a Silver-eyed Thornburg here for years and years. The last one, the one before you, was lost to us."

"Lost?"

"Yes," she said with a certain finality, and they sat for a moment in silence.

"Well," she said at last, looking out the window, "if it keeps raining like this, the Glenfaba will swell its banks and the second bridge will flood. Then we won't be able to get to Fenn House at all. Perhaps we should wait a day or two, until the weather is better."

"Would you be able to take me to Foyle? I want to visit Pixel."

Aunt Marj frowned. "How in the world did you come to be friends with that girl? Annette told me she's a Rilson."

He returned the frown. "We went to the same school in Lang. I got picked on pretty often, on account of my eyes. Pixel always defended me, and she's a good fighter. The last time I got beat up, she took me to the hospital on her bike."

His aunt looked shocked. "That explains the pink scar on your eyebrow. But where was your mother? Your father?"

"Dad was working. And Mom ... well, she doesn't go out much."

"Why?" Her expression became stern.

"Depression, I guess. Lately, she's started drinking. It all started after my brother died. And dad lost his job at the college."

"What? Isn't he a professor at the university?"

"Not anymore. He works at a diner. You know—an all-night restaurant."

"You mean he waits tables? But why did he lose his job?"

"He kept missing classes on account of Mom getting kind of sick after Daniel died. There were lots of reasons, and I've never understood them all. I don't think he was fired. I think he resigned."

"I should have asked more questions," she said, shaking her head. "But we can help them, you know. They can come and live here."

"Mom won't come."

"I expect she's afraid of what she's heard about this place. I know she read the Thornburg book after she married your father. He told me she loved all the family history, what she took to be folklore. Then you were born with silver eyes.... They didn't tell me about you at first. Not until you were two years old." She hesitated. "We can send money to your father. Surely that will help."

"Can we?" A sudden hope filled his heart, but he knew his dad. "He might not take it."

"We can at least try." Aunt Marj was silent again; then she said, "What about this girl, Pixel Rilson—she's here for the summer?"

"I don't know. However long her blood treatments take."

"Blood treatments. Oh, my dear ... Of course you must see your friend as much as you can. Even if she is a Rilson. Though I expect she'll never understand your life here." She got up, leaned down, and kissed him on the forehead. "You tell me when you want to go to Foyle, and I'll take you there myself." Then she left the kitchen.

His aunt's reaction did not make him feel better about Pixel's blood treatments. If anything, it increased the dread that sat at the bottom of his heart like a coiled snake. He sat there for a long time, staring into the fire, until he felt warm and sleepy. Leaning his head against the soft chair, he closed his eyes and gave in to the drowsiness that was stealing over him.

A sudden clatter woke him. Looking around, he saw Thrak, alone, washing pans in the sink. Outside the window above her head, steady rain fell from a leaden sky. Quietly, Peter got up and left the kitchen. He ran up the back stairs, went to his room, and put on the clean clothes already laid out for him. Then, going back into the corridor, he hesitated, wondering what to do.

The house was very quiet, and he could hear the ticktock of the grandfather clock that stood at the foot of the main staircase, the one that never showed the correct time. Three closed doors across the corridor confronted him, and in a sudden fit of curiosity, he opened the middle one. Stairs. Going up. Leaving this door ajar, he quickly opened the doors on either side, half expecting to find Aunt Marj's room or Uncle Edward's. Instead, he saw bedrooms obviously *not* lived in. Even so, the beds were made up as if guests were expected.

He passed through the middle door and took the stairs to the third floor. There was nothing of interest here: more rooms, swept and clean, with the beds all made up. Then, at the very end of the passage, he opened a door to a steep staircase. "Fourth floor," he said aloud, trying to remember how the house looked from the front. He was pretty sure there were only four stories in this building where the family lived. Aunt Marj called it the West Wing. He hadn't been told anything about the rest of the house or the stone towers.

At the top of the stairs, he found himself at the end of a long hallway. There were fewer doors here, but one was wide open and light shone out. He went straight to it and walked in.

A library. A very large one with high windows that let in the daylight, and many rows of bookcases. In the middle of the room stood a long wooden table surrounded by polished chairs, and on his right, a fire burned in a stone hearth. Peter moved toward the fire and warmed his hands, looking around.

"Can I help you, sir?"

Startled, he turned to see a very prim-looking Fenny in spectacles, standing at his elbow. Of course. He should have guessed there would be a librarian here. "Um, well ... I, uh ... I think I'm supposed to read a Thornburg book. Or something like that."

"Allow me to assist." The Fenny bowed, then hurried away among the stacks. Moments later, he returned with an enormous book. Laying it on the table, he lit a reading lamp.

Peter sat down beside the Fenny, who introduced himself as Fiak, and opened the heavy tome. No wonder Muru was bored by it! The book was a handwritten diary, and after turning a few pages, Peter realized that it was very, very old. The handwriting was difficult, the ink faded, the paper very fragile. Fiak offered to teach him how to decipher the ancient script.

"Could you just read it aloud?"

"Of course, sir." And Fiak turned back to the first page and began to read.

My name is Nathaniel Smith, though now I must go by a different name. My strange tale, surely the strangest that ever was, begins in the shipping warehouse where I once worked as a receiving clerk ...

One winter's night, I stayed late in the office to finish my accounts. Everyone else had gone home. Suddenly, the door burst open and a giant black dog entered, carrying a bristly little creature on top of his head. The hedgehog-like animal begged for help, telling me that pirates had attacked their ship. Believing that I was dreaming—how else could I hear a hedgehog speak?—I picked up my walking staff and rushed out to the wharf.

There I saw a magnificent white ship and a host of strange creatures, large and small, battling a band of ragged, half-drunk sailors. Being a strong, muscular lad, I dispatched one pirate after another with the aid of my thick wooden staff. As I fought, I heard more of the small bristly creatures crying, "Mac Lir! Mac Lir! Come to our aid!"

Finally, my staff broken, I found myself in hand-to-hand combat with a tall, dark, bearded man who kept throwing out his name, boasting that he, Ahab Rilson, was the terror of the sea and that he would avenge himself on the wizard Mac Lir.

"Rilson?" Peter interrupted. "I wonder if he's one of Pixel's ancestors."

Fiak put his finger on the place where he'd stopped. "Pixel? Who's that?"

"How long ago was this written?" Peter watched Fiak gingerly turn back a page, and there was the heading of the first journal entry. "Does that say 1599?"

Fiak nodded. "That's certainly a one, a five, and two nines."

"That's over four hundred years ago!"

"Is it?" Fiak went back to the place where he'd left off and continued reading.

With the help of the giant black dog, I fought Ahab Rilson to the end of the wharf and pushed him over the edge. As soon as the sea closed over the pirate's head, a white mist descended all around the ship. Then a strange man appeared, dressed in long silvery robes. His flashing eyes were as blue as the sky on a clear summer's day. Instinctively, I knelt before the man, who seemed to me a person of great power and majesty. The man approached, laid his hands on my head, and said, "My son, for your noble courage on behalf of my subjects, I bless thee."

I felt a burning sensation in my eyes that lasted several minutes. Moaning, I collapsed on the wooden pier and lay there until the pain ceased. When I opened my eyes, all the hedgehog creatures who had gathered around gasped, and one said, "Look! His eyes shine like silver coins!"

It was then that I perceived every creature clearly. Before, they had been more like phantoms or figures of half shadow, but now they seemed more real than the wharf on which I lay.

The old man, who called himself Mac Lir, told me that he and his subjects were voyaging to a new land where they would be safe. He urged me to come, saying that he would make me the father of a new race. And so, still believing that I was dreaming, I boarded the ship, which set sail that very night.

It was the constant seasickness, more than anything, that finally convinced me I was not dreaming. I had unwittingly left my home and all former acquaintances, bound for an unknown land, in the company of strange beasts and faerie folk.

Many days later, the ship's company sighted land, a midsized island in some northern sea. We sailed into a shallow bay, and I went ashore with Mac Lir and all the creatures. Lir claimed the island for himself, then made me the guardian.

He changed my name to Wakkenburg, which he said means "guard of my house". Now, whenever I look into still water, I see my own eyes shining back at me, like drops of molten silver. Is this an honor and a privilege that he has bestowed? To this day, I am not sure, but I have carried out my duties faithfully and feel a fondness for my strange shipmates.

Mac Lir did not stay on the island long. After his departure, I met the beautiful giants, who helped me build Wakkenburg House. Then all the creatures from the ship took to the woods and lived scattered over the island, though they visited me every so often. The following spring, I met the Merry Wanderers, a tribe of seasonal fishermen and hunters, and married the chief's daughter, and so the family line began.

"That is the end of the first entry, Mr. Peter," Fiak said, pouring himself a glass of water from the jug on the table. "And in case you're wondering, the family name changed from Wakkenburg to Thornburg somewhere along the line, though I don't remember why."

Peter nodded, looking around the paneled walls of the library, not quite believing what he had heard. Yet, in the stillness, he could almost picture Nathaniel, sitting in this very spot, dipping his quill in a pot of ink.

Then Fiak brought out a map and spread it on the table. It was hand-painted, showing the whole of the island in far more detail than the map at the ferry terminal.

"Mr. Peter, there's no mention of Fennys in this chapter. There's Bugganes and Washers and Arkan Sonney, the Moonjer Veggey and the Tarroo Ushtey. But no Fennys. I've always wondered where we come from. I've searched this library through, but there's never a mention of the Fennodyree."

"What about all the other creatures?"

"I haven't seen them for a long time. The Arkan Sonney—that would be the bristly creatures Nathaniel wrote about—were such lively little things. Curious and quick-tempered too. Always set the Christmas tree on fire, every year. It was purely accidental, of course, but everyone came to expect it.

"The Washers—according to your ancestors—kept to themselves, living up north on the Glenfaba River. Then there's the Moonjer Veggey, a proud folk, who rode white horses and bred little white hounds. Some say that when you hear the sound of wild geese in the night, it's the hounds hunting under starlight. The Tarroo Ushtey, which some used to call Mac Lir's cattle, lived in great herds along the Glenfaba.

But of the seven Bugganes there is little written. They were fierce creatures, living alone, haunting the island. We think Jonas, the second Silver, may have known them, but the bulk of his writings have never been found. There are only references to his journals in the chapters written by Maria Thornburg. And then, of course, there's the Moddey Dhoo. Maria wrote a lot about him."

"Wait." Peter paused. "Are you saying that Moody Doug came over on the ship four hundred years ago?"

"Certainly he came on the ship. We see him only when a Silver is in residence. That's how we knew you were coming. Several days before you arrived, he was scratching at the back door, wanting to be let in. I have no idea where he goes between times." Fiak tapped a hairy finger on the map. "All the other creatures are hidden in Wakken Wood, but they have not made themselves known for some time."

Peter's mind recoiled. If it weren't for the very solid presence of Moody Doug, he would think the whole tale a complete fiction. And what about Nathaniel? If his story was true, he'd been tricked. Mac Lir had changed his eyes to silver and taken him on a long sea voyage to an unknown land. Had he left behind a mother and father? A girlfriend? He got stuck in a story without being asked, and the story was still going on.

"Shall I read the next entry, Mr. Peter?" Fiak asked.

He shook his head. "Not now. We're going to damage this book. It's really fragile."

"Yes. Good thing there aren't many of you Silver-eyed or it would be in worse shape."

"Hasn't anyone made a copy?"

"Well, of course! Maria Thornburg copied it out by hand. I'll fetch that one for you."

"Yeah. You should put this one away somewhere safe. Under glass or something. A book this old shouldn't be left lying around."

"If you say so, Mr. Peter." Fiak disappeared among the stacks and reappeared a few minutes later with a leather-bound book a little smaller than the original tome. Peter opened it and saw that, indeed, it was handwritten. The title page said, "A Faithful Facsimile of the Original Diaries of Wakkenburg House, made by Maria Thornburg, 1852."

"Fiak, this is very old too. Is there no other copy?"

"Too many, if you ask me!" Fiak scowled. "Miss Marjorie made *machine* copies of Maria's copy."

Photocopies, Peter thought. *Good*. "Well, I better read one of those. My dad was a professor of history at Lang University, and he used to take me to the library's Special Collections. One thing I learned: You never, ever let ancient books like these sit around collecting dust and fingerprints. I think these two should be put under glass. Next time anyone wants to touch them, they should use cotton gloves. That's what my dad used to do."

Fiak's eyes widened at every word. "Yes sir, Mr. Peter. Under glass. Cotton gloves."

Behind Fiak, a number of other bespectacled Fennys appeared. An entire library staff!

"Do you have other books as old as these?"

"We might. Would you like me to check?"

"Yeah. They should all be preserved carefully. Don't you have a Special Collections section?"

Fiak rubbed his hands together. "No, sir. But I've always wanted to. Read about one a while back in a magazine Miss Marj brought home. I wasn't exactly sure what went into them. The oldest books, you say? We can do that." He clapped his hands, and three Fennys put on cotton gloves, lifted the ancient Thornburg book off the table, and carried it away. Two more librarians appeared and carried off Maria's edition. Then a Fenny touched Peter on the elbow and offered him a thick hardbound book. "The machine copy, sir," he said.

Fiak went off to supervise the new Special Collections Unit, and Peter opened the Thornburg book to the second chapter. Maria had written in a large, very legible hand, much easier to read. He had just come to the part where Mac Lir returned to the island after a long absence, when Fiak scurried by under a load of books.

"Is it still raining?" Peter asked.

"Yes, Mr. Peter. Like the great deluge."

He reached out and lifted six books from the load in Fiak's arms. "Don't you have a cart or something?"

"I don't know what you mean, Mr. Peter."

"A library cart. I bet the garage Fennys could build one for you."

"Thank you," Fiak said, looking slightly bewildered.

"Is there a floor plan of the house?"

The librarian's eyes gleamed. "The whole house? Even the sections that are sealed off?"

"Yeah. I . . . sealed off?"

"That's right, sir. The floor plan—I'll find it."

"Let me help you with these books."

"Oh no, sir. Just put them back on the pile."

Peter put the books back on Fiak's load and watched the little Fenny teeter away among the stacks. Then he folded up the painted map, stuffed it into his pocket, and went to the garage. He found the work crew sitting around the potbelly stove and was relieved that only one of them rose to offer a mock salute. The rest cheered and passed him the jug.

"I need something built."

"Come to the right place, mate!"

"A library cart." He described what he wanted and made a rough sketch on a paper bag. "It has to fit between the shelves without rubbing the spines. And it can't be too heavy."

"Sounds like a job for Krim." Laying hands on a fellow who still snoozed by the stove with his cap pulled over his eyes, they shook him, stood him on his feet, and put the jug between his lips. "Krim! Mr. Peter needs a spot of special work! Wake up and stop lookin' so daft!"

Krim took one look at Peter's drawing, then turned the bag over and drew a perfectly detailed model. "Of course, we'll need to take some measurements in the library."

"And we oughta stop by the kitchen for donuts," Furse added. "Shall we do that now?"

"Okay," Peter said.

Shouting and joking, the entire crew rumbled off toward the back door of the house.

The rain was still coming down. Peter sprinted to the doghouse and found Moody chewing on a bone. "There you are! Good boy!" he said and patted the great dog's head. Then, running for the back door, he bolted inside and was just passing the kitchen when he heard Norbert growl, "What do you mean 'on the way to the library *and* on the way back?' "

"That's what he said, boss. Don't blame me. Mr. Peter knows we were working hard and a bit hungry, so he sent us for eats before our next job *and* after."

Leaving the garage crew to fend for themselves, Peter ran up the back stairs, headed for his room. He could hardly wait for Dad to come and see the library. He'd be flabbergasted by the old books. Then he paused, mid-stride, in the corridor. What if Dad had already seen the library? Maybe he'd spent some summer of his youth sifting through the stacks. Maybe … And he thought of all the things his father should have told him and never did.

6

A Day in Foyle

Sometime in the night, the clouds cleared, and the day dawned bright and clear. Peter sat at his desk, trying to write with the quill. It was frustrating, and so far, he'd succeeded only in making splotches on paper and dripping ink all over his fingers. A phone rang in a distant part of the house. He put down the quill, sat back in his chair, and wiped his hands on a bit of flannel. How was it that Wakkenburg had something as modern as a telephone? Yet now that he thought of it, the whole place was an odd mix of past and present, like the electric lamp on his nightstand and the kerosene globe on his desk. The garage crew kept a push mower cheek by jowl with a large gas-powered riding mower. He'd also seen an assortment of handsaws hung up next to a power jigsaw, and about twenty hammers on a pegboard beside a cordless nail gun.

Staring idly out the window, wondering what to do next, he heard a tap at his door. He opened it, surprised by the sight of Uncle Edward.

"Good morning," Uncle Edward said politely, looking at the floor. He pulled a bony hand out of his trouser pocket and smoothed the stray hairs over his balding forehead. "Phone call for you. Annette. The phone is at the bottom of the stairs, just outside my study." Then he turned away and went down the hall to his room.

"Thanks," Peter called after him and made for the stairs.

Annette's news changed the day. "Pixel isn't well," he heard his cousin say. "She wants to see you."

"Could you bring her here?"

"No. That won't work."

"Why? Because she's a Rilson? If that's the only reason—"

"No, Peter. She can't leave Foyle. Because of the blood treatments."

"Oh." For a moment he'd imagined himself showing Pixel around Wakkenburg, maybe introducing her to Moody Doug—if she was able to see him. But it wasn't going to be like that.

"I'll pick you up in thirty minutes," Annette said and hung up.

After explanations to Aunt Marj and Uncle Edward over a hurried breakfast, he found himself speeding along Highway 20. He asked a few questions about Pixel, but Annette seemed reluctant to talk, so they rode in silence. Moody, not willing to be left behind, kept pace beside them like a black shadow passing through the trees, then disappeared before they crossed the bridge into town. As they passed the front of Thorny's, Peter saw a line of people waiting at the door.

"What's going on? A special sale?"

"There was a raid last night," Annette said. "Folks need to restock. I expect they don't have food for breakfast."

"Aunt Marj told me about the raids."

They pulled up behind the store, and Peter went through the back door, directly into the kitchen. There he found George and Mary finishing breakfast, and Pixel hunched in a chair. She looked up. "Hey, Peter."

"Hey." He was surprised by her pale face and the dark circles under her eyes. A plate of waffles sat on the table in front of her, but she wasn't eating.

"Mom, Dad," Annette said, "I'm going to open a little early. There's a line at the front door."

"That's fine, dear," Mary said, getting up to clear the dishes from the table. "Can you handle it alone? We should be back by one or two."

"Sure, but I'll need to run Peter home after dinner. Then I'd like to visit the cousins in Sweetwater. Might be home late."

George whistled. "Phew! What a night! I only hope the milk doesn't run short before we get back. Peter, sorry we can't stay to visit, but we've gotta dash. Going to Sweetwater right now for supplies."

"I can help in the store," Pixel said. "I know how to run a cash register."

"Do you? That would be a big help," Annette said. "But you better eat first."

"I'll help too," Peter said, "if you tell me what to do."

Annette tied on an apron and went through the inner door that opened directly into the store as George and Mary departed out the back.

In the sudden silence, Peter sat down next to Pixel. "Are you alright?"

She looked up with a wan smile. "Nice haircut. And new clothes. Thought I saw you in Sweetwater yesterday."

"You went shopping too? Annette told me you couldn't leave Foyle."

"Yeah." She avoided his eyes. "If I do, I have to be with Cook or Aunt Kate."

He was silent, watching her face. She was small and thin but had never looked frail before. "Is the house alright?"

"No! I'd give anything to go home!" she blurted. Then, in halting words, she told him about the hidden wing of the house and how she couldn't sleep at night because of the strange footsteps that came to her door.

"What do your cousins say? About the treatments."

"There's no one at the house but me and Aunt Kate and Cook. Aunt Kate says my cousins are in recovery, but she never says where. And another thing: My uncle Mac came around, asking about a Silver Boy."

"I know. I met him at the ferry terminal." He decided not to mention Foster.

"Peter, he's after you! He said ... Oh! I can't think straight." She put her head in her hands. "I can't eat or sleep in that house."

"These waffles look alright."

She looked up and smiled a little. "Yeah. Your cousins are nice." Then she picked up a fork. "You better wear sunglasses if you help in the store. Uncle Mac might come around."

"Don't tell me you're gonna let an old man scare you."

"I mean it, Peter. Something tells me things are worse for you on this island than they ever were in Lang." She pulled a pair of dark glasses out of her pocket and thrust them into his hand.

"Alright! Alright!" He laughed and put them on. Then, after Pixel had eaten a waffle, they went into the store.

They found Annette running back and forth between the storage room and the cash register as customers came in. She was relieved to see Peter. "Good. You're wearing sunglasses. You keep the shelves stocked from the storeroom. I've unlocked the deadbolt. Pixel, are you really feeling well enough to run the till?"

"I'm okay. But what did you mean by a raid? Were there burglars in town last night?" She moved behind the counter. "I didn't hear anything."

Before Annette could answer, a man came to the counter and banged down a carton of milk, three loaves of bread, four tins of peaches, and a box of biscuits. Pixel began to ring up his purchases.

"Morning, Mark," Annette said, bagging his groceries.

"Morning," he said without smiling.

Another customer, an older man, came to stand in line. "I always say I'm gonna move to Sweetwater, but I never do."

Mark grunted.

Turning away from the counter, Peter took off his glasses to scratch the bridge of his nose and nearly ran into a little girl. Their eyes met and she gasped. He shoved the sunglasses back onto his face, then put a finger to his lips. "Don't tell," he said quietly.

The girl backed up slowly, then turned and hurried out of the store.

A woman, with her arms full of bread and milk, got into line. "It's only been three weeks since the last one. Used to be it was manageable, you know? Once or twice a year."

"What are the police doing about it? That's what I want to know," said the older man.

"Primroses. Useless. I got five kids to feed." Mark took his bags and stomped off.

"Well," said the older man, as Annette packed his bread and milk, "I suppose it's good business for you."

"You know it isn't," Annette said. "We lose more than anyone, except from the storeroom, but we always give a discount the morning after."

The man sighed. "I know."

More customers came in. Annette left the cash register to Pixel for a few minutes to silence the bell on the door and to help Peter restock.

"It's always bread and milk," she told him as they took a load from storage. "And sweet things like cookies and tinned fruit. A few weeks ago, we had a whole case of honey disappear from the shelves, and our entire stock of coconut macaroons."

"Who does this?"

"Nobody knows. It's been going on for years, since before I was born, but it's gotten worse lately."

By noon, the milk was running low and the bread was entirely gone. A woman came in with two toddlers. She was furious.

"I already tried the bakery and they've got nothing! Not a crumb left in the shop. I've never seen anything like it! Where does it all go?"

By half past twelve, the rush was over. Annette closed the store for lunch, and Peter and Pixel helped make sandwiches in the kitchen. "I can get along on my own now," Annette said as they sat at the table. "You two should have some fun. Go to the beach or something."

When they'd done the dishes, she gave them a couple of ice cream bars and shooed them out the back door into the summer day. Taking a narrow side path, they walked around to the front of the store and stood on the sidewalk. "That's where I live," Pixel said, pointing to the Rilson house across the road.

"It looks alright."

She didn't reply.

Peter unwrapped his ice cream bar and took a bite. "Wanna see my dog?"

"Where is he?"

"Not here on Main Street. Let's try—"

"Peter!" She grabbed his arm. "It's Uncle Mac!"

Startled, he turned and saw the old man from the ferry terminal staggering down the street, his hat askew, his face unshaven. Then the man spotted Pixel. "Girl! Girl!" he shrieked. "Where is he? You know! You know!"

"Don't let him see you!" Pixel said, pushing Peter toward the door of Thorny's.

A small knot of people crossed the street and stopped to watch. Peter, glad he was wearing sunglasses, stepped quietly into the crowd.

"You know where the Silver-eyed boy is!" Mac lunged toward Pixel and she backed away but didn't run.

Then a police car stopped and two officers jumped out. "Rilson!" one of them said. "Are you making trouble again?"

Mac made another grab for Pixel, but the policemen took him by the shoulders and handcuffed him. "You're full of whiskey and moonshine," the officer said as he and his partner shoved Mac into the back of the car. They drove away and the small crowd moved off. Peter and Pixel were left alone on the front step of Thorny's.

"I don't like it," Pixel said. "This is different from bullies in Lang. He wants you for a reason."

Peter was silent. Things *were* different here on the island. He could see strange creatures, and according to Muru, he was expected to "set things right", whatever that meant. He looked at Pixel's anxious face. "Come on," he said and went around the back of the store.

Following an instinct, he crossed the gravel parking lot to the woods behind the garage. There he found a trail leading into the shadowy forest.

"Do you know where this goes?" Pixel asked.

Instead of answering, he led her a short distance down the path, then stopped and whistled. Two seconds later, he heard the sound of a large animal crashing through the undergrowth.

"Cripes! What is it?" she cried, backing up.

The crashing ceased, and a dense thicket of salmonberry parted. Out came a black snout, then a great sleek head and large pointed ears. Moody bounded onto the path and began to lick Peter's face.

He shielded himself from the giant tongue. "Argh! Get down! Sit!" The dog sat down on his haunches, quivering with joy. "Can you see him?"

Pixel stood there with her mouth hanging open.

"His name's Moody Doug, but we just call him Moody. Isn't he great?"

"He's ... he's bigger than a horse!" she stammered.

Peter grinned. "Moody, say hello to my friend Pixel."

Moody stopped bouncing and lay down at Pixel's feet. He put his head between his paws, then rolled his eyes upward and looked at her. Tentatively, she put a hand on his head and began to stroke the space between his ears. "He's so soft," she whispered. Moody's tail wagged lightly from side to side, and he uttered a deep sigh. Pixel grinned and the big dog sat up and snuffled her arm. Then, very nimbly, he started down the path.

"Hey!" Peter called.

Moody turned back, barked, wagged his great head up and down, and trotted away into the woods.

"He wants us to follow," Pixel said.

The huge dog led them deeper into the forest. When he disappeared through a clump of ash trees, they pushed past a tangle of branches and stepped into a broad, sunlit meadow.

Barking at them, Moody began racing around in quick, sharp sprints. He clipped Peter on the shoulder.

"What's he doing?" Pixel said.

"Tag!"

They raced after the great dog, darting this way and that as silver-winged dragonflies hovered overhead. Moody was impossible to catch, and the game ended when he tackled them both. They went down, laughing, breathless, rolling around in the grass. Then, leaning against Moody's flank, they lay there, panting. The giant dog's tongue lolled out, ridiculously big and pink.

"Look," Pixel said, pointing at a gap in the trees. "A river."

"I'm thirsty." Peter got up and headed for the water. Pixel followed him across the meadow and past the line of cottonwoods that stood near the river's edge. In this place, the clear water cascaded over rocks, swirling into a wide pool.

Pixel immediately took off her shoes and stepped in the water. Peter joined her, and they cupped their hands to drink, then splashed their faces.

Then Moody jumped into the pool and rolled in the shallows. When he stood up, Peter said, "Uh oh." Pixel shouted and ran back to the bank, but it was too late. There was no escaping the spray of water when the giant dog shook his coat.

After that, they went back to the meadow and flopped down on the grass to dry in the midday sun. Twirling a stalk of grass between his fingers, Peter watched blue damselflies hover among the wildflowers. Swallows swooped overhead. He followed the soaring path of an eagle as it circled above the forest in the sun-white sky. "See that tree over there? I bet we could climb it. Race you ..."

He turned. Pixel had fallen asleep with her head propped against Moody's side. Moody thumped his tail a couple of times, then put his head between his paws.

Stretching out, Peter looked up. The eagle was gone. He closed his eyes, soaking up the warmth of the sun, letting his mind drift ...

❦ ❦ ❦

"Peter!" He came awake with a start and saw Pixel leaning over him. "What time is it?"

He sat up. The sun was behind the trees. "I don't know. My watch quit working."

"I can't be late for my blood treatment."

Walking quickly, they followed Moody out of the meadow and down the trail. At the edge of the woods, he stopped and sat down, so they left him there and went across the parking lot, then around the side of the store. Before they crossed the street, Pixel said, "You better put on the sunglasses."

In the Rilson house, Aunt Kate stood waiting in the front hall. "You're right on time," she said, and then, to Peter, "Who are you?"

"This is my friend from Lang that I told you about," Pixel said.

With a look of disdain, Aunt Kate turned and went up the stairs. They followed, but on the landing, the woman turned and looked at Peter. "Where do you think you're going? Wait outside."

He saw Pixel redden at her aunt's rudeness. "I won't be long," she whispered.

Peter walked slowly down the stairs, then stopped in the front hall and looked around, curious. Through the open door on his left, he saw a bright dining room, the table set with white napkins and plates. A large vase of flowers stood on a sideboard. He recalled Pixel's dingy apartment in Lang, where the kitchen sink was often full of dirty dishes. Clearly she was in a nicer place.

Not knowing how long the treatment might take, he went outside and walked around to the back garden. Pixel had said something about a path to the sea. He found the little back gate and went through the grove of birch trees, all the way to the edge of the bluff. It was warm and there was no wind. He stood at the top of the beach stairs, looking at the sea in the white afternoon light.

Somewhere behind him, a door banged shut. Turning back to the Rilson house, he paused. *Clump, scrape, clump scrape.* Someone with a bad limp was walking on a gravel path, and he remembered Pixel's story of the mysterious nighttime footsteps. *Clump, scrape, clump, scrape.* The sound came from behind a tall hedge that grew in front of a high brick wall. Peter spotted the iron door just as a key scraped in the lock. A shrill alarm sounded in his mind as the door swung slowly outward.

"Moody! Down!" a merry voice cried.

His heart hammering, Peter turned and saw an old woman coming down the footpath. Moody Doug pranced beside her, nosing the basket on her arm. The iron door shut, and the key turned in the lock. As the woman came up beside him, the limping footsteps receded, scraping over an unseen path. A distant door slammed shut, and Peter let out a long breath.

"Are you waiting for someone?" the woman said in a low voice.

"My friend Pixel."

"Ah yes. I know Pixel."

He was distracted by the woman's staff. It was of some sturdy, light-colored wood, intricately carved with flowers and shapes of odd creatures. He watched her take a large bread roll from her basket and toss it to Moody, who swallowed the roll in one gulp. Then, pressing a bread roll into Peter's hand, she said, "Young man, if you truly love your friend, you will help her get away from this house." She looked meaningfully toward the closed garden and, without another word, walked away along the bluff.

Peter watched until she was out of sight. Then he went back through the birch grove with Moody at his heels. At the garden gate, Moody stopped and Peter went on alone, around to the front porch, where he sat down on the bottom step. Taking a bite of the soft bread, he thought it was the best he'd ever tasted and wondered whether the old woman had a bakery in town. That must be how she'd met Pixel. Then it struck him that the woman knew Moody's name, and the more he thought about this, the more it puzzled him.

A few minutes later, Pixel came out the front door looking pale. She and Peter crossed the street in silence, going around to the back door of Thorny's. George and Mary were working in the store, but Annette was in the kitchen, waiting for them. Supper was a quick and simple affair of ham sandwiches and potato salad. As they ate, Annette asked about their afternoon but didn't question them closely. Peter could tell she was preoccupied.

He said goodbye to Pixel at the back door while Annette loaded the car with a few supplies for Aunt Marj. "I'll come back as soon as I can," he said.

Pixel picked listlessly at a loose thread in her shirt. "Sure."

"I'll send you messages by dog. Big dog."

She looked up and smiled a little. "Really? Will he do that?"

"Yeah."

She started picking at the thread again. "You shouldn't come back here. It's not safe."

"I heard those weird footsteps you were talking about."

"Time to go!" Annette called.

He got in the car and Pixel waved. Then she walked away and disappeared around the side of the building.

As they drove out of the parking lot and turned onto Main Street, Peter saw her cross the Rilson lawn and go into the house. "Do you think she'll be alright?" he asked.

Annette didn't answer. She turned on the radio, and a voice said, "This is Sweetwater AM 780. Rain tomorrow and Friday, with a chance of thunderstorms."

7

The Girl in the Woods

She ran on and on, away from the lake, until her legs burned and she was out of breath. Collapsing on a bed of soft moss at the foot of a tree, she lay there, panting, listening for the sound of pursuit. The woods were silent.

She sat up, pushing the hair out of her eyes, and saw a sunlit clearing. Birds twittered and darted into the nearby trees. She got up and then waded through chest-high grass to the other side of the meadow, where bushes grew, full of big blue berries. Hungrily she ate, plucking the fruit as fast as she could until the pain in her stomach was gone. As she sucked the purple juice off her fingers, her gaze traveled inward to the place where Mother was smiling.

"Jen, we're going to the fair! Put on your new sweater!" Looking down at her too-tight sweater, she saw the little white buttons hanging by threads.

Someone grunted and she heard a twig snap. Startled, she looked up and saw a man come out of the forest. He had pointed ears and wore leather breeches and a dark vest that hardly covered his naked chest. Their eyes met. Staring helplessly at his leering face, she sank down into the tall grass.

Suddenly, a tremendous swarm of silvery hornets rose out of the bush beside her. Like a cloud, it hovered in the air, right over her head, buzzing. Then, without warning, the woods all around the clearing erupted in a fierce storm of flying sticks and lashing limbs. The buzzing rose to an angry pitch as the hornets swept toward the man. She glimpsed his mouth opened wide, heard him scream. Then a prickly branch clapped her on the shoulder. She sprang to her feet, turned, and took off running.

The forest parted to make way as the trees keened wildly. She ran and ran, and when she could run no more, she slowed to a trot, but she never stopped moving because the trees were always at her heels, closing the path behind. She halted once and sat down to rub her sore feet, but a leafy branch swept down and prodded her shoulder.

A long time later, as daylight began to fade, she stumbled wearily into a shaded clearing and flopped down on the grass. The forest moved in closer until she was surrounded by broad gray trunks and rustling leaves. Listening to the silence of the woods, she curled up on her side. "Mother?"

No one answered. Something brushed her face, and she looked up into the tendrils of an alder sapling that had drawn near. It bent over her, and she wrapped her hand around the base of its trunk and cried herself to sleep.

The next day, the trees woke her with a rain of falling leaves. A path opened under the woodland canopy, and she continued on her way.

Sometime later, feeling prickles underfoot, she looked up into the branches of dark fir and cedar. In this region, the forest was close and still, with an air of watchfulness. Once, she heard a distant buzzing and saw the cloud of silver hornets passing high overhead. Then,

toward evening, the forest ended abruptly at the edge of a dirt road. She stopped, confused, looking up and down the wide, rough track. Accustomed now to the protection of the trees, she was afraid of walking in the open. When a branch prodded her back, she stepped onto the road and turned right, keeping close to the trees until a thick cedar limb swept out and blocked her way. Doing an about-face, she walked on with the lowering sun in her eyes.

After a while, she saw the roofs of buildings in the distance. Approaching cautiously, she came to the end of the dirt road and stood on the cracked paving stones of a village square. In the very middle sat a large, smooth slab of rectangular rock, like a table, higher than her waist. The village itself stood to the right, a cluster of weather-beaten buildings hemmed in by the forest. To her left, the woods stood dense and dark, growing right to the edge of the paving stones. Directly ahead, on the far side of the square, she saw an opening in the forest and the beginning of another road.

What now? The silent trees towering on her left offered no direction. She looked at the village again. It was familiar. Into the empty air, she said, "Floden?"

She walked toward the buildings, then stopped in front of an empty shop window. The bent frame of an awning dangled over the entrance. Mounting the steps, she examined the peeling red paint on the door. Then she pushed on the latch and jumped back as the whole thing fell inward with a resounding thud, sending up a cloud of gray dust. When the air cleared, she stepped over the door and looked around. Empty shelves, broken tables, and a litter of dry leaves. Brambles reached through a hole in the roof and hung from the rafters. Something stirred in her memory.

"This was the toy store," she whispered. "There was a bear in the window. Mother said she'd buy it for me. She must have. That's why it's not here anymore."

She left the shop and walked down a side street, looking through broken window frames, straight into the empty rooms of each wooden house. Flowering brambles and weeds wrapped the rotting porches and spilled over garden walls. Up one street and down another she walked, listening to the wind as it sighed and sung through gutted doorways and roofless buildings. A loose board flapped in a sudden gust, and a flock of startled birds shot out of a crumbling chimney. She froze, her heart pounding. Then the silence returned, and she went back to the village square. Through the gap in the forest, where the road continued, she saw a horizon of shimmering sea.

Going back to the toy shop, she sat down on the doorstep. In the vastness of the empty sky, a seagull called, and its lone cry pierced her heart. “Mother?” she whispered. “I’m back. Where are you?”

8

What the Bread Lady Said

The day after Peter's visit to Foyle, Pixel lay in bed listening to the morning rain. It was very early. She glanced at the chair propped against her door. If the footsteps had come in the night, she never heard. Pushing back the quilt, she sat up, but a wave of dizziness made her clutch at the mattress. When it passed, she stood up slowly, walked to the window, and opened it.

Breathing in the rain-washed air, she looked across the street and saw Moody standing on the sidewalk in front of the store, wagging his tail. There was no one else about. She waved and he yipped, bouncing on his front feet, wagging his head up and down. He wanted her to come.

She dressed quickly and crept down the stairs, stopping once or twice to catch her breath and listen for the sounds of Cook or Aunt Kate. They must still be in bed. She opened the front door, glad that the hinges didn't squeak, shut it soundlessly, and tiptoed down the porch steps. Suddenly lightheaded, she stopped and held on to the railing until the feeling passed. Then she crossed the lawn to the other side of the street where Moody was waiting.

He greeted her joyfully, snuffling her face, then led her around the side of the building to the back of the store, where another surprise awaited. The old woman she'd seen on the bluff—the one Aunt Kate didn't like—stood under the eaves, leaning on her staff.

"Hello, Pixel! I'm glad you're an early riser. Moody has brought a message from your friend." She held out a damp wad of paper, and Pixel saw Peter's handwriting.

Taking the folded paper, she read:

Hey Pixel, I hope you like this map. Aunt Marj says she'll bring me to see you, and she also says you can come here. You have to see Moody's new doghouse. When can you come? Send reply by DOG.

"Has he invited you to his home?" the old woman asked.

Pixel looked up and nodded. "But my aunt says I can't leave Foyle."

"Never mind what your aunt says. You go to your friend's place. And in the meantime, stay out of the Rilson house as much as you can. I expect Annette will be glad to have your help in the store."

Pixel wondered how this woman knew about Peter. Then another thought came to mind. "Do you know what happened to the other Rilson girls? My cousins?"

"Yes, dear. But you have two things going for you: an inquisitive mind and your friendship with the boy. Hold on to truth and friendship." Then she gave Pixel a knobbly sack. "Keep this with you. My bread will make you strong." She kissed Pixel's forehead and stumped away across the parking lot with Moody trotting beside her.

Pixel stood there, with the sack in one hand, the map in the other, watching them disappear into the woods. "Who are you?" she whispered. "And why do you care about me?"

Sitting down on the bench beside the back door, Pixel unfolded the damp paper and gazed at the hand-painted lines and drawings. Peter knew her love for maps. She opened the sack with her other hand, took out a roll, and bit into it. Mmm! It was the best bread! Maybe the best thing she'd ever tasted. She finished the first roll, then ate two more. The lightheaded feeling passed, and Pixel smiled to herself. Peter had invited her to the Big House. And the old woman had said to go there, no matter what Aunt Kate said. "Bread Lady, if you're Moody's friend, I trust you," she whispered.

The kitchen door opened and Mary came out. "Oh! Pixel! What are you doing here so early? Are you alright?"

"I . . . I wondered if Annette needs help in the store today?" Hastily folding the map, she pushed it into the big pocket of her sweater.

"Why, of course she does! Now, you come inside and have breakfast with us first. I insist!"

"Do you ... do you have a piece of paper I could use? I need to write a letter."

"Oh yes, dear. Upstairs in the big desk in the living room. You'll find paper and envelopes and everything you need. Breakfast should be ready by the time you've finished."

So it was that Pixel found herself in Mary and George's cozy apartment above the store. She liked it right away. Everything in it was old and slightly shabby. One wall of the living room was lined with books, and another with watercolor landscapes of the island. The windows looked out onto the street, and she could see her own bedroom window across the way.

Someone was in her room, moving around.

She stood there, holding her breath, watching Aunt Kate search the room, then pull the window shut and draw the curtains. Too much a Rilson to be either shocked or terrified, Pixel went to the desk, found what she needed, and sat down to write a note to Peter.

Rain pattered on the window, and a distant gull called. The lead of her pencil broke, and she fished around in the desk for a sharpener. When she finished, she went downstairs to the kitchen just as Mary was setting a plate of eggs and sausages on the table. George and Annette came in, and they all sat down to eat.

Pixel liked helping in the store, and the day went by quickly. Her blood treatment, usually at three, had been moved to five o'clock, so she returned to the Rilson house just before dinner. Aunt Kate was waiting in the front hall. "Where have you been all day?"

"At Thorny's." Pixel hung her sweater on a wall hook, hoping the pocket, bulging with bread rolls and Peter's map, wasn't conspicuous. But Aunt Kate didn't appear to notice. Silently, she started up the stairs, and Pixel followed her to the treatment room.

As she sat down at the table, she saw Aunt Kate take two six-milliliter tubes from the rack. "Why are you taking more blood today? That's as much as the first time. Is something wrong?"

"Stop chattering. I don't like to be distracted while I work. When this is done, go straight to the dining room."

Pixel sat very still. Something about her aunt's mood frightened her more than a posse of bullies. When the treatment was finished, she got up and left the room without a word. Aunt Kate followed, walking beside her.

At the bottom of the stairs, as they passed through the front hall, her aunt said, "You should never have made friends with those Thornburgs. Especially that boy. Don't ever bring him into this house again, and stop spending so much time at the store. They probably ask a lot of questions about us, right?"

"I ... no," Pixel began, when a sharp bang on the door startled them both.

"Let me in!" a voice shouted.

It was Uncle Mac. Pixel backed away from the door as Aunt Kate yanked it open. "Get off this porch," she said sternly, "or I'll call the police!"

Mac caught sight of Pixel. "Girl! Just tell me where he is! Then they'll stop sucking your blood! His life for yours!"

"Enough!" Aunt Kate shouted, shutting the door in Mac's face. "Pixel, go to the dining room this instant." Then she picked up the phone in the hall. "Deputy? It's Kate Rilson. My uncle's drunk, giving us trouble here at the house."

Pixel moved slowly into the dining room and sat down at the table, listening to Uncle Mac hollering, hammering on the door. Then came the siren. Flashing blue lights shone on the white walls and lit up the polished silverware and glasses. She heard Aunt Kate say, "Keep him as long as you can", then the murmured replies of the police. It was almost like home, almost like her life in Lang—the car doors slamming and the sound of the engine roaring away.

As Aunt Kate entered the room and sat down at the end of the table, Cook came out of the kitchen. "What was all that about?" she asked.

"Uncle Mac," Kate replied. "The police said he was making a fuss at Thorny's too. Can you believe it? They'll keep him until I get back from Lang. He won't bother you while I'm gone."

Cook paused, one hand on the lid of a serving dish, the other holding a spoon in midair. "You're going to Lang? What about the blood treatments?"

"I'm leaving Monday night. Be back Saturday by the five o'clock ferry. Pixel will take a break from daily treatments."

"Okay," Cook said. Silently, she began serving the meal, piling Pixel's plate with roast chicken and vegetables.

Pixel felt the tension between Cook and Aunt Kate, but her mind was filled with the image of Mac's face. What did he mean by "his life for yours"? He couldn't care less about her. She knew that. But he wanted Peter for some reason. She ate a few bites, then sat there for the rest of the meal, pushing food around the plate.

After dinner, she grabbed her sweater and escaped, running to Thorny's through the rain. She went around the back, then stopped, leaning against the wall, trying to catch her breath. She took a pencil and the note from her pocket, added a postscript, and slipped it into an envelope. Then she crossed the parking lot and stepped into the woods. A few feet along the trail, she stopped and whistled.

Sure enough, Moody came crashing out of the undergrowth. She hugged him around the neck, then gave him the letter. Chirruping deep in his throat, he turned and disappeared into the woods.

She returned to the house, climbing the stairs to her room slowly, and had just passed the second-floor landing when she heard voices.

"I'm sick of the whole thing," Cook said.

"I have to get away sometimes. It's been a year! Since the last girl—"

"It's a bad business, Kate. I don't pretend to understand. While you're in Lang, see if you can talk some other Rilson into taking this job."

"You can't leave now. Think of the contract, Liza. You have two more years."

There was a silence; then Cook said, "I should never have signed that! I want out!"

"You just need some time away. When I get back, you can plan your own holiday, alright?"

Pixel stood in the dark, her heart pounding.

"I want to move to the first floor. I hate being so near the ... that end of the hallway. It's the only way I'll agree to stay, contract or no contract."

"Fine. Take one of those storage rooms by the kitchen. Good night."

Pixel heard one door shut. Then another. She tiptoed up the stairs to her room, closed the door, and leaned a chair against it.

So. Cook didn't like living here either. Looking warily around her room, she saw nothing out of place. If she hadn't seen Aunt Kate nosing around, she wouldn't know anyone had been here.

Opening the window, she leaned out into the gathering dark. Across the street, she could see the light on behind the curtains in the Thornburg living room and, below it, the sign, Thorny's Goods: Since 1891. She saw Annette's car come down the road and turn at the corner. Then it began to rain harder, so she pulled her head in, but she didn't shut the window. Somehow she couldn't stand the thought of being completely closed in the house all night.

After changing her clothes, she got into bed and pulled the lamp on the nightstand closer. Sitting in the small pool of light, she opened Peter's map and picked up a small magnifying glass she'd borrowed from George. Rain pattered against the roof. Somewhere nearby, an owl hooted. With the lens, she moved over every inch of the map as island towns came to life. In Wakken Wood someone had painted Granite Lake and the Glenfaba River. A line marked "Old Road" went from Wakkenburg House to a village called Floden on the northwest coast. And Wakkenburg House was a castle with towers! Why hadn't Peter told her that? Then, holding the lens over Foyle, she saw an exact illustration of the town as it must have been many years ago. There was Thorny's, and across the road, the artist had drawn a snake. Underneath, in tiny letters, was the title "Rilson House". That was strange.

Her eyes grew heavy. She folded the map, put it under her pillow, and switched off the lamp. Gradually, her thoughts merged with the sound of the rain. In her mind's eye, she saw Moody running through the dark woods with her letter clenched between his teeth. Then her thoughts flowed into muddled images of Mac Rilson shouting, "His life for yours!" and Cook saying with a sigh, "I wish I could go home." Into the middle of her dreams the Bread Lady appeared, holding the strangely carved staff, walking beside a big black dog over all the unmarked paths of the island.

9

Buggane

On Friday, Peter sat in the library, reading the second chapter of the Thornburg book while Fiak and the librarians scurried up and down the stacks, searching for the misplaced floor plan of the house. He had just come to Nathaniel's description of the Bugganes when Thrak hurried in and held out a damp envelope.

"Thanks," Peter said, tearing it open.

Hey Peter,

Thanks for sending Moody with the map. I met a lady who's friends with Moody. Do you know her? She knows you. I'm writing this from Mary and George's apartment. They let me use their desk. Then I'm going down to help in the store. Not much else is happening, except I got a library card yesterday so I can keep up with my book addiction.

I don't know when I can come, but thanks for the invitation.

Pixel

P.S. I just found out Aunt Kate is going to Lang for a few days and I won't have blood treatments! Could I come to Wakkenburg on Tuesday? Can't wait to hear from you by dog!

As soon as Peter had read the letter, he ran downstairs to find Aunt Marj. She wasn't in the kitchen or anywhere on the first floor. He was passing through the front hall for the second time when he thought of checking for the hearse, which was usually under the portico. If it was gone, she was probably running an errand in Foyle.

He opened the door. It was raining cats and dogs, and the hearse was nowhere in sight. Then he heard a horn blaring.

The sleek black car came tearing out of the woods, careening wildly down the drive, its wipers flapping, all the windows fogged. With a screech of brakes, it stopped under the portico and the door flew open. Aunt Marj sprang out of the driver's seat.

"Fenny!" she gasped, pointing to the back of the hearse. "Bleeding!"

Peter leapt to the rear door and yanked it open. A small figure with torn clothes and a bloody face lay on the bench. "Muru!" he hollered. Five Fennys ran out of the house. "We need a stretcher! Quick!"

Even before the house Fennys understood what was going on, the garage crew came running through the gate, crying, "That's Mr. Peter's call! Get out of the way!" Furse, Krim, and the others took one look in the back of the hearse and began shouting. "Get the old aluminum stretcher, boys! Run for the tarp! And someone bring the jug!"

"Shall I call the doctor?" Aunt Marj asked. "Should we take him to the hospital?"

"They might not be able to see him."

Moments later, Furse and the crew came out with a stretcher, followed by Norbert, six kitchen Fennys, and the entire library staff.

Then gently, oh so gently, Peter and Furse lifted the Fenny out of the hearse. As they laid him on the stretcher, he opened his eyes, saw Peter, and murmured, "Wizard. Help us." Then he passed out again. They bore him through the front door, down the back hall, and into the kitchen, where they set him before the fire.

Muru charged in. "Hot water!" she barked. "Clean towels! Move!"

"Who is this?" Peter asked.

"It's Rumun," Norbert replied. "Head of Fenn House. How did this happen?"

"Later, Norbert." Muru pushed him aside and began cutting away Rumun's shredded clothing. "Send the librarians out and keep the kitchen crew moving. If you don't pull yourself together, we'll have every Fenny in the house bawling and completely useless."

Furse appeared, holding up the jug. "This'll help. Give him a swig. He'll perk right up."

"Thanks, Furse. Put it down over there and tell Thrak we need a room. Better make it on the ground floor."

When Rumun was finally settled in a room near the kitchen with three Fennys to look after him, Peter went to find Aunt Marj. She was alone in the sitting room, having a cup of tea. "How is he?" she asked.

"He's cut up pretty bad and still isn't conscious, but Muru thinks he'll be okay. He's from Fenn House, the place you told me about the other day."

She sighed and shook her head. "For some reason, the thought of Fennys alone in that place has been bothering me for days. But you have to cross two bridges to get there, and whenever it rains like this, the second bridge floods. Today I decided to check on that second bridge, just in case. If it was clear, I was going to come back and get you."

She put her cup down and leaned forward. "You have to understand, Peter. The wipers on the hearse are old, and it was raining hard, so I couldn't see very well. Halfway to the second bridge, this huge black shape appeared in the middle of the road. Even before I put on the brakes, the car stopped. I mean ... the car was stopped ... by the thing in the road."

"You crashed into it?"

"No! The hearse was ... held. The wheels spun till I took my foot off the gas. Then the huge black thing seemed to shrink, and an old man came around and knocked on my window. When I rolled it down an inch, he said, 'Someone needs your help.' He was such an old man, and his face was so kindly. Somehow, I wasn't afraid. So I got out and followed him a little way off the road, and there was the Fenny lying in a puddle."

She stopped again and gazed at the fire. "The old man seemed to know me. He said, 'Take this fellow back to the Big House.' Then he lifted the Fenny in his arms, carried him to the hearse, and put him in the back. When I turned to thank him, he was gone. Just like that. Of course, I came straight home." She paused. "There's one more thing, Peter. As that old man laid the Fenny in the car, he gave me a message: 'Tell the Silver One we're waiting. It's time.' And then he wasn't there."

"Who is he?"

"I'm not sure, but ..." She picked up her cup, and her hand trembled slightly. "Peter, I think he might have been ... that is, I think he's ..." She stopped and bit her lip. "I think I met a Buggane."

Peter did not know what to make of his aunt's story. He sat there, looking at her lined face, not sure what to say, and was startled by the sound of someone hammering at the front door.

"Now, who could that be in this weather? Did you hear a car?" Aunt Marj got up, and Peter followed her into the front hall.

She opened the door and gasped. There, standing on the step, was an old man wearing a long gray coat but no hat. Water streamed from his hair and whiskers. Smiling sweetly, he said, "I've got two more for you, ma'am. I expect you got room."

"Two more Fennys?" Peter asked, stepping out from behind his aunt.

The man whistled. "There you are. It's you who better come. And it'll be faster in that iron beast." He motioned toward the hearse parked under the portico.

Aunt Marj fetched raincoats, and they all got into the hearse. The old man let himself into the front passenger seat, so Peter sat in the back.

"Ain't never ridden in one of these iron beasts before," the man said, as the engine started. "How fast can it go?"

"Oh," Aunt Marj faltered, "not very fast. Where are we going?"

"Same place as before. You just take the old Fenn Road, and I'll tell you when to stop."

The hearse glided down the drive into the dark, secretive woods, and as they turned right onto Wakkenburg Road, the old man seemed to grow a little bigger. When they came to a wooden sign that said Glenfaba River and crossed the first bridge, the old man definitely grew a little more. Then he turned in his seat and looked at Peter with gleaming eyes. "Well now, boy. We been waitin' for you a long time."

"You're a Buggane."

"Indeed I am. I remember your great-great-great-grandsire. The one who came over on the ship with us." He winked and vanished. In his place sat a giant mole with curved tusks.

Peter backed up against the seat, his heart pounding. Aunt Marj lost control of the steering but didn't take her foot off the gas. The hearse veered from one side of the road to the other until Peter yelled, "Stop!" Then she jammed on the brakes.

In the silence that followed, the engine sputtered. Aunt Marj whimpered, and for some reason, this made Peter mad. "What are you playing at?" he said to the Buggane. "Don't try to scare us!"

Instantly, the mole vanished, and the old man appeared, tears running down his face. "Tom forgot himself, Silver One! He won't do it again."

Keeping her eyes straight ahead, Aunt Marj took her foot off the brake and eased the car forward. When they came to a fork, she took the right-hand road.

They were deep in the woods now, trees arching overhead, blocking out the gray morning light. The Buggane leaned forward, pointing to the left. "There's where we loaded up that first fella this morning. Slow down a bit."

The hearse crawled forward until the Buggane said, "Stop. Right here." Aunt Marj turned off the engine and they all got out.

"This way," the Buggane said and led them into the woods on the right side of the road.

The rain began to let up. As Peter followed the Buggane, he became aware that the path opened as they went forward. "Funny," he said aloud. "Almost looks like the trees are moving to let us through."

" 'Course they are, now you're here," the Buggane growled. "You think they'd move for me?"

He led them to a clearing where two enormous boulders stood side by side, one leaning over the other. Set deep in the earth, they formed a sort of lean-to, almost like a cave. Farther inside the opening, Peter saw firelight and a figure sitting beside two bundles. As they approached, a big hairy man stood up. "You brought him!"

The old man began to swell and turned into the giant mole again. "Aye, Tom. We come in the iron beast."

Peter looked warily at the hairy man. Probably he was another Buggane. So far, neither one appeared unfriendly. The hairy man picked up one of the bundles and slung it over his shoulder, and the giant mole picked up the other. Then, walking on either side of Peter, they went back through the woods, Aunt Marj silently bringing up the rear.

"These Fennodyree have no sense of direction, boy," the hairy man said. "Why did you send them into the woods alone?"

"I didn't. The one you found this morning is head of Fenn House. He said something about a wizard. I bet these two are from the same place."

"A wizard! This is bad!" the mole wailed and shrank into the old man. "It means Mac Lir is back!"

"If this is true, he has come because of the Moonwitch," the hairy man said. "She is growing in power of late, and you mark my words, Silver One: She will challenge Mac Lir, and there will be war!"

When they arrived at the car, Aunt Marj got into the driver's seat and shut the door. Peter opened the back of the hearse, and the Bugganes laid the unconscious Fennys inside.

"If Mac Lir has returned and taken over Fenn House, then there will be others. Go back to the house and wait for us," the hairy man said. "We'll come when we find them." And with a bang and a theatrical puff of smoke, the Bugganes were gone.

Peter got into the car. "Aunt Marj, how many Fennys were at Fenn House?"

"Twelve." She sat there, staring into space, and he wondered whether she was alright. At last, she turned to him. "Peter, when I was a girl, I wanted adventures like this. I read our Thornburg book over and over and used to dream of meeting the creatures of the woods." She stopped, and her eyes filled with tears. "I hoped they would help us find our little sister."

"What?"

"She was only four years old when ... when she was lost. It's all so long ago. Seventy years last month." She took a deep breath. "We went to Floden, you see, for the Periwinkle Fair. One minute I was standing in front of the toy shop with Ed and Mother and Jenny. She let go of Mother's hand and ran to the window, pointing at a teddy bear. Several people came between us, and when they passed, she was gone. She just vanished. We never found a trace."

Even as he asked the question, Peter knew the answer. "Was she the last Silver-eyed?"

"Yes." Aunt Marj's eyes, fixed on the windshield, had that inward look, and he knew she was deep in memory.

Suddenly, he understood why the Fennys hovered around him, why Uncle Edward never looked him in the eye. Even Pixel sensed the danger for him on this island.

Aunt Marj put the key in the ignition and started the engine. They drove home in silence, through the rain.

❦ ❦ ❦

When Peter and Aunt Marj got back to the house and pulled up under the portico, Muru was waiting at the door. By the time the two rescued Fennys were settled, and the excitement had died down, it was three o'clock in the afternoon. Peter had to tell the story of the Bugganes to Fiak the librarian, who scribbled away as he talked. Then the garage crew demanded a recital over a jug of juice, and the kitchen Fennys insisted on a private hearing while they fed him donuts. As they set a plate of sausages on the table, Peter sat up with a jolt. "Pixel!"

He found his aunt in the sitting room having a quiet cup of tea. Uncle Edward nodded at his entrance but kept his eyes on the fire burning in the grate.

"Oh, Peter, I've been telling Ed about our little adventure."

Peter glanced at his stone-faced uncle. "Aunt Marj, I got a letter from Pixel this morning. She wants to come here on Tuesday. Can we pick her up?"

"Oh yes, dear. However did she get permission? I thought the girls at the Rilson house couldn't leave Foyle."

"Her aunt is going to Lang for a few days."

"She's sneaking off? I don't want trouble with the Rilsons."

Uncle Edward cleared his throat. "If you won't pick her up, I will," he said gruffly.

Surprised, Peter looked up and met his uncle's eye.

"She's having them dang blood treatments, right? Those Rilson girls have it pretty tough," Uncle Edward said.

There was a long pause. Then Aunt Marj said, "Oh, Peter, you tell your friend I'll pick her up Tuesday morning as early as she likes. Never mind her aunt. If there's trouble, I'll . . . I'll . . ."

"Never mind trouble," Uncle Edward muttered.

Peter went upstairs, wrote a note to Pixel, and went looking for Moody, who was nowhere to be found. What good was a messenger dog if he wasn't around? Finally, Peter called Thorny's and talked to Cousin Mary.

"Don't worry," Mary said. "I haven't seen her today, but she'll likely be here tomorrow, and I'll tell her about Tuesday."

Later that evening, Rumun woke up, calling for his Fenn House crew. When he understood what had happened, he told Peter how the wizard, Mac Lir, had come to the house and thrown the Fennys out.

"Well," Aunt Marj said when Peter told her, "three down, nine to go."

❦ ❦ ❦

The next day, it stopped raining and the sun came out, which was good because Peter was busy. He and Aunt Marj made three trips to the woods with the Bugganes, who often took on frightening forms. At first, Peter thought they were showing off, but as the hours went by in the car or on foot through the forest, he decided that their forms reflected their moods.

To make matters more interesting, a third Buggane arrived early that afternoon, in the shape of a dog-sized spider. Aunt Marj nearly fainted, and Peter found himself scolding the fierce-looking creature, but that didn't do any good. It got mad, snapped its jaws, and changed into a huge scorpion with its tail arched for attack. Peter apologized as calmly as he could and explained that his aunt was afraid of spiders. "Can't you look like something with not so many legs?" he asked.

Immediately it took the shape of a giant hedgehog.

"We didn't ask Tom to come," the old man said, "but he heard about you. He's the only Buggane in these woods that can scare the livin' daylights outa the rest of us. Normally we're a quiet lot."

In the late afternoon, Peter was in the front hall, taking off his jacket. He'd just returned from the rescue of the sixth Fenny and was hoping to eat lunch before the Bugganes returned, when he heard a knock. Putting on his jacket again, he opened the door.

Foster stood there. Peter stared at him in silence.

"Hello!" Foster said in a cheery voice, though his strange blue eyes were like ice. "Aren't you going to invite me in?"

Peter heard the creak of a door, then footsteps, and there was Uncle Edward, standing beside him. "Who are you and what brings you to my door?" his uncle said.

Foster smiled, showing all his teeth. "I'm your cousin Foster! Peter must have told you that I met him at the ferry terminal."

"Do you work there? I've never heard of you." Uncle Edward's tone was very unfriendly. Peter glanced up and saw his stony expression.

"I arrived on the island recently. I meant to drop by earlier, to reconnect with family. Aren't you going to ask me in?"

"This isn't a good time," Uncle Edward said. "Folks in the house are sick."

Foster's smile faded. "Then I'll come back when it's more convenient." He turned and walked away.

Peter moved to close the door, but his uncle stopped him. "Wait," he said.

"Is he a Thornburg, Uncle Ed?" It was a roundabout question, but Peter didn't think his uncle would believe that Foster had disappeared into thin air.

"Peter, all your cousins have dark gray eyes. Never forget that. Thornburgs have gray eyes, like the sea."

"Not me."

"True. But the last time I met a man with eyes as blue as Foster's, another child with silver eyes lived here. My little sister, Jenny."

Foster was a third of the way down the drive, walking fast.

"And I'm willing to bet that if we go inside and close the door for a second—then open it real quick—the lane out there will be empty."

"Yeah," Peter said under his breath.

His uncle looked directly into his face. "Shall we make the experiment?"

Quickly, with one last look at the figure walking down the road, they shut the door for a fraction of a second. Then Uncle Edward flung it open, and the road was empty.

Peter felt a sudden gust of wind. "Will he ... will he come back?"

"I dunno, but here comes a Buggane. Either that or a giant mole with ivory tusks. I'll drive this time. Marj is looking pretty tired."

Minutes later, Peter found himself clutching the seat of the hearse. Uncle Edward drove it like a rally car, and the Buggane, shifting between the shape of the old man and the giant mole, whooped with delight every time they struck a pothole. "I knew the beast could go faster!" he cried.

This time they drove all the way to the last bridge before Fenn House. It was flooded, as Aunt Marj had said it would be. They parked and struck a path on the right, headed east through a leafy woodland. After a while, the forest thinned, and Peter saw the sunlit marsh spreading out on the other side of the river. As he walked through the tall grass, the ground became softer, muddier. The air was alive with birdsong and the sound of wind in the reeds.

The old man led them to the riverbank, where they found the hairy man and the dog-sized spider crouched over a small campfire. Beside them, on a litter made of branches and reeds, lay a Fenny. Peter noticed her long, dank hair. Her breathing was shallow, but she was conscious. As he looked down at her, she met his gaze and gasped.

The hairy man picked her up, and they all trooped back to the car with Uncle Edward and Tom Mole in the lead. The giant spider brought up the rear.

"How many left to find, Silver One?" the hairy man asked.

"Five." Peter was watching Uncle Ed, who seemed completely unconcerned about the appearance of the giant mole walking beside him. He heard his uncle say, "No, it's only got six cylinders. Won't go as fast as you think."

The Bugganes insisted on riding back to Wakkenburg, and Peter found himself pinned in the back seat between the spider and the hairy man. Uncle Ed drove at a reckless speed, as if the devil were hot on their tail. In a fit of high spirits, the giant mole rolled down the window, stuck out his head, and whooped the whole way up the drive. Not one of the Fennys would come out, and Uncle Edward had to carry the new arrival into the house himself.

There was one more rescue that evening. Uncle Ed drove again, and when they got back, Muru led Peter to the kitchen, where she tried to feed him soup and mugwort tea. He was almost too tired to eat.

"I'm worried about you," she said. "This last trip took too long. What happened?"

"The hearse got a flat, and it took a while to fix. Then we had to hike a few miles into the woods. This Fenny told us that the wizard called a heavy fog down around Fenn House. That's why they all got separated."

"Sounds like Mac Lir, all right. Oooh! I wish I could get my hands on him!"

"What would you do?"

"Poison his tea!"

* * *

At dawn the following day—the third day of what Fiak had dubbed "the Rescue Operations"—the old man Buggane arrived, banging on the door. They had found the ninth Fenny just south of the Old Road junction. It wasn't far, but Aunt Marj was nervous about the spare tire on the hearse and drove very slowly, complaining the whole time about island road crews who refused to work in Wakken Wood. Meanwhile, the giant mole dozed in the front passenger seat, and they had to wake him up to get directions.

When Peter returned, he ate breakfast in the kitchen under Thrak's watchful eye. Then, feeling in need of cheerful company, he went to the garage and was surprised to find Uncle Ed and the entire crew bent over the engine of a blue 1969 Datsun coupe.

"Mr. Peter!" Furse cried. "Your uncle's getting his car going!"

"Haven't taken this thing out in an age and a half," Uncle Edward said, without looking up. He took a tool from Krim and made a few adjustments. "There. That should do it." He got into the driver's seat and turned the ignition. The engine rumbled to life, and the crew cheered.

"I didn't know you had another car," Peter said.

"Oh, he's got a whole fleet!" Furse ran over to a large door and slid it open. "See?"

Peter stared in amazement at the row of dusty cars lined up in the huge old coach house.

"Those aren't mine. They belong to past Thornburgs," Uncle Ed explained.

"Do they all run?"

"Mostly. Bit of a museum, ain't it?" Uncle Ed shut the hood of the Datsun and wiped his hands on a rag. "Anyway, it's about time I got this little number out on the road again. Got a hunch I'll need her. The hearse is a bit of a beast, and now it needs a tire patched."

"A tire patched, Mr. Edward? Why didn't you say so?" Furse said. "We can do that in a trice."

Uncle Ed looked at the crowd of eager faces and shrugged. "Have a go if you like, boys."

Without warning, Muru burst in, and the garage crew scattered. "Peter!" she shrieked. "Did you finish breakfast? And when was the last time you bathed? I bet you haven't changed your socks in a week!"

Peter glanced at his uncle, who began whistling and putting away his tools as if he neither saw nor heard the irate Fenny. "I ate," Peter said.

"I even tied my shoelaces this morning without your help. Happy?" He watched her closely. She was more wound up than usual.

"Well, I hope that's true 'cause there's a giant spider at the front door and your aunt doesn't look too good."

Peter and his uncle hurried to the portico, where they found Aunt Marj, white-faced, sitting in the driver's seat of the hearse. The large spider perched on the back seat waved a foreleg, and the old man in the front saluted.

"I'll drive," Uncle Edward said.

Smiling wanly, Aunt Marj got out of the hearse and went into the house.

As Peter climbed in beside the spider, Uncle Ed started the engine and said, "How many of these Fennys left to find?"

"Two more after this. Pixel's coming day after tomorrow, and I just want all this rescue stuff to be over."

Uncle Ed laughed grimly. "Even when the last Fenny is found, I doubt it'll all be over."

10

Ghost Town

"Atten-tion! Poinkers, fall out!"

The girl, who had been drowsing on the front step of the toy shop, leapt to her feet.

"Oh, cork it, Arkey!" another voice bellowed. "We ain't nobody's army."

The shouting came from the other side of the big rock table in the town square, but she saw no one. Stepping quickly into the toy shop, she crouched beneath the frame of the window.

"Time for a count off. It's your turn, Raney," the first voice said. "But use regular Manx this time. Not yer confounded mishmash."

"I'll count in any language I please!" the second voice replied. "I'll count a ways in Latin, then switch to German, then Old Norse, then Cantonese."

"Just do the countin'!" someone shouted, and a chorus of voices began to murmur loudly.

"No need to count," rumbled a deep commanding voice. "We're all here."

"Yeah and wastin' time! Let's get to the Gen Sto and eat!"

Very cautiously, the girl peered over the window frame in time to see a line of stout little creatures come marching around the side of the rock table, single file. They were about knee high, with bristly fur and pointed noses. As they crossed the square in front of the toy shop, she heard one of them say, "What's that!"

"It's comin' from the bluffs! Headed right for us!"

"Positions!" the deep voice commanded. Instantly, all of them whipped out little spears and formed a tight, bristly battalion.

Looking toward the road that led to the sea, the girl saw a small, dark figure silhouetted against the horizon. It ran into the village square, and one of the creatures exclaimed, "Hey! It's only the hermit!" They lowered their spears.

A little man with dark, wrinkled skin halted a few paces from the creatures. His clothes were ragged and hung loosely from his gaunt frame. "Poinkers should be more careful. Heard your voices a long way off."

"Forlost!" the girl gasped.

All eyes turned in the direction of the toy shop.

"Who's there!" the deep voice demanded, and the creatures raised their spears.

She rose to her feet, and a chorus of voices shrieked, "Ghost!"

Hurrying out of the shop, the girl walked right up to the little man and looked into his hairy face. They were about the same height. "Forlost?"

He stood there with his mouth open, then made a little choking sound. "Jenny?"

She nodded, and he reached up a gnarled hand and brushed her cheek with his finger.

"Is Mother here?" she asked.

He shook his head slowly. "No, Jenny. Only Forlost is waiting."

A very loud voice said, "Boss, this ain't no ghost. It's a Silver."

"You're right, Arkey," the deep voice said.

The creatures were crowded around her feet now. She looked down at their sharp little eyes, all fixed on her. The big one with the deep voice, said, "Miss, my name is Kaney, and we are the Poinkers, patrollers and protectors of this land. You are one of the Silvers from the Big House, yes?"

She wasn't sure what he meant. "I came back to Floden. To find Mother. At the toy shop."

"What do you mean, 'came back'?" Arkey said. "No one's lived here for a long time. What's your name?"

"Jen," she replied.

"How did you get here, Miss Jen?" Kaney asked.

"I walked. From the lake."

A low murmur swept through the bristly crowd, and Kaney said, "Granite Lake? That's a two-day journey from here!"

She hesitated. "There was someone bad at the lake. Following me. A man who turned into a horse. Then the trees saved me."

The Poinker chorus began to mutter, "Glashtyn! That's who she means!"

Kaney shushed them. "What do you mean by saying the trees saved you?"

"They open the way and close it behind me."

"Trees movin'! That ain't happened for ages!" the chorus murmured.

Then one of the Poinkers, the smallest of all, pushed forward. "I've got something to say."

There was a murmur of disapproval, but Kaney patted the little creature on the head. "Let Sonney speak!"

"Remember the old poem," Sonney said. " 'They have kept her ever since / deep within the lake, / on a bed of flag-leaves, / watching till she wake.' Jimmy Squarefoot read it to us."

"Oooh! Little Bridget!" the Poinker chorus gasped.

"Well, that changes things," Kaney said.

"What are you talkin' about!" Arkey cried.

A soft-voiced Poinker said, "Sonney's right. She must have been stolen out of time. Like little Bridget."

"Her name ain't Bridget!" Arkey protested, glaring at the soft-voiced Poinker, whose name was Pinkey.

"Floden's been empty for a long time," Kaney said. "If she remembers the toy shop, she's from way back."

"Look at her! She ain't old enough to be from way back," Arkey said. "And how come she knows the hermit?"

"Forlost took care of me. When I was littler." Jen hoped that would help settle the question. Something about her presence troubled them. And someone called Bridget.

The sun had nearly disappeared below the tops of the trees, and the sky was a rosy dome of color. To the south of the village, a clamor arose from the woods, like the sound of migrating geese honking and yammering.

"Cripes!" Arkey gasped. "Mooner dogs!"

Forlost, who had been silent during the discussion, came to life suddenly and grabbed Jen's arm. "Hide, hide!"

"The Mooners never come to Floden," Arkey said.

"Let's not wait to find out! If the hermit says hide, I say we hide!" Kaney bellowed, "Everyone to the Gen Sto!"

Jen ran, following the hermit down a side street and into a large building, empty and dim in the twilight.

"Cellar, cellar!" Forlost cried. "Quick!" He tugged at a ring in the floor and yanked up a door. Everyone scrambled down the ladder. Then he pulled the door shut, and they sat in total darkness.

Outside, the yammering increased until the sound was all around the village. Over their heads, hooves clattered on the floorboards and Jen heard the shrill neighing of horses.

"Ho there!" a voice thundered. "The girl's here somewhere!"

"No, no!" another voice shouted. "She's gone back to the woods! Look at the dogs! They're going that way!"

A whip cracked, and the horses thundered out of the building. Gradually, the sound of yammering dogs died away. Still the fugitives sat in the dark for a long time, waiting.

Finally, Arkey said, "I can't stand this no more." He struck a match and lit a candle.

In the light, Jen saw that Forlost and most of the Poinkers were asleep.

"Do you think it's safe?" Pinkey whispered.

"Might be. Probably is, but we may as well stay here till morning," Kaney whispered.

"Who are they looking for?" Arkey asked.

"Didn't you hear what they said?" Pinkey replied. "*The girl's here somewhere.* They're looking for Miss Jen."

"Me?" Jen stared at the three little Poinkers, who gazed at her with steady eyes.

Sonney climbed onto her shoulder and stroked her cheek. "Don't worry, Little Bridget. We'll keep you safe."

Arkey blew out the candle. Jen curled up on the stone floor and, for a long time, stared into the pitch dark, wondering about her mother.

❦ ❦ ❦

She woke in the dim cellar and sat up. Dusty light shone down through the open door at the top of the ladder. Getting up, she brushed off her sweater, which was even tighter than the day before. The last button came loose and fell to the floor.

"Forlost?" She peered into the shadowy corners and saw only broken barrels and wooden boxes. Everyone had gone away and left her alone. For a moment, she felt afraid. Then she thought, *If I wait here in Floden long enough, Mother will come.*

Climbing the ladder, she heard a hubbub of voices: "I say we get outa Floden ASAP! Somebody go wake the Silver! The morning's gettin' on!"

So they hadn't left her. They'd been waiting for her to wake up. As she walked toward the middle of the village, the loud debate continued.

"No, no. Eat here. Leave when sun overhead. Go by road," Forlost said.

"Wait till the sun's overhead?" Arkey shouted. "It'll be too hot! I say we leave this minute!"

"Now, now," said the calm, rumbling voice of Kaney. "The hermit has a valid point. The Mooners never hunt in the middle of the day. Nor do the Glashtyn. We'll be safe on the road for a while. No more arguing."

"Sure, boss. Okay, boss," the chorus muttered.

In the middle of the town square, Jen saw Forlost busy over a fire. The pack of Poinkers all turned at once and looked at her, their pointy snouts quivering.

"Little Bridget!" Sonney said, detaching himself from the crowd. "We're taking you to the Big House! Kaney says that's where all the Silvers live."

"Will Mother be there?"

"I bet she is!"

After breakfast, they left the village, going east along the dirt road by which Jen had come, tramping forward in the blazing midday heat. Enormous cedar and fir trees towered on either side, with here and there a sapling growing in the middle of the road, like a stray child.

"Are you sure this is the way to my home?" Jen asked. She walked between Kaney and Forlost. The other Poinkers were spread out on either side, a bristly honor guard. "Why didn't the trees take me there yesterday?"

"Well, obviously they wanted you to meet *us*," Arkey huffed.

"And Forlost," Kaney said thoughtfully.

"Must find Silver-eyed Jen. Don't come back till you do," Forlost chanted.

Turning back for one last look at the village, Jen noticed something on the ground. She stopped, picked up a small round disk, and held it up. "What are these silver things all over the road?" As soon as she said it, Forlost plucked a handful of leaves from a nearby bush and stuffed them into his ears.

"Well, well, Boinkey," Raney said smugly. "Seems like you're still plunkin' out them silver quarters even though *some* of us has moved beyond that."

"Oh yeah?" Boinkey cried. "I'd like to see *you* plunk out somethin' else. One o' your precious stocks-n-bonds. Go ahead."

"Yeah! We'd like to see you try!" someone else shouted.

"This ain't the time nor the place," Raney replied and sniffed in a way that unleashed a fury of debate.

Jen had no idea what they were arguing about now. It had something to do with the silver things called coins. Some Poinkers thought they should be plunking out "paper money", and some said, no, it should be "gift cards". Raney argued fiercely for a mysterious thing called stocks-n-bonds. Finally, Kaney stopped the escalating fury by holding up one paw and saying in a severe tone, "You've let yourselves become totally sidetracked. Here we are on an important mission—for a change—and you stop to argue about *fate*!"

"Okay, boss. Sorry, boss," they all muttered. Then one of them pulled out a tiny flute, a couple of drums appeared, and all the Poinkers began to sing a lively marching tune.

Once we dealt in silver coin.
Once we granted money.
Now it's nought but painted tin,
And we don't think it's funny.

Arkan Sonney we are all,
Diddled by recession.
Modern cash is so much trash,
And that's our true confession.

Arkan Sonney, keep it up,
Sonney lads and lasses;
Mind your quarters and your pence
Until the market crashes.

"Who is Arkan Sonney?" Jen asked when at last the singing died away and the instruments disappeared.

"That's us," Pinkey replied. "*We* are the Arkan Sonney. At least that's what we used to be called in the old days. Now everyone just calls us Poinkers."

"That's because we plunk things out. Get it? Plunkers, Poinkers," Arkey said.

"I don't think that's quite right," Kaney mused. "Though the term 'Plunkers' may have something to do with it, I believe 'Poinker' comes from a direct translation of 'Arkan Sonney,' which, in the colloquial, is rendered 'Lucky Piggy.' Somehow, over the ages, this changed to 'Poinker.'"

Arkey paused. "That don't make no sense. Unless maybe some idiot was standin' on his head when he said 'Lucky Piggy' and it came out backward and upside down with the sounds all jumbled. I could see how that might happen."

"Can you?" Kaney began, when an enormous black bear stepped out of the woods, right in their path. Standing up on its hind legs, it growled fiercely. Jen shrank back as all the Poinkers gathered around her knees and drew their spears.

Only Forlost ran forward, pulling leaves out of his ears. "Tom! Tom!" The bear sank onto its haunches. "Poinkers, put down your spears!" Forlost cried. "This is Tom Bear."

"One of the Bugganes!" the chorus muttered. The spears disappeared, and they crowded around Forlost, listening as the bear rumbled again.

"He says the rumor that a Silver One walks the island again has gone out through the whole woods," Forlost explained. "The Glashtyn are hunting for her, and those of the Moonjer Veggey who serve the Moonwitch."

"Yeah, we know about *them* Mooners," Arkey muttered.

"And another thing. Mac Lir has returned. Tom saw his ship off the north coast many days ago."

There was a long silence.

"I'm not sure what to do," Kaney said finally. "We must get this girl to safety, but we're no match for the Glashtyn *or* the Mooners, if they've joined forces. And I don't like the idea of taking her to Mac Lir. I don't trust him anymore, and that's a fact."

As Forlost and the Poinkers spoke with the Bear, Jen sat down in the shade at the edge of the road. All she wanted was to find Mother.

Leaning back against a tree trunk, she closed her eyes and tried to bring the memory of Mother's face into her mind. Instead, she saw a moonlit lady with stars in her hair.

"Don't be afraid, Jen!" the lady said. "Follow my path through the woods!"

Then, into Jen's mind came the sound of horses thundering across the land. Without opening her eyes, she jumped to her feet and stepped between two fir trees. Putting a hand on each trunk, she felt them tremble.

"Whoa!" she heard the chorus cry. "The trees are movin'!"

Jen opened her eyes, and there was the promised path through the woods.

❦ ❦ ❦

"Goodbye, Little Bridget," Sonney called as the Poinkers tramped away down the road. They were headed back to their patrols, and Jen watched them go with a pang of regret. Before they were out of sight, Tom Bear grunted and turned onto the new path with Forlost right behind. Reluctantly, she followed. A few steps into the woods, she felt a slight shudder and turned back. Broad tree trunks blocked the way. It was too late to go after the Poinkers.

The forest was dim and cool. For a long time, Jen walked behind the bulky black rump of Tom Bear, and after a while, she found his shaggy fur a comforting sight. "He'd beat all the Mooners," she said to herself. "Probably eat them."

Then, just as the sun sent its rays slanting lengthwise through the trees, the path veered to the left, ending abruptly at the edge of a deep dell. Tom sat down on his haunches, and Jen peered into a muddy hollow.

"Who's that?" she said.

A little woman, with her back to them, was bent over a trickling stream, collecting water in a jug. At the sound of Jen's voice, she turned and looked up. Her hair was long and wavy, but otherwise she looked a lot like Forlost, and Jen knew her at once. "Thrinn!" she called out, climbing down the bank. Forlost and Tom Bear scrambled after her.

"Who are you?" the woman cried, shrinking away, clutching the jug to her chest.

Forlost drew close to the woman until they stood nose to nose. "Me Forlost, you Thrinn. Must find Silver-eyed Jen. Don't come back till you do. That's what Mac Lir said."

The woman dropped the jug and grabbed Forlost's hand. "Oh! That's my name! Thrinn! I'd forgotten!" Then she put out a trembling hand and stroked Jen's cheek. "It *is* her! At last! Oh, child, you're ever so much bigger! You've outgrown your clothes!"

"We go home now," Forlost said.

Thrinn hesitated. "Can we? We've been gone a long time. I've marked every day on the wall, and it's past counting. Come see."

In a corner of the dell stood a huge boulder with a wide crack down the middle. They followed Thrinn into this opening, passed through a short tunnel, and came to a wide cavern lit by torches. Tiny pinpricks of light twinkled on the granite walls, and a little fire crackled in a ring of stones. Jen noticed a large picture of green fields and tall mountains painted on the smooth stone.

"Did you make that, Thrinn?"

"Not me, dear. A friend of mine comes to work on it now and then. But I made all the ticky marks!" She led the way to the back of the cave, where Jen saw a small pallet of dried leaves on the ground. Over and above it, stretching away on either side, were hundreds of tally marks. "There!" Thrinn said, looking triumphantly at Forlost. "One for every day I've been here!"

"Where's Tom Bear?" Jen realized that he hadn't followed. Running back through the tunnel entrance, she nearly fell over his huge, shaggy form lying across the doorway. "Why are you out here? Thrinn's showing us her ticky marks."

He rumbled something and she looked up. Sure enough, the path by which they'd come was now blocked by a multitude of trees, but a new path was open and waiting on the other side of the hollow. The trees rustled impatiently.

"We have to go?"

Tom grunted and stood up. Jen ran back inside. "Forlost, Thrinn! We have to go now! There's a new path."

"Not until you wash your face, child!" Thrinn scolded. "I've never seen such dirt! And look at your sweater! What happened to all those precious buttons I made?"

"Never mind that," Forlost said. "The trees know, Thrinn. If they say go, we go." He cast dirt over the fire, tamped it out, and then, taking Thrinn by the hand, pulled her out of the cave.

Jen followed, and they climbed up to the new path. Tom Bear was waiting for them, and as she reached the top, he swung around and went loping ahead.

In a little while, they came to a wide river. As they crossed over a fallen log that spanned the rushing water, a path opened on the far bank. The woods on this side of the Glenfaba were mostly pine and hemlock, with here and there a tall maple. Forlost and Thrinn brought up the rear, murmuring softly to each other, so Jen walked at Tom's side. He rumbled at her, asking how she had found Forlost, so she told him all about waking up at the lake and of her flight through the forest, all the way to Floden. He snorted with laughter at her description of the Poinkers.

On and on they went as the day dwindled and evening set in. When she stumbled in the darkening woods, Tom grunted.

"Thank you," she said and put a hand on his broad back to steady herself. His fur was warm and bristly, and she thought about the Poinkers and wondered where they were. At last, she heard the sound of rushing water again. The path made a sharp turn, and they stood on the banks of the river once more, though farther north, according to Tom. In this place, the water bubbled and swirled over flat boulders.

Into the deepening dusk, the sound of singing rose above the current. A doleful tune it seemed at first, sung by clear, deep voices whose harmonies wedded the river's tune with the song of the first star. Then little lights appeared in the woods on the opposite shore, bobbing and moving toward the water as figures emerged from the forest. Tall women, they seemed to be, wearing red cloaks with hoods that hid their faces, and sleeves rolled up to their elbows. Setting their candles on the rocks, they waded into the shallows and began to unload baskets of dirty linen.

"Who are they?" Jen whispered, her hand still on Tom's back.

He rumbled in a low voice.

"The Washers," she repeated. "Washing all the dirty laundry of the world."

Then one of the figures approached and held out a hand. "Come wash with us, child."

Tom grunted and lay down under a tree. Jen stepped into the water.

11

Ashes

After Pixel sent her note to Peter on Thursday evening, telling him that she could go to his house, she waited eagerly for the reply, but it never came. She saw Moody every day, but he carried no message, and after three days, she began to wonder.

The treatments continued, Aunt Kate drawing an extra tube of blood each afternoon. Pixel began to feel tired all the time, and no matter what delicious thing Cook made, she couldn't eat much.

On Friday and Saturday, she was too tired to help at the store and spent the day in the back garden, hanging around with Moody until it was time for the next treatment.

By Sunday, she knew that she was sicker than she had ever been before in her life. Her blood treatment had been moved to seven o'clock because Aunt Kate had gone shopping in Sweetwater. By the time Pixel left the treatment room, her head ached and she felt weak all over, but she walked out to the bluff above the beach just to get out of the house. Then she saw the Bread Lady coming down the path with Moody at her side. The old woman greeted her warmly and asked how she was.

"I sent a message to Peter, telling him I could go to his house on Tuesday," Pixel said, "but he hasn't answered. Moody must have lost my note."

The big dog whined and licked her face.

"Moody doesn't lose things," the woman said. "I asked him to look after you. Be patient. Peter has not forgotten." Then she gave Pixel another bag of bread, and they went down to the shore and walked for a while.

Pixel returned to the house feeling much better. She always did after seeing her friend and eating her bread. Then, because it was nearly dark and she wanted to take a shortcut, she went in by the back door. She had never used this entrance before because it led into a corridor at the back of the house that seemed to be Aunt Kate's private domain. Letting herself in quietly, she paused on the threshold. Another door, a little farther down the passage, swung open and Aunt Kate came out.

"Pixel, is that you? What are you doing back here?" She sounded very cross.

"I . . . I just went for a walk."

Aunt Kate switched off a light and shut the door, and Pixel heard a key turn in a lock. Then her aunt stood in front of the door, as if trying to hide it. "Go. Now. And don't let me catch you snooping again."

Hurrying out of the passage, Pixel went to the kitchen for a glass of water before going to her room and found Cook heating milk on the stove.

"Oh, there you are," Cook said. "Want some warm milk?"

"No, thanks."

She was about to ask for a glass when Cook said, in a low voice, "I've been thinking. Your aunt leaves for Lang tomorrow evening. What's to stop me from spending the week with friends in Sweetwater and you from staying somewhere else while she's away?"

Surprised, Pixel hesitated. "Nothing, I guess."

From overhead came the sound of Aunt Kate's footsteps. A door opened and shut. Then came the distant sound of water running in the bathroom.

"Listen," Cook continued. "I have to come back here for a few hours every day to look after things, but I'm not at all keen to sleep here while your aunt is away. I'm guessing you feel the same?"

Pixel nodded.

"Right. I don't want to leave you here alone, and since I know you're friends with the Thornburgs, I spoke to Mary at the store and asked if they could keep you for a few days. She agreed. What do you think? It'll be a sort of holiday. For both of us."

"Yeah. Okay."

"Good. We'll meet here next Saturday afternoon, before Kate gets back. She'll never know. It'll be our little secret. The only thing is, you'll need to hang around here tomorrow afternoon until we're sure she's on the ferry. She'll leave the house at four, but you stay here till six o'clock. Then you can lock up and leave. Just twist the knob on the front door and pull it shut."

"Why do I have to wait till six? Where will you be?"

"I'll be in Sweetwater, of course. I'm heading there right after lunch. Now listen, the five o'clock ferry is the last one. If she misses it, she'll come right back—mad as a hornet. If that happens, call me straightaway," and she held out a slip of paper with a phone number written on it. Putting it in her pocket, Pixel said good night and went up to her room, smiling.

❦ ❦ ❦

The next day, Pixel went to Thorny's as soon as they opened. She was greeted by Mary, who took her aside, into the kitchen.

"I have a message from Peter. He and Aunt Marj will come to pick you up tomorrow morning."

"Oh good!"

"He called Friday evening, and I've been waiting to see you. Where have you been?"

"I . . . I wasn't feeling too well, but I'm better now."

"Good. And you're coming to stay with us! George is looking forward to taking you fishing."

Later that afternoon, Pixel stood behind the cash register and looked at the clock on the wall for the hundredth time. One more hour, and she'd have the last blood treatment. Then Aunt Kate would leave for Lang. She sighed and began rearranging small items on the counter. Annette was at the auto shop because her car had broken down. Ordinarily, Pixel liked minding the store, but today she couldn't relax. She kept thinking about the Rilson house empty for five days. Aunt Kate would be furious if she found out. Yet it would be worse to stay there alone.

"Not alone," she said under her breath, thinking of the unseen occupant who limped around at night.

The bell on the door tinkled and Annette came in.

"How's the car?" Pixel asked.

"Not good. Expensive to fix and it won't be ready for a day or so." She sighed and sat on the stool behind the counter. "I was hoping to get to Sweetwater this evening."

"Why? Got a boyfriend there?" Pixel meant it as a joke and was surprised by the tight look on Annette's face.

"Actually, I do. Ben Rilson. I haven't told Mom and Dad because . . . well, he's a Rilson, and they're a bit funny about all that. I hope you won't mention it."

"Of course not!"

"The thing is, I'm not the first Thornburg to date a Rilson, but those other relationships were usually broken up by the family. I'm not letting that happen."

"Would your parents really make you break up?"

"I don't know. There's you, Pixel. They seem to have adopted you. That gives me hope."

"Who else in your family dated a Rilson?"

"Uncle Edward. He lives at Wakkenburg House with Peter. Once upon a time, he was engaged to Mae Rilson, but his father made him break it off. Then she ended up where you are, having blood treatments."

"Where is she now?"

"I don't know. Uncle Edward never says. I was surprised he told me as much as he did."

At five minutes to three, Pixel said goodbye to Annette and ran across the street. Aunt Kate was already in the treatment room, rummaging in the cupboard. She looked up without smiling. "You're on time."

Her aunt was sterner than usual, so Pixel sat down in the chair without speaking. She pushed up her sleeve and held her arm out on the table as Aunt Kate took two glass tubes from the rack. They were a little larger than usual, ten milliliters each.

Fifteen minutes later, Pixel was slumped at the kitchen table looking at a plate of liver and onions as her aunt poured a large glass of milk. "Eat. It will help. Then lie down and rest until dinner. Cook will be back in a little while."

Pixel heard a drawer open and shut, then the sound of her aunt walking down the hall. She tried to get up, intending to toss the liver and onions in the garbage, but as soon as she stood, the room darkened. She clutched the table and sat down, too dizzy even to think of eating. All she wanted was to get away from this place—as soon as her head stopped spinning.

The kitchen clock ticked, and somewhere nearby a fly buzzed madly. Pixel sat up and ripped the bandage away from the inside of her elbow. There was today's red dot. This time there had been the faint smell of snakes in the treatment room. She shuddered, tried a sip of milk, and retched. There was no way she could eat in this house.

Hearing footsteps in the passage, she pulled the plate close and picked up the fork as her aunt entered.

"Good. You're eating."

Pixel turned in time to see her open a drawer and deposit a single key on a ring.

"Goodbye," her aunt said coldly. "See you Saturday." And she walked out.

Wanting to see her aunt leave, just to make sure she did, Pixel stood up slowly, fighting against dizziness, and walked along the corridor with one hand on the wall so she wouldn't lose her balance. By the time she reached the front door and stepped onto the porch, her aunt was loading a suitcase into the trunk. Without a backward glance, she got in the car and drove away.

It was time to pack. Slowly, Pixel mounted the stairs, holding on to the railing. As she crossed the second-floor landing, the smell of snakes grew stronger. She gagged, then plugged her nose and forced herself up the next flight of steps.

Once in her room, she sat down on the bed and took the bread sack from the nightstand. Just the smell of the bread made her feel better. She ate one roll, then got out her duffel bag and packed all her clothes, even the new ones—still with tags—that Cook had bought for her. Looking around the room, she spied the library books on the nightstand, tossed them in, and zipped the bag shut. Closing her window, she looked over at Mary and George's apartment. She would be there tonight, looking across the street to her own dark room.

Going quickly down the stairs, she held her breath as she passed the second floor. The house was entirely silent except for the sound of her feet on the wooden steps.

In the front hall, she opened the door wide and propped her bag against it. Then she picked up the little clock by the phone and sat down on the porch to wait.

The time ticked by slowly. At five thirty, a bright blue car came down the street, and the old man at the wheel stared at the Rilson house. Pixel wondered whether he was a relative. Then he turned left at Thorny's and drove out of sight.

By six o'clock, Pixel knew what she wanted to do. She would look into the room that Aunt Kate kept locked. She'd been accused of snooping, and now she was going to do it.

On a hunch, she went to the kitchen and took the key that Aunt Kate had dropped in a drawer. Then, before she lost her nerve, she tiptoed down the main corridor, past the stairway, and into the back passage.

The first door she tried was unlocked and revealed a large sitting room furnished with wicker chairs and hanging plants. This was her aunt's private domain, and the smell of her perfume hung in the air.

The next door was locked. Pixel tried the key, the bolt slid back, and the door opened onto darkness. Feeling along the inside wall, she found a light switch and flipped it on.

It was a storage room with a bare linoleum floor. The walls were lined with rough wooden shelves holding ceramic jars of various sizes and colors. It looked like some sort of art studio. Maybe Aunt Kate was a potter.

Moving a little closer, Pixel noticed that each jar was engraved with a single name: Janice, Linda, Beth, Julie. The jars on the back wall looked very old. "Jill, Wanda, Glenda, Mae," she read aloud. "I guess Aunt Kate's a collector, not an artist. But why does she hide these? Most people who collect things put them all around the house."

Then, on a shelf beside the door, she saw three newer-looking jars named Bella, Clare, and Megan. At the name Megan, she caught her breath and thought of the cousin who had come here before her.

Trembling, though she didn't know why, she picked up the jar named Megan and lifted the lid. It was filled with a fine gray dust.

A memory flashed into her mind. Her mother and father joking at Uncle Van's funeral: "No coffin, thank goodness. No waxy dead face to look at one last time. Just ashes to ashes and dust to dust."

Shaking now, she tried to replace the lid but the jar slipped from her hands and crashed to the floor. Fine gray ash billowed up in a soft cloud as fragments of clay and bone fell at her feet. Gasping, she backed out of the room. A wave of dizziness struck, and her vision darkened. She fell to her knees, retching.

"Hello?" a voice called.

Curling herself into a tight ball, Pixel tried to still the shivering that had begun in her gut. She could feel her arms shaking and dug her nails into her palms.

"What's going on? Are you okay?"

She shook her head slightly, her breath coming in short gasps. Opening her eyes, she saw a tall man standing over her.

He crouched down beside her. "You're ill. Where's Cook?"

She couldn't speak, but she didn't have to. He looked up into the room, and she saw his face change.

Rising slowly, he stepped over the threshold. She sat up, still shivering uncontrollably, and watched him move from right to left, just as she had, reading the names on every jar. When he came to the shelf on the back wall, he picked up the jar named Mae and whispered something that Pixel could not hear, but she was suddenly aware of the clock ticking in the hall.

Finally, he straightened his shoulders and turned to her. "Let's get out of here."

He crossed the room, then reached down and gently took her arm.

His voice was gruff, but looking into his face, Pixel saw that he only wanted to help. She got to her feet unsteadily. "Who are you?"

"I'm Peter's uncle. Come to take you to Wakkenburg."

The wave of relief she felt caused her to falter, but he held her shoulder firmly. She took a deep breath, trying to stop herself from trembling. He turned out the light in the room of ashes but didn't bother to shut the door.

With one hand, he steered her out of the house. In his other hand, he cradled Mae Rilson's jar against his chest. As if she were dreaming, Pixel watched him pick up her bag and sling it over his shoulder.

"I ... I have to lock up," she stammered.

Reaching back with his free hand, he twisted the knob and pulled the door shut. Then, without a word, he led her across the street and around to the back door of Thorny's.

"Hi, Uncle Edward! I see you've met Pixel," Annette said. Then she looked at Pixel's face. "What's wrong?"

"Mary, I need to put this in a box," Uncle Edward replied. "You got one that'll fit?" Pixel watched him put the jar named Mae on the table.

"Of course. Where'd you find a thing like that? It looks like an urn from a mausoleum."

"It is. Found it over in the Rilson house."

Pixel sat down in the nearest chair and put her head in her hands. She knew the man was talking, heard Annette and Mary speaking, but couldn't take in what they said. They bustled around the kitchen, packing things. The kettle whistled. Then she felt a touch on her shoulder and sat up. Annette was offering a cup of tea. Taking it in both hands, she cradled the warmth and took a sip.

"Pixel," Annette said, "what are these treatments? Does your aunt give you medicine?"

"No. She takes blood."

"That's all?"

"She says it has to be tested."

"How much does she take?"

"Two tubes a day."

"Two tubes a day? That's not right!" Annette said. "No wonder—"

"I … I can't believe this," Mary gasped. "I … I never knew for sure … no one did."

"I'm taking Pixel to Wakkenburg. Now," Uncle Edward said.

"Oh. Yes," Mary faltered. "And you'll bring her back tomorrow, right?"

"I'm not bringing her back at all."

"But you have to. Cook thinks she's staying with us. And what about her aunt and the treatments?"

"Since when is blood sucking a treatment?"

"Mom," Annette said to Mary, "Uncle Edward is right. Pixel needs to get away from here. At least until we can find out what's really going on."

Pixel watched Uncle Edward pick up his car keys. With the sensation that all this was happening to somebody else, she put down her teacup and followed him out the back door, feeling Annette's arm around her shoulder. Then she was sitting in the passenger seat of the bright blue car, and they were driving away as Annette and Mary waved goodbye. Growling and sputtering, the car turned onto Main Street, and she had one last glimpse of the Rilson house. Uncle Edward changed gears, and they were speeding past the shops, over the bridge, and away from Foyle.

❦ ❦ ❦

"We're being followed," Uncle Edward said, pointing at her window.

She looked out and saw Moody running through the woods, parallel with the car.

"You don't seem surprised. Has Peter introduced you?"

Pixel nodded. "Last week."

"That's good. He ain't easy to explain otherwise."

They drove on in silence. The only sound was the low growl of the engine as the car hurtled deeper and deeper into the forest. The trees seemed to blot out the sky, and Pixel lost all sense of time. The shivering had ceased, and she sat looking out the window, her eyes fixed on the great black shadow that moved beside them through the woods.

"I knew a girl looked just like you, but she wore her hair long. Prettiest girl in Sweetwater."

"Mae Rilson."

"I suppose Annette told you. When Mae lived at the Rilson house, I used to go sit on the bench outside Thorny's and watch for her. Now and then she'd sit on the porch, and we'd wave and just look at each other. Then, after a few months went by, I didn't see her anymore. I never knew what happened."

"Until today," Pixel said flatly.

He didn't reply, and she turned back to the window. The dull fear that clutched her insides when she thought of the urns was relieved by the sight of Moody. There he was, keeping pace with the Datsun at sixty miles an hour.

"I don't believe in those blood treatments," Uncle Edward said.

Pixel knew the truth and didn't need to hear anyone say it.

"I mean, I don't believe they're treatments. I don't believe Mae was ever sick at all. Neither are you."

"Then what's wrong with us?"

"I don't know, but I'm gonna find out."

❦ ❦ ❦

"Did Peter tell you anything about Wakkenburg?" The woods seemed to press in, and Uncle Edward's voice, breaking a long silence, sounded sudden and harsh. They had not seen another car the entire journey.

"I saw a tiny painting on a map," Pixel said quietly. "It looked like a castle."

She saw the junction and the sign for Wakkenburg Road. Uncle Edward made a left off the highway and, after a couple of miles, turned right onto a long wooded drive. Then, quite suddenly—as if coming out of a tunnel—they drove out of the dark forest, and Pixel gasped. The sight of Wakkenburg House took her breath away.

"I guess it does look like a castle," Uncle Edward said.

She felt a sudden stab of joy. It was better than any story she'd read. Moody loped beside the car until suddenly his ears perked up and he shot across the grass toward the house and the figures standing at the front door.

12

Colliding Forces

Earlier that afternoon, just as Peter and Aunt Marj returned from rescuing the eleventh Fenny, Fiak came running down the main stairs. "Mr. Peter! We've found the floor plan!"

So, after the new Fenny was settled, Peter ate lunch and then went up to the library. He sat down on the couch, and Fiak brought out the map of Wakkenburg House, along with a number of accompanying documents that bore titles such as "The Habits and Preferences of the Average House Fenny" and "Alternative Entrances and Exits in Case of Fire, Flood, or Unwanted House Guests". Peter unrolled the plans, then rubbed his forehead and yawned. Sunlight filtered through a high window, warming his face. He leaned back against the cushion.

The sound of splashing hoofbeats came into his mind, and he saw the warrior on his white horse, riding across the sea. The mighty horse kicked up spray that shone like diamonds in the light. *Clippety-clippety*, it sped over the water, *clippety-clippety, boom, boom, boom!*

Peter sat up with a jolt as paper cascaded off his lap. *Boom, boom.* Someone was pounding on the front door. Only a Buggane could knock loud enough to be heard three floors up. The last Fenny must have been found. Peter ran down the stairs and arrived in the front hall just as Aunt Marj opened the door.

"Hurry, boy!" the old man Buggane said. "This last one made it to Floden, and he's in a real fix. Broken bones. We didn't dare move him."

"Peter, where's the hearse?" Aunt Marj asked.

"In the garage. The Fennys fixed the tire."

"Oh good! I'll drive it around." She hurried away. Peter and the Buggane stood there, looking at each other. The old man smiled benignly, folding his arms over his chest. A few minutes later, Aunt Marj returned.

"It's not ready just yet," she said. "They've fixed the tire, but now they're working on the front end. And the brakes. And something called CV joints. Krim says it's because Ed drives the hearse like a jeep and it was never meant for off-road travel. What do we do, Peter? Ed took the Datsun to Foyle, and the hearse won't be ready for an hour!"

"Why did Uncle Ed go to Foyle?"

"I don't know." Aunt Marj sounded peeved. "To pick up the mail, I guess."

"Let's wait in the kitchen," the Buggane said.

An hour later, the hearse was still not ready, and Peter now knew that, in the company of a Buggane, the kitchen was not the best place to kill time. The old man had a voracious appetite. He downed sausages and little frosted cakes by the plateful, as his form alternated between the old man and a little girl in a pink checkered dress. The Fennys worked fast, producing sausages and cake at a speed that surprised Peter, while Aunt Marj sat across the table, wide-eyed. Then, at a moment when the sausage plate was empty and the old man had turned into the giant mole, Muru stomped in.

"What's going on here?"

"I ... I think we're out of sausages," Peter said, wondering why she seemed to have no fear of the Buggane's long tusks.

"Oh, we ran out a long time ago," she snapped.

"But ... what's he been eating?"

"Listen, kid, there's things about us Fennys you don't understand. We can make illusions out of crumbs left in a pan, if we want to. It's never our first choice."

"Is that why he keeps eating and doesn't get enough?"

"Kid, all I want to know is, when are you gonna stop him? You *are* a Silver, you know! I shouldn't have to do everything around here! By the way, that car is ready. Furse is bringing it around to the front of the house." Then she stomped out, slamming the door.

The giant mole began to bang a crumpled fork on the table, but Peter turned to the Fennys at the stove. "That's enough. Stop giving him food."

"What!" the mole roared.

Bracing himself, Peter said, "No more, Buggane!"

"But I want more!" roared the mole, swelling until his head reached the rafters.

"You're here to take us to the last Fenny. The other Bugganes are waiting."

The giant mole instantly shrank into the old man and collapsed on the bench. "Oh!" he wailed. "Tom Mole has been a bad boy! Tom Spider will bite me!"

Peter took a deep breath. "He ... he doesn't have to know. It'll be our secret."

Peter led the way out of the kitchen and into the front hall, where he flung open the door and stepped under the empty portico. The approach to the house was a cobbled road that ran along the front wall, intersecting with the long paved drive to the left. At this intersection, a dirt lane went off to the right, between the west wall and the woods, ending at a back gate, where the garage was located. Furse would be coming from this lane.

"No car?" the Buggane asked.

Then Peter saw a flash of sky blue coming out of the woods. The Datsun! Uncle Ed was home. Aunt Marj came out of the house. "Oh! Thank goodness Ed's back. And look! There's Moody Doug!"

Peter's heart leapt at the sight of Moody. He whistled and the great dog sprang forward, easily outdistancing the car.

"Uh oh. There's Tom," the old man said. "He's come lookin' for us."

A great hairy spider, far larger than Moody, came running out of the woods, clacking its jaws. It was headed straight for them. Aunt Marj gasped, and the old man's form began to flash rapidly between the giant mole and the little girl. Moody saw the spider and changed course.

"No, Moody! Stop!" Peter shouted.

Then, just as the giant spider crossed the intersection, the hearse came roaring out of the lane. Peter glimpsed Furse standing on the seat, gripping the steering wheel, and through the open window heard him scream, "Brake! Hit the brakes, Krim! Now!"

It was too late. With a sickening crunch, the hearse collided with the spider, and its front end crumpled like tin foil. Instantly, the spider turned into an enormous scorpion, raising its tail over the hearse. The doors flew open and six Fennys leapt out, cursing and shouting. Again and again, the monster struck with its giant stinger. Flames shot up from the engine. Moody stood at the edge of the wreckage, howling and wagging his tail.

It was Krim who saved the hearse from complete annihilation. He opened up with a fire extinguisher, dousing flames and the Buggane's ruffled passions in a white spume of sodium bicarbonate.

The poor Fennys were beside themselves, shouting and shaking their fists at the giant scorpion. Not sure if this particular Buggane could change into anything scarier, Peter waded into the fray and set them to work, clearing up the mess. He understood their collective tirade. Here they'd spent the better part of the day repairing the hearse under time pressure, only to have it totaled less than a minute after driving it out of the garage.

Speaking gently to the Buggane, Peter calmed the poor creature, and as soon as it changed back into the spider, he began hosing off the white powder from the fire extinguisher. As he stood there, aiming the hose at Tom's legs, the Datsun pulled forward and stopped beside him. Uncle Ed rolled down his window. "I'm guessing they found the last Fenny."

Peter stood there, gaping like an idiot, the spray of the hose arcing into midair, for there was Pixel, sitting in the passenger seat, staring at him with wide eyes. Then the old man Buggane ran up. "We must go! Can't be in Floden after dark!"

"Get in," Uncle Ed said to Peter.

"Wha-wha-wait a minute," Peter stammered. "We need a stretcher. And splints."

Ten minutes later, they were on their way, the Datsun roaring down Wakkenburg Road, headed west. The forest towered above them, and it was a little like driving through a long, open-roofed tunnel. Moody loped beside the car on their left, and the giant spider ran behind on the right-hand verge, keeping his distance. Peter sat in the back seat with the old man Buggane, who kept wringing his hands, moaning, "Tom! Poor Tom! He's scared of dogs!"

As they approached the Fenn Road junction, the old man tapped Uncle Ed on the shoulder. "That way! That way!" He pointed to the left, and without slowing down, Uncle Ed turned the Datsun off the tarmac onto Old Road. It was a rough dirt track, wide enough for two cars to go side by side, but littered with fallen branches, rocks, and the occasional sapling growing in the middle. On either side, the forest was thick with undergrowth.

"Where are we going?" Peter asked, clutching the seat in front of him with both hands as Uncle Ed steered expertly around clumps of bushes and large rocks.

"To Floden," the Buggane replied.

"I saw Floden on the map," Pixel said, speaking for the first time.

What a way to be introduced to Wakkenburg, Peter thought. *Hurtling down a dirt road followed by a huge dog and an even bigger spider.* As if reading his thought, she turned and grinned.

"I'm pretty sure I'm not dreaming."

Uncle Ed cranked the steering wheel sharply, and the Datsun swerved to the right, then to the left, narrowly missing a large rock. He was driving as fast as he dared. The Buggane insisted that they be out of Floden before dark, though he hadn't said why. Fortunately it was July and sunset was after ten.

"Uncle Ed, you should be a rally car driver," Peter said.

"I suppose it's not too late. This little Datsun handles like a dream. Shoulda fixed her up years ago."

"Where *is* Floden?"

His uncle frowned. "The other side of the island. But don't ask me how many miles. I've never been sure. The odometer never works out here."

Over the roar of the engine, Pixel asked, "Are there bears in the woods?"

"No bears on the island," Peter answered automatically.

"Only Tom Bear," the old man said, as the Datsun lurched through a pothole. "Lives up north, near Spoot Voor. Ain't seen him in a long time."

At last, the derelict buildings of Floden came into view. Uncle Ed drove into the old marketplace, a paved village square, and parked beside a huge tabletop of stone. They all got out as Tom Spider scuttled off, disappearing down a side street.

Beyond the square, the road continued west toward the sea, and Peter had a good view of the sun sitting low on the horizon. The sky was a dome of turquoise and pink, with a lone gull floating in the strong breeze blowing up from the shore. To the south, rolling yellow hills spread out beyond the woods; to the north, the old village of Floden stood surrounded by dense forest.

Uncle Ed began untying the stretcher from the top of the car. He wore a closed look, and Peter remembered Aunt Marj's story. Their little sister had disappeared from this place long ago. Maybe he hadn't been here since that day. Peter took the bandages out of the trunk and followed the old man Buggane through the village lanes to a large vacant building. It was the old general store, but only a few letters remained on the sign. He looked up and read, "Gen Sto".

Inside, light shone through holes in the roof, and there was a litter of leaves and rotted wood on the plank floor. The Buggane went behind the old counter to a gaping hole and climbed down a ladder. Peter saw at once that it was the opening to a cellar.

Pixel came up beside him, one hand on Moody's neck. "I'll wait here," she said, eyeing the hole with distaste.

Uncle Ed maneuvered the stretcher down the ladder, and Peter followed. The hairy man was waiting at the bottom, holding a candle so they could see their way.

"You took a long time, Silver One. I sent Tom Spider to see if you were lost."

"Car trouble." Peter knelt and examined the unconscious Fenny, who was lying very near the foot of the ladder.

"He is badly hurt," the hairy man said. "The cellar door was open and he fell down. We think he was looking for the Hermit of Floden."

"Who?" Peter unrolled the bandages and began to wrap the Fenny's forehead. Everything he knew about first aid he'd learned from Muru in the past few days.

"The Hermit. He lived here for many years. We heard about him from the Poinkers."

"Poinkers?" Peter applied three splints; then he and his uncle lifted the Fenny onto the stretcher and strapped him down. Tilting it upward, Uncle Ed and Peter pushed from below, the Bugganes pulled from the top, and they got it up the ladder and out the cellar door. The poor Fenny moaned in pain but never woke up.

Pixel came running through the door. "Peter! That ... that spider thing came and Moody ran after him!"

"Here, take my end of the stretcher. Which way did they go?"

"They were headed for the car."

Peter took off running with the hairy man close behind. They found Moody in the town square, beside the Datsun, growling at something in the woods beyond. A giant scorpion stood close by, its stinger poised to strike.

"There is evil here," the hairy man said. "Hide, Silver One!"

Then Peter heard a large creature moving in the undergrowth, just beyond the edge of the paved square. Before he could react, Moody snarled, and the scorpion's giant tail stiffened and swung down hard. In the same instant, the hairy man swelled to a great height, twisted off his shaggy head, and threw it into the woods.

There was a tremendous explosion of sound and light. Throwing himself to the ground, Peter covered his face and heard the fierce neighing of a horse and the sound of hooves pounding through the woods. Then everything went quiet. Slowly, he got to his feet and looked around. A light breeze ruffled his hair, and several birds called. There was no sign of the explosion, no blasted crater. Moody wagged his tail and, with a *pop!*, the scorpion became a spider. The hairy man, headless now, stood with his great hands resting on his hips. Then he began to shrink. With a *ding* like the sound of a tiny bell, he became a small, ugly troll.

"You and your friends must not linger here, Silver One," the troll said in a high-pitched voice. "We will see you safe to the end of Old Road."

The old man and Uncle Edward came around the corner carrying the stretcher, Pixel trotting behind to keep up.

"What was that noise" Uncle Ed called out. "Sounded like a bomb!"

"Oh, Tom! Tom Troll! You blew up your head!" the old man cried.

"Glashtyn," Tom Troll replied.

The old man gasped. "Here?"

"Open the door," Uncle Edward said.

Peter ran to the Datsun and opened the rear door, and they slid the stretcher onto the back seat. When the Fenny was settled, Uncle Ed stood up and said, "Before we go, I'm gonna take a look around."

"There isn't time!" the troll said. "You must get out of Floden! A Glashtyn was here. More will come, and maybe other things that are worse. You must get the boy away!"

In reply, Uncle Edward held out his hand. A small pearl button, shaped like a rose, rested on his palm. "I found this back there in the cellar. The day my little sister Jenny disappeared, she was wearing a sweater with buttons just like this. They were carved by a Fenny, and there aren't any others like them. She had silver eyes too."

The old man looked at the button, and the troll sniffed it. "Yes, I remember her. But she is the Silver One that was. You must keep safe the one that *is*."

"But what if she's here?"

"When we came to Floden today, we found only the Fenny in the cellar," the old man said. "Others have been here, but they are gone."

"Others? Who?"

"Mooners. Poinkers. But they left many days ago. Before the Fenny came."

"How do you know?"

"We Bugganes know by the smell of stone and grass. And the birds tell us many things. There is no one else here, I tell you."

"But the Glashtyn will return," said the troll. "We frightened one of them away, but he may have seen the Silver One. Many more will return after nightfall."

"Glashtyn," Uncle Edward muttered. "Alright. We're going. But if you hear anything from these Poinkers about who's been livin' in Floden, I'd like to know."

"We'll come with news if we can," the old man said. "But now we must go home to recover our strength. Tom Troll won't be his hairy self for days! He's blown up his head!"

As Uncle Ed and Pixel were getting into the car, Peter paused at the door, then bowed awkwardly to the three Bugganes. "Thank you for your help. I wish there was some way to repay you."

The spider clacked its jaws, the troll inclined his head deferentially, and the old man grinned. "How about breakfast at Wakkenburg House? We've not been invited there for a long time."

Peter hesitated. What would Norbert and Muru say? Well, he couldn't refuse. "Sure. Okay. You're invited for breakfast." Then he squeezed into the front seat beside Pixel, and Uncle Ed started the car.

"What about Moody?" Pixel said as they drove away. Then his snout appeared at the window, his tongue lolling out. He barked and sped on ahead of the Datsun. Tom Spider scuttled along to the left of the bumper.

"No one will mess with us now," Peter said. "By the way, Uncle Ed, what *are* Glashtyn?"

"Horses. Or men, depending on how they feel when they catch up with you. Either way, not nice. They lure folks into the water and eat them. At least that's what I've heard."

"Ugh," Pixel said. "That's disgusting."

"But can you tell a Glashtyn from a real horse? Or from a human?" Peter asked.

"I asked Jonas that question once," Uncle Ed replied. "He was the Silver-eyed Thornburg before my little sister."

"What did he say?"

"If you meet a Glashtyn as a man, his ears will be pointy, like a horse's. And if you meet him as a horse, he'll be a beautiful stallion that you're suddenly itching to ride. But if you get on his back ... well ..."

There was no more talk. Uncle Ed turned his attention to the road, gripping the steering wheel with both hands as he dodged bushes and rocks. "Blast this road," he muttered. "Krim's gonna swear like heck when he sees this poor car."

To Peter's surprise, Pixel fell asleep, and he changed his position so she could lean on his shoulder. In the back seat, the poor splinted Fenny moaned whenever the car hit a pothole. Then, just when Peter thought his teeth would all be shaken loose, they drove onto smooth tarmac. He turned in time to see Tom Spider halt at the end of Old Road and lift a foreleg in farewell. Uncle Edward shifted into another gear and put on more speed as the twilight deepened.

"Uncle Ed," Peter said in a low voice. "We weren't supposed to pick up Pixel till tomorrow. Do you think it's okay if she spends the night?"

"She's stayin' with us for a few days," his uncle replied. "At the very least."

"What do you mean?"

Uncle Ed didn't answer. In a few minutes, they crossed the bridge, the Datsun sped over the long drive, and there was the great house under the evening sky, the lighted windows of the West Wing shining out a welcome. Overhead, the stars came out.

Pixel stirred and opened her eyes. "We're home," she said.

"Without a flat. Won't Krim be pleased," Uncle Edward said grimly.

Home, Peter thought, and for the first time in many days, he remembered Lang and his father sitting in the old armchair under the lamp, reading one of his many books. Probably he wasn't doing that. Most likely he was working the night shift at the diner. Now that he thought of it, he hadn't heard from Dad since leaving Lang.

Uncle Ed parked the Datsun under the portico, and Muru came out with the entire garage crew. As they unloaded the splinted Fenny and took him into the house, the phone in the front hall rang.

"Peter! It's for you!" Aunt Marj called. "Your dad! Shall I tell him you're busy?"

❦ ❦ ❦

Later that night, Peter met his aunt on the stairs. "Pixel's gone to bed," she said. "Muru quite likes her, and so do I. What did your dad say?"

"Asked me to send mail to the diner. Said he'd get it quicker because he's either there or at the hospital."

"Hospital?"

"Mom's in a special hospital called rehab. Dad thinks she's doing better."

Peter went to bed, tired to the bone. The Fennys from Fenn House were safe now, all accounted for. And Pixel was here. Tomorrow he'd show her around. The only thing that troubled him was the conversation with Dad. He'd sounded cheerful, but something was not quite right. Peter could tell. It had something to do with the apartment. He lay there, staring into the dark. When he finally fell asleep, he tossed and turned. Then he dreamed.

A woman with raven hair stood in the middle of Floden, her arms lifted to the sky. Six shadowy figures stood behind her, silhouetted in the orange glare, and on the edge of the firelight, a troop of little green-clad men waited, their small white horses stamping uneasily. On the old rock table, flames licked up a pool of water, all that was left of a Glashtyn.

Laughing, the woman tossed a burning brand into the village, and the dry grass ignited. Slowly the fire spread; first to the buildings, then

the nearby trees, until the flames rose like a tower into the night sky. Just before the Gen Sto collapsed, the woman and the six shadows rode away on black horses. The little men stood there for a while, watching the village burn to the ground. Then they mounted their white horses and rode north as storm clouds rushed in from the east, dumping torrents of rain. The steam from the ruin of Floden billowed high above the forest in a giant plume.

13

Waking Wakkenburg

Pixel opened her eyes. A graceful canopy hung over her head. She lay in a four-poster bed, like a girl in a storybook. Sitting up, she looked around at the matching nightstand and bureau, the armchair, the small stone hearth. Wakkenburg House. Where Peter lived.

She threw back the quilt and got up, then opened the drapes at the window and saw a gray stone tower rising over the other parts of the house. It was still early, the sky pale blue. Directly below, a Fenny with a hoe over his shoulder walked into a wide courtyard and began to dig in a large garden bed. Then she heard someone shouting and turned from the window. The voice came from down the hall. Brisk footsteps, then silence.

Her room was situated on the second floor of the West Wing, in the crook of two connecting corridors. She dressed quickly, opened her door, and looked down both passages. No one. Then, to the right, she saw a door ajar. She moved softly down the hallway, then peeked into the room. There was Peter, sitting at a wooden desk, fingering a stack of postcards. He looked up. "Hi."

"This place sure feels like home." She grinned. "Who was yelling at you just now?"

"Norbert. Moody slept in my room."

"How do we get into that tower?"

"Which one?"

"The one I can see from my window."

He got up. "Let's ask Fiak."

Without further explanation, he led her up two flights of stairs to the library. A library in a house! And here were more Fennys, all wearing spectacles and neat little vests. They were gathered around a wooden book cart, talking in loud voices to a couple of Fennys dressed in greasy coveralls. Suddenly, one of the coverall Fennys hoisted a fellow with glasses onto the cart and pushed off.

Peter started forward. "No, Furse! It's for books!" But no one heard him. They were cheering, lining up to take a turn as Furse careened up and down the aisles. Pixel watched, delighted but trying not to laugh because Peter was obviously annoyed.

"Stop!" he shouted at the top of his lungs.

All the Fennys froze except for Furse, who brought the cart to a slow halt. "What's the problem?" he protested. The Fenny on top of the cart rolled off and lay on the floor.

"It's not a go-cart. It's for books," Peter said.

The Fenny on the floor stood up and straightened his glasses. "Then we can get rid of the motor?"

"You put on a motor?"

"Just a little addition of our own, Mr. Peter," Krim said. "We thought it might go faster, but we didn't start her up 'cause we haven't worked out how to steer."

"What's all this?" Muru stood in the open doorway, fuming. "Peter! You haven't eaten breakfast, have you? Why aren't you downstairs?"

Pixel, who had seen only Muru's gentle, motherly side, looked at Peter in alarm, but he just shrugged. "I'm getting the house map. Pixel wants to go inside that big tower you can see from her bedroom."

Muru sucked in her breath. "Are you going to open the house?"

"Sure."

"Oh!" Muru threw up her hands. "Finally! I'll send breakfast up here!"

Sometime later, the leftover porridge had turned into a cold lump, the teapot was empty, and the muffins were gone. Pixel sat beside Peter, looking at the floor plan spread out on the library table.

Wakkenburg House was enormous, and she realized that the West Wing was only one section of it. There were four wings altogether, and four towers, all named for the points on a compass. Built in the shape of a rectangular horseshoe, all the wings and towers were connected by inner corridors, with the exception of the West Tower. This lone outlier stood on the west lawn, five stories high, a broad Saxon-style edifice adjoined by the high walls that surrounded the house and grounds.

About five hundred yards to the right of this tower, the West Wing faced the wide front lawns, extending a portico over the drive that sheltered the entrance: tall double doors of thick wood, carved with patterns of leaves and branches. Immediately adjacent to the West Wing, a long blank wall, stretching away to the right, hid the South Orchard and the South Wing. Only the tops of trees, the gabled roof, and the upper floors of the South Tower were visible. This much of the house Pixel had seen on her arrival, though not in detail, her attention diverted by the spectacular crushing of the hearse.

According to the floor plan, a square court named "Rose Garden" lay at the heart of the house, at the upper end of the horseshoe. This garden led onto another courtyard titled "Kitchen Gardens", which Pixel had seen from her bedroom window. Tracing a path on the diagram, she moved her finger out of the kitchen garden, to the right, past something called "Outbuildings", and around to the North Tower. She peered closely at the plan. It looked as though the only way into this tower was from inside the North Wing. Moving her finger around the corner of the tower, she then stopped it in a wide-open area with the title "Gardens and Glenny Woods". This broad section of the grounds spread along the back of the house and was enclosed by a wall labeled "North Wall". A wavering line ran along the inside of the wall and bore the name "Glenny Stream".

She traced a way back into the house, found her own room in the West Wing, and hovered over the diagram of the second floor. *Wait a minute.* The plans showed the opening to a corridor right next to the main stairs. It went directly into the South Wing and was one of the main passages that connected the whole of the house. She'd been up and down the main staircase a few times and would have noticed it.

"This can't be right," she said. "See this long hallway out of the West Wing? I haven't seen it."

"Because it's walled up, miss," Fiak replied.

Peter, who had just picked up the last piece of bacon, paused. "Walled up? Why?"

"Mr. Thornburg—that would be your Great-Aunt Marj and Great-Uncle Edward's father—wanted the West Wing sealed off from the rest of the house after his little daughter, Jenny, disappeared. In his sorrow, he tried to cut off as much contact as possible with ... with everything."

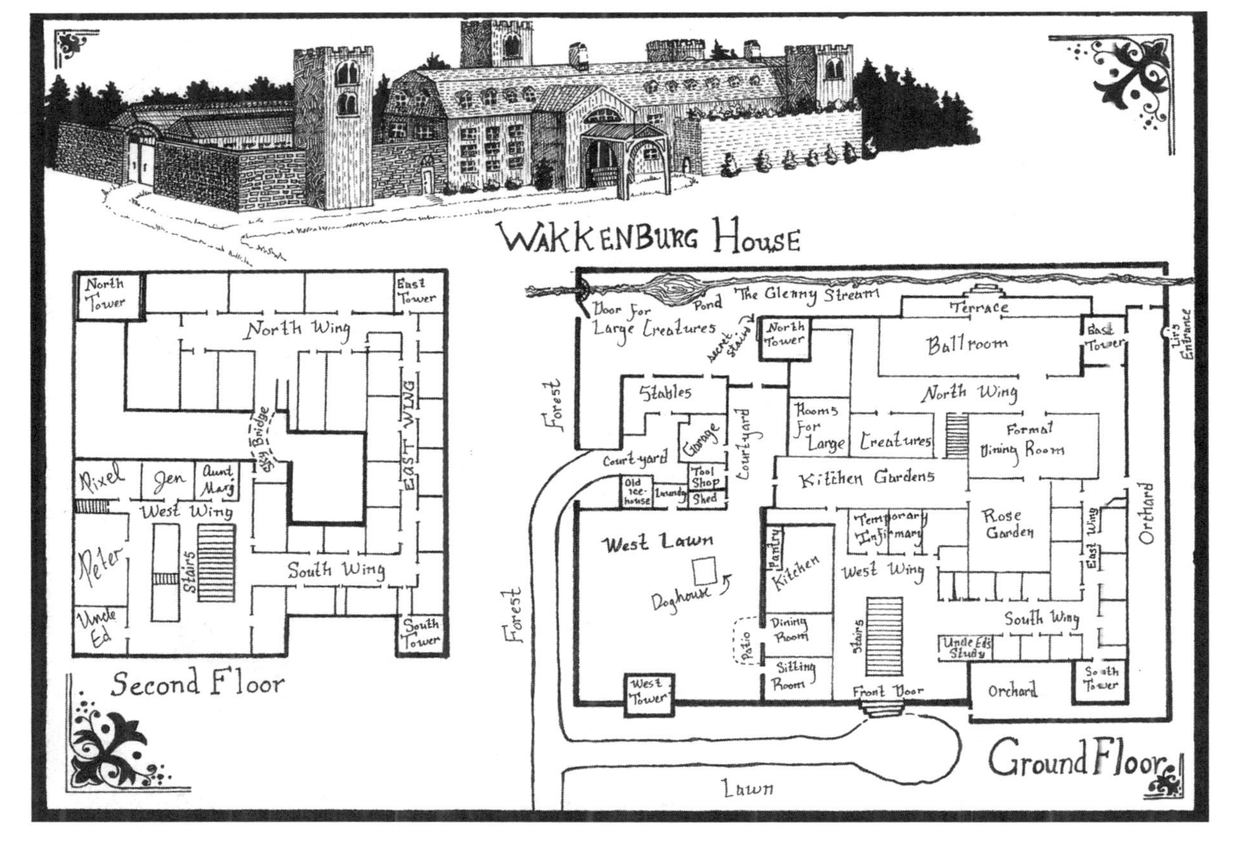
WAKKENBURG HOUSE
North Tower
East Tower
North Wing
Sky Bridge
EAST WING
Nixel
Jen
Aunt Marg
West Wing
Peter
Stairs
South Wing
Uncle Ed
South Tower
Second Floor
Door for Large Creatures
Pond
The Glenny Stream
Terrace
North Tower
secret stairs
Ballroom
East Tower
Liv's Entrance
Forest
Stables
North Wing
Rooms for Large Creatures
Formal Dining Room
Garage
Courtyard
Court-yard
Kitchen Gardens
Tool Shop
Old ice-house
Laundry
Shed
Orchard
Temporary Infirmary
Rose Garden
East Wing
West Lawn
Pantry
Kitchen
West Wing
Doghouse
Forest
South Wing
Dining Room
Patio
Stairs
Uncle Ed's Study
Sitting Room
West Tower
Front Door
Orchard
South Tower
Ground Floor
Lawn

"I think me and the boys mighta done that job," Furse said. He and Krim sat across the table. "I got a dim memory of a whole lot of plaster."

"Careful, Furse," Krim said. "You know what happened to Norbert when he remembered too much." Furse clapped a hand over his mouth.

Fiak opened a large ledger. "We Fennys have such poor memories. That's why those of us in the library try to write everything down the moment it happens." He flipped through several pages. "Yes. Here it is. Mr. Thornburg gave the order, and Norbert and his crew did the job. The gardeners also helped. It would have taken a lot of hands."

Pixel frowned. "Are you saying Norbert was on a work crew? I thought he was Head Fenny."

"Back then he wasn't Head Fenny, though I can't remember who was. But you'll find all that in the Thornburg book, Miss Pixel. In the chapter about the house."

"Do you want to see a copy, miss?" One of the librarians appeared at her elbow, looking at her hopefully.

"Okay." She watched him push the new cart away and disappear among the stacks. Minutes later he returned with a very thick book. She flipped through the pages, glancing at the slanted handwriting of Maria Thornburg.

"Okay," Peter said, "we can't get into the rest of the house through the inside corridors, I get that. We'll just use one of the outside entrances. Who has the keys?"

Furse shook his head. "All the outside entrances are bricked up."

"Yup, even the first-floor windows," Krim added. "The late Mr. Thornburg was very thorough."

"I don't get it," Pixel said. "Did he think he could make you Fennys disappear?"

"Without a Silver One in residence, we did disappear after a while," Fiak said. "That is, the family stopped seeing us.

"Wait a minute," Peter said, "if everything's bricked up, we *can't* get into the rest of the house?"

"Not without a sledgehammer," Furse replied.

"We got plenty of those in the shop," Krim added.

"I don't know what Aunt Marj would say if we started busting things up."

"As the latest Silver-eyed, you are the official head of Wakkenburg House," Fiak replied. "Your aunt and uncle know that."

"Peter!" Pixel gasped. "You own this place?"

He nodded, and the look in his eyes told her that the idea didn't thrill him. Far from it.

"If you ask me, Mr. Peter," Krim said, "we oughta start with this little door. See it here? In a corner of the kitchen gardens?" He tapped the floor plan. "It'll be the quickest way in."

Peter was silent, looking down at the table, and Pixel wondered what he was thinking. Sitting here, talking with these strange little men as if he'd known them all his life—well, he wasn't quite the same Peter from Lang. Then a movement caught her eye.

A crowd of Fennys stood in the doorway, and the entire library staff was gathered at one end of the table, watching him. When he shrugged and said, "Yeah, okay," there was a collective intake of breath, a spark in the atmosphere. The Fennys in the doorway disappeared. Krim and Furse charged out the door, and the librarians scuttled off among the stacks. Fiak smiled broadly, his spectacles glinting in the sunlight that slanted through the high windows.

"Rats," Norbert grumbled. "That's what you'll find. The whole place crawling with generations of rats! Let the past be. That's what I say."

Pixel sighed inwardly. Peter had warned her that Norbert might put a damper on things.

"But when Rumun's crew is well, you'll have plenty of help," Peter argued.

"They belong at Fenn House, and it's your job to get them back there! You'll just have to go talk to that wizard."

"Look, Norbert, Krim is just opening one door in the North Wing. If it's not too overrun with rats, it might be a good place to give that breakfast for the Bugganes."

"Breakfast for the Bugganes!" Norbert complained. "Why on earth did you invite them?"

Pixel bristled. "They saved those Fennys' lives and Peter's too!"

Norbert stared at her. "Well, I suppose you know more about it than I do. I admit that I've been preoccupied lately." He sighed. "The truth is, I was never cut out to be Head Fenny."

"Then why are you?"

"It's an old tradition, Miss Pixel. The Head Fenny never forgets. He's the repository of household customs. When the last Head Fenny was sent away, I must have said something that made everyone think I had the best memory, so I was chosen. Of course, now I wish I'd kept my mouth shut. The truth is, I don't remember much at all."

"We can't leave the house closed forever," Peter said.

"Fine," Norbert grumbled. "I suppose the whole futile project will keep that idle garage crew busy, chipping bricks and catching rats. That's the only benefit I can see." Then he marched away, grumbling under his breath.

"Listen," Peter said. "That sounds like a hammer. The crew must have started."

Pixel followed him out the back door of the West Wing, through a low archway, and into the kitchen garden. In the farthest corner of the courtyard, Krim was chipping bricks out of the wall, and already the wood of an oak door was partly visible. As soon as any debris hit the ground, Furse swept it into a wheelbarrow. Looking around, Pixel realized that the blank walls to the left of the door must conceal the first-floor windows of the North Wing. Higher up she saw the shuttered windows of its upper floors.

A number of other Fennys stood around, watching Furse and Krim. One of them said, "Sure you don't want us to start on the windows, Mr. Peter?"

He shrugged. "Okay."

"Hot dog!" There was a sudden mad scramble as ladders appeared and the crew ran for tools.

"Come on," Peter said to Pixel. "It's gonna be a while till that door's open. I'll show you the garage." He led Pixel from the kitchen garden, across a cobbled yard, and into a large workshop. A potbelly stove stood against one wall, and she saw tools lined up on pegboards. On the other side of the shop, they walked through another door, into a paved quadrangle where the wreck of the hearse lay in the sunlight. Outbuildings surrounded this courtyard. Peter and Pixel went in and out of the many doorways: a laundry, an ice house, empty stables. The outer gate of the courtyard was locked, so they went back through the garage, passed into the cobbled yard again, and turned right. Walking between the corner of the outbuildings and the West

Wing, they came out onto the west lawn. There was Moody's new doghouse, and Moody in it, chewing a bone.

On the farther side of the lawn stood the West Tower, like a solid gray rock, casting a shadow on the grass. Passing the French doors of the West Wing dining room, they approached the high garden wall adjoining the tower, and Pixel said, "This place is like a fort. Have you noticed? High walls all around and every outer gate locked."

"Well, we don't need a key for this one." Peter pulled back the bolt of a wooden door. It opened straight onto the driveway, and they were just in time to see the Datsun pass, Uncle Edward at the wheel.

Aunt Marj rushed out the front door and stood in the drive. "Oh!" they heard her exclaim. "I hope he remembers to pick up the mail!"

"Hi, Aunt Marj," Peter said. "Where's Uncle Ed going?"

"To Foyle. Says he has 'business', whatever that means," she said in a peeved voice. "By the way, Peter, what's going on out back?"

"They're opening a door to the North Wing. Is that alright?"

Her face softened. "Of course. You want to see the other parts of the house. It's been closed up since I was a child, and I hardly think of it anymore. Isn't that strange?" Then she turned abruptly and went inside.

"Look, Peter." Pixel pointed to the other side of the portico. In the garden wall that jutted out from the side of the West Wing, there was a little door, its weather-beaten wood almost the same color as the gray stone. "Where do you think that goes?"

"South Wing," Peter said, pulling a set of keys out of his pocket. Fiak had found them with the floor plan. The first key fit, and after a momentary struggle with the lock, the door opened. There wasn't much to see besides an overgrown lawn, weed-choked garden beds, and gnarled trees. Peter picked up a stick and cut his way through the tall grass as several birds took flight.

Pixel followed slowly. "Isn't this the South Orchard? I think those are green peaches."

Peter followed her gaze but didn't reply.

"I read somewhere that fruit trees have to be pruned," she said. "These look kind of old. No one's taken care of them for a long time."

"South Tower," Peter said as they rounded the corner of the house and stopped to look up. The first-floor windows were bricked over. Peter pointed to the long blank wall ahead. "That part is the

East Wing, and at the other end is the East Tower." In the distance, a tall building rose above the trees.

Continuing along the face of the East Wing, they walked down the middle of the orchard, the overgrown grass brushing their knees. Peter, leading the way, startled a few grasshoppers, and Pixel nearly trod on a bird's nest hidden in the tall weeds. It was a wild, lonely place. Now and then, they came across a stone bench or a cracked birdbath. Peter began to slash savagely at the grass, walking with his shoulders hunched forward and his head down, as if carrying a great weight on his back. When they reached the East Tower, he threw down the stick and, without a word, hoisted himself into the nearest tree.

As soon as he began climbing, Pixel felt a small tremor under her feet, then a steady vibration. Quite suddenly, the tree's branches sprang upward.

"The sea!" Peter called down. "I can see it from here. Let's walk around the outside of the wall. I bet there's a path down to the beach."

Pixel stood there, watching the leaves overhead turn a deeper shade of green. Then she looked at the other trees in the orchard. Their leaves were definitely greener, their branches now heavy with fruit.

"Pixel! Did you hear me?"

She looked up and saw his left foot hanging down, inches from a very fat yellow peach that hadn't been there a moment before. "Peter! Something's happened!"

He scrambled out of the tree, knocking several peaches from the lower branches. She caught one as he let himself down, landing beside her with a thump. "What?"

She held out the peach. "There wasn't *any* fruit growing on this tree before you climbed it. And … and look at the others! They're … they just turned green!" She stared at him, and he stared back, his strange eyes shining. Then his face paled. She watched him swallow hard once, twice. He turned pasty white, bent down, and barfed in the grass.

Coughing and retching, he leaned over, hands on knees, until the heaving stopped. Without looking at her, he stood up straight and headed for the orchard door next to the East Tower. She followed, coming up behind as he fumbled at the latch. He tried to fit a key into the lock but his hands were shaking. She grabbed the key from him, unlocked the door, and pushed it open.

They paused, looking around. Directly ahead, across a wide space of scrubby overgrown lawn, a line of trees and wild bushes stretched away to the left. Beyond that, at some distance behind the house and grounds, Pixel could see the top of an outer wall. A little wind brushed her face, stirring the tall grass. Whatever had happened to the peach trees, it had to do with Peter. Something was happening to him on this island.

"North Wing," Peter said. Turning to the left, they walked beside another long, blank wall toward the tallest building of all, the North Tower. As they passed a wide terrace, a figure rounded the tower, running toward them. It was Furse, dusty and very excited. "Mr. Peter! We got the door uncovered, and Krim's pickin' the lock."

They followed him around the corner of the tower to a little archway that had obviously just been opened. Stepping over a pile of bricks, they returned to the kitchen garden, which already looked different. Sunlight shone on the dusty glass panes of two large windows that had just been uncovered, and the little door through which they hoped to enter was now completely visible. Krim was working on the lock while, from a respectful distance, a crowd of Fennys watched.

Scowling, Norbert turned on Peter. "I suppose you're happy about this, boy!" he fumed. "Causing an uproar right before lunch."

"Look, kid," Muru added, "there's probably piles of dust in there! You'll sneeze your head off if you go in now."

Peter looked at the Fennys, biting his bottom lip, and Pixel wondered what he was thinking. "Is there a head gardener?" he finally said.

Norbert huffed and looked around. "Him."

A fellow in a green cap stepped forward. "Ulf here, Mr. Peter."

"Ulf." Peter hesitated. "Me and Pixel were walking around the other side of the house and ... well, we saw something in the East Orchard."

"Have some of the trees fallen down, sir? I wouldn't be surprised after all this time."

"Nothing like that. It's just ... well ... the trees. They didn't look so good when we went into the orchard, but ... now they do," he finished lamely.

Pixel saw a gleam come into Ulf's eye. "Did you touch any of the trees, sir?"

"I . . . I climbed one. Near the East Tower. Just to see over the wall."

"Ah. Those would be the fruit trees Mr. Jonas planted before he went away. I expect they've been asleep for a while and you came along and woke them up. But don't you worry, sir. We'll see they don't get unruly." He whistled shrilly and ran out of the courtyard followed by a third of the Fennys.

Then Krim cried, "Got it! The door's open!" and Aunt Marj came out of the West Wing, carrying three ancient flashlights.

"Peter! I thought you might need these—"

"Lunch first!" Norbert snapped, but Peter gave no indication of hearing him.

"Muru, could your house crew go in?" he said. "Maybe start on the upper floors. The windows there are only covered by shutters, so you'll have some light."

Muru, open-mouthed, stared at him. Then she grinned and pushed forward to the little door, followed by an entire brigade carrying brooms and buckets. As soon as they were gone, Peter said to Norbert, "I think Rumun and some of his crew are well enough to help you keep the West Wing going. And could you send Fiak to us? We'll need the floor plan."

"As you wish." Norbert nodded stiffly but looked relieved.

"Krim, Furse, would you and your crew mind unblocking the doors and windows all over the house? But don't kill yourselves doing it. It doesn't have to be finished today, you know."

Pixel spent the rest of the afternoon roaming the house with Peter and Aunt Marj, accompanied by Fiak, who consulted the floor plan at every turn. But Aunt Marj didn't need the aid of a house map. She guided them through the rooms and passages on every floor, saying, "Oh! I remember this" and "I know where this hallway leads!" Moody Doug followed them and sometimes ran ahead, sniffing in every dusty corner, snorting and sneezing.

"He must be looking for a long-lost bone," Pixel said.

Fiak nodded. "Probably."

The house Fennys clattered ahead with remarkable speed, throwing back shutters, opening windows to let in the summer sun, dusting, sweeping out cobwebs, wiping away decades of neglect. Pixel saw ornately carved woodwork and tiled floors everywhere. The formal dining room was furnished with a long, long table, but she was staggered by the enormous ballroom, big enough for an elephant parade.

Then, on the second floor of the North Wing, they came upon the sky bridge, a little wonder of stone masonry, built between the North and West Wings. Its many paned windows overlooked the kitchen gardens on one side and an enclosed profusion of blooms on the other.

"The Rose Garden," Aunt Marj explained as they looked down at the untamed blossoms climbing over walls and windows and winding up and around a central fountain. "Mother's favorite place. I could hear the fountain on summer nights through my bedroom window."

Pixel went to the end of the bridge and knocked on the white plaster wall. "This is one of the blocked places, isn't it?"

"Yes. Our second-floor bedrooms in the West Wing are on the other side." Aunt Marj sighed. "Jenny loved this bridge. We played here every day. Of course, we had the old playroom in the North Tower too. Father locked that up first."

Pixel looked at the stone edifice rising above the roof of the North Wing. "We haven't been to the North Tower yet."

Aunt Marj didn't reply, and in the silence, Pixel heard the muted clink of tools on stone.

"It must be five o'clock," Aunt Marj said. "I need a cup of tea."

When she was gone, Peter looked down to the courtyard, where a gardener was watering the sunflowers. "I don't understand these Fennys. They work all day and never seem tired. And whenever I offer to help or do something for myself, Muru gets really grumpy. Tells me to mind my own business."

"You know more about them than I do."

"Not really."

Taking the back stairs to the kitchen garden, they made their way to the West Wing. Then, after changing out of their dusty clothes, they had a quiet dinner with Aunt Marj on the patio outside the dining room. The sun sank behind the forest, and the shadows lengthened. Pixel listened to the immense silence behind the clink of plates and the evening twitter of birds. Gradually, their commonplace talk about the day waned, and they sat without speaking. A peaceful stillness settled over the garden.

Suddenly, Aunt Marj sat up and said, "Edward isn't back yet. He's been gone all day. I hope he hasn't had car trouble." As she spoke, they heard the distant rumble of an engine growling up the drive. It stopped, a door slammed, and Aunt Marj hurried off to meet her brother.

Pixel helped Peter pile all the dishes on a rolling cart and push it into the dining room, where a Fenny took it and wheeled it into the kitchen. Then they walked across the lawn and out the garden door by the West Tower, turning right onto the cobbled road that ran beside the front wall. Moody went with them, trotting ahead, sniffing this way and that. The road ended at the crossing where the hearse had crashed into the Buggane. To their left was the smooth paved drive; to the right, a dirt lane continued to the back gate and the garage. Directly ahead, the deep woods cast long evening shadows.

Turning right, onto the dirt lane, they walked beside the wall, under the eaves of the forest, all the way to the back gate, forgetting that it was locked. They were about to turn back when Moody stopped, tense and alert. Looking toward the forest, he uttered a low woof.

Her eyes on the deepening shadows under the trees, Pixel picked up a rock and stepped in front of Peter. Then Moody lunged forward, wagging his tail as a huge mole with ivory tusks sprang up from the undergrowth. Pixel hurled the rock with all her might. The creature caught it in his paw, growled, and stepped toward them. In blind panic, Pixel grabbed Peter's arm to pull him away, but he just stood there, laughing. Hearing a small *pop!*, she looked back, and there was the old man who had gone with them to Floden.

"Boy, I'm here with a message. We accept your invitation for breakfast. We'll come in three days' time."

"Right." Peter grinned. "Breakfast."

Pixel, still panting, stared at Peter and the strange man. In just a short time, something about her best friend had changed, and she felt as if she were seeing him again for the first time.

"Of course, we'll use our old entrance over yonder by the Glenny." He pointed down the lane. "Not that gate. The big one."

"Why not the front door?"

"Custom." Saluting, the old man turned and made for the woods. As he disappeared into the shadows of the forest, Pixel said, "Who is he?"

"A Buggane. Tom Mole. I guess you never saw him like that before."

Wondering, she followed him back to the West Wing, into the kitchen. There they found Norbert and Muru, and she listened to Peter tell them about his invitation.

Norbert scowled. "Bugganes to breakfast? What were you thinking, boy?"

"I can't go back on my word."

"Well, you'll have to! We can't bring creatures like that into the dining room!"

"The ballroom," Muru said. "Now that the North Wing is open, we can do it there."

"Not on my watch!" Norbert snapped, and he stomped out.

"It's alright, kid. Leave it to me," Muru said. "Rumun and the others from Fenn House are ready to take over duties in the West Wing. I'll see to opening the kitchen in the East Tower. It's right next to the ballroom, and it's a lot bigger than this one. And, by the way, the Buggane entrance is the Door for Large Creatures, out by Glenny Pond. It's bricked over, but I'll tell Furse to open it up. We'll be ready in three days, don't worry."

"It's a lot of work for you, Muru. Let me help," Peter said.

Muru frowned. "If I wanted your help, I'd ask."

"But it's not fair. You do all the work and we don't do anything. I know how to do laundry and ... and wash dishes."

"Did you hear me asking what's fair?" Muru scowled. "Things here don't work like they do on the mainland, kid. There's a lot you don't know about us Fennys! If it weren't for us, you Thornburgs would be dead inside a week!"

Peter shrugged. "Fine. Suit yourself."

Pixel watched Muru bustle out of the kitchen. Another Fenny filled the sink with soapy water and began to wash frying pans.

Peter rubbed the top of his head till all his hair stood up. "Beats me why they ask permission for everything and then tell me what to do."

Pixel smiled slowly. "Is life here this strange every day? I keep thinking I'll wake up and find I was dreaming."

He grinned sideways. "But will you wake up at your aunt's house or back in Lang?"

"Actually, I don't want to wake up at all. I want this dream to go on and on."

14

Lead the Way

The Washers had finished their work. As their twinkling lights disappeared in the woods on the opposite shore, Jen glanced up at the waxing moon, which hung low over the river valley.

"My, they scrub hard!" Thrinn said. "I thought they'd take my skin right off!"

Jen, her own skin still tingling, looked down at the boots she'd been given. They had bathed her, dressed her in new clothes, and done the same for her companions.

"They have washed the wasted years away," Forlost said. "I remember now. I was Head Fenny of Wakkenburg House."

Jen looked at the little man, who was now clear-eyed, no longer dressed in rags. He had come up from the water weeping.

"That's right!" Thrinn said. "And I was Head Housekeeper. But oh! No one could do the things you did, Forlost! Remember, Jenny? That time your brother teased you until you cried? Forlost came into the room and—*zing!* Little Edward was hanging in the air by the back of his shorts!"

"I have a brother?"

"Three brothers and two sisters: James, Patrick, Clare, Marjorie, and Edward. Oh! It's all coming back now! The feasts! The dancing! Remember the ballroom all lit up with candles? And the dining room filled with folk from the forest? Those were times."

"Where are my brothers and sisters now?"

"Still at Wakkenburg House, I suppose," Thrinn said carelessly. "How I had to chase you and Eddie at bath time through all those long passages! You were clever at hiding!"

"Why didn't Mother take me back there?"

"You disappeared."

"Disappeared?" Jen looked to Forlost, but he remained silent.

"That's right," Thrinn said. "One moment you were there; the next you were gone. *Poof!* That's what your brother said. *Poof!*"

"You went with your mother and little Edward and Marjorie to the Periwinkle Fair in Floden," Forlost said thoughtfully. "They came back to Wakkenburg that day, but you didn't."

Thrinn nodded. "I remember how your mother cried and cried, until I said I'd go with Forlost to find you. And here you are! But where did you go, child? You were gone a long time!"

"I ... I went back to Floden. Why didn't Mother wait for me?" Jen bit her trembling lip. All she could remember clearly was waking up at the lake.

"I thought you might return to the village," Forlost said quietly. "That's why I went there and stayed. Thrinn was to come with me, but we got separated on the way."

Jen heard a soft grunt, and Tom Bear's huge form loomed up in the darkness. He had been waiting under the eaves of the forest.

"What now?" Thrinn said, looking at the Buggane. "Is it time to go home?"

Tom rumbled a reply, and Forlost said, "I'm afraid he's right. You must lead us now, Jenny. You *are* the Silver One. I do not see an open path. What are the trees saying?"

"The trees?" She stood there on the riverbank, under the vast emptiness of the night sky, feeling an ache around her heart. The darkness pressed close, bearing down like a great weight.

"Ever of old, the Silver Ones have been able to hear the talk of the trees," Forlost said softly. "Listen, Jenny. Empty your mind of yourself."

An owl hooted in the nearby woods, and small bats swooped over the water. Jen felt her throat tighten. Squeezing her eyes shut, she tried to stop the tears, but they came anyway. More than anything, she wanted Mother, to feel her arms and to hear her voice. It had been too long, and the picture of Mother that she carried in her mind was fading. Clenching her fists, she fought against the heavy darkness that was slowly swallowing the beloved face. Harder and harder the shadows pressed, and without knowing what she was doing, she sank to her knees, bowed her head to the ground, and covered her head with her arms. "No," she moaned, pushing back against the pressure that seemed to be the very air itself. But it was too much, and with a sudden gasp, she gave way. "Oh!" She sucked in her breath, as if surfacing from under water. Lifting her head, she looked toward the forest. "I . . . I hear them!"

"What are they saying, child?" Forlost said gravely.

Jen laughed. Their voices were like the rustle of soft leaves, and wind, and pattering rain. They were singing songs about starlight and little rills of running water. She closed her eyes, listening. Then she got to her feet and pointed upriver. "That way. We're going to the mountains."

❦ ❦ ❦

Winking lights bobbed on the surface of the river. Jen stopped on the stony bank, watching a bony head rise out of the current. A creature with fiery eyes uttered a deep, lowing call.

"The Tarroo Ushtey have come to see you, Silver One," Forlost said softly. "They have heard of your return."

As he spoke, more heads appeared, and the bright red eyes moved closer, gathering near the shore where she stood.

"What are they?"

"Water bulls," Forlost said. "Some call them Mac Lir's cattle."

Tom Bear growled.

"Yes, I agree," Forlost said. "Few creatures of the Great Migration will ally themselves with the wizard now. With the exception of the Moonjer Veggey."

"Well, I heard they eat nothing more than fish, since coming to this island," Thrinn said. "So there's nothing to be afraid of."

"What did they eat before?" Jen asked.

Tom Bear growled deep in his throat, and Forlost shook his head. "Tom is right. No one from the old land behaves as they once did. We can be thankful for that."

For a time, the red eyes followed them upstream as they traveled along the riverbank, the Tarroo lowing and bellowing, spouting water. Then the way became steep. Leaving the valley behind, they toiled up a stony path beside ever-deepening ravines through which the Glenfaba flowed down from the High Hills.

On and on they went, traveling far into the night under the white stars. The air grew colder. Now and then, the birds that Thrinn called nighthawks swooped over the river, uttering their strange, rasping call. Higher and higher they climbed, out of the woodland, into the bare foothills, the silver moon lighting their way as they followed the sound of the river. Then, in the early hours before sunrise, as the moon set behind them in a bank of silver clouds, they mounted a short, steep bank. Standing in the chill light, they surveyed a wide shelf of green-gray pastureland. To their left, the river flowed almost level with the grass before it disappeared down a series of shallow falls into deep canyons.

Not far from the riverbank, Jen saw an old woman standing in the orange glow of a campfire. White hair curled around her face. She wore a blue travel-stained cloak and leaned on a wooden staff.

"Greetings, children," the woman called. "You've come a long way. It's time to rest for a while."

The voices of the trees had certainly guided Jen to this place, yet they said nothing of the woman, whether she was friend or foe. Glancing at the distant pines covering the higher foothills, Jen heard only faint, far-off songs about the coming sun. "Who are you?" she asked, drawing nearer.

Tom Bear uttered a gentle growl, and the woman laughed. "Lady of the Mountains and Shepherdess of the Hills. That is what the Bugganes call me. I am glad to see you again, Tom."

The Buggane bowed his shaggy head and sat down near the fire.

"What am I to call you?" Jen asked.

"Call me Mother if you like."

"Are those your sheep, Mother?" Thrinn said, pointing to the flock of small white creatures farther off in the meadow.

"Those are the hounds of the Moonjer Veggey."

"The Moonjer Veggey?" Forlost looked around the valley. "Have they come to you at last?"

"Only their hounds," the woman replied.

They sat down by the fire, and the woman served bread and a hot drink that tasted sharp and sweet. To the Buggane she gave a large bowl of warm milk and honey. When they were done eating, Tom rumbled his thanks, stretched out in the grass, and closed his eyes. Then Thrinn and Forlost lay down and fell instantly asleep.

"Dawn approaches, child," the woman said, softly. "Let me show you the morning star."

Jen looked up. There were so many stars. How could one be told from another? Then a faint light began to rise in the east. As the lesser stars faded, one remained, shining like a beacon.

"Is that it?" She turned her eyes from the sky and saw the most beautiful woman standing by the fire. She held the staff in her hand and wore the same cloak, but it had fallen open, revealing a deep-red garment. Dark hair fell over her shoulders, framing a face that bore no sign of age. Stars seemed to gather around her head, and suddenly Jen knew her. "Lady!" she said, kneeling in the grass.

"Yes, Jenny. We have met in dreams and visions, and now face-to-face. You have done well to come so far, child, but you have a long road still. Into the mountains you must climb, past Spoot Voor Falls and Kulifara, onto the high pass of Mount Rosknil." She turned and pointed to three stark pinnacles in the distance. "In that place, you will find the entrance to a road that goes down into the very depths of Rosknil. It is a dark path, but do not be afraid! Take that way. Deep in the mountain, you will find the lost ones."

"The lost ones?" Jen gazed at the far-off peaks, feeling suddenly weary.

"I will send someone to guide you. Listen for my voice, and all will be well."

"But ..." Jen faltered.

"But what, child?"

"I ... I want to find my mother. I went back to Floden, but she wasn't there. Is she at the Big House, as the Poinkers said?"

The Lady looked at her gravely. "She is no longer at Wakkenburg, Jenny. She went to the Inner Mountains long ago."

"The mountains! That's where you're sending me!"

"No, dear child. You are not going to the *Inner* Mountains. Not yet. I am sending you to the island mountains that you see before you."

"Then I am not to find my mother?"

"Not yet, child. You must find the lost ones. It is your first task. Will you do as I ask?"

Jen hung her head, replying in a low voice, "Yes. I'll go." Then she felt the Lady's arms around her. Leaning her head against the woman's breast, she began to weep softly, then in great heaving sighs. Sorrow overwhelmed her. She had come back to Floden too late and lost Mother. Now she must go on without her.

Gradually, her sighing ceased and she became aware of a golden light all about. Then, like a wave on the wind, birdsong came rushing over the far hills. The woman picked her up and held her close, and Jen slept.

❦ ❦ ❦

Standing over the prostrate dragon, the Lady held its head down with her foot. Thinking the beast was dead, Jen bent over to get a closer look. It opened one eye.

She sat up, instantly awake, her heart pounding. The sun was high overhead. Forlost and Thrinn were busy over the campfire, but the Lady they had met was gone. Pulling on her boots, Jen got to her feet.

Thrinn looked up. "You're taller than you were yesterday, Jenny. Your new clothes fit better."

Jen smoothed the long tunic over her skirt. She *felt* taller today. Stronger. Ready to follow the Lady's instructions.

Tom Bear came up from the riverbank with fish in his mouth. He laid them before Thrinn, who took them away to clean and cook. Then, his mouth still dripping, he grunted at Jen.

"We're going there," she said, pointing north to the three dark mountain peaks. "Past Spoot Voor to the high pass of Mount Rosknil. But ..." She lowered her arm slowly. "I don't know which one is Rosknil. Do you?"

Tom rumbled on for a bit, and Jen said, "I see. Spoot Voor Falls and the lands beyond are your territory. That's good. You'll know the way."

"Come, let us eat," Forlost said. "It is already past midday and we have far to go."

They ate quickly, put out the fire, and returned to the riverbank. Tom led them now, higher and higher into the foothills until they heard the roar of a great waterfall. Scrambling up a slope of loose stones, they came to a wide shelf and stood in the late-afternoon sun, looking down on the roaring torrent of Spoot Voor Falls.

From this high place, they could see most of the island and the Glenfaba cutting its way through the middle. On the left side of the river, south of the wooded foothills, a wide marsh glinted in the sunlight; to the right lay the golden pastures of the Tarroo Ushtey. The deep forests of Wakken Wood covered the rest of the island, except for a region of bare hills on the southwest coast, the Floden Hills, yellow under the blue sky. Encompassing all was the sea, and for the first time, Jen understood what the word "island" meant. At the urging of Forlost, she turned away and followed the others into a steep, rocky woodland.

They climbed and climbed until the trees cast long shadows and the sun sank behind the western hills. At last, toiling up a steep chute onto a forested ridge, they came to a clearing sheltered by rock walls, and here they rested. They were high up in the mountains now, and it was cold. A copse of pine trees stood just on the other side of their shelter, and Forlost gathered sticks to build a fire. As they drew close, warming their hands, twilight deepened into night. Thrinn had a few oat cakes in her pocket, given to her by the Lady. They ate these, and then the Fennys went to sleep. Tom Bear stretched out on the other side of the fire, but Jen's legs ached. She sat up, wide awake, throwing small sticks into the flames, listening to the crackle. It was the only sound in the deep quiet of the mountains. When she finally lay down between her companions, she looked up into the night sky and saw the stars—rivers and oceans of them. Then she heard the high, thin singing of the pine trees, and for a long time she listened to the beautiful music, which told her of the Milky Way and the streams of starlight beyond the reach of men.

She woke at dawn and lay for a while, gazing at the morning star. Then Forlost roused them. There was nothing to eat for breakfast, so they put out the last embers of their fire and followed Tom Bear through the pinewood onto a stony hogback, bare and open to the sky. He led them along this narrow ridge, single file. On either side, steep slopes of scree fell a mile or more to the valleys below. Jen looked down and saw a dark forest on one side; on the other, the river rushed through a rocky chasm, deep and treeless.

The ridge ended on the side of the nearest mountain, and they walked along a rocky path that skirted the southern shoulder. Then, scrambling after Tom, they climbed up a sparsely wooded slope onto another ledge that was smoother, easier to travel. By this time, it was past midday, and as the afternoon wore on, Tom Bear walked faster and faster until he was trotting. Forlost and Thrinn trudged on tirelessly, but Jen often fell behind and had to sprint to catch up. Whenever they came upon a rill of water flowing down from the heights, Tom allowed them to stop and quench their thirst, but he never let them rest for long.

Sometime in the late afternoon, after struggling past a section of the narrow ledge that threatened to crumble away beneath their feet, the travelers came around a buttress of rock and saw a wide woodland. Exhausted, Jen stumbled into the shade and sat down at the foot of a tree.

"I smell a campfire," Forlost said, looking around.

Two trees shuddered sideways, opening a new path. Tom grunted, and the others followed him into the woods.

The leafy trees gave way to dark firs growing so close together that very little light reached the forest floor. Yet the pathway continued, and the smell of a campfire grew stronger, combined with the distinct aroma of stew. Then the trail bent to the right, and they stumbled out of the deep shade into dappled sunlight. Straight ahead, Jen saw a sheer cliff face and a boy sitting at the mouth of a cave.

"Tom Bear!" The boy jumped to his feet. "At last, you're here! Greetings, old ones," he said, bowing to Forlost and Thrinn. "Welcome, Silver One."

He wasn't much taller than she was. Like her, he had dark hair, but his brown eyes were like pools of clear water whose depths are lit by the sun.

"Are you the guide the Lady spoke of?" Jen asked.

"Yes, I am. I will lead you to the Hidden Valley tomorrow."

"First, we go through the deeps of Rosknil," Jen said. "To find the lost ones."

He looked steadily into her eyes. "The lost ones? Mother did not mention this to me, but I see she has given you a special message. We will go down into Rosknil together."

They ate the stew that the boy had made and spent the remainder of that day resting. When night came, everyone but the bear wrapped themselves in blankets and slept in the cave.

In the morning, they broke camp. The boy slung a small pack across his shoulders and led them up a steep slope. All morning they scrambled over rock and root until they climbed right out of the forest and walked along a narrow ledge among sweet-smelling bushes. They were high on the mountain, looking down at forested valleys. Fat creatures called marmots poked their heads out of holes or sat up and watched the travelers pass.

Toward evening, they left the alpine scrub behind and stepped into a region of bare rock and quiet pools of clear water.

"At last, we are nearing the top of Rosknil," Jen said. "Where is the dark road the Lady spoke of?"

"It is Mount Kulifara that we have been climbing," the boy said. They went around the mountain's southwest flank onto a stony ridge, and he pointed ahead. "There is Mount Rosknil."

Jen gazed at the towering height filling the northern sky, stark and bleak. Behind it, a higher mountain lifted its craggy head into the clear summer air. Forlost and Thrinn came up beside her, and Tom Bear sat down on his haunches.

"There," the boy said, pointing to a distant crevice halfway up the eastern side of Mount Rosknil. "That is Scadoo Pass and the opening to a tunnel. I have heard it goes down to the heart of the mountain, though I have not traveled that way myself."

A high, bare hogback, like a bridge, linked Mount Kulifara with Rosknil. In the dying light of day, the boy led them across this ridge. When they reached the other side, he stopped beneath a sparse thicket of pines and picked up two stout sticks from the ground. "Torches," he said, handing one to Forlost.

The first stars appeared as the travelers came to the high, narrow entrance of Scadoo Pass, a doorway darker than night. To Jen's surprise, Tom Bear began to rumble and grunt.

"What? You're not coming with us?" she said.

He shook his shaggy head, and she put her hands on his bristly cheeks. "I understand. You have gone as far as the Lady asked, and now you have other work to do. But ... when will I see you again?"

Uttering a low growl, he touched his nose to her face, nodded to her companions, and lumbered away into the deepening shadows. Then the boy struck a flint and lit the torches, and with a pang of misgiving, Jen followed him through the dark doorway of Scadoo.

15

The Old Trouble Again

Horses whinnied fiercely, and he was falling, falling into darkness as icy hands like manacles wrapped around his arms and legs. He opened his mouth to cry out, but no sound came, and he found himself floating face down in cold water as a monstrous shape passed below. The prodigious eel looked up, saw him, and began to clash gigantic barbed teeth. *Clang, clang!* Helpless, his legs and arms bound, he watched as the monster moved upward through the pulsing current. He jerked, trying to propel himself away, and his face broke the surface as a fiery sun rose above the sea ...

He sat up gasping. Light streamed through the open window. Outside, the sound of birds mixed with the clang of hammers chipping away at old mortar and brick. Moody sat beside the bed, ears pricked forward. Peter's heart slowed, and he put out a hand, which Moody happily wrapped in his giant tongue.

Drying his hand on the sheet, Peter threw back the covers and got up. He'd grown accustomed to Muru's morning nattering, but she was somewhere in another wing of the house and had probably worked through the night.

Pushing away the terror of his dream, he pulled on yesterday's clothes, then splashed his face with cold water from the basin. If only he didn't have such vivid nightmares. He dried his face on a towel and looked around just as Moody lifted a breakfast roll from the table and swallowed it in one gulp. He laughed and the great dog attacked him, slobbering all over his face. They collapsed in a joyful heap, and the last vestige of the dream slipped away as he fought his way out from under the dog's affectionate tongue.

His next thought was of Pixel. She had three days left before her aunt returned from Lang. Then what? She'd have to go back to Foyle, to that house where she wasn't safe. Maybe they should run away to the woods. They could go to Floden and … no, not Floden. The Bugganes had warned him that neither Floden nor the woods were safe. Why? Uncle Ed had spoken of Glashtyn. He sat down at the desk and closed his eyes as his thoughts began to swirl. So much had happened in a short space of time, and he'd heard so many strange tales.

There was the young sister, Jenny, another Silver-eyed, who had disappeared in Floden seventy years ago. He felt in his pocket for her button, which Aunt Marj had given to him for some reason, then yanked open his desk drawer and tossed it in. No sense trying to figure out the past. It was the present that threatened to swamp him.

He banged the drawer shut, then fingered the stack of postcards on the desk. He'd said goodbye to his dad less than two weeks ago, but it seemed like a year. And Dad's voice hadn't sounded right on the phone. When had he called? Was it really only the night before last? Good grief. Time warped in this house. His glance fell on a small mirror hanging above the desk. The sight of his eyes, like bright silver coins, made him think of the trees in the orchard. What had happened? Ulf said something about Jonas. Who was he?

"The past again," he said aloud, standing up. "Come on, Moody. Let's find more breakfast since you've eaten mine."

In the dining room, Peter found many more rolls, a pitcher of orange juice, and a pot of tea on the table, and his uncle hunched over a cup of coffee.

"Hi, Uncle Ed." He received a grunt in reply, so he turned his attention to the food on the sideboard. There were sausages on a hot plate, peach scones, peach compote, and a salad of melon and peaches. Evidently the harvest in the East Orchard had begun. He tossed two sausages to Moody and sent him out the French doors to the patio. As he sat down at the table, Aunt Marj sailed in.

"Good morning, Peter! Oh, Edward, there you are! Is there any coffee left?"

Uncle Ed grunted at her too and poured himself another cup.

"I heard you come home yesterday, but then you locked yourself in the study. How was your trip to Foyle?"

She asked her question casually, but Peter looked up and stopped chewing when he sensed the sudden tension in the room. Into the silence that followed, a blue jay called loudly and small birds twittered in reply.

"Where's Pixel?" Uncle Edward demanded.

"I just saw her with Muru. On their way to the North Wing," Aunt Marj replied.

"Good. Then I better tell you the news."

At the tone of his voice, Peter saw his aunt sink silently into a chair.

"Night before last—same night I brought Pixel here—there was another raid in Foyle. You know about those raids, Peter?"

"Sure. There was one last week."

"Well, this one was different. No food taken. Only vandalism. The inside of Thorny's looked like a tornado hit. Boxes and cartons slashed open, jars and bottles smashed, and the front door knocked clean off its hinges."

"Oh, poor George!" Marj gasped. "What about the other shops?"

"Only Thorny's got busted up. Thorny's and the county jail. No place else. And the only thing missin' is Mac Rilson."

"He escaped?" Peter asked.

"Someone broke him out. And here's the strange thing. The guard swears he was awake all night and never heard a thing. Neither did anyone else in town. Seems mighty strange with things smashed up like they were. Not even a dog barked."

"How can that be?" Marj said.

"That's what folks are askin'. All over town. The police are completely flummoxed. Not a single clue. Some folks are sayin' they'll clear out if the police can't produce evidence that they're dealin' with regular human criminals."

"What nonsense," Marj said. "Small raids have been going on for years."

"This wasn't like them other raids, Marj. That's what I'm tryin' to tell you. Only Thorny's and the jail. And no one heard 'cause the town was under an enchanted sleep. That's what they're sayin'. Even George and Mary. That little guest room in their apartment was turned upside down, and neither George nor Mary nor Annette heard a thing. And them asleep next door!" He paused. "George and Mary are talkin' about the old days, Marj. Everyone in Foyle is. And Mac's been hollerin' all around town about a Silver-eyed Thornburg on the island again. I got some pretty dark looks."

"Oh, Peter," she said. "You visited Foyle last week!"

A chill spread over his limbs. "I kept my sunglasses on. Pixel made me." He hadn't told them about meeting Mac Rilson and Foster at the ferry terminal.

"Now let me tell you about the Rilson house." Uncle Edward lowered his voice. "I went over there and talked to Cook. Told her I knew about the room with all those urns. She was mighty upset and tried to deny it, but I told her I'd seen it and had evidence."

"Urns? What's this?" Marj said.

"Pixel didn't tell you? That evening I picked her up, I found her in a secret little mausoleum. Right there in the house. I don't suppose they wanted her to find that. It's where all them blood treatments end. Remember Mae? Found her urn in that room."

"No ..." Marj paled and fell silent.

Peter frowned. "Wait. You mean dead?"

"Whoever heard of treatments where you don't get medicine and they only take your blood?" Uncle Ed continued. "That's what Pixel said. They take lots of blood, testing for a disease no one talks about. None of them Rilson girls ever looked sick till they stepped into that house. Now we know what happens. They all disappear silently into little urns hidden away in a locked room."

The quiet dread Peter had always felt about the blood treatments resurfaced in his mind, and he felt his throat tighten. He couldn't speak, and Uncle Edward went on.

"Goodness knows how Pixel found the key. But you can bet Cook knew all along. She started packin' up all her things, and I helped load her car. Then, as we were carryin' out the last of it, a door banged upstairs. I tell you, Cook looked scared. Her hands were shakin' so bad, I had to lock the front door myself. When I asked who else was in the house, she clammed up. Wouldn't say another word. Seems to me the islanders look to us Thornburgs as being the center of weirdness, but there's somethin' strange goin' on at the Rilson house. Think about it. One day the aunt takes a trip. Cook and Pixel leave the same day. Whoever busted up Thorny's and tore up their guest room was lookin' for someone."

"Who?" Marj whispered.

"Pixel. That's what Mary thinks, puttin' two and two together. Pixel was supposed to stay with them that night, but I came and picked her up."

Peter sat there, staring at his uncle, remembering what Pixel had said about strange footsteps and someone who came to her door at night.

"But *who* went looking for Pixel?" Marj demanded. "And why?"

"I dunno for sure, but Mary's wonderin' if it's got something to do with those blood treatments. Or maybe because she's your friend, Peter. Like I said, Mac Rilson's been makin' a fuss all over town about a Silver-eyed boy."

"But why would Mac Rilson even care about Peter?"

Uncle Ed shrugged. "There's no telling. He says strange things even when he's sober."

"If you're right about all this, we can't just sit here." Aunt Marj's manner became brisk. "I think Peter had better go back to Lang on the next ferry."

Peter hesitated. He wasn't sure whether to protest or to jump at the chance. And what about Pixel?

Into the silence, his uncle said, "No. He has to stay and see this thing out."

"But we told his father we'd keep him safe!"

"I know, Marj. But don't you see? The whole of Foyle was turned upside down to find *Pixel*. It's the old trouble come back, and somehow she's mixed up in it."

"She can't go back to Foyle," Peter said quietly.

Uncle Ed laughed grimly. "I guess Pixel's aunt is in for a big surprise when she gets home. Cook cleared out, Pixel gone, and her secret room of urns wide open."

Aunt Marj drummed her fingers on the table. Finally, she said, "George and Mary should come here. Surely they'll want to get out of Foyle now."

"Oh, they're alright. Opening the store today, most likely. After I helped Cook move outa the Rilson house, I stayed a while and helped them clean up. I know they'll wanna get back to business. Trouble is, there may not be much business if the police don't come up with an explanation. People are scared, Marj. They'll move away. They've all heard their grandparents' stories. Goodness knows they're used to the local folklore, but they don't want it bustin' down their doors."

"Oh," Aunt Marj sighed, covering her face with her hands. "What if you're right? What if it's the old trouble again? I thought that was all over and done with."

"Done with! Just because things in the woods have been quiet since Jenny disappeared? Did you really think Dad could put up a few bricks, seal up the old house and—hey presto!—the trouble would be over? I knew it would come around again; that's why I've stayed, even when the rest of the family moved off the island."

"Oh, Ed. I didn't mean ... I didn't know ... Do you really think Jenny's still out there somewhere? It's been seventy years!"

Peter's sausages were cold, and he sat staring at his plate without seeing them. He was in way over his head. Pixel too. He wished they'd never left Lang.

"Oh, she's out there," his uncle was saying. "Come on, Marj. Do you really think a Silver-eyed Thornburg could just disappear like that? Remember, they're not like us. They don't die. They go off. To the mountains, or something."

Peter looked up. "What?"

There was a long silence.

"Oh, Peter," Aunt Marj said. "I thought you knew. Surely you've read the book by now."

"Of course he hasn't," Uncle Edward said bitterly. "It's a great, fat tome, and Peter's hardly had a moment to sit still." He put down his cup. "I'm sorry, boy. I shot off my mouth without thinkin'. But maybe it's better to hear it from us after all. If what the book says is true—and after what I've seen, livin' here by the woods, I've no reason to doubt it—you Silver-eyed Thornburgs have a special life. Ever since old Nathaniel came to this island, there's been one of you born every hundred years or so. You're the fourth. Usually your lives overlap here in Wakken Wood by a decade, to give time, I guess, for the newest to grow and be trained, so to speak. Maybe it was for protection too." He paused, picked up a spoon and began stirring his cold coffee. "To my mind, that was the problem for poor Jenny. She was only three years old when Jonas went off to the mountains. By rights, he should have stayed till she was at least twelve. But he was tired. Stricken, you might say. He was the guardian during the first trouble in the woods, and it seems clear to me that he didn't want no more responsibility."

"But what *is* the trouble?" Peter looked from his aunt to his uncle. "You've been talking about trouble in Foyle and in the woods, but what *is* it?"

"We've never really known," Uncle Edward said. "The Thornburg book is just a collection of diaries written by Nathaniel and Jonas, though Jonas didn't write much. It was his sister, Maria, who wrote the later chapters, but she recorded only the things Jonas told her about. She did write detailed accounts of what the house looked like and how it was run back then, but it seems Jonas wouldn't say much about whatever was goin' on in the woods."

"According to Maria, the trouble wasn't just the raids in Foyle," Aunt Marj said slowly. "It was freakish weather. In the end, Orbsen Bay burned down, and no one rebuilt much but the ferry terminal. They either left the island or went to Sweetwater."

"But ..." Peter tried to piece together the little he knew. "The raids don't happen in Sweetwater, do they?"

"Right. Have a look at one of the old maps," Uncle Ed said. "The territory of Wakken Wood covers most of the island, from the southern tip to the northern mountains beyond Spoot Voor. With the exception of Sweetwater and a narrow strip along the southeast coast, the island belongs to us Thornburgs. Well, to you, actually."

"Me?"

"You got them eyes, so you're the official guardian. Like I said, everything south of Wakkenburg Road and east of Highway 20—which includes Sweetwater—is more or less out of the domain."

"Domain?"

"The domain of, well ..."

"May as well say it, Ed, no matter how foolish it sounds," Aunt Marj cut in. "The domain of a wizard. Mac Lir."

"Oh." Peter remembered now. He'd read it ... when? Last week? Time had no meaning in this house. "Yeah. I know about him."

"So you did read the book," Aunt Marj said.

"Not much past chapter two."

"Well, then you've read enough to know as much as we know about Mac Lir," Uncle Edward said.

"Rumun told me that Mac Lir moved into Fenn House. How is that even possible? Nathaniel's story about him is a few hundred years old."

His uncle only grunted in reply, but Aunt Marj said, "Is there a reason to doubt Rumun?"

They lapsed into silence, and Peter sat there, a great weight settling over his heart. As far as he could see, they'd decided that Pixel should stay at Wakkenburg and that he would not be going back to Lang. He should "see this thing out", as his uncle had put it, though he had no idea what that meant. Suddenly, an image of the Bugganes sprang into his mind, and he remembered something they'd said.

"This is bad! It can mean only one thing: Mac Lir is back!"

"He has come because of the Moonwitch. She is growing in power of late, and you mark my words, Silver One: She will challenge Mac Lir, and there will be war!"

"The Moonwitch," he said aloud, but no one heard him.

Outside, Pixel was calling to Moody. The big dog rose from the patio and barked a friendly greeting.

"Oh!" Aunt Marj gasped. "What do we tell her?"

"Nothing," Uncle Edward said. "Not yet." He looked hard at Peter. "Not till Saturday, when she'll expect to go back to Foyle. Agreed?"

He nodded. His aunt muttered something about calling Mary and George and left the room just as Pixel appeared at the French doors.

"Pixel!" Uncle Edward said. "Come in and have something to eat."

The three of them sat together for a while, and Peter toyed with his cold sausages, watching Pixel consume a plate full of food. She had, in fact, been up for hours. The early light of dawn had drawn her outdoors.

"I looked in your room," she said to him, "but you were still asleep. Then I met Norbert in the hall, and we went to see how Muru was getting on. Do you know they've cleaned out the kitchen in the East Tower? They're already cooking. This is my second breakfast."

She was full of news, between mouthfuls. He watched her happy face and the way she ate and talked excitedly.

"I've been in the Rose Garden, and Ulf's crew has already started work there. Norbert ordered a whole lot of cut roses to be sent to the West Wing. Aunt Marj will like that, won't she?"

She wasn't sick and didn't need blood treatments. There was something bad at the Rilson house. He knew it, even without knowing what it was.

Moody lumbered in through the French doors and sat by his chair, eyeing the cold sausages. Pixel was still talking. "Furse has already unbricked the Door for Large Creatures, and now the crew is rebuilding it. I've never seen anyone work as fast as Fennys. Muru and I found the door to the North Tower. It was completely blocked, and we weren't sure it *was* the door until Furse pulled off the boards. But wouldn't you know, it's locked and we don't have the key. It's not in that bunch Fiak gave us. Muru tried them all. Boy, someone didn't want anyone to get in there."

Uncle Edward stirred his cold coffee, and Peter recognized the closed look on his face. Then, abruptly, his uncle dropped the spoon and stood up. "Let's go for a walk. I'll show you Apple Hill."

Pixel looked up, confused by his rough tone, but Peter said, "Sure. Where is it?"

"Behind the house."

Uncle Ed went out the French doors and started across the lawn. Hurrying to catch up, they followed him to the outbuildings, with Moody at their heels. They went through the garage and into the courtyard, where the hearse was still waiting to be rebuilt. Taking keys out of his pocket, Uncle Ed unlocked the gate, waited for them to come through, then locked it again. Turning right, he followed a narrow track beside the wall, and Moody took off running, nose to the ground, sniffing this way and that. They hadn't gone far when Peter heard the sound of hammers. Then he saw a gap in the high wall, and there was Furse and a few other Fennys, working away on a very large door.

"Morning, folks," Furse said, tipping his cap. "Mr. Peter, this Door for Large Creatures will be ready by the afternoon. I suppose you want the usual bolt on the inside?"

"Er, yeah, I guess." He looked around. To his left, the bordering forest stood quiet, sunlight glancing through the near trees, lighting its depths. "Why do we lock all the garden doors and gates? I mean, we're out in the middle of nowhere."

"Well," Furse hesitated. "I wouldn't like to speak for Norbert, but it really is better if we put a lock on this gate. Then we won't have to station a night watchman here. We can just stick to our regular patrol duty."

Patrol duty? Peter tried to digest this new bit of information and looked at Uncle Edward, who was turned away as if he'd rather not be part of the conversation. "Yeah. Okay. A bolt."

Furse touched his cap and went back to work. Uncle Edward led them on, and soon they came to a rushing stream that flowed out of the forest and disappeared through a culvert under the garden wall.

"Is this the Glenny?" Pixel asked.

"Yup." Stepping on large stones, Uncle Edward crossed over.

A little way past the Glenny, they came to the end of the west wall, and Peter saw, off to his right, the back wall of Wakkenburg stretching away in the distance. The path continued past this wall, through tall bushes to the top of Apple Hill, which rose out of the brushwood.

Partway up the hill, they left the shoulder-high bushes behind and walked the narrow trail through tall grass to the very top, a wide circle of bare rock where nothing grew. Peter turned slowly, gazing at the prospect in all directions. To the east, beyond a strand of woods on the bluff, the sea spread out, dotted with white-capped waves. On the western horizon lay miles of green forest as far as his eye could see. Far to the north, green foothills and dark, craggy mountains rose above the trees, but just below them, the quiet water of the marsh spread out between the river and the sea. Beyond the marsh, a mass of white clouds sat poised on the cliffs, obscuring the coast. Overhead, two seagulls floated on a high current. Peter lifted his face to the morning sun and closed his eyes, listening to the deep silence that lay on the land.

"Fenn House," he heard his uncle say.

Opening his eyes, he looked around. "Where?"

"There." Uncle Ed pointed to the strange cloud formation on the cliffs. "Strange weather for a day in July, don't you think?"

Remembering his aunt's talk about freakish weather during the last period of trouble in the woods, Peter gazed at the airy piles of white fluff but said nothing. Was there really a wizard at Fenn House? It didn't seem possible.

"That's the North Tower, isn't it?" Pixel said. "That one closest to us." She was standing a few feet away, with her back to the marsh, all her interest bent on Wakkenburg, which lay south of the hill. "Look, there's something on the roof. Is it a tree?"

Peter stared at the top of the tower. "Oh yeah. I see it. What's a tree doing up there?"

"If we can't find the key to the tower door," she said, "maybe Krim can pick the lock."

"He can't do that," Uncle Edward said abruptly.

Peter looked at his uncle's closed expression. "Why?"

"Because it's a special lock and takes a special key." Uncle Edward turned his face from the house to the vast forest in the west. "You have to understand. When Jenny disappeared, the first thing my father did was lock up the North Tower. It was our place, me and Jenny. And Marj sometimes. As a matter of fact, my mother called it the 'children's tower'. But Dad locked it up and kept the key and wouldn't let me go in, though he knew there were some things I wanted. He was half mad with grief and anger. Grief for his lost daughter and anger at the family fate. At the time, I was only six years old, and I didn't understand. So I took the key out of his desk when he wasn't looking.

"The sky bridge had already been closed off. I waited till nightfall, then snuck outside, through the kitchen garden to the little back door you went into yesterday." He paused, his eyes looking inward. "But that way into the North Wing was already bricked over. I ran around the house, thinkin' to get in by the ballroom, but it was blocked too. Every window was covered up. I hammered at the bricks, but all I did was bruise my fists. Then—I remember like it was yesterday—I was runnin' back to the West Wing when I saw them, glimmerin' like ghosts in the moonlight."

"Who?" Pixel whispered.

"The Fennys. With Jenny gone, they were already fading to my sight. But I could see them in a hazy way, all around the garden wall by the outbuildings. They were just about to brick up that little arched entrance, but they'd seen me go out, and they were waitin'. One of them stepped out of the darkness and said, 'Don't worry, Mr. Edward. We wasn't going to lock you out.' I begged them to let me into the tower, but they couldn't. It was too late." He fell silent, staring all the while at the distant trees.

"What did you do?" Pixel asked.

"I went to my room and hid the key. It wouldn't have done me much good anyway. It's a special key. Works only for a Silver-eyed. The Fennys finished their work, and after that night, I never could see them again. Not until you arrived, Peter." Reaching into his shirt pocket, he pulled out a small silver key. "Here. Take it."

Silently Peter took the key. Then he and Pixel followed Uncle Edward down the other side of the hill toward the cliffs.

At the corner of the back wall, they crossed the Glenny, which flowed out toward the sea, and struck a path leading through the woods on the bluff. They were walking along the east garden wall now. Moody ran ahead, but after a few minutes, they found him waiting at a low wooden door.

"Hey, we must have been in the orchard on the other side of this wall yesterday," Pixel said. "But I didn't see a door."

"It's probably locked." Peter tried the latch. To his surprise, it clicked and the door opened a few inches.

A thick tangle of creeper vines grew just inside, blocking the entrance. Together, the three of them pushed, and Uncle Edward, muttering to himself, got out his pocket knife and began slashing away at the branches he could reach, but they were too thick.

They were about to give up when Ulf's eyes and nose appeared between the leaves. "Oh, Mr. Peter! It's you! I completely forgot there was a door here. Hold up with the knife there, Mr. Edward. Just give us a minute and we'll have this cleared."

Then Peter heard hacking sounds and Fenny voices crying, "This thing's thick as rope! Get the machete!" and "Stand back! I'm swingin' wide!" In minutes, they had cleared the vines and opened the door. Peter followed Pixel and Uncle Ed into the orchard. Moody pushed past him, nose to the ground.

They stopped under the very tree Peter had climbed the day before. The whole place had lost its abandoned appearance. The grass was cut, and one or two Fennys were engaged in repairing a birdbath, while others chipped the bricks out of a window on the ground floor. Straight ahead, a door opened in the East Tower. Muru came out shaking a dust mop, and Pixel ran to meet her.

Uncle Ed, gazing at the uncovered windows and the Fennys pruning the apple trees farther down in the orchard, muttered, "Just like it was yesterday." Then he turned to Peter and said, "It was Jonas who planted those vines they just cut down. I remember the day he did it. Then he left and never came back."

"Why did he block the door?"

"There's no lock. Didn't want us to have unexpected visitors after he'd gone. Maybe you noticed the name carved over the door." Turning away, Uncle Ed walked off through the orchard in the direction of the South Tower.

Peter examined the wall above the entrance. Nothing. Going back through the doorway, he looked up and saw letters carved into the stone lintel: MAC LIR. He stood there, in the shadow of the trees, looking around. Then a piece of paving, barely visible in the overgrown weeds, caught his eye. Brushing the dirt aside with the toe of his sneaker, he saw another stone, then another. It was a pathway, leading from the door to the sea.

Moody came out of the orchard with his nose to the ground. He looked at Peter, snorted, then started down the path. Peter followed him through a grove of pine trees, all the way to the bluff. There he saw a wide bay, and the Glenny cascading through a stone culvert, over the side of the precipice. At his feet, a stone stairway descended to a pebbly beach, but the path continued north, along the cliff, and Peter guessed that it went all the way to the far end of the cove, where the strange white cloud formation sat. Fenn House.

Suddenly, the image of a ship came into his mind. He saw tall wooden masts and sails billowing in the wind. A man stood at the prow, and Peter could see him close up: the handsome profile, the flowing white beard and silver robes. Then the man turned and looked straight at him with eyes the color of the bluest sky.

Moody woofed, and the image vanished. Far off, at the other end of the cove, Peter noticed someone standing on the cliff, silhouetted against the strange white cloud. As he watched, the tiny figure began to move along the bluff in his direction, and Moody growled.

Seized by sudden fear, Peter ran for the house with Moody on his heels. Rushing through the door, he slammed it shut and leaned against it.

Pixel came out of the house and crossed the lawn. "Are you okay?"

"We need to lock this door. Where's Krim?"

"You need a lock this minute?"

"The vine will be faster," Ulf said quietly, coming up behind Pixel.

"How fast?" Peter said.

"Judging by this orchard, Mr. Peter, I'd say it won't take long. How about Jonas' watering method? I'll fetch a bucket."

"Sure. Okay."

With his back pressed against the door, Peter looked at Pixel, who regarded him silently. How could he explain that seeing the distant figure on the cliff had settled a question in his mind? Everything he'd heard at breakfast, everything he'd read and seen since coming to the island—all of it moved into place like pieces on a game board. He wasn't sure he understood, but he knew. The paths from the sea led to this one entrance. If he couldn't lock this door, Mac Lir—whoever he was—would one day come through it.

Ulf returned with a bucket. "If you'll just stir this water with your hands, Mr. Peter."

Stepping away from the door, he swished his hands around in the water, and Ulf poured it across the row of stumps.

Nothing happened, and suddenly Peter felt very silly. It was nuts to think that trees and vines changed at the touch of his hands. "I better find Krim," he said, and turned away.

A split second later, he heard Pixel gasp, and Ulf said, "Oh, that's capital, Mr. Peter! Faster than Mr. Jonas, if I might say so. You've really got the touch."

He looked back. The door had disappeared behind a massive growth of vine that spread out in either direction, curling up over the top of the wall. The whole thing was bigger and thicker than the old vine, complete with dainty leaves and large scented flowers.

Ulf walked over and tugged on a branch. "That's that. If you don't need anything else, Mr. Peter, there are roses that need my attention." He picked up the bucket and left the orchard, whistling.

16

In the North Tower

"Let me get this straight. That door in the wall is for the wizard Mac Lir, and you just saw him on the cliffs, heading in our direction, which is why you panicked and wanted a lock." Pixel sat across from Peter at a table in the East Kitchen, a chocolate donut poised at her mouth. All around them, Fennys were as busy as a hive of bees.

"I didn't panic."

"Yes, you did."

Peter glanced at a sniffling Fenny slicing onions at the other end of the table. Someone came by and topped off his glass of milk though he'd barely taken a sip.

"I read about Mac Lir last night," Pixel said, looking at him steadily.

A chocolate donut on a plate, proffered by a small, hairy hand, appeared under Peter's nose. He pushed it aside and swallowed hard against the bile rising in his throat.

"I don't blame you for wanting to lock up a door with his name on it," Pixel said. "Look how he sort of tricked your ancestor Nathaniel. And he had strange powers. Do you know he could make weather? Like the cloud sitting on Fenn House right now."

Sweat broke out on Peter's forehead and upper lip.

"Jonas wrote about him in chapter three, and I think—" She paused. "Peter, are you alright?"

"I ..." He closed his mouth and gulped hard, fighting a losing battle.

Then Furse's voice boomed into the room. "Mr. Peter! Mr. Peter! I heard what happened. Drink this quick!"

Peter opened his eyes and saw a bottle of purple juice in front of his face.

"Hurry! Before you upchuck!"

He grabbed the bottle and took a swig. Immediately, the nausea subsided. He gasped and took another drink. Furse's face swam into view, then Pixel's.

"Ulf was tellin' us what you did just now, and I remembered how Mr. Jonas always carried a bottle of this here berry juice around. For some reason, growin' things, and other jobs he had to do, made him feel sick. I was with him once when he upchucked his lunch, and I thought it might be the same for you."

Furse held out another bottle and Peter took it. "Thanks."

"You come to the garage for a refill whenever you want, but remember"—Furse lowered his voice—"don't drink the stuff from the kitchen. They don't make it right."

The chocolate-donut Fenny looked up and glared, but Furse only tipped his hat and walked out the door.

Peter and Pixel left the East Kitchen and passed into the North Wing. Swept and cleaned, the place looked so different. It was bright and airy with high ceilings, carved wooden paneling, and polished stone floors. Peter could hardly believe it was the same dark, neglected place he'd seen the day before. As he walked with Pixel through the wide hallway, she said, "Let's go to the North Tower now."

"Later."

"Why?"

He shrugged. With the key in his pocket, he had a feeling about the North Tower that he couldn't explain, as if something was there, waiting for him. Before he could think of a believable excuse, a commotion broke out on their left: grunts and gripes and Muru barking orders. "Not that way! More to the right! Hey, you there, pick up your end! Never mind your toe! Heave! Push! That's it!"

A huge wooden table appeared at the entrance to the formal dining room and moved slowly across the passage. It was over twelve feet long and barely fit through the doorway. A dozen Fennys pushed and pulled until, with a sudden lurching movement, the table came to life—there was no other explanation—and shot across the corridor.

"Too fast!" Muru shrieked, as it skimmed across the floor and disappeared into the ballroom with all the Fennys in pursuit. Peter and Pixel leapt to the threshold in time to see it crash through the French doors and go sailing over the terrace and down the steps, where it bumped to a stop in the grass. Muru stood in the middle of the ballroom, pulling at her hair with both hands. "Argh! Don't blame me!"

When the table was sitting quietly in the ballroom, and while Krim repaired the doors, Muru explained the plan for the Buggane breakfast.

"That's a five-course meal!" Pixel exclaimed.

"Well, of course. It's what they expect. After the last time."

"They've had breakfast here before? When?"

"Maybe a couple of hundred years ago. Fiak found an account of it in the library, so I know exactly what was served. *And* why they weren't invited again."

Peter, who had remained silent, looked at Muru. "Why?"

"You really want to know? Well, let's just say that the West Wing was a lot bigger in the old days. You can still see a part of the marble floor on the patio outside the dining room. Seems there was a fire, though that may have been the fault of the Poinkers, who were also in attendance. It's hard to say."

"Poinkers?" Pixel said.

"Small, furry creatures. Always litter the floor with silver coins."

"Are they coming too?"

Muru looked at Peter, and he shrugged. "I only invited the Bugganes."

"Right," she replied. "Well, don't blame me."

❦ ❦ ❦

Krim and Furse were eager to demolish the inner walls that blocked the corridors between the West and South Wings and were disappointed when Peter would not let them use small explosives. Yet even with hammers and crowbars, the main hallways were noisy and dusty most of the afternoon. Uncle Edward's study on the first floor was right next to the demolition. Peter figured he'd go to Foyle to get away. Then he found his uncle settled in a spacious room in the West Tower, completely removed from the hubbub in the house.

"One of your Fennys told me this place was open again." Uncle Ed sat in an armchair with lemonade and cakes at his elbow. French doors opened onto the west lawn, and a mild breeze stirred the curtains. "Maybe I'll move my study out here permanently."

As the day went on, Peter realized that opening the house and gardens had brought a measure of peace to the household. The Fennys went about their work whistling or singing songs in a strange language. It was Muru who explained the change.

"Look, kid, we might have been a bit wound up when you arrived, I admit. There hasn't been a Silver in residence for a long time, and we got used to being invisible. But we're happier being seen. And I gotta tell you that opening up the house means a lot to us. I think the West Wing was cramping our style."

Only the Fenn House crew remained disgruntled. They overcooked the food, slammed down plates, and scorched everything they ironed.

"I can't do anything with them," Norbert complained. "They won't be happy till they're back at Fenn House. And once the other wings are finished and your Buggane catastrophe is over, we can all return to our regular duties and we won't need them. There's no way around it, boy. You have to sort out that wizard!"

Grumbling under his breath, Peter went to find Rumun. "Norbert says your crew isn't happy."

"It isn't us, Mr. Peter. *He's* the one who's not happy in his work. Barks out orders and then stands at the window watching the gardeners. If you ask me, he doesn't want to be Head at all."

"Then you don't mind not being at Fenn House?"

Rumun smiled. "All will be well, Mr. Peter. You'll see. There are powers at work on this island stronger than witches and wizards."

Leaving the kitchen, Peter went looking for Norbert and found him in the sitting room with Pixel. They were standing at a side table, bent over the Thornburg book. Peter got straight to the point: "Norbert, Rumun thinks, I mean, I think that, well ..." He hesitated. "Wouldn't you be happier on the garden crew? I mean, you do a good job and all that, but maybe you'd like to ... to stop being Head Fenny."

Norbert's face was an expressionless mask. "Are you ordering me to the garden crew?"

"Well ... not exactly. Only if you want to."

Norbert threw back his shoulders as if casting off some huge weight. "I never thought I'd hear you say those words, Mr. Peter, but I've been wishing. Ever since you arrived." He smiled a wide, crooked smile. It was like seeing the real Norbert. "I don't want to be Head Fenny anymore."

"Okay." Maybe this is what it meant to put things right.

Norbert laughed, a real laugh. Hooting with joy, he went running out the door.

"How did you know?" Pixel asked.

"Rumun told me."

"Will *he* be Head now?"

"Muru, I think."

Fortunately, Muru agreed.

After supper, Peter and Pixel stood at the door to the North Tower. Evening light slanted through one or two dusty windows. The dreary corridor was the one place Muru had neglected in her marathon cleaning spree.

"Maybe we should come back tomorrow," Peter said, turning the silver key over and over in his hand. Pixel was keen to go in, but he wasn't. "It's getting late and there's not much light." He had a strange feeling about the tower. It wasn't exactly fear. More like a sharp awareness, as if he had finally come to the heart of Wakkenburg House.

"I brought a flashlight," Pixel said. "And anyway, your eyes shine like headlamps."

"Right." He fit the key into the lock. There was a tiny silver spark, and the door swung inward.

"Aaah!" Pixel cried, clutching his arm. Two shadowy ghosts stood just inside the entrance, one of them with eyes of flame.

Trembling slightly, Peter reached out and touched a large gilt mirror hanging directly in front of the doorway. "It's ... it's our reflection. See?"

Pixel let go of his arm, and they crossed the threshold into a dark passage. Dim light shone from an open door at the farther end. They went in and found a large empty room lit by an oblong window high up in the wall. In one corner, a thick metal column extended from the floor through a circular hole in the ceiling, like a fireman's pole. Several balls, a coiled rope, and two broken racquets lay scattered about. Everything was coated with a thick layer of dust. "It's a gymnasium," Peter said in a low voice.

"I bet those belonged to Uncle Edward," Pixel whispered, pointing to a pair of small shoes beside the door.

He led the way to the far end of the gym, and they climbed the stairs to the second floor, which was taken up by one large room. Windows on the north side looked out to the trees of Glenny Creek, and by the light of the lowering sun, they saw it was a playroom. Wooden blocks lay in a tumbled pile, and an electric train set was spread out beneath one window. A table was strewn with yellowing paper, pots of dried paint, and stiff brushes. In the far corner, the fire pole continued to the floor above.

Several armchairs clustered around a fireplace; on one cushion, a little picture book lay open, and a woolen cardigan hung over the back. The late Mr. Thornburg had indeed locked the tower in a great hurry. The place was a dusty time capsule. Peter wandered through the room, thinking of Uncle Ed.

Pixel, examining objects on the mantel, blew off a thick piece of paper. "Peter, look at this." It was a plain advertisement, printed in black ink. "Periwinkle Fair," she read aloud. "June 6. Auction, seafood sale, musicians, jugglers, magic show. Floden Market Square."

"Aunt Marj said Jenny disappeared on the day of the Periwinkle Fair."

"How old was she?"

"Four." He looked around at the toys, the cardigan, and the picture book laid aside on the armchair. They were hers. They must be.

"Here's something else." Pixel lifted a key from the mantle and read the tag that was attached: "For Jenny. From your Great-Uncle Jonas. Take care of it all. If you can." She held it out to Peter. "I wonder what it opens?"

It was made of silver, a little smaller than the key to the tower door. Peter put it in his pocket.

The light was waning fast.

"It'll be dark soon," Pixel said. "Maybe we should save the rest for tomorrow."

"You've got a flashlight. We might as well keep going." His initial reluctance to enter the tower was gone. Now an awareness niggled at his mind. Something was waiting for him, something he needed to see.

Mounting the stairs to the third floor, they saw rows of books lining the walls, and dusty sofas flanking a large hearth. This room was neater, but there were still books lying around on tables, one or two face down on the arms of chairs, waiting in vain for their readers to return.

"It's a three-story playroom complete with library," Pixel said. "Think it continues on the next floor?"

"Maybe not. The fire pole stops here."

The fourth floor was dark. The flashlight's beam illuminated boxes, trunks, and old furniture. Picking their way across the crowded room, they climbed the stairs to the fifth floor, where they entered a dark passage lined with shuttered windows. Peter opened one, and they looked out to the roof of the West Wing.

"There's the window of my room," Pixel said.

Down below, Fennys went in and out of the kitchen garden, pushing wheelbarrows loaded with bricks. Krim came out of the tool shop, crossed the courtyard, and went in the back door by the kitchen. On the west lawn, Aunt Marj played fetch with Moody as Uncle Edward strolled across the grass in the deepening twilight.

Pixel turned and looked around. "There's only one door in this passage." She tried the knob. "Locked."

The awareness that something waited was very strong now. "Let's get to the top," Peter said.

At the end of the passage, they climbed a spiral stairway to the sixth floor and stepped into another dark passage, this one without windows. Pixel shone the flashlight over the walls. "No more stairs. I wonder how you get onto the roof?"

"Here's a door." By the light of his eyes, Peter read the name etched into a wooden placard: "Jonas." Fishing in his pocket, he brought out the two keys and fit the smaller into the lock. Again there was the silver spark.

The door opened on a green jungle. By the last rays of the sun slanting through wide windows, he saw plants everywhere: hanging from the ceiling, clustered on shelves and tabletops; they were overgrown and wild, their leaves and flowers trailing along the floor. It was a big greenhouse.

Pushing through the branches, Pixel made her way to the north-facing windows on the other side of the room. Peter waded toward a dusty table spread with little jars containing different kinds of seeds. Then, in a small alcove to the left of the door, he found a desk cluttered with stacks of paper. Each pile was weighted down by a rock on which was painted a different word: "Flora", "Fauna", and "Fennys". One rock bore the name "Jenny". He picked up the slim diary that lay beneath and blew dust off the cover.

"Someone's been watering these plants," Pixel said.

He put down the diary and looked up. Crisscrossing the ceiling, nearly hidden under the tangle of leaf and fern, he saw a strange network of copper pipes. It was a primitive watering system.

"But how do you get on the roof?" Pixel wondered. "We saw a tree up there, remember?"

They began poking around, parting curtains of leaves, stepping over root-bound pots of bee balm and mint whose foliage had reached unnatural heights. Finally, Peter uncovered an iron ladder, every rung bound by wisteria. At the top he found a hatchway, and by the time they pried it open, the light was almost gone.

As they climbed onto the roof, the sun disappeared over the crown of the forest and the first star shone out. Below, lights came on in the great house. Peter looked over the parapet and saw Moody pawing at the back door of the West Wing. One of the kitchen Fennys opened it, peered furtively from side to side, and let him in.

"That's what catches rainwater for the pipes," Pixel said, pointing to a barrel in the middle of the roof. "And there's the tree."

A small tree, dry and prickly, stood in the northeast corner of the roof, facing Apple Hill. Its pot had burst long ago, and it clung precariously to a mound of dirt, roots stubbornly grasping the soil and stone as if daring the wind to tear it loose. Like lone outliers of some forgotten winter, a few withered leaves hung on bare branches.

"Poor thing. Its watering pipe fell apart." Pixel looked at Peter sideways. "Maybe you could do something for it."

He knew perfectly well what she meant, but he turned away. For some reason, the sight of the dead tree set all his nerves on edge. Besides that, the niggling awareness that had drawn him to the roof was now so strong it felt like something knocking against his skull. "I'll tell Ulf. He can look at it tomorrow."

Descending into the room below, they made their way through the tangle of plants. When they reached the dark passage, Pixel went first, shining her flashlight on the stairs, but Peter found that the light from his eyes allowed him to keep his footing.

Halfway through the passage on the fifth floor, Pixel stopped. "What's that noise?"

In the stillness, Peter heard a soft rustling. Pixel shone her light along the wall until it rested on the locked door. Then Peter saw something he hadn't noticed before. Someone had scratched a name across the wood, in rough lettering: Mac Lir.

"Sounds like mice," Pixel murmured.

A floorboard creaked, and they heard a swishing sound.

"Bigger than mice," Pixel whispered. "Maybe an owl got in through a window."

An alarm sounded in Peter's mind. He had no wish to open the door, even if he had the key. Putting a finger to his lips to indicate silence, he crept quietly to the end of the passage with Pixel close behind. As they reached the head of the stairs, he heard a muffled thump, then a loud clatter from inside the closed room.

He grabbed Pixel's hand and pulled her down the stairs and through the maze of boxes on the fourth floor as something banged around in the room above. When they got to the third floor, he pulled her straight to the fire pole and they went sliding, sliding, down to the gymnasium at the bottom. They landed with a thump and sat there, listening. Except for their own breathing, there were no other sounds.

"I lost the flashlight," Pixel whispered.

They got to their feet and crept out of the gymnasium, through the dark passage, past the mirror, and into the dusty corridor. His heart still pounding, Peter pulled the door shut and fumbled with the key. He heard a click and saw the silver spark. Whatever was up there, it was locked in now.

Then a bright light shone from the other end of the passage, and he saw the silhouette of Muru at the end of the corridor. "Peter! Pixel! You're supposed to be in bed! I thought Rumun had things in the West Wing under control!"

❦ ❦ ❦

That night, Peter tossed and turned, unable to sleep. Something like static had been buzzing in his head ever since he left the North Tower. Finally, he took a blanket from his bed and lay on the rug beside Moody. With his head against the dog's flank, he drifted into uneasy dreams.

He was standing on the shore of a lake, under a moonless sky. A beautiful woman with golden hair glided out of the forest and hovered over the water. She wore a scarlet dress, and her arms were bare and white.

"My daughter is calling," she said, her voice deep and sultry. "But first I will go to my old love, my ship captain. I know he misses me." Lifting her head, like a wolf picking up a scent, and with nostrils flared, she looked around the wooded shore, her eyes shining red in the darkness. "Mac Lir has returned! So *this* is why my daughter calls." She began to laugh, and the sound sent a prickle of fear through Peter. He stood there in plain sight, helpless, his feet rooted to the ground.

The woman glided a little nearer and paused over the tranquil water, gazing at her own reflection. "Oh, Lila! How beautiful you are!" She sighed and shivered.

Peter could see her face clearly now, the small, sharp fangs protruding from her sweet lips. As she reached out a graceful hand toward her mirrored image, he felt longing and desire pulse through the air.

"Now, where is the Silver Child?" she said softly. "I have need of it." She glided back to the middle of the lake. "I snatched that child from Mac Lir, and he never knew!" Peering down through the depths, she looked this way and that. "Where is it?"

The night wind said nothing. Peter waited.

"It's gone!" she whispered. "How can that be?"

The woman landed on the grassy bank, so close that he could have reached out and touched her golden hair. Crouching like a panther, she pressed her dainty nose to the ground and snuffled back and forth. When she sat back on her haunches, a dangerous light smoldered in her eyes. Lifting her face to the sky, she roared. "The *woman* has been here! How dare she meddle with me and mine!" The lake turned a sickly, luminous green as waves swept across its surface. Fish leapt high into the air as if trying to escape a boiling cauldron.

"She took my prize! Did *he* tell her she could? How like him." Wailing now, she swayed back and forth in misery. "She is nothing! Queen of small things! I should have been queen of heaven and earth!

I!" She shook her fist at the sky as the water churned and bubbled. "Someone will pay! I will not be mocked!" Then, in a burst of fire and smoke, she rose and glided away.

At her going, the troubled lake grew still. The green light faded and a mist rose from the quiet water. Peter stood there, looking around at the silent trees and the starless sky. Then a man in silvery robes stepped out of the woods, his face hidden behind the folds of a hood. He came to the edge of the lake, and Peter heard him say, "I should have known. Lila stole the Silver One, but where is the girl now?"

The trees said nothing. With a soft hiss, the man's cloak turned to white mist, and he vanished. Peter was left alone, staring into the dark water. Then the clouds parted, the moon came out, and he felt himself lifted into the wind, flying with reckless speed over the night-bound woods.

17

What Woke in the Night

"Wake up, kid! Furse says to come quick!"

Peter opened his eyes in the dark. Muru was tugging his arm.

"Something's happened! Hurry!"

He pulled on his clothes and ran downstairs, out the back door into the morning twilight. Furse met him in the cobbled yard outside the kitchen garden.

"Mr. Peter! Mr. Peter! Somethin' went crashin' through the big gate last night! The one we just rebuilt!"

"The Door for Large Creatures?"

"Me and the boys were patrollin' in the East Orchard just before dawn when we heard a loud bang. We went runnin' across the back of the house, and there was this flash of light, then a crashin' sound out past the pond. Me and Krim thought we saw something goin' through the gate, but it was too dark to see much. We got to the door and found it all bashed in!"

Running, Peter followed Furse past the pond to the western wall and saw a pile of scorched, splintered ruins, all that was left of the big door. "Was it a Buggane?"

"Could be that spider," Furse said. "Couldn't undo the bolt, so he changed into a scorpion and bashed his way through."

"But the spider hasn't been here, and you saw something going *out.*"

"Well, there's more Bugganes than the three you've met, by all accounts. Seven, so I hear. But doggone it! We gotta rebuild this gate *again*!"

"Mr. Peter! Mr. Peter!" Now Krim ran up, panting. "There's a door open in the North Tower! On the outside wall! Didn't you see it when you ran past?"

Peter turned and looked toward the North Tower in the growing light. Sure enough, there was a dark opening on the west side. Hurrying back across the garden, he saw a door on the ground, its hinges busted. Krim and Furse turned it over.

"Look, Mr. Peter! It's all of a piece with the stone wall, but it ain't made of stone," Furse said.

By this time, Fiak had come and stood gazing at the wall. "This entrance is certainly not in the floor plan."

Peter stepped into the opening and saw a long dark stairway going up. "Me and Pixel went to the top of this tower last night and heard something behind a locked door. She thought an owl got in through an open window."

Furse shook his head. "No owl could have shifted this door, Mr. Peter."

"What floor were you on?" Fiak asked.

"The fifth. There's a door there with Mac Lir's name on it. I think that's where these stairs go."

The librarian's eyes gleamed. "Ah yes. The wizard's old quarters! And this secret stairwell explains why there are no windows on this side of the tower. I did wonder."

"He lived here?"

"In Nathaniel's time, just after the house was built, the whole North Tower was given over to Mac Lir. The Thornburg book tells of strange lights and sounds from the upper floors. Often a cloud would settle on the roof. It was Jonas who changed things. When the wizard left on one of his voyages, Jonas cleared out the tower, put all Lir's things in that room on the fifth floor, and locked it up.

"He must not have known about these stairs though," Furse said.

"But what came out last night?" Peter still had an owl in his mind, and the image had grown to nightmare proportions.

"I don't know, Mr. Peter, but there are such things as portals," Fiak said. "Pictures, books, and other odds and ends through which strange creatures come and go. You'll have to go up there to find out what happened."

Furse looked horrified. "Not alone!"

"But no Fenny should go," Fiak said sternly. "We all know how Lir hates us. Probably has the place booby-trapped. No Fenny has *ever* set foot in the North Tower."

“Right,” Peter said slowly. “Maybe one of the Bugganes will come with me.” Leaving Krim and Furse to fix the big gate, he went in search of Muru, figuring she wouldn’t be pleased with the idea. He found her in the ballroom, already setting the table for the Bugganes’ breakfast the next day.

“You want them to come a day early?” she said, after hearing his plan. “You know they’ll expect to stay the night!”

“Well, I ... I can’t think of anyone else who could help in case there’s ... trouble.”

“Then you want us to get the Rooms for Large Creatures ready?” To his surprise, a gleam shone in her eye.

“Do we have rooms like that?”

“Six of them. In the North Wing. Three on the first floor, three on the second.”

“Okay, but we’ll only need two. I’ll send Moody for the hairy man and Tom Mole. Not the spider.”

“Sure, but don’t blame me.”

❦ ❦ ❦

“A secret stairway in the North Tower. Now, that’s interesting.” Uncle Edward poured himself a cup of coffee and took another muffin.

Pixel, her plate loaded with food, looked at Peter with wide eyes. “Really? And you think whatever went bashing through the gate was the thing we heard on the fifth floor? We were standing right outside the door!”

“Oh, my dears. I can hardly bear to think of it.” Aunt Marj sank heavily into her chair, sloshing tea on the tablecloth.

“I don’t know anything for sure,” Peter said. “Not until I go up and take a look around.”

Uncle Edward buttered his muffin and reached for the jam. “Even then, you may never know what was up there last night. This *is* Wakken Wood, after all.”

“Edward! Will you please take this a little more seriously?” Aunt Marj glared at her brother. “There may be other dangers in that room!”

“Well, whatever it was, it’s obviously gone now. But I suppose you should take reinforcements, Peter.”

"Oh! But this is all wrong! We can't send children into danger!" she wailed. "How did we ever come to this?"

"I'm going too," Pixel said to Peter. "You know you never won a fight without me."

He nodded, avoiding his aunt's eye. "I sent Moody to find Tom Mole and Tom Troll. They'll go into the tower with us."

Aunt Marj looked as if she might faint, but Uncle Edward smiled. "See, Marj? Take two monsters with you to find another. You have to admit there's some sense in a plan like that."

❦ ❦ ❦

Right after breakfast, while Pixel was upstairs changing into shorts, Peter went to the door of the North Tower and unlocked it with his special key. Again, he saw the silver spark when the lock clicked. Pushing open the door, he looked at his eerie reflection in the mirror, eyes shining back at him like twin moons. He walked out of the North Wing, headed for the central courtyard, and had just stepped into the kitchen garden when he heard someone calling his name.

"Mr. Peter! Mr. Peter!" Ulf came running into the courtyard. "Come quick! That dog just chased a huge spider through the gate! Right into a tree!"

"A spider?"

"Moody won't let it alone! It's shrunk now. About the size of a raccoon."

"I didn't send him to get *that* Buggane." With a sense of inevitability, Peter hurried after Ulf, past the outbuildings, all the way to Glenny Pond, whose waters lay tranquil in the morning light. A family of ducks floated among tall reeds, unruffled by the giant dog barking his head off. The spider, no longer the size of a raccoon, crouched in the fork of a tall oak, trembling. Beyond the pond, Furse, Krim, and the garage crew worked furiously to repair the Door for Large Creatures.

Peter whistled sharply and Moody backed off, still wagging his tail happily as the spider shrank to the size of a hedgehog and turned into one. Then came a shout and the other two Bugganes walked through the open gate, followed by a huge bear. The garage crew fled, leaving their tools on the ground beside the half-finished door.

Tom Troll, who had recovered his hairy man form, saluted. "We've come, Silver One! With our brother from Spoot Voor."

"Oh, Tom! Tom!" the old man wailed. Running to the tree, he lifted the little hedgehog from the branch. "We've been looking for you everywhere! But what has frightened you into this fluffy shape?"

"Er . . . I think Moody chased him into the tree," Peter said. "Sorry about that."

"It must be something more than the Moddey Dhoo," the old man said. The other Bugganes, along with Moody, crowded around, looking at the little thing cupped in his hand. Then the tiny creature sat up and began to squeak. The bear bent his snout close, listening. When the hedgehog finished, Tom Bear sat back on his haunches and uttered a few rumbling words.

The old man gasped. "You hear what he says, boy?"

"No, I . . . I don't speak bear."

"Tom Bear says that Tom Spider says that the witch set fire to Floden and the whole village burned to the ground! The very night you were there, Silver One! You left just in time!"

The hedgehog squeaked again, then cowered and shut its eyes. Tom Bear lifted his snout and growled.

"Worse and worse!" the old man gasped. "Tom Spider has also seen the Night Monster passing through the woods! Very near his own home! Can this be true?"

"The *what* monster?" Peter asked.

"If Tom is right, this is evil news," the hairy man said. "And he won't go home because of what he has seen. Do you understand, boy? He has come to you for protection!"

"Take him." The old man held out the hedgehog.

Peter took the little creature warily, wondering what the Bugganes expected him to do. He had a sudden vision of the vine in the orchard that had grown when he touched it. His hand shook and he nearly dropped the hedgehog on the ground. Then Moody snuffled the tiny thing, and it curled itself into a ball and lay still. Peter groaned inwardly, thinking of poor Aunt Marj, but he closed his fingers around the soft bristles. "Right. I guess he can stay until he feels better."

With the Bugganes close behind, Peter went to the back door of the West Wing. Asking the Toms to wait right there, and hoping to goodness they would, he went inside to find Pixel. She was in the kitchen, helping Rumun dry the dishes.

Peter set the hedgehog on the table, covered it with a tea cozy, then looked up and found Rumun and Pixel gazing at him. "The Bugganes are here," he said.

"Ah." Rumun nodded.

"What ... what happens now?" Pixel said, her eyes wide.

"You go through the tower door with Moody and the old man. Meet us in Mac Lir's room." Motioning helplessly toward the tea cozy, he said, "Rumun, I ... I ..."

"Don't worry, sir. Your little pincushion is safe with me."

Outside the back door, the Bugganes were waiting, and so was Uncle Edward! Relieved by his uncle's presence, as if a troop of reinforcements had arrived, Peter sent Pixel, Moody, and the old man to the inner entrance of the North Tower. Then he led the way to the secret stairs.

Outside the door, Tom Bear stopped, telling them in his rumbling way that he would keep watch outside.

"Then I will go first," the hairy man said, "and you last, Silver One."

Up they went, into the dark, the hairy man silent on bare feet, Uncle Ed clumping in his boots, shining a flashlight over the stone steps. The stairway ended at a narrow wooden door hanging sideways on one hinge. Beyond the threshold, it was pitch dark. Uncle Ed and the Buggane went in, and Peter followed.

The hairy man drew back the shutters, and the sudden light revealed decades of dust floating in the air. Uncle Ed began to sneeze, and Peter rushed from window to window, pushing each one wide open.

When he stopped to look around, the first thing that struck him was the emptiness of the room. He'd expected a clutter of wizard things, such as wands and cauldrons, but there was nothing like that here. A few boxes lay tumbled in a corner, and a bare wooden table stood against one wall. A large rug woven with strange signs and symbols covered the middle of the stone floor. The only other thing in the room was an enormous painting in an ugly gilt frame. It leaned against the wall not far from the door to the secret stairs. Uncle Ed and the hairy man stood looking at it.

"This is odd," Uncle Edward said. "There's nothing in this painting but the background. Looks like an unfinished work to me, though I thought artists ordinarily began with their subject."

The hairy man touched the frame, then drew his hand back as if he'd received an electric shock. "A portal!" he gasped. "It is a powerful thing! Don't touch it!"

There was a loud knock at the door to the passage. "Hey!" came Pixel's voice. "Are you in there?"

Uncle Ed unlatched the door and Pixel came in, followed by the old man. "Everything downstairs looks the same as it did last night," she said. "Aunt Marj came with us, but we left her on the third floor, crying. First, she found her little sister's shoes in the gym, then her cardigan on the second floor. Moody's with her."

"I told her she shouldn't come," Uncle Edward muttered.

Pixel looked around. "There isn't much here."

"That's what I thought, but Mr. Hairy Person says this big picture frame is a portal."

Pixel crossed the room; then she crouched down and blew dust off a silver plate at the bottom of the frame. " 'Her enchanted hair was the first gold. And still she is, young while the earth is old'," she read aloud.

"Oh, Tom!" the old man said, wringing his hands. "This is very bad! Tom Spider *did* see her!"

"Who?" Uncle Ed demanded.

"Lila," the hairy man replied. "Some call her the Night Monster, a creature fearsome and ancient. Very beautiful and very wicked. Those words on the frame confirm it is she. At one time Mac Lir united himself with her."

"And that's who came out of this frame?" Pixel asked.

Peter stood in the middle of the room, half listening to the others as an image took shape in his mind: A woman, with long golden hair, regarded herself in a mirror. He had never seen anyone so beautiful, and his heart was strangely moved. She turned to him, smiling, and he saw the points of two white fangs. It was the woman from his nightmare. With sudden realization, he knew this was Lila.

"Peter! Are you alright?"

Startled, he opened his eyes and found himself crouched in a tight ball with his arms over his head. Pixel was shaking his shoulder. Then he felt the bottoms of his feet burning and glanced down at the strange symbols on the carpet. A wizard's carpet. Lir's.

Like a springing cat, he leapt to the flagstones and stood at the open window, breathing hard.

"Peter!" Uncle Edward grasped him by the shoulders and looked into his face. "What did you just see?"

"I ... I think I saw what Tom Spider saw. By a lake in the woods. Lila. The Night Monster. It must have been her in this room last night."

No one spoke. Then Uncle Edward said, "I think we oughta burn everything here. Just in case there's any more of these dang portals."

Peter nodded and the hairy man said, "Leave it to the Bugganes."

18

Into the Mountain

Just a few steps inside the dark door of Scadoo Pass, a cold draught swept up the tunnel and nearly put out the torches. Jen and her companions stood still, listening to the wind moaning outside the mountain. "I think we are not welcome here," she whispered. Then the boy began to hum softly, a tune that reminded Jen of twinkling lights in the woods and the sky overhung with rivers of stars.

They went on, in single file, the boy first, then Jen and Thrinn, and Forlost last, carrying the second torch. Going around a bend in the tunnel, they left behind the last bit of evening light coming through the door.

For a while, their way was flat and smooth. Then it began to descend, winding down, down toward the depths of the mountain. They passed through narrow tunnels in which Jen had to shuffle sideways and through passages that sloped so steeply she had to grope along the walls for handholds to keep from sliding.

In some places, water dripped from the ceiling and there was no place to rest. There was only never-ending darkness and the *plink, plink* of water on stone. After hours of scrambling over rough paths, they came to a last treacherous descent. The road spiraled down, and together they slipped and slithered until they landed at the bottom, splashing into a puddle up to their ankles.

They had come to the deepest cavern in Rosknil, their torches like small islands of light in the empty expanse. The immense weight of the mountain pressed in on all sides. Jen's heart felt like stone, and the darkness seemed like a live thing waiting to swallow them up. Then the boy began to whistle a tune. Raising her eyes, Jen looked ahead and saw the steady flame of his torch. Beside her, Thrinn began to hum, and the sense of overpowering heaviness ebbed away. Wading carefully though the shallow pool, they followed their guide across the cavern, into a narrow tunnel.

As they moved forward, a familiar sound echoed down the passage, like the pulse of the sea, and the air became heavy with a foul odor.

"Ugh! What's that awful stink?" Thrinn said.

They went on, the sound growing louder, the smell stronger. The tunnel widened and the Fennys walked on either side of Jen, keeping close. Ahead of them, the boy held his torch high, and by its light, they saw a large gap in the wall on their left.

It was through this black hole that the mountain exhaled a stench of brine and decay, and they could hear the rhythmic boom of waves, like a beating heart echoing in some vast cavern. As they passed, water spewed from its mouth and a gust of wind blew the torches out.

"Stand still!" the boy cried.

Trembling, staring into utter darkness, Jen reached out a hand for Thrinn and found that she could see her face. Forlost moved into view, and then the boy.

"Silver One!" the boy said. "Your eyes are a light in the dark!"

The sight of his grinning face gave her courage. He struck a flint and had just lit the torches when a hoarse shriek issued from the hole.

A small figure crawled out on hands and knees, then another, and another, until seven ragged creatures crouched around the travelers, blinking in the light. Forlost pulled one to its feet. It was a little man, like him, but more than half starved.

"Lost! Lost!" the creature croaked.

Into Jen's mind came the voice of the Lady: *"Deep in the mountain, you will find the lost ones."* Then a horrible bellowing broke upon their ears. From beyond the black entrance came the sound of some huge creature thrashing in the unseen sea at the mountain's heart.

"Away! Away!" cried the lost ones. "Run!"

"Steady now," the boy called out. "Follow me." Lifting his torch, he began to sing a joyous song as he led the company from that dreadful place. The passage began to slope upward, and they left the terrible beast behind, its roar fading as they climbed.

When they finally stopped to rest, Jen was worn-out. They had come a long way, toiling up the road in the silence of the mountain. They sat down in a shallow recess of the tunnel, and the boy passed out food from his satchel.

"You are Fennodyree," he said to the lost ones. "From Cwenburgh, perhaps?"

"We do not know," one of them said. "We are lost."

Jen looked at the seven haggard faces, three men and four women. "What was that creature we heard?"

They stared at her with blank expressions.

"I think we will not speak of it," the boy said. "Let us sleep now."

It seemed to Jen that she had only just closed her eyes when she heard Thrinn say, "Get up, little one. Time to get out of this hole."

The way out became easier, the tunnel zigzagging back and forth, up and up until, at last, a speck of pale light shone in the distance. When they stepped out of the tunnel, the sun was climbing into the sky. They had gone down into the depths of Mount Rosknil on its eastern flank and come out on a high northern shelf of rock. Straight ahead, the forested heights of Mount Greeba rose into the clear air.

Ascending a short slope, they came to the High Pass, which was an arm of Mount Greeba flung out to meet her smaller brother. Unlike the bare, narrow hogback that joined Rosknil and Kulifara, this pass was wide and sheltered by great trees that seemed to grow out of the stone. Tramman trees, the boy called them, and he said they did not grow anywhere else on the island. As they walked through the forest, the light grew and many birds rustled in the branches, their calls filling the air.

Jen's spirits rose, and she felt they were walking high above the world in a place untouched by darkness or any evil thing. Only the seven Fennys wept at the sight of sunlight and the taste of clear water. Five of them never spoke a word the entire journey, and the two who did speak would only repeat, "We are lost."

"What happened to them?" Jen asked the boy.

"They have been tried, almost beyond their strength," he replied. "But many folk find healing among the giants in the Hidden Valley."

At last, they stood on the southern flank of Greeba, and Jen saw the headwaters of the Glenfaba gushing from a great hollow scooped out of the mountain's side. The torrent fell hundreds of feet into a wooded gorge, where it cut a deep channel, flowing through small valleys at the mountain's foot.

The boy led them down a well-worn path, through sloping fields of tall grass and wildflowers, until they came to the edge of a short cliff and a broad stairway cut into the rock. Below them spread a green dale and, on either side, forested hills. At its northernmost end, the valley opened onto a distant shore, where the sea shone in the sunlight.

Suddenly, the shining horizon vanished, and where the sea had been, green-clad mountains appeared, so tall their peaks were lost in the clouds. From those far-off heights came the sound of singing.

"Do you see them, little sister?" the boy said. "The Inner Mountains?"

"Oh! That's where my mother is! Are we going there?"

"Not yet."

As he spoke, the green mountains faded and the gray sea came into view once more. The boy beckoned the company forward, and Jen turned and followed him down the path, passing into the Hidden Valley, under the shadow of the trees.

19

The Trouble with Houseplants

"I've had the strangest dreams."

It was evening, after supper, and Pixel was bent over a tangle of vines, using hand clippers to cut a path through Jonas' room. Peter was on the other side of the room, by the seed table, pruning the overgrown bee balm. The Bugganes had finished dragging all of Lir's things out to the cliffs above the bay and were preparing for the bonfire.

"Last night," Pixel continued, "I dreamed I was lost in a forest. All around, I could hear horses. But mostly I have dreams about an old lady I met in Foyle. We've hung out together sometimes. I call her the Bread Lady, and in my dreams she's walking through the woods with Moody."

Peter stopped clipping and looked up. "That's not a bad dream."

"No, but it's not my normal dreams. Nothing's been normal since we came to the island. But it's better here. At Wakkenburg. I mean, I don't feel sick, you know?"

"You shouldn't go back to Foyle. Stay here."

"I don't think I get to decide. Anyway, I bet your aunt and uncle won't let me."

"How do you know? Besides, you heard what Fiak said. I'm the official head of Wakkenburg House."

Pixel laughed, wishing the answer were that easy. Then she stood up and looked out the window at the clear sky and the sun setting behind the forest. Far to the north, three jagged mountain crests rose above the sea of trees. "Do you ever think about exploring all that out there?"

"Without marked trails, I'd only get lost."

"Why *aren't* there trails? People have lived on this island a long time."

"Sounds like some pretty strange things live out there. Think of the Bugganes."

"Ahem. Mr. Peter."

Pixel turned and saw Ulf and a handful of gardeners at the door.

"We've come to see about moving that tree."

They were nervous, looking into the room with wide eyes. When Muru's housecleaning crew had come to the playrooms earlier that afternoon, it was the first time in the history of Wakkenburg House that Fennys had ever set foot in the North Tower. The housemaids were still downstairs, attacking the dust with a fury of brooms and mops. At first, they hadn't known what to make of the fire pole and kept well away, until Pixel demonstrated its use. When they saw her sliding down, whooping as she went, they all wanted to try, and for a while it was difficult for Muru to get them to do anything else.

Now that the cleaning of the North Tower had begun, the garden crew had come to see the fabled greenhouse of Jonas.

"Over here, Ulf," Peter said. "Me and Pixel cleared the ladder."

Pixel watched as the Fennys, carrying watering cans and shovels, picked their way carefully through the tangle that still covered the floor. They seemed hesitant to touch any of it. "It's alright," she said. "These are Jonas' plants, not the wizard's."

"You don't say." Ulf took a pair of hand clippers out of his vest and, wincing slightly, cut a thick vine that blocked his way. When nothing happened, the other Fennys whipped out clippers and began cutting furiously at the tangle. In five minutes, they had cleared the entire floor and pushed the debris out the open windows.

Peter and Pixel, sweaty and tired after an hour of patient pruning, looked at each other and grinned.

Ulf pocketed his clippers, dusted his hands, and said, "Now, Mr. Peter, where's that tree?"

Peter led the way onto the roof, and they all stood there in the deepening twilight, looking at the stricken thing and its broken pot.

"Poor tree," Pixel said, stroking its rough gray bark. Peter, she noticed, was looking back toward the open hatch.

"It ain't dead," Ulf replied, cutting back a lanky branch, exposing the green wick. "Looks to me like one of Jonas' special projects, though I'm wonderin' why he put it on the rooftop."

"It woulda been too tall for that plant room," one of the other gardeners said.

"True, but I guess he expected someone to get to it a lot sooner."

The other gardeners examined Jonas' watering system. One of them went down to the room below, and they could hear him shouting up the stairs, "Try sending a little water through the pipe! Oh, look! It's sprinkling!" The other Fennys dashed down the stairs, and in a minute they all came back and gathered around the rain barrel again.

"Where shall we move it, Mr. Peter?" Ulf asked.

"I don't know anything about trees."

"The easiest thing would be to take it down them straight stairs, you know, the ones that was secret, and then right out to the Glenny. We can plant it among the other trees beside the stream. It ought to do pretty well there."

"Sure." Peter moved to the hatch. "I'll be downstairs if you need me."

Pixel scowled at him. "You aren't going to help?"

He shrugged in reply and disappeared down the ladder. Then the other gardeners gathered around the tree, and Pixel, realizing she would only be in the way, followed Peter down to the plant room. She found him seated at Jonas' desk—which was now his—leafing through an old book. He looked up. "I thought *you* were going to help."

"They don't need me." She sat down on the nearest window ledge. "What's that?"

"Jonas' journal." He held up the rock painted with Jenny's name. "All this stuff was meant for her."

"Read it," Pixel said. "I want to hear."

"Okay." He lit the kerosene lantern on the desk and opened to the first page. *"It is true that the trees in the forest will move at your command, but you'll find out soon enough, if you haven't already."*

Ulf's voice came through the open hatch. "The burlap sacking, Flin! Where is it? Sure, dip it in the water. Right. We'll wrap the root ball first."

"They will naturally make way for you, which is convenient when there's no apparent path."

"Come on, fellas. What's the holdup? Mr. Peter wants it moved today, not next year!" someone shouted.

Peter glanced at the ceiling. "Maybe we should read this later."

"I can hear. Go on."

"The trees have lived here far longer than we humans. The big ones are very old. Ancient. They have seen many things we cannot imagine."

Pixel heard the sound of feet running back and forth across the roof, then Ulf's voice again: "That's right! Just use one of them pipes as a lever. Right here, under this big root."

"They will open paths where you had not planned to go, but these unexpected avenues always turn out for the best."

"Now then. One! Two! Three! Heave!"

"When they open a path for you, take it. Never hesitate. They will show you things you never thought to see."

"Frin! Flik! Finalf! What's wrong with you?"

Peter stopped reading and they looked up. Neither of them had ever heard Ulf lose patience. A shrill volley of voices replied.

Peter began reading again. *"Indeed, the trees are your allies, and they will lead you to the other creatures of Wakken Wood whom you can trust."*

Pixel realized she was holding her breath, and she let it out slowly. "Peter, do you think this is true? Will trees really move around for you?"

Strange scraping noises on the roof distracted him. He glanced up, then went on reading. *"I have recently made an experiment, Jenny. I have taken a hawthorn seed and nursed it with my own hands, feeding it with special plant food, keeping it separate from other trees. Now that it's time for me to go, I leave this seedling to you."* He stopped. "Pixel," he began, and his voice cracked. She stared at him, open-mouthed, then looked up at the ceiling. Ulf was shouting now.

"Well, I'm jiggered! This dang tree! We may as well try lifting a mountain!"

"We'll have to cut up the roof," one of the gardeners said. "Better get hold of Furse. He's got one of them power-cutter things."

"What does he say next?" Pixel whispered. The look on Peter's face smote her heart. He was in way over his head. They both were. He bent over the journal again and read in a choked voice, *"You must move this tree to the gardens before it is more than two feet high. Any larger, and it will become difficult. Already it shows signs of an unusual attachment, though I think it will respond to you as well."*

"Furse! Furse! Hey! Get up here quick! And bring that power sawzall thing of yours!"

Peter shut the book with a snap and looked around the alcove. Pixel watched him, holding her breath again. Then he opened the right-hand drawer of the desk and took out a jar labeled "Tree Food". Muttering to himself, he grabbed a watering can and stomped up the ladder.

Pixel followed slowly. When she got to the roof, Peter was sprinkling green powder on the dirt mound. Ulf and his crew took off their caps and watched respectfully. Then Peter poured water over the roots and sat back on his heels. Pixel stood behind him, hardly daring to breathe, remembering what had happened with the vines. That had taken only seconds.

There was no response. Peter put his hand on the tree's thin trunk and said in a quiet voice, "Wake up. We gotta get you off this roof." Nothing. He looked up at Ulf. "I think it's dead."

Ulf shook his head. "Ain't dead. Peeved, maybe."

Peter nodded, and Pixel heard him say, very gently, "Sorry, hawthorn. Jonas is gone. Jenny disappeared. You're stuck with me." He hung his head, and Pixel realized why he hadn't wanted anything to do with the tree in the first place. Something about Peter must be . . . part tree. That was it. And the sight of this withered one gave him the willies.

When nothing happened, she watched him stand up and turn away, his eyes fixed on the ground. He headed for the hatch, and she didn't say anything, only watched him disappear down the ladder. Then she heard a scrabbling sound on the roof.

Turning, she saw the little tree's roots curl inward and latch onto the dirt at the base of the mound. There was no other change, but Ulf said, "That's capital, Mr. Peter. It's let go. We'll be able to move it now."

"Peter!" Pixel rushed down the ladder, but it was too late. He had gone.

A sudden light flashed. To the northeast, blue flames shot up, towering over the trees on the cliff. "Oh! The Bugganes' bonfire!"

Going to the wide windows that looked out over the distant sea, Pixel watched the flames turn green, then purple. "I hope that wizard is watching," she whispered. Then, just as the blaze turned orange and sank below the treetops, the gardeners came down the ladder, lugging the tree between them. She picked up her flashlight, which she'd found on the fourth floor, and went to light their way through the dark passages.

20

Breakfast with Bugganes

The following morning, Peter stood at the door of the ballroom, waiting to welcome the Bugganes. According to Muru, they had come in just after dawn and asked to go to their rooms. She'd heard water running and assumed they were filling the large-creature baths. Then everything went very quiet. It was still quiet. Peter looked into the ballroom and saw the Fennys standing at attention, their final preparations complete. Birdsong came through the doors that opened onto the terrace.

Pixel walked in. "Peter, that hawthorn tree Ulf moved from the roof is gone! He doesn't know where it is!"

He looked at her, trying to take in her words, but at the moment a missing tree was the least of his worries. They were about to serve breakfast to four very strange creatures, one of whom was asleep on the table. He glanced at the small hedgehog curled up next to the teapot. It seemed to have shrunk in the night and was now the size of a tennis ball.

"We'll find it," Peter began. "As soon as this—"

Down the hall, three doors opened and the Bugganes emerged. The old man's hair was slicked back, and he wore an ancient coat with tails. The hairy man's long hair and beard were combed and braided, and he wore a blue cloak over his tunic and breeches. Even the bear had groomed and oiled his fur until it shone.

Peter ushered them into the ballroom and led them to seats of honor. Because he was the Silver-eyed, Muru made him sit at the head of the table with Bugganes at his right and left. Pixel sat a little farther down, beside the old man. At the far end, with paper and pen instead of a plate, Fiak was already recording the event. Places had been laid for Uncle Edward and Aunt Marj, but they did not appear.

Hoping this whole thing wasn't a mistake, Peter unfolded his napkin as he'd been told, the Bugganes did the same, and the five-course breakfast began.

Through the serving door of the East Kitchen, a troop of Fennys entered the ballroom bearing trays of fruit: sliced melons, red and green apples, grapes and peaches, blueberries and bananas. The Bugganes were unfamiliar with bananas. Peter stopped the old man just before he bit into the peel and showed him how to open it. A minute later he wished he hadn't! After one taste, the old man grabbed all the bananas, piled them on his plate, and, tossing the peels over his shoulder, stuffed the fruit into his mouth as fast as he could. The hairy man attacked the tray of grapes with abandon, and the bear climbed halfway onto the table, grunting and snuffling into every bowl. Pixel backed away from the table as banana peels, apple cores, and peach pits flew through the air.

Peter banged a spoon against an empty glass until it shattered, then jumped to his feet and thumped his fist on the table. "Bugganes!" Out of the corner of his eye, he saw Muru enter the room. "You ..." he hesitated, and she frowned. "Throwing things and climbing on the table is ... is not allowed," he said quickly, keeping his eyes on his plate. "You have to use your best manners if you ... if you want to continue this meal indoors." Expecting defiance or anger, he glanced up and was surprised to see tears in the old man's eyes. Muru was smiling.

"Oh! We Toms have been bad!" the old man wailed.

"Never mind," Peter said quickly as the Buggane's shape flickered between the old man and the little girl. "I'm sure you'll all be good for the second course. There's lots of food. You don't have to be greedy."

The Fennys removed the empty plates, swept up the mess, and brought in the second course: porridge and cream.

This time the Bugganes behaved as perfect gentlemen and even ventured to make polite conversation—except the hedgehog, who was still asleep on the table. Near the end of the porridge, the old man turned to Pixel and, in a grandfatherly way, said, "My dear, you are a newcomer to Wakkenburg, are you not?"

"Yes, I'm visiting," she replied. When she explained that she lived at the Rilson house and would be returning the next day, the hairy man said, "Do not go back there, little one. It is the place where the serpent grows."

She put down her spoon.

"A very bad place," the old man agreed. "You should not return."

Peter was about to ask what they meant when Uncle Ed entered the room. "Ah! I'm in time for the *real* breakfast," he said, as the Fennys laid clean plates and brought in veal chops and fish. Saluting the Bugganes, he sat down across from Pixel, and Peter heard him say in a loud whisper, "I hate porridge. How were the first two courses?" Pixel rolled her eyes. "I thought so. Did Muru give our guests a tongue lashing?"

"Peter did."

"Really?" He waved at Peter across the length of table and grinned.

Peter smiled wanly, glad his uncle had come. Once again, it felt like reinforcements arriving.

Besides veal and fish, the Fennys brought in boiled eggs, poached eggs, omelets, fried mushrooms, fried potatoes, muffins, popovers with butter, and coffee in delicate breakfast cups. The Bugganes took some of everything, piling their plates high, their eyes gleaming with pleasure. Peter felt his own appetite waning as the meal progressed, but he lifted his fork as he'd been instructed, and everyone dug in.

At last, when every serving dish and platter was empty, the Bugganes sat back and the old man said, "That was good. Very good. Puts me in mind of old Mooner feasts. I used to be invited on occasion, and I can tell you they have a high regard for human food, especially bread and sweets. But they have to steal it from them poor folks in Foyle."

Uncle Edward put his cup down with a thump. "Who the heck are the Mooners?"

"The Moonjer Veggey is their ancient name," the hairy man said. "At one time, their raids on the town were rare. Then during one of Mac Lir's voyages, when he was away too long, they took up with the Moonwitch. It is she who forces them to steal from the men more and more often. Especially now that the Lliannon Shee have returned."

"Yes, Tom," the old man said, "but it's because of the Shee that half the Mooners have left the witch's service. They went back to Mac Lir when they learned he'd returned to the woods."

"I met them many nights ago, Silver One," the hairy man said. "They want to know why you haven't joined the wizard."

"The wizard threw the Fennys out into the woods!" Pixel said. "Why would Peter join his side?"

"Ah!" the old man said sadly. "It is true that Mac Lir and the Mooners bear no love for the Fennys. It's a shame really, and it's their own fault."

"Whose fault?" Pixel said. "Not the Fennys. They don't run around stealing food and stirring up trouble."

"It's an old grudge," the hairy man said, "as you must know."

Fiak stopped writing, his pen poised in midair. The clatter of dishes in the kitchen ceased. There was a sudden silence in the room.

"No, we don't know," Peter said, glancing at Fiak's wide eyes. "Tell us."

"Long ago," the hairy man said, "there were no Fennys. When Mac Lir first came to the island in his great ship, he brought the Bugganes, the Moddey Dhoo, the Arkan Sonney, the Washers, the Tarroo Ushtey, the Moonjer Veggey, and Nathaniel, the first Silver One. Mac Lir believed that the island was uninhabited, so he claimed it as his domain, then sailed away again, leaving Nathaniel and all the creatures to fend for themselves.

"Now, the Moonjer Veggey, a race of small men, proud and handsome, roamed over the island, riding their white horses, hunting under starlight with little hounds. One evening, they came upon the seaside camp of the Merry Wanderers, a tribe of people who came to fish and hunt during certain seasons. The Moonjer Veggey, being curious, watched the humans from afar.

"Then, during a full moon in spring, the Moonjer Veggey, in a fit of goodwill—or perhaps loneliness—decided to show themselves and accept the people's hospitality. The Wanderers were suspicious at first, and some members of the tribe believed spirits had come among them, but when the Mooners pulled out their instruments and began to sing, all fear was forgotten and the people joined the ring of dancing.

"After that evening, two or three of the Mooner men were often seen dancing with the Merry Wanderers at twilight and walking with certain of the women along forest pathways or beside the lapping sea. They had fallen in love. These Mooners joined themselves to the human tribe and no longer rode out hunting with the other small folk.

"After many years, Mac Lir returned. When he heard of the marriage between the Moonjer Veggey and the humans, he was angry. He cursed those Mooners, their brides, and their many children. He made them ugly, condemning them to walk the forest paths in shame. 'Let them be called the Fennodyree,' he said. 'The fallen fairies, unwelcome in my domain.'

"Then the giants came, gathered the Fennodyree, and took them to the mountains to meet a certain lady. It was she who showed them the turnings of Mac Lir's curse. The ugliness, meant to make them outcasts, had strengthened them. In fact, they had become more powerful than all of Mac Lir's creatures put together. The lady told them how the wizard had tricked Nathaniel Wakkenburg, forcing him beyond the boundary of the human world, where no man was meant to live. She asked the Fennodyree to protect the Silver One and his descendants. To all this, the Fennodyree readily agreed. They moved into Wakkenburg House and formed an alliance with Nathaniel."

"And," the old man added, "now you know why them Mooners won't come near this place. They hate the whole Fenny race. And Mac Lir hates them too. If he'd had his way, he'd have routed them all out of Wakkenburg House long ago. But the lady's word proved true. Mac Lir's curse has turned out in favor of the Fennys, and there's nothing he can do about it."

Peter looked over at Fiak, who was writing like mad. Then he noticed Muru and the entire house crew gathered at the kitchen door, listening.

"It's impossible to kill the Fennodyree, as you yourselves have seen," the hairy man said. "Even the Fennys of Cwenburgh are probably still alive."

Peter frowned. "Cwenburgh?"

"Another big house," Uncle Ed replied. "On the other side of the island, a ways south of Floden. Never seen it myself. Seems it's haunted or something."

"Not haunted," the hairy man said. "The Moonwitch took it over long ago. It's one of the things lost in the battle Jonas fought."

"Then it belonged to the Thornburgs," Peter said, "like Fenn House."

"Not so, Silver One. Cwenburgh and Fenn House were here when we arrived with your ancestor, Nathaniel. The giants had built those two dwellings long before they built this place, though they never told us who had lived in them. In later years, as the family of the first Silver One increased, the giants gave both houses to Nathaniel, and there were twelve Fennys assigned to each. We do not know what happened to the Fennys of Cwenburgh when the Moonwitch moved in."

"They weren't thrown out into the woods," the old man said. "We helped Jonas hunt for them many times. No doubt the witch uses them for her own purposes."

Peter glanced at Pixel's stricken face and at the solemn house crew, who were now crowded around Fiak's end of the table.

Suddenly, Fiak stood up and bowed to the Bugganes. "We thank you, sirs. This story was unknown to us and now"—he held up his paper and pen—"it is recorded so that we will never forget. We who are born of the mingled blood of fey and humans thank you."

Moved, perhaps, by some deeper part of himself that he still didn't understand, Peter also stood and bowed to the Bugganes. "You have proved yourselves friends of . . . of this house and of . . . of me and the Fennys. We won't forget it. If no one's told you before, I say it now. You're always welcome here at Wakkenburg."

"As guests," Muru said.

Taking his cue from her alarmed face, Peter said, "Er, yes. As guests." He glanced at the bear, who was quietly pouring milk from the cream pitcher down his throat. "Muru, is there more food coming?"

The Fennys hurried back to the kitchen and reappeared with fresh plates, and the fourth course, broiled chicken with rice, began.

The Bugganes were eating contentedly when Pixel abruptly jumped to her feet, shouting, "The tree! There it is!" She dashed out to the terrace, and Peter got up and followed, with everyone else right behind.

Outside, he saw a small, leafy tree covered in white blossoms. Its thick roots were casually tearing up the bottom steps of the terrace. "This is not the tree from the roof. It can't be."

At the sound of his voice, the tree stood still, quivering, though there wasn't the slightest breeze. Peter felt an awareness pressing on his mind, hovering just outside the edge of thought.

"It is," Pixel insisted. "I looked up hawthorn trees in the library last night."

"Son of a gun," Uncle Edward murmured.

Ulf ran up, followed by three or four gardeners. "Oh, thank heavens! Here it is, boys! Tryin' to get up the stairs, followin' Mr. Peter, poor thing. Probably thinks he's Mr. Jonas come back." Then he saw Peter and took off his cap. "Mr. Peter, I thought maybe it went to the woods, and we was about to send Moody out lookin' for it, knowin' how it's kind of a special tree. You'll have to be firm with it, sir."

"What?"

"Tell it to behave. You know. Where to go and where to stay. Otherwise we'll have no end of trouble with it. We can't have it tearin' up the rose gardens or gettin' into the vegetables."

"Okay. I ... maybe ..."

Muru shooed everyone else back into the ballroom and shut the doors.

Moments later, Peter returned to the table, trying not to look at anyone. After he'd spoken to the tree, it stopped eating the stairs, but it threw prickly sticks at him, and his face and arms were covered with scratches. From across the table, he heard Uncle Ed mutter, "Stumps me why Jonas picked a pet tree with half-inch thorns."

The Fennys had cleared away the empty dishes from the fourth course, and now they brought out the grand finale: brightly colored gelatin desserts, tiered plates of pastries, and piles of waffles.

Peter had never liked gelatin for dessert and certainly didn't consider it a breakfast food, but everyone at the table, including Pixel, took generous helpings. Even the hedgehog sat up when the hairy man placed a spoonful in front of its nose. It sucked in the pink blob without opening its eyes.

Peter's uncle looked at him and winked. "Muru has played to the Wakkenburg weakness. You should try some, Peter."

Deciding to follow Uncle Ed's advice, he took a few spoonfuls of green gelatin from the nearest serving dish. Taking a tentative mouthful, he immediately regretted not taking more, but it was too late. The old man had already finished what was left, and every platter of molded gelatin on the table was empty.

Then, as the Bugganes moved on to waffles and pastry, Tom Bear turned his snout toward Peter and rumbled something. The other two Bugganes gasped and stopped eating.

"Tom! Why didn't you tell us before?"

The bear rumbled on for a while longer, then fell silent.

"This is news indeed!" the hairy man said. "Tom Bear has seen another Silver One! He thinks it is the one from before you."

The room went very quiet.

"Many days ago," the hairy man continued, "there was a rumor among the trees that a Silver One was at large. We did not know what to make of this until we saw you, boy. But now it seems that the trees were speaking of another. What is more, Tom Bear says he met this Silver Girl on the road from Floden, in the company of the Poinkers. He traveled with her into the mountains, past Spoot Voor Falls."

Uncle Ed thumped his cup on the table. "Jenny! I knew it!" He leapt up and his chair clattered to the floor. "It *was* her button I found in that cellar! But why do you call her a girl? She's about seventy years old!"

The bear made a few grunting noises, and the hairy man said, "Tom assures us that the child is indeed called Jenny. And two old ones travel with her. Fennodyree, from this very house!"

Fiak gasped. "Our old Head Fenny! The one Lir sent to find the missing Silver Child! It must be! But who is the other?"

"Thrinn," Muru said. She had come out of the kitchen and was standing at his elbow. "She was Head Housekeeper before me. Trust me, I remember."

Fiak nodded and began writing furiously.

"Well. Now we know why the Moonwitch has called the Shee," the old man said. "She is seeking this Silver Girl, putting forth all her power. And that is why the Glashtyn were in Floden."

"What I don't get," Uncle Edward said, glaring at the bear, "is why you left Jenny in the mountains. You should have brought her here!"

Tom Bear muttered a reply.

"Scadoo Pass? Oh, Tom!" the old man cried. "Why ever did she take that dark road?"

Tom Bear grunted, and the hairy man said, "This is indeed good news. The Silver Girl and her companions met the Lady of the Mountains. It was she who told the child to go to the Hidden Valley by way of Mount Rosknil. Tom was sent here to help us."

"Ah! The Lady of the Mountains!" the old man sighed. "Did you really speak with her, Tom?"

The bear put both paws on the table and hummed deep in his throat.

"Who exactly are we talkin' about here?" Uncle Ed demanded.

"The Shepherdess of the Hills!" the old man said. "Don't you know her?"

"No, I don't! And where is this Hidden Valley? Can't say I've heard of it either."

"It is the dwelling place of the giants," the hairy man replied. "We know little about it."

There was a long silence. Peter, who had been staring at his plate, listening, looked up to see the table surrounded by all the kitchen Fennys. And there was Aunt Marj! She wore a flowered apron and clutched a wooden spoon in one hand. She hadn't been hiding in her room; she'd been helping Muru the whole time! Evidently *her* courage was not failing.

"Well now. I think we understand things better," the old man said. "At last, it is clear why Mac Lir has returned. He has come to defend his claim to the island."

"And he is no longer sure of his welcome here at Wakkenburg," the hairy man added. "No doubt he remembers that Jonas turned against him, and for some reason, boy, he isn't sure of you. This is why he took Fenn House by force. It was not a good way to begin."

"Don't forget about Lila!" the old man said. "I have no doubt the wizard called her forth to aid him in the battle that will surely come."

"I ... I don't understand," Peter faltered. Then, out of the corner of his eye, he saw the hedgehog sit up. Abruptly, it turned into a teapot-sized spider, scurried down the center of the table, and came to rest on his plate, clacking its jaws. Peter backed away so fast he nearly tipped his chair.

"Oh, look!" the old man said. "Tom Spider is himself at last! But you hear what he says, boy?"

"I ... I don't speak spider."

"He's tellin' you he won't go back to his old home in the forest because it's too close to Cwenburgh! It's the *Moonwitch* who sent for Lila the Night Monster. He heard me say that it was Mac Lir who called her, and he wishes to correct me on this point."

"Wait a minute," Pixel said. "Let me get this straight. You're saying there's someone called the Moonwitch who lives in a house called Cwenburgh, and *she's* the one who called Lila the Night Monster. So it was *Lila* who came out of the portal in the North Tower, bashed in the gate, and went to join the Moonwitch?"

"That's right, little missy," said the old man.

"But when we were looking at that portal thingy, you said that Mac Lir united himself to Lila a long time ago," Pixel said. "Why didn't she go back to him?"

"These are deep waters," the old man said. "And we don't know much about Lila. Only that she is very evil."

The bear snarled and the hairy man turned to Peter. "Tom is right. You must never be in the woods alone, boy. Remember that. We may not like Mac Lir, but we'd rather have him than the Moonwitch. If she catches you, she'll enslave you and take control of the island and all us creatures."

"Why me?"

"It is believed that the Silver Ones can speak to the trees, and whoever controls the trees has dominion over all of Wakken Wood."

Peter let his mouth fall open, looking from one Buggane to the other. "But … but … that's not … true," he faltered. Then he thought of the hawthorn and glanced at Pixel, who was staring at him in dismay.

"It's finally come like I thought it would," Uncle Edward said. "Though it don't seem clear to me what to do. Should we be helping Mac Lir? He's not my idea of a savior. But"—he looked at his sister—"Marj, did you hear? Jenny's back!"

"Yes," she breathed. "And she's safe! You always believed, didn't you?"

The spider on Peter's plate grew a little more and clacked its jaws.

"Hear him, boy! He is asking permission to remain here!" the old man said. "He will guard Wakkenburg!"

Peter hesitated. "Isn't he afraid of Moody?" This probably didn't matter, but he was stalling, trying to think. Aunt Marj didn't like spiders, and Muru wasn't keen on Bugganes in the house. Still, having a giant spider around that could change into a scorpion might be useful, if everything about the Moonwitch was true.

"He is in earnest," the hairy man said. "It would not do to refuse."

"Come on, kid!" Muru snapped. "Don't be an idiot!"

Peter looked up in surprise.

"Why are you waffling?" she fumed. "After all we've heard, the obvious answer is *yes*!"

Peter and Pixel stood on the ballroom terrace, watching the three Bugganes amble away across the lawn.

"Goodbye! Goodbye!" Aunt Marj cried, waving a tea towel. Uncle Ed raised his hand in farewell. At the corner of the North Tower, Tom Bear stood up on his hind legs and roared his thanks one more time.

"Well," Aunt Marj said. "That went off rather well, don't you think?"

Uncle Edward grunted. "The house is still standing."

She handed the tea towel to her brother, then began untying her apron. "Ed, maybe you should help Muru with the dishes."

"I need a map of the island," he said, passing the towel to Peter. "Didn't that bear say something about Jenny going to Mount Rosknil? Isn't that way up north?" He looked around. "Where'd that Fiak fellow get to?"

The two of them moved into the ballroom, discussing the news about Jenny. Peter watched the Bugganes disappear through the Door for Large Creatures. Then a small figure, probably Furse, rolled the big gate shut.

"I'll help Muru," Pixel said quietly.

Her face was very pale. Even her lips were white, and she wore a closed look. She took the tea towel out of his hands and turned away, into the ballroom. Now that the Bugganes' breakfast was over, she was probably thinking of tomorrow. One more night, and she'd be back at that terrible house in Foyle. Peter wished he could say something to make her stay at Wakkenburg, but he knew her well enough. No matter how much anyone protested, she wouldn't want to lie, and she wouldn't hide from her aunt. She'd do whatever was expected—even if it killed her.

He sat down on the terrace steps, kicking at the loose bricks that the hawthorn had churned up. Maybe he should write a letter to his dad and tell him everything that was happening. "No. He'd never believe it," Peter muttered to the afternoon sunlight. Then he got up and went into the ballroom.

The swinging door to the East Kitchen was propped open. Over the clatter of dishes, he heard Ulf say, "I remember Forlost! He was Head before Norbert, right?" Then someone started whistling and another began to sing. Drawn to the happy buzz of Fennys, Peter crossed the ballroom and stood in the doorway.

There were dirty dishes piled on almost every surface. Fennys in brightly colored aprons moved among the stacks, scraping leftovers into a huge dog dish, collecting silverware, carrying cups to the sink. On the far side of the room, the back door was open, and he could see the orchard trees rustling in a mild breeze. Pixel was nowhere in sight, and he wondered whether she'd gone to her room. Then, at a table near the orchard door, he spotted Ulf, Rumun, and the garden crew sitting around a huge mound of green gelatin, one of the splendid gelatin dessert molds that had obviously fallen into ruin before it made it to the ballroom. Peter felt a twinge of jealousy. He'd tasted barely any of it. That greedy Buggane had eaten his share. With a sudden movement, he stepped over the threshold.

"Look, kid, those blood treatments you told me about sound pretty fishy!" Muru's querulous voice rose over the happy chatter, which instantly ceased. Forgetting the gelatin, Peter glanced around the room. All the Fennys had stopped what they were doing, their eyes fixed on the table nearest to him. Then, behind the highest stack of dishes he saw the top of Muru's head. Moving closer, he peered over and there was Pixel, slumped in a chair.

"You don't look sick to me!" Muru snapped, hands on hips. "At least you didn't until we started this conversation." Another Fenny set a steaming mug in front of Pixel. Probably it was mugwort, the Fenny cure-all.

"You should stay here, where you're happy," Muru continued. "I can take care of you if you wind up at death's door."

Peter smiled to himself. If anyone could convince his stubborn friend, it was Muru.

"My aunt will try to find me," Pixel said. "What if she sends the police?"

"I've just posted a giant spider at the front door! Anyway, if you really want to go, you'll have to walk. Mr. Edward and Miss Marj won't take you back to Foyle. I heard them say so."

Startled, Pixel sat up. "You ... you mean they *want* me to stay?" Then she slumped back in the chair. "I don't think *they* get to decide. Neither do I."

Muru shook her head. "It's your aunt who doesn't get to decide."

Peter moved around the end of the table, and Pixel looked up at him, her eyes large in her pale face. "No one's gonna take you back to Foyle," he said, "and you can't walk. Not with all the witches or whatever in the woods." He hadn't told her about the big raid at Thorny's and that someone, besides Aunt Kate, was definitely looking for her. Then she said something that surprised him.

"The Bread Lady told me to come here if I got the chance. No matter what Aunt Kate said."

"Bread Lady?"

"That's what I call her. She pretty much told me to sneak away from Foyle, and she was always telling me to stay out of my aunt's house as much as I could."

Quite suddenly, he pictured the old woman he'd met at the back of the Rilson house. The one with the strangely carved staff, whom Moody seemed to know quite well. What was it she'd said? *"Young man, if you truly love your friend, you will help her get away from this house."* "I think I met her."

"So ... you think it's really okay?" Her voice was doubtful, but her eyes pleaded. "Your aunt and uncle won't mind?"

He grinned. "It was their idea."

She started to get up.

"Hey! Where do you think you're going?" Muru snapped. "You haven't finished your tea!"

"I ... I was just going to help dry dishes," Pixel said, picking up the towel she'd slung over the back of the chair.

"Fine. But if you won't drink that tea, don't blame me!"

They spent the rest of the day in the East Kitchen, drying dishes, polishing silver, and sharing green gelatin dessert with the rest of the Fennys. Peter was surprised that Muru let them help with the work, but he guessed she was keeping a close eye on Pixel, just in case she changed her mind.

In the late afternoon, Aunt Marj came in, followed by Uncle Edward. Seeing the sudden doubt in Pixel's face, Peter slipped out the back door and stood on the steps. She needed to ask them, needed to hear their answer for herself.

"Oh, my dear!" Aunt Marj's voice came floating out into the sunlight. "Of course it's perfectly alright! We were hoping you'd *want* to stay!"

"And even if you didn't," Uncle Edward said, "I'd smash the Datsun's engine before I'd take you back. So don't even think about asking."

Peter turned away, smiling to himself. It was going to be alright. He jumped off the steps and walked off into the orchard, whistling for Moody.

Part II

21

Apple Hill

Pixel woke with that fluttery feeling, the one she always had before an exam. It was Saturday, the day she was supposed to return to the Rilson house in Foyle. "Aunt Kate's coming home on the evening ferry," Pixel whispered. "She'll expect me to be at the house for a blood treatment." She shuddered, thinking of the secret room where the remains of her cousins were hidden. Every Rilson girl who'd ever come to the island was in an urn in that room. And she was pretty sure that no one back home in Lang knew anything about it.

Pushing back the sheets, she sat up and looked at the needle marks on her arm. Aunt Kate had lied about the treatments. There was no cure. But why did the lab need so much blood? And if every Rilson girl with the blood disease died, what were the doctors doing? Flushing the samples down the toilet?

"But I'm not going back," she said aloud, and smiled to herself. "Aunt Marj and Uncle Ed want me to stay right here at Wakkenburg House. Muru too. And, of course, Peter."

She stood up, wriggled her toes in the soft carpet, and went to the window. It was early. The far gardens beyond the outbuildings lay in the shadow of the North Tower, but already the day was bright. Pushing up the window sash, she breathed in the cool morning air and heard the loud chorus of birdsong. As usual, it was the upward call of a thrush that drew her outside, that piping voice spiraling into the clear sky. She'd never heard one before coming to Wakken Wood. Quickly, she put on her old jeans and a T-shirt, then pulled on a sweater.

Tiptoeing down the corridor, she passed Peter's room. The door was wide open and he was not inside. A small shining object lay on the floor by his desk. Curious, she crossed the room and picked up a pearl button—the button that belonged to Jenny, the little sister who'd been missing for decades and who, according to Tom Bear, was still a child. How could that be? Thoughtfully, Pixel went down the back stairs, with the button in her pocket. She had more questions for Uncle Edward.

The lower floor of the West Wing was silent, and when she poked her head into the dining room, and then the sitting room, she found no one. Following the smell of coffee and fried ham, she went to the kitchen, where Rumun and his crew were loading the breakfast trolley.

"Do you know where Peter is?" she asked.

"He went out early, Miss Pixel."

"When you see him, could you tell him I went for a walk? I'll be back in time for breakfast." One of the kitchen Fennys pressed a little bag of donuts into her hand. Smiling her thanks, she went out the back door.

Going past the outbuildings, she went straight to the Door for Large Creatures and slid back the bolt. She tugged the door open and looked into the shadowy forest. The Bugganes had told Peter that he should never be out in the woods alone. "But I don't have silver eyes," Pixel said to the tall trees. "The Moonwitch isn't looking for me." She stepped out of the gate and followed the path beside the wall, past Glenny Stream, and up the gently sloping trail to Apple Hill.

Songbirds darted back and forth as she walked through the tall, waving grass. Raising her face to the blowing sky, she began to whistle, trying to keep in tune with the warbling birds. Shoving the bag of donuts deeper into her sweater pocket, she took off running, throwing her arms wide like a kite on the wind.

When she came to the top of the hill, she spun around and around, first quickly, then more and more slowly, taking in the view as it flashed by: sea, forest, house, and marshlands, under a blue, blue sky. All of it belonged to Peter, and she was his friend. With her head spinning pleasantly, she came to a stop facing the towers of Wakkenburg.

It had been right to come to Wakkenburg House, just as the Bread Lady had said. And it was right to stay, even if it looked like running away. Going back to Foyle would be like accepting the old Rilson dishonesty that seemed to run in the family blood. Hadn't she been fighting that all her life? To go on fighting was to run from the blood treatments, crazy as that sounded. Anyway, if she really was sick and going to die, she'd rather not spend her last months under the cold eye of Aunt Kate.

She laughed and closed her eyes, feeling the wind on her face. "I'm not going to die yet," she whispered. "I'm going to stay here at Wakkenburg as long as I can, living this strange, wonderful life." She prayed a silent thank-you to whoever might hear.

Then she opened her eyes to a world of white fog.

Where had it come from? Just a second ago, she'd been standing under a cloudless sky! Fighting panic, she stood very still. Maybe it was a freak fog blown in from the sea. In that case, it would lift again. She waited, watching droplets of mist float before her face. Then she remembered the strange cloud that was still sitting on Fenn House.

"I was facing Wakkenburg when I closed my eyes," she said aloud. "So I should turn right and walk down the hill."

Resisting the urge to run, she walked a few paces to the right, saw the path at her feet, and forced herself to walk slowly downhill. The fog was so thick she could hardly see two steps ahead. Reaching out with her hands, she felt the tall grass on either side. So far, so good. When the grass ended, the brushwood began, so she must be nearing the bottom of the hill. If she could just get to the garden wall, then she could feel her way back to the gate.

She was walking on level ground now, still on the path, and she began to go a little faster. Suddenly, her feet splashed into the stream. "The Glenny." Her voice sounded loud in the heavy fog. She crossed the stream, then took several steps before remembering to feel for the garden wall. It should be on the left. The mist clung closely about her, so that when she reached for the wall, her left hand disappeared.

The wall was not there. Taking a careful step to the left, she reached out again and felt nothing. The day Uncle Ed had taken them to Apple Hill, she'd run her hand along the stone wall as they walked the trail, so if the wall wasn't there, she'd gotten off the path. Turning around, she walked a little way, hoping to retrace her steps. If she could just find the stream again, she'd follow it to the place where it ran under the wall through a culvert. Then she'd be alright.

The white mist was growing thicker by the minute, and she'd completely lost her sense of direction. She was cold. Her clothes were damp. The cloying mist clung to her face and hair, but she kept going, listening for the sound of the stream. Branches and brambles came into view as she brushed past them. She heard the sound of flowing water and hurried forward. Then the fog thinned and she saw the beginning of a footbridge. Crossing it, she realized the waterway below was not the Glenny. It was too wide. Maybe she'd come all the way to the river. Yes. She'd seen it on a map. If she turned left and walked along the bank, she was sure to come to the road.

At the end of the footbridge, she saw the beginning of a trail. Following it, she descended a grassy knoll and plunged into the dark forest. It reminded her of the woods near the house.

"I'm getting close now. Moody! Peter!" she called. "I'm over here!"

Any moment now, the big dog would come leaping out of the fog. Even Tom Spider would be a welcome sight. But the fog grew thicker, and in the dim light of the woods, she could no longer see a path. Stumbling against a tree, she fell backward and landed on her rump. "I better stay still. Wait for the fog to go," she whispered. Crouching down against the trunk, she peered into the mist. Then she heard the whinny of a horse.

"Look! There she is!" a cold voice cried.

Suddenly, the sound of tramping hooves was all around her as dark shapes appeared in the fog. She looked up in confusion and saw an enormous black horse. Then cold hands like pincers plucked her from the forest floor, a sharp pain pierced her chest, and she fell headlong into darkness.

22

Code Red

The hawthorn tree stood in the middle of Ulf's prize calla lilies, lashing its branches.

"Do something, Mr. Peter!" Ulf pleaded. "It's gonna kill them all!"

Not quite awake, Peter stared at the unruly hawthorn. He could tell it to move, but he felt silly talking to a tree. Besides that, a strange pressure was mounting in his head. Or maybe *on* his head, like a five-pound hat. Must have something to do with the nightmare. He'd dreamed of a shadowy phantom riding through the woods on a dark horse, seeking him. In the dream, he ran, dodging through the trees as the horse closed in. Just as a cold hand grabbed him by the hair, he was jerked out of sleep by Ulf banging at his bedroom door. He still wasn't quite free of the dream's terror. Standing in the morning twilight, he shivered a little, wishing he'd put on a sweatshirt.

"Please, Mr. Peter," Ulf begged.

"Go stand by the doghouse," Peter said to the tree, pointing across the lawn. He was rewarded for this effort by a prickly slap across the cheek. Backing up, he said to Ulf, "I'll go to Jonas' room in the North Tower and get some tree food. Be right back."

By the time he returned, the tree was standing quietly by the doghouse and Ulf was repairing the damage in the flower bed. Peter fed the tree, then went upstairs to find Pixel. She wasn't in her room. She was probably in the East Tower kitchen, where the Fenny crews had their breakfast. She liked hanging out with them.

Crossing the kitchen garden, he sprinted to the East Wing, but she wasn't there. He checked the Rose Garden, but she wasn't there either. Well, maybe they'd missed each other. It was a big house.

Returning to the West Wing, he entered the dining room from the passage, just as his aunt and uncle came in through the French doors. They had taken an early walk in the South Orchard and come back by way of the front gate.

"Where's Pixel?" Uncle Ed asked.

"I haven't seen her yet," Peter replied, picking up a plate at the sideboard.

Then Rumun came in, carrying a platter of donuts. "Mr. Peter, I have a message from Miss Pixel. She went for a walk and will return for breakfast."

Peter was very hungry and had just finished two slices of toast and a large bowl of porridge when, out of the corner of his eye, he saw the hawthorn tree standing at the edge of the patio, thrashing its branches. He got up to scold it for moving when he saw a thick white cloud beyond the garden wall.

Muru stormed into the room. "Where's Pixel?"

"She went for a walk," Aunt Marj replied.

Suddenly, Moody appeared at the French doors, barking furiously. Then Ulf burst in from the passage. "Mr. Peter! Come quick! There's fog on Apple Hill and all around the west side of the house! It ain't natural! Come quick!"

"Where is Pixel?" Muru shouted.

Over the rising din, Peter heard his aunt say, "Heaven help us!" Then Uncle Edward threw open the French doors, and everyone tumbled out to the middle of the lawn.

Peter stopped abruptly at the edge of the patio and threw up his arms, shielding his face from the force that struck him. It was invisible, whatever it was, and no one else seemed to feel it. He stood there, helpless, watching Moody charge across the grass and leap over the high garden wall. He saw the fog thin as a light breeze swept up shreds of mist and blew them away.

"Well, I'm jiggered!" he heard Ulf shout. "That fog was thick and now *poof*! It's completely gone."

Then Krim and Furse came running. "The Door for Large Creatures is open!"

Peter's uncle and aunt and all the Fennys took off running this way and that, to search the house and grounds for an intruder and to find Pixel. Peter was left alone, except for the hawthorn, which thrashed about, tossing twigs and blossoms at him. As the hue and cry of the hunt moved farther away, the light of morning settled quietly around him, and the little tree beside him went still. Peter's gaze traveled over the lawn and the outbuildings, then out to the woods. The heaviness of the air increased, pressing against him, as if trying to get into his head. It was like a sixth sense shouting in a language he couldn't understand. Straining now, to grasp whatever it was, a quiet voice in his mind said, "Do not be afraid."

Quite suddenly, the weight of the air lifted, and his mind filled with the voices of whispering trees, like leaves rustling in gentle waves of wind across the vast forest. At first, he could not understand the words, for they were all speaking at once. Then he heard, quite clearly, "She's gone! Gone!" The whispering swelled, like the gathering force of a gale: "Gone! Far away!"

"Where?" he said in a low voice.

Muru came out of the house and stopped beside him. "We've looked in every corner of this place. Nothing came in the gate, but we can't find Pixel. Your uncle thinks she took a walk to Apple Hill. He and your aunt went to find her. They think she got lost in that freak fog."

The rustling whispers stopped. There was nothing more. Suddenly, the hawthorn gave a little quiver. All its blossoms fell to the ground, and Peter heard it say quite distinctly into his mind, "Shee."

"What is it?" Muru whispered.

"The Shee. They took Pixel."

Her face collapsed in anguish, but she made no sound.

"I ... I have to find the wizard, ask for help."

Muru shook her head sadly. "I know, kid. It always comes to this. Don't blame me."

❦ ❦ ❦

Upstairs in his room, Peter took a jacket from the wardrobe. No sense going to meet a weather wizard unprepared. Fighting down panic, he forced himself to stand still and think. Then Muru ran in with a backpack and began collecting socks and extra clothes from his bureau.

"Muru, I ... What are you doing?"

Shoving the backpack into his hands, she said, "Look, kid, I know more about this than you do."

"What?"

She pushed him out the door. "Get going!"

He ran down the main stairs and out the front door to the driveway, then stopped and looked around. The Fennys had gathered from all corners of the house and gardens. He realized for the first time just how many were living in Wakkenburg. It was like a small army.

Furse stepped out of the crowd. "Mr. Peter, is this a Code Red?"

Fiak, standing in a regimental row of bespectacled librarians, said, "Jonas taught us Code Red. He liked to read aloud to us. Spy thrillers. Said it broadened our minds."

"Well, it did something," Furse said. "Even *I* remember that if it's a Code Red, we get to make bows and arrows. Jonas drilled us. Said we have to be ready to defend the house."

"Too late for that," Muru said as she came out the front door. "Pixel's gone. Right from under our noses."

"So is it a Code Red, Mr. Peter?" Furse said hopefully.

"Yeah. This is definitely an emergency."

❦ ❦ ❦

Peter knew what he had to do. His mind had settled and he felt strangely calm. First, he'd go to Fenn House, talk to the wizard. Then they'd go to Cwenburgh. Since the Shee were in league with the Moonwitch, that's where they'd take Pixel. Putting his fingers to his lips, he whistled shrilly, then shouted, "Moody!"

Aunt Marj came running out of the house, took one look at the backpack on his shoulders, and said, "No, Peter! Not alone!"

"I'm taking Moody." He whistled again.

"No! You heard what the Bugganes said! You can't be alone in the woods! Where is Edward?"

The Datsun came speeding down the lane with Uncle Edward at the wheel. The crowd of Fennys parted as he pulled up to the front door and rolled down his window. "Peter, get in!"

"Edward! No!" Marj shouted. "That's not what I meant! He's got to stay here!"

"Calm down, Marj. You're hysterical. It's just to Fenn House."

"I am not hysterical! And why in heaven's name are you going to Fenn House?"

"We gotta talk to that dang wizard. Ain't that right, Peter?"

"Surely Pixel is just lost in the woods," Aunt Marj pleaded. "She got off the path and wandered out of earshot!"

Peter shook his head. “No. The Shee took Pixel. Uncle Ed’s right.”

“Get in!” Uncle Ed shouted, revving the engine.

“Don’t worry, kid,” Muru said. “We’ll take care of things around here.”

Then Moody came running across the grass. Peter hopped in the Datsun, Uncle Ed turned the car around, and they sped away with the giant dog running alongside. Peter turned to look back at the crowd of Fennys. The last thing he saw, before the Datsun shot into the woods, was the small figure of Furse waving his cap.

❦ ❦ ❦

“You know what you’re gonna say to this wizard?”

They had just crossed the first bridge, the Datsun at full throttle. Moody loped beside the car, keeping to the grassy verge.

“I have to ask for his help.”

“No good ever came of that fool’s help, I can tell you.”

“I don’t know what else to do.”

His uncle throttled down as they approached the second bridge. “Neither do I.”

❦ ❦ ❦

A mile after crossing the bridge, the trees thinned, revealing wide grasslands, and the marsh spread out under the midmorning sun. Straight ahead, Peter saw a thatched roof. Then the paved road ended and the Datsun rattled down a rutted lane, all the way to the door of Fenn House. It was a broad, one-story building with a long front and a south wing that extended toward the cliff. Wide, overgrown gardens surrounded the house. The windows were shuttered, but a wisp of smoke spiraled from the chimney.

The giant plume of cloud that had hidden the house for days was entirely gone. In fact, there was not a shred of cloud in the sky. Peter had a feeling he was expected.

His uncle shut off the engine and they got out. “Why did you bring a backpack? You plannin’ on spendin’ the night?”

Peter shrugged and slipped the pack onto his shoulders. He went to the door, then knocked and rang the bell. There was a long silence, broken only by the ascending song of a thrush that landed on the roof. Uncle Edward fidgeted, peering into the little window beside the door. Moody, nose to the ground, trotted around the side of the house.

With a growing sense of uneasiness, Peter looked over his shoulder. Someone was watching them. A gust of wind swept up his hair and sent dry leaves eddying about his feet.

Uncle Edward reached past him and rang the bell again, then pounded the door with his fist. "Mac Lir!" There was no response. "I'm goin' around back," he said.

"Wait." From somewhere nearby, Peter heard Moody rumble a warning. Another gust of wind swept over the tall yellow grass, and apprehension buzzed in his brain like a nest of hornets. "Maybe we should go."

"Nothin' doin'. We're here, and I'm gonna have some answers. Are you forgettin' that this is *your* house? Mac Lir is a squatter, as far as I'm concerned. He came here and kicked out the Fennys without so much as a by-your-leave—"

A figure appeared at the end of the lane, coming toward the house. It was Foster.

"What's he doing here?" Peter said.

"I don't know, but after the last time we saw him, I did some checkin'." Uncle Ed kept his voice low. "You don't have a cousin named Foster."

The man waved at them, but they did not return his salute. When he was in hailing distance, he called out, "Hello! What a nice surprise!" and stopped a few yards away, on the other side of the Datsun.

"What brings you here?" Uncle Edward asked.

"I was just in the neighborhood," Foster said lightly.

"Bit out of the way, don't you think? Especially for someone on foot."

"I like walking." Foster smiled, showing all his teeth. "But I wouldn't say no to a ride back to town. Or to Wakkenburg House." Foster's tone was friendly, but as Peter looked at the cold blue eyes fixed on Uncle Edward, he felt a prickle of fear.

Before his uncle could say anything else, Peter cut in: "We're looking for Pixel." Now the blue eyes were fixed on him.

"I know Pixel," Foster said. "I met her in Foyle last week. Lives at the Rilson house, right?"

"She's lost in the woods." Then something stirred in Peter's mind. "Help us find her, Mac Lir."

The man laughed and a cold wind began to blow. With the wind came a thick white fog swirling around the car. Peter saw his uncle reach out and clutch the side of the Datsun, as if it were an anchor in a rising storm. Then quite suddenly, the mist dissolved. Peter blinked in the bright sunlight.

A man in silver-gray robes, with the same blue eyes as Foster, stood by the car. "At last, you have come to seek my aid, Silver One. As you should. Indeed, I am Mac Lir, powerful and ancient as the sea, and I mean to do you good. You should have come sooner! I hope you are not like your cousin Jonas."

At the name Jonas, a cold light came into his eyes, and Peter shuddered inwardly. Uncle Edward, leaning heavily against the Datsun, rested his forehead on the roof.

"No doubt you have heard many things about me, spoken by those who do not understand the ancient gods. We see to the stars! Far beyond the petty and temporal sufferings of the present. I would that you could understand this. You have the great gift of your forefather Nathaniel, who swore allegiance to me and, in doing so, inherited this kingdom and a store of great powers. Are you like Nathaniel the Voyager, son?"

Peter figured he was indeed like Nathaniel, able to smell a skunk when it came around. Also, his knowledge of the ancient gods did not incline him in their favor. Aloud he said, "Help us find Pixel."

Mac Lir threw back his head and laughed. "Now, here is a son in whom true loyalty is found! Do you trust me?"

Peter held his tongue, waiting.

"Ah. You know exactly where Pixel is, don't you?" The wizard smiled coldly. "Come now, didn't the trees tell you? Didn't the forest whisper it into your ear? Or perhaps you dreamed."

This man was very arrogant. Peter felt a slow wrath rising.

"There is another girl that we must find, before the witch does. The Silver One who was stolen."

Glancing at his uncle slumped against the Datsun with his eyes closed, Peter guessed he was under a spell, and this made him even more angry. "Pixel first! You help us get her back from the Shee."

"It's not that easy." Mac Lir's voice became gentle, though his eyes hardened. "I can't expect you to understand my ways. No doubt you've spent your whole life running from the gifts and powers I've given you. You've seen much in a short time and been without a guide. Say you'll help me, and together we'll do great things. We'll rid the island of the Moonwitch and the Shee and all that stands in the way of peace. But first we must find the Silver One who is lost."

"I don't see why you need my help. You just said you're one of the ancient gods. Like Zeus and Apollo, right? It should be easy for you."

"It's not like that, boy. For any endeavor in this world, we great ones need the help of humans. If you will aid me against the witch, you will see mighty things accomplished."

Peter hesitated. A part of him wanted to believe this. It would be a lot easier to let Mac Lir tell him what to do. But he knew the Greek myths. Whenever a god asked for help, the humans usually got the short end of the stick. "What is it you want me to do?"

"Use your power over the trees. If you ask them, they will lead us to the lost Silver Girl. Then let me back into my tower at Wakkenburg." A look of cunning flashed across Lir's face. "I will clear the place of vermin, as I should have done long ago, and you will see great things!"

"Vermin?"

"The Fennodyree, the ugly ones. They will not aid our cause."

Muru's kind, weathered face and Krim's hairy grin floated into Peter's mind. Then he saw wrinkled hands and the face of another Fenny bending over Pixel, who lay pale and still on a stone floor. The image vanished, and he saw the cold blue eyes of Mac Lir watching him.

On a sudden impulse, he jabbed his uncle, who came awake with a jerk and said, "Foster? No one's heard of you. And you're on private property. This house belongs to Peter, and you're trespassin'." Uncle Edward blinked as he came fully awake, but even when confronted by the strange figure of Mac Lir, he never lost his head. "You get the heck out of here before we turn the dog on you."

Mac Lir smiled coldly. "The boy has come to ask for my help. He is wiser than you, old man."

Peter met his uncle's glance and shrugged. "I asked him to help us find Pixel, but he won't. Says we have to find the Silver Girl first. You know. Then let him into Wakkenburg."

"Oh, that's how it is, is it? After seventy years, you still can't find my little sister," Uncle Ed scoffed. "Great, big, powerful wizard like you. Ha! Jonas always said you were a fraud. Anyway, who says I don't know where the Silver Girl is?"

Peter saw the flicker of confusion in Lir's eyes and suddenly understood that Jenny was the only card he'd had to play.

"Just try to fight the witch yourself," Lir sneered. "Without my help, you stand no chance, and you'll certainly never see your Pixel again." As he spoke, the wind began to blow. The grass flattened as the trees at the edge of the woods swayed. Dark clouds came racing from the north.

"Is that so?" Uncle Ed continued. "Well, all I can say is, you're not much of a wizard."

"Enough, old man! Do you know what happened to Jonas? I will do the same to you!"

"You can't scare me with a few rain clouds," Uncle Ed shouted above the rising wind. "I'm not afraid of gettin' wet!"

Mac Lir stretched out his hand and shouted something in a strange tongue. Uncle Edward ducked behind the Datsun, and the blast of power aimed at his head hit the house, shattering the front windows and blowing the door off its hinges. Above the howling wind, Peter heard the sound of hoofbeats.

Smiling in triumph, the wizard turned and raised his staff, hailing the little green-clad men who came riding from the north. No taller than boys, they were mounted on small white horses the size of ponies, and they were fitting arrows to their bows, preparing to attack.

At that moment, Moody came bounding from behind the house, twice his normal size. He rushed at Mac Lir, bowled him over, and ran straight for the riders. The terror and speed of his fury caused many to fall from their rearing mounts. Little men and white horses tumbled this way and that as the wild wind swept up the grass and whistled through the sedge.

The instant Mac Lir's face was turned away, Uncle Ed slipped into the car. He started the engine, Peter jumped into the passenger's seat, and they went roaring up the rutted lane, gaining speed.

They were almost to the road when a sudden blast hit the car. Veins of white light crackled through the air, the rear window shattered, and glass flew everywhere. Peter looked back and saw the wizard standing in the lane, pointing at them, his face cold with fury. "He's going to hit us again!"

Slamming the car into third gear, Uncle Ed pressed the gas pedal to the floor. The riders were mounting their horses, urged on by the wizard.

It was raining hard. Black clouds raced overhead, and lightning cracked the sky. At the end of the lane where the woods began, the poor Datsun stalled and came to a stop. Uncle Edward pumped on the gas as her engine turned over once, twice, then died. Moody's face appeared at Peter's window.

"Go with the dog!" Uncle Edward shouted over the whining wind. "He'll get you home!"

"I'm not leaving you!"

The riders were nearly upon them.

"Get past the bridge before it floods. I'll meet you at the house. Go on! Climb onto the dog!" Reaching over him, Uncle Ed opened the passenger door and pushed Peter out.

Peter got to his feet, sprang onto Moody's back, and wrapped his arms around the great neck, and away they leapt. He thought he heard the Datsun's engine grind and take hold, but he could spare no more thought for anything. Gritting his teeth, he hung on. Moody bounded this way and that, around and over the ever-deepening puddles, faster and faster, dodging between bushes and under trees. There was only rain, furious wind, and the keening voice of the forest.

Suddenly, Moody came to a dead stop and Peter fell off. Scrambling to his feet, he saw trees moving in, their branches tossing wildly. Buzzing erupted, like the sound of a hundred chainsaws. A horse whinnied fiercely and the woods closed in. In the last gap between the trees, Peter saw a huge, shaggy man tugging at his head with both hands. There was a tremendous explosion of light and sound. The ground shook. Peter lost his balance, hit his head against a tree, and blacked out.

23

Watchman

By some miracle, the Datsun's engine came to life just as Moody sprinted away. Gunning the engine, Uncle Ed drove like fury, away from Lir and his little men. The rain was coming down hard now. "Get over the bridge before it floods," he muttered. Then a bright light flashed and a bolt of lightning hit a tree just ahead of him. As if in slow motion, a huge branch tore away from the trunk and fell. Flooring the gas pedal, he swerved. The branch came down and grazed the rear bumper, and he swore under his breath, but he'd made it. Barely.

He tore over the first bridge and around the bend, past the Old Road junction, onto Wakkenburg Road. One more bridge to go. The Datsun hiccupped and the engine rattled. With the pedal to the floor, she was only going sixty. "Come on, honey," he said as the rattle grew louder.

The second bridge came into sight, and he kept her floored. Then he was past the river and flying over the last stretch of road. He downshifted to third and made a hard left turn onto the drive. Half a mile from the front door, the Datsun coughed, sputtered, and died. He sat there, listening to the rain drumming on the roof.

Something tapped his window and he nearly jumped out of his skin. It was the giant mole. Ed rolled the window down as Tom shrank into the figure of the old man.

"Why are you stopped here?" he asked.

"Waitin' for Peter," Uncle Ed replied. "What are you doin' here?"

"We heard of your errand to Fenn House. We arrived in time to see the boy ride away on the Moddey Dhoo."

"Do you know where he is?"

"The trees hid him, but it was close! Didn't you see the Shee?"

"Shee? It was the wizard after us, and his little green guys."

"And a Shee riding a Glashtyn, I tell you!" Abruptly, the old man changed into the giant mole. "It may cross the river! You can't wait here!"

"Okay, okay! Better help me push." Ed put the car in neutral and told the Buggane what to do, and together they pushed the Datsun down the long drive.

As soon as they came within sight of the wide lawns, a host of Fennys came running. The garage crew got the car down the lane and into the courtyard, and the Buggane went back to the woods. Leaving Krim to sort out the failed engine, Ed returned to the West Wing through the pouring rain. He may as well tell Marj right away. Best to get it over with.

ꕥ ꕥ ꕥ

Hours later, the rain stopped, but a heavy bank of clouds hung over the house. Ed stood by the front door, looking out the little side window. Peter and Moody should have come home by now. What was keeping them?

The afternoon passed in a long, slow silence of waiting. As he paced the halls of the house, he saw more than one Fenny pause in his work to gaze solemnly out the window. Marj went about weeping silently, and there wasn't much he could say to comfort her.

As the day faded into a gloomy dusk, he stood at the front windows on the second floor, looking absently at the distant woods. Quite suddenly, a figure appeared at the edge of the forest, his silver robes shimmering in the twilight. Ed froze, watching, as the wizard began to walk down the long drive.

Then, like a huge and hideous flower suddenly sprung from the soil, a giant spider rose out of the lawn and turned into an enormous scorpion with its tail poised to strike. As it scuttled forward, a gigantic white-tusked mole came striding out from under the portico. The terrible creatures advanced across the lawn, and the figure at the edge of the woods melted away into the gloaming.

Ed let out a long breath. Apparently, the wizard hadn't caught Peter. And the Bugganes were on the watch. That was some comfort. He went downstairs to find Marj.

ꕥ ꕥ ꕥ

Sometime after nightfall, Ed went for a walk by Glenny Pond. He knew he'd never sleep. Restlessly, he paced the pathways, back and forth between the low hedgerows, occasionally shining his flashlight into the deeper shadows. He stopped under the big oak tree and looked out across the gardens. Suddenly, a movement caught his eye. A tall figure stood by the Door for Large Creatures. "Probably one of the Bugganes," he muttered, "but maybe I better make sure."

He switched off the light and moved stealthily down the path toward the gate, keeping to the shadowy bushes near the stream. As he paused beside the garden wall, a voice close by whispered, "Steady, Mr. Edward." He looked around and saw Furse fitting an arrow to his bow.

Soundlessly, Furse crept along the deeper shade of the garden wall, and Ed followed. Moving from bush to bush, the two of them drew near the gate. Then Furse lowered his bow, and said, "What are you doing here? You're supposed to stay by the doghouse."

It was only the hawthorn. Ed turned on the flashlight and shone it over the little tree. It tapped on the gate, then flung twigs at them. Furse hesitated. "You want out?"

The hawthorn tapped the gate again, then threw out a snaky root and tugged on the lower beams.

"Better let it out before it tears the door apart," Ed said. He helped Furse open the big gate, then stood aside as the tree sidled past. Once outside, the hawthorn stopped, its branches shifting this way and that, as if it was trying to pick up a signal.

"What's it doing?" Furse said.

"I wish I knew."

Suddenly, the little tree began pelting them with thorny twigs, and one of its roots slapped Ed's leg. "What the—" he began, when he saw a stealthy movement in the shadows beyond the gate.

A figure stepped out of the woods.

"It's Lir!" Ed hissed.

The hawthorn went still. The gray-robed figure took a step nearer.

Furse threw down his bow and tugged at the gate with all his might. Ed grabbed the handle and together they heaved it shut. As he slid the bolt into place, he heard Furse say, "I'll tell Krim! We better double the guard!"

The night wore on. One by one, the lights went out in the great house, but Ed roamed the halls of the West Wing, peering out of every window. Passing though the darkened corridor on the second floor, he saw a light in Pixel's room and heard voices. Pausing by the open door, he listened.

"Both of them gone. In one morning!" Muru said. "The trees will take care of the boy, but what about Pixel? It would have been better for her to go back to Foyle! Now she's worse off than before."

Ed heard a grating sound and guessed that someone in a foul mood was tending the fire with an iron poker.

Then Rumun said, "I believe the girl's been *sent* to Cwenburgh."

The sound of the poker ceased.

"What can you mean?"

"I believe Mara and the others are still alive. Perhaps she was sent to bring them out."

"But she's gone into the dark!"

"She is strong. Her life before she came here was not easy; anyone could see that."

Ed nodded grimly. He was about to turn and walk away, when Rumun said, "Muru, the old ones need us now."

Standing very still, Ed waited for her reply.

"If we give up and disappear, then Mac Lir will come," Rumun continued. "Mr. Edward and Miss Marj will let him in. They'll feel they have no other choice, and you know they will risk anything to get the children back."

Silence.

"Perhaps we can help bring an end to all this. I always thought Forlost would have done so when Jenny disappeared, if only Mac Lir hadn't sent him away."

"You're saying we have to do more than just housework," Muru huffed.

"That's right. Though our work keeps a binding protection over the family, there is more to taking care of a Silver One than cleaning his room and making sure he's brushed his teeth. As you well know."

This was news! Ed waited, wondering what Muru would say.

Then he heard a loud clank. Someone had thrown down the poker.

"Well, *I'm* certainly not going to let that stupid wizard into this house," Muru snapped. "Your crew is in charge of the West Wing. I hope you've secured the front door!"

Rumun chuckled. "The boy was right to choose you as Head Fenny."

"Well, don't blame me!"

❧ ❧ ❧

The next day, Ed checked on the Datsun. It was in the garage, up on blocks. The hearse sat beside it, in the early stages of restoration.

"Your little car will be ready this afternoon, Mr. Edward," Krim said, "but there's nothing we can do about the rear window."

"The auto shop in Foyle will take care of it."

"Oh, that's capital, Mr. Edward. So you're off to Foyle tomorrow?"

He grunted in reply. No doubt Pixel's aunt had returned on last night's ferry. She was probably turning the town upside down, looking for the girl. He'd have to tell her that Pixel was lost in the woods. There was no other explanation that anyone would believe.

24

Prisoner at Cwenburgh

Pixel rose to the surface of the water and felt a burning pain in her chest. Her head throbbed, and she could not feel her fingers or feet. Someone touched her brow lightly. Straining against the pain, she opened her eyes and saw a blurry face. "Muru?"

"Mara! Come quick! Her eyes aren't silver!"

Another blurred face, another voice. "She is not a little bright fish after all. The witch will be angry."

A shiver began in Pixel's gut and spread through her limbs. She began to tremble as the pain increased.

"She's taken the deep cold of the Shee. I don't know if she'll live."

"But the witch's mother and father are coming for her! What will they do if she dies?"

Someone threw a blanket over her, and a voice began to sing. The blanket grew warmer and warmer until the heat finally penetrated the biting cold. Her shivering subsided, and she floated away into a gray world of shadows.

❦ ❦ ❦

When Pixel opened her eyes again, the first thing she saw was a shaft of dusty sunlight shining through a high window. Lying very still, she let her gaze roam over the bare stone walls, the cobwebs hanging from the rafters, the row of dirty windows.

"I know what she is! She's a spy!" someone hissed.

She turned her head and saw two Fennys across the room. One was a young female, the other a very old, wrinkled woman with bent shoulders. Both were dressed in tattered gray clothes. They stared at her in silence.

"Where am I?" Pixel said. It hurt to talk.

"Don't you know?" The younger Fenny looked at her sadly. "This is the cellar of Cwenburgh. You're in the Moonwitch's house."

❦ ❦ ❦

Pixel lay on a straw pallet, looking at the cracks in the ceiling. The young Fenny bent down and laid a hand on her brow. "Her fever's gone, Mara."

The old one peered over her shoulder. "That didn't take long. Sometimes those touched by the Shee fall under the shadow. Shrivel up and die."

Pixel looked at their sad faces. "Shee?"

"It was the Shee who brought you here, riding the Glashtyn, as they do. Thought they'd caught a Silver."

By late afternoon, Pixel felt some strength returning. The Fennys had built a fire on the small hearth, and she got up and sat beside it, warming her hands. The cellar was cold and dank. The stone walls were the ugly gray of a battleship. Against one wall, a wooden staircase stopped at a closed door, the entrance to the part of the house where the witch and her cronies lived. A dark doorway on the other side of the room opened into other regions of the cellar where the Fennys slept. The main room was devoid of furniture, with the exception of a few broken chairs grouped near the fire. It was a dismal place.

The door at the top of the stairs opened, and another Fenny came down, taller and broader than any Pixel had seen at Wakkenburg. "The witch is having another feast tonight," he said to Mara. "I've prepared all the food, and Krinias has set the table."

"Good. Then she won't bother us," the young Fenny said.

"Of course not!" Mara snapped. "She's sent her spy."

"Mara, you heard the witch," the big Fenny said. "The Shee found this girl in the woods. She's no spy."

"Yes, she is!" Mara turned blazing eyes on Pixel. "Spy! Sent to haunt me! You'll never make Mara tell! Never!" Then, quite suddenly, Mara slumped to the floor, muttering.

> Steal a little silver fish, put it in your pocket.
> Steal a little silver fish and keep it in a locket.

Pixel watched as the poor creature staggered to her feet and began to dance around the room with mincing steps, chanting in a singsong voice.

> The locket is a silver lake, the fishy hidden deep
> Until the mighty Queen returns to wake her from her sleep.

The man Fenny put his arms around Mara and tried to pull her to the chair. "Quiet now. You know the witch shouldn't hear that song."

"Oh, Droat!" Mara sobbed. "This child's not a silver fish! I thought she was from Wakkenburg, but she's a spy!"

Turning back to the fire, Pixel frowned. Then she leaned forward and stared. Her friend the Bread Lady looked back at her from the blue flames. "Don't be afraid," the face said. "Fight with all your heart."

It vanished and Pixel blinked at the bright fire. The other two Fennys were bent over Mara. No one else had seen or heard. Getting up from the stool, Pixel grabbed a stick and poked at the grate. When she turned around, the Fennys were looking at her.

Standing up straight and squaring her shoulders, she said, "Mara's right. I *am* a spy."

Their eyes widened.

"I'm a spy from Wakkenburg House. I've come to help you escape."

❦ ❦ ❦

By the strangled light coming through the high windows, Pixel knew it was late evening. There had been little to eat. Droat explained that they made whole feasts for the witch every day, magicked out of crumbs from past suppers, but the Fennys themselves had pledged to eat only real food so they could remain strong. Unfortunately, there wasn't much since the Mooners had gone away, and now that the Shee and the Glashtyn were in charge of raiding Foyle, very little food made it back to Cwenburgh.

Five Fennys were gathered around the hearth, sitting on broken chairs, staring sadly into the fire: Froke, the head housemaid; Krinias and Frimlaf, the only ones left from the garden crew; Droat, the strongest of the lot, and mad little Mara, Head Fenny, the most powerful of the twelve. Except there weren't twelve Fennys anymore. Seven had disappeared long ago.

Earlier in the evening, Froke had taken Pixel aside and explained that Mara was used up. "For a long time, the witch made her do all sorts of what she called 'magic', and Mara had to make it look like the witch herself was casting spells. After a while, Mara sorta lost her mind. Now the witch is using Droat in the same way. She used to hold a knife to one of our throats to get Mara to do her bidding, but Droat just does whatever she says. He doesn't think he'll last long."

"Doesn't the witch have any power of her own?" Pixel asked.

"Nothing useful. Her only skill comes from the dark places."

Krinias reached forward and put a little more wood on the fire. It leapt up, crackling and popping, lighting up their grim faces.

Mara giggled suddenly. "I took Spy's secret."

"Mara," Droat demanded, "what did you take?"

Smiling with glee, Mara pulled a squashy packet from under her shawl and held it up.

"That belongs to the girl, Mara. Give it back," Droat said in a flat voice. When she wouldn't, he snatched the packet from her hand and returned it to Pixel. Mara turned her face away.

Pixel opened the bag: three donuts. Suddenly, she was in the West Wing kitchen with the smell of coffee and fried ham all around, and the kitchen Fenny, whose name she had forgotten, was pressing the packet into her hand. Her eyes filled with tears, but she swallowed hard and said, "Mara, you're Head Fenny, right?"

"Broken now. No use to anyone. Let Droat be Head."

"These donuts are a present from the Head Fenny of Wakkenburg. They haven't forgotten you."

She got up, pressed the packet into Mara's hands, and moved closer to the fire. What good were three donuts? What she needed was a Buggane. If only she'd had that little hedgehog in her pocket.

From somewhere overhead came a burst of raucous laughter. The witch and her crew were certainly having a good time. Shivering, Pixel shoved her fists into the pockets of her pants, and her right hand came up against a tiny, hard object. She pulled it out. The pearl button she'd picked up from the floor of Peter's room. "Mara," she said, turning quickly, "I have something else for you. From the Silver One at Wakkenburg. I came with him across the sea."

"Oh!" Mara handed the packet of donuts to Droat and stood up with her hands folded over her heart.

"It's a button from the Silver One who was lost."

Mara's face clouded over.

"It's okay. She's been found. She's alright. This button is a ... a sign of ... of help."

"Steal a little silver fish, put it in your pocket. No," Mara whispered. Her face crumpled and she began to moan. "No, no, no. I will not do this thing. Don't make me. Wait! Don't drink her blood! I'll do it! I'll do it!" She collapsed on the floor, crying, "Poor little child. Poor little Jenny."

Pixel caught her breath. "What did you say? Poor little who?"

Froke, who was watching Pixel's face, replied in a quiet voice, "She said, 'Poor little Jenny'."

"Leave Mara alone, miss," Droat said. "She gets like this sometimes. She'll come around in a bit."

Pixel persisted. "Mara, do you know something about Jenny? She was the Silver One who disappeared a long time ago."

Mara went very still. Overhead came the sound of more laughter and a loud voice bellowing something unintelligible.

Suddenly, Froke began to chant,

> Steal a little silver fish, put it in your pocket.
> Steal a little silver fish and keep it in a locket.
> The locket is a silver lake, the fishy hidden deep—

"Stop it, Froke," Droat cut in. "You'll make things worse."

"You've seen this button before," Pixel said. "Was it the witch who took Jenny?"

Mara sat up. "It wasn't the Moonwitch," she croaked. "Mara knows. She did what she did to save the child's life! She's done what she's done to keep us all alive. But what for? Slaves, always slaves. 'Do what you're told, slave.' That's what Lila said."

"Lila?" With sudden clarity, Pixel recalled the picture frame in the North Tower. The Bugganes said that someone evil had come out of it. "Are you talking about Lila the Night Monster?"

Mara nodded. "So beautiful. So cruel. She made me. Said if I didn't, she'd drink the child's blood. All of it. Every drop. Said she'd eat Froke and Droat and my pretty ones."

"What happened to Jenny?"

"Hidden. In the lake," Mara whispered. "I laid her down so gently, right at the bottom, on a soft bed of flag leaves. I used everything in me to do it, everything I had, to keep her safe."

Pixel opened her hand and held out the button. The little carved pearl shone in the firelight. "What's the rest of that song, Mara? That part about the mighty Queen?"

Mara shook her head, unable to speak. Froke sang it for her:

> The locket is a silver lake, the fishy hidden deep
> Until the mighty Queen returns to wake her from her sleep.

Gently, Pixel took Mara's hand and placed the button on her palm. "I don't know why, but Jenny isn't at the bottom of the lake anymore. She passed through Floden and dropped this button. Peter's uncle found it last week."

Mara stared at the button for a long time. Then she kissed it and held it against her heart. Reaching up to stroke Pixel's pale cheek, she whispered, "Spy, I think maybe you was sent to us. Tell us about Wakkenburg."

They drew their chairs closer together. Droat divided the donuts, and Pixel told them all she could remember. As they talked far into the night, there in the dark cellar of Cwenburgh, hope began to grow, like a small budding tree sprung from the seed of a tiny button.

❦ ❦ ❦

When Pixel woke the next morning, she tested all her limbs and decided she felt a lot better, though there was still a dull pain in her chest. She got up, folded the thin blanket, and put on her sneakers.

"Good morning, Spy," Mara said, beckoning Pixel to the hearth. "The others have eaten and gone upstairs to work, but I've saved some breakfast for you." Dipping a ladle into a pot, she filled a chipped bowl.

"Fenny porridge! It's my favorite." Pixel looked at the generous helping. "But you've given me so much."

"Everyone had enough this morning. After you went to sleep last night, Droat remembered a bag of grain stashed away in the pantry, hidden from bugs and rot. We're *all* beginning to remember. Everything is different now that you're here. Already we are stronger." As if to prove her point, Mara pulled a silver spoon out of the air and gave it to Pixel with a flourish.

While Pixel ate, Mara sat down and took up her mending. "Cwenburgh wasn't always like this, you know. Mara remembers when the house was beautiful and full of light. There were flowering vines all around the windows and shady paths that led to the sea. We kept house for the family of the Silver One. Before that, the Small One lived here. And the Queen used to come and stay sometimes."

Pixel paused with the spoon midway to her mouth. "A queen?"

"Cwenburgh means 'Queen's House'. The giants built it in her honor long before the wizard Mac Lir and the first Silver One came over the sea. I was a Merry Wanderer then ..." Her voice trailed away, and her eyes looked inward to some distant memory.

"What happened?"

"Nothing was the same after Mac Lir came. He brought trouble. First, a pirate captain in a black ship followed the wizard here, nursing some old grudge. To fight the pirate, Lir brought a mighty consort to the island, Lila, the ancient Night Monster. Together, the wizard and Lila maintained a terrible peace. Then one day he left on a voyage and was gone too long. We all had hopes that Lila would go in search of him, but instead, she took up with the pirate captain, who lived on the other side of the island. They had a child: the Moonwitch. After she was born, Lila went away and was gone a long time. Mara hoped she would never return, but she did. In the days of the Silver One called Jonas, Lila took this house by force and gave it to her daughter. We became the witch's slaves."

"What happened to the pirate captain?"

"The witch's papa lives in Foyle. He is now far past the age when humans die and has become a manserpent. The blood of the daughters of his house keeps him alive until the witch can capture a Silver One. When she does, her papa will drink the Silver One's blood and become one of the gods who live forever."

The pirate captain lived in Foyle? Pixel felt a sudden chill. "What ... what's his name?"

"Captain Rilson. That's what I heard."

Rilson. Could it be? All those tubes of blood. The room of urns. Her skin prickled as Uncle Mac's words popped into her mind: *"Just tell me where he is! Then they'll stop sucking your blood! His life for yours!"*

And she could almost hear the footsteps outside her bedroom: *clump, scrape, clump, scrape* ...

Suddenly, the door at the top of the stairs banged open, hitting the wall, and Pixel nearly jumped out of her skin. A woman came down the stairs, tall, dark-haired, brandishing a long riding whip. On the brow of her sharp-nosed face, she wore a circlet of silver with a single black gem. "Ah! Mara!" she sneered. "I see you've kept the Silver One alive! How thoughtful."

Pixel looked up as the woman approached and saw her expression shift from cool satisfaction to bewilderment, then to rage.

"What is *this*?" the woman shrieked. "You said this child had silver eyes! What have you done, Mara?" She raised her whip, but instead of striking, she howled up the stairs. "Come here this instant! All of you!"

Pixel heard the sound of running overhead. The four Fennys came first, their faces anxious; they gathered around Mara, who stood by the hearth. Then a number of handsome young men thundered down, snorting and blowing like a herd of horses: the Glashtyn.

"What is it, my lady?" the young men called out. "Fire? Flood?"

Behind them, five Shee in heavy boots descended slowly. More like shadows, they were hard to make out even in daylight. Pixel began to shiver.

"Look at this!" The witch grabbed Pixel's arm and yanked her off the chair. "Look at her brown eyes! Who is this ... this *girl*?"

Then, to Pixel's astonishment, Uncle Mac came reeling down the staircase, tripped on the last step, and collapsed in a heap. Heaving himself up, he took one look at Pixel and said, "I know this vixen! She's one o' them blood girlsh. What're you doin' here?" He pointed an accusing finger. "Yer shupposed to be in Foyle, havin' yer little treatmensh."

"This girl is one of Papa Ahab's?" the witch hissed.

"Thas right. She's a Rilson." Mac sank to the floor and started rocking back and forth. "Oh, I don't feel at all well. I'm a sick man."

"What will you do now, witch?" one of the Shee said. "Your mother and father expect to find a Silver One here when they arrive."

"I know! I know!" the witch snapped. "Let me think!"

At the sound of the Shee's hollow voice, ice crept into Pixel's fingers and toes. Her knees gave way, and the witch, with a vicious hiss, yanked her up.

"Where did you find this thing?" At the word "thing", Pixel felt the butt end of the whip on her cheek.

"A mile from Wakkenburg," the Shee said. "A long way from your papa's house in Foyle."

"This must be the girl who ran away from your father, the one we sought in the town some days ago," a horsy man said.

From somewhere in the upper regions of the house, a door slammed. Heavy footsteps crossed the floor overhead, and the sixth Shee entered the cellar, followed by another Glashtyn.

"I bring news!" the Shee said, as soon as he stepped through the door. "I saw the Silver One! The boy from Wakkenburg!"

"Where? Where?" the Glashtyn cried.

"In the northeast woods, near Fenn House. The trees have hidden him. For now."

Pixel bit her lip to keep from speaking. Peter must have gone looking for her. Dread entered her heart and darkness closed over her mind.

"You must seek him at once! My mother and father will arrive soon. You must find the Silver One before they come!"

"Fear not, witch," one of the Shee said. "Even if your father comes before we bring the Silver, this girl will serve. She is one of his own." He laughed.

"And perhaps it is best if you come hunting with us, witch," said another Shee. "This girl is small and weak. She cannot last long. Is it not likely to be your blood next if we cannot find the Silver?"

"Curse you," the witch snarled. "I know that! My snake of a father! Yet there is one thing that puzzles me." Her tone became sweetly menacing. "Why did you bring this bait to me, saying it was a Silver? Was it a trick? To bring my mother here?"

"I swear her eyes were silver when we found her in the woods," a Shee replied. "They shone like twin beacons in the fog."

The witch paused. "Fog," she said, and her eyes narrowed. "Only Mac Lir can bring down unseasonable fog. But why? It is a strange chance he took."

"Perhaps this girl knows something about the Silver One. We found her a mile from Wakkenburg House, as I said."

"Do you?" the witch demanded, shaking Pixel by the arm, prodding her cheek with the whip. "Do you know the Silver One?"

Pixel was shivering now, her breath coming in short gasps. With an oath of disgust, the witch cast her to the floor.

"Mara! Droat! You other vermin. Prepare for my mother and father's arrival!" Then she marched out of the cellar with the Shee and the Glashtyn on her heels. One of the horsemen lifted Uncle Mac by the back of his coat and dragged him up the steps. The door shut and there was silence.

Quickly, Droat added more wood to the fire, and Pixel found herself sitting before the blaze, wrapped in a warm blanket. With the exit of the Shee, the darkness was already passing from her mind, and she began to feel a little better.

Krinias tiptoed upstairs. The other Fennys drew near the hearth, listening to the tramp of horses and the shouting of harsh voices as the witch and her entourage took their leave. When all was quiet, the door to the stairs opened again and Krinias came down.

"They're gone," he said.

"All?" Mara whispered.

"Yes. Even the Witch's Man. The house is empty but for us."

"They're going to catch Peter!" Pixel moaned.

"The trees will guard him, but Spy had better think of how to save her own life," Mara said. "You should not be here when the witch's father comes!"

Mara was right. As her strength returned, Pixel's habitual grit reasserted itself, and she threw off the blanket and stood up. "Come on. Let's go."

"You mean escape?" Droat said. "No, Spy! We can't! We're bound to this house."

"No. That's not right." She stopped, trying to remember the story the Bugganes had told at that crazy breakfast, about how the Fennys had come to be. "You were humans and Mooners once. Then Mac Lir changed you into ... into what you are now. He wanted to let you die in the woods, but a lady in the mountains saved you."

"A lady in the mountains?" Krinias frowned.

"Yes," Mara whispered. "The Queen."

"Then," Pixel continued, "because Lir's curse had actually made you really strong, she asked you Fennys to protect the Silver Ones, and you said you would. You bound yourselves to *people*, not houses."

"Yes!" Mara exclaimed. "Spy is right. Mara remembers what she once was, and Mara remembers the Queen."

Pixel looked hard at Mara. "Wait. Are you saying the lady in the mountains is the Queen of . . . of Cwenburgh?"

"Yes. Mara knows."

Krinias cut in. "I heard all you said last night, Spy, but I thought we were just gonna wait here till the folks from Wakkenburg got rid of the witch."

"That's what I thought," Droat said. "Last night you gave us hope, but we Fennys know our rightful place. We take care of the house."

"But if you're with a Silver One or his family, you'll be alright! I'm Peter's friend, so I think that counts."

"Ah." Krinias nodded, the light dawning at last. "Because you're a mortal."

"The witch is mortal," Droat said.

"Only half. And she's not a Silver or the friend of one," Mara said. "Spy here is a friend of the boy."

"Then we don't have to do a thing the witch says. We can leave," Krinias said.

"Oh! Let's go!" Froke broke in.

"No, we shouldn't. She'll hunt us down and we'll die in the woods," Droat said.

"Not if we plan it right," Krinias said. "We'll need a map and . . ."

"I've always wanted to leave!" Froke was hopping up and down as Frimlaf stared at Pixel, his eyes bright.

". . . plenty of food," Krinias continued, as if they were all listening to him, "and I wonder, what did you do with that old compass, Frimlaf?"

"No!" Droat cried. "Not so fast! We can't just leave."

"Going! We're going! We'll leave the witch behind!" Froke sang.

"Stop it, Froke! Krinias, you're going too fast!" Droat shouted. "Now, all of you listen to me—"

Suddenly, there was a flash of light, and a thunderclap that nearly popped their eardrums. Froke shrieked and Pixel clapped her hands over her ears.

"All of you, listen to *me*!" Mara's eyes flashed. "Remember, Droat, I am the Head Fenny of Cwenburgh."

Droat paled. "Of course, Mara, but—"

"You think Mara is mad. Yes, she has given you good reason." Her shoulders sagged. Then she fumbled in her pocket and brought out the pearl button. Holding it up to the light, she looked at it. "We are not vermin. We are not the witch's slaves."

"Yes, Mara," Droat said, "but I don't fancy being hunted by the Shee."

"Better than sitting in their company, as we have done far too long. Put fear away, Droat. We need you. You are strongest."

Droat said nothing, and Pixel saw the indecision on his face.

"Come, Droat," Mara continued. "Together we will outwit the Shee. You and I, once free from the witch, will become ourselves again. We shall see the woodland creatures and ask their help. They were always our friends."

Droat shook his head, then laughed. He looked up at the ceiling, his eyes surveying the thick cobwebs and the dust of many years. Pixel watched him, wondering which way he would go. He looked a little like her Uncle Vernon, the only uncle to stay out of prison because he was clever and careful. At last, he said, "You're right, Mara. We should leave now. No telling when the witch's mother and father will arrive."

Frimlaf's eyes widened. Froke burst out in a high-pitched squeal, and Krinias smiled broadly.

"Gather all the food you can and meet here," Mara said. "And Krinias, find your map!"

"Hurrah!" Froke shouted, pelting up the stairs, Frimlaf and Krinias at her heels. She left the door wide open, and Pixel could hear her singing at the top of her lungs:

Going! We're going! We'll leave the witch behind!
We have a hundred names for her and none of them are kind!
Without us she will starve to death, but who on earth will mind?
We'll leave a moldy crust of bread and rotten melon rinds!

Going! We're going! We'll leave the Shee behind!
We have a hundred names for them and not a one is kind!
Without us they will live like pigs and likely lose their minds!
But we don't care! We're leaving and will never hear them whine!

25

Escape

"South," Pixel said, taking a knapsack from Froke. "The witch will expect us to head for Wakkenburg, so we'll go in the other direction. To Foyle."

"But the Shee will find us there. When the witch sends them for food," Droat said.

"We won't be there long. I have friends who will give us a ride to Wakkenburg."

She hoped her plan was a good one. The Fennys were looking at her with grim expressions, except for Froke, who was grinning, bouncing on her toes. Krinias held a map and Frimlaf clutched an ancient compass, relics of Jonas, who'd left them behind after a visit to Cwenburgh in its better days. All the Fennys carried bulging satchels of food and cooking gear, except for Mara. She had nothing but a walking stick and a small leather purse slung over one shoulder.

"Right then." Krinias consulted his map. "We take the gate out of the old rose garden. That should set us going south."

"No," Mara said, "we leave from here." She pointed at a small door to the left of the chimney. "The secret way."

"Secret way?" Droat's eyes widened. "That's the door to the wine cellar."

"Yes, Droat. Mara knows. Past the wine cellar to the secret way."

"But will it take us south?" Krinias asked.

"Not according to this compass," Frimlaf replied.

Mara smiled and tapped her head. "Old Mara has a compass right here." Then, beckoning with her finger, she went through the door. Droat and Krinias hesitated, but Pixel slipped the knapsack on and forged ahead. If Mara was having a turn of madness, they should get it over with quickly. It was already noon, and Pixel wanted to be far away by nightfall. On the other hand, Mara was Head Fenny, and Pixel had seen what she could do in her lucid moments. If she said there was a secret way, well ... best to see what she had in mind.

One dank room led to another, and Mara guided them through a maze of doorways to a long dark passage. After several turns, Pixel lost all sense of direction. When they came to a stone wall lined with shelves and ancient moldering bottles, Mara pointed to a stack of old lumber. "Move this."

Krinias and Frimlaf shifted the lumber, and there, set deep in the foundation of the house, was a low wooden door. Mara pulled a ring of ancient keys from her pocket, inserted one, and pulled the door open.

"A tunnel!" Froke exclaimed, and Pixel noticed a curious smell wafting from the interior: earth and moldy leaves with the tang of something else.

"Where does this go?" Krinias asked.

"South," Mara said. "Into the ancient Underways."

"How long have you known of this door?" Droat asked quietly.

"Head Fenny secret. Form a line, everyone. You come after me, Spy. And Droat, you bring up the rear."

"But, Mara, the witch will find this door and come after us. You know the Shee will track us through the cellar to this place."

"We will be far away by then. Watch your head, Droat. You too, Spy," Mara said. "The ceiling is low." She handed the key to Droat. "Lock the door behind you with the key and with your voice. You remember how. After that, there's nothing more we can do. Now, everyone, single file and place your hand on the one in front of you."

Pixel placed her left hand on Mara's shoulder, then turned and looked back. Froke and Frimlaf entered the tunnel, their eyes wide—whether with fear or amazement, it was hard to say. When they were all inside, Droat closed the door and fumbled with the lock, muttering a few quiet words. The darkness was complete, and Mara led them forward.

For a long time, they shuffled along in silence, linked hand to shoulder, trying not to tread on one another's heels. Occasionally Pixel stumbled over a stone, but for the most part, the path was surprisingly smooth. Now and then, Mara called back, "Spy and Droat, mind your heads!" and Pixel would feel her hair brush the roof of the tunnel. With her free hand, she often reached out to run her fingers along the wall. It was made of dirt with wooden beams spaced at regular intervals. A little later, it became rough stone. Once, her fingers touched something wet and cold that slithered away. Then they came to a place where she could sense openings on either side. Mara stopped.

"Do you know where we are?" Pixel whispered.

> One way goes to the heart of the world,
> One to the tip of the peak.
> One goes on to the great river's source,
> And one to the brink of the sea.

Mara chanted to herself, then sighed. "It is the Song of the Way. The Queen taught it to my father, Chief of the Merry Wanderers, and he taught it to me. Mara remembers now." After saying this, Mara seemed to make up her mind and they pressed on, straight ahead.

Twice during that long afternoon, they stopped to rest, crouching in the dark with their backs against the tunnel wall. Droat passed around slabs of bread spread with something sweet. This was followed by a canteen of water. But they never rested for long. On and on they walked into the darkness and silence. The only sound was the padding of their feet and the tapping of Mara's walking stick.

When it seemed as if they'd been walking for days and days in the unchanging dark, Pixel heard Mara say, "*Straight on, straight on, then walk the curve that comes before the breaking*. Ah yes!" She quickened her pace. "Here is the curve, and soon you will hear the breaking."

Running her free hand along the stone wall, Pixel felt the curve of the tunnel, first left, then right. She had a sudden sensation of going downhill and, after several steps, was sure of it. The path made a sharp left, then another long curve to the right. After that, it leveled out and went straight again. The air in the passage was cooler, and her feet splashed through a shallow puddle.

Mara stopped, Pixel stopped, and Frimlaf bumped into her heels.

"Do you hear it?" Mara said.

"Hear what?" Krinias sounded cross and tired.

"Ooh!" Froke's voice rose querulously out of the dark. "My feet are wet!"

"Mara, where are we?" Droat called from the back of the line.

"Listen!" Mara commanded.

In the silence, they heard a mute echo, a great booming that sounded far away yet close at hand.

"What is it?" Frimlaf said in a frightened voice.

"The breaking of waves on stone! It is high tide in the outer world. We are under the cliffs, south of Cwenburgh."

Salt and seaweed. That was the smell in the air. Pixel had been trying to put a name to it since they entered the door.

"A little farther and we can rest," Mara said, and then Pixel heard her say softly to herself, "A little farther and there is another door ... I hope."

After a while, Pixel was sure she saw light, though maybe her eyes were playing tricks after the long darkness. No, it was light, coming from a source high up. She heard Mara muttering over the low boom of the sea, *"Around the bend into the dark, the short way you'll be taking."* Mara repeated these lines over and over until they came up against a dripping wall below a high hole in the cliff.

"Is that the way out?" Krinias said. "How do we get up there?"

"Around the bend into the dark," Mara muttered, and she led the way through a small cleft in the left-hand wall. Pixel had to turn sideways to get through, and for a brief moment, she lost her hold on Mara as they entered another dark space.

"Wait!" She groped her way forward till she grasped Mara's arm. "Wait till everyone's here." Pixel stood still and felt Krinias take hold of her shoulder. Then after a brief sound of scuffling feet, Droat said. "We're all here."

The darkness, though complete, was temporary. After stumbling along a rough path of loose stones, Mara led them around a tight bend and through another small fissure and stopped at the bottom of a rocky ascent, lit by an opening higher up. *"Then up the stairs to the Cave of Dreams,"* she said.

"Stairs? If you say so." Droat brushed away a layer of loose stone with his foot, revealing the first step. "I guess you're right, Mara, though it looks to me like the ceiling's crumbled."

"I don't think it was the ceiling that came down," Krinias replied, looking around. "Nor the walls." He ran his hand over the smooth stone. "Looks like these rocks came from farther up."

"I wish I had a stiff broom," Droat said. "Come on, Krinias. Let's clear this rubble away."

Mara plumped down on a boulder and closed her eyes, still chanting to herself in a low voice.

> Up the stairs to the Cave of Dreams,
> Where the Small One he is making
> A little fire and a store of songs,
> For the far-off children's waking.

Pixel watched as Droat and Krinias climbed slowly, pushing aside the rocky debris that littered the stairs, making piles of loose stones on either side of each wide step. Though they worked carefully, trying to keep the rocks from falling, many small stones clattered down to the bottom. From the opening at the top of the stairs came the boom of the surf and the insistent cry of many gulls.

At last, the two Fennys reached the top of the stairs and disappeared through a doorway. Then Droat reappeared a minute later. "There's a dry cave here! Paintings all over the walls. And eggs!"

"Well, don't eat them all yourself!" Frimlaf cried as he and Froke leapt up the stairs like mountain goats.

Pixel listened to their excited voices but didn't follow right away. She picked up a jagged stone that had fallen near her foot, turning it over in her hand. It was gray and rough, but on one side someone had painted a white star. She put it in her pocket, then picked up another rock painted blue. Turning to Mara, she said, "The stairs are clear." When Mara didn't respond, Pixel touched her on the shoulder. "Are you okay?"

The old Fenny opened her eyes and smiled. "Yes. Mara feels lighter now that she is away from the Moonwitch's house."

"How far do you think we've come?"

"Many miles. Many days. Many years. Mara feels younger. Let's go up and eat Droat's eggs."

They found the others in a round, dry cave filled with light and color. Paintings of deer and whales, fish and squirrels, and many other kinds of animals crowded the walls. Tall humans with beautiful faces walked among the creatures. Yet all the figures moved and danced around one central image, the most beautiful of all: a lovely, dark-haired lady with stars in her hair. She was not the Moonwitch.

Droat had already built a fire in a small ring of stones. He was cracking eggs into a large pan, where they sizzled and popped. When he saw Mara and Pixel, he grinned. "Gull eggs. Right outside the window."

The window was a wide fissure in the cave wall through which Pixel could see white gulls soaring over the sea. The outer ledge was covered in bird droppings. Sticking her head out cautiously, she saw large nests, above and below and on either side. A gull swooped a little too near, and she pulled her head back into the cave. Droat must have reached right out to raid the nests, and the gulls were still angry. Pixel turned from the window in time to see Krinias and Frimlaf come out of a narrow passage on the other side of the cave.

"Funny this cave has two exits," she heard Frimlaf say.

"I bet this tunnel used to be the only way in and out," Krinias said. "I don't think that window to the gulls' eggs was always there. Looks to me like it was blasted open. That would explain all them stones on the stairs."

Wondering what Krinias meant by "the way in and out", Pixel stepped into the narrow passage. It wasn't dark, and it went straight on for a bit, ending right under a hole. She climbed out and found herself standing on top of the cliff.

To the west, the sea glimmered in the last rays of the sun. Behind her, a short distance away, the forest stood dark and deep in the failing light. She didn't like the idea of entering the woods and perhaps losing their way. She'd had a good look at Krinias' old map and noticed right away that there were no marked trails. How in the world could she guide them to Foyle without a path?

Back in the cave, everyone sat around the fire and shared a meal of eggs and pancakes. Droat, grinning from ear to ear, said, "This is a fine thing, Spy, cooking for ourselves with real eggs."

"We haven't eaten them for ever so long," Frimlaf added. "Droat had a few old eggshells and the crusts and rinds of other things to make the Moonwitch's meals. Imagine! All that time he fed her and the Glashtyn on illusion. Serves her right."

"What I'm worried about are the Shee coming after us," Krinias said. "They're bound to find the door to the tunnel. After that, it won't be hard to track us."

"I sent a message to the hurly burlys before we left, asking them to go into the house at twilight," Mara said. "Then I left the kitchen door open."

Krinias slapped his knee and laughed out loud, and Froke giggled.

"I don't understand," Pixel said.

Frimlaf sniggered. "The hurly burlys, or skunks, as I have heard them called, will go into Cwenburgh and spray the cellar."

"The whole house!" Mara said.

"And their stink will cover our tracks!" Frimlaf finished.

Droat smiled. "That is good, Mara. I hope you have bought us some time."

After the meal, they all lay down around the fire, tired after their escape through the Underways. Krinias took the first watch, and Pixel, wrapped in her sweater, watched the light in the window fade as the sun slipped below the sea.

❦ ❦ ❦

A huge black bird flew down from the red sky, its talons coming toward her. In blind panic, she burst from the water, scattering white feathers, and woke up. It was dark outside. By the dying light of the fire, Pixel saw Droat sitting motionless, staring into the empty air. Froke and Frimlaf were asleep, but Krinias got to his feet and crept out of the cave by the upper entrance. Mara looked at Pixel and put a finger to her lips.

A hush fell over the night. Even the sea went still. The roosting gulls stirred and beat the air with their wings. Then darkness, like a heavy weight, crept over Pixel's heart. The shadow of fear deepened, and she sat up, struggling to breathe. There was something coming. Something that would find her and drag her down, down, into the cold dark. It was very near now. Shutting her eyes, she waited for the end to find her.

All at once, a breath of wind stirred the air. The passing dread diminished, and the iron vise of fear loosened its hold over her heart. She opened her eyes and saw the fire blaze up, high and bright, lighting up the face of the woman on the wall.

Froke sat up, then Frimlaf, rubbing his eyes.

"I had the worst dream," Frimlaf said.

"Did you?" Froke said. "I did too! All about the world going black and the face of the moon bleeding."

Krinias crept back into the cave and sat down close to the fire, his face haggard, as if he had endured a month without sleep.

"What did you see?" Droat said quietly.

"Nothing," Krinias whispered, "but I felt them."

"Who?" Pixel said.

"The Moonwitch's mother and father, on their way to Cwenburgh."

Pixel blinked. "You mean Lila and ... the pirate captain?"

"The manserpent, yes. They have come from Foyle," Mara said.

Suddenly, Pixel thought of the map that Peter had sent to her, with its tiny pictures of the island towns. Every building and house in Foyle had been painted so carefully, but not the Rilson house. Instead, someone had drawn a snake. She shivered.

"We left Cwenburgh in the nick of time," Mara said. "Now let us sleep and gather our strength for tomorrow. No need to set a watch. We are held like a bird in kind hands."

26

Grist for the Rumor Mill

On Monday morning, two days after Peter and Pixel disappeared, Ed finally worked up the nerve to go to Foyle and confront Kate Rilson. He had an appointment at the auto shop anyway. Swallowing the last of the coffee, he went out without saying goodbye to anyone. As the Datsun chugged along between the wide lawns, he noticed dark rain clouds to the north, but a clear sky to the south, which was a good thing since he had no rear window.

The drive along Highway 20 was uneventful, and he arrived in Foyle a little after eight o'clock. After dropping the Datsun at the auto shop, he went to the post office and picked up the mail. A letter from Peter's dad. Heavyhearted, he turned his steps to Thorny's, hoping for a cup of coffee to bolster his sagging nerves before he talked to Pixel's aunt. As he approached the store, he looked across the street and saw the sheriff and Cousin Mary standing on Kate Rilson's front porch.

"Ed," Mary called out.

Reluctantly, he crossed the street and climbed the steps.

"Mornin', Ed."

"Mornin', Sheriff."

"I'm worried about Kate Rilson," Mary said. "She came home Saturday night, and I saw her go into the house, but I haven't seen her since."

The sheriff knocked and waited, frowning at the door. "She called me Saturday night," he said. "Told me she'd just got back from the ferry and there'd been a burglary at the house. Asked if anyone reported it. Then she says, 'Oh, never mind' and hangs up. I shoulda come over and checked things out." He knocked again. "Why don't Cook open?"

"She cleared out last Tuesday," Ed replied. "Before Kate got back."

"You mean after the jailbreak and the raid at Thorny's last week? Well, I don't blame her, but it might explain Kate's call. Them thugs who tore up the store musta come back and broke in here the next day, after Cook left. Then Kate comes home on Saturday. But why don't *she* open up?" The sheriff lifted the letter flap and looked inside. "There's a mess of mail on the floor and somebody's suitcase. I'll try around back." He clumped down the stairs.

"Maybe the burglars were still in the house when she came home," Ed said quietly.

"That's what I'm thinking," Mary whispered.

When the sheriff returned, he reported that the back door and all the windows were locked securely and the blinds drawn. As he mounted the steps, he looked up. "Hey! All the windows in that third-floor room are busted out!"

"Pixel's room," Mary said. "Why didn't I notice before?"

Then the sheriff put a shoulder to the front door and forced it open. "Cripes!" he gasped, covering his nose. "I hope she ain't dead!"

It was Ed who found her upstairs, sprawled on the bare floor of a second-story room, wearing only her nightgown and clutching a stained towel around her shoulders. She was still alive.

❦ ❦ ❦

Ed looked around the small room, guessing it was the place where the blood treatments were done. On the table, several syringes were laid out alongside a number of empty glass tubes. He bent down to look more closely at the blood smeared across the surface and noticed little dribbles on the floor. Stepping back to let the paramedics pass with the stretcher, he looked into Kate Rilson's pale face. Then his eyes rested briefly on the needle marks up both arms.

Baffled by the secret mausoleum they found in the Rilson house, the Foyle police called the superintendent, who rushed over from Sweetwater. They asked Ed one or two questions, but not about Pixel. It seemed everyone had forgotten her. Eventually, the sheriff let him go, and he trudged wearily over to Thorny's, where George and Mary waited in the kitchen. Mary gave him a bowl of soup, and he sat down at the table.

"Seems to me poor Kate wasn't alone in that house," George said thoughtfully.

Ed kept eating and didn't reply. Mary poured herself a cup of tea and sat down beside him.

George continued. "One day, when Pixel was here, lookin' pretty pale, she told us that it was mighty hard for her to sleep in that house. Said someone walked around at night and it weren't Kate nor Cook."

"I think that's why she and Cook didn't want to stay when Kate went off to Lang," Mary added.

Grunting, Ed put down his spoon. "After them paramedics took Kate Rilson out of the house, I had a quick look around. There's a whole other part of that house you can't see from the street. Smelled like snakes. I only got a peek before the police came in, but I guess you're right. There's been someone else livin' there all this time."

Outside, a sudden gust of wind shook the trees, and leaves blew across the window. It was only July, but the weather seemed to be changing already.

"There's more," George said. "After you showed us that urn you found, Annette and her boyfriend started nosin' around Harold Rilson's funeral home in Sweetwater."

"You met her boyfriend?"

"Ben Rilson. Nice guy. Works for Harold as a driver. Anyway, turns out the cremation records for those girls are kept pretty secret. I don't know how those two got on to them, but they did. I guess Harold Rilson's funeral parlor is gonna be in hot water once the police start investigatin' the remains in those urns. And then Ben's sister who works in hospital records—well, Annette got her to look for the girls' files, but you know there's not a single lab record? The whole affair was unofficial from beginning to end. What's it all about? That's what I want to know."

Mary sighed. "You're not the only one, George. People are talking. That raid on our store and on the jail last Monday has made folks mighty nervous, not to mention what happened last night."

Ed paused with his spoon in midair. "What happened last night?"

George shook his head. "I don't know, but it was weird, Ed. About nine o'clock in the evening, the electricity blinked off all over town. We opened the store to accommodate the folks who rushed in to buy candles. At half past ten, just as the sun sank, a rack of clouds swept in and the temperature dropped. And then—I don't know how else to say it, but it was like a wave of fear came in with those clouds."

"That's right," Mary said, taking up the tale. "We locked all the doors and lit every candle we could find. All over town, the dogs began to bark. I heard later that small children woke up crying for no reason."

"Not only that," George continued, "all the crows started cawin' like mad things. Chickens and roosters were squawkin'. Our cat started hissin' and crawled under the sofa. Didn't come out till this mornin'. And today I heard that eighty-four-year-old Nora Delton started shoutin' in her sleep, 'Flee from the wrath to come!' Then she started wailin' and had to be sedated. That's what her son said. Anyway, about eleven o'clock the lights came back on and it was over."

"*What* was over?" Ed asked.

Mary shivered. "I don't know, but it felt like somebody opened the gates of hell and let something bad out. This morning, Rachel Maycap told me that when her dog started barking at about ten thirty, she looked out and saw two people come out of the Rilson house and walk down the middle of Main Street. A woman with long blond hair, wearing a red dress, and a tall man with a limp. Rachel says she's never seen them in town before. Total strangers. She thinks they were ghosts."

"You can see why people are spooked. There's been strange rumors and bad feelin' in the air all week," George said. "And now this news about Kate Rilson is gonna be all over town. Then there's you, Ed, comin' down from the Big House and showin' up at the scene of the crime this mornin'. Well, it's only gonna add grist to the rumor mill."

The kitchen clock ticked, almost in time with the dripping faucet. From outside came the distant sound of a car horn. Ed sat staring absently at the table, holding an internal debate with himself. Should he tell George and Mary about Peter and Pixel? How could he explain the unexplainable? They'd want him to call the police, but what could the poor sheriff do? For a moment, he tried to imagine the sheriff meeting Tom Spider, or any of the Bugganes.

Finally, Mary sighed. "I guess we *are* living at the edge of Wakken Wood. I only half believe the old tales, like everyone else in town, but what if there's more to it all?"

"I better get goin'," Ed said. "No doubt the Datsun's done." He packed up a few supplies Marj had ordered, said goodbye, and walked to the auto shop. On his way out of town, he drove slowly past the

Rilson house. Yellow tape barricaded the porch, and several people were talking to the police on the front lawn.

A moving van passed him, going in the other direction, followed by a car full of people. "On the way to Orbsen Bay," Ed muttered. "Catchin' the afternoon ferry to Lang, no doubt. I expect they won't be the last this week." He sighed. "I dunno what's gonna happen to this town."

27

U-Turn

Pixel woke at dawn with a travel plan in her head. According to Krinias' map, Cwenburgh sat at the north end of Barrane Bay, and Foyle at the south end. The Cave of Dreams was somewhere in between. This meant that if they walked far enough south on the beach, they'd eventually get to town. Following the coastline might take longer, but at least there was no danger of getting lost in the woods.

After breakfast, they gathered their belongings and left the cave through the upper passage. As they looked around the bluff for a way to get down to the shore, Droat spied an old stone stairway, overgrown with roots, parts of it washed away by storm and tide. When they got to the bottom, Pixel looked up and saw the window to the Cave of Dreams high above their heads.

"Look! There's a painting! All around the window."

"Someone with long dark hair," Krinias said. "But the face is blasted away. Musta been struck by lightning or something."

"Not lightning," Mara said. She paused, looking at the opening in the rock. "Mara remembers now. On a night, long ago, when the moon was high, Lir's white ship sailed into the bay, carrying Lila, though we did not know it at the time. Mara saw bolts of fire come from the ship. The wizard, or maybe Lila, was firing at something—we didn't know what."

"Yes," Droat said softly. "I remember that too. I wonder whose face was painted here?"

Pixel took the stone from her pocket, the one she'd found among the rubble on the stairs. The white star painted on one side was a larger version of the stars surrounding the lady in the picture on the cave wall. Laying the stone on a little shelf in the face of the cliff, she picked up her knapsack and followed the Fennys across the sand.

The day was bright and hot with little wind. All morning they walked beneath the high rock bluff, traveling at a snail's pace. At least, that's what it seemed like to Pixel, but she tried to be patient. Freed from the slavery of Cwenburgh, the Fennys were like small children on holiday, stopping to exclaim over every shell or bird they passed. Whenever they rested—which was too often, in her opinion—they built a fire and cooked something. Pixel realized that, if not for her sense of urgency, they would be content to sit in the sand and stare at the sea all day.

Sometime in the late morning, the coastline began to change. The high cliffs began to slope downward and became low hills, gradually flattening until they disappeared altogether. By midafternoon, they were walking over sandy beaches that merged with tracts of tall grass bordered by a leafy woodland.

Because the day was so hot, Pixel suggested they walk under the trees, keeping the sea in view so they would not lose their direction. This turned out to be a good idea. It was cooler, and they found a narrow track running parallel with the shore.

"I wonder where this path leads?" Krinias said.

"And who made it?" Frimlaf added.

Berry bushes grew near the eaves of the forest, and they stopped to pick. Before long, everyone's hands and tongues were purple, and Froke's basket was filled to the brim. Continuing on, they followed the path all afternoon. Sometimes it wound between trees, and sometimes it led them back to the shore. That evening, in a grassy hollow close to the beach, they came upon a ring of stones.

"A firepit. I wonder who made it?" Froke said.

Poking around, Pixel found a stack of wood and kindling under the exposed roots of an arbutus tree. "Who left this?"

"Courteous campers," Droat remarked. Then he built a fire and cooked clams. Froke baked a berry cobbler.

As the sun began its slow descent, the air cooled and Pixel sat by the fire, gazing south along the beach. She was pretty sure they were getting close to Foyle. In the distance, the grassy shore ended abruptly at a high buttress of rock. They would have to find a way to climb up that bluff if they wanted to keep to the coastline. Then, as the sun slipped below the horizon, a great light shone from the cliff top. It flashed out, then disappeared, then flashed again. She stood up and Droat said, "That looks like fire. South a ways."

"A forest fire," Pixel said. "I wonder how it started." As they watched, flames towered above the trees and lit up the darkening sky.

Droat and Frimlaf built up the campfire, and they all sat close, watching smoke spread over the stars. The night was warm, there was no wind, and the land all around was strangely still, even the sea. Growing drowsy, Pixel lay down on the grass. The last thing she saw before drifting off to sleep was Droat, standing in the light of the campfire, his gaze turned south.

Sometime after midnight, she woke with a start to the sound of frightful howling. As she sat up, Froke clutched her arm. "What is it, Spy?"

The wailing cry rang out over the woods, and in reply, the sea began to foam and fret, as if stirred by an unseen hand. Water slapped at the shore in ever-increasing waves, and the dark night became darker as a rack of clouds swept in from the west.

"What's happening?" Krinias gasped.

"We must find shelter!" Mara shouted, and everyone began moving at once. Frimlaf kicked sand over the fire, and Droat threw all the cooking gear into his satchel. The wind, which had begun gently, now tore at their clothes and blew stray sticks into the air.

"Under the trees!" Mara said.

"We won't be safe there," Krinias cried, "not with the wind like this."

"Better than being swept out to sea!" Mara shouted as the water rushed in over their feet.

They ran for the woods as the sky let loose a torrent of rain.

"Keep together!" Mara called.

Pixel grabbed Froke's hand and kept her eyes on the back of Frimlaf's head, barely discernible in the driving rain.

They ran along the edge of the woodland, the trees groaning, limbs cracking. Then Mara led them deeper into the forest as trees crashed down beside the path and branches whipped their arms and legs. When they finally stopped, Pixel was dizzy and bleeding and soaked to the skin. "Where are we?" she panted.

"Right under that cliff we saw from the beach," Droat said. "The one you said was blocking our way to Foyle."

"Mara, we're hardly out of the rain," Krinias said.

"It's the best we can do for the rest of the night," Mara replied. "Everyone sit close."

"What was that howling?" Pixel asked, crouching down with her back to the cliff. Froke sat down beside her.

"The Dooiney-oie," Droat replied. "He was ever the herald of storms. I have not heard his call for many moons. Something has waked him."

"Well, he was right on cue. I expect the rain put out the big fire we saw away south," Krinias said.

There was nothing to do but huddle against the rock as the wind roared and the forest groaned. Toward dawn, the storm relented. The rain stopped but the trees dripped, and a thin mist rose from the forest floor. Exhausted, they fell asleep, one by one, in the quiet of the new day.

Hours later, the piping song of a wren woke Pixel. She got up stiffly, stomped her feet to shake out the numbness, then woke the others.

It took most of the day to find a path to the top of the cliff. Its surface was too smooth to climb, so they forged their way inland, through the dense woods, always keeping to the rocky wall so they would not lose their way. They got hung up in thorn bushes and bitten by mosquitoes; there wasn't enough food, and no one wanted to stop and cook. In the end, Frimlaf found a narrow track that began between two boulders and wound upward by a series of steep switchbacks. When they got to the top, it was an easy hike along the edge of the bluff. Then Pixel found a trailhead marked "Foyle". Eagerly, by the light of the lowering sun, she led the Fennys along this path, right to the edge of town.

All the buildings on Main Street were empty shells. The Rilson house was a black field of cinders. When they came to the burned-out ruins of Thorny's, Pixel sat down and stared. Then she burst into tears.

❦ ❦ ❦

"It's too late to go on," Mara said.

"Go on?" Pixel looked around helplessly. A part of her mind was fixed on the idea that George and Mary must still be around somewhere. The ashen ruins of Foyle did not seem real.

"To Wakkenburg, of course," Mara snapped. "We'll have to find a place to camp for tonight, but not in all this mess."

Pixel looked past the charred skeleton of Thorny's store and saw a few blackened timbers at the edge of the woods, all that remained of George's garage. Then a memory stirred in her mind. "I know a place," she said slowly.

"Is it far?" Mara asked.

"No."

"Good. Let's get away from here."

Pixel led the Fennys to the meadow where Peter had taken her on the day he'd visited Foyle. The place looked as it had then, though the smell of smoke hung in the air. She helped Droat and Frimlaf gather wood to build a small fire while Mara took out cooking pans. Krinias and Froke found long sticks, fashioned fishing rods, and went to the river to try their luck.

Pixel did not feel like fishing. Instead, she took a stick and began slashing at the grass. Moving aimlessly across the meadow, she came to a sodden tussock and thumped it savagely. The stick broke in half and she tossed it away. She stomped on the clump of grass and out popped a soggy wad of cloth. It was a cap. Peter's cap. Suddenly, she was back in that golden afternoon when he'd introduced her to Moody. They were rolling in the grass, splashing each other in the river's shallows ... Was it a week ago, or a hundred years? For the second time that day—the second time in her life—she sat down and cried.

❦ ❦ ❦

"The way I see it," Krinias said, unfolding his map, "if we go north, following the river, we're bound to come to Wakkenburg House. Look here at this line that says 'Glenny Stream'. Once we come to that, we turn right and follow it till we reach the house. How could we get lost?"

"But look how the river makes this big loop west," Droat said, pointing to the middle of the island. "It will take us out of our way and too close to Cwenburgh for my liking."

The sun dipped below the trees, and damselflies darted overhead in the waning light. Pixel was only half listening as she turned Peter's cap around and around near the fire, trying to make it dry faster.

"I say we go back to the cave," Froke put in. "The one with the pretty pictures on the walls. We'd be safe there and we'd always have eggs."

"We'll not move forward by going back," Mara snapped.

Everyone looked up, startled. She was sitting there with her eyes closed. Pixel thought she'd been asleep the whole time.

"Well, I guess if we go by the river, we can at least eat fish," Froke said, putting down her plate. She had caught three good-sized trout, wrestling them in with surprising finesse, while Krinias hooked two tiny bass, a tangled wrack of weed, and a mangled boot. He scowled at her.

"What does Spy say?" Mara asked, her eyes still closed.

Pixel shrugged. "We can follow the river until we get to the road, then follow that."

"What road?" Krinias slapped the map with impatience. "There are no roads south of Wakkenburg."

"Your map's out of date." Pixel brushed a patch of dry mud from the cap and decided to give it a good scrub in the river. She stood up.

"Krinias," Mara said, "that map was made long ago when Foyle was just a fishing village. The people came and went by boat."

"Is there a road?" Droat said to Pixel.

"It goes straight to Wakkenburg. That's how we were supposed to get there today."

"Today!" Krinias snorted. "According to this map, it's at least three days of walking."

"Not if you go by car."

"Car? You mean a cart and horse?" Droat asked.

"No, a—" Suddenly, Pixel realized that not one of them understood the word "car". There were no roads to Cwenburgh. She sat down again. "A car. It goes really fast. Without a horse. It—" At the sight of their uncomprehending faces, she stopped. "Look, I think Krinias is right. We should follow the river. When we come to the bridge, you'll see the road. It goes from Foyle to Wakkenburg."

Mara opened her eyes. "Spy is right. We will follow the river. When we get to the bridge, then we'll see." She shut her eyes again, and that was the end of the discussion.

The next morning, Pixel put on Peter's cap and went back into Foyle. She stood in the middle of the street, the rubble of the Rilson house on one side, the ruin of Thorny's on the other. It was eerily still. She knew the Fennys were ready to go, but she stood there for a while as the sun shone down, wishing for a car to pass, not quite believing that a whole town could disappear overnight, its inhabitants scattered like birds. Where were George and Mary? What had happened to Aunt Kate? Were they all dead?

At last, Pixel went back to the meadow where the Fennys stood waiting. Without a word, she led them to the riverbank and took a path heading north.

They came to the bridge and, after a short debate, left the river and continued on the west side of the road. Mara was suspicious of the long expanse of tarmac winding through the woods like a black snake. To please her, Pixel tried forging a path parallel with the highway until Froke got entangled in a thicket of brambles. By the time they got her out, her clothes were torn and everyone's fingers were bleeding. The undergrowth of the forest was just too thick. In the end, Pixel had to lead the Fennys along the road, whether Mara liked it or not.

On the wall at Thorny's, Pixel had seen a modern map of the island roads and knew they were walking along Highway 20. It cut north for forty miles, deep into the heart of Wakken Wood, ending at the northern junction. From there, it branched east, becoming Highway 21, which led to Sweetwater. Because she'd traveled with Uncle Ed, Pixel knew that the third road branching from the junction—though unnamed on the map—was Wakkenburg Road and would lead to the house.

In truth, Uncle Ed and Annette were the only islanders who used Highway 20. Folks preferred to drive Highway 21, which ran straight north from Orbsen Bay to Sweetwater. The main reason for avoiding Highway 20 was the belief that the bandits who raided Foyle were bivouacked in the woods nearby. And, though people didn't like to talk about it, they remembered the old tales well enough: strange creatures, eerie hauntings, and the appearance, at times, of a giant black dog on this lonely stretch of road. This was why, during two days of walking, Pixel and the Fennys didn't see a single car.

At night, they slept under broad bushes beside the road, or in some shallow dell, not daring to light a fire or make much noise. In this region of deep woods, there was an oppressive atmosphere that weighed on their spirits.

By the end of the second day out from Foyle, Pixel was sure they were nearing the northern junction. At least she hoped they were. The forest along the highway seemed endless and looked much the same from day to day. Dusk came early in the woods, and on that evening, Droat was just casting about for a place to spend the night when, out of the deep twilight under the trees, they heard the tramp of horses.

"Shee!" Pixel looked around wildly. As she pulled Froke and Mara down behind a clump of ferns, she had no doubt they'd reached the end of their journey.

Then Droat beckoned urgently from the shade of a tall fir tree: "Over here! A hollow stump!"

Hurrying toward the stump, with the other Fennys at her heels, Pixel darted into the opening and ran smack into a creature with white tusks.

"Who goes there?" he cried, bowling her over. "This is my resting place. None may enter!"

The Fennys backed away, but Pixel knew that voice. "Tom Mole! It's me!" She got to her feet. "Breakfast at Wakkenburg House. Remember? I'm Peter's friend."

Lowering his massive head, the mole put his sharp nose close to hers. She tried not to flinch as the white tusks rested on her shoulders.

"You're the girl from the serpent's house in Foyle. What are you doing out in the woods with—" He peered at Droat, who brandished a heavy stick. "Are these Fennodyree?"

"From Cwenburgh," Pixel said. "We escaped."

Tom Mole lifted his head. "Glashtyn are coming. Wait inside."

They crawled into the stump and crouched down. Pixel looked out through a gap and saw the Buggane a few feet away, like a dark shadow in the gloaming.

The horses were very close now. Suddenly, the giant mole vanished like a vapor, and all around, the trees rustled and tossed their branches as six black stallions galloped into view. They slowed their pace, stopped, and, with loud grunts and whickering, changed into men.

"Is it far?" one of them said. "Gaw! I am hungry as I've never been before!"

"Too true!" said another. "Now that the witch's slaves have gone, there is little to eat at Cwenburgh that one can stomach."

“That is not the kind of hunger I mean,” said the first Glashtyn with a leer.

“It wasn’t fair! Us having to stay behind yesterday while the others raided the men’s town. But *now* it is *our* turn!”

“Yes! By all accounts, this new town holds far more to satisfy the appetite. Foyle was small, and the folk still practiced the old ways of warding us off.”

“Listen, brothers. We cross the first road here. Then it is only a short way through the woods before we cross the second road and come to the town. I heard there is a place where much flesh can be found all through the night.”

“Then why have we stopped?”

“I feel the old stirring.”

The Glashtyn stood still, looking around.

“I feel it too, brother. There is a girl about somewhere.”

“Hush now. She is near.”

Pixel braced herself as the six Glashtyn began to move toward the stump. Droat raised his club. Then she heard a loud sniffle. A little girl in a pink checkered dress materialized in the twilight.

“No!” she whined, her eyes glowing like twin beacons. “No! I don’t care! I won’t!”

The Glashtyn lunged toward the child, who vanished and reappeared a little farther away. The men dashed after her, crying, “It is the Silver Child!” With grunts and whinnies, five changed into black stallions.

“Come now, little one!” the sixth said. “Wouldn’t you like to ride a beautiful horse?”

Leading the Glashtyn across the road, the little girl continued to whine, “I won’t, I tell you! I don’t care!” As she moved farther and farther from the hollow stump, her cry grew fainter until silence returned to the woods.

Night deepened. Stars shone out. Pixel sat down and leaned her head against the wall of the stump. Unbidden, the faces of George, Annette, and Mary came to her mind. What had happened to them? Then she thought of the Bread Lady and squeezed her eyes shut, refusing to cry. Gradually, she relaxed, letting her mind go slack.

She woke with a start. Droat and Mara stood at the gap, looking out. Trees rustled and whispered. Then she saw a black shadow looming just outside the stump. It grew larger and larger until it towered over their hiding place.

"Girl! Girl!" said a great voice.

Froke and Krinias cried out, and Mara shushed them.

"It's just the Buggane," Pixel said. She crawled out of the stump and the Fennys followed.

When the giant mole saw her, he shrank down to the form of the old man and peered at her closely. "You are bound for Wakkenburg, yes?"

She nodded.

"It is good you never arrived there."

"What? Why?"

"Wakkenburg is besieged. Covered in snow and ice. Mac Lir wants in, but they won't let him. And I hear the Head Fenny has contrived a double of the Silver One, who comes out on the roof to wave at the wizard! This is very shrewd. Mac Lir thinks the boy is in the house, and so he does not search the woods!" The Buggane giggled, then frowned. "We must hurry. The Glashtyn will stay in Sweetwater for a little while but will return before morning. You must be far from here or they'll sniff you out! Tom will take you to a safe place."

He turned and began walking away. The others picked up their bags and followed.

It was far past midnight and the woods were dark. The Buggane went at such a pace that Pixel and the Fennys had to trot, winding through the dense forest, never slowing, never stopping to rest. Pixel wondered how long the Fennys could keep up the pace, but after a while, all her thoughts were for keeping her own legs in motion. As the night wore on, her breath came short and she lagged behind.

"Not far now!" the Buggane called back. "Don't stop!"

Through a haze of weariness, Pixel kept going until at last, stumbling out of the forest, she stopped beside the Fennys on the bank of a river. The waning moon hung just above the trees, casting silver light on the water. She heard a tremendous grunt as Tom, now a giant mole, came out of the woods carrying a huge log. Tossing it over the river, he ran across and stood in the dark on the opposite side. "Hurry," he called.

Pixel went first, stepping carefully, trying to keep her balance in the dim moonlight. When everyone had reached the other side, Tom

Mole turned and trotted away. Exhausted, Pixel took no more than a few steps before her legs gave out. Droat made her climb on his back, and they kept going.

They had covered many miles in a short time when, looking past Droat's ear, Pixel saw the dark shape of two hills rising from the forest floor. Suddenly, Tom stopped. Krinias and Frimlaf crashed into his back, and the mole looked around fiercely. Then, beckoning urgently, he led them around the base of the first hill, a rocky prominence, like a cast-off child of the northern mountains. As they came around its southern side, they saw the second hill, a high mound set in a grassy clearing surrounded by tall cedars. The Buggane took them to a low door in the side of this hill and knocked.

"Who lives here?" Froke whispered.

He scowled fiercely. "I do!" He knocked again. To Pixel's surprise, the door opened, and there was the hairy man.

"Tom Mole! What took you so long?" he said.

"Look, Tom Troll," the mole replied. "I found the Silver One's friend. The one he lost. And these Fennys from Cwenburgh. Take them inside! Then we must be off." Pushing Pixel and the Fennys through the door, he shut it with a snap.

The hairy man, surprised by their sudden arrival, said, "Cwenburgh?" Then he saw Pixel. "You? We heard you were captured by the Moonwitch!"

She slid off Droat's back and stood up shakily. "I got away. Me and these Fennys."

"Only five? Where are the others?"

"There weren't any others. We went to Foyle to find my friends. I thought they would take us to Wakkenburg, but . . . Foyle is gone."

"What?"

"It burned down." Her voice cracked and she stopped.

"This is news!" the hairy man said. "But I cannot linger. I must be out with Tom. I will give you food; then you must sleep."

Tom Mole's one-room house was dark and warm, a wide dugout in the side of the hill. A small fire burned in a pit in the center of the room. There was little furniture, so Pixel and the Fennys sat down on the dirt floor. The hairy man gave them bread and a warm, sweet drink from an iron pot. Telling them to stay inside, he went out into the night.

Dead tired, Pixel lay down, right where she was. Thinking about Wakkenburg House buried under snow and ice, she fell asleep with a picture in her mind of Aunt Marj in a toque, wearing layers of mismatched sweaters.

❦ ❦ ❦

The Toms returned before dawn.

"Up! Up!" the mole cried. "We must be off at once!"

Still partly asleep, Droat leapt to his feet. "Glashtyn? Shee?"

"Shh!" Tom Mole hissed. "Don't call them! Get up, old ones! Get up, girl! We must go!"

Too weary to ask why, Pixel got to her feet and followed the Bugganes out the door, into the cold twilight.

The hairy man led them away from the twin hills and into the woods. Behind him, the Fennys trooped in single file with Pixel walking in the middle and Tom Mole bringing up the rear. It was too early for birdsong, and the woods were quiet. No one spoke, and Tom Troll took them by paths of deep moss so that their feet made little sound. Though she'd had only a few hours of sleep, gradually, as they marched, Pixel found herself coming fully awake. She felt some strength in her limbs again, though she was pretty hungry.

Slowly, the woods on her right brightened, and she thought of the sun, rising in the east. "And if that's east, then I guess we're headed north," she said under her breath. "I wonder where we're going."

As the sky lightened, birds began to call, darting across the path. The new day revealed a forest of fir and cedar, with here and there a broad maple. Pixel began to hum to keep her mind from hunger. Then, because no one shushed her, she began to sing.

> Tom, Tom, the piper's son
> Stole a pig and away did run—
> All the tune that he could play
> Was "Over the Hills and Far Away".

"That sounds like a Buggane song," Froke said.

"Do Bugganes have songs?"

"Aye, little missy," the mole said. "Teach us yours."

Accustomed to keeping her little tunes to herself, Pixel sang out tremulously. Then, feeling braver, she tried out a rhyme of her own:

Tom the Spider, Tom the Troll,
Old Tom Bear, and big Tom Mole
Joined five Fennys and a Spy
Around a campfire, eating pie.

"Oh! I like that!" And the mole fell into step beside her.

"Why do you all have the name Tom?" she asked, when they had stopped singing.

"Name?"

"You call each other Tom. Tom Spider, Tom Bear. You call the hairy man Tom Troll."

"Tom is what we are." And that was all the answer she ever got.

As the sun rose higher and the chill of early morning wore off, little brown wrens flitted through the undergrowth, flicking their upturned tails at the travelers. Then, up ahead, Pixel saw a clearing that turned out to be Old Road. She'd traveled it before, though not on foot.

The Bugganes turned left and led them west along this road. The hairy man explained that he hoped to strike a certain path that would take them north again, though Pixel had the impression he wasn't quite sure where this path might be.

"Where are we going?" she asked, walking now between the Bugganes.

"Some things should not be spoken of in the open," the hairy man replied.

She kicked a stray stone on the road. "Is it true the wizard has covered Wakkenburg House in snow? I thought he was, well, you know, kind of good. I mean, compared to the Moonwitch."

"Good?"

"Yeah. He does white magic and the Moonwitch does black magic, right?"

"They are powers of the same kind, wielded without regard for what will happen next," the hairy man said.

"But what about you and the Fennys? You do magic!"

"We Bugganes are the powers of earth and sky. Old beyond human reckoning. The Fennys are a powerful mix of ancient and new, as you have heard. I do not believe they work by what *you* call magic."

Tom Mole sighed heavily. "But what has become of the other Cwenburgh Fennys, Tom?"

"It is useless to wonder. Yet it is clear that these Fennys and the ones at Wakkenburg must be protected. If Mac Lir succeeds in destroying the witch's power once and for all, he will banish the Fennys. I have no doubt of that."

"I don't understand." Pixel kicked another rock. "If bad things happen no matter who wins, what's the point?"

"There are other powers at work in this land," the hairy man said quietly.

"As far as I can see, there are only two sides: Lir and the Moonwitch. One is bad and the other is not exactly good. But I guess it's like that in Lang too."

"Lang?"

"The place I come from. The mainland."

"Ah yes. The human world. We know little of it."

They went on in silence. The morning sun warmed their backs, and it was a perfect day for a long walk, but this was no holiday. Finally, Pixel dropped back to walk with the Fennys. Froke, still humming the Tom song, grinned at her, but she was too hungry to grin back. Then, a little way ahead, the mole stopped abruptly and pointed to the forest on their right. "Look, Tom! There it is!"

Pixel saw a shuddering movement at the edge of the road. There, between two swaying fir trees, lay the beginning of a path. Out of the corner of her eye, she saw a flash of white at the roadside, but whatever it was disappeared in the undergrowth.

"This way," the hairy man said.

Pixel hesitated. "I thought the trees only move for a Silver-eyed person."

"There is something here I do not understand," the hairy man replied. "Last night, we met a boy who told us that this path would open along Old Road."

"Who was he?"

"We do not know him, yet he seemed to know all about us," Tom Mole said in a low voice. "It was he who told us to take you and the Fennys to a secret place."

"Is it far?" Pixel asked.

The hairy man hesitated. "We will know that when we arrive."

Leaving Old Road, they returned to the deep shade of the woods.

Krinias, consulting his map, said, "I wonder which way we're headed."

"North," Pixel said.

"How do you know?"

"Because . . . well, we were walking west and then we made a right turn, so that's north."

"It must be something to have a compass in your head," Krinias said. "I wish *I* did."

The Bugganes seemed to be in a hurry, and the company marched all day, with only short rests. Sometimes a shaft of sunlight broke through the dark green canopy, and Pixel thought of Sweetwater, where people shopped and drove around in cars. It was as if she'd crossed some boundary into another world. The deeper into the woods they went, the more remote the outer world seemed. Her family and friends in Lang didn't know where she was. No one did.

As evening approached and the light began to dim, she noticed the hairy man glancing over his shoulder anxiously. It put her on edge. Sometimes she looked back too, expecting to see dark figures, but there were only trees and more trees. Then, with a start, she noticed something she hadn't before: The path behind them was disappearing. The giant cedars opened a way forward, then closed ranks as they passed.

Twilight deepened, and still the hairy man urged them forward. No one mentioned stopping for supper. In the fading light, Pixel tripped over a root and fell flat on her face. Jumping to her feet, she found that the company had stopped. Then she heard the tramp of hooves.

Before she could think *Shee*, she was scooped up by giant claws and tucked under the mole's arm, and they were running, the mole leaping like a mountain goat over roots and rocks and fallen logs. She managed to grab her cap before it fell off, then turned her head and saw the hairy man bringing up the rear. The Fennys ran in front of him, and she caught a glimpse of their panicked faces.

Quite suddenly, they stopped. Far off, a crow called. The mole put her down. "They're gone," he said in a low voice.

"For now," the hairy man replied.

"How far is it?"

"I don't know."

"But we're in your bounds, Tom!"

"In all the long years, I have never seen this part of the forest."

"Then perhaps we are close."

They went on, silent and watchful as the woods grew dark. Pixel stumbled again, and the mole picked her up and slung her across his back. She clutched at his fur and he growled a little, so she put her arms around his neck and hung on. Peering over his shoulder, she saw his great curved tusks and found the sight of them comforting.

All at once, the piercing shriek of the Dooiney-oie rang out, and Pixel heard the sound of galloping horses.

"Run!" the hairy man cried.

The trees broke out in a furious storm of flailing branches. Sticks and fir cones, stones and flurries of pine needles swirled in the air. Pixel closed her eyes and held on, burying her face in the mole's fur. Then she thought of Mara. Turning to look back, she saw the hairy man swell to an enormous size. Everyone else kept running, but he stopped and tugged at his head. She heard a fierce whinny and a cold cry, and then a loud explosion rocked the ground. A bright light flashed through the woods, and they were running, running, on and on into the darkness.

Without warning, the mole vanished. Pixel's hands clutched thin air, and she felt herself falling, landing with a thump on soft ground. She heard Droat cry out in alarm as the Fennys thumped down beside her.

Staggering to her feet, Pixel saw light a little way ahead.

"I suppose this is the place," Droat said.

"The path doesn't go any farther," Krinias replied.

Stumbling toward the light, they entered a crack in a rock and passed through a short tunnel, into a large cavern of smooth granite. On one wall, someone had painted a large mural of green fields and high mountains. In the center of the cavern, a bright fire burned in a ring of stones, and food was set out. Two logs, arranged around the fire, offered seating.

"Look!" Frimlaf exclaimed. "Someone's made supper. I call that thoughtful."

"Well now," Mara said. "This is nice."

Froke led a little girl by the hand. The child clutched a frayed teddy bear in one arm and looked around with tearful eyes. "Oh, Tom!" she wailed. "Where are you?"

"Tom Troll is leading the Shee and Glashtyn on a wild goose chase, I expect," Krinias said. He put down his bag and set to work, slicing and buttering bread. There were bowls and spoons piled on a flat rock. The Fennys began dishing up stew from the big cooking pot.

"Oh, Tom!" the little girl sobbed, throwing her teddy bear into the fire. Then Frimlaf gave her a bowl of stew, and she began to shovel in great mouthfuls.

Pixel watched the little girl, pretty sure she was Tom Mole. Sure enough, after three bowls of stew, the girl, with a small *pop!*, turned into the old man. "Ah!" he said, wiping his mouth on his sleeve. "That is good cooking." He grinned at Pixel and winked.

"Time for bed, Spy," Mara said.

Pixel did not resist. She set aside her bowl, then lay down in an open space beside the fire and allowed Mara to tuck her into a blanket. The last thing she heard before she fell asleep was the old man singing,

> Tom the Troll blew up his head,
> But that don't mean he's turned up dead.
> He's joined the Fennys, and a Spy,
> Around a campfire, eating pie!

❦ ❦ ❦

Pixel opened her eyes. The cooking fire had gone out, and everything lay in shadow except for a small pool of light on the other side of the cave. A boy stood with his back to her, bent over something. She could see his arm working vigorously, stirring a pot. A white creature with long ears sat beside him. Then he lifted a brush and began to paint the wall with swift strokes.

She was dreaming. Her eyes drooped shut and the scene dissolved.

28

Peter's Choice

Peter opened his eyes and stared at the huge silver hornet hovering above his face. It hummed gently, then rose into the air and zoomed off.

He sat up and there was Moody, watching him, thumping his tail. The ground was wet, his clothes were wet, and he could see nothing but tree trunks. Where was he? In Glenny Woods at the back of the house, right? With luck, he could get to the East Tower door, run through the house, and make it to his room before Muru saw him. She would not understand why he had fallen asleep in the rain. Why had he? Rubbing the back of his aching head, he felt a lump. When he brought his hand away, he saw blood on his fingers.

Then he remembered. He wasn't anywhere near Wakkenburg! He'd gone to Fenn House with Uncle Ed to ask for Mac Lir's help. Things had gone very badly, and he'd climbed on Moody's back to get away. He must have hit his head on a tree branch in their race through the woods.

"Can you get us home?" he asked Moody.

Moody sat upright, sneezed loudly, and wagged his tail. Then he got up, fished a backpack from between two trees, and dropped it at Peter's feet.

Muru had packed this. He rummaged around, hoping to find his cap. Moody stuck his nose in and brought out a pair of dry socks. Peter took the socks, and Moody immediately pulled out a dry shirt, dropped it in Peter's lap, and sat waiting.

Hearing a loud rustle, Peter turned and saw a trail between two trees where there had been no gap before. A line from Jonas' journal surfaced in his mind: *"When they open a path for you, take it. Never hesitate. The trees are your allies, and they will lead you to the other creatures of Wakken Wood whom you can trust."*

Then he heard voices murmuring, like the wind among leaves, rising in an oncoming gale: "Hurry, hurry!" the forest urged. "No time to lose!" Peter jumped to his feet. The trees would lead him to Pixel.

Minutes later, wearing dry clothes, he started down the path. When he looked back, the trees were almost at his heels, and a knobbly pine branch prodded his shoulder.

Hours later, he sat beside a little stream, bathing his feet. He would have stopped to rest before, but whenever he'd tried, branches poked him from behind. "I wish you weren't so pushy," he said aloud.

It was getting on toward evening. He opened his pack and pulled out a paper packet. Moody sat down expectantly. It was one of Rumun's sandwiches, loaded with everything. He gave half to Moody and then ate his portion slowly, wiggling his toes in the cool water. Trees didn't understand blisters, though in a moment of frustration he'd tried to explain.

What he could see of the sky overhead was clear and blue. The trees had led him far away from the wizard's stormy tantrum. "Do you think Uncle Ed made it back to the house alright?"

Moody thumped his tail in an encouraging way. Then the nearest tree branch struck Peter on the back of the head. He sighed and put on his socks and shoes, grumbling about the prickliness of pine needles. This made him think of the prickly hawthorn at home, and he wondered what damage it might inflict on the garden in his absence. Just for fun, he tried sending it a mental message, telling it to be good and do whatever Ulf said. Then he got up and marched on.

By nightfall, his strength was sapped. Stumbling into the darkness of a little glade, he bumped into a very broad tree trunk and heard a small sigh. Gray trunks edged closer until he was hemmed in by the forest. Evidently, the trees didn't expect him to walk all night, which was good because he wasn't used to long treks in the wilderness. Letting the pack slip from his shoulders, he sat down in the dark and felt Moody beside him. Not even bothering to take off his shoes, he leaned against the dog's flank and fell asleep in the deep silence of the woods.

Hours later, he felt a low vibration under his right ear and opened his eyes. Moody was growling, a low, ominous rumble. Peter sat up. Branches hung close over his head, and he could feel a pressure in the air, like that of an imminent storm. Then, into the silence came the tramp of hooves.

A horse whinnied.

"Silence, Glashtyn," an evil voice hissed.

The horse stopped, just on the other side of the trees, and the cold sharpened in the heavy darkness. Then, with sudden force, driving rain burst down through the tree limbs. Over the drumming downpour, Peter heard the rider curse. The horse whinnied fiercely. Then came the sound of galloping hooves.

The edge of cold diminished. Abruptly, the rain stopped and a dense fog came down. It swirled around the trees in ghostly shapes until a strong wind swept in and blew the fog away.

"It's Mac Lir's weather, isn't it?" he whispered, feeling Moody's tense posture. "The wizard's trying to flush me out." Moody uttered a short woof in reply. "But who was the rider? Was that a Shee?" Moody growled deep in his throat, then turned and licked Peter's cheek. "Yeah, I guess they're gone now." Wrapping his arms around Moody's neck, he leaned his head against the wet fur and closed his eyes against the dark. Into his mind came the sound of hoofbeats ... he saw Dad on a white horse ... no, it wasn't Dad; it was someone else—a warrior dressed in white with eyes of flame. The rider was coming over the sea, getting closer, closer ...

He fell asleep, into a deep world where the trees whispered a beautiful name and the sky shone blue. Green mountains rose out of the sea, towering higher and higher, all the way up to the Milky Way, which poured over the lip of a great cliff below a shining city.

❦ ❦ ❦

"Let me in!"

Startled out of sleep, Peter saw morning light shining into the glade. Two cedars right over his head began to thrash their branches, and a murmur arose in the woods, like wind among leaves. Raising his head from his paws, Moody looked at Peter inquiringly.

"Peasants!" Peter heard the strident voice again and realized Moody couldn't. Then the trees of their tent shifted slightly and the cedars thrashed again. A small suspicion grew in his mind. Pushing aside the branches, he got to his feet. "Better let it in," he said aloud.

The cedars parted, and there was the hawthorn. It whipped the air with its branches, then stood perfectly still as if it had been growing there all its life. Moody perked up his ears and woofed, then got to his feet. Peter heard a sudden rustle behind him. Turning, he saw a path open between the trees.

❦ ❦ ❦

That morning, he and Moody walked through an ever-brightening world of evergreens and tall, leafy trees. The early-morning storm clouds moved off, and beams of sunlight pierced the sylvan canopy, ending in pools of green-gold light on the forest floor. The woods opened the path before Peter and closed it behind him, leading him in the direction it chose. He hoped it was to Wakkenburg. The hawthorn trailed behind, mostly out of sight, but he knew it was following in its own way.

Then, about midday, he came to the banks of a broad river. At his feet, the grass sloped gently to a pebbly shore, and hazy sunlight shone over dark evergreens that stood on either side. The slow current, flowing over flat boulders, reflected the sun's rays.

A woman stood ankle deep in a shallow pool, washing a white cloth. She was dressed in a blue cloak, with the sleeves rolled up to her elbows and the hood pulled down so that Peter could see only the profile of her mouth and chin. Her walking staff lay on the flat stone at her feet. As he stood there, wondering if this was the Moonwitch, she turned and beckoned. "Come, child."

He hesitated, but Moody chirruped and sat down on the bank, his ears perked up. The hawthorn, sidling out from the eaves of the woods, prodded him with a thorny branch. So Peter slipped off his backpack, took off his shoes, and waded into the water.

As he approached the woman, she pushed back her hood with one hand, and he knew her. The old woman from Foyle.

"I ... I met you in back of the Rilson house. My friend calls you the Bread Lady."

She chuckled. "That *is* one of my names. You were nearly caught that day, but I arrived in time. There was something evil in that place, and you helped save Pixel from a terrible fate." She wrung out the white cloth, the water cascading from her hands like drops of sunlight. Then she spread it on a flat rock. "Do you know this, Peter?"

He stared at the faded cartoon logo. It was a T-shirt belonging to his mother. In the week before he left Lang, she'd worn it every day as she lay on the couch in her stupor of sorrow and gin. How had it come here? Like a lance, grief and anger stabbed his heart, and forgetting all else, he sat down in the shallows. Pushing his hands into the riverbed, he closed his fists around smooth stones, seeing only the empty bottles on the coffee table at home and his father's tired face as he came in from the night shift. He saw his brother's coffin being lowered into an open grave.

"Peter."

Startled, he looked up and saw a young woman with long dark hair and a face of such sweet beauty that his heart was pierced. She was dressed in the same blue cloak as the old woman, and he had no doubt they were one and the same person. She smiled at him and said, "Do you see that mountain there with the sharp, jagged peak?" He got to his feet as she pointed upriver to three mountains rising above the valley. "That is Mount Kulifara. Behind it you see Mount Rosknil. And the tallest mountain beyond that is called Greeba. The headwaters of this river, the Glenfaba, spring from its side. On the other side of Greeba is the Hidden Valley, home of the giants. Look now, beyond Greeba."

Gazing above the crown of the woods to the empty sky, Peter wondered what she expected him to see. Then, quite suddenly, taller mountains appeared, green as new grass, their peaks rising far higher than Greeba, beyond his range of vision. A sudden breeze flowing downriver brought to him the strong scent of cedar, and from afar he heard the sound of a thousand voices raised in song.

"The Inner Mountains. You with your silver eyes can see them sometimes."

A sudden hope rose in his heart, though he knew nothing about the place. "Am I going there?"

"You must travel dark roads first." As she said this, the vision faded. "You love this island, Silver One? They say you are the guardian."

"I . . . no, not really."

"A truthful answer. Perhaps it is a weight around your neck. As you feel your mother is."

He looked steadily into her face and nodded.

"There is another Silver One who wanders this land, besides you and Jen. He was the guardian once, carrying the burden during a time of trouble in the woods. He sought Mac Lir's help, but after many years, he came to understand that the wizard has a forked tongue. In the end, he barred Mac Lir from the house of Wakkenburg."

"Jonas?"

"Yes. And when he grew tired and disheartened, he tried to find the path to the Inner Mountains by himself. He should have come to me, but he listened once more to the wizard's half-truths. Now his appearance is much changed and he no longer uses his true name."

"I asked the wizard to help me find Pixel. I didn't know what else to do."

"It is possible to cast Mac Lir *and* the witch from this island. In doing so, Pixel will be saved. Do you wish to do that?"

He gazed at her beauty, afraid to say no, afraid to say yes.

"Peter, you do not have to serve the wizard. There is another choice. Another way, hard to understand and harder to follow. But this island will be wracked by warring powers until someone takes a chance and chooses this hidden path. Will you do this? Even at great hazard?"

"I . . . I'll do whatever you say," he stammered. "Will you help me?"

She smiled, and he thought he would do anything to keep her smiling at him. "Befriend the creatures of the wood, and anyone you meet along your path. Do not be afraid, Peter. The trees led you here, and they will lead you forward, like a voice in your dreams and a voice behind you, saying, 'This is the way, walk in it.'" Suddenly, a strong wind buffeted the forest all along the riverbank, and the woman's form began to fade.

"Don't go!" he cried. "What about Pixel?"

"I am going to her now!" And she disappeared on the wind like a wisp of cloud swept into the sky.

He stood there, staring at the place where she had been, the pang of loss sharp against his heart. Then a cloud of silver rose from the woods and hovered above his head. It was a swarm of huge hornets with transparent wings. Before he could think of running, the cloud descended, covering him, settling on his head, his arms, his outstretched hands. He felt a tingling warmth all over and heard singing, faint and far off. Looking up, he saw the Inner Mountains again, green and glorious, rising above the dark peak of Greeba. Fierce longing welled up in his breast. Then the vision faded. The silver hornets rose like a bright cloud and zoomed into the woods on the other side of the river. There, a new path lay open and waiting.

Peter looked down at his dripping pants. Then, below the clear water, he spied a small blue stone at his feet, the same color as the

Bread Lady's cloak. He picked it up and shoved it into his pocket just as a swell of water flowed over the flat boulder, taking the old T-shirt away in the current. He watched it float downstream. Then, returning to shore, he picked up his shoes, shouldered the pack, and started across the river, stepping from boulder to boulder.

"Rowrf!"

Moody came bounding through the current with the Bread Lady's walking staff in his jaws. He stopped, wagging his tail.

"Leave it, boy. She forgot. She'll come back for it."

Moody uttered a short growl. Standing on a rock in the middle of the river, Peter took the stick and felt the worn, smooth handle; he fingered the intricate carvings of leaves and flowers as a silver hornet buzzed around his head. "For me?" he whispered. The hawthorn thrashed its limbs. A fat thorny stick came flying across the water and struck him on the head.

Grasping the staff, Peter crossed to the far bank, Moody splashing beside him. A few paces into the woods, the path turned sharply to the right, parallel with the river, and he went on, wondering where he was going, but no longer anxious.

Peter and Moody stopped to rest now and then, sharing the sandwiches that Muru had packed. By late evening, when the path ended in a clearing of tall grass and wildflowers, they had eaten all the sandwiches in the bag, but even then Peter didn't worry.

There was an old firepit in the middle of the meadow. Someone had camped in this place. The Lady said Jonas wandered the island, so maybe it was he who had been here. Wondering what Jonas looked like now, Peter lay down in the grass beside Moody as twilight settled under the eaves of the forest. He was just drowsing off when a very loud voice from somewhere nearby said, "Hey! Here's a path! I ain't never seen it before."

"We *are* on patrol," a deep rumbling voice replied. "It's our duty to check it out."

A gap appeared between two poplars, and Peter sat up.

"Look! It's another Silver! And Moody Doug!"

A band of small, bristly creatures swarmed into the meadow, greeting Moody with deafening cheers. The huge dog panted happily as the creatures climbed on his head and hung from his ears. They were a little like hedgehogs, but bigger, about the size of bowling pins. Then the largest of the creatures detached itself from the crowd.

"Well now, you're the boy from Wakkenburg. We heard about you. I'm Kaney, and we're the Arkan Sonney."

"Chief! Chief!" a burly creature called. "This makes two in a month! We oughta call ourselves the Silver Squad from now on!"

"This is Arkey," Kaney continued. "You might say he's my unofficial mouthpiece. I may as well tell you, before he does, that most folks in these woods call us—"

A thorny stick sailed up from the riverbank and clumped Arkey on the head. Into Peter's mind, a voice said, "Poinkers!" Looking over his shoulder, he saw the hawthorn sidle into the meadow. When he turned back, the mob on Moody's back had stopped bouncing, and every beady eye was fixed on him.

"Uh, you're the Poinkers."

Every snout twitched but no one spoke. Peter swatted at the swarming mosquitoes, and the hawthorn rattled its branches.

"Boss, this one's travelin' with a tree," Arkey said.

"So I see. And what better guide in these woods?"

"Look, kid, what I wanna know is, what are you doin' sittin' here in the dark? You want them mosquitoes to eat you alive?"

"I, uh ..." Peter looked around, wondering what the Poinkers expected.

"Ha! You're just like the last Silver we met. Pretty near helpless."

"Now, Arkey, he probably thought better of attracting the Shee. A fire might do that, you know."

"Come on, boss. We both know he ain't got no woodcraft." Arkey turned to the mob, which had resumed bouncing on Moody's back. "Hey! We need some kindlin'! Get movin'!"

"If it's one thing we Poinkers have," Kaney explained, "it's woodcraft. We're old campaigners, we are, and—"

The hawthorn threw a fat stick at Arkey, and like a sudden outburst of rain, the trees sent down a shower of twigs over the burly Poinker's head.

A little later, Peter sat before a roaring fire, mostly mosquito-free, toasting little sausages on a stick. He had to admit the Poinkers were an efficient crew, though noisy. They had turned out his pack, and in addition to matches, they found chocolate, sausages, cheese, berry juice, Jonas' journal, a small blanket, and two jars of tree food. Good ol' Muru.

After supper, the Poinkers rolled up into bristly balls and went to sleep. Peter, with his head against Moody's flank, thought about Pixel. Where was she? Fear for her descended like a weight on his chest, yet there was nothing he could do. Maybe tomorrow the trees would lead him to wherever she was. Turning his mind toward home, he looked up at the multitude of stars and composed a letter.

Dear Dad. Me and the big dog are camping. We met the Poinkers, and they've taught me how to build a fire. Suddenly, the fact that he'd accepted their speech without thinking smote him like a thunderbolt, and he began to laugh. No, Wakken Wood was not a normal place, and this was no ordinary camping trip. *I'll write more when I get back to the house. Great-Aunt Marj and Great-Uncle Edward say hello. I hope you can come here soon. Love from Peter.* Yawning, he turned over on his side and fell asleep.

❦ ❦ ❦

The next morning, just after dawn, the trees sent down a shower of leaves and pine needles. Peter rubbed his eyes, got to his feet, and looked around for an open path. There it was, still heading along the river, toward the mountains. Moody, looking bleary-eyed, lumbered to his feet and moved toward the trail. Peter picked up his pack and followed.

A strangled snort came from the pile of Poinkers. Arkey's face surfaced, blinking. "Hey! Wait up! We're comin' with you."

By this time, all the other Poinkers were awake, shaking out their bristles, grumbling like little trolls.

"Arkey's right, Mr. Peter," Kaney said, brushing pine needles from his fur. "The trees meant for us to find you and no doubt think we should travel together."

"Right." Peter thought of the Lady's instruction: *"Befriend the creatures of the wood."* Here they were, befriending him.

"What about breakfast?" a chorus of Poinkers cried. In reply, the hawthorn pelted them with thorny twigs, and the Poinkers, muttering, followed Peter down the trail.

29

The Jool of Trollaby

Peter, Moody, and the Poinkers walked along the river for many miles before the trees let them stop to rest. It was late morning when they came to a clearing of flat, moss-covered boulders. The Poinker named Raney built a fire while several others pulled out poles—Peter couldn't tell from where—and went fishing. They caught three large bull trout, which were cooked and eaten for breakfast. Then, rummaging in his pack, Peter found a map tucked into Jonas' journal. He spread it on the ground, and the Poinkers gathered around.

"I believe we're about here," Kaney said, pointing to a spot on the western shore of the Glenfaba. "Several miles south of Spoot Voor Falls."

"Hey, kid, you never told us why you're out here in the first place," Arkey said. "Ain't it a little dangerous with them Shee and Glashtyn in the woods?"

"It wasn't my idea." And Peter told how Pixel had been captured by the Shee and how he had gone to Fenn House with Uncle Ed to ask Mac Lir for help. "But it all went wrong. Lir and some little guys on horses came after us. Me and Moody barely escaped, and I don't know what happened to my uncle."

"By all you've said, Mr. Peter, it seems to me the trees know what's happened to your uncle *and* your friend," Kaney said. "It'll all come right in the end, you'll see. The trees will show you the right way to go."

"This news about Mac Lir ain't too good," Arkey said. "I never heard that he was forceful like that with a Silver. He must be in a tight place."

"And speaking of Mac Lir," Kaney said, looking up at the sky, "here comes the rain."

The heavy clouds rushing in from the southeast brought a sudden blast of cold wind. Moody barked a warning and they scuttled under the arms of a massive cedar as the storm let loose. First came buckets of rain; then a dense fog descended, blanketing the woods. In the white mist, the Poinkers saw strange shapes that looked to them like dragons, a pack of wolves, and the Great Hairy Midge.

"Hairy Midge?"

"Ancient legend, kid. We can't say no more."

After that, an easterly wind swept the fog away, a light rain came down, and a path opened, this time under an arch of branches.

"Hey! A tunnel of trees!" Arkey exclaimed.

As he left the clearing, Peter looked back and saw the hawthorn standing perfectly still beside the moss-covered stones, its branches raised to the sky, welcoming the rain.

A little later, the clouds cleared, the sun came out, and the day became hot, though it didn't bother them much under their secret tree cover. Birds darted through the branches, and the occasional chipmunk poked its head out of a hole to note their progress. For some reason, the sight of these tiny creatures enraged Arkey, and whenever he saw one, the woods resounded with his insults.

As the sun approached its zenith, shining with a soft light over the forest, they heard the sound of a great waterfall in the distance.

"That'll be Spoot Voor," Kaney said.

Sure enough, coming around a bend in the river, Peter saw a broad torrent cascading from a ledge hundreds of feet above the river valley. Their path led right to the foot of the falls, where a deep pool, like a giant punch bowl, churned with white water. Below the rocks where they stood, the Glenfaba gushed through a deeply cut gorge.

From the base of Spoot Voor, the path began to climb into the wooded hills west of the falls.

"First come the lower foothills," Kaney told Peter, "then the High Hills, then Kulifara and Rosknil. And I must say, Mr. Peter, after hearing about the Shee capturing your friend, I'm rather glad we're headed into the mountains."

They hiked northwest on gently sloping paths at first, then into a steep country of pine and fir trees. As they trudged through the sunlit woods, Peter listened to the Poinkers argue over money, of all things. A fellow called Boinkey was for gift cards, and Raney was for stocks and bonds. Peter had, in fact, noticed that wherever the bristly crew passed, they left silver quarters scattered on the ground, but they never mentioned it, so he didn't. Then, after a particularly loud shouting match that flushed out a flock of warblers, Kaney shouted, "That's enough! You can't change fate!" and the entire band broke into song.

Mine eyes have seen the modern monetary system thrashed.
Every nation is a debtor printing money for the trash.
They've debased the worth of silver coins, as everybody knows;
Worth a fraction of a dollar, you can stick it up your nose.

Glory, glory, we're the Poinkers!
Never call us prickly oinkers.
We'll hit you in the butt with a sticky cedar nut,
And you won't disrespect us anymore.

We have seen the days of glory; we have seen the days of truth,
When all trade was done in silver coin, but that was in our youth.
Every nation's run by robbers minting money out of lead;
We'll go back to trading seashells now the dollar it is dead!

How did the Poinkers know about the state of money in the outer world? In all his time with them, Peter never got a satisfactory answer, but he collected quite a few coins.

They were nearing the crown of a steep hill, traversing a heavily wooded ridge, when they came upon a yawning hole, about three feet up the side of an embankment. The thick roots of a cedar grew around the entrance, and Peter felt an unaccountable itch to peep inside, but even he knew better. It looked like the home of some animal. The Poinkers stopped and Arkey said, "Hey now, we ain't never come across this before. And we've covered every inch of these woods."

"Not every inch," Kaney replied. "There are some things the trees keep to themselves, you know."

"Well, since we're here," Arkey said, glaring at Peter, "I suppose you better take a squinny."

"What Arkey means to say," Kaney explained, "is that the trees brought us here, Mr. Peter, so they must have it in mind for you to take a look inside."

"How do you know?" Peter felt a sudden revulsion toward the dark hole.

"An edicated guess," Arkey replied, nodding his head toward the massive cedar that blocked the way forward. They were, in fact, hemmed in by trees. "Come on, kid. Just stick your head in the hole."

"You stick your head in!"

Moody whined and the cedar tree began to thrash its arms impatiently.

"I can't believe this!" Peter huffed, but he set his staff aside, leaned against the bank, and put his head in the hole. His eyes, like flashlights, lit up a deep burrow of dry reddish dirt. There was something at the bottom. A sack. Bracing his knees against the bank, Peter pushed his head and shoulders farther in, reaching down to grab thick roots that grew like perfect handholds. As he pulled himself forward, the roots cracked. "Hold on to my legs!" he shouted, but in the same moment, a chorus of chipmunk chatter broke out high in the tree above. Arkey responded with a volley of insults, and Peter fell into the hole.

"Hey! Somethin' pulled him in!" the Poinkers yelled, and Moody began to howl.

Somehow, he landed on his back, with his feet in the air, as red earth and broken roots cascaded onto his face. Feeling a sharp pain in his shoulder, he spit out dirt and rolled over. He'd landed on the canvas sack, which contained something hard and lumpy, about the size and shape of a dinner plate. It was curiously light, so he stuffed it into his T-shirt and climbed out of the hole.

When he emerged, covered with dusty red earth, the Poinker chorus leapt back. "Ghost!" they cried as he slid down the side of the embankment and landed on his rump.

"Mr. Peter! Thank goodness you're alright!" Kaney said.

"Yeah! We thought maybe there was a dragon down there that ate you!" Boinkey said.

Peter took the sack from under his shirt, opened it, and pulled out a thing made of bright copper. As he turned it over in his hands, Moody began to whine, and the Poinker named Pinkey said, "It's a brooch! See the pin on the back? Giant jewelry."

"Set with pretty big gemstones," Kaney observed. "Two diamonds, three rubies, and six emeralds. Straight from the troll mines, I believe."

"Trolls!" the Poinker chorus gasped.

Then the cedar blocking the path shuffled aside.

"Mr. Peter, it seems clear to me that the trees wanted you to find this," Kaney said.

Arkey snorted. "It ain't a good-luck charm, that's for sure. Leave it to a Silver to find somethin' of the trolls."

Peter shoved the troll brooch into his pack, and the company went on its way, continuing north and west, into the High Hills. Thanks to the recent rain, the steep path was slippery. Everyone, even sure-footed Moody, slithered and skidded until they were muddy, covered with grit. All afternoon they toiled, and in the evening, they dropped down into a deep, wooded valley between the shoulder of the northernmost foothill and Mount Kulifara. In this region, the cedars grew tall and close, their overhanging branches draped with trailing moss. Darkness came early.

In an open area, beside the flat face of a huge boulder, their path ended. Giant cedars drew close, forming a wall of broad trunks that left no gap big enough for even a chipmunk. The Poinkers built a small fire, and everyone gathered around. As soon as Moody sat down, the Poinker band perched themselves on his broad flank and between his paws. They were strangely silent, staring at the fire, its orange light reflected in their dark little eyes. Thunder sounded in the distance, somewhere to the northwest.

"Sounds like a storm in the mountains," Peter said.

Kaney shifted uneasily. "I only wish it was."

The moon rose higher, its silver beams shining through the treetops, but no one spoke of sleeping. Peter, toasting small sticks and bits of moss, saw Moody's ears perk up.

"Woof!" The great dog rose slowly, Poinkers sliding off his back. Stealthily, he stalked past the ring of firelight, toward the wall of trees, and they all heard a crackling in the bracken.

"Stations!" Kaney hissed. Instantly, the Poinker band became a bristly phalanx of glittering spears.

Peter stood and picked up his staff, though he figured it was only some creature drawn by the light. Then a massive cedar thrashed its lower limbs and, without warning, flung a large bundle into the clearing, almost onto the fire.

"Aaah!" A man jumped to his feet, but a branch swung down and pinned him to the ground. His hat fell off and there was Mac Rilson, wide-eyed and staring. When the cedar lifted its branch, Moody stepped forward, snarling in the old man's face. "Aaah! The devil's come to take me!" Mac shrieked, scuttling back against the tree trunk. Looking around wildly, he spotted Peter and gasped, "You!"

Peter and the old man looked at each other.

"Witch's Man!" Kaney's voice rumbled, and the chorus began to mutter, closing in with their spears.

"Witch's Man?" Peter's mind returned to that day at the ferry terminal when Mac had grabbed him and said, "We've been expecting *you*."

"Every creature in the woods knows you're in her pay," Kaney continued. "Isn't that so?"

"Oh, help!" Mac whimpered. "Talkin' squirrels!"

"Answer my question," Kaney said sternly. "Aren't you in the service of the Moonwitch?" As he said this, Moody bared his teeth in the old man's face, uttering a snarl that raised the hair on the back of Peter's neck.

"Y-y-yes! No! But I . . . I thought the whole Silver-eyed thing was a crock till I seen this kid here get off the ferry."

"What do you mean by 'yes no'?" Kaney demanded. "If you're not in service to the witch, then who?" Raney hopped onto Mac's shoulder and pressed his little spear against the old man's neck.

"I . . . I ain't at liberty to say."

"Shall we scalp him, boss?" Arkey said.

"Wait." Peter remembered something he'd heard Uncle Ed say: *"Seems to me the islanders look to us Thornburgs as being the center of weirdness, but there's somethin' strange goin' on at the Rilson house."* Following a hunch, he said, "It's the person who lives in the Rilson house in Foyle. The one nobody sees or talks about. Right?"

"Aaah!" Mac squealed as Moody snarled again, his breath hot in the old man's right ear. "I may as well tell you. If you don't kill me, he will!" Then, in halting words, between sips from a pocket flask, he told Peter about Ahab Rilson, whom Mac was mortally afraid of and who was the secret inhabitant of the house in Foyle. Ahab had promised Mac untold wealth if he could catch a Silver-eyed and deliver him, or her, to the Moonwitch. For more than forty years, Mac had kept his eye on the Thornburgs, all the while carrying messages between Ahab and the witch.

Peter couldn't help but feel disgust and a little pity. It was obvious that Mac was still an unwitting slave. Kaney must have been thinking the same thing.

"Mr. Peter," he said, when Mac finished his tale, "we can't just let this creature go."

"Too true!" Arkey said. "He'd bring the Shee on us before you could say 'taxidermy'."

Remembering what the Lady had asked him to do, Peter shrugged. "Join us," he said to Mac.

"Heck no! I ain't joinin' a devil dog and a pack of talkin' squirrels!"

Sighing inwardly, Peter fished a coil of rope from the bottom of his pack (good ol' Muru), and they tied Mac Rilson to the hawthorn, which had suddenly appeared between two cedars. Then the Poinkers stoked the fire and bedded down for the night.

"Gee whiz," Arkey muttered, "what next?"

"We *are* traveling with a Silver," Kaney replied.

"Yeah. Whose idea was that?"

Toward dawn, Peter woke briefly and saw that Mac was sound asleep. Moody, who was on guard, looked up and thumped his tail happily.

❦ ❦ ❦

The next day was gray and overcast. When a path appeared, Kaney took charge of the prisoner and they marched out of the valley, climbing into a rough-and-tumble country of fallen stones and tall fir trees. The Poinkers, grim and silent, kept their spears pointed at Mac, who shambled along with Moody on his heels. They traveled west at the foot of Mount Kulifara until, climbing up and over a low pass, they descended a forested slope into a shallow canyon below the westernmost buttress of Mount Rosknil. As soon as they entered this region, the Poinker chorus began to grumble. As the day wore on, they fell silent.

Gradually, the clouds overhead broke up and the sun burned its way through. In the late afternoon, their path plunged lower, between high gray cliffs. After scrambling down the trail into a ravine of short pines, they saw a stream spilling down the rock face into a small pool. A few steps from the stream they found a wide doorway between two standing stones. It opened onto a large recess with no roof, enclosed by the cliff on one side and tall, square rock slabs on the other. A firepit, a stack of wood, and a shelf lined with stone jars made Peter think that someone lived there.

"Them big stumps make perfect chairs for a giant's behind," Arkey said, looking around. "Must be one of their regular camps."

"Giants. That's right, Arkey. Think positive," Kaney said.

For supper that evening, the Poinkers used the food from the stone jars to make pancakes, and after days of meager rations, they all ate till they were full. This put the Poinkers in a merry mood, and they took turns telling stories about little Sonney, who plunked out copper pennies instead of silver. This was the first time Peter had heard about their missing member, who had gone off with someone named Jimmy Squarefoot. Then, as soon as darkness fell, the rumbling began.

"Thunder again." Peter poked a stick into the fire. "Are dry storms common in these mountains?"

"Don't you know where we are?" Arkey said. "I suppose you ain't looked at that map for a while."

"I looked at it today. Trollaby. Below Rosknil, right?"

The Poinkers, huddled around the fire, looked at Peter with unblinking eyes. Then Raney said, "Hey! Where's the prisoner? He was sittin' here a minute ago."

"He can't have run off," Kaney said. "Mr. Peter's prickly tree is blocking the only exit."

Startled, Peter looked around. The far corners of their camp lay in shadow.

"There's our outlaw!" Boinkey cried, whipping out his spear. "Over there by the food!"

There was a general rush for the prisoner as Raney shouted, "He's gotten into your pack, Mr. Peter! Trying to pry the jewels off that giant brooch!"

Peter saw Mac drop a knife and put his hands up, and then, with the suddenness of an avalanche, several things happened at once.

Fierce whinnies broke out all around the enclosure. The hawthorn at the entrance began lashing its branches wildly, and Peter heard the sickening thunk of an axe to its trunk. Rushing to the tree's aid, he pushed past the branches and found himself grappling with someone near his size but of great strength. Things would have gone badly, but the next second Moody was beside him. The great dog pounced, grabbed the little man, and tossed him aside.

The night erupted in shouts and rattling stone. Then the whole forest was in motion. Trees swayed. Sticks and whole branches flew through the air. Peter glimpsed something massive moving overhead. The great standing stones were ripped out of the ground and tossed away like scrap wood, exposing their camp. The flames of the fire leapt high, fed by the wind. In its light, he saw a massive, horny hand reach down and close upon Mac Rilson.

"What's this?" said a rumbling voice. The night went suddenly still.

"A man! A man!"

"Get off, Willy. It's mine!"

Peter saw two giant creatures rising above the trees. They had knobbly skulls and bulgy masses of flesh that might be noses. Their mouths were great, gaping caverns of teeth, and dark, beady eyes shone in the firelight. Now he understood the meaning of the map name "Trollaby".

"You give me a bite of that man, Dolf, or I'll bang yer fat head!"

"You can eat them Moonies," Dolf said. "I'm not sharin', so there."

Peter crouched in the shadow of the hawthorn, not more than fifteen feet from the nearest troll. As he watched, Dolf held Mac Rilson near the fire and examined him closely. Mac's eyes bulged.

"Might roast this one first," Dolf said, "though he smells like a pickle."

A quiet voice from somewhere near Peter's knees said, "Shut your silly blinkers, kid. Their shinin' like headlamps." It was Arkey. He had crept into the shadow of the hawthorn, but his warning was too late.

"Oi! What's that!" Willy cried and made a swipe at the hawthorn. It whipped its branches around and delivered a prickly blow to the troll's hand. "There's a man there with glowin' eyes!"

Afraid the tree would get torn up by the roots, Peter jumped out from the shadows, brandishing his staff. "Put that man down or I'll ... I'll fight you!" Then he spied something on the ground by the fire; he picked it up and held it in front of his face like a shield. It was the giant brooch that had fallen from Mac's hands.

Willy whistled through his teeth and said in a soft voice, "Oi, where'd you get that?"

Dolf reached toward the brooch, but Peter swung his staff and shouted, "Put him down!"

Behind Peter, sixteen little spears flashed in the firelight as the Poinkers lined up at his heels. Moody rowrfed, wagging his tail as if he were watching a football match.

"Stupid dog," Arkey muttered.

"I wants to know where you got that brooch," Dolf said quietly.

"You heard what the Silver said!" Arkey shouted. "Put that feller down now or he throws it in the fire! Are you blind? There's a band of fierce warriors with their spears pointed right at you!"

"Where? What warriors?" Willy said, peering all around.

Suddenly, the night was filled with angry cries as the Poinkers screamed and clashed their little spears. Then a rain of arrows fell upon the trolls.

"Hey!" Willy bawled, pulling arrows from his scalp.

Dolf dropped Mac Rilson and clapped a hand to his eye. "Oi! Save us! Don't shoot no more!" Mac scuttled away as Dolf sank to his knees, a pathetic lump of ugly flesh. "Just tell me afore you kill me, Silver One. Where'd you get that jool?" he whimpered.

"What's it to you where we got this jewel?" Arkey said fiercely.

"It's ours! We made it for Mother Moon, and Mac Lir took it!" Willy wailed.

"That's right!" Dolf said, rising suddenly to his feet. "And we wants to know why *you* got it! Silver eyes or no, I've a mind to squeeze you! You're one of the wizard's men, just like them Mooners, ain't you?"

"Ain't you?" Willy said in a menacing voice.

"No. I ... I got it back from Mac Lir," Peter stammered, "and I'm ... I came to give it to you. Here." He laid the brooch down and stepped back, wondering what would happen.

Dolf picked up the brooch and squinted at it by the light of the fire. "It's all here, Willy. Ain't no jools missing." Then he put the brooch in his pocket, and the two trolls stumped off without a backward glance.

When they were gone, Kaney said, half laughing, "Well now, I do call that a close call."

"We ain't out of trouble just yet," Arkey said. "The Mooners is here!"

Peter saw fourteen little men step out of the woods. Each was dressed in red and green and held the reins of a small white horse. The last time he'd seen Mooners was at Fenn House, and it wasn't a happy memory. Even so, the bows slung over their shoulders explained the arrows fired at the trolls.

"Silver One!" they called, and one of them came forward and said, "Well met, child of Wakkenburg House."

"If you've come to take me to Mac Lir, I won't go without a fight," Peter replied.

"Then it's true. You do not serve the wizard."

"Excuse me, Mr. Peter," Kaney said, "I do believe these particular Mooners are with the Moonwitch. The rumor in the woods is that their hounds deserted them because of it."

"We no longer serve the witch; be assured of that," the Mooner leader said. "But we will not parley with Poinkers. Dismiss these low creatures, Silver One, and we will talk."

"The Poinkers stay," Peter said. "If you won't talk to them, you won't talk to me."

The leader looked carefully at Peter. "Very well," he began, then paused. His eyes grew wide, and, in a twinkling, all the little men and horses fled.

Into the night came the sound of tramping feet, and Peter saw a small army of trolls come marching into the valley. One of them carried an armload of wood, which he threw on the fire so that it blazed up, illuminating their ugly faces.

The largest of the trolls thumped his chest and called out, "Silver One! Dolf and Willy say you took our jool from Mac Lir, curse him." The other trolls grumbled and muttered, and the large troll thumped his chest again. "You brought it back. For this we thank you and offer our service. When you are in need, send a message to Trelly." He thumped his chest again and nodded curtly. "The crows know where to find me."

Peter thumped his chest in reply, which seemed to please Trelly, who thumped himself again and bowed. Then the trolls turned and marched away, back to the mines of Trollaby on the other side of the ridge. They chanted as they went and their voices echoed in the hills.

The woods are deep, but I am strong;
My bones are made of wood and rock.
I take an oak staff in my hand
And beat my way through stone and stock.

When the sound died away, Peter sank down on a log near the fire.

"Oh my," Pinkey said, echoing his thoughts, "what a night."

"And we still got them silly Mooners lurkin' about," Arkey said.

Peter didn't care about the Mooners. Let them call for the Moon-witch. He was tired, and hungry again. The Poinkers were of the same mind, as they so often were, and several of them scurried about, making food and bringing as much order to their camp as they could after the trolls' visit.

"Well, kid," Arkey said, as they settled down to eat, "I gotta hand it to you, pullin' that great ugly brooch out when you did. I ain't never heard of no one gettin' on the good side of them trolls. 'Cept the giants."

Peter shook his head. "It was an accident. I didn't know what I was doing."

"But you got it outa that wizard's hole in the first place."

"Accident again."

"Humph. Accident. Tell that to the trees," Raney muttered.

"I gotta say, though," Arkey continued, "right when you had them trolls eatin' outa your hand, *why* didn't you ask 'em to put this here camp back together? A small job for them, and those stone walls woulda been nice to have right now with those blasted Mooners about. I ain't gonna sleep a wink. Not that there's much sleepin' time left. Must be after midnight."

"Yes," Kaney said, "which is why those trolls didn't hang about talking."

"Where *are* the Mooners?" Peter asked.

"Ran off into the woods," Raney said. "Cowards, every one of 'em."

"Oh my. Mac Rilson is gone too," Pinkey said.

She was right. The company conducted a brief search of the ruined camp and the surrounding woods, but Mac was not to be found.

"Run off to get the Shee, no doubt," Raney said when they were gathered by the fire again. "Probably went with those Mooners straight to the witch."

"Confound that drunkard!" Arkey said. "We shoulda let those trolls eat him when we had the chance!"

"Now, now, Arkey," Kaney said. "No doubt Mr. Peter showed the proper feeling for his own kind even if Mr. Rilson is a rascal. Remember how we felt about Freddey. A low-down disloyal fink, he was, not worthy of the name Poinker, but we were all sorry when he was taxidermied."

There was nothing to be done about Mac Rilson. The hawthorn, who hadn't been hurt much by the axe, sidled over to the stream and dipped its roots into the water. As Peter gave it a little tree food, he heard one of the Poinkers mutter, "Trolls and trees! This sure ain't no ordinary patrol."

Peter set his staff within easy reach, then curled up beside Moody and fell into a deep and dreamless sleep.

30

In Ogar's Valley

Peter woke suddenly. Arkey was slapping his face.

"Kid! Look what the cat brought home."

He sat up and reached for his staff. It was the chill hour of dawn and the sky was clear, the light just reaching over the eastern edge of the valley. On the other side of a fallen standing stone, thirteen Mooners sat astride their horses. Mac Rilson, bound hand and foot, was slung over the fourteenth horse. A phalanx of Poinkers stood between, their spears pointed at the intruders.

Even in the light of morning, there was something strange and unearthly about the Mooners in their green jackets and red caps. Peter understood why the folks who saw them hunting by moonlight thought they'd seen fairies.

One of the Mooners saluted. "Silver One! I am Rathfrit, captain of the Moonjer Veggey. We caught the Moonwitch's slave." He pointed to Mac. "He is sly and fast as a fox. When we came upon him, he was preparing a signal fire to summon the Shee. This one should have been guarded more carefully." Rathfrit glanced disdainfully at the Poinkers.

"Well, it was a busy night," Arkey muttered, and Raney grumbled, "Yeah, we shoulda let the trolls eat that guy."

"Right. Thanks," Peter said. "We'll take him back." Then, remembering the Bread Lady, he said to the Mooners, "Join us for breakfast if you want."

Rathfrit nodded and his men dismounted, leaving their horses to graze on the tufts of grass that grew here and there in the clearing.

Breakfast was a solemn affair. Mac, held at spear point, lay curled up by the fire, muttering to himself and refusing all food. The Mooners remained grim and silent, and the Poinkers, ill-pleased with the presence of these guests, held their tongues. Peter, ignoring the tension, made a point of enjoying the pancakes. He ate slowly and fed Mac's share to Moody.

At the end of the meal, Kaney said, "Well, Mr. Peter, judging by that silver tree over there, I'd say it's time to go."

The hawthorn, covered root to trunk in silver hornets, stood at the beginning of a new path.

Rathfrit gazed in wonder. After a moment, he stirred and said, "Where do you go, Silver One?"

"Wherever the trees lead us."

"Obviously, that path's headed west," Arkey said curtly.

"We will go with you. Perhaps our ways lie together."

Peter frowned. "You said last night that you've left off serving the Moonwitch, but how do I know I can trust you? My friends tell me that before the witch, you were with Mac Lir."

Rathfrit shifted uneasily under Peter's gaze. "It is true. First, we served the wizard, but he sailed away so we took up with the witch. When she lured the Glashtyn to her side, we thought that was bad, but then she called the Lliannon Shee. At the Shee's coming, half our brothers went back to the service of the wizard."

"Yeah. I've met *them*," Peter said.

"We should have left too, but to my mind there wasn't much difference between the witch and the wizard. Then the Moonwitch grew displeased with us and we knew our days were numbered."

"What I want to know, Mr. Peter, is why these Mooners are in the mountains," Kaney said. "If they're headed for Fenn House, where the wizard is, there are easier paths."

"We are done with witches and wizards," Rathfrit answered. "All we want is to find our hounds, who ran away when the Shee arrived. We have come to the mountains seeking the help of the giants."

"Well now, perhaps we're after the same thing," Kaney said. "As you can see, we Arkan Sonney are in the service of Mr. Peter, though I don't think we're headed for giant country."

Peter glanced at the silver hornet buzzing in circles around his head. It was time to go. He turned to Kaney. "Is it alright with you if the Mooners come with us? You're second in command, you know."

"I'm not sure. The Moonjer Veggey have always hunted us for our silver coins. Now you're asking us to travel with them."

"I think *they're* asking you. Isn't that right?" Peter said to Rathfrit. "You want to travel with me and Moody and the Poinkers because you need our help. You're fed up with Mac Lir, you've crossed the witch, you're afraid of the Shee, and now you can't find the giants. I expect it was you who riled up the trolls last night."

"Er, well ..." began Rathfrit.

"Say no more!" Kaney said. "We Poinkers, with the help of the Silver One and Moody, will be glad to offer you our protection. We're old campaigners, we are, and if there's a way forward, we'll find it. Are you with us?"

The shadow of a grin crossed Rathfrit's face. "Since you put it so handsomely, Mr. Arkan Sonney, we accept."

"Then let bygones be bygones," Kaney said. "Mooners, if you'll kindly take charge of the prisoner, we'll be on our way."

They climbed out of the ravine, headed west through the stony trough of Trollaby. They had camped at the eastern head of this valley, and at its farthest, westernmost end lay the troll mines. But many miles before that, the trees led them south, opening a path up and over the High Hills, much to the relief of the Poinkers. For two days, under a sky of sun and swiftly moving clouds, the company scrambled down chutes of loose stone, the small, sure-footed horses picking their way carefully. At other times, they followed woodland paths that crossed and recrossed little streams tumbling down from the heights.

Sometime in the late afternoon of their second day out from Trollaby, they came to the unforested foothills. It was a gentler landscape of white granite, tall grass, and wildflowers. Bees hummed in every blossom. Directly south and east, still many miles away, lay the pastures of the Tarroo Ushtey, a broad grassland beside the Glenfaba River.

"Well, Mr. Peter," Kaney said, "there are no trees to guide us. Where do we go now?"

Peter gripped his staff and looked up at the sky. All morning and into the afternoon, he'd walked in silence, hardly listening to the chatter of the Poinkers and their conversation with the Mooners. At every stop, he'd sat alone, reading Jonas' journal with a growing sense of wonder, becoming aware of a new language. In the shifting of leaves or the swaying of branches, in bird calls and the click of insects, in the way the light fell on a pile of stones, he began to comprehend something. Some message was coming across, like words heard suddenly over the static of a radio. The static was his own mind, but if he kept quiet, the message unfolded ever more clearly. It was something to do with the light that fell in radiant waves over everything, revealing a mute conversation that wrapped the world in splendor. And yet it was also terrible because there was no escape from its embrace, unless he were to seek darkness in the depths of the earth.

He looked down at Kaney. "That way," he said, pointing.

"Southeast? Are you sure, Mr. Peter?"

"Yeah. I'm sure."

The lower hills were covered in wild daisies and red poppies, with here and there small copses of green-leafed trees. The Poinkers began looking for a place to camp.

"This seems like a good spot," Arkey would say, and Peter would reply, "Not here." He didn't know where they were going, but he knew they weren't there yet. There was no way to explain, so he closed his mouth and kept walking.

The evening sky was bright blue when they came to a meadow surrounded by grassy hills. They were getting close to their destination. He could feel its nearness. Slowing his pace, he looked from left to right. And then he saw it: the entrance to a ravine nearly hidden in a fold between two hills.

Hesitating for only a moment, Peter led them out of the sunlight into this narrow place, close and still. A hush fell over the travelers. High cliffs rose above their heads, the rock walls covered with fern and many kinds of moss. It was a dim green world of trickling water and small gray birds that chirped and twittered in low bushes. The Poinkers walked in a tight group, while the Mooners led their horses in single file, pushing Mac Rilson before them.

"What is this place?" Kaney whispered.

"I dunno," Arkey whispered back. "Here I thought we Poinkers had covered every inch of this island. This kid sure has a talent for takin' us where we ain't never been before."

"Oh my," Pinkey said. "Who's that?"

There were two entrances to this ravine, and they had come in through the southern gap, following a stony path that led right down the middle. Very close to the northern end, a high wooden door was set in the side of the hill. Before the door, an old man sat on a rock. He was large, with a grizzled beard covering his chest. When he turned toward the travelers, Peter thought it must be Silver-eyed Jonas. Then, as he drew near, he realized the old man's eyes were covered by the thick film of age.

"Who's there?" the man shouted, rising to his feet. "Who comes here?" He leaned on an ancient staff, but he was as tall as a troll and broad shouldered.

"It's us Poinkers," Arkey called out before Peter could think of what to say. "And a handful of Mooners. We've come with the Silver One and the Moddey Dhoo."

"The Silver One? Ah! At last! But Poinkers and Mooners? These names are not familiar to me. I hear the voice of the Arkan Sonney."

"That's right, sir," Kaney said. "And these others are the Moonjer Veggey."

"Ah. I see. And the Moddey Dhoo, you say? Where is he?"

Moody trotted forward happily, and the old man reached out to pat his head. Next to him, Moody looked like a regular-sized dog, which made Peter wonder.

"Welcome, friends. I am Ogar, king of the giants. I could hear and smell you as soon as you entered my little valley. But there's one among you who doesn't smell right. Who have you brought to foul up my home? Bring him here!"

At first, Peter wasn't sure whom the giant could mean. Then the Mooners pushed Mac Rilson forward. The giant stretched out his hands and took Mac by the shoulders.

"Please!" Mac muttered, overcome by fear. "Don't eat me!"

"How do you come to be traveling with the Silver One?" Ogar rumbled angrily.

"This man is our prisoner," Arkey called out. "Had to bring him with us to keep him out of trouble, if you know what I mean, Mr. Giant."

"I do indeed!" Ogar let go of Mac, who slumped to the ground in a pitiful heap. "He will come to a sorry end. He should never have gotten mixed up in the battle between the gods."

"Some of us don't have a choice," Peter said.

Ogar shook his head sadly and closed his unseeing eyes. "How well I know. In the end, none of us escapes it." Sighing, he sat down on the rock. "But now to our real business. Tell me, Silver One, what is the state of this island?"

Peter, caught off guard, looked at Ogar blankly. "What?"

"What is the state of this island? It's a plain and simple question. How do you find things?"

"Well, I ..." Peter looked helplessly at Arkey, who shrugged. "Well, it's ..."

"No need to tell me about the weather. I can tell that for myself."

Peter hesitated. How should he know the state of the island? A silver hornet buzzed down and landed on his arm. He shook it off.

"I ... I haven't been here very long," he began, "so I can't tell you much. My best friend came on the ferry with me, and she's been captured by the Shee. I thought Mac Lir would help me find her, but I had to run from him." Peter paused, wondering what it was the giant wished to hear. "The Bugganes helped rescue the Fennys when Mac Lir threw them out of Fenn House. Then someone set fire to Floden, I think. Maybe I dreamed that." At this revelation, he heard the Poinkers gasp, and the Mooners murmured, "Yes, yes, we were there."

Peter closed his eyes, trying to sort his thoughts. So much had happened in a short time. "There's a girl with silver eyes—my great-uncle's little sister. She was kidnapped a long time ago, but now she's in a place called the Hidden Valley." He opened his eyes and saw Ogar nodding. "We found the trolls' brooch and gave it back to them. And I ... I met the Bread Lady." He blew the air out of his cheeks in frustration, feeling he'd only scratched the surface and gotten it all muddled and out of order, but Ogar nodded and appeared to be satisfied.

"This Bread Lady," the giant said, "did she give you anything?"

"Her walking stick."

"Ah. I thought I smelled her. Give it to me." Ogar took Peter's staff—it looked like a twig in his hands—and ran his fingers over the curious carvings. "I see," he said. "Yes, you've done very well in a short time, and you've chosen wisely. Hmm. I must do what I can to help you." He gave the staff back to Peter and began rummaging in his pockets. "The Arkan Sonney and the Moonjer Veggey traveling together? And Bugganes helping Fennys? Yes, you *have* accomplished much. And the trolls too! Well, well." He took out a large key and went to the door. Once he'd unlocked it, he threw it open, then paused. "Is that the Vespa I hear?"

The swarm of hornets swirled down into the ravine and circled in the air above Peter's head. All the Poinkers looked up warily.

"Does this mean it's time to go?" Kaney asked.

"I ... I don't think so." Peter watched the bright cloud move sideways toward the north end of the valley. "Wait here. I ... I'll be right back." Then, ignoring the doubtful looks of the company, he and Moody followed the Vespa out of the ravine, around the foot of the hill, and up to the top. The hornets settled on his head and shoulders, but he hardly felt them. They weren't like regular insects. Behind him, the sun sat low on the horizon, and the world was still.

Something was coming. He faced east, looking toward the distant river, gripping the Lady's staff. Then, over the brow of the neighboring hill, a boy and a white dog appeared. Peter watched as they crested the summit. A crowd of small white creatures swarmed around their feet, yammering like a flock of migrating geese. The Vespa rose into the air, and the boy raised his hand to Peter and waved. Then he plunged down the hill, running.

Wondering, but not afraid, Peter stood waiting, watching the boy and the dog race up the slope toward him. As they got closer, he saw that the boy was about his own age, maybe a little older. The white dog was really a wolf, and the flock of little white creatures were hounds.

Moody began to bark as if greeting old friends, and when the group stopped, he snuffled the boy's face, then bounded around the wolf. The little white hounds nipped playfully at Moody's feet, and the wolf howled. Then all the dogs tore off across the hill, barking and rolling in the grass.

The boy grinned. "Well met, Silver One."

Peter looked at him in silence. He had never seen anyone so ... different. Yet the boy's face was ordinary enough: dark hair, dark eyes, light brown skin, a small scar on the lower jaw. "Who are you?"

"Most people call me the Small One."

Peter couldn't help staring, though he knew it was rude. The Small One's shirt and trousers were made of a fine woven material, slightly frayed at the collar, but this wasn't the thing that made him look unusual. All Peter could think was that the Small One's face was ... shiny around the edges. That was it. The boy looked shiny around the edges. Like the Lady.

"I have a message for you, Silver One. From the one you call Bread Lady. She says you are to let the Witch's Man go free."

"Mac Rilson?"

"Then go to the Hermit of Floden's house and take with you any creature of the woods who wishes to join you." The Small One laughed suddenly. "That means you'll have to take all the hounds who came with me. They belong to the Moonjer Veggey, but it's you they'll follow. I hope you like dogs!"

"The Mooners will be glad to see them."

The Small One looked at Peter for a long moment. "I've met the other one. The Silver Girl."

"You met Jen?"

"We traveled to the Hidden Valley together. I was her guide. Grandfather says you Silver Ones are like trees, injured while still saplings, with burls near your roots, though you are growing straight and tall."

"Burls?" Peter stared at the boy, trying to understand.

"Tree knots. Grandfather also told me about trees who are injured in violent ways, such as the ones struck by lightning. Perhaps you have seen a tree with a withered branch or black marks on its bark? When a tree is damaged like that, its sap runs low for a time."

"Are you saying a tree can be struck by lightning and not die?" For some reason, Peter thought of his mother, lying on the couch in their dark apartment, all the blinds drawn, the air close and musty.

"Oh yes. Those trees have been soaked by heavy rainfall and so the lightning strike does not reach their sap."

"But what if it does?"

"Then the tree will die. And yet, I have seen a strange and wonderful thing. From a withered stump, a seedling sprouts, taking what it needs from the old roots of the blasted tree."

"Yeah. I've noticed old stumps with trees growing out of the top."

The Small One grinned. "Grandfather says that I am like a sapling too, Silver One. Growing strong and always hungry. I can smell one of Ogar's stews, even from here! Let's go see if dinner is ready!" He whistled and all the dogs sprang to his side. Then Peter followed him down the hill to the giant's cave.

The Mooners were glad to see their hounds. "Twenty-eight!" Rathfrit said, counting heads. "Only fourteen belong to us. These others belong to our brothers who serve Mac Lir. Why have they come?"

The Small One chuckled. "They all wanted to be with the Silver One."

By the time they sat down to supper, Mac Rilson was gone. The sight of the Small One completely unsettled him. He called it "the last straw". "First trolls and now this!" he said. "Why bring someone like that around? He's bad for morale, if you ask me. Look at him! He ain't natural!"

When Peter told Mac he didn't have to stay, the old man wasted no time. "Ha! Justice at last. You've held me prisoner long enough and for no reason! I'm goin' to Sweetwater. A man can get decent grub there."

Peter and Kaney were the only members of the company to see Mac off. They stood at the southern end of the ravine and watched him shamble away across the meadow. He left with a pocketful of silver coins he'd been quietly collecting and a bag of food packed by Ogar.

"Do you think this is wise?" Kaney asked. "No matter what he says, he'll end up at the witch's door, you mark my words. And somehow I don't think she should know about this boy, the Small One."

Peter watched the figure of Mac disappear around the shoulder of a hill. "I hope he makes it somewhere safe."

"We felt the same about Freddey, though he was a low-down skunk. Anyway, the man is gone and we'll travel easier without him."

"Yeah. I guess we will," Peter said, turning away.

He never forgot that night around the campfire in front of Ogar's cave. The Small One told many stories that he did not understand, though he thought about them the rest of his life. Then, after hearing Ogar tell about the early days on the island, he asked, "Where is the city of the giants?"

"Spread out below Mount Greeba," the Small One answered. "If you ever go to the Hidden Valley, you may see the entrance in the Cave of Creatures."

"The Cave of Creatures?" Arkey said.

"That's where I've painted all the creatures of the island. Even you," the Small One said with a grin.

"But we ain't never met before!"

"I see many things. Sometimes from afar, and sometimes in dreams. I have often watched the Arkan Sonney and come across you in my travels, though I've chosen to keep myself hidden. And surely you'll admit that you have a voice no one can ignore, Master Arkey. Why, I can hear your patrol coming from a mile away!"

It was getting late. The Poinkers, the Mooners, and all the little dogs were asleep around the fire. Even Ogar sat with his chin on his chest. Peter knew he should go to bed, but he felt restless and wakeful. Then a large white hare loped into the firelight.

The white wolf sat up and the Small One said, "Is it time to go?"

The hare thumped its feet.

"Goodbye," the Small One said, turning to Peter.

"I thought you were coming to Floden with us."

Peter followed the Small One into Ogar's cave. They walked past brightly painted murals and rows of beds carved into the wall, and past the giant's pantry to a low opening covered by an animal skin. The Small One paused and took a small clay lamp from a shelf; then they went past the curtain and through a low tunnel. He set the lamp down in a little niche, and Peter saw a wooden door.

With his hand on the latch, the Small One stopped. The wolf and the hare waited by his side. "Goodbye, for now, Silver One."

"Where does this go?"

"To my home."

"Is it a cave or something?"

"It is the world within the world."

"How ... how far is that?"

"For you, it would be a long dark tunnel traveled for the rest of your life. Keep to your path, and I'll see you in Floden!" Then, in one swift movement, he was gone and Peter was left alone.

He looked around, at a sudden loss. The little lamp in the wall flickered and popped. Hesitantly, he opened the wooden door and looked in. All he saw were stone walls, a dirt floor, and darkness beyond.

He shut the door, then took the lamp and went back to the cave, where he stood for a long time, looking at the murals. They had been painted by the Small One. Gazing at a large picture of the Bread Lady, Peter wished he could speak with her. Everything had become tangled in his mind. He'd gone from troubles at home in Lang to even bigger troubles here. "Tree knots," he said. "Those aren't the only kind of knots."

Standing there in the dimly lit cave, wishing for something—he didn't know what—he became aware of a change. The stone walls all around the painting began to shine with small pinpricks of light, twinkling like tiny stars. Then the painting itself began to glow, as if illuminated from the inside. First the Lady's eyes, then her blue cloak. The mountains behind her became brighter, but she outshone them.

Suddenly, he noticed a black spot on her cloak. He moved closer. Had the paint chipped away? Reaching up, he put a finger on the spot and felt a hole. He drew his hand back, repelled by this unexpected gash, like a small window opening onto a dark abyss. It should be fixed. But how?

A small sigh echoed through the cave, like wind in the trees, or water flowing over stone, and the answer came to him. He reached into his pocket and pulled out the blue river stone. It was the right size. Then, into his head came the image of his mother's face as he'd last seen her. She'd been asleep and hungover, unaware that he was standing there saying goodbye, about to leave for the island. "Get better, Mom," he whispered and pushed the stone into the dark hole. For a split second, a white light blazed out, shining around the edges. Then the stone vanished and the Lady's blue cloak appeared without spot or blemish. The light in the painting faded, and Peter was alone in the dim light of the cave.

Ogar walked in. "Well now, I hope you said goodbye to the Small One for me?"

Peter nodded.

"I suppose you tried to talk him into going with you?"

"Yeah."

"I know. He has that effect on people. Not all. Mac Rilson couldn't get away from him fast enough. That's why the Small One has to be careful. If he were to go about openly, he'd just become a target for all the evil of the world. In a way, it's because of him and his ancient home that this island is a place of contention. I don't think the witch or the wizard actually know he's here, but no doubt they sense something powerful they'd love to get their hands on if they could. I guess you're leaving in the morning?"

"We're going to the Hermit of Floden's house."

"Ah. Floden. Yes. Well, don't worry. We'll have a big breakfast before you go. I'd come if I could, but a half-blind giant trailing along would be rather conspicuous, don't you think?"

"More than a giant black dog, a hawthorn tree, a swarm of silver hornets, a crowd of bickering Poinkers, and a bunch of little men on white horses?"

"Ha! I take your point. But there! You've forgotten the twenty-eight white hounds!"

31

Waiting for Stragglers

Peter woke early the next morning. Slinging on his pack, he picked up his staff and went to the south entrance of the ravine in time to see sunlight creeping over the eastern hills. The world was still except for the restless buzzing of the Vespa. They were disturbed, and he didn't know why.

Kaney trotted to his side. "We're ready to go, Mr. Peter! The Mooners are just bringing the horses— Say! What's all this?"

Three silver hornets zoomed in from the east and hovered in front of Peter's face. Then the whole swarm rose from the branches of the hawthorn and hung like a great silver cloud over his head. Above the hum of hornets, Peter heard the sound of hoofbeats.

"Battle stations!" Kaney shouted.

Eighteen Poinker spears flashed out, and behind them, fourteen Mooners drew their bows. Moody leapt forward, wagging his tail.

Three small horses came around the flank of the hill, galloping at full speed. When they saw Peter, they slowed their pace and trotted up, each one pushing forward to nuzzle his hand. They were snow white.

"Your horses got loose," he called to the Mooners.

Rathfrit ran his hands along the neck and flank of each horse. "These are not ours. They belong to our brothers who serve Mac Lir. They've been running all night."

"And where are their masters?" Arkey demanded.

"Not far behind, I suspect," Kaney said shrewdly.

Eyeing the swirling Vespa, Peter guessed he was right. The horses suddenly shied away from Rathfrit, nosing Peter's shoulders and neck. Tentatively, he scratched each one between the ears. Once again, the Lady's message came into his mind: *"Befriend the creatures of the wood."*

The three horses were in no condition to travel, so the company decided to leave later in the day. As they sat by the cave door, eating a cold lunch, Ogar turned his blind eyes to the northern gap. "Someone's coming."

Peter stood and reached for his staff as the Poinkers drew their spears. Three bedraggled Mooners limped into the ravine. When they saw him, they stopped and stared. Then a white horse trotted up and stood at his side.

"My horse!" One of the little men started forward, but the horse reared up, neighing fiercely. As if that weren't enough, three white hounds began to snarl and bark.

"Our dogs!" the little men gasped.

To Peter's surprise, the other Mooners drew their bows. "If you're here on Mac Lir's business, you'll not go far," Rathfrit said to the three. "We have joined the Silver One. He will rid the island of the witch *and* the wizard. If you want that too, then stay with us. Your horses and hounds have already chosen."

There was a long silence. Then the bright cloud of Vespa settled on Peter's head and shoulders. The three men gasped and threw down their weapons.

"I will follow the Silver Boy," one of them said, going down on one knee. "Mac Lir has done nothing about the witch. Perhaps he is not as powerful as we thought."

"He can only make snow at Wakkenburg House," said the second Mooner, kneeling beside his fellow. The third said nothing but knelt and looked at Peter in wonder.

Peter, his eyes like lamps and his shoulders covered with living silver, said, "What do you mean by 'snow at Wakkenburg House'?"

Then the three Mooners told of the deep snows at Wakkenburg and days and nights of freezing temperatures, all conjured by Mac Lir.

"And you think the wizard is doing all that to get me to join him? But I'm not even there!"

"Every few days, a boy who looks like you—at least from afar—appears on the roof and walks back and forth," said one of the three men.

"Ha, ha! Someone is tricking Mac Lir!" Ogar chuckled. "Goodness knows he deserves to sit like a buffoon in his own snow and ice."

"Not to mention all the silly Mooners who're still with him," Arkey added.

"We have all been mistaken about the wizard," Rathfrit said. "It seems the only trick he has up his sleeve is bad weather. Perhaps our brothers will follow."

"I expect we'll see their horses first," Kaney said.

Right after lunch, Peter found the hawthorn blocking the north entrance of Ogar's Valley, lashing its branches at a huge bear. When he saw Peter, the bear stood up on his hind legs, snarling and wiping blood off the end of his nose.

"It's okay!" Peter called to the tree. "He's a friend, come to join us."

Ogar was undaunted by the Buggane. "Now, now," he said to the yowling hounds, "the Moddey Dhoo isn't making a fool of himself! See! He likes Tom." Then he tipped a generous helping of honey out of a great stone jar and set it before the bear. "Really!" he said, rounding on the pack of dogs. "If you don't stop that infernal howling, that bear will turn into something much worse!"

In the early afternoon, the company was preparing to leave by the south entrance when the Mooners happened to count the hounds and discovered that seven were missing.

"They must have taken fright at the bear and run off," Rathfrit said, and he sent out search parties.

Then Peter realized that Moody Doug was missing too. "Wasn't he just here?" He whistled and called but the great dog did not appear.

"Maybe he went to find the hounds," Kaney said. "Does anyone remember seeing him leave?"

Two hours later, the search parties returned to the cave, where Peter was sitting with Ogar.

"We can't even find their trail!" Rathfrit said. "I don't know what came over them to leave like that or where they could be!"

When Moody and the hounds did not return for supper, Arkey and a couple of Mooners went in search of them again. The other Poinkers wiled away the time by sharpening their little spears.

"I could use your help with a few chores," Ogar said to Peter. "They're hard to do with my eyesight as it is."

"What can you see, Ogar?"

"Shapes, shadow. Light. I need someone with sharp eyes to take an inventory of my pantry. I must send a message to my friends in the giants' city for more supplies."

Helping Ogar took the rest of the evening, and the giant had just lit the lamps when Peter looked up and saw a dark shape at the back of the cave. "Moody!"

Moody wagged his tail. Behind him, the curtain covering the Small One's entrance swayed, and the seven lost hounds appeared.

"Bless me! Where did they come from?" Ogar cried.

Moody picked up something on the ground and brought it to Peter. It was a thin piece of bark on which someone had drawn a picture of seven hounds following a wolf, a boy, and a hare into a garden. On the other side, a big black dog was leading the little hounds away.

When Ogar heard Peter's description of the drawing, he laughed. "It explains everything. Those scoundrels followed the wolf all the way to the ancient place, and Moody led them back again. I guess the Small One didn't shut the door properly last night."

"Ancient place?"

"The heart of the earth and the world's treasure. I am guardian of the seventh entrance."

That night, Peter dreamed of the Small One. He was standing in a pool of light, painting a stone wall. The white hare sat at his feet, and someone else was there. In the dream, he thought it might be Pixel, but she was hidden in the shadows beyond the light. After that, he fell into darker dreams. A dragon appeared at the head of a shadowy army as the sea seethed with serpents. Yet above all that, he heard again the whinny of a great horse and the sound of clashing steel. Over the sea, the white warrior came riding. Peter sighed in his sleep and turned over.

❦ ❦ ❦

He was summoned at dawn. Three more horses had arrived in the wee hours, and Kaney said they may as well put off their departure. Sure enough, in the late afternoon, three Mooners appeared. So that evening, Peter, Ogar, and the Poinkers held a council in the cave.

"More will come tomorrow. You mark my words," Kaney said.

"But how many?" Raney asked.

Arkey scowled. "We won't know till they show up."

"I only ask," Raney said, "because if all fourteen are gonna make their way here, two or three at a time, we could be here for days! I thought we was supposed to get to Floden."

"Well, we aren't waitin' for fourteen now," Arkey said. "Six has already come."

"I know, I know," Raney said. "I can add!"

"But can you subtract?" Arkey said. "Seems to me like those who've set their sights on stocks-n-bonds can't be too good at minusin'."

Kaney held up a paw, stopping the debate before it could go further. "There's one thing that worries me. Won't Mac Lir follow the Mooners here?"

"As to that," Ogar replied, "one of the newcomers told me they were camped in the woods just outside Wakkenburg, spread out all around the house to keep the occupants from escaping. They hardly saw Mac Lir, who stays up on Apple Hill working his weather spells. Apparently, there's so much snow and fog and hard rain that nobody can see anything, so it was easy for the horses to slip away."

"Is there a chance these new Mooners will leave us and go back to him?" Kaney asked.

"I believe they are loyal to the Silver One," Ogar said. "And there is this: If they tried to go back to Mac Lir, they would have to go on foot. Their horses have made that clear enough."

"Then the only question now is, Will the rest of the Mooners come? And how long do we wait for them to show up?"

"They'll follow their horses," said Ogar. "And the horses will all come to Peter, or I'm a Buggane."

"What do *you* say, kid?" Arkey asked.

Peter glanced up and saw everyone looking at him. Two large hornets landed in his hair, and he brushed them away for the umpteenth time. "We stay till the last Mooner comes. I don't see what the hurry is." At these words, the hornets zoomed out of the cave. Free at last from the annoyance, he looked around and saw the Poinkers gazing at him silently.

"Good!" Ogar said. "I'm delighted you're staying. After days and years of solitary watching, I shall be sad when you do go. But if you don't mind some advice, I think you should take a different way when you do depart. Not south and west to Old Road, as you planned. It's too dangerous, walking in plain sight across the pastures of the Tarroo Ushtey. Mac Lir and the Shee would spot you before you ever reached the cover of the southern woods.

"There is a path, north of here. A longer route, to be sure, but hidden. It winds through the ravines that lie between the lower foothills and the High Hills and goes all the way to the cliffs of the western seacoast. There you'll find a stairway to the giants' road, which goes south along the shore, right to the Hermit's House. I haven't been that way for ages, and the land may have changed. Do you know of this, Mr. Kaney?"

"Ah yes!" Kaney said, his eyes bright. "I'd forgotten that road. We haven't patrolled those shores for a long time. It's a good idea, Mr. Ogar."

❦ ❦ ❦

Peter rose early the next morning and found Ogar standing at the head of the valley, a safe distance from the hawthorn and the agitated hornets.

"Listen," the giant said. "Five more."

Sure enough, five white horses came galloping around the side of the hill, and one of them had a bloody gash on its flank. All the Mooners came running and took the horses away to dress their wounds and give them warm mash.

"How do they know to come here?" Peter asked.

"The Vespa are calling the creatures to you," Ogar said. "It is time."

As Peter watched the buzzing swarm, he saw several hornets separate from the rest and zoom away to the east. He tried to follow their movements, but the light of the rising sun got in his eyes.

Two Mooners arrived at supper, ragged and weary. At nightfall, three more.

Raney ticked them off on his paws. "That makes eleven, and three to go. See! I can do minusin'."

"Well, ain't that a surprise," Arkey muttered.

All the Poinkers were on edge, except for the ever-equitable Kaney. The Mooners, what with attending to the daily arrival of weary horses and comrades, had plenty to keep them occupied, but the Poinkers were restless. Peter knew they weren't used to staying in one place for long. They tried going on a patrol in the nearby hills, but the agitated Vespa followed and more than one Poinker nursed a swollen sting. There was nothing Peter could do about it, and he got some pretty dark looks.

"What's wrong with those overgrown flies?" Arkey complained. "Anyone would think they was herdin' us like sheep!"

"Well, of course they are!" Ogar replied, coming to Peter's rescue. "Here they go to all the trouble of gathering, and you Poinkers go traipsing off like ninnyheads!"

"I am not a ninnyhead!" Arkey fumed.

"Well, of course not," Ogar said. "But try to be patient. This little valley's getting crowded, and we can't afford to lose our tempers, Mr. Arkey."

When the last three horses arrived the next morning, followed by their masters at midday, Peter watched the hornets settle down quietly in the hawthorn tree. He wished to stay in the safety and peace of the giant's valley, but he was pretty sure the Vespa would soon be buzzing around his head, telling him to get moving. On a blank page at the end of Jonas' journal, he recorded the day with the stub of a pencil: five days with Ogar, and ten days since he'd left Wakkenburg.

That evening, they held a last feast before the door of Ogar's cave. For a little while, listening to the giant's tales of happier times, Peter forgot the island's trouble. As the evening waned and stars wheeled overhead, he dozed, slipping into pleasant dreams.

Sometime later, he felt someone tucking him into bed. Dad hadn't done that for a long time. He opened his eyes and, in the torchlight of the cave, saw Ogar bending over him.

"At last, this is the one," the giant said softly. "And when it's over, I will be free to go home. Soon now. Soon." The giant's voice was like the murmur of the sea, and Peter slipped into deeper dreams of water lapping the shore and Poinkers paddling little round boats upon the waves.

In the morning, thin clouds raced across a windy sky. Everyone was gathered outside the cave door, eating a hasty breakfast. Peter looked up from his bowl of porridge, and there, right at his feet, sat the white hare. As he looked into its gold-green eyes, he became aware of a sudden silence.

Then Ogar said, "Young man! What a delight to see you!" And there was the Small One, coming out the cave door, followed by the white wolf. Moody pushed his way forward and greeted his old friend.

"Silver One!" the Small One said. "I have seen the girl you seek. She is safe."

"Pixel? Where?"

"In the cave of Thrinn beyond the pastures of the Tarroo Ushtey. She is in the care of five Fennys and a Buggane."

Peter slung on his pack and picked up his staff. "Is there a path to this cave? Kaney, do you know where it is?"

"Wait a minute, Mr. Peter," Kaney said. "If we go that way, we're sure to meet the Shee."

Tom Bear lumbered over, put his nose close to Peter's, and began rumbling, but Peter thumped his staff impatiently. "I don't see why we should be afraid of the Shee. I heard there are only six of them. We outnumber them by a long way."

Ogar stood and thumped his own staff. "Didn't you hear a word the Buggane said, boy?"

"I don't speak bear." A hornet hovered down, landing on his arm. He brushed it away.

"The Buggane is right, Silver One. You cannot knowingly lead these creatures into danger," the Small One said.

"Then I'll go alone. Kaney, you can get everyone to Floden, right? I'll meet you there."

The Small One shook his head. "That is not the path appointed for you."

"I left Wakkenburg to find Pixel, and now you're telling me where she is!"

"That is not why you were led from Wakkenburg, Silver One. I have come to tell you she is safe so that you can travel with one less worry."

"Pixel is in trouble because of me. I have to take care of her!"

"That is not why you were brought to this island."

"I know why I came to this island! Because I'm a freak! These silver eyes got me in too much trouble! Everyone beat me up and my dad was sick of it, so he sent me here." Peter felt something sharp brush his cheek. The hawthorn had pushed its way through the crowd and stood beside him. The hornets sat silently in its uppermost branches, waiting. He glanced around at the solemn Poinkers and the grim faces of the Mooners, then closed his eyes to shut them out.

In the silence, a figure came into his mind: the shining warrior on the white horse who had haunted his dreams for as long as he could remember. The warrior spurred his horse and stopped, raising his sword in salute, and Peter was looking into his face. He saw the snow-white beard beneath the helm, the eyes like flame. It was like looking into the shining sun. He gasped and opened his eyes.

The Small One was watching him, his dark eyes neither accusing nor pitying. "Your friend is in the keeping of the Lady."

Peter hung his head. "Yeah. Okay. Are you going to see her again?"

The Small One nodded.

Peter took off his pack and rummaged around inside. "Will you give her this?" He handed over a little flashlight.

The Small One pushed the button. "It shines!"

"Yeah, but I'm not sure how much battery is left. Don't waste it." Peter shouldered his pack. "Will you tell her I'm alright?"

"I'll tell her."

Without another word, Peter saluted Ogar, then picked up his staff, turned his face to the north, and started walking. He didn't look back. From behind, he heard Kaney call out, "Fall in!" and then Arkey and the other Poinkers were shouting their thanks to the giant.

"Come again, my merry Poinkers!" Ogar said. "And you Mooners too! The sooner the better!"

Peter felt a nudge at his elbow, and there was Moody Doug with several hornets resting on top of his head and a bevy of little white hounds surging around his feet. Kaney and the Poinkers fell into step on his left, and the horses came trotting close behind as the Mooners shouted at them, "Hey now! Wait for us!" Peter looked straight ahead and kept walking.

As they approached the nearest hill, he finally looked back. Across the open grassland, lit by the slanting rays of the morning sun, the narrow entrance to the valley lay in shadow. He saw the figure of the Small One beside the white wolf, and the tall form of the giant standing in the gap with his arm raised in a farewell salute.

Peter raised his staff in answer, then, turning his back on the valley, walked into the shadows of the morning between the northern foothills.

32

A Winter House Party

"Pass the mince pies, Marj."

"Mince pies. It's the thirtieth of July! What are those Fennys thinking? I expect they'll want to set up the Christmas tree next."

"Well, it does look like December out there." It was early morning, four days after Ed's last visit to Foyle and the finding of Kate Rilson. The west lawn was covered in five feet of snow and had been ever since the wizard's siege began two days before. Pouring himself another cup of coffee, Ed looked up as Muru stomped into the room. "Muru! How is our little ruse goin'? Will Peter appear on the roof again today?"

"Oh sure. Furse hates having to shave his face, though. And of course, all that stage makeup is itchy. But the wig looks pretty good, don't you think?"

"It seems like a great risk to me," Marj said. "Isn't he afraid something will happen?"

"You mean a bolt of lightning? It's possible, but I don't suppose that wizard, stupid as he is, will want to zap Peter. Not when he needs to use him first."

Marj poured herself a cup of tea and stirred in a little milk. "Now, Muru, what's the news from the rest of the house?"

"Not much. Ulf keeps hanging around the kitchen, eating too many donuts. He's depressed about the state of the vegetable garden under all this snow. And with all that guard duty in foul weather, the Buggane has a head cold."

"*Can* a spider have a head cold?" Edward asked.

"Judging by the sniffling, I'd say yes. He's in one of the Rooms for Large Creatures on the second floor of the North Wing, if you want to visit him, Miss Marj."

Shaking his head, Ed watched his sister unfold a piece of paper and spread it on the table. "Whatcha got there?"

"Oh," she sighed. "It's the letter you picked up in Foyle the other day. From Peter's father. Martin asks how his son is and says, very politely, 'I'm sure he's having too good a time to write.' Oh, Ed! Peter disappeared nearly a week ago, and I've put off calling Martin because I don't know what to say! How do I explain what's happened? *And* that there's nothing to be done? He won't believe me!"

"It'll come as a blow, that's for sure. From what you've told me, Martin's already up to his neck in problems. Isn't Peter's mother in the hospital?"

"I wasn't sure what Peter meant by rehab, but Martin says here that she's in an alcohol recovery clinic. Oh! Peter told me that she was drunk most days. What a mess. And, Edward, I think Martin has lost his apartment. He doesn't say, but reading between the lines ... well, he wants mail sent to the diner. And the phone number he's given is for the diner."

"Diner?"

"That's where he works. The night shift. It's one of those twenty-four-hour restaurants."

"I thought he was a professor at the university in Lang?"

"Didn't I explain? Everything fell apart after their oldest son died."

Edward turned in his chair and looked out the French doors. Snow was falling again. "I guess you better call him, Marj. Tell him—"

From the other side of the West Wing, the telephone rang, shrill and discordant, even from a distance.

"I'll get it," Ed said, rising from the table. "If it's Martin, I'll just tell him the truth. He's a Thornburg. Father of a Silver-eyed. He may not be surprised."

Ten minutes later, Ed returned to the dining room and stood in the doorway. Muru had laid more cups and saucers on the table and poured tea into five cups, none of which was being used by anyone.

Marj turned in her chair and looked at him. "What ..." she faltered. "Ed? What is it?" She rose to her feet, and Muru paused to stare at him.

"Bad news, Marj." He drew in a deep breath. "That was George. Foyle's gone. Burned to the ground."

She gasped and sank into her chair.

"Happened four days ago. Monday night, just hours after I was there." He felt a lump rise in his throat and swallowed hard. "Whole town gone. Nothin' left."

"What about Mary? Annette?"

"They're okay. Everyone in town's alright. In Sweetwater now. Annette's already found a job."

"I ... I can hardly believe it! Foyle gone? Just like that?"

"I know. It ... it don't seem real. But that was George, callin' us from a hotel in Sweetwater. Wonders if he and Mary can come here to stay for a while. No place else to go."

"Of course! Oh!" She closed her eyes and he saw tears running down her lined face. His own eyes were wet. So much lost.

"What are you saying, Mr. Edward? You want to go to town and bring back guests?" Muru said.

"George said they lost their car, but they got quite a bit out of their apartment before it caught fire. Krim finished repairs on the hearse yesterday. I could pick them up this morning if the work crews can shovel a way out through all this snow."

"They want to live here?" Muru persisted.

"Is that alright? Since Peter opened the house, we've got plenty of room."

"Is that alright? Yes! I'll cut a way through the snow myself!" She picked up the teapot and ran out the door, crying, "Thrak! Weetha! The South Wing! We need rooms ready *today*!"

When she was gone, Ed said, "That's not all, Marj. You were wonderin' if this bad weather covered the whole island. Well, it don't. It's a perfect sunny day in Sweetwater. George said so. Not only that—there was a raid on the stores in town, just like in Foyle, but bigger. He didn't give me all the details. Then, just after I told him I'd be there in a couple of hours, our phone connection cut out. I guess with this blasted Wakkenburg winter, our lines have gone down. So you can't call Martin. Better start writin' to him now. I'll post the letter from Sweetwater."

"Oh!" she said, hurrying out of the room. "So much trouble! What's going to happen next?"

❦ ❦ ❦

That night, Ed tore along Highway 21 in the hearse, going as fast as he dared. It was nearing eleven o'clock, and he'd told Muru and Marj to expect him hours ago. The delay was the result of a dinner invitation. After George and Mary checked out of their hotel and loaded the hearse, they wanted to have supper with Annette, who got off work at five. Ed understood. George and Mary were reluctant to say goodbye and leave their only daughter in Sweetwater, where anything might happen. So here they were, speeding into the woods long after nightfall. Ed couldn't help wishing for one of the Bugganes in the back seat. There wasn't another car on the road, and the hearse's headlights did little to illuminate the dark road. He flicked on the brights, but that didn't help, except to reveal the trees reaching long arms over the tarmac.

"Does anyone know what started the fire in Foyle?" he asked.

"I told the fire chief how it started," George said. "Arson. At the Rilson house. The only surprise was how fast it spread."

"The news about Kate's secret room of ashes was all over town," Mary added. "After you left that day, Ed, people were coming into the store asking questions all afternoon." She sat huddled in the back among boxes of books and bags of clothing they'd rescued from their apartment in Foyle.

"That's right," George cut in. "Some folks were talkin' about murdered Rilson girls, puttin' that together with the long-time raids. I told 'em they weren't bein' logical, but they were spooked. Anyway, that same evening, Kate Rilson's house went up in flames. Then a big storm came along. Wind fed the fire, and driving rain put it out. But by the time the rain finally let loose, it was too late."

"Folks in town lost nearly everything they owned," Mary said. "When it was over, some took the first ferry to Lang. Others went to Sweetwater. Lucky for us, Annette was staying with the Maycap cousins, and she came down from their farm and picked us up."

"Have you heard anything about Kate Rilson?" Ed asked.

"That poor woman." Mary sighed. "She's in the psychiatric ward at the Sweetwater Hospital. I saw Cook in the shoe store the other day and she told me that Kate hasn't said a word. Just sits in a chair and stares out the window all day. At night, she has to be sedated."

"I bet Cook knows what happened to her," Ed muttered. "Or at least she's got some idea."

"Imagine her and Kate living there all that time, pretending there was nothing wrong," Mary said. "I suppose they did it for the money. Seems there was plenty of it."

Uncle Ed shook his head, thinking of poor Pixel. "And what about the raid in Sweetwater?"

"That was Wednesday night, just a couple days after we got there," Mary said quietly. "I tell you, no place feels safe anymore."

"It was a lot worse than anything I ever saw in Foyle," George added. "The supermarket must have lost ten thousand dollars' worth of goods. All those fancy little food shops on Main Street cleaned out! Who coulda done it?"

"And people disappearing too," Mary said. "From both bars and the pub. I heard there were a bunch of handsome strangers in town that night, but later, when the police were asking questions, no one could remember much about them except their looks."

"I could maybe put a name to 'em," Ed muttered under his breath, thinking of the Glashtyn. He took the speed up a notch, just to see what the old hearse could do. The engine purred as if asking for more. Krim was a genius. At the highway junction, Ed swerved to the right, onto Wakkenburg Road. Then, less than a mile from the turnoff to the house, he heard a loud thump and felt a strong vibration. The steering wheel pulled to the right as the hearse made a flapping sound. "Dang nabbit!" Letting the car slow down, he pulled her to the side of the road. "A flat tire. Just what I need," he grumbled.

"You got a flashlight?" George asked.

"In the glove box."

Ed put the hearse in park and left the engine running and the headlights on. When he looked out the windshield at the dark eaves of the forest, a strong reluctance to get out of the car took hold of him, but he gritted his teeth and opened the door. George got out too, and together they inspected the right front tire under the flashlight's beam.

"Blown it," George said. "Musta been the pothole back there. This road's pretty rough."

Ed moved to the back of the hearse and opened the rear door.

"Listen!" George hissed. "Who's that?"

Over the idling engine, Ed heard quick steps coming down the road, like bare feet slapping the pavement. Then a figure appeared in the headlights, running toward them. Ed heard Mary's muffled shriek as a man approached, waving long arms. "Go! Go!" he called out in a high, squeaky voice.

When Ed saw the pointed head and big ears, the bulbous nose and warty chin, the tension went out of his arms and legs and he leaned on the car door. "Buggane," he gasped as Tom Troll ran up.

"B-b- ... What?" George stammered, backing up, still holding the flashlight's beam on Tom's ugly face.

"Why are you stopped?" Tom Troll squeaked.

"Got a flat," Ed grunted.

"But you must fly! They are coming!"

Ed didn't ask who "they" were. He didn't want to know. Better to change the tire quickly. "George! Shine that light in here!" He pulled out the spare tire and the lug wrench, then reached for the jack. "Dang nabbit! No jack!"

"Where is he?" Tom asked.

"I dunno but I need it!"

"Why?"

"To lift this beast!"

With one hand on the bumper, Tom lifted both back tires clear off the road. George whimpered and the yellow beam wobbled. Ed glanced up and saw Mary's white face and wide eyes looking at him from the back seat.

"Yeah, yeah," he said. "Come around this side, Tom. The flat's on the front tire. Get a grip, George, and hold that light steady so I can get these lug nuts off! Mary! Turn off the engine!" He glimpsed her climbing over the seat. The headlights went out and the engine stopped.

Tom put down the back end, then went around to the front, where Ed was removing the wheel nuts. "Ah," Tom said. "I see now. The iron beast's forepaw is broken."

While Tom held the front of the hearse off the ground, Ed worked fast, his nerves on edge, alert to every rustle in the woods at his back. When he was done, Tom set the car down and, without a word, scuttled into the forest. Ed stowed the flat tire and the tools in the back, thinking maybe he'd set some kind of pit-stop record. "George! Get in, quick!" Ed jumped into the driver's seat and started the engine, and they were off, speeding down the dark road as fast as he dared on that dang spare tire.

"Ed," George said quietly, "did I hear you say 'Buggane'?"

"Yup. Guess I shoulda told you. Things are different. Since Peter came." They were approaching the last turn, and he slowed down.

"Snow!" George gasped.

"Five feet on the lawn when I left this morning. Not much here, but . . ." The hearse turned onto Wakkenburg Road and rolled over a light dusting of snow. It became deeper and deeper until the woods ended and they were confronted by a wall of white. Ed stopped the car and thumped the steering wheel. "That dang wizard!"

A strong wind swept down, whipping up flurries. Long icicles hanging from the trees shone in the headlights as small white flakes fell onto the windshield.

"Holy mackerel!" George said. "This ain't happenin'."

"And me in my sandals," Mary said, digging through a bag of clothing for socks and a sweater. "What do we do now?"

"Muru's gonna clear it. She did this morning." Ed tooted the horn a few times, and quite suddenly, the wall of snow in front of them vanished. He gunned the engine and the hearse leapt forward down a white lane. "Whoop-de-doo! Hang on tight!" He saw George clutch the dash, wide-eyed, as the hearse careened down the tunnel of snow, faster and faster. The small flakes increased and became a blizzard. Ed flipped on the wipers. "That dang wizard!"

On they went at breakneck speed. He heard George mutter something about a smashup.

"Look!" Mary cried. "Look!"

Bobbing lights came into view.

"Hold on!" With a sharp turn of the wheel, the hearse swung to the right and spun sideways. Then she righted herself and leapt forward. Small figures with lights appeared at either side of an open gate. Ed took his foot off the gas and let the car slow to a creeping pace. A large door opened and the hearse pulled sedately into a cavernous garage. He turned off the engine. Behind them, great doors slid shut on a world of furious snow.

"Who are they?" George gasped, as the garage crew opened the back of the hearse and began unloading.

"Fennys. Best darned mechanics on the island. Best cooks too."

A little later, while George and Mary were settling into the South Wing under the direction of Muru, Ed went to the kitchen and found

Tom Troll eating supper. The Buggane moved over, and Ed sat down across the table from Marj. She poured herself a cup of tea as he told her the news from Sweetwater.

"Those folks who disappeared—you really think that the Glashtyn ate them? Oh, Ed! Annette should have come!"

"I invited her. Told her to bring the cousins too, if things got bad." He turned to the Buggane. "I don't suppose you've heard anything about Peter?"

Tom looked up from his plate. "The trees have hidden the boy. You can be sure he's safe."

"I hope you're right," Marj said. "But, oh! Pixel! Is she still alive?"

"She is safe," Tom replied. "I left her with Tom a little while ago."

"What?" Ed let his mouth fall open.

"It's true. The girl escaped from the witch's house with five Fennys. Tom Mole found them in the woods. This very evening, we took them to safety, but on the way, just after sundown, the Shee came after us. I had to blow up my head, which is why you see me as I am."

"Oh!" Marj gasped, putting a hand over her mouth as tears of relief ran down her face. Ed let out a long breath.

"The girl and the Fennys went on with Tom and must have reached the haven, but I could not follow. By the time I led the Shee away and returned, the trees had hidden the path. So I came here. And a good thing! I met you on the road just in time."

"That's right!" The kitchen door banged open and Muru stomped in. "You certainly took your time getting back here, Mr. Edward."

"Now, Muru, it wasn't like that. We got a flat!"

Her voice rose. "You barely made it. Don't you know that lot will freeze your blood! They were practically on your bumper!"

"Who, Muru?" Marj said. "You mean those little men?"

"Mooners! I'm not talking about the silly Mooners! I'm talking about the Shee!"

Ed stood up. "Shee? Are you saying they're here? Now?"

"Take a look for yourself!" She stomped out of the room.

They followed her up the main stairs to the wide landing on the second floor, where a row of windows fronted the house. Candles gleamed on every sill, and by their light, Ed saw all the house Fennys gathered, grim faced and silent. Outside, ranged across the snow-covered lawn, six figures stood, dark against the wintry night. Ed shivered at the sight of the strange, menacing creatures. The blizzard had stopped, but a strong wind blew and masses of heavy clouds sped across the sky. No doubt the wizard was clearing the air to get a better view of this new challenge to his power.

"What are those ... those phantoms?" Marj whispered.

"The Lliannon Shee," Fiak said. His entire library crew stood beside him in a neat line. One of them was taking notes. "They are powerful creatures who can appear in the form of your darkest desire or your deepest sorrow. They are the offspring of Lila, and, like her, they crave the domination of all humankind. I expect the Glashtyn are here too, though they won't like this weather."

Another figure appeared, coming slowly down the snow-packed drive, riding a great black horse. It was a woman, in flowing robes of silver.

Fiak let out a low hiss and said, "The Moonwitch, I presume. Come to assault the house."

She stopped just below the windows and held up her hand palm out in a gesture of defiance. Ed shuddered as cold fear crept into the room. The candles flickered. Until this moment, he had never really believed there was a witch. Perhaps it would be wise to seek the help of Mac Lir after all.

"The witch and the Shee at the front door, Mac Lir at the back," Fiak said. "And us caught right smack in the middle."

"That's right!" Muru glared at Fiak. "No need to be glum about it. They still believe the kid is here, and we've got to keep it that way."

"Peter!" Marj exclaimed. "Of course. If they're all *here* trying to get at him, then ..."

Ed watched the witch dismount and move toward the portico. "She'll break down the door."

"Not when a Fenny has locked it," Muru snapped. She turned from the window and began issuing orders. "One of you find Furse. It's time for Peter to make an appearance. Tell Krim to get out his old catapult. And we'll need a few fireworks."

Librarians began to run this way and that. Housemaids giggled. Such a Head Fenny they had!

Ed looked down at the small, wizened face of Muru. The icy fear clutching his gut suddenly evaporated. "Just what do you have in mind, Muru?"

"I think we'll give the witch a little show, since she's come all this way. It would be a shame to disappoint her."

❦ ❦ ❦

Sure enough, as soon as Furse in his Peter wig and makeup began parading back and forth on the roof of the West Tower, the witch and her vultures drew near. Smiling to himself, Ed lit the fuses of the dynamite loaded into Krim's catapult. The trick was to time it so that they blew up the witch, but not the house or the drive. Muru had been very clear about that.

The first explosion blasted craters in the deep snow, right at the Shee's feet. Ed watched in satisfaction as the witch clung desperately to her maddened horse, screaming commands. Fiak, who had climbed the tower to record the event, whooped like a schoolboy.

After the second blast, the Moonwitch, screaming curses, gained control of her horse and rode away. The Shee simply melted into the night like shifting smoke.

"I guess we can't expect to blow up creatures like that," Ed muttered.

"But at least the witch knows she can't just walk in and take Mr. Peter," Krim said.

❦ ❦ ❦

The following day, as the weather worsened, Ed sat in the West Wing kitchen, glumly tossing pinecones into the fire. Tom Troll sat at the table, still eating sausages as if his life depended on it. The hedgehog, looking like a gray pincushion, slept beside the saltcellar, while Rumun calmly assembled sandwiches for lunch. Outside, thunder boomed and lightning flashed. Since early morning, they'd had snow, then hail, then more snow. Ed wondered how it would all end—if it ever did.

George and Mary were charmed by the Fennys, and especially by Muru, who had given them a tour of the entire house. Ed figured the Wakkenburg oddities were a good distraction from their losses in Foyle. Marj, however, was closed in her room. Ed had picked up another letter from Martin at the Sweetwater post office, where all island mail was now delivered, and the sight of the postmark had cast her into gloom.

Ed heard a loud *pop!*, and there was Tom Troll, back to his usual hairy man self.

"Ah! At last! Many thanks, Rumun," the Buggane said in his deep voice and then went on eating.

The very next morning, when Ed woke, he threw off the covers in spite of the biting cold, shuffled to the window, and drew the curtains. It was so dark he couldn't see anything but the sill. "Fog! That dang wizard!"

"This is not fog, Mr. Edward." Startled, Ed turned and saw Rumun kneeling at the grate, lighting a fire. "This is the dark of the Lliannon Shee. Soon they will bring down the deep cold." He stood up. "The coffee is ready, and your sister is waiting at the breakfast table." He bowed, then left the room.

Ed dressed quickly, in his warmest clothes, and went downstairs, straight to the dining room.

"Oh, Edward! Isn't this darkness awful?" Marj wore a fantastic array of sweaters and scarves layered one on top of the other. The dining room was lit by a multitude of candles, and a fire burned in the hearth.

"What's happened to the electricity?"

"Muru says the power lines have gone down and Krim's having trouble with the generator."

Grunting, Ed helped himself to coffee, thankful that the lack of electricity had not slowed things down in the kitchen. At the sideboard, he piled his plate with donuts and fried eggs and sat down at the table. "Are George and Mary up?"

"Muru took breakfast to their rooms. I'm just glad their suite overlooks the central courtyard. Maybe they won't see the faces."

"Faces?"

She pointed at the French doors behind him and he turned to look. "Mom!" he gasped.

There was Mother, standing outside, covered in white frost. Her mouth moved, and though he couldn't hear her voice, he knew she was begging to be let in out of the freezing cold. He stood up and moved toward the door.

"No, Ed!" Marj cried. "Mother is dead!"

He reached for the doorknob as a stern voice said, "Don't open it, Mr. Edward." Rumun appeared at his side and pulled the curtains over the glass, shutting out Mother's face. "The Shee are trying to get inside this house, but they can enter only if invited. They are using all their powers of deception."

Ed looked down at Rumun's solemn face. "I ... I think I'll go to my study." He went back to the table and picked up his coffee cup, but his hand shook, so he put it down and walked out.

His study was dark and cold, and his dead brother's face looked in the window. He shut the door and stood in the front hall, blinking. The West Wing kitchen would be safe. There'd be a fire on the hearth and the company of Fennys. He turned, and there in the small window on one side of the front door, he saw his father's face, white with frost. As he stared at the apparition, it changed, and he saw Mae Rilson. When little Jenny appeared, crying in the snow, he turned his eyes away and walked blindly through the hall and into the sitting room.

Marj sat near the fire, reading by the light of a candle. She looked up from her book but didn't say anything. Ed sat down on the other end of the sofa, opened a newspaper, and held it in front of his face. All morning, Fennys came and went, tending the sitting-room fire, lighting more and more candles all around the room as the darkness of the Shee seeped in through the cracks. Now and then, Ed looked up and noticed one housemaid or another, standing very still, with a box of matches, or a duster in one hand, gazing helplessly at a window. He wondered what they saw.

Finally, Muru stomped into the sitting room. "Those darn Shee!" she fumed. "If we're not careful, they'll notice the kid isn't in the house. I had to make Furse dress up again and sit in the kitchen. He gets grumpy when he has to shave his face!" She ran around the room, yanking down blinds, then stormed out.

"Why didn't we think of that?" Marj said.

Ed folded his paper and tossed it onto the table. "Them Shee appear as our fondest wish, and who's ever strong enough to shut that out? But I tell you, this ain't my idea of how to spend a Sunday morning!"

He was about to get up and leave when George and Mary came in, bundled up in winter clothes. They sat down on the other sofa, closer to the hearth.

"Muru told us you two were in here," George said. "Some fog out there, eh? And I think there's a blizzard goin'!"

"Oh!" Mary said, rubbing her hands together. "The island never gets cold like this, not even in the middle of winter."

Suddenly realizing just how cold it had become and that he could see George and Mary's breath as they spoke, Ed got up and put another log on the fire.

"We need more layers!" Marj said and hurried out the door. A few minutes later, she returned with an armful of heavy coats. Behind her, a house Fenny came in with a pile of hats and mittens.

Ed put on his thickest jacket and pulled a knitted cap over his head, but it didn't help much. "I had no idea things would turn out like this when I picked you up in Sweetwater," he said.

"It's alright." George helped Mary into a wool coat. "One of the Fennys explained everything."

Before Ed could ask which Fenny and what had been explained, Muru bustled in, followed by Fiak.

"Yes, yes, I know! I don't need you to tell me, Fiak. It's getting colder, and you can thank the Shee." She stopped in the middle of the room with her hands on her hips. "Tea will be served," she snapped.

Ed shrugged. Could be time for elevenses. Without daylight, it was impossible to know for sure.

Marj glanced at him sideways. "Thank you," she said uncertainly.

Thunder boomed over the house and everyone jumped.

"Good grief!" George exclaimed. "That was close!"

"Ooh! That wizard!" Muru seethed and stormed out of the room.

"This," Fiak said, with the air of a professor addressing his pupils, "is a classic case of the struggle for power between two opposing forces."

"Classic!" Ed flinched as another roll of thunder sounded. "I'd like to know what's classic about a weather war!"

"Weather war! That's it!" Fiak whipped out a pen and notebook and began to scribble furiously. "Thanks, Mr. Edward. I've been trying to think of a title for this chapter." Then he took a large thermometer out of his breast pocket. "We are now at minus fifteen degrees and falling," he announced.

The very air in the room seemed to darken as a wild wind whined through the rafters. Mary moaned, pulling her heavy coat closer.

"Minus twenty," Fiak said.

"Bet my nose is blue," Ed grumbled, stuffing his hands into his pockets. "Here I am wearing three sweaters and a coat indoors. In the middle of July! That dang wizard!"

He stood up and stamped his feet. Marj was pacing back and forth before the French doors, muttering words in connection with the Shee, words she didn't normally use in polite company.

"Minus twenty-five," Fiak announced.

Muru came rattling into the room pushing a loaded tea cart.

"Get out the tea table!" she barked. Five house Fennys dashed into the room, pulled a low table before the fire, spread a cloth, and dashed out again. Two kitchen Fennys came in bearing plates of cakes and biscuits. Muru laid out cups and saucers for twelve.

"Muru," Marj said, hesitating, "are we expecting company?"

"No. Milk and sugar?"

"Minus thirty," Fiak said, his eyes on the thermometer as the mercury plunged with each passing moment.

Ed watched as Muru tried to pour milk from a jug. Of course, its contents were frozen solid.

"Those darn Shee!" She scowled and tried pouring tea from the pot, but the tea was frozen too. Thumping the pot down on the table, she stomped her foot. "Oooh! I hate it when this happens." She glared at the teapot and jug, her eyes blazing with anger.

"Minus forty and falling," Fiak said, in the tone of a station master announcing the arrival and departure of trains. He was wearing neither coat nor mittens. Ed wondered how he could stand the cold in just his shirtsleeves. It was the same with Muru, who wore a short-sleeved dress under her apron.

Suddenly, Muru picked up the teapot and began pouring tea. Ed watched in amazement as steam rose from the cup. She handed it to Mary, who said thank you without noticing the impossibility.

"Minus fifty!" Fiak said.

"Ooh! That's torn it!" Muru seethed. "Much too cold!" She waved a hand as if swatting away a fly, and the candles seemed to burn more brightly.

Fiak looked from the thermometer to Muru, his eyes widening. "Minus thirty now and holding."

A roll of thunder shook the house, then another. Muru stamped her foot in fury, then poured another cup of tea.

"Thank you," George said, taking the cup from her. He set it down and held his mittened hands over the rising steam.

Muru poured tea for Marj, and the darkness at the windows turned a murky gray. Then, as she poured a cup for Ed, he said, "I don't suppose you've got any coffee?"

"Coffee? No!" She glared at him, and he meekly took his cup of milky tea. The howling wind died and there was a moment of silence.

"Minus—"

"Oh, cork it, Fiak! Go tell Furse to get off his duff and start clearing up all this snow. We should be able to look out the first-floor windows, you know."

Fiak ran off, leaving his thermometer behind. Ed picked it up. The mercury was now at zero degrees.

Muru poured a fifth cup of tea, and the light in the windows brightened noticeably. "Well? Aren't you going to eat something?" she said, glaring at the pile of cakes.

Marj took off her mittens and filled a plate. "Thank you, Muru. I *am* hungry."

"Ten degrees above zero," Ed said, winking at Muru. He took off his coat and helped himself to a large slice of gingerbread. "Mary, try these coconut biscuits. We call 'em Little Snowballs."

"Snowballs! Oooh! That darn wizard!" Muru poured four more cups of tea.

Ed handed the thermometer to George, then took off his cap and peeled away two sweaters.

"Look, Mary. This is a Celsius thermometer. Says thirteen now. A few more degrees and it'll be spring again." George helped her take off her coat. Laughing, she unwrapped layers of scarves and pulled off three sweaters.

"At last!" Marj threw her winter coat on a chair. "I wondered just how far you'd let them push you, Muru."

"Listen! What's that noise?" Mary said. It sounded like a thousand mice pattering across a wooden floor.

"Rain," Muru snapped. "As if we haven't had enough weather." She poured more tea. Mary tried to drink each cup, either to be polite or because she was terribly thirsty, but as soon as she emptied a cup, Muru filled it again.

Then, from somewhere overhead came a tremendous grinding sound. Ed heard someone outside shout, "Look out below!" Ulf appeared at the French doors, his small frame squeezed between the snow and the glass. Springing to the door, Ed opened it, and Ulf tumbled inside, along with a mountain of snow.

"Thrak! Weetha!" Muru called. "Get this mess cleaned up!" Two Fennys ran in with shovels and buckets and began clearing the snow from the sitting-room floor.

Ed helped Ulf to his feet and made him drink a cup of tea.

"The snow on the roof came down all of a piece," the little gardener said. "A great wide slab."

"Ulf! You're dripping all over the carpet!" Muru snapped.

"Well, of course I am," he snapped back. "You would be too if you were ordered to go outside and clear six feet of slushy snow in a thaw!"

Ed gave him another cup of tea and a piece of pink cake.

Ulf winked at him and gulped down the tea. "By the way," he said in an undertone, "that little tree never did come back."

"Peter's tree?"

"Furse told me that you and him let it out the big gate on the same day Mr. Peter disappeared. I think it went after the boy."

"No kiddin'!"

"I wish it well, being a gardener and all, but I sure won't miss it tearing up the flower beds."

All at once, the room grew brighter as the snow that had been banked against the house fell from the windows. Outside, it was a clear day.

"Shall I put out the candles?" George asked.

Marj threw off the last sweater she was wearing. "Thank you! I think the snuffer is on the mantle."

Ed watched Muru, who was still pouring tea with furious concentration, though Mary had ceased to drink it. One of the house Fennys set out fresh cups and saucers as fast as Muru poured from her seemingly bottomless pot.

"It's stopped raining!" said Mary, looking out at the west lawn. "But look there—at the edge of the woods beyond the wall. It's still dark. And snowing!"

"How can it be sunny here and stormy less than half a mile away?" George said.

"Well, I can't be responsible for every square foot of this island," Muru snapped. "Ulf! Don't you have something to do besides dripping on the carpet?"

"Can *you* see the flower beds yet? When I can see the flower beds, then I'll be out there doin' my job." He winked at Ed, gave him his teacup, and left the room.

"See? See what all this has done?" Muru said, glaring after him. "Everyone grumpy and all I get is back talk. Ooh! I'd like to give that witch and wizard a piece of my mind!" She thumped the teapot down on the table, took hold of the cart, and stormed out of the room. Thrak looked around in surprise, then stacked all the extra teacups on a tray, picked it up, and ran out.

Tentatively, George lifted the lid of the teapot. "Empty," he said and picked up another biscuit.

"I'm going to my room." Marj picked up a pile of coats and sweaters. "I have got to take off these wool socks and find my sandals!"

❦ ❦ ❦

By late afternoon, the snow was gone. Ed stood on the patio holding a glass of lemonade and looking across the green lawn. Bees buzzed around new blossoms on the lilac tree, and yellow poppies nodded on the borders of the grass. Flowers of a second spring seemed to open as he watched, but beyond the west wall, the snow-covered forest was still shrouded in the Shee's clinging darkness.

For the rest of the day, bolts of lightning flashed over Apple Hill, and the woods all around the house writhed in the storm. It was too much for George and Mary. They spent the rest of the day in the South Wing, looking out the windows at the peaceful, sunny orchard, or walking in the Rose Garden, where the outside world was not visible. Ed understood and left them alone.

Sometime before midnight, he looked out his bedroom window. The woods were wrapped in darkness, but there was no snow, no rain. He padded downstairs to the sitting room and found Marj stoking the fire. She nodded to him but did not speak. He went through the French doors and stood on the patio. The night sky to the west was clear and full of stars. A warm breeze touched his cheek and stirred the lilac tree, but a thick mist sat on Apple Hill. He returned to the sitting room. "That wizard's up to something."

"I know. And the Bugganes are gone. Oh, Ed, I wish we knew what's happening."

Neither of them could sleep. They spent the small hours of the morning by the fire, waiting for something, though they didn't know what. Then, just before dawn, Ed said, "Let's go see the sunrise."

They went out the sitting-room doors, crossed the lawn to the outbuildings, and walked through the courtyard to Glenny Pond. The air was still, with only the slight chill that comes before daybreak. Darkness hung over the land, but the morning star shone brightly. The weather war was over.

"I'd like to see the light come over the eastern sea," Marj said. "I wish we were up on the hill."

"Me too, but not for that reason."

"Give Mac Lir a piece of your mind, would you?"

They stood at the edge of the pond as the darkness lightened ever so slowly. Then, all at once, the birdsong began.

"Remember that time Patrick pushed you into the water?" she said. "Told Father he was teaching you to swim."

"I remember. And the nurses used to bring Mother out to hear the birds."

"Yes. Before she died. You were only eight. And remember— What's that? Is it a tree branch? There, hanging over the big gate."

Ed turned to look. The Door for Large Creatures was a hundred yards away, and nothing was clear in the twilight.

"Look, Ed. It's moving!"

"That's a spider leg!"

They began to run. Before they reached the gate, a large bundle wrapped in spun silk came flying over the wall. With a thump and a muffled cry, it landed in the grass. It looked like a giant grub, wriggling and twisting on the ground.

"Oh! It's caught something!"

"Some*one*. Wearin' a hat."

Ed tugged the gate open, and the giant spider came in, clacking its jaws rapidly. To Ed's amazement, Marj began to translate. Evidently she'd been spending more time with Tom Spider than he knew. But the tale that unfolded was even more surprising.

As soon as the storm cleared, both Bugganes had gone out to gather news. Tom Spider, disguised as a dung beetle, climbed up through the mist on Apple Hill and found the wizard sitting in a clearing before a small fire. The Buggane hid in a tuft of grass and waited to see what would happen. Sometime after midnight, an old man stumbled into camp. The wizard seemed to know him, called him "Witch's Man", and gave him a purple flask, from which he drank greedily. The old man told Lir a long, rambling tale about traveling with the Silver Boy into the mountains. According to his account, he'd been taken prisoner by the boy, a vicious dog, and a band of savage porcupines who'd tried to feed him to the trolls. After that, he'd been force-marched to a place called Ogar's Valley, where he'd seen a person who "wasn't natural". At the description of this person, the wizard began to ask many questions but could get no more than "He's a fiend! But I escaped! Been on the run for days!" Finally, an hour before dawn, the Witch's Man fell asleep and the wizard walked away northward into the mist. Then Tom changed into a spider, wrapped the Witch's Man in sticky threads, and carried him away.

"Oh, Ed," Marj said, when the spider stopped clacking, "do you realize what this means? The wizard knows! He's gone after Peter!"

"Witch's Man." Ed crouched beside the inert bundle. "I wonder." Pulling away the webbing from the man's face, he gasped. "Mac Rilson!"

"You lemmee go! I ain't done nothin'!" Mac swore, struggling against his bonds, and Ed pulled the web back over his mouth.

Suddenly, a strong breeze kicked up, scattering dry leaves. The gate creaked and the hairy man stepped through. "Foolish to leave the gate open!" the Buggane said, pulling it shut and fastening the bolt. "Foolish with the Shee so close. I have seen them! On Apple Hill! The Moonwitch tried to ambush Lir's camp, Tom! You narrowly escaped!"

The great spider clacked its jaws and cowered.

"Never mind! You have the Witch's Man, I see. That is good. She knows he was on the hill with Lir and has given orders to kill him on sight." At this news, Mac Rilson stopped wiggling and lay very still. "She also believes the wizard has captured the Silver One and has sent the Shee in pursuit."

"You followed the witch to Apple Hill?" Ed said. "Didn't she see you?"

"I was a tiny sparrow, hidden in the leaves of a berry bush. We Bugganes leave neither track nor scent." He paused and looked down at the wormlike form of Mac Rilson. "This man has done much harm. What will you do with him?"

"Lock him in the tower." Edward said this for Mac's benefit and was rewarded by the wild squirming of the prisoner.

"I suppose Muru will know what to do with him," Marj said.

"Yes! I suppose she will!" said a loud voice. It was Muru, headed toward them like a battleship at full throttle. A crowd of gardeners followed her. They glanced nervously at the giant spider, but no doubt they'd follow their Head Fenny into a dragon's lair.

"Muru," Edward said, "allow me to introduce our newest guest. This is Mac Rilson, otherwise known as the Witch's Man. Rilson, this is Muru, our warden."

The figure on the ground lay very still.

Muru wrinkled her nose. "He smells like a rotten pickle. Take him to the West Wing and put him in the infirmary." The gardeners hoisted the inert bundle onto their shoulders and bore him away.

Then she said to the giant spider towering over her head, "Make yourself small, for goodness' sake! Don't try getting into the kitchen like that!" And she marched back to the house. Before she was out of sight, Tom Spider had changed into a small hedgehog. Marj picked it up. "At least you're over that head cold."

"Where are you going?" Edward said, as the hairy man drew back the bolt on the gate.

"I must keep watch on our enemies." He saluted and let himself out the Door for Large Creatures.

Ed fastened the bolt, then looked around as the light in the east spread across the sky. Overhead, a seagull called as the summer dawn unfolded in shades of green and gold. It felt like the ominous calm before an approaching storm.

33

Three Enemies and a Cat

Peter squeezed his eyes shut to block out the hornet circling his head and calculated the date. The seventh of August. He'd been away from Wakkenburg for two weeks. He took out his pencil stub and made a note in the journal. Then, unfolding Jonas' map, he put his finger on a spot to the southwest of Mount Rosknil. For five days now, they'd been walking at the bottom of a narrow gulch with the lower foothills on the left and the steeply wooded High Hills on the right.

"I think we're right about here," he said to Moody, making a little x. "Getting near the coast."

Moody thumped his tail, flicking off the hornets trying to settle on his rump.

Between the horses, which needed time to graze, and the Poinkers, who insisted on time to cook, their progress was slow. At least that's how it seemed to Peter. Time was of little importance to these creatures. They lived from one full moon to the next, taking the seasons as they came. There was no telling how long this roundabout route to Floden might take.

Their path lay beside a rushing stream, so water wasn't a problem, but food was getting low. Though the hounds were always tearing off, chasing anything that moved, they had found neither ducks nor rabbits—not even a chipmunk in this region tucked between the hills.

The midday sun slanted straight into the canyon, and Peter's shirt clung damply to his chest. The hornet circling his head landed on his arm, and another buzzed loudly in his left ear. "Alright! Alright!" He snapped the journal shut, folded the map, and stuffed them into his pack. Getting to his feet, he picked up his staff and signaled the company. The hawthorn, which stood at the stream with its roots in the water, rattled its branches, and two crows—messengers sent by Trelly the troll—flapped up from the rocks and perched in its branches.

"I thought maybe we was gonna camp here," Arkey said, coming up beside Peter.

"Not unless you want to get stung by a hornet."

Shouldering his pack, he moved forward, following Kaney. By now, he'd grown accustomed to long hikes, and anyway, it was easier to think while he walked, easier to hear the murmur of distant trees growing on the heights above the gulch. In sudden eddies of wind that sometimes swept through the canyon, he heard their talk of starlight and weather and secret springs of clear water.

They were coming to the end of the narrow ravine now. Looking back, he saw the company strung out behind for some way, with Tom Bear bringing up the rear. After a while, the path began to climb, ascending slowly until, in the late afternoon, Kaney led them up a steep, rocky slope onto a tableland. Except for a lone tree, it was covered in scrub grass. To the left, wooded slopes spread out below them, and on the right, a gray cliff wall rose above the plateau, the last bastion of the High Hills. Straight ahead, to the west, stretched the blue-gray line of the sea, still some miles distant.

"Well now," Kaney said, "seems like we ought to be looking out for some place to spend the night."

"What about over there, under that tree?" Peter suggested.

"A Tramman tree," Kaney said. "I've never seen such a big one growing south of Mount Greeba."

After hours of traveling in the hot sun, Peter was glad to get into the shade of the huge tree. Yet when the Mooners tried to lead the horses under its branches, they reared up, pulling away from their masters. The two crows squawked loudly and flapped off toward the mountains. Then the hounds began to whine, and even Moody would not go near.

"Sorry, Mr. Peter," Rathfrit said. "I don't know why they're so spooked."

"Never mind," Kaney said. "We'll set up camp under the cliff, if that's alright with you, Mr. Peter."

"Sure." Peter thought he should help with the cooking, but they probably didn't need him, and a shady place apart from yipping hounds and bickering Poinkers suited him very well. He watched the

Mooners lead the horses and hounds away, the Poinker band trailing behind. Yawning, he sat down on the soft moss beneath the tree, leaned back against the broad trunk, and drifted off to sleep.

He woke suddenly, with a loud buzzing in his ears, and sat up. There were no hornets around. The sun had dipped below the rim of the sea, and beyond the deep shade cast by the tree, a gentle twilight covered the land. Then he felt a tremor in the earth.

Mac Lir appeared in the shadows, transparent, bent over the ground, a ghostly glimmer of water at his feet. He moved slowly along a riverbank, tracking something. Then the land began to race by, blown by some otherworldly wind, and Peter saw Lir on the rocks beneath Spoot Voor Falls. The scene flowed away, and there was Mac Lir standing at the entrance to Ogar's Valley. Then the wizard began to run.

His heart racing, Peter grabbed the Lady's staff and jumped to his feet. All around him leaves rustled, and a voice said, "I see you, Silver One. I see you! How dare you run from the one who can save us! It's not too late! He is coming."

The tree began to sway. Giant, snakelike roots seethed under his feet. One of them wrapped itself around his ankle, and he felt it pulling him into the earth. With all his strength, he struck the root with his staff.

Instantly, the tree was gone—roots, trunk, branches, all. Breathing hard, Peter found himself looking at the starlit sky. A lone hound began to yap, and there was a sudden burst of laughter from the camp.

"Oh, my beasty bones! Oh, my shriveled stumpers!"

Startled, Peter looked around and saw a little man rolling on the ground a few feet away, dressed in a tweed suit, of all things.

"What a walloping wallop! What a whack to the windpipe! Oh!" Abruptly, the man sat up. His face was craggy and clean-shaven, with a hooked nose. "What's your name, boy?"

"What's *your* name?" Peter frowned at the neatly combed hair, the bulging eyes alight with cunning.

"Ah!" The man sprang to his feet and rubbed his hands together. "How about a little wager, sonny? Winner keeps that little stick of yours and—"

Moody came charging from the camp with the entire company in his wake. Springing to Peter's side, he snarled, and all the Mooner hounds surrounded the little man, baring their teeth. Tom Bear sat down outside the ring of dogs, rumbling in anger. Then a great shout echoed in the High Hills. Into the night came the sound of tramping feet. Big feet, heavy feet. The little man whimpered, "Oh, my hairs and straws! Oh, my feckless little frittles!"

"Trolls!" Arkey hissed.

Indeed, it was the trolls. They came tramping down from the cliff onto the scrubland, like a slow-moving avalanche of living stone. The crow messengers rode high on Trelly's shoulders. Stopping before the company, Trelly thumped his chest. "Silver One! The crows tell us you're bound for Floden."

Peter looked up at the towering figures, feeling very small, but he thumped his chest and nodded.

"They also say you may be in trouble, and we have come to your aid." Then Trelly looked at the little man cowering near Peter's feet, and his face became very ugly. "What is this?" He bent down until his face was level with the tweedy man. "Garool?" At this name, the Poinkers and Mooners began to mutter.

"Now, boys," the little man said, through chattering teeth, "I never meant no harm. I never meant nothing by it. It was just a silly jewel!"

"Silly jool, my eye! You robbed us!" Trelly swelled with anger. "We made that jool for Mother Moon, and you stole it for the wizard!"

The other trolls began to grumble and growl. One of them lifted a club and said, "We been lookin' for *you*!"

Tom Bear snarled and Trelly shouted, "A tree? You been hidin' right here as that old Tramman tree?"

"Listen, boys! It was a long time ago!" the little man whined.

Trelly slammed his club down next to Garool's head, and the earth shook. "Well now. We got our jool back," the troll said in a soft, menacing voice that made the hair on Peter's arms rise. "But what I want to know is, what are you doin' here with the Silver One?" He looked at Peter, and his face was far from friendly.

Before Peter could open his mouth, the little man vanished and the great Tramman tree towered above the trolls, its roots writhing. Lashing the air, its branches drove the trolls back, scattering Poinkers and Mooners. Horses screamed; dogs yowled. With a deafening roar, Tom Bear made a rush for the tree's trunk, but an enormous root wrapped itself around his throat and began to squeeze. As thick roots coiled around Peter's legs, he mustered all his strength and thumped the staff down hard.

In an instant, the world went still. The tree was gone. The little man lay at his feet, moaning in pain. "Moody," Peter commanded. The great dog leapt up and stood over Garool, his jaws at the little man's throat.

The trolls picked themselves up off the ground, muttering. Trelly, who had a nasty cut on his forehead, glared at Peter. Then, into the ominous silence, the crows flapped down onto Peter's shoulders. One of them uttered a low squawk.

"Is he your prisoner?" Trelly said, pointing to the little man.

Peter nodded. "Yeah."

"Do you know who he is?"

"One of the Bugganes."

Tom Bear snarled, and Kaney said, "Mr. Peter, I do believe this particular Buggane is in the same class as our Freddey: a low-down skunk. We used to call him Garool the Great."

The bear snarled again, and Kaney said, "Well, I heard that too. He's very powerful in his way and helped Mac Lir drive the Shee out of the woods during the last trouble. I suppose he's useful. If you can trust him."

In spite of the bared teeth inches from his neck, the little man had not lost his look of cunning. Peter suspected that he was not at all afraid of Moody. He was only afraid of the Lady's staff. Twice now it had stopped him in his tracks. No doubt he'd like to get his hands on it.

"Come now, boy," Garool said softly. "You can't run from Mac Lir."

"I'm not."

"Then what are you doing out here, leading the wizard's folk astray? Gone and joined the Moonwitch, have you? I bet she's the one who gave you that stick!"

"You're out of your reckoning, Mr. Garool," Rathfrit said. "We don't want Mac Lir or the witch. We've joined Mr. Peter here because he's willing to lead us against them."

"Aye, aye," the trolls rumbled.

"Against Mac Lir *and* the Moonwitch?" Garool laughed. "You think you can take on the ancient powers in these woods by following a boy with a magic stick?"

"The real question is what we're to do with this Buggane," Kaney said. "It seems clear to me that he'll be off to find the wizard the moment we turn our backs."

Peter saw the look of hatred, mingled with fear, on Garool's face. Still, for the sake of the Lady's command, he had to try. "Join us," he said simply.

With a puff of smoke, the little man vanished. Everyone gasped, and the trolls began to grumble and growl. Peter thumped the staff on the ground. "Trelly," he called out, "we're taking a route along the coast. Are you coming with us?"

"We can't walk in daylight. We'll follow you in our own way. Goodbye for now, Silver One. Until we meet in Floden!" He thumped his chest and bowed, and the trolls marched back to the mountains.

The next morning, Peter woke to a faint buzz in his ears, like radio static. Kaney and Rathfrit had roused the company early, and the Poinkers were making porridge with the last of the oats. A thin fog lay over the land. Rathfrit attributed the turn of weather to Mac Lir. "Let us be off!" he said. "I do not wish to linger in this place."

"Hey! What's with Trelly's crows?" Arkey cried. They were squawking and flapping around an old log that lay a little apart from the camp, pecking at it savagely.

"Rathfrit's right," Kaney said. "I think we'll all feel better when we've gotten away from this place."

Quickly, they broke camp. As Peter slung on his pack and picked up the staff, the static in his head increased until even Arkey's voice had a muffled sound. Gritting his teeth, he followed Kaney.

As soon as they climbed down from the plateau, the static in his head cleared. All that day, they walked the northwest reaches, a flat country of low gray bushes and few trees. There was no path in that gray waste. Kaney led them forward, trusting his native Poinker instincts because the mist never lifted. It blotted out hills, mountains, the sea, anything that might tell them their direction. Then, in the late afternoon, the mist turned to heavy rain, and they spent a miserable night huddled under a thicket of brambles. The fire would not light, everything was damp, and no one had quite enough to eat.

Sometime after midnight, as he lay on the hard ground, Peter fell into a dream. He was in a cove of dark water surrounded by sheer cliffs. Near the water's edge, a dead deer lay on a rock, and high above, a woman with long raven hair stood at the top of the precipice. The sea began to churn, and rising waves slapped the sides of the secret inlet. Then a tremendous, snakelike head erupted from the water, opening jaws of spear-like teeth. Calling to the beast in a shrill voice, the woman picked up something from the ground near her feet and swung it over the water. Peter saw the thing falling, legs splayed, right into the sea monster's cavernous mouth. The woman tossed another dead creature over the cliff, and another. The monster clashed its teeth and, spying the dead deer on the rock, lunged. Peter woke up shouting.

Poinkers and Mooners leapt to their feet. Hounds began to bark. When the company heard that he'd only been dreaming, they lay down again, grumbling. Only Arkey said, "Somethin's comin', ain't it? Get some rest, kid. I'll keep watch." Peter went back to sleep with his head on Moody's flank and the Lady's staff in his hand.

The morning brought more mist and steady rain. Kaney led them northwest in nearly a straight line. He was making for a small grove of arbutus trees that marked the stairs that led down to the giants' road. "If this confounded fog would lift, we could probably see those trees from here," he said. "We've got to find them. Otherwise, we'll have to walk in the open, all the way to Floden, for there isn't another way down to the shore until you get to the Hermit's House."

When they arrived at the edge of the bluff, there wasn't a tree in sight, large or small. Peter could hear the surf far below, but the whole world was gray, and it was hard to see anything in the driving rain.

After a short debate, Kaney decided to send scouting parties for two miles in either direction. Peter suggested Tom Bear until he realized no one had seen him since their camp on the plateau. So Rathfrit took a party of Mooners on horseback south along the bluff. Kaney and Arkey went north perched on Moody's back.

After a while, the rain stopped and Peter sat on the edge of the cliff, kicking his heels on the rock. Then he saw Rathfrit and his men returning. They had not found the stairs, but as Peter stood talking with them, a shout rang out, and a happy bark. Moody and the two Poinkers appeared out of the mist.

"Found them trees!" Arkey exclaimed. "Hardly a mile away!"

The company set off again, Kaney leading the way at a brisk pace. Halfway there, Peter felt something sharp in his shoe and dropped back to take it out. Moody grunted and sat down beside him. Struggling with the waterlogged lace of his sneaker, he glanced up as the Mooners, who were bringing up the rear, disappeared into the fog. By the time he got the rock out of his shoe, he could no longer hear the yipping hounds. He and Moody started off again, listening to the booming surf on the fogbound shore.

At last, he saw half a dozen red trees growing right at the edge of the bluff. Must be the ones Kaney meant. Then Moody began to growl. From somewhere farther ahead, a shrill voice rose out of the fog, and he heard the clop of many hooves. A whip cracked. The Mooners didn't use whips.

With a low woof, Moody leapt over the edge of the cliff. Peter scrambled to the brink between two trees, looked down, and saw a long stairway. It was carved into the side of the rock, made for people with longer legs than his. Moody waited below.

The horses were close now, though still hidden by mist. Clutching his staff, Peter jumped to the first stair, slipped on wet stone, lost his balance, and went tumbling down. He would certainly have dropped to his death, but Moody blocked his fall and grasped him by the belt. As he got to his feet, a shower of rocks and dirt cascaded over the ledge as a mass of moving roots tore up the top step. The hawthorn lurched out of the mist right above his head. Into his mind came the command "Hide!"

Horses whinnied. A woman shouted, "Korman! The wizard's cat! There in that tree! Catch him!"

Peter pressed himself against the rock. Twigs snapped.

Above him, a gruff voice swore, and a man said, "It has climbed out of reach! And I'll swear this tree lashed me with its branches!"

"Are you men or are you Glashtyn?" the woman shrieked. "Get that cat! I must return with a prize. Mother is angry. She says it's my fault we lost the Silver Boy."

Glashtyn! This must be the Moonwitch, right above his head! Peter glanced at Moody, who stood still as stone.

"Your mother does not appear pleased with all you have done, my lady. And if the Shee do not find Lir and capture the Silver One, your father will need feeding."

"Curse you, Korman! I don't need to be reminded!"

"And yet," Korman said in a softer voice, "there may be another way. Perhaps your ladyship should join the wizard."

There was a long pause; then the witch said, "That thought is also in my mind."

"I have no doubt that, together, you and the wizard could drive your mother and father from the island. After that, it would be easy to wrest the Silver Boy from Mac Lir. With our help."

"You have read my very thoughts, Korman. How clever of you. But how shall this be done?"

"We should go east, my lady. It is in the bay below the cliffs of Fenn House that Mac Lir keeps his ship. We must speak with him before he sails for Cwenburgh, as he surely will."

"And the Shee? We are to meet them in Floden tomorrow."

"They are your mother's slaves."

"True enough! Let us ride south with all haste and take the Old Path east. It is the quickest way to Fenn House. Goodbye, kitty!" the witch called out. "We go to your master. Shall we give him your greeting?"

A cat yowled and hissed. Then the witch gave a shrill command, and the horses galloped away.

Peter slumped down on the step, trembling, as fear drained away. A little brown wren landed beside his shoe. It twittered and Moody grunted. Then it hopped down to the next step, and *pop!*, there was Tom Bear, rumbling, pawing the ground. The hawthorn sent down a shower of thorny sticks.

"Okay, okay," Peter said. He got up and followed the Buggane and Moody down the long flight of stairs.

At the bottom, he saw the beginning of the giants' road, cut deep into the rocky cliff so that it lay under a wide overhang, out of the rain. On the right, three feet below the path, sea grass grew against the cliff, but a heavy mist sat on the shore, blotting out a view of the beach.

Half a mile from the stairs, they found the rest of the company in a wide, airy cavern, preparing supper over a small fire. Peter stumbled in behind Moody, sat down, and let his pack slide off his shoulders. Hounds skittered back and forth across the stony floor, chasing rumors of mice, and no one paid him any mind until Arkey looked up from the cooking pot and said, "Hey, kid! What took you so long?" Then Tom Bear began to rumble. As the tale of the witch unfolded, everyone gathered around.

"Cripes! That was a close shave, kid!" Arkey said. "We shouldn't ever let you out of our sight!"

"Still, no harm done," Kaney mused, "and now we know her plans. Who would have thought? The witch gone off to join Lir! Goodness knows, those two deserve each other."

"But the cat in the tree is undoubtedly Tufkals," Rathfrit said. "I remember when he parted from Mac Lir, just after the witch's last uprising, and on the very day the Silver Girl went missing. The wizard was in a terrible mood. Slammed the door on the cat's tail and cut it clean off."

"Poor, poor Tuffy," Kaney said. "In my opinion, Mac Lir hasn't come up to snuff since. That cat's got more power in him than ... well, certainly more than the wizard has now."

"I agree," Rathfrit said. "But Tufkals is ashamed of his missing tail, I think. Keeps to himself. Sometimes he shows up at our campfire and begs a little food. Always polite, though I doubt he'll ever trust anybody again."

The company sat down to a supper of stale bread and a thin soup made of dried peas and shriveled apples. Rations were certainly low, but the Poinkers spoke of clamming and fishing along the coast, hoping for heartier meals in the days to come. After that, they all sat around in companionable silence, warm and snug for the first time in days. The fire burned low, and one by one, they dropped off to sleep.

In the middle of the night, Moody uttered a low woof, and Peter came awake. He sat up and saw a large cat at the cave entrance. By the light of his eyes, he saw gray fur, a white star on its chest, and blue eyes staring at him. He fetched a bowl of leftover soup from the pot by the fire and set it down. The cat sauntered over, rubbed against Peter's leg, then began to eat.

Picking up his staff, Peter went out and stood on the road, listening to the surf. The fog was breaking up, and though it was a dark night with no moon, he could see the tide line in the distance. A cool wind cut across the shore, and he was just turning away to go back to bed when a terrible shriek rent the air.

Moody leapt to the road, howling, and the hounds began to bay as all the Poinkers and Mooners jumped up and ran to the cave entrance with their weapons drawn. Again and again, the wild cry rang out.

"It's the Dooiney-oie," Kaney said grimly. "I wonder what's disturbed him?"

As if in answer, the waves began to surge, booming and crashing up the shore as the head of a gigantic snake burst from the dark sea. Poinkers and Mooners cried out in alarm. Tuffy began to hiss. But Peter knew this monster. He'd seen it in a dream. Higher and higher its long white neck rose out of the sea, its bulbous green eyes looking this way and that, shining with a pale light. Lifting its snout to the night, the beast clashed its teeth and bellowed. Then it dove, and Peter saw the huge folds of its body undulating through the water. As it passed, the Dooiney-oie shrieked again and didn't stop until the last coil sank beneath the waves. The company stood there in stunned silence until the heavy breakers subsided.

"Mrroww!" Tuffy said, somehow expressing what everyone felt.

"Our clammin' days is over!" Raney whimpered. "I ain't never gettin' closer to the sea than I am right now."

"I want to know where that monster comes from," Kaney said.

"The mountains," Peter replied. "I saw the witch feeding it."

No one spoke. Then Kaney shook his head. "Well, well. So that's the Moonwitch's pet. We heard about it. And it explains why she was in this region today."

"Kid," Arkey added, "I'm glad I don't have your dreams."

The company went back to bed, though they agreed to set a watch, so Raney and a Mooner took up posts on either side of the entrance. To everyone's surprise, Tuffy followed Moody into the cave, rubbing against his legs, purring. Moody grumbled a bit but eventually gave it up and settled down beside the quivering hounds. Then the cat curled up next to Peter and closed his eyes.

"I think that cat's joinin' our side," Arkey observed.

"My, my," Kaney said. "Will wonders never cease?"

"I wish they would," Rathfrit muttered, and Peter silently agreed.

Toward dawn, Peter woke again, this time to the sound of loud whispering. "That big eel passed by again, farther out to sea. Goin' north." It was Arkey speaking.

"Well, no need to tell the others," Kaney rumbled. "I expect it was heading to its home under the mountains. You heard what the boy said."

"But what's it doing? Fishing? And for what, I wonder." This was the voice of a Mooner.

"Trouble, no doubt. But mark my words," Kaney said, "it won't pass by again tonight."

"And you mark mine, boss," Arkey hissed. "We ain't seen the last of that sea snake."

Peter looked at the shifting shadows on the rocky ceiling; then his fingers curled around the staff and he fell into untroubled sleep.

34

The Way Through the Woods

Pixel sat in the torchlight, turning a jagged flint over in her hand. She'd been stuck in this place for a week—caged in with a melancholy Buggane and five Fennys who seemed to think the dirt-floored cave was now their home. All day, every day, they busied themselves with chores. Droat gathered firewood, Mara and Froke mended clothes, Frimlaf scrubbed their one water bucket over and over, and Krinias counted the mysterious tick marks on the back wall of the cavern. Every morning and evening, he counted a section of the wall and hadn't much more to go. "Someone lived here before us," he kept telling them, "one mark for every day."

Pixel got up and went through a narrow stone passage and out the door, which was a wide crack in a rock face. She stood at the bottom of the muddy hollow and looked up at the tall fir trees rooted around the lip. They were so tightly packed that not even a squirrel could get through, and the branches overhead formed a roof that blocked the daylight. Beside the cave door, a little stream trickled down the side of the gully into a pebbly pool hardly big enough to wet your feet.

She went back inside and crouched down beside the wall, just under the bright mural. With the flint, she added the eighth tick mark to her own count of days.

"Oh, Tom!" The little girl sitting by the fire began to sob again, twisting the arms of her teddy bear. She had a new one each morning and, by bedtime, had torn off its legs and thrown it into the flames. Would the girl ever turn back into the old man or the giant mole again? Tom Troll had not returned and maybe never would. It was possible that after he'd blown up his head, the Shee had caught him. She shuddered, recalling their icy clutch, and dread bloomed in her heart like a dark flower. What if the witch had already captured Peter? By the time the stubborn trees let her out, there would be nothing left of Wakken Wood. She saw herself wandering a burnt-out land, looking for Uncle Ed, Aunt Marj, and Peter. Everything she loved, demolished by the terrible Shee. Feeling suddenly sapped of strength, she went to the fire and sat down beside the weeping Buggane.

"Look!" Froke pointed to the mural. "It's finished!"

"Yes, but don't stand there gawking." Droat handed her the bucket. "We need water for tea."

When they'd arrived eight nights ago, the mural had been a landscape of mountains, but every morning, they woke up to find something new added to the painting. Today, Pixel saw the startling likeness of her friend the Bread Lady from Foyle. By some trick of the light or maybe the paint, the old woman's eyes seemed alive, watching.

Mara, who sat across the fire from the sad Buggane, glanced up from her mending. "Oh! Look at that picture of wide-open sky! I'd like to walk in that field, feel the wind and the sun."

"Those few days of camping by the seashore were grand, weren't they?" Droat said. "This cave is good, but I'm beginning to feel like a prisoner."

"No, Droat. Never that. We are looked after here."

"True, but by whom? That's what I'd like to know."

Suddenly, Krinias whooped and snapped his fingers. "Done!" he cried, from the back of the cave. "There are 25,550 marks on this wall. I think that's how long someone lived here. And see the way the tick marks slant? That's Fenny writing."

"You can't tell by little lines," Droat said, adding more wood to the fire.

"But think how *clean* this cave was when we found it. No cobwebs and the cooking pots scrubbed, dishes stacked. And the water bucket without holes! I'm telling you, at least one Fenny lived here. Maybe one of our lost ones from Cwenburgh."

"I don't know," Droat said thoughtfully. "I remember when the witch marched them away to serve Tegi the Enchantress in the mountains. How could any of them escape to find their way here?"

"Well, someone with a tidy mind lived here before us," Krinias insisted. "And it's not the person who brings us food, cuz he don't add new tick marks to the wall. I wish we knew what it's all about."

"And I wanna know what's behind that wooden door," Frimlaf added. At the very back of the cave, a short, narrow tunnel branched to the left, ending at a locked door. Pixel had often stood with her ear against it, listening.

"I think it's the nighttime painter who brings the food," Froke said. "I've seen him. Or maybe ..." she faltered. "Maybe it was a dream."

"I dream him," Pixel said. "And a white hare."

"Yes! The white hare!" Froke exclaimed. "You've seen it too?"

"Could be the Small One," Mara said.

Everyone paused and Krinias said, "Who?"

"The ancient one who paints everything that was, is, and will be." She threaded a needle and began to stitch the seam of a torn shirt.

Froke put down the bucket. "Tell us!"

Mara looked up, her needle poised in midair. "I thought you knew. The Small One is the child of the first folks, born in the morning of the world. That's what my people said."

"*Your* people?" Something clicked in Pixel's mind, and she sat up straight, suddenly wide awake. "Do you mean the Merry Wanderers?"

"That's right. I wasn't always a Fenny, you know." There was a short silence.

"But to get back to the Small One," Krinias said.

"He roams the island painting pictures. You saw the Cave of Dreams, where we ate eggs."

"The song!" Pixel said. "The one you sang in the tunnel." She began to chant quietly.

One way goes to the heart of the world,
One to the tip of the peak.
One goes on to the great river's source,
And one to the brink of the sea.

Straight on, straight on, then walk the curve
That comes before the breaking;
Around the bend into the dark,
The short way you'll be taking.

Then up the stairs to the Cave of Dreams,
Where the Small One he is making
A little fire and a store of songs,
For the far-off children's waking.

Mara began to stitch again. "However did you remember that, Spy? I forgot as soon as we left the tunnel."

Wondering, Pixel turned back to the mural. Against a background of tall mountains, her friend from Foyle walked in a green field, surrounded by a flock of small white sheep. A single lily grew at her feet, and a golden bird flew overhead. Beside her stood a huge black dog. "The Bread Lady and Moody."

"What did you say, Spy?" Mara jabbed her needle into the cloth. "Why do you call *her* Bread Lady? That's the Queen! Wearing traveling clothes, in the company of the Moddey Dhoo. Just as I saw her long ago."

"Queen? No, no. I met her in Foyle. She's a baker. She . . ." Pixel trailed off and there was a long silence as she and Mara gaped at each other.

"You've walked and talked with *her*?" Mara said in a hushed voice. "I have longed to do that for many a year. I thought she left the island!"

"It can't be the same person," Pixel said.

"But it is!" A new light shone in Mara's eyes. "Spy, you *were* sent to us! By the Queen herself!"

"I don't think the Bread Lady sent me," Pixel began, but she fell silent as Mara stood up and kicked aside her mending.

"Nonsense! Enough doubt! Get up, Spy! You have chores to do!"

Whatever the mural on the wall might mean, by evening they were still stuck in the cave, and the trees outside had not moved one inch. The day's chores were done, the Buggane had thrown another teddy into the flames, and everyone else was asleep. Pixel sat with her back to the dwindling fire, gazing absently at the painting. A heavy weight of sadness pressed against her heart, keeping her awake. Then, out of the corner of her eye, she glimpsed a flash of white at the back of the cave, and the painted lily began to shine.

A snow-white hare loped out of the shadows. Standing up on its hind legs, it looked directly at her, then came forward and sat at her feet. Wondering, Pixel rubbed its nose. It moved closer and she scratched between its ears.

"He likes you," said a voice, and she nearly jumped out of her skin. A boy stood before her, smiling. His eyes shone with a clear light, like a distant star, and for a split second she had the impression of seeing him through the lens of a telescope. Then he pulled a little flashlight from his pocket. "The Silver One sends you this. See what it does?" He pushed the button and shone the beam around the cave. "But he said not to waste batteries."

Switching off the light, he held it out and she took it in her hands. "You ... you've seen him?"

"Oh yes. He is on his way to the Hermit of Floden's house. I was in the Valley of Ogar and saw him go. You are not to worry. He is safe—in the keeping of the Lady." The boy slipped a satchel off his shoulder, opened it, and took out paintbrushes. "I've decided to add one or two things." He went to the back of the cavern where the mysterious tunnel began, then returned with pots of paint and a small lamp. He set these things under the mural and lit the lamp with a brand from the fire.

Everything was still but for the muffled snore of the Buggane and the soft rustle of the boy's movements. Pixel watched him pick up a knife and dip it into a pot. Deftly, he added several colors to a palette. After a moment, she said, "Are you the Small One?"

"Some people call me that."

"How do you know her?" She pointed to the figure of the Bread Lady on the wall.

"She is my mother. She told me that you met in Foyle."

"The Bread Lady is your mother? Mara says she's the old Queen of Cwenburgh."

He chose a brush and swirled it on the palette. "That's right. The Queen is my mother in the same way that she is your mother, and the mother of all. My first mother—and my father—were lost, taking an inner road that led away from me. I remember that day. Grandfather called and called, but they had gone." Slowly, under his brush, two more figures took shape, standing beside the Bread Lady. "I was sad for a while. For the same reason that you are sad right now. You think you have been left behind like a lost purse. Yet you are not forgotten." With a skillful stroke, Peter's face emerged, and the clear, shining eyes she knew so well. "The Silver One wanted to come straight here when I told him where you were. He would have abandoned the work he's been given to do. That would not be right."

A sudden hope rose in Pixel's heart. "Can you take me to him? He never won a fight without me."

He turned and looked at her, and she faltered under his gaze. "He has set himself to follow the Lady." He pointed to the picture of her friend. "It is she who will fight for him. Just as she fights for you and guards you closely." He picked up another brush and, with his back to her, began painting again, adding color to the second figure, which was not yet clearly defined. "Mother, your friend, says you have done well, even if you do not think so. If not for you, Mara and the Fennys would still be at Cwenburgh. If not for you, the Silver One would still be in the house, besieged by the wizard, or perhaps by now doing the wizard's bidding. As it is, things go well. The creatures are gathering to the Silver One, and all things proceed toward the desired end."

He dabbed his brush on the palette and turned to look at her again. His eyes were like probing lights, and she thought once again of a distant star. "It is time for you to rest now," he said. "Tomorrow will be a long day. Good night, Little White Shadow."

"Good night." Without protesting, she lay down on her bed and slept.

Someone called her name. Pixel opened her eyes and looked around. The Fennys were still asleep. The white hare and the boy were gone, but his lamp still burned. She got up and stood before the mural. Beside the figure of Peter, she saw her own face, her short blond hair sticking up all over, her arms spread wide to greet the Bread Lady.

"I'm in the story too," she whispered, gazing in wonder. The white lily at the Lady's feet shone out again, reminding her of the Small One's bright eyes. When the lily dimmed, Pixel suddenly felt so tired she could hardly stand. She stumbled to her bed and fell instantly into a dreamless sleep.

Coffee. She smelled coffee. And someone was chopping vegetables. At least, that's what it sounded like. Pixel sat up, and there was the Small One beside the fire, cutting up carrots, of all things. She watched him give a slice to the white hare and throw the rest into a black pot. The little girl sat beside him gnawing a melon rind and clutching a new teddy under one arm. Then Pixel saw a white wolf curled up at the boy's feet, watching every move he made. Its eyes turned to her and it growled softly. The boy looked up.

"Good morning!" he said cheerily.

Mara and Froke sat up among the bedclothes.

"I knew you weren't a dream!" Froke cried, hopping up.

Mara, her eyes wide, clutched a blanket around her neck, like an old housewife caught in her pajamas at midday. "Small One!" she croaked.

"Well met, faithful one!" the boy said to her. "Mother sends greetings." Then he motioned toward Droat, Krinias, and Frimlaf, still rolled in their blankets. "Do you think they're going to sleep all day? It's past noon, and this meal is nearly ready."

"Noon!" Mara threw the blanket over her head.

Froke looked into the pot on the fire. "I told Krinias it was you who brought the food."

"Yes. From my garden." The Small One gave her an apple slice, then turned to Pixel. "Little White Shadow, perhaps you should wake the others. Then help the old one wash and dress. She seems unwell today."

"Not sick!" came the cry from under the blanket.

"I'll wake the others," Froke said and began to sing at the top of her lungs.

> Snoring! You're snoring! You sleepyheads will find
> That I have eaten all the food and left you melon rinds!
> Wake up! Wake up! Get out of bed! It's way past breakfast time!

At the last line, Droat leapt out of bed and stood wide-eyed, looking around the cave. "Trolls? Glashtyn?"

After several more rounds of her ear-splitting song, Froke finally stripped Frimlaf and Krinias of their blankets and splashed their faces with cold water.

"They aren't usually this sleepy," Pixel said to the Small One.

"Perhaps a special rest was granted to them before we begin our journey."

"Journey?" the Buggane said, then hiccupped. Mara uncovered her head, and Froke stopped singing.

"We are going to Floden," the Small One said eagerly. "To the Hermit's House. Mother asked me to lead you through the woods."

Pixel caught her breath. “Isn’t that where Peter’s going?”

“Yes. Grandfather says we must go there too.”

“Your grandfather?” Mara gasped. “But he knows what Mara has done!”

The Small One laughed. “He told me all about Jenny. He said you did a brave thing in a tight place and that it’s turned out better than you imagined. But come and eat, old one. Then we’ll prepare to leave.”

Tears welled up in the little girl’s eyes. “Tom?” She looked at the Small One, pleading. “Cake?”

“Yes, Buggane! Mother is thinking of you too!” He pulled a bundle from the basket at his feet and uncovered a large vanilla cake.

The girl threw her last teddy onto the fire and, with a loud *pop!*, became the old man again.

Preparing to leave was not as simple as Pixel had hoped. Not with the Fennys. They’d made a home and weren’t about to leave without a thorough cleaning. Working like fury, they swept, washed pots, and shook out blankets. When at last they were ready to go, they shouldered their bags, went out the doorway for the last time, and stood looking up at the tightly packed forest. A loud rustling noise broke out overhead as twigs and fir cones showered down and a gap opened between two trees.

“Here we go!” the Buggane said, helping Mara up the steep slope. They all climbed to the top and stood at the beginning of a narrow trail. Then Pixel saw a shuddering movement as the trees closed ranks.

“Why do they hide the cave?” she asked, falling in behind the Small One. The path was so narrow that they went single file, and even then they had to push past branches and step over roots.

“The trees are the guardians,” he replied. “Of this entrance and three more.”

“Entrances to where?”

“Shush, missy,” the Buggane said. “We don’t talk about the seven doorways. Not in the open.”

The trail led them north for about a mile until it joined another path.

“Which way?” Krinias held out the old compass, squinting at the wavering needle.

“West,” the Small One said, turning left. “This is the Old Path, and it runs right across the woods, from the marsh in the east to Floden in the west. The Merry Wanderers made it long ago.”

"Do the trees move it around?" Pixel asked. The trail from the cave had already disappeared.

"Only if they must," the Small One replied. "The trees who guard this way are very old. And yet the trees in my home are more ancient still. Many a seedling I brought up to the sunlight and planted before even the Merry Wanderers were afoot."

"Ah!" the old man sighed. "West! I could point the way with my eyes closed. Can you smell it?"

"West? You can smell west?" Krinias cried.

"Oh yes! The western sea! The Floden Hills! The ancient cedars of the woods!" The Buggane lifted his nose to the air and breathed deeply.

"It's something to have a compass in your head like that," Droat said.

"His compass is in his nose!" the Small One said with a laugh.

As the company ambled along the wide path, little birds darted through the branches, calling out to one another, and somewhere to their right, a stream burbled away. Morning sun, slanting through the dense forest, shed a greenish light. It was good to be moving again, to be out in the open and to feel the cool breeze. Pixel's heart lifted and she began to hum. Then she looked back and saw Mara's drooping shoulders and sorrowful expression. Falling into step beside Froke, she said, "What's wrong with Mara? Is she sick?"

"She's afflicted with a sharp sense of justice. That's what Droat says."

"What does he mean?"

"No idea."

The forest began to change, as fir gave way to maple and alder. Then, a short distance off to their right, the woodland thinned, and for the first time, they saw the stream they had been following.

"The Dorry Doont," the Small One said, by way of introduction. "The name means 'back door', and we will walk beside him nearly all the way to the Hermit's House."

Beyond the stream, they began to see sunny clearings of tall grass and flowering foxglove. Passing a clump of oak saplings, they walked into a meadow with here and there a large gray boulder standing among the wildflowers. Suddenly, from a patch of tall grass, red eyes looked at Pixel, and she gasped.

"Moo!" a voice bellowed.

The Small One turned back, laughing. "Ah! Baby Tarroo! I did not see you hiding there!" A smooth gray head moved toward him, waggling little round ears. It looked something like a calf, but its eyes were fiery red. The Small One stroked its snout. "Where is your mother?"

A far larger head popped up nearby. It nickered like a horse, and the calf swung away and went lumbering across the stream to join its mother. Pixel and the Fennys stared after the pair.

"Not boulders!" Pixel said faintly.

Krinias whistled. "Phew! Never thought I'd see an Ushtey. But I guess they aren't dangerous."

In the late afternoon, they came to the foot of a hill. The Old Path and the Dorry Doont skirted this slope on its south side.

"Come," the Small One said. "We have walked far enough today. We will camp here." And he led them to the right, over the stream and up the hill.

Stopping on the northern edge of the summit, they looked over the vast grazing grounds of the Tarroo Ushtey. Far away, east of the pastures, the Glenfaba River gleamed in the sunlight. Straight ahead, on the far side of the yellow-green grassland, rolling foothills spread across the northern horizon, then higher hills, and beyond that, the peaks of three mountains. A cool evening breeze swept across the bluff, and Froke shivered. "Brrr!" The Small One and the Fennys turned away from the view, but Pixel remained, gazing north.

Suddenly, for a fraction of time, she saw emerald mountains towering high above the island. From these heights came a warm wind and the sound of singing. Then, in the blink of an eye, the vision vanished. Pixel stood very still, wondering what she had just seen. The strong scent of cedar hung in the air, and she was struck by a sharp pang of loss. With a small sigh, she followed the others into a copse of short trees.

Coming to a round clearing, the first thing she saw was a neat stack of cut wood beside a ring of stones. "This reminds me of that place we camped on Barrane Bay. Someone left firewood there too."

"No doubt it was the Arkan Sonney who were here last," the Small One replied as he laid down his satchel. "This is one of the usual resting places."

Droat built a fire, and they had a good supper of pancakes and roast apples. All that evening, Mara remained silent and ate very little, but the others talked and laughed about the Tarroo. The Small One told them stories of the strange river cattle that had come in Mac Lir's ship long ago. Then they went to sleep in the fading light, listening to the murmur of the Dorry.

Late that night, Pixel woke from a troubled dream. It fled as soon as she opened her eyes and felt the soft fur of the white wolf, which lay beside her. The fire had gone out, and there was no light greater than a slim crescent of waning moon.

"Little White Shadow," the Small One spoke in a low voice, "come look at the stars." He was sitting just beyond the trees, having taken the second watch. Pixel got up and went to sit beside him.

"There," he said, pointing straight ahead, "do you see it? The North Star. And over there"—he turned and pointed to a bright point of light just visible between the branches behind them—"is Jupiter."

"How do you know their names?"

"Grandfather taught me long ago, when they were very young."

"We can't see the stars in the city. Not so many, like this."

"And yet they are there whether you see them or not."

She looked over the dark field to the north. The tall grass looked like a low forest in the moonlight. Suddenly, a small red light blinked out, then another and another. Red lights winked and blinked all around the base of the hill. "What are they?"

"Only the Tarroo. There is nothing to fear, Little White Shadow. Grandfather is nearer than you think. And Mother too."

"I never really understand what you say."

He laughed softly. "Yet I do not speak in riddles."

She went back to her spot beside Froke and lay down. The wolf nudged her with his nose, and she scratched the top of his head. Gradually, she drifted into sleep.

The next morning dawned bright and clear. Pixel got up early and went down the hill to fetch water from the stream. When she returned, the Small One was lighting the fire and talking quietly to Mara. He had got her to look at him, which was progress, but still she wouldn't speak. For breakfast, they had bread and tea and one more slice of cake apiece. As they were finishing the last crumbs, a golden thrush flew down and perched on a rock beside the Small One. Pixel had never seen such a beautiful bird. It twittered and the Small One nodded. Then she saw his face change.

"This is news indeed," he said. "The Shee are hunting in the woods around Floden."

Froke gasped and said, "They're after Spy!"

"Humph! Not Spy," Mara said, speaking for the first time since leaving the cave. "Mark my words, Small One! The Shee have not come to this island by accident. Neither have the wizard and Lila. Something draws them!"

"What is that, old one?"

"You! The ancient realm where you live and its hidden power! They will find your doorways! You should not be out in the woods!" She spoke with a sudden vehemence that startled even Pixel.

The Small One looked at Mara gravely. "No doubt Grandfather is the power you speak of. Yet why should I walk in fear when he takes care of all things? But I suspect the Shee are hunting for sport, or maybe to feed the witch's pet."

Pixel stared at him and again had the strangest feeling. Though he sat beside her, he was remote somehow and alive in a way she did not understand. He held out his finger, and the thrush hopped up, regarding him with a bright eye. "You stay close now, little one. The Shee would shoot a bright target such as you for pleasure."

With a flutter, the bird alighted on the top of Mara's staff.

"Are you ready now?" the Small One asked her.

She did not reply. The golden thrush jumped onto her shoulder, and, as if that were the signal, the company broke camp and began its march.

The Small One led them down the hill and back to the Old Path. For several miles, they walked in the light of morning, the stream on their right, thickets of leafy trees on their left. A little way ahead, Pixel saw dark evergreens rising like a high wall from the forest floor, and almost before she knew it, the path plunged straight into these woods. It was like walking through a door into a room where all the shutters were closed against the light and heat. Solemn cedars and fir trees grew in rank upon rank as far as she could see, with tall ferns and thickets of vine maple at their feet. There were no breezes playing among the branches. Even the murmur of the stream was muted as it flowed between banks of deep moss. The Buggane changed into the giant mole, and Pixel noticed the Fennys glancing anxiously from side to side. When she felt her nerves couldn't take it any longer, she began to sing quietly.

The woods are deep, but I am strong;
My bones are made of wood and rock.
I take an oak staff in my hand
And beat my way through stone and stock.

Tramp, tramp! Stamp, stamp!
Step it lively, ancient bones!
Tread upon the silver snake
And take the narrow pathway home!

The Small One stopped in his tracks and turned around. "What are you singing?"

She shrugged. "Something my granny sang. To get me to sleep."

"That's no lullaby! That's a troll song if ever I heard one!" the Small One said.

"Sing it again!" Froke demanded. "It sounds like a good one for walking."

So, while they walked, Pixel taught them her granny's song.

My roots go down into the ground,
Under the forest, far beneath,
Below the crust and granite bones,
Into the silent, secret deeps.

And I am strong, my bones of stone;
My skull is thick, a mountainside;
You shall not crush me with your stick,
And swords shall never pierce my hide!

Tramp, tramp! Stamp, stamp!
Step it lively, ancient bones!
Tread upon the silver snake
And take the narrow pathway home!

"Little missy, that granny of yours is a Buggane," Tom Mole said.

Pixel laughed. That was Granny alright. Always telling stories of unlikely heroes who climbed mountains, lived in deep caves, or held magnificent banquets in stone castles.

"When was she here on the island?" the Small One asked.

Startled by the thought, Pixel frowned. "I don't think she ever was. She never said so."

All that day, as they moved deeper into the woods, there was a strange feeling in the air, as if the whole forest held its breath. The white wolf and the hare walked in front with the Small One, and the five Fennys came behind, the golden thrush still riding on Mara's shoulder. Pixel brought up the rear with Tom Mole. His long white tusks were comforting, and sometimes he hummed the Tom song and she hummed with him.

Then, in the late afternoon, as they passed through a gloomy stretch of forest, they heard a commotion in the bracken off to their left. Some large creature blundered through the trees, and everyone froze.

"This way!" the Small One hissed. He dove off the path, to the right, into a thicket of tall sword fern beside the stream. They crouched down, except Tom, who stood behind the nearest tree, looking out.

A stag came bounding across the path, headed right for them. When it caught sight of the Buggane, it veered sharply away, leapt over the stream, and plunged into the woods. Fierce neighing broke out, and a rider on a dark horse thundered by in pursuit. At his passing, Pixel felt an icy hand clutch her heart and she began to shiver. When all was quiet, the Small One led them back to the path and they went on their way, warily.

Pixel, still shivering a little, fell into step beside the Small One and was surprised to hear him humming.

"Aren't you afraid?" she whispered.

"No. Grandfather knows all about us."

"Does he know about the Shee?"

"Oh yes. They are old enemies."

She glanced at his calm face. "How old are you?"

"I am firstborn in the circles of your time, but I did not let go of Grandfather's hand, so he holds me in place."

"Does that locked door at the back of the cave lead to your home and your grandfather?"

He grinned. "Yes, it does."

"If he knows all about us and the Shee, why didn't we go there?"

"For me, it is a few steps from that door to my home in the heart of the world, but your way to that place is still a long road. You will be traveling it for the rest of your life."

Pixel frowned, trying to sort this out. "Couldn't your grandfather come here? Then I could meet him. And would he ... could he travel with us? Or is he too old?"

"The earth is his footstool, Little White Shadow. The tip of his smallest finger would crush this whole island."

"But ... you go to him, through that door."

"He is not so easily explained. And as for his coming here to meet you, that will have to wait for another day."

After the passing of the stag hunt, Pixel found herself short of breath, as if the Shee had left something behind in the air that was too thick for her lungs. As the company marched on into the evening, she kept close to Tom, and when she stumbled in the fading light, he reached out a great claw and steadied her.

At last, they stopped and found a place to camp a little way off the path, next to the Dorry. The Small One would not let them light a fire, so they sat in the twilight under the cover of salmonberry bushes, eating apples and oatcakes, talking in low voices. Finally, when it was too dark to see one another's faces, they lay down, and Tom Mole kept watch, his great bulk hunkered down beside them. Pixel lay awake for a long time, listening to the stream's burbling night tune. When she finally drifted into sleep, she dreamed of red vultures peering down at her from every branch.

The next morning, a thin fog rolled in from the east. White mist hung in the air, and the trees looked ghostly. After a hurried meal, they returned to the path, and the Small One led them at a quicker pace than the day before, on and on into the fogbound forest. There were no sunbeams piercing the gray-green canopy; only cold mist that clung to their hair and clothes. Sometimes, far off in the forest, Pixel heard a horse whinny, and she tried to walk as quietly as she knew how, wincing every time a twig snapped under her foot. Tom Mole stumped along at the rear of the company muttering to himself, "This fog is the wizard's doing!"

They had been walking for some time when shrill laughter pierced the silence of the woods.

"The Moonwitch!" Mara said. "Ahead of us, on the path!"

Hurrying between the cedars on their right, the company crossed the Dorry, climbed over a huge fallen tree, and hid behind it. As Pixel crouched there, panting and shivering, she looked up and saw the Buggane perched on top of the log, perfectly still. First, she heard the tramp of hooves, then the snorts and whinnies of many horses. It went on for several minutes, and when the sounds faded into the distance, Tom Mole looked down and said, "She's headed east, a troop of Glashtyn with her. Do you think it's safe?"

The Small One got to his feet and picked up his satchel. "We must go warily while it is still light."

The fog grew thicker around them as they trudged forward, and by the time they stopped for the night, it hung like a shroud over the Dorry. They crossed the stream again and made a cheerless camp under the branches of a spreading vine maple. Tom paced restlessly back and forth until he finally stumped away, saying he was off to reconnoiter. Pixel hoped he wouldn't go far. Exhausted, she lay awake for a long time, staring into the mist, her head and joints aching.

❦ ❦ ❦

"Well met, brother!" a cold voice called. Startled out of sleep, Pixel lay still, listening.

"You were to meet us in Floden a day ago!" a hollow voice said. "Where are the others?"

"We came upon the Silver Boy's trail east of the river. Where is the witch? Still in the mountains feeding her pet?"

"She returned yesterday but has gone on some errand of her own and would not speak of it."

"Ha! She is avoiding her father. But tell me. Did you ever find the blood girl who escaped the witch's house?"

"Not even her corpse."

Pixel heard the sound of an animal lapping water and realized that the Glashtyn and Shee were on the other side of the Dorry, just a few feet away. She began to tremble.

"Will you wait here for the witch? Or join me in the hunt for the Silver Boy?"

"I will go with you. Come, little Glashtyn. You have had your fill of water." A whip cracked, a horse whinnied fiercely, and then came the stamp of hooves in the undergrowth and the sound of horses galloping away.

Shivering uncontrollably, Pixel clenched her jaw shut to keep her teeth from chattering. After a little while, she heard someone whisper, "It's alright. Didn't you hear? All the Shee have left the woods now. We can go." Then she felt a hand on her arm, and Froke said, "Spy? Are you alright?"

Tom's snout appeared inches from her face. "Missy is not well. I will carry her."

He picked her up and they crossed the stream. As they returned to the path, it began to rain, softly at first, and then harder. Pixel closed her eyes, leaning her head against the mole's velvet fur. In her mind, she saw the red vultures of her dream again, but it was hard to be afraid in the arms of Tom Mole.

By late morning, Pixel knew she could not walk even if she wanted to. Her eyes burned, and everything—even Mara's face bent close to hers—seemed remote and hazy. Yet her sense of hearing was sharper. Voices were too loud, and small noises made her wince. At Mara's command, someone wrapped her in blankets, but it didn't stop the shivering.

With her eyes half open, she saw branches overhead, gray sky, and Tom Mole's snout. She felt the constant rhythm of his gait.

"Why is she so ill?" Froke's voice said, and the Small One replied, "It is the cold poison of the Shee in her blood and the evil of the house in Foyle where she lived." Then he spoke her name and said, "Drink this." Tom had stopped moving. A cup touched her lips, and she swallowed something cool and sweet. She was so thirsty. A cold, wet nose pressed against her cheek, and the white wolf whimpered in her ear. She tried to lift her hand to pat him but found she couldn't move.

"Time to go," Tom growled.

Pixel felt rain on her face, and always the pain in her head and joints, every nerve raw. She heard herself wheezing. Then, after a long while, Tom stopped. "My, my! What a terrible sight!"

"What?" she rasped, unable to open her eyes.

"Floden," he said sadly. "What's left of it." He began to move again, and Pixel heard the rain pattering in puddles. Her clothes were wet, or maybe she was trapped in ice. She shivered harder and Tom tightened his hold. "You hang on, little Buggane!" Then he began to sing her granny's song. *"The woods are deep, but I am strong; my bones are made of wood and rock. I take an oak staff in my hand . . ."*

She tried to sing with him, but her voice made no sound, and she couldn't remember the words. All that came back was *tramp, tramp, stamp, stamp*, to the steady rhythm of Tom's tread. Gradually, the shivering subsided and she felt nothing. Not even pain. Then Tom said, "Here we are!"

Lifting heavy eyelids, Pixel saw Annette. Wait. Annette didn't have silver eyes, did she? Had Tom Mole brought her to Foyle? They'd made it to Thorny's! She could phone Peter. Uncle Ed would come and take her home. Making a sudden effort to move, she felt a stab of pain near her heart and fell into a whirl of dark water that crashed about her ears and sucked her under.

35

The Last Mile

Peter and the company of creatures traveled along the seacoast for a number of days, sometimes walking on the giants' road, sometimes over broad grasslands with the sea on their right and the high cliffs on their left. The sky remained clear and the weather warm, with a mild breeze blowing over the shore. In this region, there was plenty of good grazing for the horses and little rivulets of fresh water running across the sand. The Poinkers caught small fish in these streams and collected beach peas for supper. As they moved south, they came upon groves of spruce trees growing at the base of the cliffs, screening the giants' road from view. There were many small caves in which the Poinkers found old firepits they'd made, and Peter learned much about their past patrols.

Most nights, they heard the Dooiney-oie's cry, and though they never saw him, they did see the witch's pet passing through the dark sea. Sometimes Peter grabbed his staff and sprinted across the sand, where he would stand alone to watch the sea monster swimming just beyond the shoal. Yet the bright days always dispelled their nighttime fear, and as the company marched over the turf or along the stone road, they sang old island tunes while the hounds chased one another over sandy beaches. The Mooners learned the marching music of the Arkan Sonney, though Peter guessed the little men understood nothing about money, which was the subject of every Poinker song.

Tuffy showed no sign of leaving the company. The hounds, suspicious at first, as any dog might be, soon grew accustomed to their feline companion, accepting the cat as part of the pack. The hawthorn traveled in its own way, falling behind by day and moving far ahead while the company slept. Whenever they passed the tree, its branches alive with glittering hornets, Peter waved.

"Slowpokes!" it would reply, and Peter thought this laughable until he recalled how fast it could move.

On the fourth evening, after a long day's march, they set up camp in a woodland beside a little stream. The sky was clear, and Peter fell asleep looking at the stars. Then, in the small hours of the morning, he woke with a start. Someone had called his name. He sat up, and Moody lifted his head and looked around. The other members of the company were sound asleep around the dying embers of the campfire, and no one stirred, not even a hound. A waxing crescent moon shone silver over the shore, and beyond the trees, Peter could see the figures of a Mooner and a Poinker keeping watch.

Wondering who had summoned him, and why, Peter picked up his knapsack and stole away to another part of the woodland, accompanied by Moody. In a sandy hollow, he built a small fire, and as the flames blazed up, Tuffy appeared out of the shadows. A few minutes later, the hawthorn sidled up with the Vespa in its branches, and a picture flashed across Peter's inner vision of a leafless tree drooping in the hot sun.

"Yeah, right," he muttered. After taking a jar from his pack, he applied a little tree food with a generous amount of water from his canteen, and the tree quivered with delight. Then, into his mind, it said, "Dooney!"

Peter looked up as a man with a pale, thin face stepped into the firelight. He was dressed all in black like an undertaker, and long white fingers fluttered from his sleeves. Moody woofed a friendly greeting, and Tuffy rubbed against his legs, purring like an engine.

"Oh, Silver One! Why do you linger so nigh the shore, in the path of Leviathan?" The man's voice was curiously raspy, as if he had a bad case of laryngitis.

Peter stared at him until the hawthorn prodded his mind. "Stupid. Dooney hungry!" So he opened his pack and took out stale bread and an old apple. It was all he had.

The man sat down and began to eat quickly, gulping and smacking his lips. When he finished, he belched loudly and looked up with tragic eyes. "Always, I wander this cursed land, looking in every corner for the light of the world," he rasped. "For a time, I thought it was the light of you Silver Ones, but you bear only a flicker of the lost light." His voice trailed away. Then suddenly he jumped to his feet, let out a piercing shriek, and took off running.

Peter got up slowly and picked up his staff. Dooney must be the Dooiney-oie, herald of bad tidings. He stood there, listening to the anguished wailing and the crashing surf. Sure enough, there was the monster's head, rising above the waves. Sick of the sight of it, Peter lay down beside the fire and covered his ears to block out the torment of the sea.

When he woke again, it was nearly dawn. There sat the Dooiney-oie, feeding the fire with small sticks and twigs. Tuffy sat in his lap.

"The night is over, Silver One, and we have won through! Though darkness seemed to prevail, we did not lose hope and have lived to see a new day!"

"Yeah. Okay." Peter rubbed his eyes and went to wash in the stream. On his way, he passed the hawthorn. It tapped him with a prickly branch and said into his mind, "Dooney join you!"

"Sure," Peter replied aloud. "But what are we gonna do with a guy like that?"

If the company was surprised to see the Dooiney-oie at breakfast, they didn't say so. The Poinkers stared at him with wary eyes and the Mooners gazed uneasily, but the hounds flocked around his knees, whining and vying for attention. Tuffy sat on his shoulder, purring, and Moody stood by, waving his tail happily. Even the little brown wren sitting in the hawthorn twittered and chirped, paying his respects to Dooney.

Then, toward the end of breakfast, a cold wind began to blow, sweeping though the woodland, blowing stray twigs into the air. Breakers pounded the shore as a bank of dark clouds descended, covering the sun.

Dooney looked up from his plate. "It is an ill wizard's wind that blows no good, but fear not the coming gale! It's only rain, wind, and more rain. Perhaps a little lightning, a little thunder."

Peter stared at Dooney, then jumped to his feet and grabbed his staff. Everyone scrambled to break camp as the wind began to moan and thunder boomed. Before the company could get back to the shelter of the giants' road, the rain came down in torrents.

As the morning wore on, the storm's intensity increased. At midday, they stopped for a hurried meal, huddled against the cliff wall. Wind fretted and whined, and rain sluiced sideways so that the overhang above the road was no protection. Peter watched the poor horses, chafing and stamping. Yet the fiercer the gale, the happier Moody became, wagging his tail from side to side, snorting merrily at every peal of thunder. The hounds were glad to huddle under his cheerful bulk, though Arkey was heard to mutter "Dumb dog" more than once that afternoon.

By evening, everyone was bone-tired, cold, and wet. Peter hoped to find a small cave where they could rest and build a fire, but there were none in that region of high, smooth cliffs. Instead, the sandy shore diminished until the road was only a stone's throw from the incoming tide on their right. Then the sand vanished under the waves, and the sea licked the edge of their path. In the fading light of that cloud-heavy day, they came to the end of the road, hemmed in by lapping water, and Peter looked up and saw a flight of stairs carved into the face of the bluff.

"We've come farther today than I ever expected." Kaney said, obviously pleased. "We're less than half a day's march from the Hermit's House." Without hesitation, he led them up the short stairway to a broad, crescent-shaped shelf, halfway up the side of the cliff.

"Look, kid! There it is!" Arkey pointed to a dark hole bored into the headland. "Through that tunnel, then in and out of Grondle's Gap to the back door."

"Our horses are tired," Rathfrit said. "And we've got a mare that's lost her hind shoe."

"Then we better camp here," Kaney said. "This ledge is wide enough for all of us. We'll go on tomorrow."

Peter looked around the bare, rocky shelf. The cliff was at their back, with the high headland, like a rocky buttress on one side, but there was no real shelter from the wind. They were perched on a ledge that hung out over the waves, and if the sea monster came by tonight, it would pass dangerously close. "There's still a little daylight," he said, looking up at the gray sky. "Can't we keep going?"

But no one heard him. The Poinkers were already building a fire by the tunnel door, and the Mooners were settling the horses for the night. Arkey cooked supper, and it wasn't until they were all sitting around the campfire that anyone thought of the sea monster. Then the Poinkers huddled together in a tight knot of bristles with here and there the glint of a spear, and the Mooners stared silently into the flames, tense and uneasy.

"We're like sittin' ducks," Arkey muttered. "Why didn't the boss think of that? We oughta camp in the tunnel."

"Too narrow," Kaney said. "And damp. Water drips from the ceiling."

Unexpectedly, the Dooiney-oie came to the rescue. All day he had marched at the rear of the company, with Tuffy on his shoulder. Now he sat down beside Kaney. "Dooney can hear the stars," he began in his raspy voice. "He can hear them singing high overhead, above the whirl and fret of the sea." Then he began to chant a thin, wavering song. The hounds grew still, and the horses, standing beyond the circle of creatures, ceased their restless stamping.

Peter closed his eyes, listening, and saw long boats coming over the sea. In the stern of one, a man with flaxen hair and silver eyes plied his oar. A beautiful woman sat in the bow. Peter could hear the beat of a drum and a deep voice calling out the stroke. Then the tune changed slightly, and he saw the Silver-eyed man and the woman come walking out of the woods carrying a baby. After that, images came in quick succession: men and women, tall and beautiful as gods, laboring to build a great stone house; little men on white horses hunting over the hills; firelight in a great room where many folk feasted and where gray-eyed children collected silver coins scattered across the polished floor.

Gradually, the song took a melancholy turn, and Peter saw two great ships, one with a black flag and the other with white sails, driving before a steady wind. They landed on a wooded shore, and after that the island seethed with fire and terrible storms. Peter thought he could hear the trees wailing as the creatures of the wood scattered to hide in dark holes. Then softly, softly, the tune changed again, unwinding like a glittering stream. He saw himself at the head of a large company, walking through a green valley. Green mountains, whose names he had never been told, rose in height upon height toward the bright stars.

He opened his eyes and saw all the others blinking in the firelight and silence. Then Kaney pointed in the direction of the sea. A thick white mist had come down like a curtain, between their camp and the water. Peter listened, hearing only the sound of waves slapping the side of the cliff.

"Did you do that?" Arkey whispered.

"Nay, my little friend," Dooney replied. "Call it an unlooked-for mercy. We have been spared the sight of Leviathan. Indeed, it has already passed. Lie down and sleep in peace. Dooney will watch tonight."

Without a word, the company settled down right where they were. The last thing Peter saw as he drifted off to sleep was Dooney, with Tuffy on his shoulder, standing at the edge of the impenetrable white fog, facing the sea.

Peter woke at dawn, static buzzing in his head like a rasping handsaw. He sat up and there was Dooney adding wood to the fire. Everyone else was still asleep. The white mist had lifted sometime during the night, but the sky was gray.

"Ah, Silver One! Your little tree passed this way, carrying the glittering hornets. It entered the tunnel before the sun rose, and the Vespa went whirling and swirling like a hundred stars, right over the headland. Dooney thinks they are waiting at the Hermit's House."

The static grew louder and Peter rubbed his forehead. He could no longer hear the waves slapping or gulls calling. Dazed, he watched two crows flap down to the rock near his feet, pecking at this and that. A log, borne on the swells, floated close to the cliff, and the crows swooped down and attacked it, landing on the rough bark, pecking furiously. Then a little wren appeared and hopped onto his shoe. He raked his hair roughly. There was something important about the wren, but he couldn't think what. All he could hear was the sound of a chainsaw roaring in his ears.

Suddenly, Moody and all the hounds woke up and started baying. Then the horses began to whinny, and the Poinkers and Mooners leapt to their feet. Gritting his teeth, Peter clamped his hands over his ears as the static rose to a crescendo. And then, quite suddenly, it stopped. He opened his eyes. Everyone was looking at him. The hounds wagged their tails and scurried off, noses to the ground. The crows flapped away, over the headland, and the company began breaking camp.

Only Kaney said, very quietly, "Are you unwell, Mr. Peter?"

"I'm okay." Absently, he picked up his staff and looked at the empty waves. Something had just happened, but what?

The company marched into the tunnel, the Mooners carrying torches and the Poinkers holding spears ready, but they met no one. There was nothing to see in the flickering light but wet rock walls and puddles. They came out the other end, into the deep bay called Grondle's Gap. Immediately to his right, Peter saw a long flight of steps going down to the sand. On his left, the giants' road continued high above the shore, skirting the entire cove, right to the top of another headland.

"This is the last mile," Kaney said, leading the way forward.

Into the stillness of the Gap, the overcast sky shed a lonely light. Peter looked over the low parapet that sheltered the road and saw driftwood scattered over white sand. A flock of wading birds stood at the water's edge, dipping long beaks into the lapping surf. "In and out of Grondle's Gap to the back door," he murmured, repeating what Arkey had said. When they came to the end of the road, he saw another long flight of stairs.

"Ah!" Kaney said. "Here we are at last."

Beyond the headland where they stood, the coastline bent inward again, forming a shallow crescent of sand and foaming surf. At the top of a craggy cliff face, Peter saw low humps and hillocks covered in yellow grass and wildflowers. "Where's the house?"

"You're looking at it! Built right into the earth and indistinguishable from the hills."

Wondering, Peter followed Kaney down the stairs to the shore and saw a swift stream gushing from a hole in the base of the cliff. A few yards before the stream, they turned left and passed through an arched cleft in the rock, and Peter found himself in a deep ravine. A fine mist hung in the air. Little ferns and green moss sprouted from the high rock walls, and from farther back in that secret canyon came the sound of a waterfall. A path led through sandy grass to a stone bridge that crossed the stream. At the end of the path, standing against the canyon wall, the hawthorn waited, with the Vespa in its branches humming a welcome. Kaney stopped beside the tree, picked up a large stone, and thumped it against the wall. The outline of a door appeared and swung inward, revealing a dim passage and a smooth stone floor sloping gently upward. A Fenny stood beside the open door, holding a flickering candle.

"Krinias, at your service, Mr. Peter," the Fenny said. "We've been expecting you. Come this way."

Up the long passage they went, sea wind blowing through narrow lancet windows, the company marching solemnly, even the Poinkers and the little hounds, with the horses clip-clopping behind, and Dooney bringing up the rear. With every step, Peter had the sense of walking deeper into the heart of the world, whatever that meant, while outside, the gray sea and sky merged. Though it was midmorning, he fell into a sort of waking dream: He was in the green valley again, climbing a narrow road with a great company. Emerald mountains towered above him and he heard the roar of a great waterfall. Gradually, the sound faded from his mind, and he found himself standing at a wooden door. In the sudden silence, he glanced back and saw that his companions were no longer with him. "Where is everyone?"

"Gone to their quarters, sir. In the lower passages." Krinias stood with his hand on the latch. "Droat thought you might like to stop in and see her before going to the Silver Wing. The fever broke last night. I don't think she's come around yet, but she's out of danger."

He pushed open the door and Peter walked in, wondering whom Krinias wanted him to see.

The first thing he noticed was a row of windows looking out toward the overcast sky. Someone sat on a bench beneath the windows, and when Peter saw her face, he froze. Her eyes shone silver, like piercing lights.

Gasping, she jumped to her feet. "Oh! You ... you're Peter!"

His heart slowed. "Jenny?"

She nodded, her eyes fixed on his. "Call me Jen." Then she pointed. "Your friend."

Realizing he stood at the foot of a bed, he turned and saw someone lying in it, pale and thin, with white lips and dark circles under the closed eyelids. One arm lay on the coverlet, old needle marks still visible in the crook of her elbow. "Pixel!" he said, his throat tight. "What happened?"

"The answer to that is a long tale, Mr. Peter," Krinias said in a low voice. He remained in the doorway holding a candle. "She takes to shiverin' and passin' out whenever the Shee get too close, and they was doggin' our steps all through the woods. But don't you worry! Like Froke says, our Spy is made of flint and fire. We'd never have gotten away from Cwenburgh without her." He bowed and went out, closing the door behind him.

Peter stood still, watching Pixel breathe, her coverlet rising and falling gently. Then, shrugging off his pack, he set his staff against the wall and sat down on the edge of the bed. "Will she be alright?" he asked Jen.

"The Lady says so."

"You've seen the Lady?"

Jen smiled. "She was here and saved your friend, who was very near death."

Peter reached out and took Pixel's hand. Sea wind blew into the room, accompanied by the insistent murmur of waves. He closed his eyes, listening. Then, above the voice of the sea, he heard a sound like a smooth engine and looked up. Tuffy sat on the window ledge. The cat hopped down to the bench and rubbed against Jen's arm.

She scratched him between the ears and glanced at Peter. "Who's this?"

Before he could reply, Tuffy leapt onto the bed and put his whiskers in Pixel's face. Her eyelids twitched, then opened slowly. She looked at Tuffy, and then her eyes met Peter's. "You got a cat," she said in a hoarse whisper, then swallowed and licked her lips.

"Tuffy."

Her eyes closed. A moment later, she opened them again. "I can't go yet."

"What?"

"To the green hills. I was halfway up, and she said not yet 'cause you were waiting. Down in the valley. So I came back."

The Inner Mountains flashed into his mind, and he nodded, his throat still tight. "Yeah. That's good."

She sighed softly. "The music. I wanted to hear it again."

"I know."

She lifted her arm slowly and reached out to touch the cat. Tuffy nosed her fingers, then curled up in the crook of her arm. Glancing toward the windows, she saw Jen. "Oh!" she croaked. "Who ...? Where am I?"

"I'm Jen. We're in the Hermit of Floden's house." Jen got up, poured a cup of juice from the jug on the table, and picked up a slice of bread from a plate. "Can you sit up?"

Pixel licked her lips and made an effort to move. Peter helped her lean forward, stuffing pillows behind her back. When she was settled, she took the cup and sipped, coughing a little.

Peter grinned. "Berry juice?"

She nodded and took another sip; then Jen gave her the bread. "The Lady says you should eat this."

Pixel nodded, taking a bite and chewing slowly as color came into her cheeks. When she had finished, she gave the cup to Jen. "You look like Annette."

Peter laughed, and Jen cocked her head sideways. "Who?"

Before either of them could explain, they heard a squawk and two crows flapped down to the ledge outside the windows. A brown wren joined them, chirping and twittering. At Jen's inquiring look, Peter said, "The trolls' messenger crows, and Tom Bear."

"Oh! Tom Bear!" Jen said, saluting the wren.

"You know him?" Peter asked.

"We traveled together. But what's that?"

The sound of singing floated into the room.

"The Poinkers too!" Jen knelt on the wooden bench and leaned out the window, holding out her finger to the wren as the singing grew louder.

> The woods are deep, but I am strong;
> My bones are made of wood and rock.
> I take an oak staff in my hand
> And beat my way through stone and stock.

Pixel, her eyes wide, stared at Peter. "That's the Poinkers?"

A bristly snout appeared at the window casement. Then Kaney came walking across the wide, grassy sill, followed by the entire Poinker band. In single file, they trooped past Jen and the birds, still singing, then jumped through the window one by one and hopped down to the wooden bench. Peter grinned, watching Pixel's surprised face. Then she said something unexpected.

"That's Granny's song!"

The singing stopped and the Poinkers stared at her with keen black eyes.

"Who's this?" Arkey asked.

"I do believe this is Spy," Kaney said. "Old Tom Mole and that Fenny, Krinias, were just telling us about you."

"She's my friend. Pixel," Peter said. "Pixel Rilson."

"Rilson? Well now, are you related to—"

"Yeah, Mac's her great-uncle."

"Sheesh!" Raney complained. "Ain't the plot thick enough already?"

"Well, whoever you are, Pixie, or whatever your name is," Arkey said, "I gotta hand it to you. Thin and scrawny as you are, you managed to outwit them Shee and clear out of the witch's house with five Fennys. Not bad."

The chorus began to cheer, and Kaney shushed them.

"But what I wanna know," Arkey continued, "is where the rest of them Fennys came from. The ones in the kitchen that don't speak."

"They arrived a few days ago, with me and Forlost and Thrinn," Jen replied. "We found them under a mountain, and they went with us to the Hidden Valley. They're from Cwenburgh too. Droat said so."

"Where *is* Droat?" Pixel said. "And Froke? And Mara?"

"*All* the Cwenburgh Fennys are here," Jen replied. "They're the Hermit House Fennys now."

"Wait a minute," Peter said to Pixel. "Back to your granny's song. We heard the trolls sing that."

"I did wonder about it, Mr. Peter," Kaney said. "We Poinkers have always steered clear of Trollaby, but we learned that tune from a girl we met in the mountains. What was her name?"

"Lily! Lily!" the chorus replied.

Pixel frowned at the Poinker band. "But . . . but that's my granny's name."

Peter grinned, shaking his head in wonder, and Kaney said, "Well now, Miss Pixel, maybe you aren't the first Rilson girl to escape that house in Foyle."

36

In the Hermit's House

"Out! Every one of you! This is a sick room! She's at death's door!"

"I am *not* at death's door!" Pixel's voice cracked and she scowled at Mara.

"Out! Now!"

Poinkers and birds fled out the window. Tuffy hissed and jumped under the bed. Peter picked up his staff and pack and moved quickly out the door. It snapped shut, and he was standing in the corridor with Jen.

"Our new Head Fenny, Mara," she said, her eyes alight with amusement. Then her face sobered. "You look pretty tired, Peter. Let's go to the Silver Wing. Forlost is probably there, and he'll know where your room is."

"Silver Wing?"

She grinned. "You can see it from here." Leading him down the hall, she pointed out a narrow lancet window. He looked and saw a rocky headland rising over the south end of the shallow bay. It was roughly the shape of a stone tower, and there were windows carved into its face. In one or two, a light burned.

"Come with me," she said. "It's easy to get lost in this house."

He followed her through a long passage lit by clay lamps. They turned left, then right, then left again. In several corridors, they passed wooden doors, and in others, nothing more than the occasional window cut into the cliff. The walls were of whitewashed stone, and Peter started thinking of rabbit warrens in books he'd read, and Mole in the home of Mr. Badger. After many more turns, and three or four short flights of stairs, they entered a wide room lit by torches on the walls.

"Forlost?" Jen called.

When no one answered, she led Peter up a spiral staircase to a landing, as dim as the room below.

"Forlost?" she called again.

A Fenny came out of a nearby door, wiping his hands on a towel. His face was more wrinkled than any Fenny Peter had seen before, and he guessed that the little man was very old.

"Ah! Mr. Peter! I had not heard of your arrival. I hope you will forgive us. You should have been shown to your room right away. Mara is the newly appointed Head of this house, but she doesn't yet know her way around. Thrinn and I are retired from regular duties, but we have agreed to help for a while. Please come this way."

"I'll see you later, Peter," Jen said and turned down another passage.

Forlost led him to the left, down a narrow corridor all the way to the end. There, he opened a wooden door. "Here we are, Mr. Peter."

They stepped into a plain room with few furnishings. A bed stood against one wall. Across from that, a chair and a small table stood near the fireplace, and at the other end he saw a little door with a round window. Otherwise, there were no pictures, no other decorations—not even a small rug.

Forlost knelt at the grate and lit a fire. "Mr. Peter, as the former Head of Wakkenburg House, I always looked after the Silver Ones. I still do. Please let me know if you need anything."

"Thanks."

"And about your staff: Where did you get it?"

"From the Lady."

"I thought as much. You should never be without it. Indoors, but especially outside this house." Forlost bowed and went out, shutting the door.

Peter put down his knapsack and set the staff against the wall; then he went to the door with the window and looked out. Upon seeing a wide ledge, like a balcony, he opened the door and stepped into the misty rain. He was at the very top of the tower Jen called the Silver Wing. From this vantage point, he could see the rest of the house—now that he knew what he was looking at. Four windows in a row near the top of the cliff face must be Pixel's room, and from her ledge, he saw a narrow trail winding up to the top of the bluff. So that's how

Tuffy and the Poinkers had gotten in. Far below his feet, there was nothing but gray sand and a line of white foam marking the tide. A gull swooped out of the mist and landed on the beach, then another and another. At the base of the cliff, near the opening to the ravine, Tom Bear stood and shook himself. Peter stepped back into the room, shut the door, and went to the fire.

He stood there, warming his hands, feeling very tired but also restless. Finally, he took off his damp sneakers and set them near the grate, then turned his knapsack upside down, letting the contents spill onto the floor. Picking through the pile for a pair of dry socks and a clean T-shirt, he found there were none, and the odor reminded him that he hadn't washed any of his clothes since leaving Ogar's Valley. Glad that Muru couldn't see the state of his socks—yet, at the same time, wishing she could—he separated other odds and ends from the heap of dirty clothes. Everything was damp and smelled like a campfire, even the small coil of rope.

He picked up Jonas' map and journal and spread them on the table to dry. Then he sat down on the edge of the bed. Well, here he was, in the Hermit's House. Now what? Then the door bumped open and Moody Doug pranced in.

"I wondered where you were!" he said, as the great dog snuffled his face.

Like a whooshing vacuum sweeper, Moody sniffed around the room. When he came to the pile of smelly clothes, he grumbled deep in his throat and sneezed. Then, turning to the wall beside the fireplace, he banged his great paw against the wood paneling and a door popped open. Surprised, Peter followed Moody into a dim passage. Past a small lamp set into the wall, they came to a door on which a sign was posted.

Peace, peace far and near,
Hope to all who enter here.

Wondering, Peter put his hand on the latch, pushed the door open, and found himself at the top of a steep stairway. It led straight down to a huge round room where a fire crackled in a stone hearth. Lamps burned in long windows set here and there between the floor and ceiling.

The shape of the room reminded him of the old lighthouse in north Lang, a place he and his dad used to go on sunny weekends. But this was certainly not meant to be a lighthouse. The whole thing had been chiseled out of the headland, and nearly every square inch of wall space was covered in a bright mural. Having spent time in Ogar's cave, he immediately recognized the artist.

It was a huge picture of a garden. Flowering bushes and trees of every kind filled the foreground. Set among the trees, all sorts of animals walked or sat on the grass. In the background, emerald mountains towered over the garden, rising into a deep-blue sky set with stars. Directly over the fireplace, the Lady stood with the staff in her hand, a white lamb at her feet, and a golden thrush resting on her shoulder. About ten feet to the right of the fireplace, near the floor, the bright colors were broken by the image of tumbled gray rocks and a brown door, very different from the other paintings. Peter stood at the top of the stairs, gazing down at this oddity, when suddenly the brown door opened and Forlost walked in.

As if he'd expected to find Peter in this place, he nodded, went to the fireplace, and added another log. He opened a cupboard and took out a pitcher, a cup, and a plate with bread and cheese. He placed these on a table near the fire. "Will there be anything else, Mr. Peter?"

"Uh, whose room is this?"

"It belongs to the Hermit of Floden."

"And the Small One painted these pictures for him, right?"

"The Small One *is* the Hermit. At one time, the Arkan Sonney thought I was the Hermit. I couldn't remember who I was, so one name was as good as another. But I am Forlost. It is the Hermit who welcomes you to this house, Silver One." Then he bowed himself out and closed the door.

The Small One was the Hermit. Why hadn't he said so?

Moody had gone back into the passage, so Peter went down the stairs alone and stood in the middle of the room, looking around. Through an open window, he heard the insistent boom and call of the sea and the cry of gulls. Then he noticed one picture he hadn't been able to see from the high doorway: the image of an old man, larger-than-life, painted on the wall under the stairs. Peter stood very still under the joyful eyes of that bearded face, knowing that, somehow, this person was aware of him.

After a time, the old man's eyes released him, and Peter sat down at the table. In addition to bread and cheese, Forlost had laid out butter, jam, a warm omelet under a covered dish, and a bowl of shelled nuts. After many days of traveling with short rations, he ate hungrily.

It was only after he'd finished eating that his eye fell on a small book lying beside the pitcher of berry juice. Curious, he picked it up, running his fingers over the rough brown cover. It felt like the bark of a cedar tree. The first few pages were sketches of a garden, obviously made by the Small One. Then several pages of neat handwriting followed.

The giants have asked me to paint all the creatures of the island on the walls of the entrance to their city. It is a great task! I will begin with the trolls and their home, Trollaby. For this I will need slate gray.

I mix this pigment only when I must, for it makes me sad, reminding me of the day my parents left. Long ago, I watched them pass through the gate at the place of the broken stones, their faces gray and lightless. They never came back.

It was the Unwelcome Visitor who tricked them. He made them believe they'd be happier apart from Grandfather. And me.

Peter glanced at the image of tumbled gray rocks and the wooden door through which Forlost had come. Wondering, he turned to the next page.

I will also need black paint, but that will pose no problem. Here in the upper lands, the materials to make the ebony pigment are abundant—ever since the Unwelcome Visitor left his footprints over the new green fields. It was right after my parents went away. Grandfather and I tracked the creature from the gate of broken stones, straight through the green woods, all the way to my home. We found him there, in the hollow of the hill, blackening the grass at my door.

His robes were dirty white, and patches of glistening scales shone on his face and neck, though I have heard that once, long ago, he was a great and beautiful prince. He cursed Grandfather in the most terrible language, claiming the world as his kingdom.

"You are mine too," he said to me.

"Never! Not in a million years!" I told him.

After that, Grandfather hid me in the deep hollow of the earth and told me to wait for the sign of the lily. I did not know what he meant until one day, at the edge of the woods, a new flower appeared, with white petals and a long, slender stalk.

The deep hollow of the earth. That's where the Small One's mysterious door must lead, the one at the back of Ogar's cave. But who was Grandfather? The Small One always spoke of him with great affection. For a moment, he stared hard at the painting of the old man on the wall; then he turned the page.

What came next were sketches of the trolls and a number of pages devoted to the Mooners' hounds, followed by various studies of their horses. Peter flipped past drawings of Poinkers and several of Moody in different poses. In the middle of the book, he found another entry.

First the lily, and then the Warrior all in white.

The Warrior was always a great friend, coming and going from my home. He never stayed long, for he has always been about his father's work. Then one day, he rode through the gate at the place of the broken stones, and in that moment, a great silence began. I wondered if—like my parents—he had gone away, never to return.

But of course he came back, and with many wounds from a great battle. It was he who opened the way to the upper world for me, just as Grandfather wished.

Ah! I remember that glorious day so well. He took me riding on his tall white horse! First, we went to see the sky and say hello to the golden sun and the silver moon. Then he showed me all around the island, which is to be my home when I choose to go to the upper lands. After that, we rode to the City of Giants and feasted there.

He has also shown me the Inner Mountains and has charged me with painting all that I see. Best of all, he introduced me to his mother, who has taken me under her care.

A warrior on a tall white horse. Peter thought of his dream and the horseman with eyes of flame, riding across the sea. For a split second, he heard the splashing of hooves on water. Then a gust of wind blew through the open window, ruffling the pages of the book. He lost his place and couldn't find it again, but soon he became absorbed in sketches of a beautiful city. Then, toward the back of the book, he found one last handwritten entry.

I wish to paint the Inner Mountains on the wall of the cave by the river, the one where the old Fenny lives. This will require the color of newborn green from the world's morning—a difficult color to mix. I must use berries and leaves from home, for there is no combination of materials in the upper lands that comes near to that first green. Not anymore.

Grandfather says that one day, this particular shade of green will return to the island as one of the primary colors, and from this place it will spread out to all corners of the earth. Then the whole world will be home.

Peter sat there, staring at the last few words. The Small One's home seemed to be something outside history, and yet perhaps the seed of it. As he closed the book, he wondered what his dad would think.

Suddenly bone weary, he laid the book aside and got up from the table. Lying down on the bench in front of the old man's picture, he fell asleep.

❦ ❦ ❦

Sometime later, deep in a dream of flowering hills on the edge of a sunlit sea, he heard someone call his name. The hills receded and he opened his eyes. It was dark outside, but the room was aglow with lamplight. He got up and stoked the fire, adding a few sticks. Warming his hands, he wondered about the time. Then the sense of being called came again. He climbed the stairs to his room, then opened the little door and stepped onto the ledge.

The air was cool. He could hear the lapping waves and see the dark bulk of the cliff stretching north. A bank of clouds sat over the sea, but the eastern sky was clear and many stars were visible. He noticed one blazing brighter than the others. It seemed to sit on top of the cliff, directly over the house. He gazed at it for a long time until a faint light spread across the sky. The bright star faded, and he knew it was dawn. He had slept all night in the Hermit's room.

A movement near the top of the cliff caught his eye. In the hollow above Pixel's window, a figure appeared, thrashing its limbs, and into his mind came the command "Feed me!" Smiling, he picked up his staff and headed for the main part of the house.

After wandering through many corridors, he found himself in a dead-end passage. There was a stone bench under a little window. Kneeling on the seat, he looked out. The sky was the color of lead, and he could hear breakers pounding the sand. The sound of whistling wind brought a stab of homesickness, and he thought of Dad, sleeping off his night shift or sitting at the hospital with Mom. At this last thought, he waited for the usual anger to rise, but it didn't. "Stop drinking, Mom," he said aloud to the wind. "Get better. I need you too."

"Hi, Peter," said a quiet voice.

Startled, he looked around and saw Jen's shining eyes.

"Lost your way?" she asked.

"Yeah."

She came up beside him and looked out. A gust of wind blew the hair from her face. "The trees love this kind of weather."

"You hear them too?"

She laughed. "Oh yes. I met your friend the hawthorn standing outside the front door."

"Yeah. It follows me everywhere." He looked at Jen out of the corner of his eye, wondering how old she was. Maybe the age of the university students who used to visit the house in the old days when Dad was a professor.

"Peter, do you ever wish to be free of this ... this silverness? Everyone thinks we know what to do—although the Poinkers don't think I'm very bright," she mused. "The first time I met them, I couldn't remember where I was from. I—" Heavy footsteps sounded in a distant corridor. Alarmed, she got to her feet. "What's that?"

Then, with a skitter and thump, Moody came around the corner and nearly knocked her down in his joyful greeting.

"Down, boy!" Peter commanded, and the great dog sat back on his haunches, quivering with joy.

"I saw him in the hall earlier this morning and ran from him," she said, half laughing. "He acts like he knows me." She reached out a tentative hand to stroke the long snout.

"Well, Moody sort of belongs to us Silvers. At least *he* thinks he does. I bet he lived at Wakkenburg House when you were there."

She scratched Moody behind one ear and grimaced when he lapped her face with his tongue. "I don't remember anything about Wakkenburg, though Forlost and Thrinn do. They're always talking about the old days when I was a little girl. By the way, I meant to give you a message from the Lady. Just before you arrived, she went through the Nowhere Door—"

"The what?"

"The door that leads to the Hermit's real home. It goes nowhere for us. But about the Lady's message: We're to watch for the morning star while she's gone, and after eight days she'll return. That's eight days counting yesterday, so we have seven days to go."

"The morning star? Eight days?" Peter pondered this, remembering the bright star he'd seen at dawn. "What does that mean?"

Jen shrugged. "Maybe the giants know. Are you coming to breakfast?"

"I have to feed the hawthorn first. Did you say it's at the front door?"

He followed Jen and Moody to the main part of the house. As they passed Pixel's door, Mara came out scowling, so they hurried on. A little farther down the corridor, a wide doorway on the right opened into a sitting room with a little fireplace and a sofa. A round window offered a view of grass, and beside it was the front door.

Jen opened it and there was the hawthorn, standing in the rain. The Vespa in its branches began to hum. Peter spread a little tree food around the roots. When he stood up and looked around, he noticed that the door was set in the side of a low hill. At his feet, yellow-gold grass grew ankle high in a secluded hollow surrounded by other hills. Three well-worn tracks led away from the clearing. "Where do those trails go?"

"That one over there goes to the top of the Silver Wing," Jen said, indicating the trail on the right. "And that one directly in front of us goes through the hills all the way to the woods. That's what Forlost told me. The one over there"—she waved a hand to the wider path on the left—"goes to Floden. But no one lives there now."

"The Mooners told us it burned down."

"That's right," she said and turned away into the house.

Peter followed her back to the main corridor, past a kitchen on the right, and through a doorway on the left, into the large dining room. Tall windows, floor to ceiling, faced the sea. A long wooden table, flanked by chairs and benches, stood in the center of the room, and at its farthest end, two armchairs sat in front of a big stone hearth.

Peter had just enough time to take all this in when a Fenny with long graying locks grabbed his elbow and steered him across the room.

"Oh! You're just in time! Sitting at the head of the table is what Silvers do!" She pushed him into a chair and he sat there, still clutching his staff. "And now we have *two* Silvers! One at this head, one at the other head! Perfect!"

"No, Thrinn," Jen said, but the Fenny frowned and pointed to a chair at the opposite end. Across the long expanse of table, Peter watched Jen take a deep breath and sit down. Moody trotted to the hearth and stretched himself out on a rug in front of the fire. Then the Fenny struck a bell.

Before the sound began to fade, Dooney walked in, with all the hounds swarming around his feet, and the Poinker band right behind. The Mooners followed, with Rathfrit in the lead. Everyone sat down as the hounds scurried under the table. Last came Tom Mole, in his old man form. He took a chair at Peter's right hand.

"Am I late?"

Before Peter could reply, Mara marched in at the head of the Fenny crew just as Jen called out across the room, "Thrinn, did I know Moody when I was little? At Wakkenburg House?"

In an instant, the windows and whitewashed walls vanished, and Peter found himself sitting on a broken chair in a dank gray room strung with cobwebs. The hearth and the furniture were gone. Poinkers and Mooners sprawled on the floor with the hounds, blinking. Tom Mole, now a little girl, sat on a three-legged stool, clutching a brown teddy bear. Peter looked at the girl; then he looked across the space where the table had been. Jen, her mouth open, clung to a tipsy chair.

A moment later, Pixel appeared in the doorway, leaning on Froke's arm. She stood there, staring. "No, Mara! Not Cwenburgh!"

Peter rose to his feet at the sight of her pale face. She was crying! He had never seen Pixel Rilson cry. "What's going on?"

"Not the cellar!" She wiped tears from her face with the back of her hand. "We escaped!" Her voice broke. "Didn't we?"

"Mara is always here," the old Fenny said in a toneless voice. She stood there, stone-faced, her lavender dress replaced by gray rags.

"That's not true," Jen said. "We're in the Hermit's House. Put things back as they are, Mara."

"Once a slave, always a slave," the old Fenny croaked. "Mara is no Head. She's a fool! A cheat!"

Ripping the legs off her teddy bear, the little girl began to sob, and the hounds whimpered.

Droat stepped out from the line of Fennys and put a hand on Mara's shoulder. "You have to tell her," he said softly. "You won't feel right till you do."

Mara did not reply, and into the silence Froke began to chant, "Steal a little silver fish, put it in your pocket."

Mara covered her face with her hands and sank to her knees.

"Froke, that's enough!" Droat said sharply.

Wondering what they were talking about, Peter thumped his staff in frustration, and a little spark of green light shot across the room.

In a quiet voice, Pixel said, "It was Lila who kidnapped Jen. She made Mara hide her at the bottom of a lake."

Mara rose to her feet and pointed at Jen. "It can't be her. She's a grown woman! I laid a little child down under those waters."

Thrinn shook her head sadly, "Oh, it's her alright."

Jen stood there, her eyes wide, looking back and forth between the two Fennys.

"Wait a minute." Peter thumped his staff again. Another green spark sped over the floor and up the wall. "Pixel, did you just say that Lila kidnapped Jen? Isn't that the monster who came out of that portal in the North Tower?"

"Yeah. She's the Moonwitch's mother. And Ahab Rilson, who lived in Aunt Kate's house, is the witch's father. He was a pirate."

Peter stared at her. "And that's the person you heard walking around at night?"

Her face crumpled. "Our ... our blood. Us Rilson girls. He drank it."

Peter's mind reeled, trying to grasp at some handhold of understanding. "But ... why?"

"To keep him alive. Until he can drink the blood of a Silver One. Then he'll live forever."

There was a long silence. The Mooners and Poinkers were staring at Peter and the staff. They had all seen the room begin to change, but he hadn't noticed. Neither had Jen or Pixel. Like peeling wallpaper, the gray cellar was falling away in tatters. Mara, no longer dressed in rags, looked askance at her new blue dress.

When the last shred of Cwenburgh had dissolved, Thrinn smiled at them all. "So that's what happened to our Jenny! Hidden at the bottom of a lake. Goodness knows why Lila didn't give our little

Silver Girl to Ahab back then. But she didn't! And now we have you back, child!"

"But ... but how did she get *out* of the lake?" Peter said. The Poinkers and the Mooners, sitting on chairs and benches again, gaped at him.

"How should I know?" Thrinn exclaimed. "But this is not the time for questions. Let's eat!"

There was a loud *pop!* Startled, Peter saw the old man smiling at him benignly, with a fork in one fist and a spoon in the other. Winking, the Buggane said in a loud whisper, "Do you think we'll have cake?"

❦ ❦ ❦

The following evening, after supper, Peter and Jen sat by the hearth in the dining room. It had rained for two days. Now, with the old armchairs turned toward the windows, they watched the storm break up, torn billows of red and gold clouds moving slowly across the horizon. Everyone else had gone to their quarters, and Pixel was in bed. The Fennys were tending fires or washing up after the meal, and in the silence, their clatter echoed down the passage. Then Jen began to speak of her journey into Rosknil with the Small One and her time with the giants in the Hidden Valley. It was a strange tale, and when she finished, Peter said, "I heard the giants are all around the hills now, guarding the Hermit's House. That's what Arkey said."

Jen looked thoughtfully into the fire. "Some of them are here, keeping watch. But not in the way Arkey thinks. You should go see them, Peter."

Tramping feet sounded in the doorway, and the voice of Rathfrit called out, "Silver Ones!" All twenty-eight Mooners, wearing their green jackets, filed around the long dining table and gathered in front of Peter and Jen.

"It is time," Rathfrit said. "All the creatures of the wood are gathered in one place. Never, since the Great Migration of Lir, has this happened. We must make plans."

Forlost entered the room carrying a tray. After setting it down on the end of the table near the hearth, he served cocoa to Peter and Jen. He offered it to the Mooners but was met with looks of disdain and stony silence. Undaunted, he poured some for himself, then moved a wooden chair to the hearth and sat down between the two Silvers.

The Mooners began to mutter, and Rathfrit said, "We cannot sit here, idly drinking cocoa. We must make plans. No doubt Garool has already spied out our position. Mac Lir could arrive at any time."

"This house is protected," Jen said. "The wizard will not find it."

"Protected? By whom?" Rathfrit glowered. "A handful of weak Fennys? *We* are the ones who must protect this house!"

Weak Fennys? This was too much. Peter got to his feet. Turning from the Mooners, he said, "I'm going to see the giants."

Jen nodded, trying to hide her smile, but Forlost looked at him sternly. "Not without your staff."

Taking the staff, which leaned against the back of his chair, Peter left the room without acknowledging the Mooners. He knew it was rude, but their contempt for the Fennys made him mad.

He opened the front door and looked out. The sky was clear. A cool breeze stirred the yellow grass. Closing his eyes, he listened. "Oh. Right," he said aloud. Then he walked across the hollow and took the trail through the Hills of Floden, guided by nothing more than the voice of the wind.

In the deep blue of evening, he stopped at the edge of a shallow valley and gazed in wonder. Western sunlight lay golden on the hills, but the grass of this valley shone emerald green, and giants, tall as cedars and beautiful as gods, came walking barefoot to meet him.

"Greetings, Silver One! We wondered if you'd come!"

He followed them to the center of the valley, where a large fire—its flames blue, green, and yellow—burned in a shallow depression of grass. Twelve giants, seven men and five women, seated themselves around the fire. Peter sat down between a fair-haired man who introduced himself as Gregor and a woman with dark braids who was called Bridget.

The fire burned without sound, and gradually Peter became aware of the silence. At first, it reminded him of that split second of relief after coming into a house straight out of a storm. Then he felt it, like a torrent of water pouring through him, scouring the rough grit of days. No, that wasn't quite right. There was no movement. He closed his eyes, feeling silence press close, a living presence whose heaviness might crush him, but only if he resisted. Floating, empty, in a white light that buoyed him upward, he heard a voice singing.

Softly the music began. As another voice joined, then another, it swelled to a piercing sweetness, and Peter recognized the melody from his visions of the Inner Mountains. He opened his eyes and saw a circle of radiant faces. Night had fallen, and the moon, almost at her full, cast a silver light over the hills.

When the singing stopped, silence filled the hollow again. Leaning forward, he looked into the firepit and saw a mass of color heaped at the bottom. What in the world was it? Not wood. Instead of smoke, a sweet scent rose from the flames.

Then Bridget, as if reading his thoughts, said, "This time of year we burn the fallen blossoms from the ancient place, see?" She held out a large basket, and Peter saw flowers, more colorful than any he'd ever seen. The woman scooped out a handful and tossed them into the flames. As they tumbled onto the burning heap, they did not turn black. There were no ashes. They burned but were not consumed.

"Now, Silver One. Why have you come to us?" Bridget said. "What is it you seek?"

Turning from the strange fire, Peter looked into her face. "I ... Jen told me I should come," he stammered. "And the Lady gave us a message. Something about the morning star for eight days. Do you know what that means?"

"During the octave of August, we hail the morning star each dawn," the woman replied. "And on the eighth day, we celebrate her coronation."

"Yet, before that, a hard time is coming, Silver One," said Gregor, who sat on his right. "You and your friends will be tested, and what you choose may decide the fate of this island."

"Me?"

"Not just you. You are not so important as that. *All* of you, humans and creatures of the woods alike, must choose. Either this island continues in its agony of contention, or it is freed and left to its long history of hiddenness and peace."

"I don't understand."

"And yet you carry the Lady's staff."

"I think she only lent it to me," he said slowly, "but I don't know why."

"Then go on as you have been," Gregor said, "turning away from those powers that your instinct tells you are false. More than that, I cannot say. We see some things from afar, yet we don't know how all will end."

"Can you tell me how to fight Mac Lir?" As Peter said it, he realized that this is what he had really come to ask.

Bridget smiled. "Tell me, do you have command over the trees of this wood?"

"No! They're the ones always pushing me around, showing me where to go."

"Then, as Gregor said, go on as you have begun. Listen and wait. Strength and the knowledge to act will come. Your hope lies in quietness and trust."

"But what about the Shee?" Peter asked.

"We know of the Lliannon Shee, though we do not fear them," Gregor said. "Their hunger runs deeper than oceans. They are ever restless, always hunting, and far more dangerous than the Moonwitch, who is only the half-human child of Lila."

"Then why do they do what the witch wants?"

"Because her father is someone they fear."

"Ahab Rilson? Why are the Shee afraid of him?"

"What remains of that man has shrunk into a far corner, you can be sure of that. And unless I am mistaken," Gregor said sadly, "he is finding that the immortality he has sought is nothing more than slavery. Do you understand, Silver One?"

"No."

Gregor nodded. "And why should you? Yet I tell you that Ahab Rilson is never alone. One day, the counselor he has taken to himself will overwhelm and destroy him."

"I still don't know why he needed Pixel's blood. And why does he want mine?"

"Neither the witch nor the wizard, nor any creature, has *real* power over you, Silver One, or your friend. That is only an illusion. The manserpent, Ahab, would gain nothing by capturing you unless he could enslave your mind. There is nothing to fear, don't you know?"

"Yeah, when I listen to the trees, they're always telling me not to be afraid."

"The stars say so too, and the wind. Can you hear them?"

Peter laughed. "I can hear the hawthorn! It's hungry again."

"Look, child. Dawn approaches." Bridget pointed to a faint light in the eastern sky. "We are glad you've kept vigil with us.

"One more thing," Peter began.

Gregor grinned. "Only one?"

"Who *are* you? Jen calls you giants, but you're not like any I've ever read about."

"We are those who live in the Inner Mountains, where you will go one day. Yet we come to this borderland when we are called. For now, this island, these woods, are the only place where we are visible to you."

Suddenly, a bright star blazed in the east. All the giants rose to their feet, lifted their arms, and began to sing a new song. Gazing in wonder at the star's pure brightness, Peter forgot everything else. Then, when the full light of the sun rose into the sky, the star faded and the song ended. Peter stood and picked up his staff.

"Farewell, Silver One!" Bridget placed her hand on his shoulder. "Go with all our blessing. And no matter what happens, remember to watch for the morning star. May we meet again in the green hills!"

"Goodbye, Peter," Gregor said. "I'll be seeing you."

Peter turned and saw the little hawthorn standing at the entrance to the valley. The hornets resting in its branches glittered like stars. As Peter drew near, the Vespa rose and surrounded him in their silvery swarm, and he knew they would lead him over the winding paths to the Hermit's House. He had only to follow.

There was no one about when he entered the house. Slipping quickly through the dim passages, he went to the Silver Wing and into the Small One's painted room. He took off his shoes, set his staff against the wall, and lay down on a bench, his head propped on a pillow, so he could gaze on the face of Grandfather.

37

Driving Old Road

"Dang nabbit!" Ed scowled and slammed the back door on the shouting match between Muru and Mac Rilson. From the moment Mac arrived two weeks ago, he'd been a dratted nuisance that only the spider Buggane could keep in check. Muru did her best, but Mac made her cranky, and the fact that he'd told the wizard where Peter was—all for a bottle of rum—still rankled.

Ed stood in the late-afternoon sunshine, scowling at the trees of the forest, which rose like scorched skeletons beyond the far garden wall. Seven nights ago—according to the hairy man—the Moon-witch had gone to Fenn House demanding that the wizard join forces with her. When he'd refused, rudely departing in his ship behind a cloak of mist, she'd set fire to Fenn House. Then she'd ridden south with the Glashtyn, lighting fires in the woods around Wakkenburg and all the way to Sweetwater. "Blasted witch!" Ed muttered, crossing the courtyard.

He surveyed the sandbags still piled in the yard. For several hours the witch's fires had spread through the forest until the flames licked the outer garden walls. No doubt the wizard had seen the rising smoke from the vantage of his ship, and his reply to the witch, in the form of torrential rains, had caused floods from Wakkenburg to Sweetwater. "Dang wizard," Ed fumed.

Muru, of course, wasn't about to let that stupid wizard control the weather of Wakkenburg again. As soon as the fires were out, she'd cleared the clouds over the house, but storms continued unabated over the rest of the island. George brought out his transistor radio and tuned in to Sweetwater AM 780, and they all sat in the West Wing kitchen, listening to the news of floods, missing persons, wild stallions running loose in town, and rumors of ghosts.

"Those stallions were Glashtyn!" Ed snarled as he paused by the garage door. "The Shee were in Sweetwater!"

After the floods, blinding blizzards had dumped four feet of snow on the beleaguered town. All regular programming was suspended; AM 780 kept up a running commentary on the deepening subzero temperatures and ice-bound roads. Doggedly, the radio announcer kept at it, transmitting interviews and accounts of the people leaving town, headed for the mainland and never coming back.

Mary and George had grown distracted. They could not reach Annette by phone. Finally, on August 15, the radio announcer, his voice trembling, told the world that he was taking the last car to Orbsen Bay to board the last ferry. He signed off the airwaves, the radio went to static, and that was all. Ed leaned against the doorpost of the garage, remembering that moment again, the long silence in the kitchen, broken only by the quiet sobbing of Mary. Then, Furse had burst through the door.

"Cars! A whole line! Coming up the drive!"

Annette had come, bringing friends and distant relations: Maycaps and Deltons and Thornburg cousins two or three times removed. And that's how the Sweetwater Invasion had begun. At first the refugees were amazed by the size of the house; then they were scared of the Fennys. Ed had wondered how to explain the presence of the little hairy people, but he hadn't had to. In the end, it was the Fennys themselves and their natural charm that had overcome all fear and suspicion.

Today was the third day of the invasion. The house seemed overrun with guests, and already Ed was tired of company. He went into the garage, picked up a wrench, and began a tune-up on the Datsun. The balmy afternoon had become a warm summer evening, and the shop doors stood wide open. Krim and a few of the boys stood around, ready to lend a hand, but no one spoke. They seemed to understand his need for silence.

"Oh! There you are, Ed!"

Startled, he bumped his head on the hood. "Dang nabbit!" The wrench slipped out of his hand and clattered down into the engine. Krim made a dive for it.

"Ed." Marj's voice trembled and he looked up, surprised to see Muru there too, and an old woman in a blue, travel-stained cloak.

"Ed, this is ..." Marj hesitated. Tears ran down her face as she looked at the woman in blue.

"I have many names," the old woman said. "Pixel calls me the Bread Lady."

Ed searched her face. "How do you know Pixel?"

"We met in Foyle. And now all things move toward Floden."

"Do you ... do you mean Pixel's there?" Marj asked.

"Floden?" Ed said. "I heard it burned down. Like Foyle."

"There is one place in Floden that remains," the woman said. "Will you go there? It is time."

For a moment, no one spoke. Then Muru said, "Yes, they'll go. Krim and Fiak too."

The wrench in Krim's hand clattered to the floor, and he stood gaping.

"It is well," the old woman said. She reached into the bag on her shoulder, withdrew a white lily, and gave it to Muru. She placed a loaf of bread in Marj's hand. Then she walked out the shop door. Ed watched her pass through the courtyard and out the gate, which opened for her of its own accord.

For several seconds, they stood like statues. Muru looked solemnly at the lily in her hand; then, without a word, she left the garage and went back to the house, Krim trailing behind.

"Who is that woman, Marj?"

Marj ran a trembling hand over the bread. "You remember when Jenny disappeared. Mother weeping, father shouting orders, everyone running this way and that."

"Sure. I remember."

"*She* was there. That woman, looking just the same. She told me not to be afraid. Then she gave me a bread roll and kissed me. I watched her walk away, out of Floden, into the woods, and knew that Jenny would be found."

"She *has* been found."

"Yes. So much has happened since the Bugganes came to breakfast and we heard that she's alive."

"And every dang thing began that day in Floden, didn't it?"

"Long before that, Ed. But for us it began that day."

"What did she mean by 'all things move toward Floden'?" he asked.

"I hardly know. But here"—she broke the loaf and gave half to him—"I think this is for both of us."

❦ ❦ ❦

The next morning, as the Sweetwater folks were sitting down to breakfast in the East Tower, Ed and Fiak loaded the last bag into the back of the Datsun. Krim was still arguing with Muru.

"Krim, I wouldn't send you if I didn't think you'd be alright."

"But won't we go mad away from the house? That's what I've always heard about us Fennys."

"You're mad already," Ed muttered. "And why have we packed all this luggage, Muru? I thought this was just a day trip."

"Look, Mr. Edward," she said, stuffing one last bag into the trunk. "I know more about this than you do."

Marj came into the garage, hastily shoving something into her pocket, and got into the car. Ed started the engine, and the Datsun pulled out of the garage and stood idling in the courtyard. Fiak was already scribbling away, determined to record every minute of the momentous trip. Then Muru, surrounded by the garage crew, leaned through the open window on Marj's side. "Krim! Fiak! Take care of these two!"

"We can take care of ourselves, thank you," Ed said. "Goodbye." Releasing the hand brake, he steered the Datsun through the gate.

Furse and Norbert ran alongside, shouting, "Good luck, Krim! Don't use all your ink in the first hour, Fiak! Goodbye! Goodbye!"

They drove past the wide lawns, serene under the late-morning sun. Turning right onto Wakkenburg Road, Ed put on more speed as they passed through the woods.

"You're going awfully fast, Mr. Edward," Krim said, leaning forward to look at the speedometer. "I didn't think she could go over fifty."

"Krim, you genius, she can go faster than this. Watch." Ed stepped on the gas and took the speed up to eighty. Krim's eyes widened.

"Look to the weather!" Fiak said sharply as the first bridge came into view.

Ed slowed the car, then brought her to a stop a few feet from the bridge. On the far side, they saw a leaden sky and the forest bent under wild wind and sheeting rain. They all got out of the car and stood looking at the storm.

"Here ends the domain of Muru," Marj said, looking up at the bright day directly overhead. "I should have guessed the Glenfaba was the barrier."

Silently, they got back in the car and rolled up the windows as the Datsun chugged into the heavy rain. Ed drove slowly, wondering about potholes. When they reached the junction, he stopped the car again and sat looking ahead into the gloom. To their right, the tarmac of Fenn Road stretched away north, fairly smooth and even. But straight ahead, the Old Road, which had never been paved, looked pretty rough.

"It wasn't this bad a month ago," Ed muttered. "Dang wizard's weather."

"How far is it to Floden?" Fiak asked.

"I don't know. The odometer acts funny out here in the woods. But when I came with Peter, we got there in an hour." Ed released the hand brake and took the Datsun down the short, sharp incline.

By swerving cautiously from one side of the road to the other, he managed to avoid rocks and wide puddles of unknown depth, but it was a slow business. He bent over the steering wheel, grumbling. "At this rate we'll be lucky to make it by lunchtime."

"Let's hope to make it before nightfall," Fiak said.

As if these words were an omen, they heard a loud *kathunk*. The Datsun faltered, lurching sideways. Marj groaned and Ed turned off the ignition, grinding his teeth.

"A flat!" Krim said bitterly. "And we won't get far on the spare."

Ed watched the rain sluice down the window and wished a Buggane would appear. "I'll jack her up," he said, opening the door.

By the time they finished changing the tire, he and Krim were completely soaked and covered in mud. No one spoke as Ed started the car. The Datsun crawled forward to the *flap, flap* of the wipers, and after a while, Marj leaned her head back and dozed. Glancing in the rearview mirror, Ed saw Fiak slumped in his seat, his pen still. But Krim sat bolt upright, cringing every time they drove through a pothole, and once, when the car scraped over a rock, he uttered a long string of words in a strange language. *Fenny swear words*, Ed thought, adding a few of his own.

At last, when he could take it no longer, he stopped and turned off the engine. Closing his eyes, he leaned his head against the steering wheel. He felt as if he'd been gone for years, though he guessed that hardly half a day had passed.

"Ed," Marj said.

He opened his eyes and looked at her.

"Listen! I think the rain stopped, but what's that humming sound?"

"It's a gas leak!" Krim said. "I knew that last rock ripped her open!"

"It's more like a cat purring on the roof." Fiak thumped the ceiling with his fist.

The hum grew louder as a swarm of large insects circled the Datsun. They landed on the car, covering the windshield. Ed could feel the vibration of their buzzing. "What the devil?"

"Silver hornets," Marj said softly. "I remember seeing them in the orchard once, when Jenny was a baby. Mother told me they're the sign of the Silver One."

As soon as she said these words, the hornets rose into the air and sped off westward. Everyone got out of the car.

"Look at that!" Ed said. The road ahead was a sobering sight. Wide potholes and fallen branches blocked the way, not to mention innumerable rocks, all large enough to put a significant dent in the Datsun's undercarriage.

"But look at the way we've come!" Marj said. "Why, anyone would think you'd had a guide, Ed. Somehow you drove the only possible way through this mess."

"Good grief, you're right." He gazed back at the zigzagging tracks of the Datsun.

Then, as scattered rain began, Krim said, "Let me drive."

"I saw you driving the hearse with Furse down on the floor pushin' pedals. That didn't end too well."

"Oh, we'd have been fine if that darn spider hadn't attacked," Krim said. "I can reach the pedals in this car."

"Let him drive," Marj said. "You can sit in back and take a little nap, Ed."

"A nap? You think I can take a nap now?" But at everyone's urging, he changed places and watched Krim move the driver's seat as far forward as it would go. The engine started and the Datsun eased forward.

The road narrowed, curving gently north. Though he could barely see over the steering wheel, somehow Krim managed to steer the Datsun skillfully, winding slowly in and out between thickets of young saplings that had spread out from the forest. The clouds passed and the sun came out. Small birds darted across the road, disturbed by the unfamiliar sound of an engine in the woods. Ed rolled down the window. He'd traveled Old Road a number of times in his life, yet it always bore the strange quality of going deeper and deeper into dream. Breathing in the warm scent of wet trees and deep green moss, he let his head fall back against the seat and closed his eyes.

❦ ❦ ❦

"Ed! We're here!"

Startled out of sleep, Ed sat up and saw a wooden door in a hill. The silver hornets were hanging like a cloud above the idling car, and he watched them land in the branches of a little tree that stood beside the door. "That's Peter's hawthorn!"

"The Vespa led us here," Marj said in a hushed voice, and Krim shut off the engine.

A golden thrush landed on the hillock above the tree and let out a song that seemed to rise, twirling into the azure twilight. As if this were a cue, the door opened and a lovely young woman with long dark hair stepped out. "Small One?" she called. "Is that you? I hear your bird!" Then she saw the Datsun. "What is that?"

At the sight of the woman, Ed thought his heart would crack wide open.

"Jenny!" Marj said and opened the car door. But before anyone else could move, several things happened at once.

First came a piercing wail, like the voice of some soul in torment. The hawthorn began lashing its branches violently, and the huge hornets rose in a towering cloud. Buzzing angrily, they swept over the bluff toward the sea.

"That's Dooney! Something's happened!" Jen cried. She ran back into the house, leaving the door wide open.

Ed, Marj, and the Fennys scrambled out of the car and stood staring at the open front door. Then, like a stage curtain dropping suddenly out of the sky, white mist enveloped the Datsun. The hill and door vanished. Instinctively, Ed reached out, felt the side mirror of the car, and held on.

"Oh, Ed! Help!"

"Hold still, Marj! And keep talking!" With one hand on the Datsun, he groped his way around the front end, toward the sound of his sister's voice. Grasping her arm, he steered her toward the open door. At least, he hoped they were heading toward the door. "Krim! Fiak! Where are you?"

"Right behind you, sir," Krim said.

A lamp shone out of the dank mist, held by a small, gnarled hand, and a wrinkled face appeared in the halo of light. "Good evening, Miss Marjorie, Mr. Edward. Goodness! Here's little Krim and Fiak too! Come in. The door is right here."

Pulling Marj after him, Ed followed the Fenny over the threshold into firelight.

"What the devil's going on?" he demanded.

The elderly Fenny shook his head. "Oh, Mr. Edward, you're just in time to be too late. But welcome to the Hermit of Floden's house."

38

Tricky Tree

Peter woke from a dream of the warrior riding across the open sea. With the sound of hoofbeats still ringing in his ears, he blinked in the afternoon sunlight shining on the image of Grandfather. Sea wind blew through the window of the Hermit's room. Peter had been asleep most of the day. As he lay there, thinking about his all-night visit to the giants, a buzzing static began. It sounded like someone running a chainsaw far away. He got up and closed the window, and the noise became faint. Maybe this sporadic sound in his head was some peculiar side effect of having silver eyes. He'd never thought of that. Better ask Jen about it.

He put on his shoes, then picked up his staff and left the Silver Wing. In the main part of the house, he went first to Pixel's room, expecting to find her there. She was getting stronger, but the Head Fenny, Mara, made her rest a lot. To his surprise, her room was empty. Guessing it might be teatime, he hurried to the dining room and found her standing at the window with Jen.

"Peter! There you are! Look at the hawthorn out there on the Hermit's beach! And the tide's coming in."

"I tried talking to it, but it doesn't listen to me," Jen added.

Sure enough, the hawthorn was standing below the Silver Wing, right where the headland met the water. Even at low tide there was only a narrow stretch of sand. Peter turned his thoughts to the tree. "What are you doing out there?"

"Waiting for you, silly."

"But why there?"

"Hungry!"

"Alright. I'm coming. But can't you move away from the water?"

"Water? Stupid!"

He grimaced, wishing trees were more reasonable. Then he caught Jen's eye.

"I heard that," she said with a laugh.

He shrugged. "Maybe if I feed it, it'll move."

"I'll come with you," Pixel said. "Mara told me I should get some fresh air."

They stopped in the kitchen, where he'd left a jar of tree food handy. Then, matching his pace to Pixel's, he led her down the sloping beach passage. As they approached the back door, the faint buzz in his head increased, growing louder as they passed out of the ravine onto the open shore. Halfway across the beach, he heard Pixel say, "Look! The tide's reached its trunk! Saltwater can't be good for it."

He rubbed his forehead hard, then looked up and caught her eye.

"Are you okay?" she asked.

"I get this weird buzz in my head sometimes."

The hawthorn had moved up the beach, just out of the lapping sea.

"Hello!" Pixel called, and the tree waved its branches. "Did it say something?" she asked.

"I don't know." The rasping grew louder, and Peter gritted his teeth.

Walking ahead, Pixel got to the tree first, just as two crows flapped down into its branches. Squawking like mad, they began ripping off leaves and twigs. Pixel shooed them away, and the birds rose into the air, circling the tree, cawing harshly.

Peter squinted in the sunlight. The static was overpowering now, like a roaring chainsaw. Forcing himself to keep going, he reached the end of the headland and stopped near the tree. Water lapped his feet. "Here. Hold this," he said, and he handed his staff to Pixel as the metallic roar intensified.

"What's with you?" she cried as a crow flew down and beat its wings in her face. He knew something about these crows but couldn't think what. Now she was waving the staff in the air, trying to fend off the birds. He could see her through half-closed eyes, the rasping buzz tearing at his nerves. He should help her; he should ... Why was he here? *The tree; feed the tree.*

Fumbling with the lid of the jar, he felt a thump on his head and heard, very faintly, the shriek of a crow. The roaring static drowned out all other sound now. The noise swelled until the pain of it was so great that he dropped the jar and squeezed his eyes shut. He pressed his hands against his head as if to keep it from exploding.

Then, quite suddenly, the static stopped.

He opened his eyes. The ground rumbled under his feet, and the roots of the hawthorn began to writhe in the sand. He heard a low laugh.

"Run!" he shouted at Pixel.

The world slowed. He saw her mouth open in horror, felt a slippery root wrap itself around his middle, and looked up into the mouth of a giant fish. As the huge jaws closed over him, a vivid scene flashed into his mind: his dad standing at the bow of a boat in the open sea. "Dad! Help!" Then darkness swallowed him.

39

Meanwhile, in Lang

Martin Thornburg woke with a start. That was Peter's voice. Or ... or maybe it was a dream. Getting up from his chair, he looked around. There was no one else in the diner. Switching on the radio, he stood at the counter, listening.

"Eight days ago, on August eleventh, the island station Sweetwater AM 780 reported torrential rain and extensive flooding, hours after forest fires swept through the area," a voice said. "More recent reports indicate unseasonal and extreme weather patterns. The rain in Sweetwater was followed by heavy snowfall and subzero temperatures, causing treacherous road conditions. Ferry service has been temporarily discontinued ..."

The bell on the diner door sounded, and Martin turned off the radio. A man dressed in greasy coveralls walked in.

"You Peter's dad?" the man said.

"Yes. Martin Thornburg. Do I know you?" He looked at the man's hardened expression, wondering what this was about.

"Tommy Rilson. Pixel's dad. She told me you worked here." He sat down at the counter and jerked his thumb at the radio. "You heard the reports about the island lately?"

Martin nodded. Then, to his complete surprise, Tommy put his face in his hands and groaned. "I never shoulda sent my little girl there! And that nurse. That Kate Rilson." He thumped his fist on the counter. "She never called like she said she would. We never heard nothin' about how them treatments were goin'! Then the whole of Foyle burnt down! That's where she was livin' and I ain't heard a word about her!"

There were tears in the man's eyes. Pouring him a cup of coffee, Martin thought of the short, evasive letter he'd received from

Great-Aunt Marj. It had arrived yesterday but was dated July 30, almost three weeks ago. She'd mentioned "the tragic fire in Foyle" and then had gone on to say, "All things considered", she "hoped Peter was well". What did that mean? Didn't she know? "I haven't heard from my son either," he said aloud. "I'm not sure what to do, now that there's no ferry service."

Tommy paused with the cup to his lips. "Whaddya mean, no ferry service?"

"I heard it on the news a few minutes ago. Ferry service to the island has been temporarily discontinued because of the strange weather patterns."

"You're kiddin'!" Tommy set the cup down hard, sloshing coffee on the counter. "And here the wife and me been workin' extra hours, savin' money, hopin' to go to the island and find our kid."

A siren wailed in the distance, the lonely sound fading into the hum of traffic. "Don't give up yet. Ferry service to the island is sure to resume. As soon as it does, I plan to go."

"I sure hope you're right. Pixel's baby brother has been cryin' himself to sleep every night since she left."

"I'll let you know if I hear anything."

"Okay. I work down at Al's Garage, a coupla blocks from here. Thanks for the coffee."

"Sure." Martin watched Pixel's dad go out the door and disappear down the street.

He stood at the counter, looking absently out the window. The streetlamps flicked on, and a police car cruised by slowly. Something about the radio reports niggled at his mind. Wasn't there a connection between strange weather and the family folklore? Some mythic figure who commanded storms. Martin stood there, biting his thumbnail, wishing he hadn't sold *all* his books. It had been necessary to pay the last hospital bill, but the copy of his family's history hadn't fetched more than a few dollars.

The Thornburg book. He wished now that he'd kept it.

40

Move the Datsun

The house was deathly still. Standing at the open window, Pixel listened to the waves far below. There was nothing to be seen but mist, thick and impenetrable.

Peter was gone. Snatched from the beach, right under her nose. She felt like weeks had passed since that moment, but she was pretty sure it was the same day. Over and over, the scene replayed itself in her mind. The giant fish swallowing him and plunging into the sea. Moody Doug tearing across the sand as she ran, screaming at the top of her lungs. Tom Mole picking her up and carrying her indoors. She remembered little after that—only Uncle Edward's voice shouting, "Dang nabbit!" but that must have been a dream.

She shivered and reached for her sweater. Then she slipped on her shoes and went to the front door. When she opened it, the hawthorn waved a branch and struck her gently on the side of the head.

"That wasn't you on the beach, was it?" she whispered.

The little tree shuddered. Then a large figure loomed out of the mist.

"Little missy?" Tom Mole sat down and blocked her way. "You're not to come out. Strict orders from the Head."

"I just want to know about ... about ..."

"Kidnapped!" Tom growled.

"Oh! He's not dead!" The surge of relief left her wobbly, and she leaned on the doorpost.

"Of course not! Tom Bear saw it all. Thinks it was Garool the Great. Who else could make himself look like a tree and then a fish." The Buggane leaned forward until his tusks almost rested on her shoulders. "Little missy, go back inside. You leave news gathering to the Poinkers and Mooners!"

She frowned at him and stomped her foot but retreated and shut the door. Feeling a little breathless, she sat down on the sofa. Peter was a prisoner! Somewhere . . .

"Pixel!"

She looked up, and there was Uncle Ed! He stood in the hall, holding a plate in one hand. She went to him, wrapped her arms around his waist, and hung on.

"When did you get here?" she asked.

"A few hours ago. Just after Peter was nabbed. Thank goodness *you're* alright," he said, patting her back awkwardly. "We been worried. You was delirious when Tom Mole brought you in; then you passed out. Where's Marj?"

Pixel tilted her head back. "She's here too?"

"Been sittin' at your bedside. I went to find us some food. This place was total pandemonium when we got here. Where's the kitchen?"

She let go and led him down the corridor. To her surprise, there was not a single Fenny in the kitchen. Uncle Ed clapped the plate down on the table. "Dang scones are full of pepper."

Pixel nodded. "Droat says we have to make allowances 'cause they're still settling in."

"Who?"

"The seven Fennys who got lost under a mountain or something."

"Well, I can make allowances, but my digestion won't. Is there anything edible around here?"

Rummaging in the larder, Pixel found a few apples, a round of cheese, and a ginger cake that turned out to be delicious. They ate in silence until Uncle Edward said, "George and Mary say hello."

"They're alive? Foyle was gone by the time we got there."

His eyes widened. "You went to Foyle?"

Before she could answer, they heard a loud sigh in the corridor. A tall, lanky figure passed the kitchen door. "Lost!" it moaned. "We shall never get back! Lost!"

"Who the devil is that?" Uncle Ed said as the figure moved out of sight.

"The Dooiney-oie. We call him Dooney."

"Friend of yours?"

"More Peter's friend than mine."

Dooney's sighs had hardly faded when a door slammed and a voice began scolding.

"Uh oh. That's Thrinn," Pixel whispered. She was about to hide under the table when Jen ducked into the doorway, flattened herself against the wall, and put a finger to her lips. She wore a red woolly scarf and carried Peter's staff.

"Don't you run away from me!" Thrinn cried. Still scolding, the Fenny passed the doorway, her voice carrying up and down the corridor. When she was gone, Jen relaxed and took a piece of cake from the table. Then she noticed Uncle Ed. "Who are you?"

He gaped at Jen and reached out his hand. Pixel saw his face crumple. "I ... I'm your big brother!"

Jen stared at him. "From Wakkenburg?"

He bristled, blinking back tears. "Of course from Wakkenburg! Where the devil have you been?"

"I ... I was just ..." Jen frowned at him. "Which brother *are* you? Thrinn says I have three."

"I'm Edward." His face softened, and he pulled her into a tight hug. They stood like that, Jen stiff and awkward, Pixel looking at them from the corner of her eye. Then Jen withdrew herself and Uncle Edward said, "But to answer *my* question, where have you been? Our old Head Fenny, Forlost, has been lookin' all over the house for you!"

"Down at the beach," Jen said, still frowning. "I found Peter's staff. Then a long green arm came out of the waves and grabbed my ankle."

"Jen!" Pixel gasped.

"It's alright. I hit it with this staff and it disappeared."

"Good grief!" Uncle Ed muttered. "No wonder that Fenny was yellin' at you."

"We've got to do something about that Buggane," Jen said.

Ed frowned. "Which one?"

"Garool! The fish who captured Peter! The tree who tricked us! That's who tried to grab me! The other Toms say he's a friend of the wizard." She wrapped the woolly scarf tighter around her neck. "I'm going to see the giants. Maybe they'll help."

"But you just told us a renegade Buggane is after you!" Ed snapped. "You can't go out there! If he nearly caught you on the beach, he'll come lookin', and it won't be long before he finds the front door!"

"This house is protected. He won't find it."

"Sisters, blisters! I don't see how he can miss this place! I got a bright blue car out front!"

"Ahem."

Pixel turned and saw Forlost standing in the doorway, flanked by Krinias and Krim.

Krinias grinned. "Feelin' better, Spy?"

Pixel put down her slice of cake and prepared to be scolded, but Forlost had other things on his mind.

"Mr. Edward," he said, "you are exactly right. You must move your car. Immediately. There's a workroom near the back door, at the bottom of the beach passage."

"But how's he gonna get it down to the ravine?" Krinias said.

"Through the tunnel at the back of the canyon. The giants made it long ago when the tide sometimes covered the stairs to the Gap. I lived in it for years, while I was waiting for Jenny."

Minutes later, Pixel found herself squashed in the back seat of the Datsun between Krim and Krinias, surprised that Forlost let her come at all. Jen sat in front, watching her brother start the engine.

"I'll drive," she said to him.

He scowled. "Not on your life."

The Datsun followed Tom Mole, chugging slowly through the thick fog, its headlights illuminating his broad back. There were no visible landmarks in the swirling white mist, only the sense of the car traveling straight, then curving right, then a sharp descent into darkness. They were in the tunnel now. It was high and wide. In the glow of the Datsun's lights, Pixel saw wet, glistening walls and a sandy floor. Then, over the hum of the engine, she heard the sound of a waterfall, and they drove into the mist again. The car went bumping over a rough track in the foggy darkness. Branches scraped across the windows. Then, with a revving roar, the Datsun stopped moving and Uncle Ed exclaimed, "Dang nabbit! She's stuck in the sand!"

They all got out, Uncle Ed issuing orders. "Pixel! You steer. Everybody push! You too, Tom Mole!"

Pixel hopped into the driver's seat and looked through the windshield in time to see Tom swell until his head disappeared in the mist. The next thing she knew, he had picked up the Datsun with her in it. She clung to the steering wheel, laughing and listening to the panicked shouts of Uncle Ed and Krim as Tom walked away. Then he set the car down, and after a volley of distant shouts and cries—"Over here! Stick together!" and "Why didn't we ask him to do that in the first place!"—everyone converged at the Datsun. According to Tom, he'd set it right on the back step.

When Uncle Ed opened the driver's door, he was still muttering, and Pixel scooted over to the passenger's seat. As he started the engine, the sound of brash voices resounded through the canyon.

"It's the Arkan Sonney!" Tom shouted.

Pixel heard Moody barking, and when his big snout appeared at her window, she rolled it down. He licked her face, then shook his head, jowls flapping. A small bristly bundle fell into her lap, and she saw a little thing like a pincushion unroll itself.

"Ditched!" the tiny Poinker fumed. "Jimmy ditched me! So they found Lir's ship! So what! That's no reason to swim off with Arkey and leave *me* behind! I am *not too small*!"

41

Sisters and Toms

Jen opened the door to the ledge outside her room and stepped into thick white mist. Lifting her eyes to the east, where the morning star must be shining, she thought about the Poinkers' news of the night before. They had found Lir's ship anchored in Grondle's Gap and sent Arkey to find out whether Peter was on board. It was the logical place to look, Kaney said. Someone named Jimmy Squarefoot had gone with Arkey, swimming across the cove. If they found Peter, they would arrange for his escape. "Help us," Jen whispered to the unseen star.

She went inside, dressed, and took a jar of tree food from her nightstand. Forlost had told her never to be without Peter's staff, so she picked it up and left the Silver Wing, walking swiftly through the corridors. From every window, the mist shone bright white, cloaking the sunrise. And yet ... maybe the fog was thinning.

In the front room, she stopped at the round window that faced the hollow and looked out. Yes, the fog was certainly thinning. Hearing a footstep behind her, she turned and saw a tall woman with long, wiry limbs standing in the doorway. Her short gray curls framed a lined face and sea-gray eyes. Stretching out her arms, the woman said, "Jenny! At last!"

"Mother?"

"Not Mother, though maybe I look something like her now. I'm Marj. Your sister." She came forward and placed her hands on Jen's shoulders. She was only a little taller. "How I've missed you! You were only four years old the last time I saw you, but I'd know you anywhere!"

Jen searched the woman's face and saw the likeness to Edward. "Mother is gone, isn't she? The Lady told me she went to the Inner Mountains."

"Did she say that? This is her staff, isn't it?" Reverently, Marj ran her finger over the intricate carvings. "I've seen that woman only twice in my life. The first time was moments after you disappeared. She was carrying this very walking stick, I'm sure of it. She's the one who told us that 'all things move toward Floden', and she was right! Here you are!"

Jen felt herself embraced in strong arms, and she leaned against her sister's shoulder. Then Marj stiffened. "Who is that tweedy little man?"

Startled, Jen turned and looked out the window. The mist was gone, and a man stood in the hollow, examining the Datsun's tire marks. Suddenly, he looked up, and she saw his eyes widen. A swirling silver cloud descended, and he began to wave his arms. Rushing to the window, she looked out in time to see him run off with the swarm of hornets in pursuit.

Jen opened the door cautiously. The hawthorn blocked the threshold. A large spider sat in its branches, winding a fly in a sticky web. When it saw her, it grew a little larger and began to clack its jaws. "Garool?" she said.

Marj leaned over her shoulder. "This is Tom Spider. Tom came in the car with us. Don't tell Ed."

The spider clacked its jaws again.

"What's it saying?" Jen asked.

"Tom says that tweedy little man is Garool and that you should call the Bugganes. All of them."

Jen stared at the spider. "Are there others besides Tom Bear and Tom Mole?"

"Let's see." Marj counted on her fingers. "Tom Spider, Tom Mole, Tom Bear, Tom Troll. That's four." The spider crawled along the branch, a little nearer to Marj's face, and clacked its jaws. "Two more? Really? How interesting. I never knew."

The Buggane wound another strand of silk around its little fly. The hawthorn quivered, and Jen heard it say, "Aha! Clever spider!" Steadily, like a small stream flowing through the woods, its thoughts came into her mind. She smiled grimly. Then it put out a prickly branch and rapped her on the head. "Feed me!"

❦ ❦ ❦

Jen and Marj went to the dining room, hoping for breakfast. As they stepped through the doorway, Marj said, "Oh! There's Fiak!", and

Jen saw a bespectacled Fenny sitting at a small writing table against the far wall. He was interviewing Froke, scribbling on a notepad as she talked. Jen heard her say, "That's right. We escaped from the witch's house through a secret tunnel."

Then Marj said, "Oh look, there's Tom Troll!"

A large man with wild brown hair and a long, tangled beard sat at the farthest end of the dining table. Beside him sat Tom Mole, in his old man form, eating porridge. Next to the hearth, Mara slept in an armchair, and a very tiny Poinker stood on the table near her elbow, helping himself to scones and jam.

"Excuse me, miss," a voice said from behind. Marj grabbed Jen's elbow and drew her aside as Rathfrit entered, followed by all the Mooners.

They went straight to the hearth and surrounded Mara's chair. The old Fenny opened her eyes.

"Was it you who lifted the wizard's mist?" Rathfrit said.

Mara's face was expressionless. "Yes."

"And you serve the Lady? Mr. Peter's Lady?"

Mara nodded. "We Fennys have always known the *real* Queen."

Since their arrival, the Mooners had avoided the Fennys as much as possible. They couldn't hide their contempt, and for the past four days, Jen had felt the tension in the dining room at every meal. She wondered which way this conversation would go. Then, to her amazement, Rathfrit swept off his cap and went down on one knee.

"Mistress Mara, we are at your service. Tell us what to do." As he spoke, all the other Mooners knelt before the Fenny.

"Good!" Jen said under her breath, and Marj squeezed her arm.

"Keep watch over this house," Mara said. "There is a renegade Buggane on the loose. He is searching the hills."

"He has already captured the Silver One," Rathfrit said. "What else does he seek?"

"Me," Jen said.

All the Mooners turned and stared at her.

"Look!" one of them said. "She carries the boy's staff!"

Rathfrit stood and bowed to Mara. "It will be as you command." Then the Mooners left the dining room, saluting Jen as they passed.

As she and Marj moved toward the far end of the table, the hairy man got up, brushing crumbs from his beard. "Come, Tom. Enough breakfast. We must go to Floden now. Tom Wolf and Tom Hag will meet us there. And with your permission"—he bowed to Mara—"we will bring them here."

"Oh good!" Marj cried. "Tom Spider said to gather the Bugganes."

"Ah. Then he thought of it too," the hairy man said, and Jen nodded.

"Thought of what?" Marj asked, sitting down near the tiny Poinker and the scones.

"More trouble is coming," Mara said. "I feel it in my bones. Your brother Toms are welcome."

As the Bugganes hurried out, Marj picked up a knife and the jam pot. "Well, Jenny. Sounds like we're going to have a busy day! How about breakfast first?" She paused. "Though I see all the scones are gone."

The tiny Poinker held the last scone in his little paws and blinked at her.

❦ ❦ ❦

After dinner, Jen and Pixel sat in the front room looking out the small round window. Twilight had settled over the hollow. The branches of the hawthorn blocked most of the view, but now and then a silver hornet hovered in front of the glass, coming from its evening patrol to rest in the little tree. The tiny Poinker, whose name was Sonney, sat curled on Pixel's shoulder, tucked against her neck. Guarding her was his special assignment because he was too runty for a hero's job. Kaney had confided all this to Jen earlier that day, just before taking the Poinker band on a scouting mission to the Gap.

"Why can't those other Cwenburgh Fennys cook?" Pixel asked. "And they hardly talk. What happened to them?"

"They spent many years as slaves in the deep labyrinths below a mountain," Jen replied.

Pixel frowned. "Froke says they lived with a sea monster."

"That's right. Peter told me it's the Moonwitch's pet."

"What if Peter doesn't come back tonight?" Pixel asked. "What if he's decided to help the wizard?"

Jen looked into Pixel's anxious face, heard her wheezy breathing. "Surely your time with Small One taught you one thing."

"Yeah. Don't be afraid." She puffed out her cheeks and exhaled slowly. "It's not as easy as it sounds."

"Spy!"

"Uh oh." Pixel sighed and stood up as Mara marched into the room.

"What do you think you're doing? Still up at this hour! Just as if you're not at death's door!"

Pixel started coughing, then sucked in her breath. "I'm *not* at death's door."

"Straight to bed, and none of your sass!"

"But Aunt Marj said I could stay up with her and wait for Peter," Pixel said as she followed Mara out of the room.

Jen listened to the argument as it proceeded into the corridor. Then a door shut and there was silence. She got up and went to the Silver Wing to fetch her woolly scarf. She was going with Ed to Grondle's Gap, the appointed place for the rendezvous with the Poinkers and Peter.

Striding quickly through the stone passages, Jen heard the sound of crows cawing. It came from her sister's room. She stopped in the doorway and saw Marj sitting at a table with her fingers in her ears. Two crows perched at the open window, bobbing their heads, squawking insistently. Tom Spider, the size of a tea cozy, sat beside a blue teapot, winding a dainty ham sandwich in silk.

Jen stepped into the room, and Marj looked up. "Oh, Jenny! These crows won't leave me alone! I tried feeding them, but they don't seem interested in food."

The crows flapped from the ledge to the table. One of them uttered a low "Cr-o-ck." The spider put down the sandwich and clacked its jaws. Marj took her fingers out of her ears. "What's this? Slow down!"

Jen watched the crows bob and squawk. Tom clacked, and Marj nodded.

"I see. I see," she said. "You must be out of your minds with worry." She turned to Jen. "These birds came with Peter. They say the mountain trolls are coming here to meet him. Did you know that?"

"He mentioned it."

"The crows are afraid the trolls have gotten lost in the ... what did they call it? The Underways. They want someone to go look for them."

"Ah. I traveled the Underways myself. From the Hidden Valley to the back door of this house. The paths are difficult to navigate." Jen looked into Marj's face, weathered by years of waiting, and suddenly knew she had an unexpected task ahead.

The crows cawed and flapped their wings. Tom Spider clacked again and picked up the sandwich, as Marj's eyes widened. "Not tonight! I promised Pixel!"

"No, you shouldn't go tonight," Jen said.

"But . . . but what will Ed say?"

"Does it matter?"

Marj smiled weakly. "I think maybe I won't mention it to him. Not just yet."

42

Do Something Stupid

Peter lay flat on his back, looking up at a mast. "A boat," he whispered. "How ...?" Boards creaked and he heard waves lapping the ship's side as he stared at limp sails. All around, thick mist, like white walls, enclosed the deck. Hearing the cry of a seagull, he sat up and saw an old man in a silver cloak. Mac Lir.

"Well, well. We meet again. I'd introduce you to Garool, but I hear you've met."

Garool. The tree on the beach. The giant fish. Peter clenched his fists.

"He told me how you were gallivanting through the hills, boy. Leading astray my most faithful creatures until there is no one left to defend the island. Why have you turned against me?"

Well, there were a lot of reasons. Peter held his tongue.

"But you're here now, and you will bring all the creatures back to me. You'll see that I am merciful and good to all."

Anger ignited in Peter's mind, and he got to his feet. "Merciful? Like when you gave Pixel to the Shee?"

"She's a Rilson girl. She was going to die anyway."

There was a loud splash on the port side. "Let down the rope!" a voice called.

Mac Lir went to the rail and threw a rope ladder over the side. Up climbed Garool. He shook himself like a dog, then smoothed down his tweed suit, straightened his tie, and said, "I saw the Silver Girl with the boy's magic stick. She hit me with it! Garrotted my gumboils! Sliced my spleen! Oh!" He pressed his hands to his temples. "Pain! Agony!"

"You saw the Silver Girl?" Lir turned to Peter. "What do you know about this? And where did you get a magic staff?"

Peter looked steadily into Lir's blue eyes but remained silent.

The wizard thumped his staff on the deck. "I see that you know far more than you are willing to say. Stubborn and misguided, that's what you are. But you will do as I say in the end. Garool, take him to a cabin and lock him in."

"Not so strong! Not so tough!" the Buggane gloated as he pushed Peter down the passageway. "Without your stick, you're no match for old Garool. Hee hee!"

They stopped at a narrow door, and the Buggane's voice softened. "Come, boy. Garool would like to be friends. Show you're on Mac Lir's side and we can do great things together! Think on it!" He shoved Peter through the door, banged it shut, locked it, and went away whistling.

Peter surveyed his narrow prison. A bunk stood against one wall and that was the only piece of furniture. In three steps, he crossed the floor to the porthole and opened it. Somewhere in the distance a gull cried. There was nothing to see but white fog, though he could tell it was still daylight. Peter guessed that Garool had scooped him off the beach not more than a couple of hours ago. What he wouldn't give at that moment to have Moody at his side, or Arkey, or even a couple of silver hornets. But Jen had his staff. Good. Pixel must have given it to her. Lying down on the bed, he curled up on his side, listening to the waves and thinking of his dad far away in Lang.

He woke in the white light cast by his eyes. Outside the porthole it was dark, and he wondered about the time. Then he heard a light tapping at the door and something scrabbling at the latch. Rising stealthily, he put an eye to the keyhole and heard a low chuckle.

"Keep yer blinker on the hole, kid."

Peter grinned, stifling the urge to whoop aloud. With his ear so close to the lock, he heard the click and stepped back as the door swung open silently. Sure enough, there was the small, burly form of Arkey and a tall, block-footed man with the head of a pig.

"We ain't got much time," Arkey whispered. "Garool will be back any minute, and it'll spoil everything if we get caught. We come to see if you're goin' over to Mac Lir's side. Jimmy here thinks you oughta."

"No!"

"I told you so, Jimmy," Arkey said. "Look, kid, you gotta get yourself put in the hold."

"The what?"

"The hold!" Arkey huffed. "You know. In the bottom of this ship where they keep prisoners. That's where we're hidin' out."

"How do I do that?"

"Do somethin' stupid! Come on, kid, do I gotta tell you everythin'?" Arkey scowled.

"You mean get myself in trouble."

A board above them creaked. Someone was on the quarterdeck. The creature named Jimmy pulled the door shut. The lock clicked, and Peter lay down on the bed and closed his eyes.

Stealthy footsteps stopped at his door. After several minutes, whoever it was stole quietly away, and Peter lay awake for a long time, thinking.

ꕤ ꕤ ꕤ

He woke suddenly, from the dream of the warrior riding over the sea. Sitting up, he threw off his blanket. The cabin was lit by a cold light from the porthole. He opened it and stuck his nose into the mist. It was impossible to tell the exact time of day, but having gained some experience traveling with the Poinkers, he guessed it to be morning.

"Hey! Wake up!" he shouted. He crossed the room and pounded on the door, calling at the top of his lungs, "Hey! I need water! Get up, you lazy wizard!"

Loud footsteps sounded in the passage, and a voice said, "Locks and lashes! Oooh! I could lash him! With whips and ropes and … hang it all, this lock's rusty!" The door burst open, and Peter saw Garool's tweed suit torn in several places. His hair was ruffled like the feathers of a disturbed hen, and there were red welts all over his face. "Crab pots and weasel butts!" Garool snarled. "How did you do it! I made three ginger cakes and you've stolen one! And me hard-pressed and hungry. Pecked by crows! Stung by hornets! While you've been sitting here doing what?"

"Starving."

"Lumping liar! Callow cake snatcher!" Garool began to change. Slowly the tweed, hook nose, and smooth white hands disappeared. In place of the natty little man, a huge, dark creature rose up, claw-footed and fanged, its red eyes leering down. Peter shrank back from the doorway.

"How do you like it? The true Garool, greatest of the Bugganes," said the monster. "If you weren't under Mac Lir's protection, I'd finish you this instant! Not even your magic stick could save you!"

At the mention of the stick, Peter remembered the Lady. When the Buggane reached out with enormous snapping claws, Peter widened his eyes and said, "I'm not afraid of you."

For some reason, this unnerved the Buggane. He slammed the door, locked it, and stomped away, his footsteps pounding down the passage. Peter counted to ten, then began singing at the top of his lungs. "Boggering your breakfast because you've boggered mine! Ginger cake and bacon, you dirty little swine." He sang this verse over and over as he pounded on the door.

At last, he heard a key in the lock. The door opened, and Mac Lir thrust in his staff. A stream of water shot out the tip, but Peter, who was behind the door, pushed it hard against the wizard's outstretched arm. Surprised, Lir lost his grip. Peter grabbed the staff and pushed it through the porthole. There was a splash, followed by silence. Without a word, Lir pulled the door shut, locked it, and went striding down the passage, shouting, "Garool!"

Peter sat down on the bed and waited. After what he'd just done, he'd be put in the hold real quick. Anyway, he was hungry and hoped Arkey had regular meals figured out. Then he heard a big splash and smiled in satisfaction. Garool had been sent to find the staff.

A long time later, he heard the key in the lock and jumped to his feet. An angry Garool grabbed him up in wiry arms and carried him out to the main deck, muttering curses and threats. "He don't even want to see you, boy! He won't see you for a good long while, not even if you begs!"

I won't beg, Peter wanted to shout, but Garool had a hand clamped over his mouth. He was carried down the hatch to the lower deck, then down another ladder to the bottom of the ship. There, he was put on his feet and frog-marched across the wooden planks to the farthest end, where there was no light. Garool opened a heavy door, pushed him in, and banged it shut. Peter heard the click of a padlock. Uttering a string of curses, the Buggane stomped away.

In the silence, Peter looked around the bare room by the light of his eyes and saw a few feet of floor space, with a curved wall on one side. He must be in the bow, in the very depths of the ship. If he screamed at the top of his lungs, he would probably not be heard. Leaning back against the door, he smiled to himself. As Garool had carried him across the deck, he'd seen blue sky high above the ship. The mist was thinning. Lir wasn't having things all his own way.

He sat there for some time, listening to the creak of ship timbers. Then he heard Arkey say, "Good grief, kid! You got yerself in a pickle. He musta really hated your song to put you all the way back here." Bending down with his face near the floor, Peter peered through the inch-high gap under the door. There was Arkey's twitching snout.

"I pushed his staff through the porthole," Peter said.

"No kiddin'! Yer lucky you ain't in chains!"

"But how did *you* get here?"

"When we heard it was Garool who carried you off, us Poinkers figured he'd take you straight to the wizard. So we did a bit of scoutin' and it warn't hard to tell that Lir was moored in Grondle's Gap. As we was discussin' how to get on the ship, up pops Jimmy Squarefoot—the pig-headed guy you saw last night. He says he can swim, so along about midnight, I hopped on his head, he swum out, and here we are."

"Do you have an escape plan?"

"Sure, sure. But we can't do it till tonight. Anyway, I brought you some grub. You eat and I'll find somethin' to pick this lock. Then I'll come keep you company."

A tin plate came sliding under the door. Peter grinned. Two thick slices of ginger cake.

❦ ❦ ❦

Arkey found something to pick the old padlock, and he joined Peter in the prison cell. He brought more food and news from the Hermit's House, which was how Peter heard of his uncle and aunt's arrival. All through the long hours, they munched on Garool's cake and other things pinched from the galley. Then, shortly before midnight, they crept up to the main deck.

Except for the sound of distant breakers, all was silent, though they could hear Mac Lir behind the door of his cabin, pacing, muttering to himself.

Stealthily they tiptoed to the railing, and Jimmy Squarefoot came to meet them, his strange form rising from behind a barrel. He was dressed in dark trousers and a ragged shirt that barely covered his broad chest and muscular arms. Thick layers of calico cloth wrapped his feet, giving them an odd square-shaped appearance. His little piggy eyes blinked, and he extended a hand in greeting. Peter took his hand and, for a split second, saw the face of a man with shining eyes. Gasping, he let go, and there was the pig face again.

"Any sign of Garool?" Arkey whispered.

"Lir sent him to look for the girl again," Jimmy replied.

"Okay then. Over we go."

As Jimmy threw one leg over the railing, a piercing shriek echoed through the Gap. The companions froze. Then the sea began to surge around the ship's hull.

"Oiks!" Arkey gasped. "The sea monster!"

Behind them, a door banged open and Lir swept out of his cabin. The three companions stood rigid at the port rail, in full view, but the wizard never saw them. Striding swiftly to the opposite side, he pointed his staff out to sea and sent a shock of lightning over the waves.

Peter nudged Jimmy. Together with Arkey, they ducked into a dark corner behind a barrel and crouched there, listening, as Lir fired bolt after bolt across the water.

"He'll make it mad," Peter muttered.

Sure enough, the sea monster surfaced one hundred feet from the starboard side, bellowing. Lir aimed a blast, which struck its head, and the monster dove. There was an ominous silence.

The air, heavy with the stink of rotting kelp, pulsed around Peter's ears. "It's coming," he whispered.

With a tremendous roar, the monster's head rose alongside the ship. Water cascaded from its jaws. Lir slipped, rolled across the wooden planks, then jumped to his feet and sent another bolt at the monster. The beast clashed its teeth, plunging beneath the waves as Dooney's wild cry echoed over the Gap. Suddenly, the monster surfaced near the stern. Higher and higher its neck rose, far above the main mast. Lunging, it tore at the sails, sending a shower of seawater over the deck. Peter hung on to a ladder as the ship pitched like a cork. He saw the creature bite into the forecastle, ripping off the upper deck. Wooden beams flew. The ship lurched and tipped on its side, and he saw Jimmy go sliding down the deck as a huge wave crashed over the rail and swept him overboard.

The ship rolled upright, and Mac Lir shot another bolt at the monster and blasted its eye. Roaring in pain, the creature lunged toward the wizard, and Peter saw its terrible jaws right above his own head. He crawled toward the hatch and then ducked behind a fallen beam, watching the wizard take aim.

But a flying spar knocked the staff out of Lir's hand, and it landed on the deck near Peter's feet. He looked up and met the wizard's eye.

"Help me!" Lir shouted.

Peter picked up the staff as the monster roared and tore up the rigging. In the sudden rain of block and tackle, Lir went down. Then the air was a whirlwind of debris. In blind panic, Peter tugged at the hatch door, but something struck the side of his head and everything went black.

43

Finding Trolls

The following morning, Uncle Ed went down to the workroom alone. Crouching by the rear wheel of the Datsun, he ran his hand over the scraped side panels. She hadn't *quite* fit through the back door. "Dang nabbit," he muttered, thinking more about the sight of Lir's ship getting torn apart and Peter being swallowed by that great, fat eel. As long as he lived, he'd never forget it. His throat tightened and he swore. Getting to his feet, he saw someone passing in the corridor. "Marj!"

She came and stood in the doorway. "Good morning, Ed."

He looked at her carefully, noting the khaki trousers, the walking shoes, and a knapsack on her back. "Where are *you* going?"

"I'm just out for a walk."

"A *walk*? You're not plannin' to go alone, surely. Not with Garool on the loose."

She frowned defiantly; then her face brightened. "Oh, Ed! Peter's alive! Pixel told me that Jen told her that the hawthorn heard from him quite early this morning."

Ed sank down on the Datsun's bumper. "If that ain't the best news in a month of Sundays! Still, somethin's got to be done about Garool. Me and Jen saw him on the beach last night, big as a house and uglier than your worst dream, doing nothin' to save the ship. I tell you, no one's safe with that Buggane hangin' around."

"Oh, Ed," Marj huffed. "I think our little sister is up to something. She's been awfully tight-lipped since yesterday. Pixel thinks it's to do with the Bugganes and Garool."

"Sisters, blisters!" he complained. "I guess we can't stop her doing somethin' dangerous, and after all, she *is* a Silver-eyed. But you still haven't told me where *you're* going."

"I ... I'm going to ... to ..." she faltered, but then her defiance returned. "I'm going after the trolls! I don't care what you say, Ed, or how foolish you think it is! They'll help Peter!"

"Does Jenny know about this?"

"She's the one who told me to go out the back door."

He stood up and crossed the room. Then he pulled the pack from his sister's shoulders and put it on. "Okay. I'll come too. Better than sittin' around bitin' my nails."

Side by side, they went into the beach passage and out the back door.

"Caw! Caw!" Two crows swooped into the ravine and landed in a bush, bobbing their heads.

"There you are," Marj said to them. "Well, lead the way!"

Ed watched the crows fly ahead, deeper into the canyon. Every ten feet or so, they'd land on a bush and caw at Marj. "Just how far do you think we'll have to go to find these trolls?" he asked.

"I have no idea, Ed. And the crows don't know either. Somewhere in the Underways."

"What's that?"

"Tunnels, I guess. Jenny didn't really say."

Soon they heard the sound of cascading water and came to the base of the Back Door Falls, a frothy pool surrounded by flowering vines. The two birds flew to a rocky overhang above the pool, not six inches from the falling water.

"Oh look," Marj cried, "steps!"

Sure enough, there was a short flight of stairs cut into the rock beside the falls. Parting a curtain of tiny roses, they stepped onto a smooth ledge behind the cataract of water.

"Marvelous!" Marj breathed.

Ed stood beside her, watching water pour over the rock, till he heard a low "Cr-o-ck!" Turning, he saw one of the crows hopping around in a dark opening. It bobbed and pecked the ground. "Look, Marj. A cave. Or do you think it's the Underways?"

"Cr-o-ck," the crow said again.

Ed rummaged through the knapsack and pulled out a flashlight. "Here's what's been knockin' against my spine. Well, come on. Let's get this over with."

Saying goodbye to the crow, they entered the tunnel, and Ed was relieved to find that it was high and wide.

"I suppose the giants built this," Marj commented.

"Did you ever read that part about the trolls in the Thornburg book?"

"Yes, and I know what you're thinking. But they didn't eat Peter, so I guess it'll be alright."

"I wish them crows had come with us. Who else is gonna explain that we aren't dinner?"

"Oh, stop grousing."

The floor of the tunnel was smooth and sloped gently downward for a while, going deeper and deeper into the earth.

"I wonder how far underground we are," Marj said. "Do you think there are bats?"

He heard the little quaver in her voice. "Most likely they're hangin' from the ceiling."

There was a short pause; then she muttered, "Can't be. No bat poop on the floor. Thank goodness."

Sometime later, the tunnel leveled out. Suddenly, Marj stopped. "Ed, I feel a draft. Is there an opening here?"

He shone the light around, revealing a doorway on their right. "That's headin' east."

"How in the world can you tell it's east? I've completely lost my bearings in the dark."

"Might go to Floden."

She sighed. "Let's stick to this main tunnel. If we don't find them, we'll come back and try that branch."

They went on for a while, and then she said, "I need a rest. By the way, is there food in that knapsack?"

"Don't you know what's in here?" He slipped the pack off his shoulders, and they sat down against the wall.

"Droat gave it to me as I passed the kitchen this morning. Hold that light here for a minute, will you? Oh look. Candles, matches, water, a cup. And sandwiches! You eat the ham on rye. I'll eat the liverwurst. And remember, that flashlight won't last forever."

"I suppose that explains the candles." He switched it off, and they sat on the stone floor in the dark, but it was hardly comfortable. When they finished eating, they got up and trudged on, the flashlight's beam growing dimmer with each mile. After a while, they passed another opening and Ed shone the light around. "South, I think. And west. See how it curves away?"

"Well, let's keep going. Seems like we're on the main route."

They both realized it would be easy to get lost in these dark Underways, but neither of them said as much aloud. Ed began to wonder what the end of this journey might be. He had come along to keep Marj company but hadn't really thought what it would mean to find the trolls. "Have we been walking for hours or days?" he asked.

Marj only stopped and said, "Listen. Is that the sea?"

Faint and far away, he heard a sonorous rumble. "Don't sound quite like that."

"It's been going on for a while. Whatever it is, we're getting closer."

On they went, side by side in the dark, the rumble growing louder and louder. Then, quite suddenly, it ceased and there was a space of silence. They stood there in the darkness, waiting, and then a deafening clamor broke out.

"Sounds like babies bawling!" Marj shouted.

"It's them, ain't it?"

She clutched his hand. "Oh, Ed! What do we do?"

"I dunno. This was your idea. But we oughta do somethin' before they start an earthquake."

They went around a bend, and Ed saw the opening to a yawning hole, certainly the source of the howling. Without stopping to think, he stepped in and shone the flashlight around. Abruptly, the wailing ceased and a voice said, "Ghosts!"

Shining the light in the direction of the voice, Ed saw more than a dozen pairs of enormous eyes and huge, ugly faces. They could only be the trolls. They were sitting around the walls of a great cavern littered with boulders. No, not boulders. Legs and feet stretched out across the floor! In the center of the room, he glimpsed the remains of a wood fire gone cold.

"That ain't ghosts!" said a rough voice, and one of the figures got to its feet. "Mick, light the torches, quick!"

"Can't, Trelly. No torches. Dolf and Willy burnt 'em all when we cooked them moles and little beetles."

"Dumb idea, Dolf!" Trelly said, and he thunked one of the trolls on the head. A scuffle followed.

Ed stepped back into the doorway, trying to push Marj behind him, but she hustled him aside. "What are you doing?" he whispered. "Do you wanna get squashed?"

She huffed and grabbed the flashlight out of his hand. "Stop this at once!" she shouted, holding the dimming beam to her face.

The fighting stopped. Ed held his breath as the trolls got a look at his sister.

"The crows sent us to find you," she said in a loud voice. "Me and my brother."

Ed flinched when she shone the light on his face.

"Crows?" the one named Trelly rumbled. "They're supposed to be with the Silver One."

"They were, but the wizard kidnapped him," Marj said. "He needs your help! That's why we've come."

Trelly thumped his chest. "Kind lady—if that's what you are—how do we know this ain't some trap of Mac Lir's? He's tricked us 'afore, sendin' us folks as a bribe—"

"We are *not* a bribe! And we are *not* your dinner!" Marj shouted, stamping her foot. "If you eat us, who's going to lead you out of here? You *promised* to help the Silver One, and if you don't, that stupid wizard will take over this island. Or maybe the witch will! Do you want *that* to happen?"

One or two of the trolls grumbled something about "a long time since we last et" and Ed saw one pick up a club.

"Marj," he said in a low voice, "maybe we better go."

She snorted at him. Snorted! He'd never seen his peaceful, ladylike sister behave this way. Then, to his everlasting surprise, the troll called Trelly thumped his chest and bowed.

"Lady, you is right. We're lost. If you can lead us out of here, we promise not to eat you."

"Or my brother!"

"Boss, we can't go now!" one of the trolls whined. "It's daylight above ground!"

"How do you know?" Marj cried. "You have no idea how long you've been sitting in the dark. Admit it!"

"That's true enough, lady," Trelly replied humbly, "but we trolls feel the day and night in our bones."

"You promised Peter! He's stuck on that wretched ship with Mac Lir and Garool. Who knows what might happen! You must come now, before it's too late!"

"She's right, boys. We've wasted enough time gettin' lost," Trelly said. "You remember how the Silver One gave us back our jool that the wizard stole. If he needs our help, we better go! The sun don't shine down here. Everybody up!"

Lumbering to their feet, they picked up huge clubs, and Marj said under her breath, "Imagine them in the light of day! But I suppose if the old legends are true, they turn to stone in daylight."

Ed backed into the tunnel as Trelly and his boys stumped toward the doorway. Their huge faces loomed overhead, and then the flashlight gave out. In the sudden darkness, one of the trolls said, "Hey! They're gone!"

"Musta been a dream. Probly 'cause we're so hungry."

"Hold still," Marj called out. "My brother has candles."

Fumbling with the knapsack, Ed felt for a candle and the matchbox, grumbling at himself because his hands were shaking so hard. When he finally got the candle lit, he handed it to Marj.

"You trolls come with us," she commanded. Holding the small flame aloft, she led the way into the tunnel, and the trolls followed.

44

The Wizard's Staff

Peter woke with a dull pain in the side of his head. He lay flat on his back, looking up at the dawn twilight. The sea monster was gone, and he was still alive. A wide-winged heron, passing over the ship, crossed his vision, and he turned his head to follow its flight. Then he saw the morning star sitting low on the horizon. Its lone beauty smote his heart, and he thought of Jimmy and Arkey washed overboard. "Help me," he whispered.

He lay there, gazing at the bright star as the light grew. Then a gull called, a gust of wind blew over the sea, and the star faded into the dawn sky. He sat up slowly and looked around.

The main deck was a wreck of torn sails and broken beams. Half the mainmast was shorn away. He wondered how the ship was still afloat. And where was the wizard? Under a pile of rubble, he guessed.

Without warning, a hairy claw went around his throat.

"Gotcha!" a voice hissed into his ear. "Thought you'd get away from me, did you?" Garool the monster yanked him to his feet. "Buckets and broken necks! Who will help you now, boy? Not Lir! I have little hope for your chances. Hee hee!"

The claw tightened, and Peter's vision began to darken. Then, quite suddenly, the Buggane shrieked and let go. Peter fell to the deck, gasping.

"Aaah! I been pronged! I been prinked!" The fearsome, red-eyed beast shrank into the tweedy little man. Forcing himself to move, Peter scrambled to the opposite rail, stumbling over drifts of broken rigging, never taking his eyes off the Buggane.

"Oh! My comely calf all netter-bunted!" Garool wailed, rolling around the deck. Then suddenly he stopped and pulled a six-inch spear from the back of his leg. Peter knew what it was, but there was no time to think. The Buggane was on his feet. "You stabbed Garool! You skewered him, boy!" His eyes flashed red. The tweeds vanished, and there stood the fanged beast.

Peter knew Garool would kill this time, so he picked up a short piece of wood with a sharp, splintered end. He would have to stab upward. He would have to—

A small movement caught his eye, low down amid the debris, but he forced his attention back to the slowly approaching Buggane. Garool was enjoying himself, a cat stalking a cornered mouse. There was nowhere to go but overboard, a useless option when faced with a creature who could turn into a huge fish. Peter braced himself and brandished the stick.

A quiet voice said, "Steady, kid. Hold his eye." Then the Buggane was upon him, yanking the stick out of his hands. Just when he thought his life was over, the hideous creature stopped, stone still. His red eyes widened, and he let out a tremendous shriek that shook the timbers of the ship. Glancing down, Peter saw Garool's great clawed foot pinned to the deck with a small spear.

"Pins and pincers! Darts and devils!" the monster wailed. "Help me!"

"I didn't do that," Peter said, backing out of the way.

"Garool!"

To Peter's surprise, the door to the quarterdeck banged open and Mac Lir came out, disheveled and angry. "What's all this noise?"

"He pinned me to the floor!" Garool shrieked, pointing at Peter.

"Are you a man or a Buggane? Where is my staff?"

"Nowhere," Garool snapped. "I haven't seen it. Ask your escaped prisoner."

"The pigman helped him," Lir said. "Must have boarded the ship while you were away yesterday."

"Jimmy Squarefoot? Where is he now?"

"Washed overboard," Lir said. "Oh! I've got a lump the size of a gull's egg on the back of my head. Still, we're lucky. I have no idea why that monster didn't finish the ship."

"Snip, snap! Clamped its jaws on man-pork, that's why!" Garool cackled.

"Clear this mess off the deck and make the boy help. When you're done, put him in the hold. We can't take any chances." He pointed at Peter. "You won't escape again. No friend to help you now." Then he went into his cabin and shut the door.

Garool reached down and pulled the spear from his foot. The wound closed instantly, and Peter noticed there was no blood. Then the Buggane shook his fur, and suddenly he was the tweedy little man again. "Get moving, boy. Throw the rubble overboard, but if you find the wizard's staff"—a crafty look crossed his face—"give it to me."

"Double-crosser," Peter muttered, turning away in disgust. He was hungry and tired, and his head hurt. Touching the sore place above his temple, he felt a large bump, and his fingers came away bloody. He looked toward the shore and the densely wooded ridge of Grondle's Gap and thought a message to the hawthorn. Then he began throwing debris over the rail, working his way toward the open hatch. That's where Lir's staff had fallen last night. He remembered now.

"Clear the deck, clean the wreck." Garool picked up a stick here, a fallen spar there, inspecting each piece carefully before tossing it seaward. Peter watched him, then picked up as big a pile of timber as he could lift and pushed it over the rail.

"Boy!" Garool shouted. "Are you looking for his staff? Careful you don't tip it overboard by mistake!"

"I know what his staff looks like. Anyway, he was over there last night, where you're standing now, shooting lightning at the sea monster."

"Oh ho!" Garool began picking carefully through a pile of timber near his feet.

As soon as the Buggane's back was turned, Peter stepped quietly across the deck, picked up Lir's staff, which was lying next to the hatch, and added a couple of broken spars about the same length. He carried this load to the starboard side and pushed it over. As he stood there, watching the staff float out to sea with the rest of the timber, a thought niggled at his mind. The hawthorn.

"What are you looking at, boy?" Garool was watching him carefully.

"Nothing." He turned away and went back to work.

By the time the decks were clear, the sun was directly overhead. Peter lay by the open hatch, bound hand and foot. Mac Lir stood over him, holding a long knife.

"Sticks and staves! It's gone! What will you do now? You've no time to fashion a new staff," Garool said.

"What about the boy's stick? You've said it has some power."

"Oh no. Rattle my bones! I am not going on another goose chase, and you can't make me!"

"You could not rule this island without me," Mac Lir sneered. "And you know nothing of the power coming soon from Cwenburgh."

"Garool is not frightened by the Moonwitch or her little Shee friends."

"Have you never heard of Lila?"

The Buggane paused and a strange look passed over his face. "Are you saying Lila has returned?" His voice was unnaturally quiet.

"Of course. She is the witch's mother," Lir replied.

"And who is the witch's father?"

An ugly smirk crossed Lir's face. "I believe Captain Rilson has that honor. Remember him, Garool? The third-rate pirate who thought he was my rival. Powerful in a small way, though at an enormous cost to his family." Then Lir stooped down and held the knife at Peter's throat. "Tell us where to find the Silver Girl. We know she's got your stick."

Thanks to the hawthorn, Peter was prepared for this moment. "She's at our camp south of Grondle's Gap."

"Where? Where is this camp?"

Peter felt the cold steel against his neck. "South of the Gap, like I said. At the back of a hidden ravine. The Mooners are there with a couple of Bugganes."

Lir looked up at Garool. "Do you know the place?"

"He's making it up!"

The knife pressed harder. "Tell the truth, boy."

"Stairs go down from the giants' road in Grondle's Gap. Straight down to the shore. The opening is at the bottom. A small tree grows at the entrance."

"He's talking about that shallow little bay south of the Gap," Mac Lir said. "Didn't you find him there? On the beach?"

"I know, I know," Garool fumed. "I saw the Silver Girl there too. But swabs and sorcerers! Look at him! He's not afraid!"

"Enough, Garool! Put him in the hold and go."

"Why don't *you* go?"

Mac Lir let go of Peter and stood up. Wizard and Buggane regarded each other.

Then Garool shuddered. "Alright! Alright." He untied Peter's legs, yanked him to his feet, and forced him to the lower deck and into the hold. With his hands still tied behind his back, Peter marched blindly through the sudden dark, stumbling against barrels and boxes.

When they reached the prison door, Garool jerked it open, and Peter said, "Who is Lila?"

The Buggane let out a small, involuntary sigh. "Queen of the world, they say." His voice hardened. "She was Lir's mistress."

"And yours?"

"You're made of trouble, boy!" Snarling, he pushed Peter to the floor of the cell, banged the door shut, and locked it.

Peter lay still, listening to Garool cross the hold and stomp up the ladder. Then he rolled over and scooted toward the door until he was looking out the gap at the bottom. Sure enough, there was Arkey's whiskery snout.

"Gimmee a minute to pick this lock, kid; then I'll cut you free."

A few minutes later, Arkey was pulling out a spear and cutting the ropes that bound Peter's arms. Rubbing his wrists, Peter said, "I knew those were your spears in Garool's foot. Thanks."

Arkey paused, his little eyes glittering. "You was pretty cool at knifepoint. I heard the whole thing. A smart bit of work sendin' Garool to the Bugganes."

"It was the hawthorn's idea. But what will the Bugganes do?"

"Didn't ol' pricklethorn tell you? Look, kid, even Bugganes has got rules. Layin' hands on a human, for instance, is taboo, not to mention that business with the trolls. Garool is a Buggane gone sour, make no mistake. I expect they're gonna snuff him."

"Kill him? Is that even possible?"

"They'll undo him, though it'll take all six, I'm sure."

Peter looked at Arkey thoughtfully, and then he pulled something out of his pocket. "I saved your spears."

"And you cleaned 'em too! Thanks."

"Yeah. Garool dropped his hanky, so I used that."

"Gee whiz, kid. You're somethin' else."

❦ ❦ ❦

The more Peter thought about it, the more anxious he was to get off the ship. With no masts and no sails, they were like a great sitting duck, and the Moonwitch was bound to come around eventually. Yet even with the prospect of Garool's undoing, Arkey wasn't willing to swim across the shallow bay of Grondle's Gap in broad daylight. Mac Lir might not have his staff, but there was no telling what he was capable of. So Arkey robbed the galley and brought back Garool's last ginger cake, a bottle of ginger beer, and several small apples. He and Peter sat in the open prison cell and ate; then Arkey went up to the main deck to keep watch. Down in the bottom of the ship, Peter could not hear the hawthorn or the voice of the woods. He spent the rest of that long day alone, dozing, drifting in and out of uneasy dreams.

Sometime later, he woke with a start and sat bolt upright. Arkey was tugging at his arm. "Come on, kid. We gotta go."

Rubbing his face, Peter followed Arkey out of the cell. They crept across the hold and stood at the bottom of the ladder.

"Did Garool come back?" Peter asked.

"Nope."

Peter put out his hand and let Arkey hop onto his shoulder. Then he climbed the ladder, put his head out the open hatch, and looked around. It was very still, and the night was lit by a billion stars and a full moon riding high overhead. Cautiously, Peter stepped onto the deck and crept to the port-side rail. Looking toward the distant ridge of Grondle's Gap, he saw lights among the trees and heard the distant *thud, thud* of an axe. An angry murmur arose in the woods. "The Glashtyn are up there. Cutting down trees!" he hissed.

"Glashtyn at the Gap," Arkey muttered. "I dunno if we oughta make a run for it now. Let's hide behind that ladder over by the quarterdeck and wait."

Arkey hopped off his shoulder, and they crept into the shadows. The sound of axes continued for a long time. What were the Glashtyn doing? Then the ship lifted on a swell. Far out to sea, the monster passed.

When the waves subsided, Arkey hopped up to the rail and peeked over. "Take a look at this cloud what's comin'."

Peering over the rail, Peter saw a strange shadow rising out of the south, creeping over the stars, speeding toward the silver moon. In a very short time, the night was black.

"Come on, kid! It's now or never!"

Arkey jumped onto his shoulder, and Peter ran to the side where the rope ladder was tied. He flung himself over the rail and began to descend as a door on the main deck banged open.

"Get a move on, kid! He's comin'!"

Lowering himself as fast as he dared, Peter heard a woman's voice ring out across the Gap: "Mac Lir!"

Was that the Moonwitch? He stopped and looked over his shoulder, but Grondle's Gap lay in darkness.

Then the wizard appeared at the rail, right above his head.

"Mac Lir!" the woman called sweetly, her powerful voice cutting through the night. "You have the Silver Boy. I want him. Now."

"Lila!" the wizard muttered, and Peter recalled, with sudden clarity, the terrible Night Monster of his dream. He flattened himself against the ship's side, hoping to go unnoticed.

"What do you give in return?" Lir shouted back.

"Why should I give you anything?" Her voice sounded pained, like one unjustly treated. "You abandoned me! And now I ask this one little thing and you refuse?"

"If I do this, you must leave the island," Lir shouted. "It is my only price, Lila." Then Lir looked down and met Peter's eye.

"You have until dawn to bring the boy to me," she said. "And if you try any tricks, beware! I will destroy this little island of yours. With fire!"

Peter had two choices: He could get back on the ship and help Mac Lir, or he could swim to Grondle's Gap and try to get around the headland to the Hermit's beach. In the split second left to him, he decided to swim and started down the ladder. But it was no good. The wizard reached down and grabbed him by the back of the shirt. Arkey yelped and fell off his shoulder. Lir dragged Peter over the rail, set him on his feet, and clamped one hand around his throat. Then the wizard raised his other arm to the sky and uttered a few terse words.

Like a lance through the chest, Peter felt the spell's piercing power as a bolt of white light streamed from Lir's upraised hand. He fell to his knees, wracked with pain, but the wizard held on. Again and again, the incantations tore through Peter, until, with one final spell, Lir released him.

Peter fell to the deck, helpless. Struggling to breathe, he curled up on his side, clutching at his heart, which heaved in his chest unsteadily. His whole body burned with fiery heat. Then rough hands picked him up, carried him into a cabin, and dumped him on a bed. A door slammed shut. He lay in the dark, shivering. "Help me," he gasped. Overcome with pain, he passed into dark dreams.

45

Witching Hour

Pixel woke from a good dream gone bad. She couldn't remember the good part, only the dark birds that came fluttering down on wide wings. The room was dark and very still. Then she glanced at the row of open windows and saw the Poinkers lined up like ninepins, silhouetted against the starry sky.

"What—" she began, when a distant pounding resounded through the house.

She heard Kaney say, "Hush now. Someone's here." There was a rustling movement; then the door of her room opened a crack. She sat up and saw the outline of Kaney's small, stout figure in the light from the outer passage.

Footsteps sounded in the corridor.

"What is it?" came Tom Mole's voice.

"I must speak with the Silver One." That was the hairy man.

There were more footsteps, and then she heard Jen's voice. "Who's there? Peter?"

"It's Tom Troll," Forlost said. "What news, Buggane?"

"I bring strange tidings. I have seen Lila the Night Monster in Floden! She came with the Moonwitch and a man, riding down the road on tall horses. They stopped in the middle of the town square at the table of stone. Lila brought out wine and food, as if to make merry. Then she unsheathed a long knife, took the witch by the hair, and slit her throat! 'Come,' she said to the man, 'you are weak now, but drink of this and you will have power for the end.' The man drank the witch's blood, and as he did, he changed! I know him now. The most ancient of foes." Pixel heard the hairy man's voice tremble. "We did not stay to watch the vile revels of Lila and the manserpent. I hurried here to warn you. Without doubt, they will go to the Gap to wait on the wizard."

"Did you meet Peter?" Jen asked. "I thought he might try to escape again."

"No! We did not see him! But Tom Hag and Tom Wolf are waiting for me in the ravine. We will watch for the boy."

Very quietly, Kaney shut the door. Pixel could hear him moving around the room. Then someone struck a match and lit the candle. The other Poinkers were still lined up at the window, looking out.

"Miss Pixel," Kaney began. He was standing on the table. "I hope you don't mind this intrusion ..."

"Jeepers creepers," Raney said. "What's this muck?"

Kaney hopped up to the sill. "Oh no! The Shee are here!"

Pixel got out of bed and climbed onto the window bench. A black fog was stealing over the sky, blotting out the starlight. More than a cloud, it was a deep darkness, alive and crawling over land and sea. She watched in horror as the evil mist came creeping over the sill.

"Keep it out! Quick!" Kaney cried. In a mad rush, they slammed the windows shut. The foul vapor billowed and swirled against the glass. The Poinkers hopped off the ledge in a panic, and Pixel collapsed on the floor, shivering.

"Hey! Pixie's in trouble!" Sonney shouted. "Somebody get Mara!"

Then Froke ran in. Pixel saw her anxious face through a haze of pain. Closing her eyes, she felt herself lifted onto the bed and wrapped in blankets. In spite of her confusion and the hubbub in the room, she knew when Mara entered. The old Fenny began to croon, and Pixel felt a cloud of heat envelop her body. Gradually, the pain receded and she was floating away from the darkness, over far green hills.

46

The Pigman Returns

"Wake up, kid. You gotta drink this."

Pushing up through layers of sand and gravel, Peter opened his eyes and saw Arkey's snout and whiskers silhouetted in the light of the porthole. He held a cup between his paws. Slowly, painfully, Peter sat up, took the small cup, and tipped it back. Thick, grainy silt ran over his tongue, tasting like the woods after rain. He gasped and began to cough.

"Shhh!" Arkey hissed, pouring another cupful. "It's from Jimmy. He thinks tree food'll get you back on your feet."

Fully awake now, Peter drank from the cup again. "Lir used me like a wizard's staff."

"I know, kid. Me and Jimmy saw it all."

"Jimmy's alive?"

"He was waitin' for us at the bottom of the ladder. When I fell off your shoulder, he fished me outa the drink. Then he scrambled up the side of the ship quick as a squirrel. But it was too late to save you."

"What happened?"

"You didn't see? Four bolts and this ol' ship was good as new. New masts, new sails. Everything that sea snake tore up came back, just like that. Then Lir raised a wind, the black clouds cleared, and we set sail. But just after we got past Grondle's Gap and around the headland, the wind stopped. Dead calm. And you'll never guess where we're parked. Right offshore from the Hermit's House." Arkey paused. "Cripes! He's comin'!" And he dove through a hole in the base of the wall.

A key turned in the lock, and the door opened. The first thing Peter saw was a long knife, then the wizard's grim face. "No trouble, boy." Lir tied Peter's wrists behind his back and pushed him into the passage and out to the main deck. Then he gripped Peter's shoulder, raised one arm to the sky, and murmured a spell.

The Lady's face flashed into Peter's mind, and he held her image there as the spell blazed through him like a lightning strike. Fiery pain tore at every nerve and sinew. When a strong wind lifted the sails, Lir pushed him up the ladder to the quarterdeck and took the tiller with one hand.

The ship was underway for hardly a moment when the wind died completely. Lir cursed aloud as every sail went slack. He cast another spell and the wind picked up, only to die a minute later. Twice more he tried, and each time Peter held the Lady's face in his mind. Somehow, it made the burning pain easier to bear. Even so, his heart beat unsteadily, and he dropped to his knees.

"Lila!" Lir shouted angrily. "This is her meddling!" With one hand on Peter's head, he turned toward the shore and sent a spell over the water. Dark clouds appeared out of nowhere, gathering over Grondle's Gap. "You're better than my staff, boy," he said with a laugh.

Thunder boomed, and through a haze of pain, Peter saw the storm clouds building, rising in dark towers over the Hermit's House.

"That will teach her." The words were hardly out of Lir's mouth when the clouds vanished, like a puff of smoke on the wind. He grabbed Peter by the hair. "It's you!" he hissed, raising his knife.

"Stop!" cried a loud voice, and there was Arkey standing on the rail by the tiller, a tiny spear pointed at the wizard. "Let 'im go or I skewer you."

Out of the corner of his eye, Peter saw a movement, but the wizard was intent on the Poinker. "Skewer me? Ha! Pinprick from a pincushion!" Then, with quiet suddenness, an arm caught Lir around the neck, a hand wrenched the knife away, and there was Jimmy Squarefoot, holding the wizard in a firm headlock. Peter collapsed on the deck.

"Let me go!" Lir gasped, struggling against the pigman's iron grip. "I am lord of the sea! You cannot overmaster me!"

Jimmy grunted, his snout close to the wizard's ear. "Do you not know who I am, wizard? Jimmy Squarefoot is not my real name. Long ago, you deserted me in the labyrinth under Rosknil, knowing I would meet Tegi the Enchantress. Her curse changed me, but it did not weaken me, as you hoped. I still retain the powers of a Silver One, as well as great strength. Greater now than yours."

Lir strove to free himself. "Garool! Garool!"

"Garool will never come again. The Bugganes have finished him."

The wizard went very still.

"Yesterday, as I watched your ship from the Gap, a hideous monster came ashore. He climbed to the giants' road and I followed, down the stairs and into a hidden ravine. He grew very tall as he moved deeper into that canyon. Then six birds fluttered in a bush and became six Toms. The Silver Girl came out of a door in the rock, carrying the boy's staff. They followed the monster, but I hid myself and waited. What do you think happened, O lord of the sea? The girl and six Toms returned, but not Garool. You have no friends now, wizard."

"We cannot win against Lila unless we hand over the boy," Lir said softly. "Once we do, we'll sail to the island of my true home, where a certain tree grows. From it I will fashion a new staff and change your form to what it once was, Jonas."

Jonas? Peter raised his head and looked at Jimmy Squarefoot's piggy ears and snout.

"Sail to your true home?" Jimmy laughed softly. "You are a liar. All you want is to save yourself."

"You do not know Lila," Lir said. "She will get what she wants in the end."

"What is it she wants?"

"A Silver One. To feed to her lover, the manserpent."

Peter laid his aching head on the deck, listening.

"Who exactly are you talkin' about?" Arkey said.

"The ancient enemy of the world. He has fastened upon the pirate Captain Rilson. But he needs to drink the blood of an unstained soul to completely possess the pirate's body."

"And the blood of a Silver One will do this?" Jimmy asked.

"No," Lir said. "Lila believes that in the Silver Ones I have wiped away the stain of death and brought back the pure blood of the first humans. Yet it is only a trick of the light."

"What you're sayin' is, you double-crossed her and landed us all in a pickle," Arkey muttered.

"But listen! What if I told you one of the ancient unstained still lives?" Lir lowered his voice. "It has long been rumored that a child from the dawn of time was hidden away. Kept safe from the enemy. It is not something you humans would know. Only those of us sprung from Earth's elements."

The shipped rocked uneasily in a sudden gust of wind.

"This island holds many secrets," Lir continued, "and if I read the signs aright, the child dwells on this very island."

"And you believe this hidden child will help us?" Jimmy said.

"I believe he is the answer to our present difficulty."

"Because he will have some power over Lila and the old enemy?"

"Because he is a pure, unstained soul."

There was a long pause; then Arkey roused himself. "Let me get this straight. You wanna find this unknown child and hand him over to Lila so her evil lover can take over a human body and do somethin' nasty?"

"You should stick to sharpening your spears, pincushion," the wizard sneered.

"I aim to, though if you think I ain't hit on your exact meanin', it's only your *wits* that want sharpenin'."

"The old man, Mac Rilson, has met this child. And so has the boy." The wizard looked down at Peter. "Is that not so? In the valley of Ogar?"

"You can't get the Small One," Peter croaked. His lips were parched and his throat burned.

"You *have* seen him! Where?" Lir made a sudden movement, but Jimmy held him fast.

"He's protected. By his Grandfather. And the Lady."

"Protected by an old man and a lady?" Lir scoffed. "Where? Where is he?"

With sudden harshness, the voice of Lila rang out from the Hermit's beach. "I see you, Lir! Trying to get away from me, are you? Where is the boy?"

"Sail! We must sail away or hide!" Lir cried, trying to pull himself free.

"You will kill the boy with your spells," Jimmy said. "But I am strong. Use me."

"No! You are only a pig!"

"Don't help him, Jimmy," Peter murmured, but the pigman forced the wizard's arm upward. Lir struggled, then gave up and uttered a few words. A strong wind began to blow but died in an instant.

"Call up your mist, old man," Jimmy commanded.

The wizard spoke and fog rose up, all around the ship. "Let me go," Lir said. "You have proved yourself. I will not use the boy."

Jimmy put his hand into the wizard's pocket, fished out a ring of keys, and tossed them to Arkey. "Take Peter inside."

Arkey picked up the keys and trotted to Peter's side, cutting the ropes that bound his wrists. Forcing himself to his knees, Peter crawled slowly across the quarterdeck and down the ladder. At the bottom, he stopped to catch his breath and heard Lir say, "The mist is turning black! It is the Shee calling forth darkness."

Arkey hopped down the ladder and landed at Peter's side. "Come on, kid. We gotta get you someplace else. You're startin' to shiver."

By the time Peter staggered to his feet and followed Arkey into the cabin, daylight had disappeared behind a black fog. He crawled onto a bunk and drew a blanket over himself. Arkey hustled in with a small lantern and a cup. "Have a little more of Jimmy's tree food, kid."

Peter drank it down, then lay back, listening to thunder cannon overhead, the opening overtures of another weather war.

A long time later, Peter came awake to the rat-a-tat of rain beating against the ship. "Arkey?" There was no reply. He sat up, groaning, his joints stiff and painful. No light came through the porthole, but a lantern sat on a small table next to the bed, illuminating a jar of tree food, a spoon, and a cup. Peter swung his legs off the bunk, then poured water from a small jug, mixed himself a drink, and swallowed it, grimacing. His legs felt like lead, but he forced himself to move. Wrapping a blanket around his shoulders, he went out into the passage.

There was no one about. He made his way to the outer door, pulled it open, and stepped out into a smokelike darkness. Instinctively, he backed up into the doorway of the cabin, out of the sluicing rain. Lightning flashed, and in the brief glare, he saw Arkey standing on a barrel with his spear poised to strike. Over the beating rain, voices shouted. Another flash, and he saw a tall man with ears like a horse, running across the deck. Glashtyn!

A sudden shriek pierced the dark, then a hubbub of screams and shouts. Heavy footfalls and thuds pounded the wooden planks. Arkey came scurrying out of the fume.

"What're you doing here, kid? Get back inside!" he yelled. Behind him, a large figure emerged from the black mist. Arkey turned and flung a spear, and Peter glimpsed a half-horse creature. It clapped a hand to its eye and fell to the deck, howling. Then Jimmy appeared, like a phantom in the vaporous air. In one swift movement, he picked up the fallen Glashtyn and ran toward the side of the ship. Peter saw him vanish into the smoke, then heard a loud splash.

Suddenly, a caterwaul tore the air, and Arkey said, "Cripes! What now?" Rushing back into the reek, he disappeared.

Aware that his shining eyes would draw the enemy, Peter retreated two steps into the passage but did not shut the door. He heard Lir shout, "Thundering herds!" A black stallion reared out of the dark, screaming, its front hooves flailing the air. A fierce gray creature clung to its head, clawing like a mad thing. The stallion went down in front of the cabin door, and Lir leapt upon it, stabbing with his knife. Hissing, the gray thing darted away into the black fog. Then Jimmy appeared again, shouting something at Lir, and they hurried off, swallowed up by the black murk. Peter stood there, horrified, as the dead horse began to melt away in the driving rain, like a thing of ice, until there was nothing left but bare boards.

A moment later, from somewhere close at hand, he heard Lir muttering, and the rain turned to white snowflakes falling like dull stars out of the gloom. Straining his ears, Peter listened for the sound of more fighting but heard only the wind and waves slapping the hull.

Then the gray creature stalked out of the dark, its sopping fur plastered down so that Peter could not tell what it was. He backed up as it stepped into the passage and looked up at him with blue eyes. "Tuffy!" Crouching down, he wrapped the cat in the blanket and began rubbing his fur. "How did you get here?"

The cat gave him a piercing look, and a curious scene flashed into Peter's mind: He was following a tall, lanky figure down a dark passage. A door opened onto a beach and someone with long white hands set a flat piece of driftwood on the water. Stepping onto the driftwood, Peter felt himself afloat. Then he was looking back at the shore where Dooney stood, waving sadly. Swells of ocean rose all around. A sheet of blinding rain came down, and there was only water on all sides. In an awed voice, he said, "You were sent here. By Dooney." Tuffy began to purr.

The pain in his joints returned. Going back to his bunk, he set Tuffy down, took another dose of tree food, and sat on the bed. Tuffy hopped onto the mattress and curled up beside him. There was nothing to see from the porthole but black fog. In the quiet of the cabin, Peter began to wonder what would become of his friends, the island, himself. The Lady had asked him to follow the truth, but what *was* truth, here on Lir's ship? "Jimmy's letting himself be used as a staff to save me," he whispered, and as soon as he said it, he thought, *If* I *were braver, I'd give myself up to Lila and end this.* He imagined climbing over the side of the ship and quietly, very quietly, swimming off across the dark water.

Tuffy's whiskers tickled his arm, and the purring ceased. Suddenly, the gray cat sat bolt upright and his fur stood on end, electrified. Hissing, he leapt to the floor and bolted into the passage. Peter got up and followed slowly. Moving down the corridor to the open door, he heard fierce mewling, then shouts and the sound of something being dragged across the wooden planks. Going out on deck, he saw Tuffy disappear down the hatch and Jimmy pull Lir to his feet.

"Bring the keys to the prison cell, Arkey," Jimmy called, and he forced the wizard down into the hold.

Peter stood under the quarterdeck looking around as a gust of wind lifted his hair. The inky fog was breaking up. Shreds of black mist floated by, swirling and blowing out to sea. The forecastle appeared, then the top of the main mast. Looking straight up, he saw one or two stars shining. The ship rose on a sudden swell, her timbers creaking, and he wondered whether they were far out at sea. Then he heard the baying of hounds. "The Mooners are hunting tonight," he said aloud.

Arkey and Jimmy climbed out of the hatch.

"Would you believe it?" Arkey said. "MacMoron tried to make a getaway in the dinghy! And we didn't see him cuz of this Shee muck. Good thing Tuffy raised the alarm."

Jimmy lifted his snout and sniffed. "There is a change in the air. The black fog is lifting."

The words were hardly out of his mouth when a wild lament pierced the stillness.

"That's Dooney," Peter said. "Do you think—"

"Douse the lamps!" Jimmy commanded, as Tuffy crawled out of the hold, hissing.

Arkey ran for the lights, and then they all climbed to the quarter-deck and stood at the stern, looking north to the darkness of Grondle's Gap. The wind grew stronger, lifting from the sea, pushing the roof of darkness up and up. With one strong breath that seemed to come from the island itself, the black fog was swept away. Stars appeared with the full moon riding high, casting silver light on the waves and the far shore. Again they heard Dooney's voice ring out.

Then harsh laughter cut through the night, and Lila called from the Hermit's beach, "My little pet is coming! You will not escape tonight, Lir, and I will pluck the Silver One from the wreck of your ship!" An arc of light came streaming across the water and burst in a shower of sparks high over the ship.

"She's baitin' it!" Arkey cried.

The old ship rocked, and heavy swells surged against her hull. A mile distant, at the mouth of the Gap, Peter saw the monster's coils rise above the sea. They were right in its path.

"Steady," Arkey murmured.

Another blast of light burst over their heads, accompanied by shrill laughter.

Then, into the night came an unexpected sound: grunts and angry bellowing as if a tribe of bears were quarrelling in the Gap. Suddenly, the shallow bay of Grondle's exploded in a clash of white waves and foaming spray. Above the riotous clamor, Peter could hear the triumphant howl of the Dooiney-oie, high-pitched and wild.

The ship heaved and pitched in the oncoming waves; then the tumult subsided and a light sprang up in the Gap.

"A bonfire!" Arkey said. "I wish we knew what's happenin' out there."

Peter reached out in his mind toward the hawthorn, but all that came back was a shimmer of laughter and a picture of the small tree, covered in silver hornets, glimmering in the starlight as it stood at the Hermit's door.

47

Barbecue

Ed listened to the trolls, grunting and muttering behind him, clumping and stumping along the stone passage. Trelly rewarded any verbal complaints with a cuff on the side of the head—at least, Ed guessed it was their heads by the hollow thumping sound. He didn't dare look back.

Marj was certainly a trooper. He'd had no idea his sister had so much pluck, though he guessed she was longing for a cup of tea. They'd been walking for hours, probably their second straight day of walking. Or maybe it was the middle of the night. Who knew? His joints ached, but since it seemed dangerous to take even a short rest in the presence of so many hungry trolls, he never suggested stopping.

After a while, he sensed a slight change in the air and noticed the tunnel curving more sharply to the right. "Marj, I think we've taken a wrong turn. That passage we come in by was pretty straight, and this one's got a sea smell. I bet we end up on a beach."

"What's that?" Trelly rumbled.

"He said, doesn't it smell like the beach," Marj called back. She sounded tired. Definitely grumpy.

"That means clams!" someone said.

"Aye, and fish cooked slow over the fire," another added.

"Food is certainly the wrong subject," Marj muttered. Then, in a louder voice she said, "Does anyone know a walking song?"

To Ed's surprise, the huge creatures started humming, a rough, guttural sound, echoing off the tunnel walls. Then their leader, Trelly, began to sing in a strange language. As he trudged through the dark, listening, Ed thought he understood a word here and there that set him thinking of mountains and rocks, hills and raw stone. Gradually, the tune changed and Trelly began to sing of one called Mother Moon. The humming rumble took on a joyous note that put Ed in mind of soft light and silver lamps, and fortunate hunting under the stars.

"Oi, what's that?"

The singing stopped abruptly, and Ed felt sand under his feet and a breath of night air. It must be the end of the tunnel, but it was pitch black ahead. Everyone stopped, and Marj said, "We're here, wherever 'here' is. I think you're right about taking a wrong turn back there, Ed. I expect we're not at the Hermit's House."

"Why's it so dark?" Trelly murmured. "It's nighttime, but this ain't regular dark."

Ed stood close to Marj in the light of their last candle, wondering what to do with a tribe of trolls on a black night. Then the trolls began to mutter and grunt, and Marj said, "This feels just like the Shee darkness, doesn't it, Ed?"

"Come on, boys," Trelly said. "Let's see what's out there."

Ed pulled Marj aside as the trolls picked up their heavy clubs. They stumped out of the tunnel, and their huge figures were swallowed up in darkness. Then a little puff of wind put the candle out. Ed stood there, listening to the sound of waves.

"Oh, Ed!" Marj sighed. "This is turning out all wrong! Where are we?" As she spoke, a faint wind picked up, stirring the air like a soft breath. It grew a little stronger and a little stronger, until, quite suddenly, the black fog rolled away. Ed saw the trolls, standing at the edge of the sea, broad and tall as a line of hills in the starlight. Marj grabbed his hand and pulled him across the sand. "Come on!"

They ran, stopping at the tide line as the last shred of mist sailed away. Overhead, the silver moon shone, and Trelly cried, "Look up, boys! It's Mother!"

There she was, the full moon, and for a moment, Ed saw what the trolls saw. Within the enormous circle, a young woman stood on the head of a big snake, holding it down with her toe.

"It's a sign, boys," Trelly said.

"But what does it mean?" Mick cried.

Suddenly, a wailing shriek rent the air, and somewhere above the Gap, the Mooner hounds began to bay.

"Moon almighty!" Mick bellowed. "It's the Dooiney-oie a-howlin'!"

"Dang nabbit! I know where we are!" Ed shouted at the trolls. "Grondle's Gap! But where's Lir's ship?"

Then, out of the dark night, they heard a familiar bark. Moody Doug came down from the giants' road, followed hard by Tom Spider, grown to the size of a baby elephant. Stopping beside the trolls, Moody began to snarl, and the spider clacked its jaws fiercely.

"I know what it is! That dang sea monster's comin'!" Ed shouted.

"Sea monster?" Mick hissed. "You mean the great stupid eel we seen in Cronk's Chasm?"

"That'll be the witch's pet!" Trelly hollered, and all the trolls began to mutter angrily.

Then, to the south, a shower of light appeared in the sky.

"I think someone's callin' the monster on," Mick snarled, "and I bet I know who!"

"Boys!" Trelly cried, wading into the breakers. "Look up and see what Mother Moon's tellin' us!" The other trolls shouldered their great clubs and followed. Even Moody Doug leapt into the water, his teeth bared. Ed heard a loud *pop!*, and where Tom Spider had stood, a gigantic scorpion raised its deadly tail. Waves began to surge and slap against the shore. Ed backed away but Marj did not. He watched her pick up a big stone.

"Marj! Whaddya think you're doin'?"

"I've been waiting all my life!" she shouted.

Then an enormous snakelike head reared up from the seething sea, the folds of its white scaly body stretching out behind. Even the huge trolls were dwarfed by the mammoth creature.

"Beast!" Trelly roared, lifting his club in defiance as he waded farther into the surf.

Ed watched the monster's bulbous eyes turn to the shore. It saw Trelly and opened gaping jaws full of long, barbed teeth. Bellowing, it lunged, and Trelly swung his club.

The bay erupted in a tumult of roiling water as all the trolls rushed to their captain's aid. Ed heard them growling and grunting and Trelly's voice rising above the din, roaring something that sounded like "Mother Moon!"

The great monster's head rose above the wild waves, and Ed saw the figure of Moody Doug, dangling from the beast's neck, his powerful jaws clamped on its throat.

"Dang dog!" Ed cried. Suddenly, hardly knowing what he was doing, Ed began to run toward the water's edge where Marj was shaking her fists, shrieking terrible war cries. He stumbled over a stone, then stooped to pick it up. With the stone in his hand, he splashed into the water and threw it as far as he could. He stood there, panting, wishing he could do more than throw rocks. The trolls were swinging their clubs like hammers, pounding the monster's coils. Tom, now a scorpion the size of a ship, struck at the sea monster again and again.

"They're killing it, Ed!" Marj shrieked. She was still throwing stones, scooping them up from the sand, throwing them by the handful.

Sure enough, the trolls were slowly pulling the terrible beast toward the shore, pounding it as the scorpion thrust its stinger in and out of the scaly hide. Ed backed out of the water as Trelly and Mick dropped their clubs in the shallows and throttled the creature with bare hands. At last, it went limp. The trolls dragged it onto the sand, where it lay bleak and breathless, the end of its long body still trailing into the sea.

Moody trotted out of the surf, wagging his tail. He nosed Marj's shoulder, then licked Ed's face.

"Dang dog!" Ed rubbed Moody's snout, and Marj laughed as the great dog shook the water from his fur.

Hearing a low chuckle, Ed looked up and saw Trelly's toothy grin. All the trolls were standing on the shore now, dripping, rumbling with laughter in their triumph, gloating over the hideous beast.

"Oi, boss," Dolf said, leaning on his club. "Are we gonna hafta bury this thing?"

Willy grunted. "It'll take a mighty big hole."

"I say we push it back into the sea," Mick said.

"No!" Ed piped up. "Don't do that! Let's cook the dang thing!"

So the trolls built a huge bonfire at the north end of the beach, dragging up driftwood from under the cliff. The Mooners and Dooney came down from the bluff to help, and Ed was glad to see a crowd of folks closer to his own size. Knowing a thing or two about barbecue, he told Trelly how to cut the thing up and roast it on a spit. By the time the monster was done, Ed thought he might try a slice just to see how it tasted. Marj asked for a small helping too.

Trelly carved up the roast beast and handed it around, throwing the giant jawbone to Moody and the hounds. "It's a whole lot more fillin' than the moles and beetles in the tunnels," he observed.

"You can say that again," Mick grunted.

"Maybe we oughta thank the witch for fattenin' up this beast," Willy said.

The trolls roared with laughter. Then, from the far side of the Gap came a loud rumble. Every troll jumped to his feet, and the Mooners picked up their bows. Trelly lifted his club as a huge figure loomed up in the dark.

"It's just Tom Bear," Marj said, not even turning around.

Tom came to the fireside, accepted a slab of meat from Ed, then turned his small black eyes on Marj and grunted.

"Did he say somethin' Marj?"

"He thinks you and I are Bugganes," she said, chuckling.

The spider clacked its jaws and Trelly grinned. "Buggane or troll, lady. Take your pick. You and the little man are one of us now."

48

The Eighth Day

The sea monster never came. Peter stood on the quarterdeck with Tuffy, gazing at the far-off twinkle of firelight in the Gap. Wrapping himself in a blanket, he sat down beside Arkey on a pile of rope and looked up at the full moon. Jimmy stood at the port-side rail, watching the Hermit's beach. No one felt like sleeping, not with the menace of Lila so near.

The night wore on while the moon swung slowly into the west. As dawn approached, Peter looked up and there was the morning star, like a beacon on the eastern horizon, blazing right over the roof of the Hermit's House. He got to his feet and moved to the rail, drawn by the star's light. Far to the south, he noticed a gray pall covering the sky and brown billows of smoke rising above the Floden Hills. Wakken Wood was burning.

Then, down on the beach, all six Shee came to the water's edge. They raised their arms toward the ship, and Peter could feel their ill will like a palpable force. Instead of black fog, he saw a white hoarfrost spread from their feet and move slowly over the shallow water of the bay. Little wavelets froze, like tips of icing on a cake. The frost crept up the side of the ship, over the rail and across the decks. Masts and rigging turned snow white and every sail stiffened.

With a slight crackling sound, frost crawled across the wooden planks of the quarterdeck toward the stern, where the four companions stood. Tuffy arched his back, hissing, as Arkey's bristles turned white. Peter backed up against the railing, but there was no escape. It began with the tips of his shoes, then the laces. He watched the glaze of frost creep up his pants and sweatshirt. Then he felt his hair stiffen as the horrid ice stung his nose. He looked up and saw the frost-white piggy face of Jimmy blinking at him.

"We must see what Lir can do before we perish," Jimmy said.

"No. Wait." Shivering now, Peter glanced at the fading star in the east. "What day is it? The Lady said something about eight days and—"

"I lost track of days and nights long ago, Silver One. It is Lila who is here, and not your Lady." Then Jimmy went down the ladder to the main deck and into the hold.

Turning his mind to the hawthorn, Peter was met with a whimper of fear and the image of burning trees. He pushed this away, searching the shore for some sign of help. Then a bright light pulsed from a window of the Silver Wing.

In an instant, he was groping through a dim place of leaves and branches, the lilting song of a thrush in his ears. He followed the sound, pressing forward toward a winking red light. The woodland gave way and he stood at the mouth of a cave.

A ravishing woman in a scarlet dress sat beside a fire, her golden hair glowing. She held a wide bowl of clear water and gazed at her reflection with intense desire. Beside her stood a man with a black beard, the skin of his naked chest shifting continually from flesh to the scaly armor of a snake. His goat-shaped legs were covered with black hair, and a long, horned tail stretched out behind him. His face was an agony of pain and raw fear. Then a rasping voice came out of the man's mouth, though his lips did not move.

"I must have *this*!" He thumped his chest, pulled at his hair. "It must be before she is crowned!"

"*Her* crowned? It is *I* who am queen of the world!" the woman shrieked, her eyes fixed on her reflection. "Your enemy has lost his head over a thing of clay!" Then she laid the bowl aside and rose to her feet. Lifting bare arms, she cried, "Black blood running, as black as red! Destruction upon all hearth and home! Come, naked fire! Come, deepest cold! Come, desolation and dark dread!"

The manserpent laughed, then screamed in terror. Flames broke out in the woods, crackling all around Peter as thunder crashed upon his ears. The two creatures leapt into the air, soaring over his head, and the roots of trees trembled.

Then the flames died and a great silence fell. A path appeared in the twilight wood, and Peter began to walk. All around, in the outer field of his vision, he saw small and large creatures flocking near the edge of the path, though he could not see them clearly. As he passed, they fell in behind him in silent procession. On and on he went through the woods, the rustle of creatures behind, the twilight ahead. He did not know where he was going or why. For a while, he thought that he had lost something but could not remember what.

The path ended at the side of a sheer cliff, where a river of light poured from a hole in the rock. Stepping forward, he put his face to the hole and saw a golden room, roofless and with an immensity of stars overhead. He seemed to be looking from offstage, as it were, and sensed an enormous crowd of onlookers just beyond his range of vision.

On the other side of the room, a door opened and an old woman appeared. He had seen her somewhere before. Then a man whose face and hair were bright as lightning came to meet her. He took her hand and, with a loud voice, presented her to the crowd of witnesses, who began to sing. Quietly at first, and then swelling like an ocean wave, the song rose until it seemed the heavens were singing too. The man reached up and plucked twelve stars, the nearest and brightest in that cloudless sky. Weaving them into a circlet of silver, he placed the crown on the old woman's head.

All at once, she changed. Now she was the Lady, dark-haired and beautiful, dressed in white. The room became brighter and brighter until it hurt his eyes. Squinting in the unbearable light, trying to see her face, Peter called, "Lady!" Then he saw her turn in his direction. She took the crown from her head, passed it into unseen hands, and came toward him with gladness and welcome shining on her face. The thrush began to sing.

Peter blinked and she was gone. The sound of the thrush faded. He stood there in the deep silence of a frozen sea that shone like dull crystal. His fingers were numb, and his feet ached with cold. Timber groaned and snapped. Tuffy let out a sad mew, and Arkey shivered.

"Help us," Peter whispered, his breath a thin white wisp in the red twilight.

49

Battle Stations

A little before dawn, as Peter stood at the ship's rail looking at the morning star, Jen went to the Hermit's room to talk to Grandfather. She knew it was only a painting, but there was an awareness in his eyes and a kindness that encouraged trust.

"Yesterday, during that weather war, I thought the Fennys had gone mad. Droat and his crew made so much food, even though there was no one around to eat it. And it looked like Mara and Forlost were asleep all day in the dining room. But you know what? It was those two Heads and the busy kitchen crew who kept Lir from sailing away! That's right! When the Shee fog finally cleared, there was the ship, still in the bay.

"But Wakken Wood is on fire." She gripped the Lady's staff harder. "Last night, right after the sea monster didn't come, and the Glashtyn failed to build a boat, Lila went off and started burning the forest all around the island!" Jen thumped her staff in anger, and it seemed to her that a light pulsed out of those eyes that watched her from the wall. "When I heard her voice yesterday, I remembered how she kidnapped me when I was little. I would have been afraid, but she makes me so mad I could hit her! With this stick!" She thumped the staff again, and there it was: starlight flashing from Grandfather's face. Then Forlost walked through the door of painted gray stones.

"Miss Jen, the Bugganes bring good news! It was the trolls who killed the sea monster last night. Your brother and sister brought them to Grondle's Gap in the nick of time."

"Oh! That's where Ed went! I was pretty sure. Then they're alright!"

"Oh yes, but Pixel is unwell, though she's up and dressed against Droat's wishes. Mara is occupied, and he asks you to come."

Clutching the staff, she followed him out the door. Together, they left the Silver Wing and went swiftly through the long passages. Forlost went on to the dining room, and Jen stopped at Pixel's door. She had just put her hand on the knob when the door was yanked open and Kaney stuck his head out. "Do you smell smoke?"

She paused, and her eyes widened as an urgent command pushed all other thought from her mind.

"Come!" the hawthorn pleaded. "Come!"

She raced to the front room and flung open the door. There was the hawthorn on the threshold. The little tree trembled as the Vespa swirled above it in a maddened swarm. Across the hollow, flames licked the near hills, spreading fast.

"Move away from the grass!" Jen shouted.

Lifting its roots, the hawthorn scuttled to a patch of bare dirt in the middle of the hollow, and Jen followed. Suddenly, the hornets landed in the tree and their humming ceased. Seeing a huge shadow on the ground, Jen looked up. A woman passed over, screeching with laughter, her red dress and golden hair streaming in the wind. Then came a rasping sound, like a giant lizard among stones, and a man with a long tail skimmed over the hills. The pair touched down on the roof above the door and disappeared over the crest of the hill. Buzzing angrily, the Vespa rose in a silver cloud as the hawthorn and the entire cliff top burst into red flames.

"Look to the tree!" a voice cried, and Dooney came running out of the house with a bucket of water. He doused the hawthorn, and then Froke and Frimlaf came out with more buckets.

Leaving the burning tree to the Fennys, Jen ran back into the house just as heavy footsteps pounded up the passage.

"Battle stations!" Tom Mole shouted. "To the back door!"

She rushed to the main corridor in time to see Droat and the seven speechless Fennys come out of the kitchen and go running down the beach passage.

She crossed to Pixel's room and saw the Poinkers lined up on the sill, looking down toward the shore. Pixel, who should have been in bed, stood on the bench beneath the windows. She turned a pale face to Jen. "Lila's back."

"Right above our heads," Kaney added, as dirt and small stones cascaded onto the outer windowsill. Outside, they could hear Lila's shrill laughter.

Kneeling on the bench beside Pixel, Jen looked out and caught her breath. "Is that ice?"

"The Shee brought down the deep cold just after dawn," Kaney said, and Jen knew it had happened while she'd been in the Hermit's room.

Smoke from the hills wafted over the beach, but a southeast wind pushed it back so that Jen could see the six Shee who stood at the edge of the frozen sea. Locked in ice and covered by frost, Lir's ship shone like a phantom. "What's happened to the light?"

"It started a while ago," Kaney replied. "Dooney says something is eating the sun."

Suddenly, a flash of forked lightning shot from the ship, straight for the house.

"Aaah!" the chorus cried as the Poinkers leapt off the sill. Jen and Pixel ducked as the bolt struck the roof above the windows. Dirt and clods of grass flew, and small stones rattled against the glass.

"That was meant for Lila!" Kaney said.

Jen stood up warily and looked out. "She's returning Lir's fire!"

Pixel got up on the bench and the Poinkers scrambled back to the ledge in time to see a fish-tailed ball of flame sail over the bay and hit the ship.

They stood there in silence, watching the topsails burn. Tears ran down Pixel's face, and Jen could hear her wheezing. Then the door behind them opened and Fiak walked in. "Do you mind?" he asked. "I don't want to watch alone."

"Aren't Mara and Thrinn in the dining room?"

"They went to the back door with the others. Forlost too. In case there are ... casualties." He got up on the bench as the Poinkers moved over, set his notebook and ink pot on the wide sill, and began to write.

Though she could hardly bear to watch, Jen turned her eyes to the battle down on the beach and saw the hairy man wielding a great club. He was hard-pressed by a ring of horse-eared men with swords and black stallions kicking with hard hooves. Jen watched as they closed in around the Buggane.

Pixel pounded her fist on the sill. "Tom! Blow up your head!"

Then Moody, three times his normal size and baying like a hell-hound, broke through the line of men. The great dog darted under the stallions, snapping legs in half, tearing out throats, scattering them like flies.

But the fight at the north end of the beach was not going well. At the door of the ravine, Tom Bear and Tom Wolf battled a host of Glashtyn. It seemed to Jen that when one went down, two more came up out of the sea. The Bugganes fought valiantly with teeth and claws, but they were outnumbered three to one. Without warning, a deafening blast issued from the base of the cliff. Rocks and sand flew up, and she heard a noise like the honking of geese. The Glashtyn mob quailed, wavering with uncertainty. Then the Mooner hounds swarmed out of the ravine, teeth bared, jaws snapping. Close behind came the Mooner men on their white horses, firing a rain of arrows as another bomb exploded at the feet of the witless Glashtyn.

"The catapult!" Raney whooped.

"Hooray for Krim and Krinias!" the chorus shouted, but Kaney shushed them.

For the dynamite had drawn the attention of the Shee. Jen watched in horror as the six shadowy figures turned their backs on the burning ship and moved swiftly across the sand, firing long black arrows.

"No!" she moaned, as one Mooner after another went down. Their little horses screamed in terror as the creatures of fear bore down upon them. When the Shee reached the place where the Glashtyn were grouped, another burst of dynamite exploded. Several horse-men fell, but the Shee pressed forward as if there had been no explosion at all.

Then Tom Bear, fierce and terrible, rose on his hind legs and advanced. The shadowy figures loosed arrow after arrow into his chest until he looked like a roaring pincushion. He was joined by Tom Wolf, who snarled and snapped, his huge jaws tearing at the few Glashtyn who dared to join the attack. Jen watched, biting her lip. Then a gigantic scorpion mushroomed out of the sand, its stinger poised high. "Oh no!" she gasped.

But Pixel croaked, "Tom Spider!" and the Poinkers cheered as the fierce creature crushed the remaining Glashtyn with one mighty blow of its tail. Yet it was clear to Jen that even three very terrible

Bugganes could not hold back the six Shee. Step by step, they gained ground, moving toward the line of Mooners.

Suddenly, with a roar that echoed off the cliffs, Tom Mole leapt out of the ravine, eyes ablaze, white tusks gleaming. He rushed at the Shee, and they scattered, but not before he'd wrenched away one of their longbows. Stooping to scoop up fallen arrows, he took aim and a black shaft went home, piercing one of the Shee. It staggered but did not fall. The others sent a rain of arrows, many of which pierced the mole's hide, but he only pulled them out of his flank and used them to shoot. "That's the way to fight!" Sonney shrieked, and Pixel beat her fist on the sill, crying, "Tom! Tom!" He shot two more Shee, and they faltered. Then one of them uttered a piercing shriek.

In answer to that call, a red figure leapt down from the roof, hurtling past the window. Lila landed on the beach beside the Shee, swinging a great mace. Like a tidal wave, she fell upon the Bugganes, pressing them back as the few remaining Mooners shot their last arrows. From overhead, Jen and the Poinkers heard a terrible hissing laugh.

"This is the end," Kaney whispered.

Jen stared in horror at the burning ship. Pixel moaned and fell sideways. Jen caught her as she slid to the floor. She lifted Pixel onto the bench, then wrapped her arms around the shivering girl and listened to her labored breathing. The light in the window darkened. Into Jen's mind came the shuddering sigh of the hawthorn, then silence. Tears stung her eyes as she looked around the room. Fiak stood staring at the smoky twilight, the idle pen in his hand dripping ink on the floor. The Poinkers, fearing the worst, had gathered by the door, their little spears drawn. Lila would come into the house now. *She'll find me*, Jen thought, *but I'll fight her first.* Holding Pixel with one arm, she reached out and took the staff in her hand.

In that moment, as she listened for the footfall of the enemy, a strange sound rose out of the day's defeat. Someone, somewhere, was singing. The door opened, and in walked a gray-haired old woman in a blue cloak. The crowd of Poinkers lowered their spears and stepped aside as she went straight to Pixel and touched her brow.

Pixel stopped shivering. She took a deep breath, sat up, and said to the woman, "I knew you'd come."

And suddenly Jen remembered the night she'd met this woman in the foothills.

"Lady!" she said, bowing and holding out the staff.

"You have done all I asked, Silver One," the old woman said. She took the staff, and in that instant her appearance changed. Once again, Jen saw the beautiful dark-haired Lady of the Mountains. "Come, children," the Lady said. "There is still work to do." Taking Jen by the hand, she turned and went out the door, the Poinkers and Fiak and Pixel coming behind. Then, in the corridor, she stopped. "What's this?"

There was Dooney on his knees. "At last," he wept, "at last! I knew I would find you."

"Oh, Dooney," the Lady said, "your reason for weeping was over long ago."

"But the lost light! How is it that you—"

"It's a long tale, and I cannot tell it now." She smiled at the Fennys who came crowding into the passage and at Mara, whose face was radiant with joy. Then the whole company followed her out the front door and into the hollow where the Small One and the beautiful giants stood singing. The Vespa swirled down, hovering over her head like a crown of stars. Still leading Jen by the hand, the Lady went up a little path to the high headland of the Silver Wing. She did not hurry, as if there were all the time in the world, though the Hills of Floden burned and the cry of the forest went up in smoke and fire.

50

Fire and Rain

Peter shivered, trying to hold on to the image of the Lady and the sound of the thrush, but the vison he'd had was fading fast. Across the bay, the Shee stood on the shore, calling down the deep cold.

"Cripes! What now?" Arkey cried. "Looks like somethin's eatin' the sun!"

Hearing the fear in Arkey's voice, Peter glanced up, his eyelids stinging with cold. "An eclipse, I guess," he muttered. This explained the slow darkening of the day, but, like Arkey, he wondered what would happen next.

"Come on, kid," Arkey said. "Let's get to the galley and stoke up the stove. I've had enough of this killin' frost!"

Slipping and sliding across the quarterdeck, the companions climbed down the ladder just as Jimmy and Lir emerged from the hold. Peter watched the pigman push the wizard to the ship's rail. Then, before Lir could cast a single spell, two figures leapt to the roof of the Hermit's House and the entire cliff top burst into flame.

"That's Lila!" Lir gasped. "She's come to finish me!" He turned a furious face to Peter. "This is your fault, boy!"

"*My* fault!" Peter shouted, fighting down panic. "*You* brought her here! I saw the empty painting in the North Tower."

"She will feed you to her lover," Lir said bitterly. "See him there?"

In the lurid light of the grassfires, Peter saw a man standing on the bluff beside Lila, and he guessed it was the manserpent, Ahab Rilson. Ahab cast a huge shadow, like a dragon with its mouth open wide to swallow the world. Dread crept into Peter's heart. Tuffy uttered a low hiss.

Cursing, Lir clapped one hand on Jimmy's shoulder, lifted his other hand in the air, and pointed at Lila. A shaft of lightning streaked across the bay and struck the cliff at her feet. She jumped back, raised one arm, and hurled a pale green ball of fire.

For a fraction of time, Peter gaped stupidly at the approaching missile. Then he dropped to the deck, shouting, "Duck!" High above, the topsail burst into flames, sending a shower of sparks everywhere. The ice had no effect on the sickly green fire, and little flares sprang up all over the ship, as if fueled by the frost.

"Rain!" Jimmy shouted at Lir.

The wizard muttered another spell, and clouds appeared right over the ship. Driving rain came down, but it did nothing to quench the fire. Peter watched in dismay as the topsail continued to burn and the flames spread. Suddenly, Lir's storm clouds vanished on a puff of wind, as another fireball struck the bowsprit.

"This is witch fire!" Arkey cried. "Get below!"

He ran for the hatch, and Peter was right behind, but he slipped and fell. Scrabbling to his feet, he looked up just as a burning spar broke from the rigging.

The beam fell on Arkey. Sparks and fiery brands fell like rain. "No!" Peter shrieked and propelled himself across the slippery planks with frantic speed. The spar lay tilted across the hatch, and its lower end held Arkey pinned to the deck. With a burst of strength, Peter dragged the broken timber aside, lifted the Poinker out of the flames, and made a beeline for the cabin. He kicked open the door, then took two steps into the passage and sank to his knees, overcome by fear and exhaustion. Tuffy ran in.

"Help me, Tuffy! Is he breathing?"

The cat put his face close to Arkey's snout. Uttering a low trill, he trotted into the galley and returned with a small canteen clenched in his jaws.

Peter unscrewed the lid and sniffed. It was tree food. He tipped a few drops into Arkey's mouth, and the Poinker stirred slightly.

Tuffy trilled again.

"Oh!" Peter gasped. "He's alive!"

Arkey was in bad shape. His forepaw was crushed, an ear was torn, and his little back legs were broken. His breathing was very shallow.

"You hang on," Peter groaned and shifted the small limp form into the crook of his arm.

Not knowing what else to do, Peter sat in the passage with his friend in his arms. His joints ached and he was stiff with cold. Through the open door of the cabin, he heard the roar of flames as the ship burned. No doubt Lir was still casting lightning bolts, using up Jimmy's strength, but what was the use? Letting go of his last hope for rescue, Peter closed his eyes wearily, steeling himself for the end. An image of Pixel floated into his mind's eye, followed by swift memories of his father and mother. Grief welled up. If only he could see them again.

The sound of hoofbeats broke into his thoughts. He opened his eyes and blinked. "Must have fallen asleep," he murmured. But there it was again, the sound of a horse galloping on water, just like his old dream of the warrior riding over the sea. Wondering, he got to his feet, careful not to jostle Arkey, and moved to the open door. Pale green flames crackled all over the ship. Standing on the threshold, he looked up past the smoke and the burning mast to a patch of clear sky. For some reason, the sight of it reminded him of the day he'd met the Lady at the river.

"Boy!" A rough hand grabbed his shoulder, and he jerked away, thinking only of Arkey and how he must not drop him.

"Leave it! It's dead!"

"No!" Peter struggled against the wizard, trying to hold on to Arkey, and suddenly with a fierce howl, Tuffy bounded out of the passage, electric light shooting from his bristled fur. He leapt at Lir's face, scratching and hissing. Lir staggered back, trying to fight the cat off, but Tuffy hung on, tearing at the wizard's hair and beard.

Holding tight to Arkey, Peter backed away from the violent brawl, and then, there it was again—that sound of hoofbeats. Where was it coming from? Moving warily through the fire and smoke, Peter saw the inert form of Jimmy lying by the ship's rail. There was nothing he could do, so he passed on and climbed the ladder to the quarterdeck. Listening intently, he stopped at the stern, looked across the open sea, and saw a white speck in the distance.

The daylight grew brighter. On an impulse, as if hearing a call, he turned around just as the main mast cracked. Its top half, and all the rigging, collapsed over the side of the ship in fiery ruin. And now, across the water, high above the Hermit's beach, he could see someone standing on the headland of the Silver Wing. The Lady! She had come! Peter's heart lifted in sudden hope. Sure enough, she raised her staff, the last shadow passed from the sun's face, and the ice vanished.

Then Peter heard the sound of hoofbeats plainly. He looked back and saw the figure who had haunted his dreams all his life. Down from the north the Warrior came, riding a white horse over the sea. Peter stared, half believing he was asleep, until he glanced down at Arkey's singed bristles. "No," he said aloud. "It's not a dream this time."

Speeding swiftly over the water, the great horse kicked up spray like sparks of light. As it drew closer, Peter could see the silver eyes of the Warrior piercing even the brightness of day. His upraised sword caught and reflected the fire of the sun as he swept past the port side of the burning ship.

Peter ran across the quarterdeck in time to hear the Shee uttering shrill commands. He saw a band of Glashtyn rush into the oncoming tide, brandishing swords and clubs. Then the Warrior was upon them. He met the assault head-on, striking blow after blow as his bright sword flashed up and down. He slew all the Glashtyn and left them lying in the sea. Hard on the heels of the defeated Glashtyn, the Shee pressed toward the Rider, urged on by Lila, who was still fighting the Bugganes outside the ravine. The Shee drew their bows and loosed a rain of arrows as the Warrior reined in his horse and spoke aloud a single word. Instantly, the six Shee turned to stone, and all their arrows splashed harmlessly into the shallows. Dumbstruck, Peter gazed at the Warrior, who sat calmly in the saddle, holding his eager horse in check.

Then, from the top of the cliff, a hideous voice cursed. Ahab Rilson, the manserpent, stood alone on the roof of the Hermit's House, dwarfed by his monstrous shadow. His will was bent upon the Lady and a smaller figure who stood exposed on the top of the headland.

"That boy is mine!" Ahab called in a voice that carried across the water. "Give him to me and I will spare the rest!"

There followed an ominous silence, as if the island, even the sea, awaited a reply. Peter held his breath. Suddenly, the Lady laughed and the Small One's voice called out, "No! Nothing is *yours*."

The manserpent's menacing shadow swelled to a great height, stooped over, and tore Ahab from its heart as the living man uttered one last piercing shriek. Then the shadow turned into a terrible dragon. Roaring in rage, it leapt toward the headland where the Small One stood. Even as it opened huge jaws to snatch up its prey, the Lady struck it over the head with a mighty blow of her staff. For a split second, the world stood still as the dragon teetered on the edge of the cliff. Then, with a noise like an avalanche, it toppled over the brink and smashed on the beach, sending up a blast of sand and rock.

In that same moment, Lila charged across the shore and leapt toward the Warrior, shrieking curses and swinging her mace. Peter quailed at the fierce hatred in her voice. The Warrior spurred his horse and bore down upon her, singing as he raised his sword. With one swift stroke, he cut off her head.

Before Peter could blink, a loud crack echoed off the cliffs. A rent appeared in the sky. With a shrieking whine like the unoiled gears of some ancient engine, an iron door opened over the shore. The dragon and Lila were sucked into darkness. Then the door shut with a clang and vanished in a burst of foul smoke. All that remained was the body of Ahab, cast down from the height, a broken wreck in the sand.

The Warrior turned and pointed his sword at the ship. To Peter's surprise, Lir appeared at the rail, cowering. The Rider spoke one quiet word, and with a small puffing sound, the wizard turned into a huge wheel with spokes like human legs. Whirring, it rose from the deck and went spinning across the sea into the west.

When it was gone, the great Horseman stood up in his stirrups and raised his sword to the Lady. She lifted her staff, and the Small One stretched up his arms. Then, though there were no clouds in the sky, it began to rain.

With his white horse pawing and prancing on the sea, the Warrior drew near to the side of the ship. He stopped below the quarterdeck and looked up. For the space of a heartbeat, Peter gazed into those piercing silver eyes. And though the eyes sifted him, Peter did not look away. "Well done," a quiet voice said into his mind. He felt a surge of joy. Then the Rider saluted him and, with a mighty shout, wheeled about and rode north across the sea.

Peter watched until the Horseman passed into Grondle's Gap; then he raised his face to the rain, letting it mingle with his tears. "It's over," he whispered.

He saw the sun shining behind a sparkling curtain and knew it was raining all over the island, a steady shower of liquid starlight falling over Wakken Wood, quenching every last spark of witch fire.

51

Book Return

Peter's dad stood in front of the library, looking at the window. He wasn't looking *into* the library. He was looking at the reflection in the glass. Like a mirror, it showed him the recovery clinic across the street, the gray walls, the few visitors coming and going from the main entrance.

This was the morning of his wife's discharge. The doctors had given her the all clear. Martin hoped they were right. He really did wish her the best.

Suddenly, he stiffened and his heart constricted. There she was, coming out the door, pulling his old rolling suitcase. She was followed by her sister. As Martin watched, a taxi pulled up, the two women got in, and the cab drove away. It happened so fast. He turned from the plate glass window, raised a hand in farewell, and stood there on the sidewalk, watching till the back of the cab disappeared in traffic.

Picking up his duffel bag, he walked quickly in the opposite direction. After half a mile, he began to jog. There wasn't really any hurry. He was simply trying to outrun grief.

He arrived at the ferry terminal, breathless but determined. The hope of finding Peter was all he had left. He *must* get to the island. Surely ferry service had resumed.

The line in the booking office was long. When it was finally his turn, he asked for a ticket to Orbsen Bay.

"Service to the island has stopped," the ticket agent replied.

"When will it start again?"

"Ferries to Orbsen Bay have been suspended indefinitely. Next!"

Angry at this peremptory dismissal, Martin walked out and stood at the curb, looking up and down the street. What he ought to do was go back in and demand to speak to a manager, a ferry captain, the port authority … someone. But he didn't. It required more confidence than he had at present. He was no longer a man of the world. The collars of all his shirts were frayed. Everything he owned was in the duffel bag on his shoulder. The only thing left to his name was his job at the diner.

Pushing all this aside, he forced himself to think. There must be a way to get to the island. There had to be a way … What about a fishing boat? Right.

The docks weren't far. As he jogged through the streets, the smell of the wharf grew stronger. Creosote and the sea. He'd always had a hankering for the sea—it must be his island roots.

His first stop, Atlas Adventure Fishing. Expensive. Then Finley's Charter Yachts. More expensive. Patiently, he went from door to door, up one end of the wharf and down the other. One thing he learned: He did not have nearly enough money. And even if he did, no one was keen to go to the island.

His last stop was an old warehouse at the farthest end of the docks. It bore the title "Island Fishing and Trading", and the sign in the window said "Open". This looked promising at first, but the door was locked, and when he peered through the dirty glass, he saw that the lights were out.

He became aware of an old woman sitting on a bench not far from the warehouse. A thick wooden walking stick sat across her lap, and she was watching him. Knowing the wharves were home to all sorts, he approached her cautiously. "Excuse me. Do you know when this fishing company opens?"

"It's gone out of business."

"When?"

"Coupla weeks ago."

"Okay. Thanks." Martin paused, looking out to sea. He bit his lip, fighting a feeling of helplessness.

Perhaps the woman read something in his face. "What're you after, son?"

Martin looked at her weathered skin, her watery eyes. "I … I'm trying to get to Orbsen Bay."

"Why do you wanna go there? Ain't you heard the reports? Orbsen burnt to the ground. Even the pier. That's what I heard."

"Burned … are you sure? But what about the people who are still on the island?"

"Everyone cleared out of Sweetwater is what I heard. Foyle burnt down, and then there was freak storms. The last ferry arrived 'bout a week ago. Had all the survivors on board. That's what I heard."

"But ... my son ... He ... he's there ..."

"You tryin' to charter a boat?"

"I ... I don't have enough money for that. I thought maybe ... maybe I could work for my passage on a fishing boat." He wasn't sure why he was telling her this. She was a complete stranger, but she'd asked. "Do you know the fishermen around here?"

"A few."

"Would you ... would you let me know if you hear of anyone who'd be willing to go to the island? I work at the diner. On 87th Street.

"Sure, mister. What's your name."

"Thornburg. Martin Thornburg. I work the night shift."

"Thornburg," she repeated, narrowing her eyes, giving him a long look. She ran one hand over her walking stick, then got to her feet. "I'll send word if I hear something."

Martin thanked her and walked away, heavyhearted. Orbsen Bay burned down. Sweetwater abandoned. The last ferry from the island ... He hadn't known all this, but now he understood why Sweetwater AM 780 had vanished from the airwaves.

By the time he reached the diner, he hadn't an ounce of hope left. Even if he did manage to find a fishing boat willing to take him to the island, what point was there in going? The last survivors had returned to Lang. He should never have sent Peter away. If only he'd waited. He could have had Peter transferred to another school. He could have ...

Pushing open the diner door, Martin was relieved to see that it was nearly empty. His shift didn't start for an hour. He went behind the counter and poured himself a cup of coffee, then went to the hatch and asked the cook for a bowl of soup. Sitting down in a booth, he forced himself to eat.

Mrs. Murdle came bustling out of the kitchen. "Oh, Martin! I'm glad you're here! Can you start early? Do you mind? My hubby got tickets for the theater, and I gotta get home and change!"

Martin took his dishes behind the counter, then stowed his duffel bag under the coatrack and tied on an apron.

"Oh thank you, darlin'! Hey! How's your wife? Happy to get home, I bet."

He nodded, not trusting himself to speak.

"Tell me all about it tomorrow! And you got some mail. Just one thing. I put it over there, by the cash register."

He forced himself to smile and nod as she put on a hat and hurried out. Then he picked up his mail. For a moment, he allowed himself to hope that Great-Aunt Marj had sent a letter, until he saw the return address. It was from the recovery clinic. One final bill. Of course. Good thing he hadn't purchased a ferry ticket.

There were only two customers in the diner. A young couple lingering over coffee and pie, both of them reading. He walked over and refilled their coffee cups. They looked up at him and stared.

"Evening," he said. There was something familiar about them. They weren't regulars, but maybe they'd stopped in once or twice before. Martin had a pretty good memory for faces, but tonight he simply didn't care. As he moved to the next booth to wipe the table, he heard the woman whispering. He glanced over and found her staring at him. Then she reddened and looked away.

He went back behind the counter, sat on a stool, and looked absently out the window. Somewhere in the distance, a siren wailed over the rumble of traffic. His thoughts turned to his wife and then to Peter. The sharp edge of grief pressed against his heart. He shook himself and stood up.

The young couple were leaving. As Martin rang up their bill, he noticed that they avoided looking at him. Then the man picked up a leather satchel, and something in Martin's mind clicked. These people were former students. That's where he'd seen them. And they had recognized him but didn't know what to say. Well, what was there to say?

Putting it out of his mind, Martin began bussing their booth. They'd left an unusually large tip. He carried away the dishes, then came back to wipe the table and noticed a book on the seat. One of them had left it behind. He hurried out the door and looked up and down the street. They were gone, of course. Well, he'd put it aside for them. Probably they'd come back for it tomorrow.

The book was lying face down. He picked it up. It was certainly hefty. Then he turned it over and caught his breath. Not quite believing, he opened the cover and sure enough, there was his name on the flyleaf, in his own handwriting. When he'd given up the apartment and sold his library, it was the one volume of all his collection he wished he'd kept. The Thornburg book.

His heart beating fast, he laid it on the counter and finished cleaning the table. Then he washed the few dishes, dried his hands, and picked up the book. It had been ages since he'd read it. Where to start? He leafed through the pages. That's right. It was a facsimile. Wondering briefly whether the original still existed, he flipped ahead, glancing at the drawings of strange creatures. Let's see. There was something about a mythical character who controlled weather ... There was something about ... ah, here was a reference to the Silver-eyed. He cast a practiced eye over the archaic handwriting, running his finger down the page as he read ... Wait.

What was this? *"The Silver-eyed do not experience death as we know it. They live on until it is time to go on a mountainous journey ..."*

Martin stared into the empty air. Was this true? Was it even possible? And if it was ...

The bell tinkled as the door opened. A large man entered and came straight to the counter. "Thornburg? Are you Martin Thornburg?"

Martin looked at the man's friendly face, his knitted cap, his ... fishing bibs.

"Lily Rilson sent me to find you. Says you're wantin' to go to the island."

52

Repairs Begin

The sparkling rain fell for several hours after the Warrior rode away to Grondle's Gap. In the early evening, a rescue crew came to get Peter and everyone off the ship. They arrived on a raft that Krim and Krinias had made. It was powered by an outboard motor pieced together from parts off the Datsun. Dooney piloted the raft, bringing Fiak and all the Poinkers. Peter was very glad to see them.

They came aboard the ship, and after a noisy greeting, the entire Poinker band disappeared into the hold. Dooney, with the help of Peter and Fiak, lifted poor Jimmy from the deck where he lay and managed to get him down the rope ladder and onto the raft. Then Peter and Fiak strapped Arkey to a makeshift stretcher and lowered him over the side. Rain continued to fall from the bright, cloudless sky. A warm rain, scented faintly of afternoon cedar and the woods under a summer sun.

"Are they done yet?" Dooney called from the bottom of the ladder.

As Fiak turned from the rail and looked toward the hatch, there was a sudden clamor of voices and a muffled crash from below. "Not yet," he called down.

After that, Peter found himself giving Fiak a hurried tour of the upper decks. They crawled under scorched timbers and climbed over piles of rubble while the Fenny scribbled away, trying to keep his notepad out of the rain. "She's sustained a great deal of damage, and a diagram will have to be made." Then he paused and cupped a hand to his ear.

Peter wondered what they were listening for. All he could hear was rain pattering on the deck. Then Dooney called from the raft, "Aren't they finished?"

"Finished what?" Peter asked.

Raney's strident voice came from the hold. "She's got a snout like a dragon! Roll her over here!"

"Nearly done!" Fiak shouted. He stuffed the notepad into his pocket and said, "Thank you, Mr. Peter. Time to go." Then he ran to the rail and clambered down the ladder to the raft.

Peter went to the hatch door and stood there, listening.

"Shove that bag of powder down her nose! Oi! Gimmee that box of sticks!"

Curious, he started down the ladder. Halfway, he nearly stepped on Pinkey. "What are you doing in there?" he asked, but she pushed past him and scuttled out of the hatch.

In the dim light of the lower deck, Tuffy sat at the edge of the dark opening to the hold, peering down. Peter stopped beside him.

"Okay! All set!" Raney cried.

Kaney's voice boomed out, "Now!"

Peter heard a soft hiss and a pop, then a crackling sound.

"Well, boys," Kaney said, "I guess that's what 'fire in the hole' means."

"Sure, boss," came Raney's voice, "but don't you think we better scoot?"

Poinkers came scrambling up the ladder, two and three at a time. Kaney was the last to appear. "All accounted for? Oh, Mr. Peter! I thought you'd be on the raft!"

Without warning, a tremendous report sounded in the hold, followed by a crashing boom. The old ship rocked.

"Whoa!" the chorus cried. "She musta recoiled out the other side!"

Peter heard the sound of gushing water and watched in astonishment as the sea surged into the hold. Tuffy turned and fled.

"We gotta get offa here!" Raney hollered, and everyone swarmed out of the hatch. Helter-skelter they ran across the main deck and flung themselves over the rail. Peter scrambled down the rope ladder, Poinkers clinging to his shoulders and arms. They hung off his belt loops, but he didn't stop to think. He dropped to the raft, then *splash! splash!* and Fiak was fishing Poinkers out of the water with a net. Dooney revved the idling motor as Kaney counted and recounted his scattered band. The raft pulled away and began to move toward shore.

Jimmy coughed slightly and opened his eyes. He turned his face from the rain and looked at Peter. "Was that a cannon shot?"

Peter stared at the crowd of twitching Poinker snouts. "You fired a cannon in the hold!"

"Yup. We scuttled the ship," Raney said proudly. "It was Forlost's idea. He figured there'd be a cannon on board."

Dooney cut the motor and they sat in silence, watching the wizard's ship go slowly down into the deep.

"It is well," Fiak said. "He will never return."

Jimmy lifted his head in time to see the quarterdeck disappear beneath the waves. "So ends the realm of Mannon Mac Lir," he said, and Tuffy began to purr.

Dooney started the engine and the raft moved smoothly over the quiet water. When it reached the shallows, he cut the motor and ran the raft right up onto the sand. Then Peter picked up Arkey and stepped onto the beach, glad to feel solid earth again. Fiak and Dooney helped Jimmy to his feet and across the shore, toward the Hermit's House. They were surrounded by the Poinkers, still noisily congratulating themselves.

As the company approached the ravine, a crowd surged out the entrance and Peter was suddenly overwhelmed by a giant tongue and the affectionate greeting of Moody. Hounds yapped; horses whinnied. The Fennys carried Jimmy into the house. Jen appeared, pushing her way past Moody. She gave Peter a quick hug and took charge of Arkey. Then Peter looked up, and there was Pixel.

He went to her and put his arms around her frail shoulders. She heaved a great sigh, and when he pulled away, she searched his face. "Are you okay?" she asked.

He shrugged. "Yeah. But I'll have to get used to it."

She smiled and then, with a final burst of liquid sun that cascaded over their heads, the rain stopped. Peter lifted his wet face to the sky and laughed. Then he heard someone else laughing, and there was the Lady, standing by the ravine door. She came and wrapped her arms around him, covering him with her blue cloak, and he knew that he was home.

❦ ❦ ❦

What remained of Ahab Rilson the Bugganes buried on the headland of Grondle's Gap. They set up a stone marker on which Krinias etched, "Capt. A. Rilson landed here", a saying that all the creatures agreed upon, though Peter wondered how they knew. "He came from the west," Rathfrit explained. "We saw his ship on a moonless night. Let him rest, if he can, facing his homeland."

After that, the healing of Wakken Wood began, and Peter, in later years, always said it started with the hawthorn. That evening of his return, before eating or doing anything else, he took the canteen of tree food that he'd saved from the ship and headed for the front door.

"Mr. Peter," Forlost said, stopping him in the passage. "Did anyone tell you? Your tree got hurt in the fires."

"What?" Peter stared into Forlost's solemn face; then he took off running. When he got to the front room, he threw open the door and there stood a blackened tree trunk beside the threshold. Two branches with singed leaves stuck out from one side, and on the other hung lifeless stubs. He could hardly believe it was the hawthorn. It made him think of a dog he'd once seen lying in the middle of the street: two legs working to get up, two legs smashed by a speeding car.

"Why didn't you tell me?"

Into his mind came a faint voice: "Your sap low."

"Not as low as yours!" He was angry now—at Lila, at stupid Lir. "And where are the Vespa?" Looking around helplessly, he saw the black hills rising above the hollow, the grass burned to the ground. Then the hornets appeared, swarming above the doorway. "Can't you do anything but sting Poinkers?" he cried.

Like falling stars, they landed all over him, covering his hair and shoulders and arms. Ignoring them, he pulled the little canteen from his pocket and with a helpless feeling bent down and emptied it over the tree's roots. Then, shooing off the gentle hornets, which rose and landed on his hands again, he stroked the hawthorn's charred bark. "I'm sorry. I don't know what else to do."

Straightening up, he saw Pixel standing in the open doorway, looking at him with wide eyes. "It's alright," he mumbled. "They don't sting."

"That's not what the Poinkers say," said another voice, and Jen stepped over the threshold.

All at once, the Vespa began to buzz loudly. Rising from his shoulders, they hovered in the air as a voice like a bell sounded in his mind. He turned in time to see fresh bark spreading upward from the hawthorn's roots, like a wave lapping the sand. New branches sprouted, grew, and burst into green leaves. The tree sprang upright, and Peter heard its joyful voice in his mind. "Sap!"

"Wow," Pixel said, "that's good. Just like the big vine at home. But are you gonna barf?"

Jen laughed. "Peter! Do you think *I* can do that?"

He stood there, staring at the tree, trying to understand what had just happened. Then, for the first time since the battle with Lila, he turned his mind to the voice of the woods but found only a strange silence. A mild wind, blowing over the hollow, stirred his hair, and suddenly he caught the sound of one faint sigh, then another. Slowly, the lament of the trees came into his mind.

"What is it, Peter?" Pixel said.

"So many trees have died. And a lot more are hurt."

"I know," Jen said, her face solemn. "But Wakken Wood will be healed. By time and the strong power of root and seed. That's what Small One says."

A thorny branch tapped the top of his head, and he ducked to get out of the way.

That evening, Uncle Ed and Aunt Marj returned, trudging stiffly up the beach passage and into the dining room, right in the middle of supper. They were greeted by cheers and a large pot of tea. Of all the stories Peter heard, theirs was the strangest, but it certainly explained the disappearance of the sea monster.

Later, when supper was over and Aunt Marj had gone to take a bath, Peter and his uncle remained at the table, sipping cups of Forlost's cocoa.

"Them trolls aren't too bright, that's for sure," Uncle Ed said, "but the Rider on the white horse called them his warriors, so I guess they're alright."

Peter caught his breath. "You met him?"

Uncle Ed grinned. "Oh sure. After he finished off them Shee and that giant gorgon, me and Marj saw him head for the Gap—"

"You saw all that?"

"Oh yeah. Saw the whole battle on the beach from the top of them giants' stairs. Those Bugganes are heroes, that's for sure. Anyway, like I was sayin', we ran back to the Gap and saw his horse parked in front of the tunnel, so we went in and there he was, talkin' with them trolls like they were best of friends."

"Trelly knows him?"

"Trelly was down on one knee in front of him, like he was gettin' knighted or somethin'. Called the guy Hælend."

"Hælend." Peter repeated the name slowly. "But what did he say to them?"

"Well, they wanted to go to some place they call the everlasting hills, but he told 'em there was still work to do on the island. Asked 'em to clear up the rubble in Floden. What I hope is that they'll fix up Old Road so we can get home."

"Was that all he said?"

"He invited them to a big feast in the City of Giants, in their honor. That woman who clubbed the dragon over the head is gonna be there too. They call her Mother, but I still don't know why. Anyway, when he was done talkin' to Trelly, Hælend turns to me and Marj and asks us to take the trolls through the Underways to a door near the ravine. 'Escort my warriors' is what he said. So we did. I expect he thought they woulda got lost again otherwise."

"Then what happened?"

"Well, he said goodbye and we followed him out the end of the tunnel, and he got on his horse and rode away over the sea. Just like that. Then Marj started yellin' at the trolls—"

"Aunt Marj was yelling?"

"Yeah, she's got a knack with big creatures, that's for sure. Anyway, she starts yellin', and them trolls get up and light a bunch of torches, and off we go, back through the tunnels. But it was a lot different with more light, I can tell you. Them Underways are somethin' else! I might go back someday. Smooth, wide passages with carved pillars and pictures everywhere, and every crossroad marked with arrows and words made outa colored jewels. Me and Marj never saw all that on our way in, not with one measly little flashlight. And the whole time we walked, Trelly and his boys were singin' songs to Mother Moon, whoever that is."

"The Lady who clubbed the dragon."

"No kiddin'! That explains a lot. Anyway, when we got near the Back Door Falls, Marj saw a trapdoor near the end of the tunnel—another thing we missed on our way in. Trelly pulled it open, and we saw lights below, and a big stairway goin' down. All them trolls went in, and Trelly was about to close the door when he said, 'Ain't you comin', lady and little man?' I sure wanted to go down, but all Marj could think of was tea and a bath, and anyway, Hælend was pretty clear that we had to get back to the house. But now I'll always wonder."

The following morning, a little while after dawn, Jen met Peter in the Hermit's room. "Come with me," she said. "I want to show you something in the ravine." Together, they walked through the quiet house and down the beach passage. When she opened the back door, they were confronted by a short, scraggly tree in the middle of the threshold. Suddenly, from farther up the passage, they heard a sound like yammering geese, and the entire pack of Mooner hounds surged around their feet, leapt over the tree's roots, and ran outside.

With a *pop!*, the tree changed into an old hag with stringy gray hair. Then a huge wolf trotted up and, in a blink, became a very tall ogre with a stubbled chin. Both creatures stared at Peter.

"Are you Bugganes?" he asked.

"You're the one that got caught by Garool, ain't you?" the hag said.

Then the ogre looked wistfully past Jen's shoulder. "Is it nice in there?"

The hounds returned with a rush, oblivious of the two strange creatures. As they poured over the threshold, the ogre became a wolf again and trotted away. By the time all the hounds were inside, the hag had turned back into the old tree.

"Excuse us," Jen said, pushing past the branches. "We're going out. And I don't think there's any need to guard the door so closely."

Peter followed her over the threshold, wondering what would happen if he trod on the Buggane's roots. He decided not to risk it.

Crossing the bridge, Jen led him to the back of the ravine, where a few stunted trees grew just outside a cave. She stopped before a dry, leafless bush. As Peter reached out to break off a twig, she said, "This is Garool." He drew his hand back.

"The Bugganes undid him. He'll never be anything more than this. They wanted you to know. He's gone and he can't come back."

Peter nodded, remembering the sly tweedy man and the feel of Garool's monster claws squeezing his throat. Then he reached down, broke off a branch with a loud snap, and tossed it into the fern brake.

On their way back to the house, a piercing cry echoed through the canyon. "Oh, Tom! Oh, Tom! He's dead!" Running down the path, past the waterfall, they found a little girl in a pink checkered dress standing barefoot in the sandy grass. She tore the legs off her teddy bear and then began to weep. Aunt Marj and Uncle Ed were crouched beside a teapot-sized spider that lay on its back with its legs curled inward. The other Bugganes stood around them in a solemn circle.

"Oh, my dear!" Aunt Marj said, picking up the stiff spider and turning it right side up. Peter, leaning over her shoulder, could see its shuttered eyes. "Oh! Poor Tom! He fought the Glashtyn and the Shee so bravely, and this is what happened!"

Her tears dripped onto the spider's back, and it made a small jerking movement.

Uncle Ed stood up and backed away. "I don't think its *quite* dead."

The spider jerked again and clacked its jaws once, and Aunt Marj began to scold. "Oh! Stuff and nonsense! Didn't you help kill a sea monster? Stop these amateur dramatics!"

With a small *pop!*, the spider became a little hedgehog. Peter saw its black eyes looking at his aunt; then the hedgehog blinked, yawned, and curled up in a ball.

"Well, isn't that dandy," she snapped, shoving the creature into her pocket. "And you!" She turned on the rest of the Toms. "Are you sissies or Bugganes? Look at you, with your slings and dressings! Anyone would think you're actually bleeding!"

The little girl wailed and tore the head off her teddy bear. Tom Bear snarled, but he and the hairy man kicked off their bandages and splints. Then they stumped off toward the back door, and Peter followed, grinning. The Bugganes hadn't changed. And yet ... something was different. It niggled at the back of his mind. Shrugging it off, he strolled up the beach passage, listening to Uncle Ed tease his sisters. They went off to the dining room for coffee, but he stopped at the kitchen and found Pixel there, eating a pink frosted donut. Droat sat beside her at the table, staring bleakly into his teacup.

"Here," Pixel said, pushing the plate of donuts toward Peter. "We're celebrating Mara's retirement."

Peter glanced at Droat's glum face. "If Mara's retired, who's the new Head Fenny?"

"Me." Droat picked up a donut and sighed.

Peter took a chocolate frosted donut and bit into it. "Wow! These are better than the ones at Wakkenburg House, Droat. Did you make them? You'll be an excellent Head."

"I can't be Head Fenny of the Hermit's House!" Droat moaned, shredding his donut to bits.

"You'll be a perfect Head," Pixel said calmly, and Peter noticed that Droat looked up and smiled when she spoke. She had the same effect on all Fennys.

"If you say so, Spy. But don't blame me."

ꕥ ꕥ ꕥ

A few days later, the company assembled for supper at the long dining room table. Everyone but the horses was there: Mooners; Fennys; all six Bugganes; Dooney; the entire Poinker band, including Arkey, who sat in a little rolling chair that Krinias had made; Uncle Ed; Jen; Pixel; Sonney; the Small One; Aunt Marj; and the hedgehog by her teacup. The Lady sat at one end of the table, and Jimmy Squarefoot sat at the other with Tuffy on his lap. Moody stretched out near the hearth, and the hounds lay beside him.

Before the meal began, the Lady stood and tapped her staff three times on the floor. There was a spark of green light, and everyone looked up.

"Silver Ones," she said, "you have been given great gifts. Though Mac Lir did not intend it so, a large part of his old powers were transferred to you. With great gifts come obligations, and you are charged with forestry work, a long task that will take many seasons."

Peter glanced at Jen and she grinned. "Can I do what Peter does? If we can heal trees, we won't have to plant so many."

"Healing *and* planting. And when Jonas is not working with you, he will direct the repair and rebuilding of Floden."

"Jonas?" Uncle Ed said. "Where?"

"Isn't it time you were healed?" the Lady asked, looking at Jimmy Squarefoot.

His piggy eyes blinked, but he did not speak.

"Jonas, do you want to be *healed*?" the Lady said gently.

The pigman stared at her, so she asked again, "Do you *want* to be healed?"

"I want to be myself, Lady. I've no wish to be Jimmy Squarefoot the Wanderer anymore."

"Then unwrap your feet and stretch them out."

There was dead silence. Tuffy hopped off his lap, and Jimmy pushed back from the table and began fumbling with the long bands of ugly calico.

"Help him, Peter," the Lady commanded.

Leaving his place, Peter knelt down and began to unwind the tightly bound cloth, uncovering small cloven hooves at the end of thin, spindly shanks. Then, in a twinkling, they were transformed to a man's feet and a man's legs. Startled, Peter looked up to find keen silver eyes gazing at him out of a bearded face. Jonas' hair hung to his shoulders, black and gray. Every trace of pig was gone.

"It *is* you!" Uncle Ed cried, and Aunt Marj gasped. "Jonas! We thought you were dead!"

Jonas rose to his feet, then bowed to the Lady. "Thank you, ma'am. I should have come to you before. And you," he said, turning to the Small One. "You taught me how to make tree food once. I hope you will help us again."

The Small One smiled. "Oh yes. Seeds and seedlings. These I can bring from home."

"From home?" Pixel's eyes widened in awe, and Peter realized that she must know something about the Small One too.

Then Dooney said, "Lady, it is good to celebrate our victory and to make amends for our losses, but I can't help thinking of the time to come. I have seen how evil always returns, no matter the good intentions."

"That dragon will not come back to this island," the Small One said. "Not until the end of the age. Grandfather will see to it. Besides, you saw the way Mother popped him one on the head."

"I did not 'pop him one'!" the Lady said.

"Oh yes, Mother! You walloped him!"

"Yeah! You sure did, Lady!" the chorus cried. "We saw it all! What an arm you got!"

Peter saw her mouth twitch but she did not reply.

"Hey, Dooney, you oughta come on patrol with us," Raney said. "We're goin' back out tomorrow. See what it's like havin' peace in these woods."

"Yeah! We're gonna try a Peas Patrol!" the chorus cheered.

"That's right," Kaney mused. "A patrol without fear or trouble ahead—"

"That's it!" Peter thundered, jumping to his feet. He thumped the table so hard it rattled from end to end.

"Peter!" Aunt Marj pressed a hand to her heart. "Really!"

"Well, I knew there was something," he said, looking around the table at the surprised faces.

Pixel frowned. "Something what?"

"Something missing. It's been bothering me since I got off the ship. Leave it to the Poinkers to know."

There was a short silence as he sat down. Everyone stared at him. Even the Lady gazed at him wide-eyed.

Finally, Jen said, "Peter, *what* is it that's missing?"

"Trouble," he said simply. "We can go for a walk in the woods with no fear. Just like Kaney said."

The Lady left for the giants' city the next day. Everyone felt a little deflated at her departure, but in the time that followed, they settled into a happy routine of meals, rest, and work. Under the direction of Droat, the seven speechless Fennys became excellent cooks. Peter's health returned quickly because, as Thrinn liked to say, "You can't keep a Silver down." Pixel and Jonas grew stronger, the hawthorn put out a mass of white blooms, and the Silver Ones took up their tasks.

On a morning of wind and bright sun, Peter found himself trailing out the front door behind Jonas—no one, not even the Poinkers, called him Jimmy Squarefoot anymore. Along with Pixel and Jen, they followed the Small One, climbing to the top of a hill. From this high place, they looked over a rolling landscape of burnt grass, black as far as the eye could see.

"Did Lila set fire to the *whole* island?" Pixel said in a small voice.

"Not all," the Small One replied. "The mountains and foothills she could not touch. Also, Wakkenburg House is under strong protection."

"This is work for many seasons," Jonas said, sighing. "How shall we begin?"

"Here." The Small One reached into his pocket and drew out a fistful of something, which he put into Peter's hands. "Grandfather sent these."

"Seeds," Peter said. They were tinier than grains of sand.

"Oh!" Pixel gasped. "These are from your home?"

"Yes," the Small One said and grinned. He pulled a handful of seeds from another pocket and poured them into her hands. Then he gave more to Jen and to Jonas.

"What kind are they?" Jen asked, her face full of awe.

"Grandfather didn't say, but I expect they're his favorite flowers. Maybe grass seed too. Anyway, it's much too late in the year for tomatoes and peas!" As he spoke, a strong breeze blew from the southwest, bringing the smell of the sea.

"Come on, Pixel!" Peter said and tossed his seeds high in the air.

Pixel threw hers up too, and so did Jen and Jonas. Then a great gust of wind sent all the seeds blowing, scattering them far and wide over the clean hills of cinder.

After that, the three Silver Ones and Moody went into the woods around Floden every day, healing the trees that could be saved, cutting down those beyond aid. Tom Mole and Krinias often helped with the felling of the blasted trees, laying them to rest on the forest floor.

One afternoon, Peter and Jen were working on the banks of the Dorry Doont just north of the ravine. In this region, the Glashtyn had damaged many trees and cut down many more in an attempt to build a boat for Lila.

"I sure wish we had tree seeds," Peter said. He laid his hand on a deep gash near the roots of an old cedar. As he watched the cut fill in with new wood and bark, he heard someone whistling. It was the Small One coming along the stream. He was followed by a donkey wearing a packsaddle with large open bags hanging on either side.

"Did you bring lunch?" Jen called out.

"I bring a friend from home," he replied. "Meet Finlo."

The donkey whinnied softly.

"And he carries something better than lunch to you foresters." The Small One removed the bags from the saddle and laid them on the wide stump of a cedar. "Saplings."

Peter drew near and looked in. "Baby trees!"

Jen pulled one out of the bag very gently. It was less than a foot high. Peter watched her dig a little hole near the cedar stump, set the sapling in, and tamp the dirt down. "There," she said, giving it a playful tap. "You grow up big and strong— Whoa!" She was thrown onto her backside as the tree went shooting up, its trunk widening in the blink of an eye. Peter gasped at the young cedar that stood before them, spreading forth branches and leaves as they watched. It thrashed about, then stood still and straight, as if it had been growing there for a long time.

Jen looked at the Small One. "Did ... did you know it would do that?"

"Grandfather expected it," he said, chuckling. "But I'm glad I saw for myself."

53

Going Home

The late August days had given way to September. The sunlight sharpened and the morning air grew crisp. Uncle Ed and Aunt Marj sometimes talked about going home to Wakkenburg House, but no one was in a hurry to return. In between forestry work, there were lazy afternoons and picnics on the beach. The Poinkers and Mooners held rock-throwing competitions, which reduced the Shee statues to piles of crumbly stone. Many evenings, they built campfires under the stars, and Peter learned the songs of the island that the Merry Wanderers had sung long ago. Then the Small One taught them new songs of starlight in ages past and sprightly tunes that reminded Peter of the roots and leaves of all growing things.

One afternoon, as he stood alone on the headland of the Silver Wing, looking over the Hills of Floden, Peter knew he would have to leave the island. The thought of Dad and Mom had been nagging at him for days. If he returned to Lang, he could get a job and help with money. No doubt Mrs. Murdle would hire him to bus tables at the diner. And then, slowly, he'd convince Mom that life on the island would be better. He imagined her living at Wakkenburg House, walking in the Rose Garden, becoming herself again under the wise mothering of Muru. He saw his father, free of worry, roaming the stacks of Fiak's library. His decision made, Peter returned to the little hollow, where he found the Datsun parked and Krim working under the hood.

"You've put the engine back together."

Krim looked up and grinned. "Well, we can't very well take the raft back to Wakkenburg, though Krinias did suggest it."

Peter's heart felt like lead. For him, Wakkenburg was the first stop before Lang. "When are we leaving?"

"Soon, I think. Muru and all the folks from Sweetwater are expecting us any day now."

"What do you mean, 'all the folks from Sweetwater'?"

"Cousins, from what I gather. And others from the men's town. They moved in right before we left."

Peter was silent, digesting this news. Clearly there was a lot his aunt and uncle hadn't yet told him. "Will you be glad to get back?"

"It's been a grand adventure, Mr. Peter, but I *will* be glad to get back to my own garage." Then Krim stuck his head back under the hood and went on with his work.

At supper, Jonas told the assembled company that the trolls had made great progress removing the rubble in Floden. *And* they'd cleared and smoothed Old Road. "It's time to mark out building sites and meet with the giants. Peter and Jen, you will have to go to Wakkenburg House without me."

"But I don't understand," Jen said. "Who is it that will live in Floden?"

"All the folks who didn't leave the island after the trouble in Foyle and Sweetwater," Uncle Ed explained. And he told them about the fires and floods and terrible weather that had destroyed the two towns.

"Orbsen Bay is gone too," Aunt Marj said. "We heard on the radio that ferry service to the island stopped just days before we arrived here. I don't know when it will start again."

"It won't," Jonas said. "The Lady explained to me that this island has become a hidden place. No doubt people in the outer world are already forgetting its existence, and soon it will no longer appear on maps. The Small One's grandfather is arranging this."

"But ... but what about people who want to get to the mainland?" Peter asked.

"Some of the folks who've stayed have fishing boats," Uncle Ed said. "And I imagine we'll build a new pier at Grondle's Gap."

"Peter, I don't see why you want to go back to Lang," Pixel said. "I'm never going back there. Aunt Marj says I can live at Wakkenburg, and I'm going to tell my family to come. Jonas said they can have a house in Floden."

"Speakin' of the folks at home," Ed said, "Krim finished puttin' the car back together, so I guess we can head for Wakkenburg anytime."

"But, Ed, the Datsun is too small for everyone to go in one trip," Aunt Marj said. "Have you thought about that?"

Peter listened absently to the conversation that followed. Jonas had already said he wasn't going, and none of the Cwenburgh Fennys wanted to leave. The Small One said he would pay a visit to Peter when there were fewer guests at Wakkenburg. And then it came out that most of the creatures would be returning to their homes in the woods.

After everyone had decided, Uncle Ed counted on his fingers. "Me, Marj, Jen, Peter, Pixel, Fiak, Krim. That makes seven. It'll be a squeeze, but we can do it."

When supper had ended, the Mooners rose from the table.

"It's time again for hunting under moonlight and starshine," Rathfrit declared. "But look for us again! Remember us, Droat, when you find gifts laid at your door! For we Moonjer Veggey have changed! Now we know who is the real Queen."

Peter watched them go, the last hound trailing out of the room. A little later, as he and Jen stood in the twilight outside the front door, they heard from far off a sound like rushing wind and flights of wild geese.

Then all six Bugganes came marching out of the house.

"Silver Ones," the hairy man said solemnly. "We, too, must take our leave and return to our own work."

"But Tom hopes you will visit him soon," the old man said. "The trees of the Twin Hills need your aid!" With a *pop!*, he turned into a blackbird, and suddenly the hollow was filled with a noise like bursting fireworks. The other Bugganes vanished, and a sparrow, a hummingbird, a swallow, a robin, and a brown wren fluttered in the air. With a rush of wings, they flew over the hill.

Jen went into the house, but Peter stood beside the hawthorn, listening to the silence. Suddenly, the hornets began to hum. They rose from the branches of the tree and swirled around him, the wind of their many wings like a breath on his face. The hum rose to a mighty buzz as they gathered themselves over his head and hovered there. He looked up at the swarm, glittering like stars. Then, like a wind-driven cloud, the Vespa swept away, over the far hills.

"Gone," the hawthorn said into his mind.

"Will we see them again?" he whispered.

"Not like that." The little tree shuddered, and Peter knew it would miss the Vespa's company. He thought he might miss them too.

Tired of goodbyes, he went looking for Pixel and found her in the dining room, playing fetch with Moody.

"Not in the house, Miss Pixel," Droat said.

So they went down to the ravine and played hide-and-seek among the bushes and boulders.

The next morning, right after breakfast, Kaney said to Peter, "Arkey's casts came off yesterday, and now that he's well, we're going back to our patrols. We'll come by here again, but I suppose you'll be gone."

Peter nodded, unable to speak.

"Then we'll say goodbye, for now," Kaney rumbled.

"See ya when we see ya, kid!" Arkey called.

Peter, Pixel, the Small One, and Jen followed the Poinkers to the front door, then stood together, watching the bristly band cross the hollow. They disappeared in a fold of the hills as the chorus chanted, "Peas! Peas! Peas Patrol!"

"Is everything going back to the way it was?" Peter said, when the sound of their voices faded.

"No," Jen replied. "Not the way it was. Say instead, the way it should be."

Pixel and the Small One grinned at each other. "Peas!" they cried in unison.

ꝏ ꝏ ꝏ

That same evening, they left for Wakkenburg House.

"Two Silvers going home," Thrinn commented. She stood at the front door with the Small One and Dooney. Jonas, holding Tuffy in his arms, waited by the hawthorn as Aunt Marj and Uncle Ed loaded the Datsun's trunk.

Mara rushed out, followed by all the Fennys. "Wait! Wait!" She fumbled in the pocket of her apron, then grabbed Jen's hand. "This is your button, Jenny." Trembling, she opened Jen's fingers and placed a tiny thing in her palm. "Mara remembers that day when she put you in the lake. She is sorry."

For a long moment, Jen looked at the pearl button. Then she put it in her pocket and cupped Mara's face in her hands. "Little Jenny says thank you. Thank you for saving my life." She kissed Mara's forehead and got in the car, squeezing into the back seat with Peter, Fiak, and Krim.

Pixel was already perched between the two front seats, with Uncle Ed and Aunt Marj on either side. They rolled down all the windows, and Uncle Ed started the engine.

"Krinias!" Krim called out the window. "I'll send a few things over for your shop!"

"You got an extra car?"

"As a matter of fact, we do," Uncle Ed said, and Peter thought of the ancient dusty cars lined up in the Wakkenburg garage.

Now they were on their way, waving, looking back at the crowd by the front door.

"Going!" Peter heard the hawthorn say.

"I'll be back soon."

The hawthorn didn't reply, but in his mind Peter heard a whispering sigh like the rustle of leaves in the wind.

The road wound through the hills, and as the Datsun rumbled along, Pixel called out, "Look! The grass is starting to grow!" Sure enough, a thin haze of green was sprouting over the hills. Then they went around a bend and there was Floden, the ground cleared, waiting for the rebuilding to begin.

As they passed through the old village square, Jen called out, "What's that? On top of the old stone?"

A large brown sack sat on the rock table, with a big piece of white bark sticking out the top. Ed stopped the car and got out. He picked up the bag and looked inside, and they heard him say, "I'll be darned." When he came back to the car, he was holding a large, colorful object.

"That's a troll brooch!" Peter said.

"And this is a note." Uncle Ed handed the piece of bark to Peter. Someone had scrawled letters in charcoal. "Giv to hir wot savd us. An the litl man," Peter read aloud. "Who is 'her what saved us'?"

"Marj, of course." Jen reached over Peter and took the troll brooch from her brother. It was a little larger than her hand, inlaid with gold and precious stones. She passed it to Marj, who ran her fingers over the smooth setting.

"Oh! I think it's carved from a tooth of that sea monster! But what about the little man? Did they make something for you too, Ed?"

He reached into the sack and brought out a dagger with rubies and amethysts in the handle. "I'll be danged," he muttered. "Those trolls are somethin' else."

He got back in the car and started the engine, and they drove out of Floden and down Old Road.

They were cruising slowly along, passing through the fire-damaged forest, and Peter was thinking what a lot of work there was to do, when Krim hissed, "What is *that*?"

Startled, Peter looked out the window and saw a huge black shape in the woods, running parallel with the car. "It's Moody! I wondered where he was!" And his mind went back to his very first day on the island, when Annette had driven him to Wakkenburg and he'd had his first glimpse of the great dog, huge and mysterious. It seemed like forever ago.

"Must be clocking fifty." Uncle Ed chuckled as Moody leapt onto the road directly in front of the Datsun. Then, in a burst of speed, he disappeared into the distance.

A little while later, the old dirt track ended and they were spinning along the tarmac of Wakkenburg Road. A few minutes more, and they were crossing the bridge, turning left onto the long drive. Then the Datsun sped out of the woods, and Peter heard Jen's gasp of astonishment. Uncle Ed let up on the gas and they passed slowly between the wide lawns in the deepening twilight. The house, with all its windows alight, shone like a jewel.

"Jenny, you're comin' back after seventy years! Shall we make a grand entrance at the front door or go in by the garage?" Uncle Ed asked.

"No grand entrances, please," Jen said quietly.

"Home at last," Pixel murmured as the Datsun turned down the back lane and into the courtyard.

Peter smiled grimly. "Yeah, but we sure traveled a long way to get here."

54

Peas in Our Time

The garage crew escorted them in triumph right to the back door of the West Wing, everyone laughing and talking at once. Peter came last. In his mind, Wakkenburg was just one step closer to Lang. He could already see himself on a fishing boat, working for his passage. As the company moved down the corridor, he slipped up the back stairs and went straight to his room.

Everything was just as he'd left it. Opening the window, he looked out over the west lawn in the fading light. One or two stars shone above the charred trees. There had been a battle here too. Looking down at the lawn, he saw a family taking an evening stroll. Must be people from Sweetwater. They stopped suddenly, and he heard the mother gasp. On the other side of the lawn, Moody Doug, huge and oblivious, sat in the doorway of his giant doghouse, chewing happily on a large bone. Peter stifled a laugh until he heard one of the children say, "Look, Mom! Up there! It's the Silver Boy!" He shut the window and turned away, fumbling with a small lamp on the table.

"Don't bother to say hi or anything."

He looked up, and there was Muru standing in the doorway, hands on hips. "Don't bother to greet your friends who've been worried sick about you."

"Hi, Muru. I, uh ..."

"Save the apologies for your father, kid. Him come all this way, driven by worry, thinking you're dead! And you up here, mooning about like a lost orphan!"

Peter stared at her. "What ... what did you say?"

"Don't blame me if he never talks to you again! I'm not sure I will!"

Then Dad was there, standing behind Muru, and Peter couldn't speak, couldn't breathe. Tears stung his eyes as Dad rushed in. He felt the strong arms around his shoulders, the familiar kiss on his forehead, and he was shaking, sobbing, and couldn't stop. His dad held him tight and did not let go.

❦ ❦ ❦

They were alone in the kitchen, except for Thrak, who was making coffee at the stove. Peter poured hot cocoa into two mugs and pushed one across the table toward his father, then took a donut.

"I heard about the fires on the island, and how Foyle and Orbsen Bay burned down. A woman I met on the docks told me," Dad said.

"You came on a fishing boat, right? Is that how we'll get back?"

Dad paused. "Do you want to go back to Lang?"

Absently, Peter began shredding his donut. "Not really. No. But what about Mom? Is she alright? Will she come here?"

Martin let out a long breath and put his cup down. "She's fine. Made it through detox. Discharged three weeks ago."

"Then she's at home?"

"Not exactly." His dad hesitated.

"Where is she?"

"At her sister's place. In Bellarmeen. Where she lived before she met me."

"Then we're going to Bellarmeen?"

"No, Peter. She ... she filed for divorce."

Sorrow was written in every line of Dad's face. In all the wreck of their lives, Peter had never imagined this. He sat there, feeling some part of him tear away, as if someone were removing part of the background scenery of his life. He didn't know what to say.

"I'm sorry, Peter. Right now she believes that living happily ever after means walking away from me. From us."

He knew how his mom felt about him. "I'm the Silver freak."

"Peter, your life, your silver eyes, are not the reason she's going. The real reasons are inside her, and you can't do anything about that."

Into his mind came an image of the Small One. He had lost his mother *and* father. They had walked away from him and their home, and there had been no way back. Then the Lady's face rose to the surface of his jumbled thoughts. “Do you think Mom could change her mind someday? Start missing us?”

Dad smiled sadly. “I sure hope so.”

* * *

The next morning was busy for Peter, but Dad stuck close, which made things easier. First, Thrak came running down the passage. “Mr. Peter! That man, Mac Rilson! He’s run off!”

“Mac Rilson?” Peter stared at her.

“He just ran out the front door, I tell you! I don’t know what Muru’s going to say!”

“What she says is good riddance!” Muru sailed into the corridor with a duster in one hand. “He’s been impossible since Tom Spider left. Anyway, there’s no point keeping him now.”

“But ... but what was Mac Rilson doing here?”

“It’s a long story, kid, but even if he comes back in a few days, he’s off my hands for the party.”

“Party? What party?”

“Isn’t it your birthday today?”

“That’s correct,” Dad said, grinning. “September twelfth.”

“The party starts at three o’clock sharp. And since Pixel’s birthday is in three days, we’re doing your parties together. Your suit’s all laid out on your bed. Don’t be late, kid.”

On the way to breakfast, Peter met a flustered Ulf in the passage outside the kitchen. “That giant dog of yours is gonna bury his big bone in the gardens. I know it!”

Peter stepped to the back door and whistled. When Moody appeared, he told him to bury his bone on the other side of the Glenny. Ulf ran off, extremely grateful, and then Krim turned up, talking excitedly about bicycles. Thinking of donuts and not really listening, Peter said, “Okay,” and Krim ran off toward the garage, whooping.

“Is it always like this?” his dad asked. “Everyone asking you what to do?”

Peter shrugged. “It’s my job. I’m one of the Silvers. But I sure hope Jen will start helping out soon.”

After breakfast, he took his dad to the library and introduced him to Fiak.

"Martin Thornburg? A trained historian?" Fiak exclaimed. "Mr. Martin, I'd be very grateful if you'd help me organize my notes."

"Notes?"

"Everything that happened this summer. To Mr. Peter and Miss Pixel and everyone. You see, we must add a new chapter to the Thornburg book!"

Peter left his dad happily absorbed and went to find Pixel. He wanted to tell her that he was staying. His mom's decision made it bittersweet, but he still couldn't help being glad. "No Lang for me!" he said to himself as he stepped out the back door into the sunlight.

ೲ ೲ ೲ

Later that day, Peter sat stiffly at the high table on the ballroom terrace with Moody sitting up tall and straight behind his chair. Dad sat on his right, and Pixel on his left. Below the terrace, at cloth-covered tables, about twenty adults were assembled, plus a few teenagers and a handful of children. These were all the islanders who had come from Foyle and Sweetwater. Beyond the small crowd, the woods of Glenny Stream swayed in the breeze.

Muru had made him wear a rather old-fashioned suit that once belonged to Jonas. He would have felt silly wearing it, but Pixel had put on an elegant dress. In fact, everyone wore beautiful, old-fashioned clothes, all borrowed from the attics, according to Muru. Generations of Thornburg attire, brought out of boxes and chests, had been aired and pressed for the occasion. At a table on the other side of the terrace, he saw Aunt Marj wearing the big troll brooch on her shoulder. Jen, in a white gown that had belonged to her mother, wore the pearl button on a fine chain. Then Uncle Ed sauntered out of the ballroom wearing a magnificent tuxedo with tails, and a top hat cocked sideways on his head.

Standing just inside the French doors of the ballroom, a host of prim, uniformed Fennys lined up beside a beaming Muru, awaiting commands.

Dad, arrayed in a tweed suit befitting the rank of historian, leaned over and said, "By the way, why didn't I see them before?"

"The Fennys? Dad, how often have you been here?"

"We visited once when I was young. For my grandfather's funeral. But where were these Fennys then?"

"They were here but ... Aunt Jen wasn't. They're invisible without a Silver One."

"Ah. A Silver One. I'm beginning to understand. Where was Aunt Jen?"

"At the bottom of a lake. It's all in Fiak's notes." He glanced at Jen, who was sitting at the head of her table, laughing and talking with her brother and sister. George and Mary also sat at that table with Cousin Annette and her boyfriend, Ben.

"Mr. Thornburg," Pixel said, "how did you get here? I heard the ferry from Lang stopped."

"Tim Maycap." Dad pointed to a large man sitting at a table with a little girl on his lap. "I came on his fishing boat."

"How in the world did you meet him, Dad? At the diner?"

"Lily Rilson sent him to find me. Whoever she is. Must have been the woman I met at the docks."

"Lily Rilson!" Pixel sat up. "My granny? Mr. Thornburg, you met my granny?"

A bell sounded. The assembled crowd grew quiet and turned toward the terrace. Slowly, Peter pushed back his chair and got to his feet.

"Are you giving a speech?" Pixel's eyes widened in concern.

His collar suddenly felt like a noose. Then Fiak hurried out the ballroom door and thrust a paper into his hands. "Sorry, Mr. Peter! Last-minute alterations!"

Looking over Fiak's neat writing, which appeared to be swimming all over the page, Peter cleared his throat and was about to begin when there was a sudden commotion.

"No! No!" came the urgent plea, shouted into the afternoon silence. It was Ulf. He came running across the garden, past the North Tower, followed by half a dozen gardeners in pursuit of a fast-moving tree. The hawthorn! Peter couldn't help feeling glad, even if it *was* tearing up Ulf's manicured lawn. Many of the guests stood up in alarm, and a child began to cry. Moody whined and snuffled Peter's coat sleeve.

"Stop," Peter said under his breath. The little tree halted, waving its branches in protest, scattering white blossoms.

"Come too!" it shouted into his mind.

Ulf ran up to the edge of the terrace. "Mr. Peter, it's back! Won't listen to a thing I say!"

"Better let it stand here by me." He leaned over the rail and pointed to an open space in the garden border.

"But you know how it tears up brickwork!"

"It's alright, Ulf." Looking at the tree, Peter said, "Come and stand here. And be good. No eating bricks."

The little tree obeyed, coming to stand at the end of the terrace, its branches poised over Peter's head. Many people grinned, and not a few applauded.

"Can we get on now?" Muru huffed. "The tea's getting cold."

Peter cleared his throat again. "Today we celebrate the birthdays of ... of me and Pixel." Pixel waved at the crowd. "And we also rejoice in the defeat of the witch and those evil forces that have caused so much trouble on our island. With the advent of peas, uh, I mean peace"—he heard Pixel giggle—"we begin anew, here and in Floden."

He pulled at his collar as the crowd cheered. Yet the next part of Fiak's speech surprised him. "As so many of you have read the Thornburg book and heard the truth of recent events from Miss Marj and Mr. Edward ..." He paused, looked out over the crowd, and saw people nodding and smiling. The teenagers grouped at a near table gave him a thumbs-up.

"I will not," he continued, "repeat what you already know. I only wish to assure you again that the witch is dead and the wizard cast off this island, as I saw with my own eyes." There was more clapping and cheering. A few of the older children began to chant, "Silver! Silver!" but were hushed by their elders.

Peter went on, "In our victory, many things were destroyed, but many more made well. Allow me to introduce my great-aunt Jenny Thornburg, who has returned to us after so many years in exile." He looked over at Jen, who stood and waved at the crowd. Everyone broke into cheers and whistles and calls of "Welcome home!"

He was coming to the end now. "After tea, there will be dancing in the ballroom and games on the west lawn, and fireworks after dinner." He grinned, thinking of the garage crew. "Lastly, I wish to call your attention to a special announcement. Wakkenburg House is pleased to host a wedding on October the sixteenth, to which you are all invited. Congratulations to Miss Annette Thornburg and Mr. Ben Rilson." He read this last bit in happy surprise as the couple stood and waved to the assembly. Cheers and wolf whistles and tremendous applause erupted. He saw Uncle Ed clapping, a wistful smile on his face.

As Peter sat down, Pixel said, "I'm glad our family feud is over."

There was only one thing missing that day, though Peter would never have said so to Muru. As the afternoon merged into evening and people trailed off to their rooms to rest and freshen up for dinner, he sat under the hawthorn with Pixel and Moody. The tree had been very good, and he thought it needed company.

Muru, on some errand, stopped when she saw them. "You two having a happy birthday?" she asked.

"It's great, Muru," Peter replied.

"Yeah," Pixel said. "But, Muru, at tea there were empty seats at our table. Are they for the Bugganes?"

"No. They won't make an appearance with so many people around. But the hairy guy stopped by the garage this morning and told Krim to expect some other guests."

"Who?"

"Didn't say. Maybe they aren't coming after all. Don't blame me!"

The sun sank below the western woods, and a bell sounded from the East Tower. It was the summons for dinner. There were fancy candlestands on all the tables, and the Fennys had set out the best silver and china. Peter sat down at the head of his table, right under the hawthorn's branches, and watched the crowd assemble again. His dad joined him, just as Pixel came up the terrace steps with Moody.

"Where are the mystery guests?" she asked.

Peter shrugged. "I guess they aren't coming."

The bell pealed again, a signal for the feast to begin. Everything went quiet, and Peter wondered whether Jen would have to give a speech. Then the sound of shrill piping floated over the lawn, and the sharp rat-a-tat of a drum. Wondering, the assembled company looked toward the woods, and the very thing Peter had wished for all day marched around the corner of the North Tower.

We done traveled half the night
Through boggy, burnt-out forest
Just to sing this little song,
A happy birthday chorus!

Happy birthday, Silver Kid!
Happy birthday, Pixie!
Mind yer spendin' habits 'cause
The market's gettin' tricksy!

Hearing one voice he knew quite well, Peter jumped from his seat and stood at the rail. "Arkey!"

As the bristly band marched through the crowd and onto the terrace, people stood and watched in amazement. They clapped and cheered, and several children cried, "Look, Mom! It's the Poinkers! Just like in the book!"

Peter turned and saw Muru grinning at him. "I guessed who was coming," she said. "You may not have noticed, but there aren't candles on *your* table."

When the Poinkers were settled, Jen stood and raised her glass. Her clear voice rang out over the garden. "To the island! And the Lady who has brought peace in our time."

"To the Lady!" Peter said, raising his cup, and beside him the chorus cried, "Lady's Peas!"

Oh, let us lift our eyes to the heights, to the snow.
Oh, let our voices rise; let us go.
For one day we'll be free.
We'll sing and merry be.
We'll take the upward climb, we will go, we will go,
Through forests and the snow, we will go.

The mountains and the hills lead us on, lead us on,
With courage and goodwill, lead us on.
We journey and endure
Till all our hearts are pure,
Like eagles in the heights, we'll live on, we'll live on,
Where mountain meets the sky, we'll live on.

PRONUNCIATION GUIDE TO THE NAMES AND PLACES OF WAKKEN WOOD

Arkan Sonney: ARK-an SOWN-ay
Buggane: boo-GANE
Dooiney-oie: DOH-in-yeh OY
Fennodyree: fen-ODD-ore-EE
Floden: FLOE-den
Foyle: foil
Glashtyn: GLASH-tin
Glenfaba: glen-FAW-ba
Kulifara: kool-i-FAW-ra
Lliannon Shee: LEE-an-on SHAY
Moddey Dhoo: MOD-ay DOO
Moonjer Veggey: MOON-jer VEJ-ay
Rosknil: ROSK-nil
Shee: shay
Tarroo Ushtey: TAR-oo OOSH-chuh
Wakken: WOK-in

THE CREATURES OF WAKKEN WOOD

During a period of political upheaval, the wizard Mac Lir and a band of creatures sailed to Wakken Wood in a voyage known as the Great Migration. These strange companions journeyed from the land of the Manx people, called the Isle of Man, which lies in the middle of the Irish Sea.

These creatures came to Wakken Wood with Manx names, and they gave Manx place-names to many locations on the island. As might be expected, language variants developed over the centuries. By the time this glossary was compiled, under the direction of Fiak the librarian, the variants of old Manx were in common usage all over the island. No doubt these changes were the direct result of other influences in Wakken Wood: the Anglo-Saxon dialect spoken by the trolls and the giants, the tribal languages of the Merry Wanderers, and the languages spoken by nineteenth-century immigrants from the mainland cities of Lang and Bellarmeen. All given spellings and pronunciations are taken from the Thornburg Book.

Arkan Sonney (ARK-an SOWN-ay) [MANX *lucky pig*]: A tribe of hedgehog-like creatures that go about on two legs and stand about fifteen inches high. They plunk out silver coins that used to be of great value. On coming to Wakken Wood, they developed unique customs and habits apart from their relatives, who remain on the Isle of Man. Sometimes referred to as "prickly oinkers" (or "squeakers", though it is dangerous to use this title), by the time of Peter Thornburg, they had become known as the Poinkers.

Bugganes (boo-GANES): These creatures are fearsome shape-shifters that haunt the highways and woods, terrorizing lone travelers. The Bugganes who came with Mac Lir in the Great Migration are seven: Tom Mole, Tom Troll (or the hairy man), Tom Spider, Tom Bear, Tom Hag, Tom Wolf, and Garool the Great. Each Buggane occupies his own region of the woods and guards his territory fiercely.

Dooiney-oie (DOH-in-yeh OY) [MANX *Night Man*]: The Dooiney-oie—or Dooney, as he came to be known by the time of Peter Thornburg—bears some resemblance in nature to the mythical Irish banshee. He wails at the foundering of ships and the onset of storms. No one knows why Mac Lir brought the Dooiney-oie on his ship. Many of the creatures speculate that Dooney had a terrible case of laryngitis and wanted to take the sea air.

Fennodyree (fen-ODD-ore-EE) [MANX *fallen fairy*]: At the time of the third Silver One, Jonas Wakkenburg, the race of Fennodyree was already known, colloquially, as the Fennys. The Fennys are small men and women, usually dark-skinned and hairy all over (though the females have less facial hair), with wrinkled hands and faces. In Wakken Wood, they originated from the union of Moonjer Veggey and the human tribes once known as the Merry Wanderers. A similar race exists on the Isle of Man, the original domain of Mac Lir, where they were once known as the Phynnodderee.

Glashtyn (GLASH-tin) [MANX *water horse*]: The Glashtyn were always a blight on the Isle of Man, luring people to their death in the sea. They appeared as beautiful horses, but woe to the human who dared to mount them! The creatures of Wakken Wood all swear that the Glashtyn did not come to the island in the Great Migration. It is rumored, however, that once his domain was established in Wakken Wood, Mac Lir went back to his Manx homeland and returned to Wakken with his mistress, Tegi the Enchantress. The Mooners believe it was she who brought the Glashtyn to haunt Granite Lake and the shores of the sea.

Lliannon Shee (LEE-an-on SHAY) [MANX *evil fairies*]: Known colloquially as the Shee, these tall, dark, shadowy figures often take the form of a person's hidden desire or sorrow. They are the incubi offspring of Lila (also known as the Night Monster). Summoned by Lila, they appeared during the first trouble in the woods, and they departed with her. Called by the Moonwitch, they reappeared during the guardianship of Peter Thornburg for the second battle over Wakken Wood.

Mac Lir: A minor sea god who ruled the faerie island now known as the Isle of Man. He was a great navigator and wizard and could call down mists to hide himself or great storms to punish his enemies. It was sometimes said that he rolled on three legs, like a wheel (this, in fact, became the insignia on Manx coins). He called himself king, and his queen was Fand, but Lir was ever unfaithful. During a time of invasion, he fled his domain with certain creatures (the journey known as the Great Migration) and established himself in the secret land called Wakken Wood.

Moddey Dhoo (MOD-ay DOO) [MANX *black dog*]: A huge black dog that, at one time, haunted the environs of Peel Castle on the Isle of Man. To see him meant that your death was very near. He came to Wakken Wood at the time of the Great Migration and, for reasons still unknown, lost his reputation as a harbinger of death. Over time, he became known familiarly as Moody Doug and attached himself to the Silver Thornburgs.

Moonjer Veggey (MOON-jer VEJ-ay) [MANX *little people*]: These small folk are very like mortals in feature. Wearing red caps and green jackets, they are sometimes seen on moonlit nights, hunting on horseback, followed by a pack of little white hounds. By the time of Peter Thornburg, the Moonjer Veggey were known, colloquially, as the Mooners. Perhaps this rather vulgar title was given to them by the Arkan Sonney, who had good reason to resent these "little people".

Moonwitch: The daughter of Lila and Ahab, she is part lilin and part human. Tall and dark-haired like her father, she is more human than she wishes to be and has few supernatural powers. When she was fourteen, she left her father's house in Orbsen Bay and returned to the woods, where she lived in a small hut on the outskirts of Floden. After a long absence, her mother returned and laid claim to the house named Cwenburgh, wresting it from Jonas the Silver One. She gave the house to her daughter, called the young Moonwitch "Queen of the Woods", and commanded the Glashtyn to serve her.

Tarroo Ushtey (TAR-oo OOSH-chuh) (MANX *water bull*): Sometimes called Mac Lir's cattle, these bovine creatures are light gray with smooth skin; short, round ears that waggle back and forth; bony knobs on the tops of their heads; and glowing red eyes. In the old country, they ate cattle and sometimes horses, but not men. In the Wakken domain, they live in a watershed area north of Old Road and can sometimes be seen swimming in the Glenfaba River, where they consume large quantities of fish.